DEATH MAKES ONE

A Novel

SOL GATOS

ISBN: 0692925082
ISBN 13: 9780692925089
Library of Congress Control Number: 2017949976
Sol Gatos, Lemoore, CA

For those that we have lost:
Your lives inspired us,
Your deaths awakened us.

Dedicated to the Truth

CHAPTER 1

The drive to Fresno was how it all began. The man had asked one of his oldest clients for a ride to the airport to pick up the rental car. The client had a fixation with loud music and fast driving. He was a genuine guy, but like most, wasn't always quite right in the head.

The man knew all too well about mental illness. He had been called crazy since a child and had come to live with it. The two enjoyed the strange friendship they shared with each other. They were completely different people, but somehow shared the same core beliefs. Both held a deep reverence for the other. Respect was the trait they followed.

This attitude was not a usual thing in these modern days of social media. Respect was a dying feature of the human race. Most people now were just concerned with themselves and how they portrayed themselves on their social media sites. They had no time to look at a fellow human and understand that they were the same. All were just beings trying to get by in a world which was against them. If they could only see, respect was what was going to save the planet.

The music was getting to the man. Conversation was impossible. The constant headache he had endured thumped to the beat of the speakers. It was a headache he was all too familiar with for the last two years. Tragedy had struck his family and some close friends. Death had haunted the man and his family over and over for the last couple of years. This trip was meant to reconnect with the rest of his sisters and a few friends who had remained loyal. Mostly it was to reconnect with their souls and heal their broken beings. So much death had crippled the family and now it was time to walk on.

These were the thoughts going through the man's mind as he drifted off to sleep. Years of military service in the era of his youth had trained him to sleep through anything. He tried over and over to rid his thoughts of the pain but there was so much of it. It flooded his soul like a tsunami. He was aware of his friend driving exceptionally fast, but he did not care. Death was not something he was afraid of. He had learned that we

1

all go when it is our time. Some cosmic calling of the numbers that was to be embraced, not feared.

The sound of screeching brakes and a loud air horn jolted the man from his near sleep. His dreams had been of the turbulent kind when you are just on the edge of sleep. It seemed as if he were hurtling through space and hit an invisible wall. The last thing the man saw was the grill of the semi-truck. It was the only thing in his vision when he came out of his sleep. The truck slammed into the car in an explosion which witnesses would later testify seemed more excessive than it should have been. They also would say the color of the flames was a color their eyes couldn't identify with. It was as if a new spectrum of color were visible that was invisible before.

The cars around the mayhem all came to a screeching stop. Many jumped from their vehicles to help while others just sat in the safety of their cars sobbing. It had been a horrendous sight. The 'would be' rescuers were helpless as they watched the vehicles burning. They got as close as possible but the heat was too intense. Some of them later told their family members that it seemed as if the people in the burning wreckage had disappeared for some time before reappearing. When they reappeared, they seemed to be smiling and laughing and not in the least bit of pain, although they were engulfed in a terrible inferno.

More than a few of the people who stayed in the safety of their cars also spoke of the first responders. They would speak of the ambulance crew fading in and out of existence. Others would say that the firemen were making odd movements which did not seem human. It was almost as if they were changing shapes into different animals. All these stories were ridiculed by family members and anyone else who had heard them. This had prevented the witnesses from talking more about their experiences. Some of the witnesses could never forget, nor accept, the things they had seen. Some had even ended up in mental institutions or dead at their own hands. This tragedy, as all do, had a terrible impact on many people and their families. Sometimes, things happen that are so bad, they burn a hole in your being that will never be filled. This was the case for every one of these witnesses.

After seeing the grill of the semi-truck, the man saw an explosion of light like nothing he had ever seen. The explosion hurtled him into space. He was shooting through the universe like a comet. His mind had completely separated from his body. He had left his earthly flesh pod. Solar systems, then whole galaxies, flew by him at a speed much faster than light. Everything was so beautiful to the man. All his senses were absorbing the sensations being thrust upon his being. There seemed to be a light at the end of the darkness but he didn't seem to be getting any closer. Not that he was in any hurry, the lights zinging by, all around him, were godlike. His thoughts understood this. Patterns were everywhere, combining in an endless web of cycles.

After what seemed like an eternity in a spiritual state, the light was suddenly large and enveloping the man. The effulgence was warm and buttery feeling. It had a taste and smell of tropical fruit. His existence had never felt so pure and right. All the answers to the questions he had ever pondered were flooding into his thoughts. The answers were an explosion of emotions in the man. The whole universe and all of existence were nothing like anyone could imagine. This was the beginning of everything, and it was also the end of everything. This was pure. This was "The One".

Suddenly, the light was gone and only darkness remained. The man seemed unable to move or to focus his thoughts. There was just a terrible sense of loss. He didn't want to move away from the light, but he had no control over anything. Something very bad was coming his way, but he couldn't pinpoint what it was or even where the thoughts were coming from. He seemed to be flying through space again, but this time backwards. Combined with a sense of dread, he also felt a serious sense of purpose. The man had been chosen for a mission. He had been chosen as a small child. Now this was the next step in the journey to fulfilling the destiny. The answers were clear.

The man jerked awake in response to a bad dream. Obviously, he had been able to block the loud music which continued to blast through the speakers. The driver seemed to be rocking out to the music in his own world, a cigarette in hand and foot heavy on the pedal. The man would be happy to arrive at the airport and get his own car. He had always liked this guy, but since all the death around him, he preferred to be alone or with his remaining family.

A flash of silver caught his attention out of the corner of his eye. He looked up to see a diesel truck headed on a ninety-degree collision course with their car. The man backhanded the driver's elbow, causing the cigarette to fall into the seats. He glared over at the man and saw the truck headed their way. Both drivers slammed on their brakes and skidded in an obscene way around each other. The accident was narrowly avoided by mere inches. The man was slammed back into the reality of the consciousness.

While both drivers exchanged angry words and gestures, the man noticed a family in a minivan drive by. There were four passengers in the van and they all seemed to be wearing masks. As the family passed by their stalled vehicle, the man noticed that the masks were of skulls, but not a human variety. Also, there were two animals in the car that looked like a mix between a monkey, dog, and octopus. The man shook his head to clear his eyes, but the image remained. The passengers in the minivan were impervious to the scene around them and kept their eyes straight ahead. The man thought that one of the small animals changed into a humanoid looking creature but convinced himself that the near accident had stirred up his imagination. He also was still trying to wake up and told himself that it was not real. The man had seen many things in his life and had told himself the same thing many times. But so many times the things he had seen were real, sometimes terribly so.

The rest of the trip to the airport was filled with angry words from the driver. He couldn't let go of the fact that accidents sometimes happen. The man explained this to him over and over but the driver did not fully understand. He always felt like everything was directed at him, as if it were a personal attack. At least the music wasn't so loud and he was driving more sanely. There seemed to be a car following them to the airport, the driver warned, but the man told him he was just being paranoid. "Not everyone was out to get him," the man had told him.

The air and sky seemed to be different to the man. It seemed much warmer before and now there were a few clouds in the sky. "Something very unusual for this region, for this time of year," the man had thought. The air had seemed so thick with humidity before, and now a cool breeze made it enjoyable. There seemed to be many chemical trails in the sky. It gave the atmosphere a strange brown hue. The air felt good but the man had a very bad feeling about things.

At last they arrived at their destination. The man insisted on going in alone to handle his business; much to the chagrin of the driver. He was a guy who liked to help, but the man needed his thoughts focused on his agenda. This also was going to be the only time in the next month that he would have any time alone, and he was going to cherish it. Alone time was not common to the man. His job dealt with the public in an intimate way, and he was around family whenever not at work. So, when it happened, it was well accepted.

The rental car booth and contract agreement went very smoothly. The man had taken care of all the business on the internet months before, and now it had paid off. After grabbing the keys, the man thought it best to use the airport restroom. The terminal was very sparse with people, as this airport often was. It was one of the reasons the man liked it so much. Walking into the expansive bathroom, the man noticed the lack of people in the facilities. He took care of his business in solitude and turned to wash his hands. He couldn't help but shake the feeling that someone or something was looking at him. He looked in the mirror but there were just toilet stalls behind him. A movement in one of them caught his eye in the mirror. He spun around and focused on the spot where he had seen the action.

Above the stall door was a black top hat suspended on the head of an unseen voyeur. The sight was very unusual and unnerving to the man. His heart thumped a little harder than usual. However, he had lived his life fighting any feelings of fear and now stepped towards the stall door. The energy coming from behind the door was very dark and made the man feel uneasy, somehow full of dread. It also made him light headed, almost like he would be sick or even pass out. He had felt this feeling before and knew all about it. He did not fear it, but he had a dark respect for stepping well around this energy. It was in a realm of reality the man had steered clear of his whole life. It had called him over and over in his days but he fought this darkness with all his being.

It almost felt like taking apart two magnets as he tore himself from in front of the door and left the restroom. The feelings of dread evaporated immediately. The energies had been separated.

The man had known strange things were going to happen on this trip but he had not planned on them coming this quick. He had visions of the future his whole life but they were not always decipherable. These premonitions were knowledge of things to come through feelings deep in his being, not in his mind.

He made his way to the rental car lot and found his vehicle for the next ten thousand miles. It was a nice new minivan. He took pictures of it and sent it to the other three who would be calling this car home for the next month. The trip was about to begin. The last six months of hard work for the man and his family were coming into reality. It was time to get home and get this adventure on the road.

The drive back to the man's house was filled with oddities. Some of the music on the radio he had never heard of before, although he prided himself on knowing so many styles of music. The songs that were familiar seemed to have different lyrics than before, or the beats were slightly different. Some of the cars on the road also seemed strange. The man had never seen some of them before and some made movements that didn't seem possible. Some almost seemed to have an organic feel to them like they were machines but alive at the same time.

The man thought he just needed to get home and rest some before the others arrived. His wife and Grandson were to be arriving hours later after going to visit her mother. This would give the man time to gather his thoughts and focus on the trip ahead without distractions.

There seemed to be a large black crow flying around the van. The man would spot it every few miles or so. He could swear that they had made eye contact a few times and somehow had a mutual bond of energy. The bird's wings would catch the sun just right at times and appear brown in color. The man had never seen a crow so large before. It seemed to be familiar with him. Somehow, the bird was also in his memory. There was a strong sense of déjà vu with this creature.

Down the highway some, there was a congestion of traffic. "Must be an accident" the man had thought. Traffic crawled along for some time before he could see what had happened. A diesel truck had crashed through the railing of an overpass, falling on the highway below. A minivan had hit the truck and there was a lot of fire. There was just a shell of the vehicles now but the people were still inside them. The minivan had four people in it when it had crashed. They were still in a sitting position but the fire had completely burned all the skin from their bodies. Their faces were just skulls, twisted into an unrecognizable mess of charred bone. There seemed to be movement in the backseat. Shadows of unrecognizable shapes, twisting through the inferno, filled the rear of the vehicle.

The man made the connection immediately. This was the family which had driven by him earlier. Had he had a premonition of their fate? He had always been slightly psychic but nothing like this. He was startled out of his reverie by movement to the right. He thought it was a cop waving him on but when he looked he realized he was wrong. The movement had been caused by the large crow which had been shadowing the man. It flew directly in front of the minivan's windshield and looked straight into the man's eyes. They shared a moment of 'One".

The crow made a strange movement of wings and flew towards the wreckage. In its beak, tendrils hanging, was an eyeball. It seemed to look right at the man. The bird seemed to fade into the smoke coming from the wreckage. It dropped something into the burning car and vanished in the smoke.

This was the beginning.

Chapter 2

The family spent all day Sunday preparing the van for travels and enjoying one last cooked meal before a month and a half of eating out. The man took pride in his cooking. Barbecuing was the way they would feast on this day. The next home cooked meal would be at his sister's house in Texas, many miles and days down the road. The excitement was high, but the family maintained well. They were of a mellow type, trying their best not to get worked up over things.

The journey would take them from the gold country of California to East Texas, up the Mississippi river into Minnesota, back across the plains to the coast, and down the west coast back to sweet Mountain Ranch. It was a time to put the hard road behind them and be adventurous. Through this, the man spoke of true enlightenment. A purging of the gone and accepting of the next. It was time to cleanse the souls of all the death. It was time to get back to the light.

The niece arrived in the early afternoon. She was one who was always on time and could be counted on for anything. Her way was as a true member of the family spirit. The man, woman, and boy all greeted her warmly. This trip had been planned many months before and the anticipation had been building since. The energy created between the four beings was especially strong. They had all been close before, but now that bond would grow even stronger.

The girl and her uncle had come up with this idea the year before. The man had spent the last six months cleaning out his mother's house and trying to prepare it for sale. It was the second time in two years he'd had to clean a house out after family members had died. The year before, his brother's wife, brother and their son had all been tragically killed in an accident. The girl had lost her entire family in one twisted moment. The families had been very close. The man had taken care of his brother's personal business upon his death. The elder had been a collector of everything interesting and had a house full of collectibles. The man would not squander his treasures, nor let it be abused.

They had stored the family's household at the man's mother's house. She had moved into an assisted living facility some years before, and her house had remained vacant. The man dreamed that someday she would be able to move back into her house and spend her last days there, but this never happened. The house was secure and made a great storage for the belongings of the brother and his family. The man knew his brother's wishes and was safeguarding the future of his niece.

After his mother's death, it was time for the man to prepare the house for sale. First was to repack his brother's things for safe storage. After finding secure storage, they had the task of moving everything from the mother's house to its new home. Next was packing up the remainder of his mother's belongings and putting those into storage also. His mother had given away most of her possessions long before her loss of memory. It was almost as if she was aware of the dementia creeping into her brain and wanted to be the least burden possible. This had always been a fear of the man's mother, 'being a burden'.

Finally, the house had been cleared out and the painting and repairs could be done. The mother had only lived in this house for ten years, and then it was vacant for another three. She was not hard on her house nor was her husband, as he spent the last years of his life there. The repairs would be minimal.

After getting multiple bids, the man decided he would do the work himself. He and his son had done this kind of work together before, and now they would do it again for their family. The man and his sister made agreements on the costs and materials and the job was done efficiently. The man also paid his niece to come in and do all the cleaning. She had worked with her mother at their cleaning service, and she would be perfect. So, all the work got done, the family got to be together during the Christmas holidays, and the money stayed in the family. It was a fraction of all the other bids and saved the family in the long run. It had also paid off. The house sold after one day on the market.

It was the day after Christmas that this idea had first come up. The man had an allergy to the paint and was feeling very sick for the past couple days. The job had to be done though, so sickness was not even an issue. The man and girl said they should take a trip to go see the family and reconnect their people. It had been many years since they had seen each other and it would be good for all their healing processes. "That's what my parents would want us to do," the man had said.

When he was a child, the man's parents would take him and their family on cross country trips every couple of years to see family. His parents were very strong family people and it was important for them to stay in contact with theirs, and get their children to know their kin. It was very fond memories the man had of these trips; some of the best of his life. He remembered his family and the adventures they had. The trips had ended as they got older. After raising seven kids, they began to do more of their own thing. And of course, the kids were doing their own thing also, sometimes with disastrous results.

The plans had been started that day. The family members were not ones to say they would do something and not do it. The man had a very creative mind and understood everything happened in steps. The first step was to come up with an idea, the second was to make it happen, and the third was end results. This is how he had been so productive in his artwork. Most humans spoke of things and never did them. This was the normal. The man pitied this in people. That Christmas night, mentioning this to his wife, she was fully on board from the first words. She also knew that their family needed something different, and this was a perfect step towards healing.

Extra hours at the man's tattoo shop, and being thrifty, made everything a reality. The man had inherited some money from his parent's estate but thought it would benefit his family best by putting it towards paying off their house. It took three years off their payments, which would benefit them greatly in the future. The man had saved money over the past twenty years and had decided to use some of this money for the trip. He was not one to take anything he had not worked for, and this trip would be all the sweeter from his, his wife's, and his niece's hard work.

In March, the man's sister had died of cancer. It had come upon her quickly, and now she was gone. The loss to the family just deepened. The man had purchased some head-stones for his family members, and now there was to be a new one. He and his sister had decided to bury the family's ashes on the man's land and had markers made to grace the spots. It had been a somber, cloudy day when the family buried their people. The man had brought the family Gong out to the spot, and they had all took turns ringing the spiritual sounds through the hillside. A crow had flown above the spot all the while. That week, the man began to make all the plans for the rental car. The trip was going to happen. The family needed this medicine.

That was all behind them now. Today was the first day of holiday and they were all so ready. The boy had spent his entire life around his grandparents. His mother had been on drugs intermittently throughout his life and his father pretty much had nothing to do with him. The boy's other grandparents had raised him half of his life. The woman had always spent much time with the boy. The son of her son, she took an instant bond to her grandson. Without her, the boy would never had known his father. The woman felt the importance of having him in his son's life and did her best for the two to bond.

As a little boy, the grandson would come to the man and woman's house every Sunday. They had lived in the country at that time too, but in the San Joaquin valley. The boy had loved coming to the house in the middle of the corn fields, riding the lawn tractor and catching frogs. Their bond had started at an early age and continued. It had been an easy decision for the man, woman, and niece to invite the boy on this trip. The lad lived with his other grandparents, and they were all moving to Crescent City from Visalia. The boy would be spending his high school days on the coast. The man and woman were very happy for him and his grandparents. Where they were moving was beautiful and there was not a gang problem. It would mean much less time of seeing him, but he would be living in a much better place than the central valley of California.

The family spoke over dinner with an excitement seldom seen in adults. The man promised an adventure of the mind and soul, which would recharge their energies and strengths that had been stolen from their lives. They spoke about the strange events which would take place on the road and how they would shape their experiences. Strange things always happened when their family got together and now this would be multiplied. Cosmic situations were coming their way.

The barbecue bacon cheeseburgers were very popular. It was always a favorite of the woman's. The man tried to do nice things for the woman because he knew he was not always easy to be around. He had major mood swings dictated by the severity of the everlasting headache. His peace of mind came from painting and creating. The woman and man had been married for many years. They had met when both their children were still young and both had come from heartache. They had been friends for many years, with their boys sharing that friendship, and then they had fallen in love.

They had worked hard together in their family tattoo shop. The man made the tattoos alongside his son and another friend, and the woman made the piercing. Together they had built a very successful business. They had built this house in the mountains after the purchase of the land. The last twenty-two years had been devoted to this business and the time and effort had paid off for the two. It was a unity which was in both of their destinies. Their love was a strong one. They had been through a lot together and would be through so much more, side by side.

After dinner, the four spent some time outside enjoying the sunset. The man told the others how the sunset would be different when they got back, and this was the last one they would ever see here like this. The others asked what he meant, and he said everything was about to change. This reality was just another reality in a timeline of events without time. The things happening right now have happened over and over countless times, just with slight variations each time. "You will understand this better when we are reborn on the coast," the man told the others.

"You're always talking some madness," the boy said to his grandpa.

"Just because you do not see does not make me crazy. I think you and all like you are the crazy ones, because you go through life with your eyes open but you cannot see. Your mind is the true sight and most have theirs closed. Things are about to happen which you will not be able to comprehend, unless you let your mind relax its restrictions. In this way, you will be truly free."

The words were punctuated by the cawing of the crow flying overhead. It had its eye locked onto the man's eye. The man noticed something in the bird's talons, and then it was falling towards him. He reached out his hand and grabbed the object when it was about waist high. It was a round object, flat on both sides, slightly larger than a golf ball. It seemed to be a metallic stone and had a symbol somewhat of a sun drilled completely through it. The man had never seen material like this. He had worked on aircraft in the Navy and thought he had seen all forms of metal. This one was foreign.

"What is that," asked the boy.

"It's the key," replied the man. The others looked at the object with awe. It seemed to be pulsing a strange light in the man's hand. It felt cool to his touch. The man knew this symbol somehow but could not remember the full extent of it. He knew in his heart that he had held this stone before and used it for something. The stone went into the man's pocket. The vibration from the object pulsed through his leg and then his body.

Hours passed while they worshipped the stars. The new moon was hidden on this eve to their trip. They spent some hours in the tree house that the family had built together earlier in the year. The view of the stars through the branches of the large valley Oak was astounding.

The man told the others how their trip would encompass one whole moon cycle and a half. This new moon was to be the beginning.

The man knew of the moon cycles and understood their powers. Most times, he could predict the positive or negative effects of the cycle. This cycle was tugging on the man's thoughts greater than ever before. This cycle was to be a new brighter chapter in their epic lives. All the other moon cycles had built to this one, gathering the energy for this new beginning. The man spoke of rebirth and a new time. The object in his pocket pulsed. The family felt as one.

It was late when the family came into the house. It hadn't seemed like it, but more than four hours had passed since they had climbed into the tree house. They were all in wonder of the loss of time. They were all hungry again, like they hadn't even eaten earlier. Their energy seemed depleted. The four took turns taking showers and getting into sleep. They wanted to be on the road early, daybreak if possible. They had wanted to get a good sleep this night but now, with the loss of time, would only get a few hours. There were no worries for them, though. They were ready and excited. The trip that they had created was about to come to reality. It was time to begin healing. This adventure was the way to do just that.

The man put the stone from the crow on his dresser, right on top of his wallet. He didn't know what it was just yet, but he didn't want to leave it behind. There was importance in this object. It was going to be something they needed on this trip. The man's imagination was already running wild with the adventures that lie ahead. His mind was filled with these dreams until his conscious thoughts gave way to the subconscious.

The journey ahead was far greater than he ever could have imagined.

Chapter 3

Just after sunrise, the family was on the road. The journey had begun. The idea of having the car the day before, parked in the driveway, was a good one. It had enabled the family to pack the vehicle and take care of all the last-minute details. Now, all they had to do was make some sandwiches and get their two small dogs into the car.

Getting up early had been no problem. They had been anticipating this trip for a very long time and were ready to get started. The trips when he was a child were the same. His father would rouse up the seven kids and his wife. They would be on the road at sunrise. Pulling out of the drive, the man was thinking how everything had already started out very smoothly.

There had been no debate about bringing the dogs along. They were part of the family. The contributions they had provided in the last two years towards the family's mental state was exceptional. They had provided companionship and friendship, and there was no way they would be left behind. The teacup Yorkshire and the Chihuahua Terrier mix were also best of friends. They would enjoy this adventure as they enjoyed all the adventures they were part of. They were happiest when with their people. Their bond was solid.

The man's dreams the night before were of an odd nature. He had dreamed of a stone that was speaking to him. The stone was only about an inch across and had two eyes. The eyes seemed to give off a light, greenish in color. It was on top of a body that looked to be made of a metallic flesh. It was only about ten inches tall with long wiry arms and legs. Its head looked much too small for the body. Like the head was from another being, borrowing this pod for its purposes.

The being did not have a mouth to speak from. His words were transmitted to the man's mind. It told the man that its name was Toomey. He had come to this planet long before any of the species now present. He had seen all the changes on this planet over hundreds of millions of years. He knew the secrets of the Earth and the universe.

When the man had awoken from these dreams, the stone from the bird was in his hand.

The man was disoriented when he awakened that morning. He had felt as if he were in a different place. There seemed to be a strange energy in the house, but then he remembered the others sleeping over. There was a faint smell of roses in the air. His sleep was not so restful the last hours of the morning; the images of the dream nagging at him. He was not one to get excited about things to the point of losing sleep. This was not the problem. It was the sense of premonition from the dream which kept him awake. Something was coming their way and the boy had tried to tell them.

His dreams, before, had been so vivid and far flung from normalcy. In the last two years, after the coming of death, his dreams had almost stopped completely but for occasional bursts of madness. Last night, his dreams had been one of these bursts. His dreams, when he did have them now, were of a premonition state. Things seemed so real in his visions. Sometimes, next day events would happen that would mirror the dreams from the night before. At times, it almost got difficult to distinguish what was really happening in the conscious from the subconscious.

The man knew all too well about madness. He had seen it first hand with so many of the people who had come and gone through his life. He had seen it mostly in his own family. He would never let himself fall into that pit. Instead, he used the dreams to give him ideas for his paintings and tattoos. Maybe a little something to fuel the mind for a story. He saw the visions more as a tool. They were something to use as a benefit and enjoyment, almost like watching strange movies.

The images kept playing through his mind as he rode down Mountain Ranch Road towards Highway 49. His dreams from the night before were of other times of his life. Things were the same, but different in ways. Some of the memories didn't seem to be his, but they were in his dreams like they were his memories. His wife in the dream was the same wife as he was married to now, but her eyes were green instead of brown. Her hair was also of a different tint, as was her skin, which was without tattoos. In reality, his wife had a full body suit of tattoos. The woman in his dream also spoke with an Australian accent. There were two moons in the sky; one full, the other a crescent.

His grandson in the dream also seemed taller and much older. He spoke with a strong voice and told the man a story. It had been a story about traveling through dimensions and time. How the stars and planets all lined up for the man to follow. The man and his dream wife had listened to the words, even as the grandson grew to fill the sky and then faded away. Yet still his voice spoke of the next time. The two were sitting atop a waterfall, below was a single being, sitting on a rock by the spring. The man could see the aura of the figure and knew it was his niece. He had seen her aura before and was familiar with it. He called to her but had no voice. His wife held his hand and looked at him with knowing eyes. He looked back to his niece in time to see her aura shifting into a large bird. The bird took the shape of a crow and flew toward the man and his wife. It landed between the two of them at their feet. This is when the man had awoken.

A backup of cars snapped the man out of his reverie. A crow flew in front of the windshield, casting a shadow on the man and woman. There were flashing lights and many cars. Looked like an accident up ahead. Funny, he thought, ten minutes down the road and already something out of the ordinary. The highway patrol was very efficient in these parts of the country. Accidents were a way of life on the twisted roads of the Mother Lode.

The traffic moved along smoothly. It was just minutes before the family passed by the scene of the wreck. A big rig, loaded down with logs, had taken a curve too fast and tipped off the side of the road. Logs were scattered all down the embankment. The driver stood by sheepishly while the authorities tried to get a handle on things. Funny, the man thought to himself, the second diesel accident in two days.

The man hadn't told the others about the accident yesterday, nor the events associated with it. He was very happy at this moment that he had kept it to himself. It had been a very disconcerting chain of events. The man was still trying to figure out just what had happened.

Luckily the delay this morning was minimal. No one got hurt. The road hadn't been blocked by the truck. They were back on the open road in no time. The crow, sitting atop the cab of the crashed truck, took flight as they passed by.

Soon they were on the highway. The woman had driven first so the man could get the stereo set up with his IPOD, and get the maps organized. It would be many miles in this car and being organized would be a benefit. They had decided to stay on back roads and highways whenever possible. The main interstates would be bypassed as would all major cities. The family knew if they were going to see real America, they would have to get off the interstate. They were not ones to fall for the corporate greed. Small business was who they were and small business was what they supported. This would be way more prevalent in small towns and hidden places. This is where they would find the real people of America.

The next couple of hours were beautiful. After leaving Sonora, it was all high Sierra from there. After crossing Sonora Pass, it was time to find a spot for lunch. At nine thousand feet elevation, this pass is one of beauty. The view was filled with waterfalls in every direction, and mammoth cliffs of granite. The Yellow Belly Marmots are abundant at this elevation and the family thrilled in seeing these creatures. A pullout by the river was the spot they were looking for. The family hiked off into different directions, happy to be out of the car for a bit. The dogs found it particularly fun to chase the marmots around, barking their happiness.

The family all gathered to take some pictures before having lunch. They had brought a small camera and were going to take turns taking pictures with it. Today was the man's turn and he got some good group shots. The water was rushing behind them. The man told the boy to be careful. Sometimes, his grandson was careless around dangerous situations; it made the man uneasy. The boy had crawled up a large rock next to the river and the man snapped the picture. "This was the first picture of many on this trip," he thought, and it was a great one. He continued to snap picture after picture, even as the boy came charging at him, flying from his boulder with a look of panic on his face.

The sound of the river had made the man's hearing distorted. A big rig full of logs had taken a curve too fast and was now spilling down the embankment. It was the same scenario as earlier in the day, except now they were downhill of the logs. The family had seen countless logging trucks already in the last couple of hours, and more than once someone in the car observed that the trucks were overloaded. The greed overshadowed any notions of safety. Now the family was about to pay the price for somebody's carelessness.

The boy had seen everything so clearly. With his grandma and cousin standing ten feet below him, their sight was blocked by the large boulder which was directly behind his grandpa, who was taking pictures of the three. He saw the truck take the turn too fast and roll on its side. He yelled, but there was too much noise for anyone to hear him. He jumped off the rock onto the rock his grandpa was on, twenty feet away, just in time to push his grandpa out of the way. His cousin later said it looked as if he had super human strength when he jumped because it was such a long distance.

The man landed at the base of the boulder very startled. He made eye contact with his grandson just before the log hit the boy. In the brief exchange, the two saw their entire relationship flash before their eyes. All the memories of their existence together came flooding through their beings at once. It was a look of knowing and deep respect.

The log carried the boy into the river like a cannon ball. It exploded in splinters as it smashed into rock after rock. The woman and girl saw what was happening and ducked behind a rock. The logs tumbled down the hillside like Lincoln logs thrown by an angry child. Splinters of wood were hurled everywhere. The sound of crashing was so loud it overwhelmed the sound of the river. Hell had come visiting the family once again. The dark shadows, hidden for a bit, encompassed their beings. Familiar feelings of dread, washed upon their souls.

The wood had barely settled onto the earth when the man leaped from his hiding spot. Why had he even thought to bring his family on this trip. He knew things were going to happen but he had pushed fate and went anyway. An explosion of pain rocked his right knee but the adrenaline pumping through his blood pushed him. He jumped to the bottom of the rocks where his wife and niece had jumped to. At the bottom of the boulders lay the two. They were well beat up but alive. One of the logs broke in two and a piece had jackknifed into the spot right next to the them. The log had exploded like a grenade and sent shrapnel into the two women.

The man jumped down and assessed the wounds. It appeared the woman's wrist was broken and she had a six-inch splinter sticking out of her calf. The niece's leg was bent at a strange angle and her arm had taken a very hard impact. Both had small splinters sticking out of their skin. They seemed to be going into shock. The man knew they needed immediate medical attention but the boy needed him even more at this moment. "Okay, you are both going to be okay, I have to go find the boy," the man shouted. The woman yelled something at the man but his mind was focused on rescuing the boy. It was all he could think of at this moment.

He climbed up on the rock nearest the water and began to frantically look for his grandson. His eyes were very distorted. Everything around him was foreign. There was a strange energy in the air that was unknown to the man. It almost seemed like a dream but the pain in his knee told him otherwise.

Downstream, about fifteen feet, he could see the lifeless body of the boy, stuck on a tree trunk which was wedged in the river. Movement to the left of the boy caught the man's eye. He could have sworn he saw a shadowy figure standing by the side of the water but now it was gone.

Through the blackberry brambles and poison oak, the man quickly made his way to where the boy floated, mangled in the water. He shimmied his way out onto the tree trunk and made his way to his grandson. The wood felt as if it could cut loose at any time and wash down the fast-moving rapids, but the man had to get to the boy. Maybe, by an act of God, he had survived this terrible ordeal. The man grabbed the boy's wrist and pulled. The boy flipped over and the man saw his face. Where his eyes had been, there were now just blank sockets. The boy's face was also pretty beat up but the man could tell something was wrong. This was not his grandson. This boy had a different nose and hair color than his grandson. Also, this boy weighed maybe one hundred pounds. His grandson had seventy pounds on this kid. This kid seemed to be wearing the same exact clothes.

The man looked in all directions to see if there was another body. Maybe there were multiple people at this spot and they just had not seen them. This boy was obviously dead, but the man tried to pull him to shore anyhow. About halfway back on the log, the boy got stuck on something. It seemed to the man as if something in the water had a hold on the boy and was playing a sick kind of tug of war. He pulled as hard as he could, but on the third yank, the tree came free and went careening down the river. The man barely had time to grab onto a low hanging branch and pull himself to the safety of the shore as the log and corpse were swiftly swept away.

Once, when the boy was small, the man and woman had taken him to the Sequoia National Park for hiking. They had gone to a bridge at Potwisha which was a favorite of the family. The boy had found a stick and was playing in the water with it. He had gotten so close the man was worried he would fall in. He told the boy to back away some but he had just laughed. The man took the stick from the boy and threw it into the water. It was quickly washed away. He had told the boy that would be what happened to him if he fell in. The boy could only see red from his grandpa throwing his prized stick. He rushed the man and hit him at the knees. The man fell directly into the river. Luckily, he had always had fast reflexes and had grabbed onto the rock. The water was to his waist and pulling him. The woman saw what was happening and instantly was there, pulling the man from the water. That day had ended at that moment.

The pain of his knee brought him back to reality. He must have passed out or something. It was as if he had just dreamed of that day so long ago but he didn't remember passing out. He sat on the bank and looked at the bloody mess before him. His knee looked like it had a terrible road rash which extended halfway up his thigh and halfway down his calf. It looked like a lawn mower had run it over. The man had to lay back and rest for a minute. This was all way too much to happen in a short time. His brain needed to process it all.

Instantly he remembered the others. They were a team and would need each other more than ever. He hobbled over to their spot to find they had already come out of their hiding place and were laying on the rocks on top of the wood splinters. Both women looked very distraught and pale. They looked like they were in and out of consciousness, as if they had concussions. The man was sure they had been hurt very badly and expected concussions to be one of their maladies. "Did you find him?" asked the woman, groggily.

"I looked all over but could not find him. I saw him get hit by that log and don't think he could have survived that. Let me get my breath, and I will go up to get some help," the man answered. He thought it best not to tell the others what had just happened with the other boy. He was not sure what happened himself. He didn't know if it was just a dream, delirium, or some form of madness. Either way, the woman and girl were in no condition to hear that story. The shock of the situation was overpowering their senses. It was all they could do to take the next breath. The man knew his mission up the hill was urgent.

The family hugged tightly. The tears flowed freely. At one time in his life, the man thought it would be impossible to ever cry again. The last couple of years had been so hard. How many tears could one person cry. But now he knew that was not true. The pain from so much death came flooding back into their souls with this new loss. Another tragedy in a string of misfortunes so common they seemed like they were scripted, like a test on the soul and mind. The boy had saved his grandpa's life, sacrificing his own in the process. The boy was a hero.

"Mourning will have to come later," the girl said to her aunt and uncle with a quavering voice. "Auntie is badly hurt and so am I. I think I have internal bleeding and need help quick. Your knee is mangled. If we are to survive this, we are going to have to get back up to the road. For all we know, no one even saw that truck go over the side. I suggest we all make our way together up the hill."

There was no way the man was going to let the others die. He could not even imagine losing these two also. The group had been spiritual guides for each other in the last two years. He knew he would be lost without them. The man reasoned with the others that it should be him that went. They should stay behind and rest. That way, they could be there in case they saw the boy. With these words, the two women reluctantly stayed behind.

As he climbed up the rocks on one leg and both hands, the two women had called out to be careful. Over the first rock, he found the dogs. They were hidden in a crevice in the rocks, and a pine branch had trapped them inside. When the man moved the branch, the two dogs jumped all over him with delight. Their tails moved so fast they were a blur. They didn't seem injured in the least. Their quick reflexes and senses had prevented injury. The man pointed to the women, and the dogs took off in pursuit. They loved their mommas, and their mommas loved them. It was what all four needed; a conjoining of energies that would make one strong collective.

The trek up the rocks was grueling. It took all the man's willpower to take each baby step. Halfway up, he came to the cab of the diesel truck. It had been nearly split in two with the impact of the rocks and trees. The driver hung lifeless over the steering wheel, suspended three feet off the forest floor. A marmot was under the rig ripping out wires. The man approached the cab and beat on its side. The drivers head rolled to the side and looked directly at the man. He would have fallen over if he had not been on his hands and feet. The driver's eye sockets were empty, as if they contained sight so long before but had been vacant for some time. His mouth sagged open and the man noticed his shiny set of gold teeth. Odd for a truck driver the man thought to himself. The familiar feeling of dread surrounded this corpse. The forest began to spin in the man's head. He felt as if he would be sick. The man circled widely around the truck, freeing himself of the dark sensations.

At long last, he made it to the top of the hill. It was maybe only forty feet to the river, but it had seemed like many miles in his condition. There in front of him sat the car. It seemed as if the truck had missed it entirely, but the man thought this would be impossible. How had the truck gone off the road and not hit their minivan? It was almost as if it had passed right through it. There was no sign even that anything had happened. No one driving by would have a clue about the destruction below.

As the man made his way to the front of the van, he noticed the large crow on the hood of the vehicle. The bird was eating something, using the hood as its dinner plate. As the man got closer, he saw the bird was dining on a strange object. It seemed to be a humanoid type creature but it was only about eight inches tall. The object was a gray metallic color. Its head seemed too large for its body. It looked just like the creature in the dreams of the man the night before. The figure seemed to be moving and making some sort of sound, like a whistling. It seemed to be trying to get away from the crow. The bird held the creature in a death grip with its black talons.

The man noticed the crow had an unusually green eye. The eye seemed to be casting a strange light from within it. The man made direct eye contact with the crow and suddenly he understood. The light from the bird's eye held knowledge. The man was very familiar and close to this knowledge. Also, this light was oh so familiar. It was the strongest sense of déjà vu the man had ever encountered. The knowledge and light seemed to be part of the man's being. It had always been. The man knew everything was going to be okay. The good energy always came with the bad energy. They existed together, just like everything else.

He got into the vehicle and fished around for his cell phone. The crow continued to look at the man, all the while enjoying its feast. The creature it was eating was still alive and would shape shift sometimes into something else. Once it looked like a lizard and another time like a small pica. The man knew he was in shock and was beginning to seriously doubt if the crow were even real. The sky had changed into a strange shade of orange. The air seemed to stand still.

The man tried to use his phone but there was no signal. Typical cell phone, he thought; only worked if it were meaningless. He dropped the phone into the center console and drifted into his subconscious. He thought of the time he was a child and had jumped off the benches in a steam room at his aunt and uncle's apartment. He had smashed his head against the hot rocks and given himself a concussion. He had laid around all day on the couch while his family had fun in the pool. His conscious and subconscious had become one that day. It was the day he first knew about the other dimensions, hidden away in our subconscious, blocked by an unseen force in our minds.

Now he was having that same feeling. Conscious and subconscious thought had become one and the man was stuck in limbo. He was helpless to get out of the vehicle. It felt as if he were dreaming, yet he was awake. His conscious thoughts of effort were intertwined with the subconscious memories of already fulfilling those efforts. He needed some water very badly.

The cell phone ringing began in the distance and moved closer as if in a tunnel. After the fifth or sixth ring, the sound was unbearable and the man forced himself back to reality. He fumbled for the phone, dropped in the console, and peered at the screen. On the phone in big blue letters were the words "Drink Up".

The man looked up, bewildered, to see a wall of water coming his way. The raging rapids were all around him. "How had he ended up in the river?" he frantically thought. The minivan was poised on the edge of a rock and now it was slipping into the river. Water was splashing all around the vehicle. Had he accidentally put the car in gear he wondered. "What happened" were the thoughts racing through his mind. He had been resting, awaiting his turn to drive and now he wakes up to this. The car was now floating in the fast-moving water on a collision course with destiny. It quickly began to fill with water as the man was tossed around inside. The water was so very cold.

Abruptly, the car came to a halt. It had wedged itself between two large boulders which were luckily in the middle of the river. The impact threw the man forward and he hit his head on the windshield, shattering the glass and his bones.

He was awakened from unconsciousness by the sound of tapping on the window. He looked around for the source of the sound, expecting a branch or something banging against the floating minivan. What he saw shocked him even more. Standing around the outside of the minivan were his family. His wife, niece, and grandson were all there and all seemed perfectly healthy.

"What's wrong grandpa?" the boy asked, "you look like you've seen a ghost."

"Aren't you going to eat your sandwich?" asked the woman, "you came back up here to eat and check on some things. What did you do, take a nap or something?"

"I guess I did," replied the man. He got out of the minivan thinking his knee would fail him, but it was perfectly normal. It must have been a dream, the man thought. It was a fucked-up dream, he also thought. His wife said he looked pale and was shaking. Things seemed to be spinning in the man's mind. He smelled a faint smoke in the air.

His appetite was gone but he knew he would need the energy. Something had just taken a huge part of his energy. It had been stolen from the man's soul.

As he was eating his sandwich, his thoughts began to come back to reality. The memories of what just happened fading like any other dream. Thoughts shifting back to the subconscious where they came from and are so well kept.

He noticed the others milling about together. The dogs were also with them. They seemed to be creating a strange shadow. It was like an echo of their every movement was repeated for a split second. It was almost like some computer programs that the man had used that weren't fast enough to keep up with the graphics. Even the dogs were leaving behind these strange trails. Shadows followed the groups every movement.

The man quickly finished his sandwich and got the others in the car. He was ready to leave this spot. Something was not quite right in this little oasis on Sonora pass. It was just the first stop of many, anyway, and they were all ready to get down the road to the next destination. Pulling away, the man looked in the rear-view mirror. Standing by the path to the river stood a tall figure dressed in black. Its face had no features. On its shoulder sat a large black crow. Behind the figures, the man could just make out the twisted wreckage of a diesel truck. The man sped off from this spot in a cloud of dirt. He did not look back again.

CHAPTER 4

The boy woke with a startled shiver. In his dream, he had fallen off a dam and was hurtling towards the rocks below. Something large had struck the boy from behind and sent him free falling. It all seemed so very real. Even the details of the bricks in the dam seemed so vivid to the teenager. Something was falling all around him, almost like snow. He woke up right before smashing into the bottom of the chasm. He was sweating profusely.

"Where are we?" the boy asked groggily. This was the first day of their trip but the car was already getting very uncomfortable for him. He was fourteen going on fifteen and growing rapidly. He was the second biggest kid in his school. Nothing seemed comfortable at this stage in the boy's life. All he wanted to do was play sports and have adventure, hopefully with girls. Drugs and alcohol hadn't entered his life. He was just a normal kid with a dream of being strong. A dream he followed.

"We're just now rolling into Bodie," answered his grandma. "We're going to go check out this little ghost town for a bit and let the dogs run around."

The family parked and made their way through the town. All the streets here were dirt. Most had become one with the earth. The buildings were from the 1800's and very worn, but still livable. There were a few park employees wandering around, but mostly tourists. The man was happy to see there were not an abundance of either.

The sun was plentiful, as were the spectral spirits. The man saw movement out of the corner of his eyes around just about every corner. Some of the windows to the old houses or hotels seemed to have voyeurs which were watching over the town. The energies did not seem bad nor menacing to the man. This was just a place where people had lived many years ago. Now they had left behind some of their energies. The man believed this is where all spirits came from. Kind of like a photograph of a past event left behind in energy that the living didn't understand.

It seemed to have been a hard life, mining on the eastern side of the Sierra Nevada. The weather extremes alone would have driven most sane men down the trail. Gold was a fever that got into people's minds. It was an addiction worse than heroin. So many lives had been destroyed in these mining towns. So much energy had been left behind. Mostly sorrowful.

The girl commented on the size of the town. There were at least a hundred buildings spread over about a ten-acre area. Houses were to the south, while the town was to the north. Many large mines intermixed with the two. The family hiked through both areas. The old houses seemed occupied still, as the businesses seemed like they were only closed for lunch. This place was still very much alive.

The family enjoyed looking for objects and interesting rocks. It was like a treasure hunt for them. They were a creative group who liked to make things out of found items. This place was only for looking, though. These artifacts were all to be left behind for future generations.

Walking through the old town streets, they came across the ruins of Bodie's bank. The walls were mostly crumbled, but there was enough intact to explore. The boy, being fourteen, was a master explorer. His imagination running wild, he was way ahead of the others. He had found a hole in the back of the bank and imagined robbers blasting their way out of a holdup. There was a small hill outside the hole, and the boy could almost see the horses there, awaiting their getaway.

Something nagged in his mind to go up the hill. He had ideas in his head before, which paid off for the better: Random ideas that seemed to tell him what to do: Some unseen force guiding his thoughts and actions. This, again, was one of those feelings. Almost like someone else telling him what to do or where to go. The feeling always got him very excited. They always led to adventure.

He climbed the fifteen feet to the top of the hill and was stopped by a fence. Along the fence on this side was much debris scattered about. There was so much old glass, twisted into strange shapes by the heat of the sun. So many old tin cans, most with their lids opened but still attached. The boy had visions of the miners eating their canned food from the can after a long day in the mines. Probably all they had energy for, he thought. Not even enough concern to take the lids all the way off.

The movement of a snake by his foot caught the boy's attention. He wasn't afraid of snakes, but had a serious respect for them. His grandpa had taught him long ago not to pick up snakes and not to make sudden movements.

Slowly he tilted his head towards the ground. Confusion was in his mind. There wasn't a snake anywhere around him. He looked more closely for a crevice or hole the snake could have gone into, but there was no snake. Again, by his foot, he saw movement. He squatted down quickly this time and spotted a pica hiding in the smallest of holes. How had he not seen this before? The pica seemed to have something in its tiny hands. The boy waved his hand at the small rodent and it raced off. Left behind was the object the creature had been protecting. It was a small skeleton key.

The boy could not believe his luck. The key was only about one and a half inches long, but it was in very good condition. It didn't seem to have any rust or wear. The rodent was protecting a very valuable item. The key swiftly went into his pocket. It seemed to have a strange feel to it against his leg. Almost like a vibration was being emitted from the object. Also, a strange warmth seemed to spread through the boy's being, emanating from his found item.

The boy had always been very adept at finding treasure. The man and woman had orchestrated elaborate treasure hunts for the boy when he was younger. They would make a map and bury treasures throughout the property. A made-up story about the discovery of the map, and the boy would be bubbling with excitement. Of course, he knew it was make believe when he got older, but at that time of his life, it was magic. The situation with parents on drugs and putting their lives first is hard on all those who have lived that life. The two felt a very close bond with the boy and wanted to push his imagination. They believed a busy mind was a healthy mind. Drugs were for those who didn't use their brains to the fullest. Clouding the brain was not the way to enlightenment.

By now, the others had joined the boy on the hill. He showed them enthusiastically the key he had found. The others were very impressed and began their own search of the area. There was so much debris scattered around. They reasoned that this might have been the dump or something similar. They were all having a good time poking around, nonetheless. Maybe another key would turn up.

Their friend, the crow, had returned. It's brown hue reflecting golden in the sun light. The man asked the others if they realized they had a guide. The crow had been following them all day. The girl said she had noticed this too. They looked at each other with a knowing glance. The bird made a clicking sound. The air had seemed to join the energies of the family and the crow. Their auras flowed together like a breeze of mist in the dry desert air.

The man made clicking sounds from his throat. He had long ago learned to speak the language of the crow. They were an interesting animal. He showed them a deep respect and observed their ways and words. The bird made eye contact with the man. It began to make strange movements with its head and beak. It seemed to be pointing them towards something in the distance. Its beak opened and closed, but no sound came from it. They looked in the direction the bird was gesturing; it was a course that they knew should be navigated.

The key in the boy's pocket began to take on a magnetic pull. It was guiding him in the same direction as the crow was gesturing. "Come on," the boy shouted, as he bound from the crumbled walls of the bank. He ran out into the clearing and only slowed enough to turn back to the others and wave them on. He had never felt anything like this before. There was treasure ahead and this time it wasn't make believe. He felt as if his heart was going to beat out of his chest.

The others were very joyful to see the happiness in the boy. It was his family too who had perished. The toll had been hard on each of them in their own ways. The group understood this in each other. They had all had hard lives, as all common people of this planet do. The situations of life brought on by living, taking a toll on all creatures. Theirs was made so much worse with the shadow of death lurking behind them at every waking thought. Mental anguish was a part of being human. With the good always came bad. With the bad always came good. This is what made the happy times all that much better. This family knew this all so well. The times had been so happy and fun in the past. The last years were shadowed much more dark and solemn. Adventure, once prolific, came so seldom any more.

The three spoke about how proud of the boy that they were. He had come from a broken home with no repair in sight. Luckily, he had two sets of grandparents who loved him and wanted him to succeed. The deaths in their family could have completely disabled many people for the rest of their lives. The family knew things though, deep thoughts lost to most humans. Their entire family had always been different than others. They were ones to see the truth.

They had decided at the beginning of the end to get on with their new lives. They knew nothing would ever be the same. This was truly a new beginning for the entire family. Strength amongst them all would create the ONE. This was the new way. The boy fit perfectly into this way. This trip was the final road to enlightenment. It was the end to such a long journey. Once again to embrace the beginning and the path their lives would be on for the next cycle.

The boy jumped into a small ravine and spun around. The key had a very strong pull now. He could not have ignored it if he had tried. A large tree trunk lay across the ravine and the boy ducked below it. On the other side was a washed-out area dotted with old bricks. It kind of looked like an oven but it seemed a strange place in the middle of a ravine. The boy poked at the brick with a tree branch. He was excited but kept his patience. He didn't want to get bitten by a rattlesnake.

A brick came tumbling down through a cloud of dust. The dust began to take on the shape of a strange creature. It seemed to move with reason and became aware of the boy. The boy felt suddenly sick. He thought he might throw up or even pass out. He stepped back and sat on the fallen tree branch. Looking skyward, he saw the behemoth of a tree which had once held this branch. The base of the dead tree was bigger than their car. The boy thought he saw a dark figure hanging from one of the tree branches, suspended from a shadow rope.

A strong breeze came from the silence. It blew the shadows the boy was seeing into oblivion. Also, the dust creature seemed to be writhing in agony and fighting for its existence. The boy watched as it became one with the desert, once again. The boy felt instantly better. He had felt the dark energy in his presence but now the good had returned.

The crow was sitting on the branch that he had seen the shadow figure. It was looking directly at him.

"Are you okay?" the woman asked from the top of the ravine. The others had all arrived just in time to see the boy stumble away from the fissure and sit wearily down.

"Yeah, I'm good," answered the boy. "I didn't feel good there for a minute but feel great now. Sorry if you guys think I'm a queeb."

"What is that?" the girl exclaimed, pointing to an object a few feet to the boy's left. The loose brick had unearthed something metallic.

The boy jumped to the spot and started digging with his hands in the loose soil. He had dreamed of this moment so many times in so many scenarios. He pulled his treasure from the earth. It was a small metal box about six inches by four inches by two inches high. It seemed to be of a strange metal which didn't seem corroded like all the other objects the boy had found. This box almost looked to be made of gold but there was a strange patina of green on it. In the center, engraved in a Jewelers precision, was an eye. The center of the eye, the pupil, was where the key hole was situated. On each corner, was an indentation of a crescent moon. The indentations looked like they had held small orbs at one time.

"What is it?" asked the man. He could see the boy holding a metal object, but his eyes couldn't focus correctly. He couldn't discern what the object was. The boy seemed to be blurry, and almost seemed to fade out of existence a couple of times. The man thought the sun was playing tricks on his eyes. Everything else around him looked normal. It looked kind of like the boy had found a portal and was crossing back and forth through it. The others saw the same thing. They too thought it was just the shadows from the tree playing tricks on their eyes.

"It's an old box," answered the boy. "And I have the key." There was no question in the boy's mind that the key in his pocket was the same as the one for the box. The key seemed to jump into his hand when he reached into his pocket. Bringing it into its familiar light, the key flew from the boy's hand into the center of the eye. The box sprung open like a jack in the box. The boy had to shake his head in disbelief. What just happened? The box in his hand seemed to be vibrating his entire being. It seemed as if the energy from the box and his aura were merging into one. It didn't seem like an inanimate object, but more like a living being.

The box held only one item. It was a tooth. It was a tooth like the boy had never seen before. It looked kind of like a fang from a big cat, but was much different. His uncle had given him a tiger tooth when he was little. He had a fascination with teeth since. The tooth in the box had strange ridges on the sides that seemed to be miniature teeth themselves. The tip seemed to be open, almost like a mouth. It too was ringed with miniature teeth. "It's a tooth of some kind," the boy reported to the others.

He looked up as he finished speaking these words to see the large dark shadow descending on the others. It came up right behind them and spoke in a commanding voice. "What are you doing over here?"

The boy stashed the box in his pocket before the park ranger even looked his way. "And what are you doing down there? A little treasure hunting?" The sun behind the man blocked his features from the boy but there was something disturbing about the stranger.

"We're just looking around" answered the man. "Is it not cool to be over here?" he asked.

The park ranger answered, "You can go anywhere as long as you aren't taking anything that could get you into trouble. Do you know what I mean?" The man felt very uncomfortable in the ranger's presence. Something was very wrong with the man. He wouldn't look at the group. He just kept his eyes on the ground.

"We're not taking anything," the boy said as he climbed out of the ravine. "I saw a lizard and tried to catch it and ended up in the ravine. I know the rules." The boy's being was solid again and fully in this reality. The man thought they had better get going. Nothing seemed right here. It was like they had come here for a reason and now they had fulfilled that quest. They were no longer welcome, if they ever had been.

When the ranger looked at him, the boy knew. This man's eyes were solid black. He had an expression on his face like he was a robot. He peered at the boy intensely for thirty seconds before turning away. He looked at the man and said "you folks need to stay here. There's someone who wants to talk to you." His long stride away struck the man as odd, surreal almost. Like he had stilts for legs.

"We better get going," the boy told the others urgently. "There was something wrong with that guy and we are about to get wrapped up in something that is not going to be good. We all know about the dark cloud and it is coming our way as we speak."

All the others knew exactly what he was speaking of. The dark cloud had been following them for a few years and they were vigilant of its presence. They were aware of the fact to steer clear of this energy. It only brought on hardship and sorrow. When they were given the choice, the decision was easy. They wouldn't have to get far away from this dread before they would once again find the light.

The group all headed into the direction of the car. The crow flew above them, cawing its racket. It seemed to be warning them of something while also warning some unseen forces to step aside. Apparitions and spirits of a time long past began to appear with the four. Almost as if they were guiding them on their path. There almost seemed a frantic urgency in some of their movements.

The four hurried along through the dirt streets. The car loomed ahead. A long, piercing shriek cut through the dry desert air. The group had never heard such sound. The man looked around. There stood the park ranger, both hands raised grotesquely above his head. The sound was coming from a device he held in his gnarled, long hands. The man couldn't make out what the object was, it was too far away. He just wished it would stop making that noise. The sound made his will come to an end and made him feel like giving up. The pull was to lay down in the desert and become one with the other spirits.

A strong wind brought him out of his daze. The energies around the group began to materialize. The family could see they were being helped by the long-ago inhabitants of this town. Women, children, and men, all dressed in their eighteen-hundred era clothes, encompassed the group. Even some spirits of dogs were with the group. The whole town had come to the aid of the clan. The spirits seemed to bring the family's thoughts back into reality.

What had the man been thinking? He had never given up on anything in his life and this would not be the start. The wind turned the perverse sound into a strange kind of garbled music; almost soothing after their nerves had been assaulted before.

The four were upon the car immediately and wasted no time getting in and speeding away. The group was very shaken. They had to focus their thoughts and energy to get out of there. There was no time to lag.

They approached the gate at the exit to the town. It was closed, and a park ranger was standing in front of the barricade with a shotgun and a very angry look on his face. The man began to slow the van, to plan his next move. This is when he saw the spirits of the town mob onto the security guard. They seemed to be dashing into his body. Light from the beings entered the man, only to exit as shadows. The ranger began to shake and shift appearance. He seemed to become different beings, morphing in and out of its' own dimensions. Finally, the creature succumbed to the barrage of spirits, and it, too, dissipated into a dust cloud, once again returning to the desert. The gate came open at the same time. The man passed by the guard house. The whole inside was carnage; like a living being had been torn apart. On the roof sat the crow. They passed through the exit with no more problems. A ray of sun touched their car, poking out of the dissipating darkness.

The road back to the 395 seemed to pass very fast. The family talked about how, when you went somewhere, the trip there always seemed so much longer than the trip back. Still, the man could not shake the feeling like they were being followed, or watched. His energy receptors were very strong. His senses told him something was out of the ordinary. There also seemed to be a different energy in the car also. Almost as if they had picked up a hitchhiker and were sharing the cockpit. The energy did not seem foreign to the man at all. It was as if it were supposed to be with the group. The family never once spoke of it, but this energy accompanied them the entire trip.

On the interstate, the man asked to see what the boy had found. The boy pulled the box from his pants, while explaining to the others how the key had dropped somewhere and he had not realized it. It had been lost back to the desert. He handed the box to the woman. All eyes in the car were on the box, as its eye, emblazoned on the top, was upon all of them. They seemed to have a connection to this box. Déjà vu was what the girl said it seemed like. Almost like we have held this box before and something strange happened then, too. It's like it has come around full circle into our existence again.

The box, and the thoughts it provoked in the group, filled the conversation for the next miles. The connection they felt towards this object was profound. Mono Lake was to be the next stopover. It would not be too far to get there. They had a loose agenda and were on no time constraints. They could stop as many times as they wanted. With the dogs, it would be necessary. The purpose of this trip was to see things and experience America; to have adventure once again. Having a set agenda would only create stress, and that was what they were getting away from.

The lake was a wasteland in an oasis of the past. Humans had come here and destroyed this land for the greed of a few. This place had once been a paradise for the creatures who called it home, and now it was a home to nothing.

The group spoke of the destruction the greed had created upon this planet. The few had destroyed beloved Pachymama. All for gain with no regard for the people.

It had been the same with longing for power. The greedy were the ones who made the rules for everybody else. These rules did not apply to them. They were the real villains: The destroyers of everything good and the bringers of the bad: The ones who twisted the people into their way of thinking through fear: Controlling the masses with fear, when the only fear should be of them, the ones in charge. The self-proclaimed One Percent.

The family did not stay long at Mono Lake. The group felt bad for the destruction, which their species had created on this planet. They all spoke of the desire to change things. The man told his niece and grandson that they were young. They might be the ones who made a direct impact. For all they knew, they might be the ones who changed everything; the ones who made everything right for the first time in thousands of years.

The group was very aware of atrocities towards the people of earth. They spoke of it often and on this day the talk was no different. They believed if no one ever talked about things, then things would never change. They would only get worse and worse. Deepening chasms of shadows where thoughts were forbidden. The talk was frowned upon by some who believed politics and religion should not be discussed in most environments. The group felt this was attributed to the fear and control put upon these people.

They could not see through it. Most humans were blind to the true things happening around them. They just went along with everything they heard or saw with their eyes.

The man always spoke of observing with our eyes and seeing with our brains. Our third eye was the true sight in our beings. Our First sense of the six senses. One most humans would never be aware of.

The talk carried them into Bishop, California. The crow seemed to appear sporadically throughout the drive. They were here to stay a couple of days. The man and woman had decided the first stop on the journey would be here. A close friend they had met through tattooing lived here and they had not seen him in a couple of years. The man and woman had come here once before and met up with the friend and his lady. It was a friendship which had no falseness. The fishing had been great, as well as the hospitality. It was an easy choice to make this the first stop.

Introductions were made to the niece and grandson. The friend had met the grandson many years before when he was just a toddler. It was as if they had all seen each other the week before. The true friendships always picked up right where they left off. Seamless stitches on the fabric of our lives. No expectations, nor worries, about the time in between. The only thing true friends want from each other is companionship.

Within ten minutes of arriving, the group was headed off into the desert in two cars. The friend and his lady were outdoor people and were guaranteed to provide adventure. Their jeep was a much more suitable vehicle for the trail through the desert than the minivan, but the family had no complaints. The van did surprisingly good for what it was. The trail was dry and the desert beautiful. They drove past some mammoth satellite dishes that were pointing to the heavens. The man explained how they were satellites in search of extraterrestrials and their communications. He had always had a strong curiosity about the true purpose of these large dishes.

There was a pickup truck parked by one of the satellites. A door to a small brick building at the base of the structure was open. The man saw a figure standing in the doorway. It seemed to be dressed all in black with a black top hat. The man couldn't make out any features, except the creature was unusually tall and very thin. He thought maybe it was just a shadow from within the enclosure he was seeing. The sight seemed so unreal to him. "Watch out!" the woman said with an exclamation.

The man's attention snapped back to the trail just in time to see the deep rut ahead. He spun the car to the left, gliding through the sandy soil around the grooves, up a small embankment and back onto the path. The man righted the car and promised himself to stop daydreaming and pay attention to the trail.

The car in front of them was creating a storm of dust. It would be forty-five minutes before they reached their destination. Although they had air conditioning to block the dust, the family would be very happy to be out of the vehicle. It already had been a very long day.

The place they arrived at was a pool cut into the earth in the middle of nowhere. The water was crystal clear and about four feet deep. Being in the desert, the temperature of the water was about eighty degrees. The boy said he thought he had been here before, but it was not possible. He had never been to Bishop. Still, he told the others how this place had seemed so familiar to him. He spoke of some carvings on a rock just over the ridge, pointing his finger lazily in the direction. He said the carvings were of a sun, kind of like the rock his grandpa had acquired earlier. The other was of an eye, almost exactly like the one on the box he had found in Bodie. The others all laughed it off and focused on the very pleasant swim they were about to enjoy.

A couple of hours had passed in the water. The group was enjoying the time together in such a pleasant place. They were all a spiritual sort. They knew where to find God; right out here in the middle of nature.

The boy could not get the thought of déjà vu out of his head. Finally, he put on his shoes and walked the short distance. He knew he was retracing steps he had taken before. Over the bluff, there was a small outcropping of rocks forming a small shelter. The boy knew. He went straight to the rocks, laid on his back and looked up. As he knew, carved into the stone overhang, were the symbols he had told the others about. He didn't know how he had known about the markings. It was a memory that was unknown in origin to him.

He ran back to the others and told them what he had found. They all laughed and said, "yeah right", but the boy was adamant. He convinced his grandpa and cousin to follow him into the desert. At the outcrop, he told the two to lie down and check it out. The two had full trust in the boy and did as he said. There, before their eyes, were the symbols the boy had spoken about. The man asked the boy, with wonder, "How did you know?"

"I'm telling you", he replied "I've been here before. I don't know how, but I have." The man pulled the stone that the crow had given him out of his pocket. He held the object next to the symbol on the rocks in front of him. It was exactly the same. The boy already had the box out and was handing it to his cousin. They need not have even compared the two. They already knew that the eye on the box was the same exact as that on the rocks.

On the short hike back, the man told the other two to keep this to themselves and not tell the others. The man explained that the others might think they were crazy. The girl already had the knowledge about their family but the boy did not. She knew the prophetic nature their family held. She also trusted her uncle's thoughts. The boy was of a different blood than the man and girl. His family genetics were different than theirs. He tried to understand the things his grandpa and niece told him, but he thought a lot of the time they were just crazy.

It was the job of his grandpa and cousin to teach the boy their way.

The man and his niece were different than other humans. The man and his brother had spoken of this often for many years, and their offspring were the same. They had always seen things differently than most and conducted themselves in their own ways. Their family had never been followers. They were not in the least manipulated with fear. They fed on the good energy around them and shit out the bad. They came from a clan of pure at heart people. These beings were true shamans who cherished the planet and respected other beings. Others could not ever understand this. They saw and knew things others couldn't even imagine.

When they got back to the swim hole, they all jumped in the warm water to cool down some. The slight breeze made the air slightly cold on their warm skin. The others asked what they had found. The man said the boy had a great imagination and had showed them some rocks with cracks that looked like symbols. He had been encouraged by his grandpa since an early age to use his imagination and make up stories and this was one of them. He had used this knowledge to foster his creativity.

The man told the others how proud of the boy he was. The use of your imagination was the most important aspect of your being. Being creative was being one with God.

Sunset was approaching, and it was time to get back. The drive back seemed much shorter. They saw a large gopher snake next to the road and the man seemed to get a calm vibe from the creature. They seemed to have a common bond of existence. The snake seemed to change color to the man but he knew this was impossible. The thought made him realize just how tired he was.

On the drive through the desert, the three told the woman about the symbols in the desert. She asked them why they had lied about it. The man told her about the strangeness of this and asked how they would be able to explain it. She said the others would understand, but the other three in the car agreed. It would be easier to keep it as it was.

The family checked into a motel a couple of blocks from the friend's house. It was a nice motel and the lady at the desk was pleasant. The man knew when she handed him the key that this was to be the first hotel key of many. This scenario would be repeated many more times in the next month. This would be the only hotel clerk on the entire trip that was holding a baby. It was fitting the man had thought. The trip was young and some young energy needed to be thrown into the mix.

Some pizzas and swimming ended the day. The man had stopped drinking when his family had passed. Alcohol had been a problem in the lives of his brother and their family. The man had seen the destructive powers of the bottle. A heavy drinker himself, he had stopped and never looked back. He had no cravings for alcohol and the thought of the taste somehow disgusted him. The others were not drinkers either. They were all smokers of the fine herb. A soothing of the brain, not a clouding was what they sought. Smoking was a tool to stoke the imagination and conversation. It was a gift from the earth that the greed had tried to suppress for so very long.

Conversation was much better without the cloudiness of alcohol. The man and friend talked about their lives in the last couple of years. Still, the man did not speak of the death of his family. It was not something he spoke of often, not even to his close friends. He had never been one to have many friends anyhow. His family was where his focus had always been. He had raised his son by himself for many years, and it had taught him the importance of family first and friends second.

The women had been in their own talks this whole time too. The group flowed very well together in the joining of auras. A very small crevice of moon was visible descending the night sky. It was time to call it a night. It had been such a long day. It was just the first day and it was already filled with so much madness. The family bid their friends farewell and headed to their room. This was an older hotel. It had a very cool character to it, the man had thought. It reminded him of the places his dad would choose on their childhood vacations.

After showers, the family was ready for a little lounge time. The man and woman hadn't had television in fifteen years. Every time they would rent a hotel, the man loved to have the television on. It would quickly remind him of why he got rid of the annoyance in the first place. It was all mind control by the greed. He had no time for this false reality. For background noise in this hotel, though, it was just what he needed.

The man had bought some blank books for all the travelers and pens for himself and grandson. The plan was for everyone to write some, every night, about the day. Write about their thoughts or just write nonsense. Just to use their creativity. When they got home, they could share their stories and maybe make a story from them all. Keeping their minds busy with imagination would be important during these days, the man had told the others. They would be experiencing so many things. They should use these events as tools to fuel their thoughts.

The man opened his book and was shocked to see some writings already on the pages. It was his writing, but he did not remember starting the book yet. He read through the words and noticed it was almost an exact account of the day's events. He had been thinking about what to write all day and this seemed to be all his thoughts, already written in words. Everything was there, up until the moment he opened the book. It was a strange paradox in the man's mind, which made his thoughts swirl in confusion. How had the story stopped when he opened the book? It should stop when he closed the book.

He opened the pen case he had purchased for the trip. He would write this ending to the first day. He had to find out what would happen when his pen touched the paper.

Inside the pen case, where he had safely stored it, was the stone he had received from the crow. The sun inscription in the middle seemed to cast a strange red glow. He had not remembered putting the stone in this case. Next to it lay another object. It was the key from Bodie. "How had it got into the pen case?" The man wondered. "Look what I found!" he exclaimed gleefully.

The others all looked up from their books at the object in the man's hand. "No way!" exclaimed the boy. "Where did you get that?"

"It was in my pen case, next to the sun stone. I was getting ready to write and there it was. Let's see that box you found."

The boy pulled the box from the safe hiding in his backpack. He handed the object to the man and looked on with wonder as the key was once again drawn into the eye. The box sprang open again. There was a warm glow coming from the enclosure that the man could feel in his mind. The object seemed to vibrate in his hands. He examined the inside of the box more closely. The tooth seemed to be fitted into the inside of the box with molding carved out of a strange substance. The molding was organic, but not wood or stone. It seemed to be a mix of wood and plastic and flesh. It felt a little soft to the man's touch.

The tooth was not the only object that had been in the box. There was also a circular shape depression and a spot for a spear kind of shape. The tooth looked very odd to the man. This could not have been of this earth. It looked to be part bone, part metal. Whatever it was, it was a tooth from an animal the family would not want to meet. The box seemed ancient. Maybe this was a fossil the miners had unearthed. Whatever it was, the man sensed enlightenment in the object. This box was tied into their trip somehow.

A flash from the sun stone stole the man's eyes away from the tooth. It was like a flash bulb had gone off. "I think that thing just took your picture," the woman joked.

The man knew. The object had just told him the truth. He picked up the stone and placed it perfectly in the vacant spot in the box. The box made a sound like a gong ringing in the distance. It put off an energy that was felt by all the beings in the room. The warmth assaulted all their senses. It encompassed their auras into its encompassing embrace. For a moment, all the beings in the room became one with the box.

The lid snapped shut. Just as it had opened, the box was now closed. The key had disappeared from the center of the eye. There seemed to be more of the green corrosion on the outside of the box. It was as if it were growing stone on its surface. The family looked at each other in bewilderment. "Wow" said the girl, "what just happened?"

The man answered, "we were just shown the truth. We can't fully understand it yet, but that is what has happened. This is one of the first events to happen to us on the road. Much more strangeness is going to occur and we must be ready. Mostly, we must open our minds and allow the truth to come through. Our thoughts have been blocked for way too long and it is time to take back our minds and souls. We have been chosen. We will see the true way. We have become stronger than the greed. They already know about us. They are scared. Our time is upon us. We will charge our souls through the miles and be reborn on the coast. We will be the ONE!"

The rest drifted off to sleep thinking about the man's words. Everything that had happened already had been unusual and the man seemed to understand it. They were going to have an adventure like no adventure ever before.

The man stayed awake all night. He couldn't get over the feeling that something was following them and watching their actions. He needed to keep vigilant. Sleep would come later when he was resting at home again. He picked up his book to write the last of the night's events. The words were once again already written. The account was again almost exact but there were slight variations in the true events. Almost like he had written it and then rewrote it again later. Whatever the case, it was very strange.

It was on this night the man decided to write the second book. He would write about the day, when they were all chilling around the hotel. After the others would go to sleep, he would write another tale. A story about the fight of good and bad. About the light and the dark and how the planet could still be saved from the greed. He would write a story about how all the creatures could co-exist together in harmony. This would be a story about Pachymama, the true god, and the people inhabiting her soils. He would talk about the defeat of the dark forces which had brought so much terror to the beings on this planet. This would be a book that future generations might use as a guide towards living with peace and unrestricted freedom. The man imagined the influence a book like this could have on the dying spirituality of a once proud species. He saw most humans as already defeated spiritually, but there were some who knew and wanted to turn our mother earth back into the utopia she once was. There were some who understood.

This would be a book for them. It would be a guide, a companion, a way to the righteous path. This book would be about only one thing.

The book would be about the truth.

CHAPTER 5

The girl was the first to wake. Sleep had been so abnormal to her in the last two years. Exhaustion made sleep come easy every night. The clincher though was the cookies her uncle would make for her. His baking skills were therapeutic. He would make marijuana infused cookies and it was all night sleep for whoever was lucky enough to partake. Anything to help sleep was welcome to the girl. The nights she would eat one of these edibles were the ones she slept fully and with rest. This was the true medicine of the planet. The herbs from Mother Earth.

It had been hard on the girl after the death of her family. Only months before, she had turned eighteen. She had gone down to her uncle's tattoo shop, in the valley, with her mom for her birthday. Her uncle had tattooed her while one of the other guys tattooed her mom. It had been such a great time for the family. That night they had gone back to the aunt and uncle's apartment and smoked up some good herb and drank some beers. The girl had never been much of a drinker, and tonight would be no exception. She left the drinking to the others. They were the professionals. She was happy with the herb.

The girl and her mom were sidekicks to each other. They worked together in their family business and hung out the rest of the time. They were more like best of friends. The girl was also very close with her dad and her brother. They had all formed a friendship throughout their lives, and as teenagers fit right in with their parents' odd ways. The girl's parents loved to party. The booze flowed freely in their house, as did the prescription pills. Throw a little marijuana in the mix, and the dad would speak in tongues. He had been a Seer who thought that the drugs opened his eyes to the reality. In truth, they had masked his true calling for the wisdom.

The mom had been prescribed pain killers by her doctor for pain in her back from a minor traffic accident. The doctor never took her off the pills, and stepped up the strength and dosage over the years. He had turned a normal soccer mom into a zombie. It was not his first time either. He had a reputation. It was all part of the greed. This guy destroyed other people's lives so he could have his nice house in Hawaii.

People talked of conspiracies while they were victims of conspiracies themselves.

The oldest daughter did not help the situation. She decided that a drug addict was not the kind of mom she had envisioned, and disowned her. It was a sad situation. It broke the mother's heart. She had always been the best mother to her children. When she needed them most, they did not all reciprocate. It takes many factors to destroy a person. Losing your family is one of the fastest ways to that destruction.

The brother and sister helped keep the household together. The four of them created the ONE. It was not normal living, but it worked. The four had so much bickering and fighting always breaking out. It was their way of communicating. When you saw through that small outside personification, you could see a very strong bond. This family was very close, and would remain so. They needed each other and relied on each other.

The accident had shaken the rest of the family. The girl had been over at her aunt and uncle's house celebrating an early new year with their grandson. About twelve thirty in the morning, the girl and her uncle became very uneasy. Something bad had happened or was about to happen. They could see the familiar feeling in each other's eyes.

The two had grown close throughout the girl's teenage years. She had become part of the hang out crew in her family's garage. Her uncle was a frequent visitor, coming over every Sunday to pick up her dad. They would go and see their mom in Stockton on Sundays. It was their time together and they chose to share it with their mother. They would bring back their stories and treasures from the day. They would leave real early and hit every yard sale on the way. The girl and her brother were always waiting for these times. They would be there every Sunday before the trip to Stockton and after. The bond had strengthened.

There was no need for words. The girl and her uncle both were headed inside to use the phone. Something was very wrong. It was tugging very hard at their thoughts. The man dialed his brother's number and waited with patience that came from deep within. The girl thought that it was probably the longest minute of her life. There was no answer. Not even the answering machine.

Cell phone service in these parts was not so well but his brother's cellular worked at his house. He only got his brothers symphony of sounds and barks which was his voice message. Something very bad had happened. It ripped at their beings. The man and girl sped to the car. They barely waved to the others as they raced out the gravel driveway. They flew the fifteen minutes to the girl's house.

They saw the lights from the police before they even turned into the driveway. The girl and her uncle knew they had just lost their family. They could feel it in their hearts. The police would later say that it was an execution style killing that took their family's lives. The man had demanded answers that never came. There was never a single lead in the murder of his family. There was not even a single bit of evidence and not the smallest of motives. The police had decided that it was a random killing. The man and his niece knew better. They would find out who had killed their family if it took the rest of their lives.

The two had spent the entire night and half the next day in the front yard. The police would not let them in the house and had many questions for the two. The girl kept repeating, through the tears, about how she didn't know what she would do now. The man tried to be the best help to his niece as he could, but his heart had been broken also. He had not cried since he was so young, but now the tears flowed like a river. This was by far the worst day of his life. Not only did he just lose his brother, sister and nephew, he had seen his niece's spirit die, too; along with his own.

It had been a long, hard road to get to this point in their lives. Almost two years had passed since that fateful night. The girl and her uncle spoke much about her future. He told her how all our decisions now would affect our future somehow. He would also talk about when bad things happened, it would be so much sorrow and confusion. It would be hard to think your life could ever be good again. But then a few years go by, and you are doing well. Happy times are back in your life. You realize that you wouldn't be having these good times now if all the things in your past hadn't happened. Good and bad. It's all a part of the cosmic game that all living creatures must play.

The trip had been very much anticipated by the girl. Her uncle knew the way. It was the time of rebirth. The shedding of the old. She was beginning to understand the cycles of life. She knew she was different than most. She could see it since she was a small child. Now things seemed to be clearer than ever before. It seemed to her, sometimes, that she held the knowledge of all her family. It had been passed to her that night two years before. Her strength seemed to grow since that night. Her family's energies had become hers.

She looked across to her uncle, lying in the other bed with her aunt. He was staring at the ceiling, but the girl couldn't tell if he was awake or asleep. It was still dark. There was just the soft glow coming from the digital clock on the nightstand. She woke up early every day at home and was ready to go. She felt like you could only sleep so much, and then the rest was wasting your day. "I see you," said an eerie voice out of the darkness.

The sound made her laugh softly. She and her uncle were always making jokes. "You ready to go" he asked her from the dark.

"Five minutes for me" she said back.

Minutes later the two were walking down the back street of Bishop toward the 395. The woman and boy could easily sleep longer, something their DNA differed on with these two.

The man hadn't even slept the night before. He had written the truth until the early hours and then rested his mind until his niece woke up. He felt meditating was just as good as sleep sometimes, but not a substitute all the time. In the meditative state, he was more alert to the surroundings while still resting. In this state, he was between the conscious and the subconscious.

They made their way to a convenience store, their dogs following closely. The small town at this hour, just after sunrise, was quiet. Later in the day, the traffic from the main interstate would bring many more tourists and travelers. The man and girl enjoyed the solitude while it was present. Entering the store, the man greeted the clerk standing just inside the door. He laughingly realized the man was a cutout poster of a beer commercial. He turned to the clerk and was relieved to see that she had not noticed the man's silliness.

The girl stayed outside with the dogs. They started to growl an angry growl that the girl had never heard from them. A tall man in a black suit approached her and asked for a cigarette. He kept his head towards the ground. The man had a terrible smell to him. It reminded her of the compost bin at her uncle's house. She told the man she didn't have a cigarette and he turned and shuffled off. The girl caught a glimpse of his face as he turned and saw that he had very wrinkled skin. His eye sockets seemed to be just deep canyons of wrinkles.

The dogs were still growling when the man came out of the store. He told the girl about the mistake inside when he said hello to the poster. They both laughed. He asked his niece why the dogs had been growling, but she just gave him a blank look. "I don't know," she stammered. "I can't remember. Something really weird just happened, but I can't remember what." The two looked about but nothing seemed out of the ordinary. They were the only two patrons at this store at such an early hour.

The girl walked with her uncle through the streets of Bishop. She commented on how she really liked this small town and could see herself living here in the future. The man agreed. The town held a very nice charm. The air seemed so clean here. The people were nice. There were hundreds of miles of desert in every direction, holding so many hidden gems. There seemed to be something else in the air here that drew the two. They spoke of this, but could not focus their thoughts enough to pinpoint what it was. The truth was just out of their grasp.

After a couple of blocks, the two were ready to head back and get the others ready for the day. When they arrived back at the hotel, the woman and boy were outside and obviously ready to go on an adventure. The friends had also arrived. They seemed to be a little irritated at the two as they walked up, coffees in hand. The woman asked, "Where have you guys been?"

"Just walking through town, checking things out," replied the man. "Sorry, we didn't know you were up already and ready to go."

"Well, no big deal, let's get going," the friend said. "It's already getting late, and we need to use all the daylight we still have."

"What time is it?" the man asked.

"It's past one o'clock," the woman replied with irritation in her voice. The man knew now why they all seemed so pissed.

"That's impossible," replied the man, "We went and got coffee and walked around for about an hour. That was at six this morning. Look, my coffee is still warm." He held out his coffee, but there were no hands reaching back to feel it.

"Well it's One now, and we are ready to go," the woman said. Her irritation was already subsiding. She was used to her husband and his strange ways. When he got with his niece, there was no telling what kind of oddities were going to happen.

The family hopped into the minivan and followed the friends once again. The man and girl spoke about the loss of time this day. What had happened to the hours after they got their coffee. They had no recollection of walking for over seven hours. And how had their coffee remained hot. The whole situation was very disturbing to the man. So many strange things had happened already in just the last few days. Had he been imagining it all or was some cosmic twilight zone being pulled on him.

The woman turned the van into the entrance to a very large park. Trees and ponds were in every direction. The man wasn't even offered a chance behind the wheel. The woman saw that he was acting very strangely and wasn't going to chance the safety of the rest of the group. The last few days she had observed many oddities in her husband's actions. He had always acted strangely, but this was different. His actions were of a schizophrenic nature. Mixing reality and fantasy, and not knowing where the line of either stopped. He had been talking about strange events coming their way. He also spoke of odd things that had already happened to the group along the way that the others did not remember.

The two groups found a secluded spot in the corner of the park. The man had been dreaming of fishing for some time, and here they were. The family had always enjoyed fishing together and planned on angling as much as possible on this trip. They had not had many opportunities over the past years. Now was the time to make up for lost fish. The man had a worm in the water before all the bags had been placed on the table.

The first fish came before anyone else got a line in the water. This place was going to be a good one. Every cast after that was filled with action. The whole family and friends got into this fishing frenzy. They were just catching bluegill, but it was the action they were out for. "Trophy fish only come after catching hundreds of small fish," the man reasoned to the others.

The boy wandered off in his own direction as the adults stayed close to the picnic area. This is where the smoking pit would be. The boy was not old enough to smoke, and the grandparents did not want to influence him into it. He was a sportsman. The grandpa had explained to him that sports and pot did not go together. Most kids that started smoking pot, quit playing sports. The man, nor woman, wanted to be responsible for that. Their grandson had a dream, and they wanted him to follow it.

Hours had passed before the boy came back. He had brought a flotation device and was floating while fishing. He told the others that he had found a cave that went under the water. The friend told him to be careful. There were large snapping turtles out here. The boy laughed in the cynical style of a teenager and said it was no turtle cave.

"Come on," the boy said, "I'll show you". The man and girl, once again, got to their feet to follow the boy. After seeing the symbols, the day before, there was no way they could not check this out. The boy led them to a point of land protruding into the water. There was a large tree fallen into the water making a small dam. At first it looked like a beaver dam, but the man noticed Mother Nature had made this blockage. "Over here," the boy said over his shoulder as he hiked to the far side of the fallen tree.

On the bank of the pond, hidden by the tree, was an opening. "In there," the boy pointed. The man and girl stuck their heads into the enclosure. The whole opening was about three feet around. It took their eyes a bit to adjust, and then they saw the finger marks. Like someone had dug this cave out with their bare hands.

They could not tell how deep the cave was. The man asked the girl, "you got your lighter?"

Light from the Bic illuminated the inside of the cave. It was about fifteen feet deep and had a small hill in the middle. They could see to the back of the cave, but only the top. The bottom was blocked by the small uprising of soil. "I'm going in," the girl said as she was breaching the entrance. She climbed swiftly through the small tunnel until the man could only see the bottom of her feet. The girl's feet began to shake violently. At the same time, a sound was emitting from her throat that made the man's skin crawl. The man leaped into action to help his niece. He was jumping into the entrance when the sound she was emitting suddenly stopped. The next sound was her voice rumbling from the back of the tunnel. "Found something!"

The man watched the girl slither backwards until she was next to him again. "Check this out," she said laughing. "I bet I had you all worried, kicking my feet like that and screaming." The two laughed, with the boy joining in. A good joke was never passed up by the family.

In her hand was a small piece of silver. It looked kind of like a cigarette holder, but it was solid. It had strange symbols carved throughout it. The object gave off a warm vibration to the girl. It seemed so familiar to her. Her dad had been a collector of so many things odd. His obsessive collecting of the odd had worn off on the man and girl. They too were always on the lookout for 'the score'. "This looks like one of my dad's treasures," she told her uncle and cousin.

The two were looking at the girl with wonder. Her hair, blond before, was now pure white. The object in her hand reflected light onto the girl's face, which made it seem to be shape shifting. Her face was becoming other people's faces and then changing back into her own. The girl's aura seemed also to be moving in a weird series of patterns. The man grabbed the object from the girl's hand and thrust it into his pocket. He told the girl that this thing was a part of it all and needed to be safe guarded. It was not meant to be held like that.

The words were punctuated by the burning sensation the object was making in his pocket. It felt almost like a hot coal. The man, no matter how much pain, could not take the object out of his pocket. It had to be kept from the others for the time being, until he understood it more. The effect it had just had on his niece deeply concerned the man. As soon as the object left the girl's hand, her hair turned blonde once again.

The man felt bad about the new round of lies he told the others. He said it was just a beaver dam the boy had found and nothing more. He spoke nothing of the object the girl had found. The family spent the rest of the day in the park playing Frisbee and fishing. The object burned in the man's pocket all day. It had made him begin to feel ill. He thought through his imagination that the thing was giving him radiation poisoning or something.

The sun was setting, and it was time to go. It had been a great day. The family had feasted throughout the day while the dogs ran all over. They got all the excess energy out of their little beings. The group was ready for the next round of adventure.

After packing up and grabbing some gear, the group headed for the cars. Halfway there, the man remembered he had forgot one of the fishing poles leaning up against a tree. He ran back to fetch it and discovered something floating in the water. It seemed to be a boy's body. This all seemed so familiar to the man. It was stuck on a branch that was floating in the water. The man fished for the log with his pole and pulled it closer. The body broke free just before it came to shore and was pulled to the depths of the water by some unseen forces. The man looked and looked but could not see any trace of a body. He knew he had always been a little crazy, but this was a whole new level.

The next few hours were a much-needed rest around the hotel. The women and boy spent the time around the pool. The man and his friend stayed in the room and shared tales of their lives. The man had been working on an epic project for the last two and a half years. It was a book of "masks, shamans, and other oddities of human unkind". He had worked on it every week for the past one hundred and thirty and was to continue through this trip. The book had been a kind of therapy for the man. A way of dealing with so much death while bringing out his spirituality. He had used his extensive library of reference for the project. Masks and spiritual beings from the planet were represented, along with some from the man's imagination. Painting and creating taught the man so very much. It was when he truly felt at one with all things around him. He understood the power of creation. It was the wisdom.

The friend now flipped through the book. Some people were uninterested in projects like this, barely giving it a glance. This friend was not like that though. They had been friends for many years. They had created together in the past. Theirs was one of mutual respect as humans and creators. They were of a breed of Tattooers unlike most others. They were not looking for fame or glory. They just wanted to create things and be one with God. They knew that spirituality did not come from the opinions of others.

The story came flooding from the man's mind. He had already said so much before he realized the words had formed from his mouth. It was the story that the man had held in for too long. Of course, his family had known about the tragedies that had happened. None of the man's friends did. It was not something the man spoke freely of. Until now. The pain and hurt were ebbing away with every word. The friend looked at the man with the look of anguish and horror. He continued to page through the book as the words assaulted his thoughts.

The man had lit a large joint that he had rolled earlier. The sun rays coming through the blinds cast a life into the smoke. Creatures and spirits were all around them, they just couldn't see them. With the smoke clinging to the energy, the spirits were clearly visible. The last word came from the man's mouth as his friend closed the book. The timing was exact. The smoke dissipated and floated into the suction of the air conditioner. Silence overtook the room. It felt almost as if the two had just finished watching a movie in which they were the characters.

Some time had passed when the friend suddenly jumped to his feet. "We've gotta go" he exclaimed excitedly. The sunlight coming through the blinds had been replaced by the sporadic glow of the hotels ancient neon. The red glow reminded the man of the hotels from his youth. The door flew open and there were the others. They asked if anyone was hungry and the friend said he had a plan. It was time for an adventure none of them would ever forget. "And since it's your last night," the friend had said, "it's going to be great!"

Off to the desert for the next round; grabbing some sandwiches on the way to build up their strength for the madness which was coming their way. They arrived in an open spot away from everything. The slight sliver of moon provided the only light. It was a natural hot spring they had come to. The hot water came from the hills above and ran into these pools. It flowed from one pocket to the other. The water became cooler down the stream. Once again, it was a magical spot in the middle of the desert. Their sorrows this night would be washed away in the mineral baths.

Power lines above the pools seemed very out of place out here in the middle of nothing. But there they were. Arcing their electric current like tendrils in the night. You could feel the electricity in the air as well as see it and smell it. Somehow, it just all added to the mystique of this place. The energy here was like no other place the family had ever been.

The water was very warm. The whole group got into the first pool, but the man and girl decided it was too warm for them. They headed down to the fourth pool, where the water was a tolerable ninety-five degrees. Basking in the solitude of their warm tub, the two admired the night sky. The Milky Way was very bright here, as were the stars. The absence of light from the city made all the difference.

The two talked about how the trip had been nice so far. So many cool things had already happened and they looked forward to more. They spoke about how they had earned this trip and paid such a dear price to make it happen. All the hard work was paying off. This was the beginning. The man spoke about how the moon was in a new phase, just like their lives. He told the girl how this moon phase was going to follow them their whole trip. "It's a good moon," he had told her.

Light to the left caught their attention. "What's that," hissed the girl. The family was always looking to the sky to see objects; they saw them quite often. This was no surprise to the man, nor was it something that created fear. He was always fascinated with the lights when he saw them. This one was no exception. It was a solid white light. It made very erratic movements in the sky. It almost seemed to be sending a signal through its movement. Whatever it was doing, it was moving all around the night sky very fast.

The object seemed to appear and disappear in ways the man had never seen. It was at one point and then another with no trail in between.

The light began to make a more pronounced motion. It was flying around in a circular orbit that covered most of the sky. As it sped up in this motion, the circle got tighter and tighter. The light became more and more one solid elliptical beam. When it had spun into the tightest of circles, it was hovering directly over the man and his niece. The intensity of the spinning light could be felt by the two below it. It seemed to be radiating an energy that the two had never felt before. It felt as if the light was penetrating their bodies, merging them into one.

With a flash, the light shot onto the ground below, encompassing the girl. The whole pool lit up with a green explosion of light. The man looked straight up into the light. It seemed to be a hollow tube of light going straight into the stars. The heat it produced was hot yet cold at the same time. It made the man feel like his soul was separating away from his body.

The water surrounding him brought him back. He must have fallen from the light and the water had brought him back to consciousness. The beam was still there, and the girl was suspended. She seemed to be paralyzed by the force. The girl made eye contact with her uncle. "Wake up," he heard the girl say in his head. The man sprung to his feet and grabbed the girl by her feet. She had begun to ascend into the stars. He held on with all his strength. He couldn't lose his niece too. She was one of the last. The water from the pool shot into the air like a hand and grabbed the man back to earth. Unseen energy held him in the green glowing water. He watched helplessly as his niece was sucked up into the light.

The man felt her thoughts tugging at his subconscious. "Help me uncle!"

He watched with hatred and vengeance as the light and his niece faded away. He thought with all his energy focused toward his niece, "I'm gonna get you back." The man's connection with the girl was fading. They had taken the last of this line of his family. She had been spared from the same fate as her family by the intuition of her uncle. He had been the one to convince her to come to his house that night two years before. He had tried to get the others to come as well, but they had declined the invitation. He had felt something terrible was going to happen, but none had listened except his niece. Now, they had taken her away after all.

He had made an oath to his brother and their whole family that he would take care of the children if anything happened to them. He had not taken that oath lightly. He would get the girl back.

The others woke him with shaking hands and anxiety in their voices. He was still in the water, but his niece was not around. He barely had a recollection of what had happened. The others were so full of questions. "Where was the girl?" they wanted to know. "Where have you been?" was the other question.

The man told the others that they were just kicking it and had seen something like a meteor or something. The man told them how they had risen to their feet, standing in the hot water, to get a better look at the light in the sky. That was the last thing that he remembered until they had awoken him.

The others told the man how he and his niece had wandered off about four hours before. The group had been frantically searching for the man and girl for the past three hours. They had passed by this pool numerous times and it was empty until this time. They had found the man sleeping in the corner, pressed against some rocks.

"Help me get out of here," the man said. The boy jumped into the water and steadied the man. He seemed to have no energy, a rag doll. The boy mostly dragged his grandpa out of the water and onto the rocks with the others. He laid him in a sitting position on the stones and the others could immediately see. The man's face had strange markings on it, symbols of a different people. His whole face was covered in these signs.

On the back of his neck was a strange incision. It was in the shape of a sun. It looked like the stone the man had been given by the crow, the boy thought to himself. The incision was deep yet seemed to be a scar already, like it had some super healing properties.

"How and when had the man got these scars and symbols?" the woman asked aloud. The group was perplexed.

"Let's get him back to the car," the woman said. The others helped the man walk the one hundred feet back to the car. It seemed like such a long walk to the man. His body felt like it had lost its density and was now just an empty pod. Finally, they had arrived back to the parking area. The woman opened the back of the minivan, and there, laying back on the seats, was the girl.

The girl did not look so well. It looked like she had lost fifty pounds from a body that was not overweight. Her hair had turned white again, and there was dried blood around her eyes, nose and mouth. The girl was having a hard time breathing. She went into a coughing fit and slumped forward. It was then that the woman saw the marking on the back of her neck. It was the same as the one on the man's neck. The girl opened her mouth to speak but just guttural moans came out. It sounded the same as her father used to speak when he was very drunk and high. A language long lost to the people of this planet.

"We've gotta go right now," the woman shouted. The boy gathered the man into the van while the woman got behind the wheel. The boy barely had his door closed as the grandma was speeding away. At the edge of the highway, she pulled alongside their friends and came to a screeching halt. With wide eyes, she said she would see them tomorrow.

"Where are you going," they asked her, but she was already speeding off into the desert night.

CHAPTER 6

The man saw the light before the sonic boom thundered the car. The others woke up with a jolt as the military fighter jet zipped by in pursuit of the object. They had been driving through Death Valley for over an hour. They had already stopped and looked at some of the awesome sights that the landscape provided. Death Valley was way more than the group had expected. Its painted hillsides and vast expanses of rocks were incredible.

The woman had drifted off to sleep before the others. It had been a hectic night for her. After her husband's episode, back at the hot springs, she had not gotten much sleep. She had tried to sleep after returning to the room, but the man was obsessed with his writings. He had stayed up all night and wrote in his many books. She didn't know what he was writing about, but she was happy to see her husband keeping his mind busy. He was consumed with whatever project he was working on. This was normal behavior for her partner.

The woman's life had been a hard one. She was widowed from an early age. Strangely enough, her husband had also died under mysterious circumstances. There had been a fire at the apartment where they lived. Many people would have died, but the woman's husband had gone door to door and alerted everyone. He had also carried many to safety that were unable to help themselves. After getting his wife and two small children to safety, he turned into a superhero and went into action. The papers hailed the man as a hero. No other lives had been lost. The fire had been arson, but no arrests were ever made. The woman had felt proud of her husband, but that did not help raise their kids. It had been a very hard road, widowed at such an early age, raising two small children on your own.

The woman was strong though, and had taken care of business. She had met this man a few years later and had fallen in love and married. With his child and her two, there was a full house. The experiences she had, losing her husband, had helped her understanding of what her current husband and niece were going through. She too was

47

close to their family. She and her kids had been accepted by this clan from the first introductions. Now she was there with the family, helping them through the hardest of times.

The times had been very hard. Her husband, an artist, had always been different than others. It was one of the things that had attracted her to him in the first place. Since his family's death, he had become somewhat schizophrenic. She had kept a close eye on him and seen the changes. Some had been subtle, others profound. Sometimes he would be almost normal and others he would be ranting about some notion that popped into his head. He had a hard time telling the difference between fantasy and reality.

Last night had been no exception. They had gone to the hot springs and everything was fine. Then the man started speaking of the electricity coming from the lines above. He was relentless in his conspiracies about everything. This was no different. He had wandered off with his niece in search of a safe place. They were gone for hours. The woman, boy and friends had become so worried. They searched the desert for hours only to find the two in the van, sound asleep. This, also, was the second time in one day that the two had disappeared for hours, only to show up and act like all was normal.

After she had gotten them back to the hotel, it was already three in the morning. The man ranted on about someone writing in his book. He had become so paranoid in the last years. Like someone was out to get him. He wrote all night in his book anyhow. She didn't know what he was writing about, but his hands were a blur as they sped over the paper.

After a few hours of sleep, a couple cups of strong coffee and loading the car, it was time to get back on the road. The woman was happy the man was going to drive first. She needed the rest that was lacking from the night before. They stopped at their friends' house for a quick goodbye.

The friends were concerned about the man. They took the woman aside and asked if she was going to be able to handle the situation. She told them that somehow her destiny had brought her into the path of this family. She didn't know why, but it was all meant to be. The things she had encountered in her life had prepared her to help deal with the things in her husband's life. It was all meant to be, she had told them. The two looked at the woman with admiration. The journey ahead was going to be a long, crazy one, they told her. They gave the woman and her family good energy and hugs for the road.

The sonic boom woke the woman. She had been having very strange dreams and had been deep in sleep. In it, she had been flying somehow, almost like hovering. There was a sound of loud buzzing and an obtrusive light in her dream that was very intense. The sound from the aircraft morphed her unconscious into her conscious. She sat up straight just in time to see the fighter jet pass by at a very fast speed. It barely was registering in her mind when the girl shouted from the back seat, "What the fuck was that?" There seemed to be a frantic energy in the car.

"It was a fighter jet, my guess an F-15. There must be an Air Force base close by. They probably use this area for their practice," the man said. His job in the Navy was working with jets from all branches of the military. He knew quite a bit about the aircraft. The light once again zipped by. The first time he saw it, the man thought maybe it was his imagination. But this time, there was no mistaking the orb that passed just above their car. It was bright white with a greenish tint of color. It was very fast and flying low.

The object was maybe only two hundred feet off the ground when it passed over the family. It was followed by a fighter jet, which passed by seconds later. It looked to be in pursuit but there was no way the aircraft was going to catch the orb. They were both flying so close to the ground. Being on an aircraft carrier, the man had seen many exhibitions of flight. This was different though, like something out of a movie. The sky had taken on a strange brown tint. Shadows were all about.

They had been traveling through a narrow canyon and now were emerging. The orb made one last pass with the fighter in pursuit. As the car vanished from the canyon, so did the flying objects disappear from the sky. The man pulled into the first turnout he could find. He scanned the sky with his eyes, but there was no trace of anything out of the ordinary. Nothing but that strange brown aura being filtered through the sun rays. He wondered where the aircraft had gone. He could have sworn they had come out of the canyon just as they were.

The man realized they hadn't seen another car in quite some time. He told the family they were going to stop for a bit and walk around. They needed to take in some of these awesome sights and stretch the pods out. Everyone piled out of the car, including the dogs. The man strained his ears, trying to hear anything, but the valley was deathly quiet. Even the wind had stopped. Everything felt very still.

"What just happened?" the woman asked. She was looking at the man with a very odd look.

"I don't know what that was," replied the man, "but I've never seen anything like it. Why are you looking at me like that?"

"Did you bump your head or something?" the woman asked.

"No. Why, do I look funny?" the man asked back.

"You are very pale," she said, "and you have a red bump right in the middle of your forehead."

"The bump was on my head this morning. I noticed it when I was brushing my teeth. I've been wearing my hat all day and forgot about it until you said something. By the way, where is my hat? I don't remember taking it off."

The group searched the car for the man's hat but could not find it. Maybe it had blown out the window when the aircraft had flown by. The man had rolled down his window to get a better look. Again, it was early and the man was already behaving oddly.

The woman awoke in the early hours of the night to see him staring at something in the book he was writing. She didn't think he had gotten any sleep all night. Now he was going on about his hat or something. She didn't really remember him wearing any hat that morning. For all she knew, it could have gotten lost the night before during all that mayhem.

The bump on the man's head was only visible because he had become so pale. Now he was gaining his color back, and it was becoming much more blended with the rest of his skin. He must have gotten it the night before, the woman reasoned. There seemed to be a pulse under the affected area. The bump seemed to throb to the man's heart beat.

The woman wondered often why strange things always happened to her husband. Her twenty-five years of companionship with the man had brought so much oddities and strangeness to her life. The extensive travels they had made together were a gateway for cosmic energies to be presented to the couple.

The family emerged from Death Valley. The clock in the car said eight but the man knew this was impossible. They had left Bishop at six thirty and it had taken them an hour and a half to get to Death Valley. They had even stopped for gas and sandwiches. The drive through Death Valley had taken them almost three hours the man would guess. They had stopped numerous times to take pictures, let the dogs wander and sight see. They had even stopped once long enough to eat some lunch. The man asked aloud, "how could it now just be eight? It's almost like Death Valley really didn't happen."

The group looked for the next highway marker and pulled over. The man checked the map and realized they were on the eastern side of Death Valley, headed toward the Las Vegas area. "So strange," he thought. "What had happened to the time?"

The girl asked her uncle how long they had all been sleeping. He told her that they had slept for the last couple of hours. The man's mind was trying to comprehend what was happening. Everything seemed so surreal. A strong breeze blew across his skin. It cleared his energy and his thoughts. This was all part of it. He had known it would be weird but had signed on anyway. The crow's caw drew his eyes toward the sky. The sun had a rainbow around it. The bird seemed to fly in and out of the color spectrum, its brown feathers reflecting the many colors. Its eyes were connected to the man's eyes, even at the great distance between the two beings.

A gust of wind blew the bird's hypnotic flow into chaos. It also brought the man out of his day dream. He shook his head to get his bearings again. There seemed to be a shadow of a man standing behind his grandson. The apparition dissipated in the strong gust of wind. The man looked at the others. How had they just slept this whole time, he wondered. The woman was looking at him now like she was about to have him committed to an asylum. The others too looked at him like he had done something odd. "Oh well," the man thought to himself, "I'm always doing something someone doesn't like anyway."

"Let's go," he said to the others. "We still have a long way to go today and had better get moving."

The family packed themselves back into the minivan for the rest of the day's miles. The woman couldn't stop thinking about the man's newest bout with insanity. He had insisted on getting on the road at four this morning. They had to leave the hot springs early last night just so they could get a few hours of sleep. No one had wanted to leave early, though. The desert air mixed with the warm waters was a great way to get ready for the many miles ahead. The man had also been on one of his story telling kicks and had entertained the group of desert revelers until just after midnight.

The family had returned to the hotel and drifted off to sleep. After they had all gone to bed, the man had gone outside with his writing books. The woman didn't know how long he had been out there. She woke up once around two, and he was not next to her. The man had awakened the rest of the group early. They hadn't even said goodbye to their friends because it was so early. The woman, girl, and boy had enjoyed much needed sleep the entire trip through Death Valley. They all hoped that the man wasn't going to keep them on this neurotic pace the whole trip.

The man insisted on driving some more. It was fine with the woman. After the lack of sleep last night, she would take as much rest as possible. The group passed by Indian Wells Air Force base. The man said that was where the fighter jet was probably from. The others asked what he meant. He told them about the jet flying over their car when they drove through Death Valley. None of the others seemed to remember. The man was getting a little irritated by it all. It seemed like the rest of the group was fucking with his head or something. Their memories were not the same as his, yet they were experiencing the same things.

The crew stopped at a gas station to let the dogs run about and get some drinks. They had just passed into Nevada. It felt good for the group to get out of California. The second state on the journey. The trip was becoming more and more real. The man and his niece went in the store first. With dogs to be looked after, the group would be taking turns on this trip many times. Someone would have to stay with the animals. After using the restroom, the man skirted around the slot machines that were calling to every sucker thinking they would win. The man had lived in Nevada for some years while with the Navy and had learned all about the gambling. It was built on greed and fed off greed; something the man had no time nor desire for. He worked hard for his money and would spend it wisely.

The man always bought something if he were to use the restroom. He felt this was the right way to be. Have respect for your fellow man and respect would follow. Many people could never understand this and many times the gestures would be unnoticed. The man didn't conduct himself in an honorable manner for recognition though. It was just the way to be. Treat people the way you want to be treated yourself. This is also how the man and woman ran their business. It is why their tattoo shop would be turning twenty-two years old on this trip. It had been lots of hard work and lots of respect for the people coming in through the doors. Egos had no place in their lives.

This store had coconut water. It was a favorite of the family. Approaching the counter, the clerk was looking very strangely at the man. She was a woman of about fifty, the same age as the man. She said good morning and the man replied. He asked her how far Las Vegas was but the woman just looked at him like she didn't understand. She gave the man his change and they exchanged pleasantries. The girl approached and tried to give the man money for the supplies but he told her no. She asked the man if he wanted help carrying the waters but he said he had it. On the way out the door, the man said to have a nice day, as did his niece. The woman looked so oddly at the man but returned the girl' and s comments with niceness in her voice.

After the others returned, it was off through Nevada. It wouldn't be too long of a drive through this state. They were going to pass to the north of Vegas and bounce right into Arizona. The woman spoke to the man about scaring the people in the stores. He asked her what she was talking about and she said, "The woman in the store said you were speaking in some sort of strange tongue. It was a language like she had never heard before, almost like it wasn't from this planet. I know you and your brother used to talk like this amongst yourselves but it really does freak people out."

"I wasn't talking in tongues back there. I was talking to the lady at the counter normal. I asked her how far Las Vegas was and she looked at me like I was crazy. Maybe she doesn't understand English well," the man said.

"Yeah," the girl said from behind. "Uncle was talking normal to the lady but she didn't understand. She talked to me normal though." The woman looked at her husband with annoyance. He was pushing this game a little too far.

The skyline in the distance was the sight the woman woke to. Her husband had been fumbling around with the map trying to figure out something or another and had begun to grumble. The woman and girl both brought out their cell phones and offered assistance. The family was not addicted to cell phones like most folks. They used them as tools to make everyday life all the easier. This was one time the phone was most handy. After finding the way around construction zones and through the highway cutting north of the city, the family crossed into Arizona. It had been a team effort to get to this junction. It was also the third state on this trip.

It was the first time for the girl or boy to be in Arizona. The man and woman had both been to this state but had never drove through it together. It turned out to be a beautiful place. The rock formations and windswept cliffs made its views magical. Around every turn was a new place of beauty.

The views were beginning to absorb the energies from the family's thoughts. Like going to an art museum, and after a few hours you are exhausted. You wonder how you could get so tired from standing around, but the thoughts from within your head absorb more energy from your being than anything else. It's almost visual overload. Then, you think about what you saw for months after trying to wrap your mind around the beauty you witnessed. Traveling through this beautiful countryside was the same draw on their energy.

With depleted energies comes hunger. The hunger in the car became an epic distraction. Tempers inside the vehicle heated up as the temperatures outside did the same. The pains of the stomach will make anger come faster than anything else. They were in the middle of nowhere. There would be no place to eat for quite some miles.

The man knew it was time to stop. A turnout at Feather River was what he was looking for. The wind had kicked up considerably. That and the dry air would make this a stop that wouldn't be lengthy. They just needed a bit of time to get their heads straight and the blood flowing throughout their bodies. Food was on the horizon anyway; it would not be a long stay. The group walked around looking at rocks and cactus. There is so much beauty on mother earth. Most people were too caught up in their lazy lives, they had no time to enjoy what Pachymama had to offer.

The woman found a rock with what looked like an eye in it. It reminded the man of a bird skull. She showed her niece, who was nearby, and the girl agreed that it looked like a head. The crow swooped down, almost flying between the two. It looked over its shoulder and made a strange twist of its wings, almost as if it were calling to them. Something fell from its claws. It was another rock. The girl caught it before it hit the ground. This rock was in the shape of an egg. A very small egg like from a tiny bird. It was all black with one red spot on it. The crow cawed and flew over the hill. The man saw, past the hill, a dark figure standing out by the highway. It seemed to be looking at the group. The man saw no cars or other vehicles near the figure. It was just there.

"I'm starving," exclaimed the man, "let's get the hell out of here." Down the road they rolled, passing into Utah for their fourth state on the trip. They would be bouncing in between Arizona and Utah for the next couple of days checking, out the awesome sights these two states held. This was all new territory to the entire group. They hungered for adventure almost as much as the hunger in their guts.

Outside of St. George, Utah, the man spotted a barbecue joint. This was exactly what he had been hoping to find. The family raced in and got their order going. It was cool enough in this spot to leave the dogs in the car. After getting their brisket sandwiches and side dishes, the group decided to eat in the car. Funny, the woman had thought to herself, they had been in the car all day and now they were eating their very late lunch in the little box. Nothing was normal in this family, nor on this trip.

The barbecue had been fantastic and very fulfilling. It had been the perfect amount, the man thought. The energy in the car returned to the easy level. Everyone had recharged their batteries and their moods. Now they could start thinking about a destination for the night. Sagacious plans were much easier to make correctly with sensible thinking. Intelligent thinking only came when you had fuel in your vessel.

The woman and girl used the maps and their phones to book a hotel room in Kanab, Utah. The town seemed small, which was what the group wanted. It was also close to the Grand Canyon, less than two hours. It would be an ideal place for the night. The family was going to the Canyon the next day anyhow, and now they would be close. The town being only about another hour away from their current location sealed the room confirmation.

Kanab turned out to be a very pleasant town. It was not difficult to find the hotel. The town was mostly two highways which crossed in the middle of its limits. This junction was Kanab. After unloading the car, the man, girl, and boy went for a walk to explore this little gem of a town. They were not disappointed. They stopped at a gas station to get some small cigars. The man and girl smoked these little turds on occasion, and this seemed like a perfect occasion. The drive today had been long and stressful. The walk back with a stogie would make things very pleasant.

The store they entered had a live bee hive in glass boxes and tubes connecting them. You could see the workings of the inner hive. The man had seen something like this before in Victoria, British Columbia. It was at an insect zoo he had visited with the woman. In that case though, it had been Leaf Cutter Ants and their tubes of highways had covered every wall. This bee enclosure was much smaller, but equally impressive to the man. He got closer to get a better look. The bees began to make a strange humming sound as the man got closer. They also seemed to be congregating in the corner closest to where the man stood. They were all buzzing their little wings as fast as they could.

"What are they doing," asked the girl.

"I don't know, something got them all worked up," replied her uncle.

"What's going on over there?" The clerk shouted from behind her register. There had been an old-timer sitting in the corner, next to the counter when the three had come in. He had not gotten out of his seat, even when the group was trying to look at some stone orbs sitting on the shelves behind him. Now the old dude had no problem getting up and lurking on the man. The bee hive had begun to vibrate, and the glass seemed like it might break. The lady behind the counter suddenly appeared on the other side of the man. Like a ghost, she was there. Her energy, combined with the old-timer's, seemed to envelope the man's being. He felt that familiar feeling of dread. It felt as if his body temperature had doubled. He thought he was going to be sick or maybe even pass out.

The boy's hand pulled the man out of the dark circle with a yank. The boy had a strong grip on the man's shoulder. They were at the door before the man could even wrap his mind around what had happened. The clerk and the old-timer stared at the group with their blank, dark eyes. A small sound that sounded like a screech escaped the old-timer's lips. The boy had pulled his grandpa and niece out of the store, just as the piercing cry emitted from the two in the store. He heard sounds of breaking glass inside the shrill. The screeching seemed to fill his senses. The door to the store slammed shut behind them, and only the sound of a few cars could be heard in the desert sunset. The crow flew so close by the group, the boy could hear its feathers whispering in the breeze.

"What happened?" the man asked, a little shaken up. He looked to the girl and she seemed to be in the same state of mind as he was in. They were both covered in sweat.

"You almost knocked that bee hive over," said the boy. "I was looking at something on the shelf and heard a weird rumbling. I turned around and you guys had your faces up to the glass on that beehive and were making strange sounds. It sounded like you were making them from your throats. The bees started getting all crazy. They all came together in the front chamber and made it all lopsided. That is when the clerk and that old dude came running over. They were very pissed at you guys."

The three decided it was best to get back to the hotel and rest up a bit. Too many crazy things were happening, and most couldn't be explained. They talked about the bee incident during the short walk back to the hotel. The man told the boy the way the situation inside the store had happened in his mind. The girl confirmed the story. The man told the boy about the bad energy the two in the store brought upon him, and the boy laughed. "You would have hit them both if I wouldn't have grabbed you," the boy said. "You were chanting in a weird language, and cousin was singing in. You had hatred in your eyes for the other two".

"It's because they were evil," the man said. The girl nodded her head ever so slightly.

"Whatever." The boy answered with sarcasm.

On the walk back, the man and girl convinced the boy not to tell his grandma about what had happened. His bond was strong with his grandma and he wouldn't lie, he told the others. It wouldn't be lying, they told him, just not telling. The boy had reluctantly agreed to the deception of the two.

The pool at this hotel provided a much-needed wake up. The setting sun turned the sky a magical array of colors; almost like the sky was one large prism. The water was a bit cold, but the extremely hot jacuzzi made a nice balance. The group met a few other fellow travelers and made new friends. A man from Wisconsin talked about the places he and his wife had been. They were on their way home. Another man and his wife spoke of the places they were going and where they had been. It was the middle of their trip.

The man and woman spoke about how this was the first part of their journey. They spoke about how they had planned to see so many things and visit family also. The more the three families spoke, the more the man thought how well they all flowed. Like they were all fish of a same group meeting up to swim upriver. The man understood about how energy flowed. He knew that some people's energy flowed perfectly with his while others repelled it.

The man believed this energy came from a long lineage. He saw the similarities in his family. He could see the traits which were common in their genetic group. But human genetics went way into the past and many people we met might share in the same DNA and ancestry as each other. Or maybe just their energy was appealing to one another. The kind of attraction auras would have. Whatever it was, the group bonded in a short time. The tree understood its roots.

The man really enjoyed speaking with these other travelers. They gave him and his group little tidbits of information that they would not have found from other sources; bits of advice on where to go that would pay off more than once in the future. At dark, the family was ready to get some more food. They bid their farewells and were headed back to the room when the man from Wisconsin stopped the man.

He told the man, in his northern lakes accent, about a quickening. He said that the man and his family were a part of this happening, and they should be prepared. As the Wisconsin man turned to go back into the pool area, the man saw the scar on the back of his neck. It was a strange sun shape. It seemed so familiar to the man. Beyond the gate, in the hot tub they had all just shared, was the lone figure of a man in a dark suit. He seemed to be just a shadow in the waning light, but also seemed to be looking directly at the man.

His wife calling after him brought his attention back. He hurried after the others. He had the key to the room. "What were you doing by that gate?" the woman asked her husband.

"I was talking to that guy from Wisconsin," he replied. "He stopped me after we left and said something but I couldn't really hear him."

"I didn't see anyone there," the woman said with doubt in her voice.

It was getting late. Living in small towns for the last thirty years, the man knew they better get some food before it was too late. He changed into some comfy clothes and grabbed his niece and grandson once again. They had seen a grocery store earlier and would go get some supplies. The fifteen-minute walk was filled with conversation. They spoke of the pool and how nice the people they had met had been. They also spoke of all the good times that were ahead of them.

After loading up on sandwich making items, it was a quick walk back to the hotel. There were many people out and about. The man talked about how he liked this town. It had a very nice vibe to it. Not to mention the beautiful views surrounding the entire valley. As they were soaking it all in, the man said he was getting a very bad feeling. He said it felt as though something very bad was going to happen. He had this feeling before. It was very familiar to him. It always ended the same. He had this feeling for the two weeks before his family had died. If only he knew more details about the sensation. Maybe he could have prevented his family's death, and the others before. His premonitions had always been vague, though. All he knew is when he got it, bad things were coming.

As they walked into the hotel parking lot, they noticed so many more cars than had been there before. Also, two tour buses were now present, and over a hundred tourists poured out like cattle. The man almost felt sorry for them. Crossing the lot, the group saw the dogs running in the grassed in area outside their room. The area was large, and the family had hung out there earlier with the dogs. They had loved running around, stretching their little canine legs.

The dogs were not running around playfully now, though. They seemed very agitated. They were shaking wildly as they jumped into their family's arms. It was obvious they were very happy to be back with their pack. The man looked all around for the woman but she was not in the yard. He called her name with no answer. It was not like the woman to let the dogs be out here by themselves. A serious sense of dread was washing over the man's being. Something very dark was going on here.

The three raced up the stairs, with the boy in the lead. The crow was perched on the railing, directly outside their room. The bird barely flinched as the three ran by it. The man noticed something in the bird's beak as he passed. He could have sworn that it was the tooth the boy had found back in Bodie. He could not be sure though, he had more pressing things to think about. The bird kept its spot on the railing, as if checking to see what the family would do.

The door to the room was ajar when they rushed inside. The table in the corner was knocked over. Again, the man called the woman's name. He rushed to the bathroom, but it was the same, empty. The boy said, "What's this?" He was crouched down in between the beds, looking at something. It was the woman's purse and its contents. They were scattered across the small space between the beds. Everything in the room was covered in a strange film. It was like the old 8mm film from when the man was a kid, but it wasn't in strips. It seemed to be formed over everything, like it was a laminate on reality.

The man told the others to wait there in case the woman showed up. He went to the office, two buildings away, and looked around for the woman. The office was full of tourists trying to check into their rooms. The man would not have a problem spotting his wife. She was covered in tattoos and had a full head of thick greyish black hair.

Heading back to the room with frustration and worry, a smell in the parking lot stopped the man. It was the perfume the woman always wore. They had been soul mates for a very long time. His senses were at one with the woman's. He called her name with no response. A flash of light in the distance made the lot light up with an eerie light. The man saw the woman standing over by the minivan. He only saw her in the brief flash of light, but it was enough to know she was distraught. She was looking as if she needed his help.

It was mere seconds before he made it to the vehicle. The woman was not in sight. Again, the man smelled her essence but could not see her. Again, the light flashed from above. The first one had caught the man off guard. How could there be lightning, there were no clouds in the sky. This flash he could perceive. It had come out of nowhere and filled the entire sky and air. It was greenish gray in color. The man could feel the light too. It felt almost damp and cool in the dry desert air. It felt very unnerving.

This time, the man could not see the woman in the light. Every other detail of his vision had been enhanced though. He could see, just for that one moment, the inner workings of everything around him. He understood in that moment. Everything was binary. It had all been prearranged. There were no trees or buildings, just series of numbers. Everything was a series of numbers which made up reality.

The sheriff did not arrive until the next day in the early afternoon. Something about not coming out on a missing person report for twenty-four hours. The man had explained the situation with the purse and knocked over table, but the police were of no use. Obviously, they had much more crime in this sleepy little town to worry about.

What did finally bring the cops was when the man was told he had to leave the next day. The hotel was filled up this day, and he couldn't keep the room. The rest of the family had stayed in the room the night before, hoping the woman would return. When the man had returned after seeing the light, the film that had been in the room was gone. His niece and grandson were both fast asleep, each sprawled on the opposite beds. The dogs were cuddled up next to them. Many hours had passed since the man had gone to the office. It was early morning now. Where had the time gone, he wondered. He spent the last hours of dark writing. He was obsessed, the truth needed to be told. Forces were trying to stop the story, but the man had a mission. He was not one to give up.

At first light, the man went to the office and explained to the clerk about the disappearance of his wife. The clerk had no sympathy for the man. He said he had a job to do and was going to do it. The clerk spoke to the sheriff when they arrived, before the man got a chance to. Strange, the man had thought, why would the cops speak to the heartless clerk first, when he was the one who had called. His thoughts were answered when he saw the face of the sheriff. The man had known this look from law enforcement before. You are a victim, but now they are going to make you the perpetrator.

They would turn it like you did something wrong. It was a scenario that had played out many times before with the man's dealings with the cops.

"Mind telling me what's going on here?" barked the big man. His shiny cop glasses and over starched shirt almost made the man laugh. These guys always put on this big guy personification. It was one of the reasons people disliked them so much. Nobody likes a bully.

The man was not intimidated. He spoke with confidence and respect. His speech and manners caught the lawman off guard. The cop felt something from this man that gave him fear. "I called you last night about my wife," the man said aggressively. "She's been missing since last night and we need to find her. I explained it all to you last night about the table and her purse. I really don't know why you just showed up now."

"I'll show up when I want to," growled the cop. "Now why won't you leave this place?"

It was then that the man saw the policeman's eyes, or where his eyes should have been. There were just blank sockets hidden behind the glasses. The man knew. "I'm sorry sir, you're right. We will load up now and wait around town until we find out about my wife. Sorry to be of a burden to you."

"Okay then, get a moving," was the thanks.

The man loaded the van with his niece and grandson in a hurry. He dropped the keys at the front desk, to the glaring stares of the desk clerk. "Have a good day," the man said with sincerity. The clerk's face cringed at his words.

When he got back in the van, the others asked what the plan was. "Well," he told them, "first, we've gotta get out of this town. This place is about to be very unsafe for us. Then we can figure out what we're going to do."

The man's words were topped off by the crow cawing as it flew next to the open windows. It would show them the way. The man felt it from the creature; it was their guide. It would show them the light. As the bird passed by, the man kept his eye locked to the green one staring back from the socket in the crow's skull. In the animal's beak was the tooth.

Calm returned to the family. Everything was going to be okay.

CHAPTER 7

The flash of lightning and awes from the family brought the woman back into consciousness. The dream she was having was difficult to fully grasp. It seemed to flow seamlessly into reality. Something seemed so familiar to her about this place she awoke to. Her heart was racing. The constant headache she experienced for so many years of her life had now gotten worse; much worse. She went to wipe her forehead and saw the small cut on the back of her hand. She didn't remember how she got it. It didn't seem to be painful, just an odd shape. The sky was a color like she had never seen. The hues were those of a rainbow. The entire sky was aglow with color. Everything seemed so odd.

"Where are we?" the woman asked the others. They all seemed to be so awake and full of energy. She felt as though she was still in the middle of sleep and fighting to get out. It seemed like she was still stuck halfway in her dream.

"We're just now turning onto the highway 67," the man answered. "We're going to the Grand Canyon."

The woman asked groggily, "What happened to me? I feel like I was drugged or something. I don't remember anything after checking into the hotel last night. I was having a dream about bees or something, and some light. I must have been exhausted. I don't even remember getting out of bed this morning."

"Funny," said the man, "you were the first one up and ready to go. You were so excited this morning. You said that you had looked forward to this day your whole life, and you were going to get the most out of it."

"Yeah, grandma," said the boy, "you went to sleep right after those grubbin good burgers. We all watched a little T.V., and then me and cousin fell asleep. Grandpa was writing and looking at maps when I fell asleep. We all wanted to get an early start."

The woman tried to understand what the others were saying. She had just been flung into this dimension from one in which things were happening slightly different. She did not know then, but it would all come to light as the miles passed. Many dimensions existed next to each other. She had just crossed paths with another.

The whole family had been very excited about going to the Grand Canyon. It would be the first time for all four of them. So many stories had been told to each of them over the years. This place was going to be magic. The energy in the car was at a bursting point, but very patient. It would be a long day and they would have to put up with a lot of tourists. They were going to need all the energy they could muster up now on the drive.

The family had decided to go to the North Rim. The man and woman had researched the trip extensively. Books from the thrift store were inexpensive and full of knowledge. The girl had brought a cache of maps, and the trip was planned. They had ideas about certain places to go. These tools they had obtained would help them make wise decisions. This is how they had heard about the north rim being much less crowded than the south. A little time dedicated to research would pay off on the whole trip.

They didn't have an agenda, but they still needed to make plans. There were things they had wanted to see their whole lives and this trip would be the perfect time to see them. Without basic plans, they would miss out on so much. Their homework prevented them from driving by sites in oblivion, like the usual tourist.

A herd of buffalo was a nice greeting upon entering the park. The lack of cars had made the journey pleasant. They had learned through their travels that buying a season park pass would be the best way. They did plan on going to many national parks on this trip. A large Crow seemed to be showing the family the path through the park. A couple of deer, some chipmunks, and a golden eagle finished the welcoming party. The park ranger gave the man a strange look as he handed him his annual pass and I.D. card back. It was a look that seemed to say the family was expected.

The first stop in the park was Imperial Point. The small road sign pointing to the left, and the lack of cars going in that direction, confirmed this to be the way. The drive to the first scenic sights took about twenty minutes, but it was beautiful the entire drive. Twisting roads of high pines lined the highway.

The first glimpse of the canyon took the family's breath away. Their excitement for the day had only increased since they had arrived. It was everything they had heard about, and so much more. The air was so fresh and clean; it was about sixty-five degrees. The sky held so many shades of blue, but it was nothing compared to the multitude of green surrounding everything.

Stop after stop proved to be better and better. The family was very happy they had come here. They all agreed that it was the most beautiful place they had ever been. The views from every angle were equally as nice as the ones before. The family spent some quality time at the turnouts. The traffic and tourists were very minimal. The family was surprised by this. The books had said to get there early, and they had been correct.

After more than a thousand pictures, the family was back down the road. Cape Royal was passed on. The junction to the left said twenty miles, but it would have to wait until another time. The main attraction here was the village, and they would head there. They had no idea how long they would be there and didn't want to miss out. It was a short drive to their destination. The beauty of the landscape was worth every minute of driving.

The parking lot at the village was mostly full, which was not promising. The other place had been such few people, while this was so many. The family decided they could check it out and didn't have to stay all that long. Although being full of cars, the group had expected so many more people than this. The man had thought there would be tens of thousands of people, and there were maybe a few thousand. There were a lot of cars, but there could be so many more. It didn't take long to find a space. It happened to be all the way at the end of the lot, but it wasn't a problem for them.

After parking and getting situated, the family headed off to the tourist spots. "All of the people appeared to be in a good mood here," the man thought to himself. He could see why. It was spectacular; awesome views in every direction. This was some of the most beautiful land in America; in the world, for that matter.

The trails did not allow dogs. The group would have to split into two. They knew this would happen at some places and they had made up their plan. They would just take turns wherever they went. On occasion, someone might have to sacrifice going some-place. They would have no choice but to stay with the little ones. They would deal with that or anything else that came up. They knew there would be some hardships associated with the decision to bring the dogs. It was well worth any inconvenience to have their canine homies with them.

The man and girl would go on the first adventure this day. The trail was nicely main-tained. It was surprisingly not very congested. If not for the Chinese tourists, the trail would be almost empty. They were in abundance: So many were taking photos: Some in very precarious ways. The man told the girl that it looked dangerous. Some of the Chinese tourists were even carrying their suitcases with them. The two tried to figure out why you would have your luggage by your side on this trail, in this beautiful place. They could not figure it out. It must be the greed, they reasoned. They were afraid of losing their stuff.

The man told his niece that these Chinese tourists were not regular folks. The aver-age person in China could never afford to come here. These were the rich from their country. They were part of the greed who took from the working people just to live ex-travagant lifestyles. All the while, the average person in their country worked long hours just to barely survive. It was the same the world over.

The sights of the canyon were incomprehensible in beauty and depth. The man had never seen anything like this in all his years. He had traveled extensively, but this was different. The two took so many pictures. Around every bend of the trail was another gem. They felt like little kids with the excitement. A fire on the other rim of the canyon obscured the view a bit. A couple of the other tourists were complaining. One even said he would ask for his money back. The man liked the smoke from the fire. He thought that it added to the ambiance of the place. He told the complaining tourists this and they agreed, reluctantly. There were many ways to see everything. No matter how awesome, the man knew that there were always going to be humans who complained.

As the man and his niece walked, they spoke of the road that had brought them here. They spoke about how their conversation had always drifted toward the path. How every decision affected your future. How bad things would somehow turn into good. They spoke of the healing that was already going on in their hearts and souls. The wounds had been deep. The family had been strong. They had helped each other. They had spent the time together healing their souls. The Grand Canyon was a part of that healing. The entire trip was part of the path.

On the way back to the others, the man began to speak to an older gent. The two appeared to the girl to become instant friends. They spoke to each other about where they had been and where they were going. They shared some travel tips they had learned along the way. The man felt a strong bond to this older man. He understood about energy and aura, and knew this man's energy flowed with his. Soon, the fact that they were both veterans came up. The friendship was set.

Walking back together with the man and his niece, the gent gave them some great advice. He said that Cape Royal was very beautiful and a place not to miss. He also said that the tour buses couldn't get up the road so there was much less of the problem with crowds. The two said they would be heading back up that way. A group of crows had been flying around directly behind the man's new friend. They seemed to be mimicking some of the tourists. They were acting with vanity, mocking the scenes before them. The man and girl did not let the birds' actions go unnoticed. They were the only two who had seen the beauty and strangeness of nature in front of them. They understood the animals and the animals understood them.

Passing by a large rock that was above their heads, the group was disgusted by the sight. A Chinese girl was poised on the rock, unsafely, while others took pictures of her from below. It looked very dangerous to the three as they passed. One of the crows flew close to the model and spooked her a bit. Suddenly, a rock shifted, the young girl came tumbling down. Her mirrored sunglasses shattered as they bounced down after her. Her too tight mini skirt split in two, revealing her hello kitty panties. Her red rayon top, once skin tight, was shredded. Her bra was see through. Like Saran Wrap, thought the man. She had no nipples. The girl made a grotesque cartwheel and was over the safety railing. At the last minute, her hand grabbed the bottom of the railing, leaving her dangling above the chasm below.

The man, girl and new friend saw it all. The young model had gained too much speed as she careened down the embankment. There was nothing the three could do as the woman slid past them. The girl sped past the group as they reached helplessly toward her. All the other tourists were standing around watching the spectacle in front of them. Most of them had their phones out recording the whole scene.

As soon as the woman went over the rail, the niece jumped into action. Her reflexes were lightning fast. She grabbed hold of the dangling woman's wrist and held on with a death grip. At the same moment, the woman lost her grip on the railing. The man was instantly at the side of his niece, grabbing the other hand of the woman. Together the two pulled the terrified woman to safety. She wasn't very big. She just came right over the rail and was on her feet, safely on the path again.

She just kept babbling on and on and saying thank you over and over. She wouldn't stop hugging the two. Her near naked form was forgotten in her mind. She had just narrowly escaped death. Without these two people, she would be dead on the rocks below. The other tourists all applauded the girl and her uncle. The girl was a hero. She had saved the other woman's life. She had seemed to possess superhuman powers for those few minutes. The gentleman they had been walking with, hugged the two and said that had been amazing. The other Chinese tourists never stopped taking pictures.

The caw of the crow sounded like laughter, echoing on the wind, dancing through the smoke-filled canyon.

The woman and boy were waiting for the man and girl as they approached. There was not a bad place to sit, so they were not worried about the wait. The man told the two about what had happened back on the trail. He told them how the girl was a hero. The other two seemed skeptical. They knew the others had wild imaginations and this place would fuel them. They also told them about their new friend, but he was nowhere in sight. The woman said they would talk about it after they got back from their own hike.

The man and his niece talked about the experience while they waited for the others to return from their hike. They spoke about how everyone was so fast to judge each other and didn't want to help their fellow man. They commented on how many people stood around while the lady went over the edge. So many of them could have just stuck out a hand, but they didn't. They would rather videotape other people's misfortune, so they could put it on the internet that night. These people took comfort in seeing others in misery. If others failed, they could feel better about themselves. They had chosen their paths very poorly.

These same people would talk about you but not know anything about you. They would be the self-proclaimed critics of everyone else. If they could judge everyone else, then they wouldn't have to adjudicate themselves. At the end of the day, when they were home alone looking in the mirror, that is when the truth came out. You can't lie to yourself.

After a time, people's words would brand you into something you are not. Then, you are like them in their minds, something they are not. They would try to make you seem like the bad person to the world, when in truth they are the bad. Then, something bad happens that need other people's assistance. It is always the blamed who are the first to help. One minute they are bad people, the next, heroes. It's sad how people were caught up in their own little spheres. "You have to be stronger than them," the man told his niece. "Be the one, not the many. The good carry the blame from the many, the bad. The good have no time to blame others. They are too busy creating."

The girl was thinking about her uncle's words as the others approached. A crow flew over the two, casting them in its shadow. She was happy they had all made this trip together. Their family had always been strong. Her aunt and uncle had proven this to her countless times in the past, and continued to show her the way. Their way was one of truth. A false face was not to be worn in public. A false face would come off anyway, and the person wearing it would be faced with the truth. So why not always strive to be the same person? A good person!

The woman and boy approached with huge smiles on their faces. They too found the beauty of this place enlightening. The woman made a comment about no one talking of the accident on the trail. She pointed out that people should have been talking about it. The man just reasoned with her that the Chinese had all probably gotten back on the bus, and the rest of the tourists probably just didn't care.

She looked at the man with a skeptical eye he was very familiar with.

It was time to head back to the car, but none of the group was in any hurry. They stopped inside the market and got some free water that came from the canyon. It was very refreshing. Some coffee at the same spot, and they were off. Crossing towards the parking lot, the man wondered to himself why he had worn sandals this day. He was not one to ever wear sandals or shorts. Today he wore both.

These sandals had belonged to his brother. The man had taken his brother to the shoe store a couple of years before, on a Sunday, to purchase them. His brother always complained to the man about a sore back but would do nothing about it. So, the man had taken him to buy new shoes after going to see their mother.

Then, the man had bought his brother and family an inversion table. If they weren't going to help their health, he would. The man had kept the sandals after his brother had died. They fit him perfectly and reminded him of that awesome day. This way, he could truly walk in his brother's shoes.

The family spoke about the rescue back on the cliffs while walking through the parking lot. Their car was at the far end. Second to the last spot. They quickly noticed all the different license plates. It distracted them from their talk of rescue. At least thirty-five states were represented. It was amazing to think that all these people came from all those places for this spot.

Finally, they arrived at their car. The dogs were very ready to hit the road. They were not very fond of groups of people, nor of cars. While getting situated, the people in the SUV next to them rolled down their window and gave a hello. The man and girl were surprised to see that it was the man they had met on the trail earlier. What were the odds of that happening, they wondered aloud. So many people here and so many cars and they meet the one guy, on the trail, who is parked next to them. Their friendship was meant to be, the man told his niece.

Introductions were made all around. The older man introduced the girl excitedly to his wife. He told her that the girl was the one he had been telling her about. "She's the one who saved that woman from falling into the canyon." The girl's aunt looked at her niece and then to her husband, first with shock, then with apology. They had been telling the truth. The boy also looked to the others with the look of knowing.

The gent's wife looked at the girl with admiration in her eye. She took kindly to the girl. Theirs was an instant bond. They had encountered an ancient relative from another existence. The gent turned out to be a double bronze star recipient. The man and woman felt an instant bonding to the older folks. It was as if their energies had crossed before. Their paths had been thrust together today.

While he was arranging something in the back of the van, the older gent approached with a stealth that made the man jump. "It's alright, boy," the older man said, "I just have to tell you something. Nothing is ever coincidence. Everything happens for some reason, but we are not usually sure about that reason. Our destinies have been planned since long, long ago to meet up today, in this place, in this very spot, for that matter. Even our cars being parked together was planned so very long ago. I knew your dad. He was a radioman in the unit I was in. He had received a bronze star for the same campaign that I did. It was at Bikini Atoll. That is all I can tell you now. The truth is coming your way. You are on the right path. Others also know you are on the path, though, and your group are making them uneasy. Things have been going this way for a very long time, and they don't want the change they fear you are bringing. You and your group have a strong power. It's as powerful as theirs, maybe stronger. So, stand solid my friend, our bond goes deep."

The older man was around the other side of his vehicle and backing out before the man even noticed he had gone. What an odd thing to say to him, the man had thought. Just one more brick in the road to madness, he concluded. He knew where this road was headed. He had been on it for a very long time.

The drive back up to Cape Royal had been well worth the extra time. The woman and boy apologized to the man and girl for doubting their story before. She told them it seemed so hard to believe, but she shouldn't have doubted them. The two were not upset at all. They told her that it was a hard story to believe anyway. They were having a hard time believing it themselves, and they were there.

The sights at this place were majestic. There were enough turnouts that the tourists never became a problem. The trails and vistas were flowing. The family enjoyed every turnout and trail they came across. Cape Royal had been worth the drive. They had passed on it earlier, but the lack of tourists away from the village called them back. The views from this area were much different than before. The tourists were so minimal, it almost seemed surreal. They met up with the older gentleman and his wife at least half of the stops; their paths keep crossing.

On one trail, a woman of about sixty was yelling at a Chinese woman to talk softer and watch where she was going. The Chinese did talk loud and were not concerned much with personal space. "But," the man had told the angry woman "this is just how it is where they live. It is how they live their everyday since they were born. They are not trying to offend you or anyone else. They just come from a place with way too many people. Personal space to them is not known like here".

The tourist was amazed that the man had told her the truth. At first, she had thought it was just some nut who was coming up upon her. But the man knew. He had an aura around him that was very soothing and trusting. The tattoos covering his body were a deception to his true being. The woman understood all this with the touch of his hand in her hand. She would never judge another person in her entire life. The lady had even called her husband and their friends over to meet the man. The man felt as if this all just added to the experience of the Grand Canyon: This awesome exchange of energy with some complete strangers.

At one of the last stops, the boy climbed out on a ledge. It worried the family. They called him to come back but were not ones to be frantic. The girl had stayed behind, talking with the older couple they had befriended. The rocks below the boy's feet began to crumble. He jumped back to the safety of the cliff. The overhang of rock didn't tumble away, but it looked like it might at any moment.

When he got back to his grandparents, his grandma told the boy not to do crazy things like that ever again. She was upset that the boy had put himself in danger. The family needed each other more now than ever before. The boy told his grandma not to worry. He would never do anything like that again. It had scared him. Secretly, his grandpa thought proudly of him for this. He had overcome his fears.

The family was exhausted after their long day at the Grand Canyon. After lunch and a few more sights, they were back on the road. They had experienced this amazing place. They had come early and were leaving early. They were passing the toll booth at two in the afternoon, there were hundreds of cars. Earlier in the day, there had only been a handful of cars in front of them when they had arrived. "Thank god we read those tour books," the woman said. They all agreed.

The drive through the desert continued to be beautiful. Smaller canyons, carved by thousands of years, dotted the landscape. Giant fissures opening the desert floor. They had heard about a bridge that crossed over the Colorado River that you could walk across. The cell phones did not tell about the spot nor did the maps. They would just have to ask around and keep their eyes open.

A small spot called cliff dweller called to the group. There wasn't much there but maybe it would give them some answers. There was a bar and grill and a bunch of mobile homes. The rest of the town seemed to be parking. The earth was very red at this place. The air was also very dry. The dogs would not get out of the car. The woman stayed in the running vehicle while the others wandered around. It quickly felt like all the moisture was being sucked from their beings. They were mummifying. The three were back in the car in minutes. This was not a place for adventure.

Down the road about ten miles was Marble Canyon. There was a sign for a native American cultural center. There would be answers at this place. The woman went right for the bathroom while the boy stayed with the dogs. The girl and man made their way into the building. There, to the left, was the bridge they had been looking for. They had just stumbled upon it.

The man and his niece both went inside first and enjoyed the very cool air. The boy soon joined them and they wandered through the small museum. The man would be on the lookout for native American books throughout their journey. He used them for reference in his drawings, and for the spiritual aspects. This place had some very good books. The lady at the desk could sense the energy from the group. They in turn could sense her energy. It was a good flow of auras. The clerk normally did not trust tourists, or white people, but these folks were different. These people knew. The man touched the clerk's hand when he gave her the money. She felt the light immediately. It was the ONE. She had read the prophecies. Now they were coming true.

The group left the museum feeling great. The lady's energy was very strong. They seemed to all share some of their energy with each other. The woman's hand gave off a very strong vibration, the man thought. She was special. One who was at one with the One.

The bridge crossing the Colorado river was impressive. The woman went back to the car quickly. The sun was so hot out here. The wind also was very strong, so wearing a hat was impossible. The man's head already was sunburned, along with his feet in those sandals. The view from the middle of the bridge was one of a kind. The height of the chasms was an impressive testament to the powers of the planet. It wasn't a long stopover, but was worth the time. The sun would not allow more. It was a place they would have to come back to someday, when it wasn't summer.

It was soon determined that it was time to find some place to stay for the night. Lake Powell seemed like the closest spot that would have hotels. This area of the country didn't have many people or hotels. The family liked that just fine. They weren't here to see people, just nature. The cell phone service had been sporadic all day. Now was no exception. It took some time, but the woman got a room reserved for the group for that night. Now they just had to get there.

The sun was setting as they rolled into Lake Powell. A tourist spot in the middle of the desert, split by the river, the town was a perfect place to stop. The side of town they were staying on was the more local side, not the tourist side. Cell phones guided the family right to their destination without any problems. They noticed a burger spot across the street and all was set. This room, not as nice as the others, would do. They were happy to find any place that accepted dogs. The man didn't understand, their dogs weren't destructive at all. He knew the destructive powers of children, yet they were welcome at every hotel.

The burger spot was everything they had hoped. It had a small-town feel, staffed by locals. The burgers were great, as was the service. They were happy to see breakfast burritos offered. They knew where they would be coming back to in the morning. While they were waiting for their order, the man and girl went outside to smoke. There were so many flies at this place. A terrible stench from the street corner caught their attention. There, motionless, stood the dark figure the man had been seeing. It seemed to stare at the two, but had no eyes. "Who is that?" asked the girl.

"That's the boogie man," replied the man, distantly, "watch out for that fucker."

"Watch out for who?" the woman said behind them. They turned to look at her and then back, but the figure was gone. "You guys alright?"

"We're fine, just a long day. Let's go get down on them burgers," the man replied. The girl had chills running down her spine from what she had just seen. What her uncle had just told her filled her being with dread.

Walking back to the hotel, the family noticed all the colors in the sky. The sun had set and now it was casting a myriad of colors. The man grabbed his camera while the woman and girl settled in to eat. The boy said he was going with his grandpa. He couldn't pass this up. About the third or fourth picture, a crow flew in front of the camera. "I got it," the man had yelled at his grandson. The crow was captured perfectly in the viewer. Its eye seemed to be looking directly at the lens.

The man continued to snap away. Suddenly, a very bright light enveloped the two. The man looked up just in time. He dropped his camera while grabbing the boy. "Run!" he yelled, but it was too late. The light had taken them. The big rig crashed into the hotel parking lot with a thunder like an earthquake. The entire building shook with the threat of collapse. There was an explosion, and then everything was eerily silent.

The woman and her niece ran onto the balcony to see what had happened. The others had been outside taking pictures somewhere, but they could not be seen in the wreckage. The entire parking lot of the hotel was torn up like a demolition derby. Even their minivan was a crumbled mess. It had all happened so swiftly. They had heard the crashing and ran to the balcony. By the time they got outside, the truck was coming to a rest right in front of the hotel. It was only ten feet from the woman and her niece.

It took many hours to clean up the wreckage. The fireman and auto wreckers worked tirelessly. Miraculously, no one had been killed. The truck driver had been slightly wounded, but that was it. He said he was swerving to miss a tall man and small boy who were standing in the road. They seemed to be staring towards the stars and had not seen the truck coming their way. He thought for sure that he had hit the two, but no bodies had been found in the mayhem.

The man and boy were the only two missing.

It was three in the morning when the fire department gave the okay to go back to the rooms. The guys still hadn't come back. The woman and girl were very worried about them. They had tried calling them on their cell phones over and over, but neither answered. They just kept getting their voice mail and the message was odd. It didn't sound like their normal message. Like someone else had recorded their greeting for them. The language almost didn't sound like English. The phone reception was poor though, and they couldn't be sure what they were hearing.

All the guests made the way back to their rooms. The other hotels in town had been filled, so people had no choice but to wait it out here. Fumbling for the room key, the woman heard the television. She pushed into the room to find the man and boy sprawled out on either bed, watching television. The man was writing in his book, and the boy was fidgeting with something. The room seemed like a crime scene re-enactment from the movies. Everything seemed so surreal. The television was playing a news segment about the accident earlier. So much footage had been taped. "Are you guys watching this?" asked the woman, pointing at the screen. The television suddenly went blue. The screen was blank.

"Where you guys been?" asked the man. "We were worried about you." He had laid his pen down to talk to the others when he saw the condition they were in.

"What do you mean, where have we been?" said the woman, "you guys went outside to take pictures and then that accident happened. Now here you are".

"I don't know what accident you're talking about. You guys left to get some ketchup for your burgers, and that was like three hours ago. Now you come back looking like that."

The woman raced into the bathroom to look in the mirror. What had happened? Her hair, normally gray, was now a bright green; her clothes were made of a metallic looking material and were of a style like she had never seen. How had she gotten into these clothes? She came out of the bathroom with the look of guilt. The others looked at her as though nothing was wrong. They were sitting in various locations throughout the room, quietly eating their burgers.

"Better hurry up, your burger is getting cold," the man said between bites. "It sure is a good one."

The woman glanced into the mirror over the dresser where the burgers sat. Her hair was normal again. Her clothes were the same as what she had been wearing before. She went out on the balcony to clear her head. She was awestruck with the colors of the sky, illuminated by the ending sun. She thought to herself that possibly the things her husband had been telling her hadn't been so crazy. Maybe he was having premonitions. Maybe things were coming their way. Movement in the parking lot caught the woman's eye. It was right next to their vehicle. She could only make out a shape, the shape of a tall figure, standing, looking directly at the woman. She noticed that the figure had no face, just a shadow where his features should have been.

A crow, cawing, drew her attention away. The large, brown bird was on top of their car. She felt good, comfortable, when she looked at the bird. It was contrary to the way the shadow had made her feel. It had made her uneasy. If filled her with a sense of dread and almost made her sick. The crow made all those feelings go away.

"You gonna eat that burger?" the man called from inside. The crow took flight as the woman was passing through the doorway to the room. The two creatures made eye contact.

The woman knew.

The truth was coming.

CHAPTER 8

The family was happy to find the burger spot open at such an early hour. Once again, there were many things to see this day, and they would need an early start. They noticed some police tape in the parking lot which wasn't there the night before. The lady behind the counter was very nice to the group. She told them the story from the previous night. A drifter had been stalking the patrons all day. Sometime, just after sunset, he had forcibly assaulted a young woman of about twenty years of age. The girl's dad saw what was happening and rushed outside. He beat that drifter to death with his bare hands. When the police arrived, they saw the condition the young girl was in and didn't charge her father with a crime. It had been justified.

The burritos were everything the family had expected. With the quality of the burgers the night before, they knew this was their place. They spoke about what happened after they had left the burger spot. The girl asked her uncle if he thought the drifter had been the man they had seen the night before. He told the girl that he wouldn't doubt it. That man was bad. Luckily, he hadn't tried anything funny with their group.

Things would be much different now around this area. There had been many drifters wandering the city. Now they would think twice before doing anything stupid.

When they went to leave, the man realized that he had been standing inside the tape on the ground marking the crime. He laughed to himself. Some creatures did not earn the respect to live.

The caustic smell that had assailed their senses the night before lingered in the air.

The man turned the music off for a few minutes to listen to the news. He liked to keep up on what was happening in the world. He felt the need to be informed was very important. His information came from so many different sources. Long ago, he had made a book of collages. He used different newspapers and magazines for the images and words. He had realized immediately that the different newspapers would slightly change stories. So, all the information put out there was basically the same, with slight variations. He realized that it was all fake in its own way. Just like the history he had been taught in school. It was then that the man decided to get his information from as many sources as possible. He would make his own decisions about what he read and heard. The man saw how easy the human herd was manipulated. The media, part of the greed, were masters of the manipulation. Theirs was a control entirely through fear.

A story on the radio talked about an accident in Albuquerque the night before. A big rig had crashed into a hotel there, killing four. Miraculously, more people hadn't been hurt, the reporter said. "Funny", the boy said, "I had a dream almost exactly like that last night. I don't remember much, but I do remember the truck and running for our lives. In my dream, grandpa, you jumped in front of the truck and made it lose control."

The woman said, "I, too, had a dream about a big rig crashing into a hotel. In my dream, I had been woken up from the sounds outside and ran out to see the hotel across the street in an inferno. You guys were standing in front of the blaze, watching its destructive forces." The family all spoke of the common dream. They believed that their thoughts were connected somehow. In the subconscious, their thoughts intertwined with each other, forming a different reality. In the subconscious world, they thought, they were in a different dimension.

The rest of the news was filled with the events at the burger stand the night before. People were calling in to give their opinions. Most agreed, the father was justified in beating the drifter to near death. He had tried to harm his daughter. How many other people had this nomad done this to? The police had said they couldn't find any info on the perpetrator. He had no identification, and his fingerprints were not in the system. It was like he never existed at all.

The news was quickly forgotten in favor of music once again. The family did not care about all the people's opinions about a crime, nor anything else. He was open to other opinions when he encountered them, but not to stranger's voices on the radio. It was nice to be informed, but the news and radio got old very quickly.

The drive through northern Arizona and southern Utah was spectacular. The road wove in and out of beautiful countryside. There were not many cars in this corner of Arizona. Most tourists were farther south at the Grand Canyon. Their destination this morning was Monument valley. One of the travelers they had met on the road had told them about the Valley of the Gods. The man had said there was much less people there. He had told the family that they should go there instead of Monument Valley. He had also said the entrance was free. The family would be on the road to the Gods.

The roads got confusing, and the signs pointed the cars in one direction. They were funneled into the tourist spot. Out of nowhere, they were driving up to the fee window at Monument Valley. They had never been here before so thought this was just the way to get to the Valley of the Gods. They were wrong. The dirt road led them through the valley. There were many other cars and jeeps with tourists and their guides. Everyone seemed very respectful of each other, though. People would pull out and let others pass with a wave. There were so many places to stop and take pictures. There was no need for a crowd in any one spot.

Tour guides, natives of the area, were driving the tourists around in open jeeps. The man thought highly of these guides. They had a respect like he didn't see in most humans. Whenever they stopped, the man would speak with these native people about the way. They knew the truth. They were the truth. The natives enhanced the experience for the family. This place was one of beauty and the people were part of it, not the tourists.

The sights of the valley outweighed any bad points. Overall, for a tourist destination, the family felt as if it were very nice. The rock formations, painted by the hand of God, towered above the tiny roads. Around every corner was a monolith of epic proportions. The three-hour drive seemed to pass quickly. The family had stopped numerous times to take in the sights. The sky seemed to be of a very deep blue, with clouds floating by. It was truly a place of beauty.

More than once, the man saw a flash of metal in the sky. Each time, he would search for the object but it would not exist. He saw the flash in the sky more than a dozen times when they were in this park, each time for just a split second. He had even taken off his sunglasses to make sure that there were no blemishes which may have caused a reflection. He told the others but only the girl confirmed that she had seen the same thing from time to time. It almost seemed like something was taking their picture from the sky. The feeling of being watched was very profound.

This place felt like magic to the family. It was so amazing, it seemed surreal. The dust and ruts in the road were the only bad part. The family had to go slow, which was fine with them. There was too much beauty to take in around every bend. They would miss so much if they were driving fast. After a time, the dirt road began to make the drive very uncomfortable. The discomfort began to overtake the majesty of the place, and the family could not enjoy it the same. It was time to get back to the highway.

As they were leaving the park, the road twisted up around the main parking lot and wound out to the highway. As they were passing the fee booth from this direction, they saw that there were hundreds of cars lined up to get into the park. It had been like the Grand Canyon the day before; getting there early had paid off. A flash of metal just over the booth caught the man's eye. It was the same flash he had been seeing for the last few hours. This time, when he looked, the object was briefly in the sky. It was visible just long enough for him to make out the shape of a disc. It seemed to be hovering in the blue, before disappearing into a cloud.

The woman shook the man back into reality. He had almost run into the metal guard post used to close off the park at night. He had been looking to the sky, which was not unusual for the woman's husband; getting them killed while doing it, though, was unacceptable. His eyes seemed far away as he looked back to the road. The woman knew that it was another part of the man's fantasy, spilling into his reality. She could see it by the look on his face.

Less than five miles down the road, the family saw the sign for the Valley of the Gods. It was a small sign in the middle of nowhere. Nothing like the trap they had just been to. If only they would have stayed on the highway. They would have found this place and had it all to themselves.

The man told the others how he did not mind paying to see such beauty. The native people deserved to make some money off their lands. The rich man of this world had desecrated the indigenous man wherever the two met. So many resources had been taken from the many to fuel the greed. The greed had no regard for the planet or its people. The natives deserved whatever they could get. They had protected the land for thousands of years. Without the indigenous people, there would be no Monument Valley.

The next stop on their agenda was to be Canyon de Chelley. The man and woman had read about this place in their books and thought it was a must see. The drive there was long, after the many hours on the dirt road. A couple of times, the group almost decided to pass on the Canyon, but in the eventually, they decided to go. They knew that they may never be in this region again and thought it best to go while they were here. They had read so much about this place, they had to see it and feel its energy. The man told the others if they weren't exhausted, then they weren't doing their vacation right. At the end of the trip, they could rest all they wanted.

Canyon de Chelley was what they were hoping for. The ruins of the native people's dwellings, tucked into the cliffs, was a dream come true for the man and woman to see. The binoculars they had brought along would prove to once again be very handy. The cliffs were quite some distance from the observation platform. It was hard to make out with the naked eye. Even without the binoculars, it was a sight to behold. Like always, the family took turns with the two sets of spectacles.

The feel that this place gave off was magical. The people had chosen well when they had made their settlements here, thousands of years earlier. The vibe was one of welcoming. The man felt at one with this place. The man and woman talked about how it seemed like people still lived here. It felt as if they would look to the cliffs and see people about their daily life. This place had energy left over from many former occupants. The family all had a sense that they had been here before. They all spoke about features of the canyon, only to see them at the next trail. Their knowledge of the area made it seem like this was a familiar place.

The large, brown crow was swooping in and out of the valley. It seemed to be performing for the group. A natural tour guide showing them the real way. It was then that the man realized that this was the same crow they had been seeing all along. The birds eye was green like the one before. It seemed to have a knowing connection with the man when they made eye contact. The man didn't know how this could be. They had traveled over a thousand miles already. It was very impossible to think that the same bird could be with them. But there it was. The man knew the connection. He knew that green eye.

As the day was getting late, the group decided they had better go. They would have liked to stay in this place longer, but it was not in their calling. The day's events had worn them out already. The yellow line stretched on as they passed out of the valley. Storm clouds were brewing on the horizon, and they all hoped for rain. The family paid attention to the desert plants as they raced by. There were so many species of cactus and other desert plants. The desert, seemingly dead, was full of life. This planet was full of life.

A hitchhiker drew the family's attention. There were not many cars on this small stretch of highway. The man said the guy was going to be waiting a long time for a ride. He decided, much to the complaints of the others, to give the stranger a ride. The figure was hard to make out on the side of the road. The sun was just beginning to set, and cast strange shadows throughout the desert. All they could see was a tall shadow with his thumb sticking out. The man slowed to a crawl as he pulled up to the hitchhiker. It was then that the man saw the stranger's face. It was dried up and vacant. Where the eyes once had been, now there were two dried up empty holes. The figure seemed to be frozen in time. It looked like it hadn't moved in a very long time. The mouth of the figure began to move as if it were trying to say something. This is when the man sped off. He had just been slowing to a stop and switched his foot to accelerating. The others were very happy to sidestep the nightmare they had felt in their souls.

At sunset, the family rolled into Gallup, New Mexico. The woman, on the road, had lined up a hotel room with a suite. This night the boy would have his own bed. They had brought an air mattress for the boy, but sleeping on the ground got old for anyone quickly.

This night they would also have more space for their own personal use. The group was all very happy for this. Being in the small car all day, then in small hotels at night, could get very cramped. Personal space would not be a thing in abundance on this trip. The family would have to work hard on not being frustrated with each other.

The hotel room was another mediocre spot to rest the bodies and minds. The space inside the room was large, though, and there was the couch for the boy. Two guys in the room next to the family brought distrust in the man. Something was not right about the two. They had a work truck outside their room, and they were sitting on the tail gate drinking beers and smoking cigarettes. They spoke in Spanish, which the man could understand bits and pieces of. The man had never looked at any other man in a lesser way just because of their looks. He felt that people who judged others by the color of their skin or what they wore were fools. The only color that mattered was that of their aura.

He made all his decisions on the way the people acted. Their true colors were hidden inside their minds and projected through their actions.

These two kept looking at the man's niece with bad intent. The man couldn't get over the feeling that something was very wrong. The crow had returned and was sitting on the light pole in the parking lot. It was making a shrill kind of clicking sound that was completely foreign to the man's ears. The two workers also noticed the crow. They looked to the man and saw something in his eyes that made them cautious. The man knew. The two men ambled off their tailgate and made their way into their room. There was a very thick tension in the air. War was about to break out in the parking lot.

The man gathered up the others and went in search of a restaurant. They had purposely booked a room on the historic route 66. Now they would dine on this fine highway, glorified by many. It wouldn't take them long to find a nice Mexican place. The man explained to the others about how Mexican food in the southwest was different than the food they got in their home state. It was called Tex Mex here. They used more tomatoes in their food here. The others loved the different foods they had been experiencing. This was no different. The food was delicious. The people at the restaurant were so friendly, dinner was a success.

Pulling back into the parking lot at the hotel, the man noticed the truck parked next door was gone. "Hope those guys didn't go driving after all those beers," he said to the others. After parking, they saw that the two men next door had left a pair of shoes outside their door. It was an old pair of shoes, obviously used for many years of work. They thought it to be strange that the guys would leave their shoes, but reasoned they must be coming back.

After getting situated in the hotel, and resting a bit, the man and girl said they were going to walk to the store. It would give them a chance to smoke a cigar together and get a camera card. The first had been filled up already with the thousand pictures the man had taken. The man also spoke of a firework stand he had seen on the way in. He had told the others that he would be buying fireworks at the first place he could, and he had meant it. Now was that time.

The walk, after dinner, would be much needed. It was less than a mile. There were no sidewalks on this stretch of the 66, but it did not matter. The two loved to experience parts of history. This place was historic in a greed kind of way. It didn't matter to the two. They needed to know aspects of everything. Opinions came from experiences, as did knowledge. If you didn't experience as much as possible, you were cheating yourself.

The store with the fireworks was closed. It was a convenience store, and the two thought it strange that it would be closed at such an hour. It was only ten and it was Friday. The drug store was open though, so half their mission would be complete. A very friendly store clerk helped the man look for the card they needed. It was five minutes of talking while the clerk looked for the right one. The man and girl did not mind in the least. They had come on this trip to experience America and its people. Anyone who wanted to tell them their story, they were happy to listen. It all added to the knowledge.

Unfortunately, the store did not have the camera card the man needed. All around, they had not gotten anything they had come for. But they had gotten something, the man had told his niece. They had gotten conversation. They had also left positive energy with the clerk. They would have to find a card the next day. While the two were talking to the clerk about SD cards, a local policeman came through the doors.

The cop had an issue with the man and girl from the time he had seen them walking into the store. He had been sitting in his cruiser in the parking lot of the store and had been lurking on the two. It wasn't often they saw heavily tattooed people in these parts of the country. The two were up to no good and the deputy was going to put an end to it. He had been waiting outside for over ten minutes and had got fed up with the wait. This was not a guy to wait on anything.

The man saw the cop walk into the store right away. He had dealt with many cops over the years who thought they were something they were not. Their training made them think they were better than everyone else. Their job was to uphold the law of the greed but there was no need for them to abide by it, in their minds. Most cops, the man had dealt with, were bullies. This guy was no different.

The officer stood behind the two as they spoke to the cashier. They could feel the bully's eyes boring holes into the back of their heads. The girl was becoming slightly agitated. She was young. This is how they would get you. They controlled you by creating a fear in your head. The man did not bow to fear. He accepted this as a part of life. He turned to head for the door and made eye contact with the officer. The cop was standing in an aggressive stance. He had his hand on his gun. "Good evening officer," the man said with sincerity. "We love your fine city of Gallup."

The cop looked at the man in disbelief. The anger in his face quickly changed to one of admiration. He hadn't known. It was them. The cop stammered out some lame apology like they always did. The man discounted these apologies. He had no time for bullies or their ways. Just because this cop could see the truth now didn't mean he wouldn't harass someone later. "Outer respect begins with inner respect," the man told the cop. The officer broke down in tears. The man and girl ignored the large uniformed figure as they stepped around him and out the door.

"You're a trip, uncle" the girl said. The man laughed loudly.

In the parking lot, the two saw a diesel truck with Jesus wrote on the entire side of it in some fancy computer print. They were laughing at the truck and the events in the store when the door of the truck opened ominously. Out of the cab crawled a tall thin man dressed all in black. His skin was very pale. His hat looked like it belonged to the guy's great grandfather, it was so old and dusty. The man and girl got a very bad feeling from this guy. The familiar feeling of dread had returned. Their bodies and minds put up their defenses.

The tall figure approached the two. There was no direction they could go to bypass the stranger. His truck was blocking their paths. The store was behind them but all the lights were off now. They were on a collision course with the bad. The trucker stopped when he was ten feet away from the two. The man had raised his hand in a stopping motion when the stranger was getting too close. The trucker had heeded the man's warning. The man felt a strange energy pulsing through his body. It felt as if he had the strength of many. The strong energy radiating from the girl met with the man's energy. The two had become one. The good!

The feeling of dread the two had been having turned to one of pity. This game had been played over and over since the beginning of this planet. The bad and the good battled over their differences for eternity.

The trucker spoke in a voice that came from deep within the being. It was a guttural growl that reminded the man of Tibetan throat singing. The voice asked the other two if they knew the way. The creature seemed to stare through the other two as it spoke. It kept its hands in its pockets.

The girl and her uncle laughed simultaneously. "We are the way," the two spoke in unison. Their voice together was projected through the night air like a megaphone.

The dark figure stumbled back a few steps. The words from the two seemed to have shaken the creature. It brought its hands out of its pockets, and the man saw. Its hands were gnarled up pieces of flesh and bone. They looked like a burl off an olive tree. They seemed to move stiffly and were encircled around an object. The man tried to make out what the creature was holding, but the being seemed to be fading in and out of existence. The creature's gnarled hand opened, and the man saw what it was holding. It was the same object the crow had dropped into his hand at the beginning of the trip. How had this creature gotten it?

The trucker raised the object towards the other two in a very menacing manner. The man raised his hands at the same exact time as the girl. They moved as one. A soft glow of green light radiated from the two beings' hands. The trucker seemed to be hit with a bolt of lightning. His body began to convulse and twist into shapes not humanly possible. The man and girl kept their hands raised even as they watched the other being twist in pain and finally disappear. There could be no empathy for the bad. They felt no remorse.

The two talked about so many things on the walk back. They spoke about how strange things always happened whenever they were together. The man told his niece that it was the way their families had always been. Strong energy abounded when they were united. Once again, the talk turned to the dissimilarities their family had to most other humans. They had been looked at like crazies their whole lives. How could the family see things when most had their eyes shut? The man told the girl again about using the eye that is inside your head to make your perceptions, not the ones on the outside. They were just for seeing. The eye inside was for knowing.

The man asked the girl if she ever thought about the concept that we die all the time. Maybe that is where our dreams come from. We die and then wake up in a slightly different reality. Everything is the same with slight changes. The man told her that we come so close to death all the time. Maybe we were really dying. Maybe our people who had died were now just in another dimension, with us, living like nothing had ever happened. The man told his niece about the strangeness with the truck driver. How his life had ended, or had it? It seemed to the man that the trucker had just disappeared into another realm. The two had felt his energy evaporate, like it was sucked out by a vacuum. Maybe it was just another dimension claiming its prize.

"You always talk some trippy shit," the girl told her uncle. "I'm so happy we hang out together."

Their talk could have gone on all night, but they were coming up on the hotel.

The lights were off in the hotel parking lot. Dark shadows were cast throughout the open expanse. There had been only three or four cars here earlier and now it looked like no more had joined them. The man and girl made their way through the shadows to the far corner of the building. There was a strange energy in the parking lot that the two had not detected before. It felt as though hundreds of souls had joined them. The parking lot was filled with spirits, almost like a cosmic party was going on. It was not menacing to the man and girl. They liked the feeling. They were always ready for anything weird that came up, and would embrace the oddities.

As they came up by the car, the two noticed that the pair of shoes from the guys next door were still sitting there, waiting for their owner's return. Their truck had not returned. Everything seemed so quiet. Not even crickets could be heard.

The door to their room flew open as they approached. The woman's face had a look of relief at the sight of her fellow travelers. The boy was quickly past his grandma, rushing to embrace the two. "What's wrong?" asked the girl, "why are you guys acting like this?"

The woman and boy looked at each other with a common knowledge. They had been talking about the strange actions of the man and girl all night. They had both been a witness to the other two acting as if they belonged in a mental institution. It was like they were living in a movie that they were writing as the miles stretched on. Their reality was being made up in their heads as they went along. Their creativity had always been profound, but this was something far deeper than that. When you believed your imagination, you had problems. The woman and boy had agreed.

The boy and his grandma got the other two into the room. The man asked again what was wrong. He could detect animosity coming from his wife and grandson. They seemed to be very angry at the man and his niece.

The woman spoke with hurt in her voice. She was not angry. The actions of the other two were crazy and erratic. This only made her worried about them. She cared for her family deeply. "You guys have been gone for six hours. We thought you would be right back, but you weren't. I don't know what you guys think you are doing being gone for so long, but it needs to stop. This is not funny."

The man and girl assured the others that they did not know what they were talking about. Finally, after a small discussion, the woman said it was time to get as much sleep as possible. There were only a few more hours left of dark and she was going to take advantage of it. The others agreed, bedding down for the night. Snoring filled the room within minutes.

Everyone was quickly asleep, except the man. The storyteller inside his head would have a lot to say on this night. So many things had happened this day, as in all the other days. He was scratching away with his pen as the others drifted off to sleep. The pages, mostly filled by his own phantom hand, just needed the finishing touches. It boggled his mind how the book was written in every night when he picked it up to write the day's events. Every night, the story ended right where he picked up the book and opened its pages.

The man thought this must be a sign or something. He was not one to look for signs or to follow the path of a sign. Sometimes though, the sign was so profound that you could not ignore it. That was the case. He interpreted the sign simply. It meant the story about the path they were on was already written. They just had to follow it, like the script of a movie. Everything had been predestined. Just like the man at the Grand Canyon had told him.

The other book was the one that had to be written. It was also predestined, but in a different way. It was not scripted like the other book. This one would be channeled through the man to teach the people of the earth the truth: The better way of living, in harmony.

The man needed the others in the group to help fulfill this destiny. Together they would form the ONE. Together they would bring the knowledge to so many others. Some would be happy to know. Most would not believe. It was the way. The way of the One taught to the masses. They could make their own decisions from there. The balance of choice was given to all of us, as a player's piece in the game of life. Choose wisely and live well. Choose foolishly and live poorly.

The man wanted to show only one way.

There was only one way.

It was the way of the wisdom.

It was the way of the ONE!

CHAPTER 9

Every day of this trip had started oddly. Something out of the ordinary was the way each morning began. Day six would be no different. The family had decided to sleep in a little later today, until seven or eight. Every other day, the mornings had been much earlier. They had been on the road every day by six. The man felt like they could sleep anytime. This was a once in a lifetime opportunity they were experiencing and had to get the most of it. The others had reluctantly agreed.

This had been the first night on the entire trip that the man had slept for more than an hour or two. This night, he felt like he had gotten at least four hours of good sleep. It had been much needed. He felt as though he was losing his mind. After returning from the store the night before, the family had watched television while the man wrote. They had all gone to sleep early but the man had a lot of things to say this night. The Jesus truck they had seen earlier fueled the man's story.

His sleep had been filled with the same dream. He was with his new friend Toomey. The small stone head and dangling body was a companion through the man's subconscious. Like the tour guides at Monument Valley, this creature was showing the man something that was very important. On this night, he had been with Toomey walking about Gallup. They had not seen a single car on the Highway 66. This town was deserted.

In the dream, when they had gotten back to the room, the police were there. The man had been missing for three days. The woman had called the police to file a missing persons' report. The dream had seemed so real. Even the look on the woman's face when they arrived at the hotel seemed so real.

A loud banging on the door woke the family. The dogs went into a barking and running around frenzy. The man, not asleep, was quick to respond. He had been lying next to his wife thinking about his dreams and the events that were happening to them. He felt something nagging at him the whole time. He felt like he needed to be alert and ready. Something was going to happen and now it had.

The man jumped from bed to answer the door, only to find no one there. He looked around the parking lot and up and down the walkway. No one was around, except his friend the crow. The bird was perched on top of their minivan. It was as if the animal was calling to the man to get on the road. "Who was it?" asked the woman as the man closed the door behind him. She was still half asleep.

"No one was there" replied the man.

"Who was knocking then," asked the woman, "just some asshole thought it was time to wake us up?"

"I don't know who it was" answered the man. The whole thing seemed very odd to him. The sun had come up on that side of the building and had been shining through the drapes. There was a window on either side of the door. The man had been staring at the dust particles floating through the rays of light when the knock came. He had not seen a shadow at either window.

The family was not happy about being woken up so early. They agreed that since they were already awake, they may as well go and do something. The man had read in the local paper the night before about a flea market in town. It was on this day, Saturday. The family thought that it would be a good time. They were all looking for different jewelry items and any other treasures they could find. The man said this would be the best place to find what they were looking for.

It was early when the group arrived at the sale. They had kept their room. They planned on coming back to use the toilet and pack the car after the sale. Checkout was at eleven so they had all morning to browse through the local wares. Most of the booths were still vacant or in the process of setting up. The man noticed that all the vendors were native peoples. He was impressed with this. The peoples of this region were a proud people with honorable ancestors. Their paths were in tune with Pachymama. They were happy to be happy. They were not part of the greed.

The family walked through many booths. They all found some jewelry which fit their tastes. It was a good time by them all. Meeting the vendors and getting to know the culture some was enlightening. At one booth, the family met a man selling herbs. He was also selling mountain tobacco. The man and his niece were very interested in herbs and their healing abilities. They struck up a conversation with the vendor. The older man was very doubtful and not trusting of the tourists. He seemed to not want anything to do with them. This changed when he heard the words of the man. The man spoke of the time of the earth returning to the solar system. He spoke about the healing which was coming. He also spoke about how the people of this region would be very important figures in the coming events. The man talked of the cycle.

The medicine man looked at the man and his niece with wonder. The prophecies had told of this to the healer. How had these two known about this. The auras surrounding the two people also seemed to be of a broad spectrum of colors. They seemed to be connecting and intertwining. The medicine man knew. These people were special. He had known of their coming for so very long. It had been in his visions and dreams since he was a small child. He had never doubted those visions once. They had been confirmed in his mind since they began. Now he was seeing all those visions in the now, the reality of the moment. He was with the One.

The man thanked the native healer for his time and turned to walk away. "One moment, friend" the vendor called out. The man turned back to the booth. In the vendors hands were bags of the mountain tobacco. "Take as many as you like. I'm sorry I doubted you before."

The man took one bag from the vendors hand and thanked the man sincerely. "One is all we need. We are not greedy people. We will enjoy your tobacco I am sure. The visions it gives us will be a gift from you. Thank you, my friend. You know the truth. Peace is truly in your heart."

The medicine man watched the family walk away towards the parking lot. A small smile crept onto his very weathered face. It was the first time he had smiled in a very long time. The time had come.

On the way back to the motel, the family stopped at a store to get the camera chip. This time they found it without a problem. It was a windy morning and the low clouds blocked the sun. The shopping center where they got the card seemed ran down. Trash blew through its asphalt expanse. It didn't matter to the family. They liked the people of this town. They felt a repression of the people here and an underlying darkness. These folks were being held back from happiness. Sadness and hopelessness permeated everywhere the family ventured to in the city.

There were many treasure shops in Gallup selling native jewelry and crafts. The family stopped and checked out a few of these stores. They were impressed with the workmanship put into some of the artwork. The jewelry was awesome and the blankets were like none they had ever seen. The stores were a bit too expensive for the family though so they stuck to just looking. The family was not impressed with the vendors at the stores. They were all older white women who were obviously well off. The prices were three times as much as the same items at the flea market. This was the greed in all its glory. Taking the best things from the natives and selling them for much higher profits. These were speculators. This profession was the true embodiment of the greed. These shops were the last places the family would be spending their money.

They stopped back at the Mexican food place from the night before and got some breakfast plates to go. A quick stop at the gas station, which also conveniently sold fireworks, and the family was ready to get the car packed and on the road. Now they would have the addition of some nice explosives for a time on the road when they might feel like putting on a fireworks display.

Rolling into the parking lot, they noticed the work truck from the night before parked in front of their room. No one seemed to be around when they backed in next to the vehicle. The pair of shoes left out front were now gone. Strange the man thought, the work shoes were here when the truck was not and now the truck is here but no shoes. He put it swiftly out of his head. It was already after ten and there were a lot of miles to cover this day.

As the others gathered up their bags, the man scrolled through the pictures on his camera before inserting the fresh disc. There were so many pictures of the Grand Canyon and Monument Valley. As he got more and more into the pictures, he began to see some that he did not remember taking. Some of the pictures were even of things he did not remember even seeing. In one photo, the whole group was standing in front of a rock formation. Who had taken that picture he wondered. He had not given his camera to anyone.

Another picture was one he remembered well. In it, his wife, grandson and niece were all making faces like they were choking. What was different though was the tall dark man in the group photo. The man had not remembered seeing anyone there when he took that picture. He couldn't make out the man's face but it seemed as if he was sporting a very broad grin. On the man's shoulder sat the crow. The bird was perfectly clear in the photo. The man could even see its green eye.

Another photo showed a burning building. It looked to be a large two-story building and was engulfed with fire. One of them even showed the boy in the photo with the burning building in the background. The strangest photo of all though was one of the man and woman standing in front of a geyser. They were obviously at Yellowstone in the photo. The problem was, they had never been to Yellowstone before. That was to be many miles down the road.

The man thought about these strange pictures the whole time he loaded the car. The family ate breakfast at the same time as packing. They were very good at multitasking. They also worked very well together. The woman had made a second pot of coffee for the road and they were ready. The man was torn in his mind. He knew he should tell the others about the strange pictures on his camera. He also knew they thought he was losing his mind. In the end, he decided not to tell the others what he was seeing. Some things were better left unsaid. They left the hotel and all the weirdness of Gallup behind.

A few miles down the highway, a car was off the road. As they got closer, the man saw that it was a police SUV that had intentionally parked. The back of the vehicle was open. Behind it was the officer. She was dragging a body towards the open police cruiser. She was having a hard time dragging the dead weight. The man couldn't make out the features. It just seemed to be dressed in dark clothes. Shadows danced around the officer. The sky had been a strange gray all day with hints of pink speckled throughout. It only added to the madness before them. It truly looked like they were watching a movie from the safety of their vehicle.

The officer was oblivious to the passing cars. The man was just fine with that. There were very few cars out on the back ways of New Mexico on a Saturday. They would be happy just to be on their way. Peacefully on their way was not an option for what they had just seen. Miraculously, the woman and boy had seen nothing. The woman had been looking at the map and the boy at his phone. The man and girl were the only witnesses in this car to the grisly scene behind them.

The family talked about the last few days and all the things they had done. It had been so many miles but just a fraction of the miles they would travel. Down the road they rolled. Through towns like Fence Lake and Quemado and some so small they had no name. The signs for Pie Town stretched on for many miles. They were making the group very hungry. The signs all spoke of a legendary Pie Lady of Pie Town. They all knew there would be no way they wouldn't stop here.

Pie Town was about eight buildings lining its streets. All the buildings seemed to be cafes. They all had advertisements boasting about their pie skills. In the end, the family ended up going to the last place on the left. It was the home of the Pie Lady. Walking through the doors was like walking back in time. The feel was from the fifties and the employees fit right in with the atmosphere. By the slice or whole pie was the motto at this place. There were only two pies in the display. The man chose the apple pie. It was already sold, the waitress sadly told him. He had to settle for the triple chocolate fudge brownie pie with chili. The waitress asked him more than once if he didn't want to stay and wait for an apple pie but they were happy with this purchase. The man and girl headed out the door while the woman and boy used the bathroom. On the way out, the waitress called out after to two by name, and told them to have a nice day.

"How had that waitress known our names?" asked the girl.

"She must have overheard us talking to each other or something." answered her uncle. "It sure was weird."

"That waitress knew our names," said the woman as she came out the swinging doors. "Did you guys tell her?"

"She knew our names too" answered the girl. "Something was wrong with that girl and with that place. I got a weird vibe in there. Not a bad vibe, just weird."

"It was a weird place but I didn't feel bad vibes either. It felt more like going into the twilight zone for a brief visit. Besides, the pie sure does look good," the man said. The others all agreed.

The miles passed one by one. The man didn't mind driving. It was beautiful country-side they were passing through. He had never been to any of these places and was making the most of it. In his mind, he was keeping notes on the story to write that night. He knew he didn't have to remember the day's events, that was being done for him. What he took notes on were his thoughts. The stories that were weaving in his mind as the days progressed. They would collect in his mind all day like a dammed river. Later, those stories would be flooded onto the paper when everyone went to bed. The true story was unfolding.

A stop at some lava beds woke the woman and boy. The woman said she was dreaming of traveling through space on a beam of light or something. There was another creature with her, a guide showing the way. A light at the end of the universe was there and so close but so far away at the same time. The dream had made her feel very good. It filled her being with hope.

The boy said no way. He had been having the same exact dream. The feelings when he woke up mirrored those of his Grandma. They had just had the same experience. Toomey had come to them also. They both said they could feel the light in their dreams. All their senses had been working in their subconscious.

The man told the others that they were on a mission. Their initial trip had been planned to heal the wounds of so much death. But maybe the death happened just to prepare them for the things that were happening to them now. The tragedy had brought out all their inner strengths and the collective strength. They were ready for anything. Nothing could ever happen to the family that was worse than what had already happened. Many strange things were going to continue to happen. This trip had been predestined long ago. It was the time and they were ONE.

The family hiked around the lava beds for a time. The dogs seemed to like this spot also. The satellite dishes from SETI formed an awesome line stretching off into the desert. One of the discs seemed to be emitting a ray of light that was more a shadow. It was barely perceptive with the eye. The puffy clouds floating through the sky were the backdrop that enabled the group to see the ray. At the cloud, the beam went into a different direction until it stretched from horizon to horizon. It looked like a black void crossing through the sky. It looked like a line in the sky where realities met. Maybe even the line separating the light from the dark.

Another of the discs seemed to be rotating slightly. It looked like it was humming and receiving transmissions. "Is it normal?" the boy asked the others. They all agreed that they truly did not know. This was all very foreign to them. The discs stretched on as far as the eye could see. There must have been fifty of them. They did not look inexpensive to the family. They wondered who had put the devices here, in the middle of the New Mexico desert. It looked like they were in a science fiction movie.

Coming out of the lava beds back onto the shoulder of the road, the boy tripped. He fell backward and stumbled awkwardly a couple of times before regaining his balance. The others all told him later that it looked like he was doing a strange ballet act.

Miraculously he had not been hurt. Climbing onto the road, something fell out of the boy's pocket. It was headed towards a fissure in the rocks and oblivion when the man snatched it from mid-air, just inches from the rocks. His balance was lost when he bent so fast and now was tumbling backward into certain pain.

The hand of his grandson caught his shirt just as he was passing the point of no return. The boy yanked the man to the asphalt and back to safety. "Let me see that" was the first thing the boy said to the man.

The man produced the object like a magician pulling a rabbit out of his hat. The object was silver. It was about the size of a cigarette. It seemed to be slightly tapered at one end. There were strange carvings on it. The object looked very familiar to the man. He was so sure he had just seen and held one of these very recently. The object seemed to be vibrating but in a way the man couldn't describe. "Where did you get it?" he asked the boy. "It was in your back pocket."

"I don't know," the boy replied, "I've never seen it before."

The man put the object in the console of the car with the other treasures they had acquired along the way. There were rocks, square nails, feathers and an alien skull. All the objects had been found for a reason. The man knew there was something going on and all these objects were coming to them at the opportune times. Everything they found was a little piece to the puzzle. Just like every person and everything that happened. It was all part of a puzzle that was being pieced together with every passing mile. The farther along they went, the more complete the puzzle would be.

The sun was beginning to get low in the sky. So many miles had been covered this day once again. The woman had booked a room in Roswell for the night. The man and woman had always wanted to stay in this town. They were both interested in UFOs and the like and this place was famous for their own story.

In this part of New Mexico, there weren't many towns close together. They were happy to pull into a small town for a much-needed rest for the humans and dogs. The town was deserted. Not a single soul could be seen. The family heard some loud voices coming from an area adjacent to where they had parked. The voices were loud at first but tapered into the wind. Silence followed.

There were no other cars in the unpaved lot. The man and girl walked to where they had heard the voices. An enclosure used for re-enactments of battles was through a tall fence. The two stepped through the small entrance but the place was deserted. Nobody had used this place for a very long time. The girl asked her uncle where he thought those voices had come from. He told the girl that they had come from another time. They had been left over here like the recording of your favorite music. Your ears just had to be able to hear it.

The name of the town had struck the man as familiar but he could not put his finger on it. There were no modern buildings in this town. It was like it had been frozen here since the eighteen-hundreds. The saloons and boarding houses were all intact as was the general merchandise. It looked like a replica, it was so authentic.

Walking through the town, the man realized why this place was familiar. It was Lincoln. This is where Billie the Kid fought the Lincoln wars. They were in a very cool little place of United States history. The boy hollered for the others to come over. He had found a concrete slab in the ground. It told about Billie the Kid killing some guy on this very spot on the eleventh of June 1876 at seven p.m. The man pulled his phone from his pocket. Today was June eleventh. This had happened one hundred forty years ago today. Furthermore, it was just now seven p.m.

A loud gunshot startled the group. Strange flowers began to float through the air. The man looked to see where the shot had been fired from but the flowers were obscuring his vision. The flowers seemed to be cherry blossoms but the man saw no trees to support this. It was not the season for blossoms anyhow. The flowers seemed to be making everything surreal. It was like the man was in a movie. When the air began to clear, they were no longer in the center of town. They were now in the Lincoln cemetery. The group was perplexed on how they had got there. They had passed this cemetery coming into town but it was at least a mile away.

The tombstones were old. Some were just rocks. There was a strange flower growing in the yard which the man had never seen before. He realized now where the flowers had come from before. These pods were puffing into the air with every breeze. They were a beautiful small white flower that seemed to float on the air like paper airplanes. They had no smell, just beauty. They were abundant in the air but nothing like moments before. They had gotten so thick, the family could not see for a few minutes. Then they had ended up here.

Many of the graves had collapsed. They looked dangerous. The man was just about to caution the others when the boy yelled out in pain. He had fallen into a collapsed grave. The others raced to his rescue. His lower body was buried as he clawed to get out. The boy was frantic. He was screaming that something had his leg. It was clawing at him and trying to pull him deeper.

The man pulled the boy as hard as he could. The boys leg tore free of his pants and he came out of the hole. The relief was evident in the boy. The man had never seen his grandson scared like that before. His pants had been shredded. On his leg was a hand print. It seemed to be burned into the boy's leg. It looked more like a claw than a hand. It only had three fingers. The burn was a deep red but was lightening quickly in the sunlight.

The man and girl both looked to the heavens and opened their mouths. Their eyes rolled back into their heads. They both saw. There had been a crash of a flying disc at this place in 1897. It had crashed into the farm on the North side of town. The locals had found a creature which had been killed in the accident. They had taken the creature and buried it in their cemetery, "like any God-fearing folk would do". The craft had disintegrated over a period of a few months. The story had been passed on as folklore for many years but had died off as the town had. The tale had been lost to time, until now.

The boy grabbed his niece as the woman grabbed her man. The look on the faces of the two had frightened the woman and her grandson. They needed to get out of here and fast. The two had looked like they were possessed or something. Whatever had happened, it was not good.

They turned to go and saw the minivan sitting outside the gate to the cemetery. The boy and his grandma were relieved to see the safety of their vessel so close. "They must have drove here after all," the woman thought. As soon as they took a step or two, the man and girl were perfectly normal. They both had questions to what had just happened. It was like they had lost time or something. They remembered walking through town and then the others were waking them from some daydream. They both clearly remembered the vision they had just had.

They helped the boy but the youngster said he could walk just fine. The man turned back to see the collapsed grave. The earth was normal again. It looked like nothing had ever happened. The flowers he had seen before had been white in the setting sun. Now they were now the blackest of black. He caught up to the others and got everyone back in the car. As he was closing his door, he glanced once more at the grave where his grandson had fallen in. Standing there was the dark figure which seemed to be shadowing them on this trip. The man felt dread when he saw this creature. Strange things always seemed to come with its sighting.

It was not much farther before they got to Roswell. The man and girl told the others about what they had seen at the graveyard. Their vision had been correct. Their subconscious had gone back to more than a hundred years before and seen the truth. What they didn't tell the others was that the visions they had were not visions. They were memories. The two had been at that spot the day the extraterrestrial was buried. The man had been the one to dig its hole.

It would be a much-needed rest in Roswell. The hotel had a swimming pool so the group could unwind a bit. The temperature was perfect for swimming and no one else was around. The pie proved to be a perfect dinner for all four of the weary travelers. Pie town lived up to every bit of hype they had seen in its advertisement. The family spoke of the rarity of that these days. It was rare to get something as good as it was advertised.

After pie and showers, the boy asked the man to see the object. The man told the boy he didn't know what happened to it. He had it in his pocket earlier but it was gone after they got back from swimming.

"I bet I know where it will be" the girl said excitedly as she bound off the bed. She reached into the boy's backpack and pulled out the box with the eye on it. The eye etched into the box was emitting a soft green glow. The girl set it on the table in the middle of the room and they all looked at the object.

"We all need to touch it at the same time" the woman said. The group all extended their hands and touched the box at the same exact moment. The box made a deep tuba kind of sound, vibrated twice and popped open. Inside the box, fitted in their own little niches, was the key and the sun stone. Also in the box was the metal cylinder they had found at the lava beds. It had found its way home. The man remembered why the object looked so familiar. It was the same artifact that the girl had found back in bishop. The man had carried it in his pocket all day but had forgotten about it. He had not thought about the object again until just now, seeing it in the box of treasure.

The man examined the new object. It seemed to be a machine or mechanical object but the man did not know. He had seen a lot of things in his years but nothing like this. The object seemed cool yet warm to his touch. It had a strange metallic smell to it. It also seemed to emit a low hum that was barely perceivable to the human ear. It was something that all the man's senses were aware of. The markings on the side seemed to be an ancient language. It told a story that the man knew he would understand very soon.

The boy asked what happened to the tooth that was in the box when he found it. The man told him that he had seen the crow with it in its beak a few days before. The creature must have pilfered it from the family when they were unaware. "The crow is a tricky little bird" the man told the others.

"If the crow has it, it is safe. Our friend is just using it for something now but will return it when it is time." The girl said with a sound to her voice that seemed different to the others. The man looked to his niece and saw that her eyes were green, like the crows had been. They faded back to their normal hazel color as her words tapered off. The man felt like the crow had just spoken to them through the girl. The bird was part of the circle.

The objects went back into the box and it closed itself. The items seemed to have a magnetic pull to the receptacle. The contents would only come out when it was time. Otherwise, the box would keep its treasures hidden. The family said that the box seemed to have a mind of its own, like it was making its own decisions. They did not understand how the objects had gotten inside its locked enclosure, but they had. The boy put the metal container back into his backpack. The green glow had vanished.

It had been a very long day. Many more were ahead. The man told the family they needed to get as much rest as possible. Adventure awaited them the next day, as it had every day. They were asleep as their heads hit the pillow.

The man had a lot of writing to do this night. This object they had found was something so familiar to the man. It had already come to them twice on this trip. Just like the stone with the sun in it. Something in his mind told him that they had encountered this stone again and again on this trip. It was a part of the story. It was tearing his mind up trying to figure out the connections of the objects. The box the boy had found only deepened the mystery in the man's mind. The knowledge was right there but he could not grasp it.

There were many shadows in this room. They were in every corner and were not even trying to be hidden. The man knew about shadows. They did not scare him. It was just another part of existence. Another being that was coexisting in our everyday world, living their own existence in their own dimension. He realized that the shadows really came out late at night, when the mind was tired. This is when the bridge between conscious and subconscious would begin to narrow. This is when you could see into the other dimensions around you.

The man's hand became a blur as it raced across the pages. It didn't even feel like he was the one writing the story exclusively. It felt as though others were telling the story through his being. Not the shadows in the room, it was a much greater force moving his hand. It was as if a higher being was speaking through the man. All he had to do was put the pen in his hand and the being spoke. The truth was being told.

The man knew that the dimensions were merging. The objects they had been encountering confirmed the story. The One was becoming whole again. Things were coming together like so many times before. It had been so very long but there was no stopping it. The cycle always came around. The entire universe was a cycle and everything in it was on that sequence. From the grandest of the universe to the smallest of life, everything was on a cycle.

Once again, just like at the end of every cycle, was the beginning.

CHAPTER 10

The end of the first week was upon them. The family spoke of all the adventure they had, and how there was going to be so much more. They had been happy to stay in Roswell the night before. The man and woman knew the details of Roswell very well. It was a place they had both always wanted to visit. They were a family who was intrigued by the unknown. This, too, was a night the man had slept. It had only been for a couple of hours, but it was sleep. This place seemed very comfortable to the group.

The dreams, while the man had them, were of his new friend Toomey. The creature in his dream this night took him on an aerial view of the White Sands nuclear test sites. Alamagordo was below, what was left anyway, after it had been leveled with an atomic weapon. Flying over the Roswell crash site was the last of the tour given by Toomey this night. On this part of the trip though, the man was back in time to 1947. The craft had just made impact with the Earth and the astronauts were flung in different directions. All three of the beings were still alive, but in serious need of help. The man had watched as black helicopters converged on the scene. There were no markings on their craft. The man watched as hundreds of these helicopters came from the sky, landing in a geometric pattern on the ground. The creatures that got out of these flying black machines were tall and dressed in black. The man thought, in his dream, that they all looked the same. The beings converged on the astronauts and shot them with a green laser that came out of something they held in their hands. The visitors were motionless after that. The men in suits began to take apart the space ship and put it into a larger craft that had landed after the others. This is when they had spotted the man, hovering above. They all pointed to the man and Toomey while looking straight at them. A sound came from their beings that reminded the man of the sound he had heard in Bodie. It was deafening and made him feel like his head would explode. The noise made him lose all his will. He felt like he was not going to make it out of this dream.

Movement in the hotel room brought the man back to consciousness. His niece had saved him from doom in his subconscious by awakening early.

The girl was the first out of bed this morning. She was done in the bathroom as the man was finishing getting dressed. The others were awake in minutes. The experiences of their lives had brought them here. All the weird things throughout their existence led them to this moment. Maybe this place would give them some of the answers they were looking for. They were all excited to get to the museum. This was Roswell, their museum was world renown.

The man had very many experiences with the paranormal since being a small child. When he was very young, him and his brother had seen a cosmic serpent in their bedroom late at night. It was not a onetime event. The experiences terrified the young boys at first, but over time they became accustomed to them. The spirits in this house ran rampant. The experiences with these spirits were on many different levels. There was good energy here, but also a very dark energy. The cosmic serpents protected the family. The boys were the only ones who knew. They were the only ones who could see.

The stories were countless from the time in this house. It was the house the man grew up in until he was eighteen and joined the service.

As a teenager, the experiences heightened. The dreams the man had then were very realistic. He would always dream of different houses which also held spirits. He would be in these houses experiencing strange occurrences. Almost like he was a medium going around checking out haunted houses. But he was just a boy. Some of his dreams found him in a possessed state. These ones were particularly disturbing to him. Other beings would on occasion occupy his subconscious. These beings would take all his own thoughts and will out of him. The memories of these dreams remained the rest of his life.

He was seventeen when he saw his first UFO. He had met a girl and she seemed to be in touch with things, just like he was. She too had strange experiences at his house. On this night, at the park they frequented almost every night, it was about ten. A bright light came from the horizon and instantly was in the sky. It stopped, made a sweeping motion, and blinked off. The light was so bright, the man and woman felt its blue intensity. The news had said it was a rocket, but they knew better. The man had felt what the craft had truly been.

After this, the man saw many other strange lights in the sky and on the ground. His senses were very in tune to the things most people didn't understand. Then one night on the way home from the tattoo shop at about three in the morning, the man saw IT along with his son. They had turned onto the dirt road leading to their house, on the man's three-wheel motorcycle. They passed by the large stand of eucalyptus at the neighbor's house, and it was there, in the sky, as they came into the clearing. The craft had to be at least a mile in diameter. It seemed to be very close to the ground, maybe five thousand feet or less. The craft looked sort of organic in a mechanical way, on the bottom. It made the sound of a fan. The man and boy asked each other over and over if this was real. They had never seen anything like this. The man, while in the navy, worked on many aircraft. This was nothing built by humans. The two watched the object pass over and continue its path towards the north. It had a very bright white light and a very bright red light. The lights did not blink. The man and boy were awestruck.

Fifteen years after this incident, the man and his brother were driving to the city to see their mother. The two passed by the county dump. "It was here that I saw that UFO," the brother had said.

"Yeah, what did it look like?" the man had asked him. There was not a shred of doubt in his voice.

His brother's reply had been incredible. He described, exactly, the same thing the man and his son had seen. He too had been with someone else and said he probably wouldn't have believed it then or now if someone else hadn't been present. The man said he felt the same. He thought of the strangeness of this. How had they seen the same exact thing? What was it and why weren't others seeing the same craft. It was much too large to go unnoticed.

The man saw this object one more time. It was about a week after his brother had died. He had taken his dog outside in the middle of the night. He would use these times to have a little relief himself and look at the stars. On this night, in the distance, were the same exact lights he had seen with his son. They were many miles away, but not at a high elevation. The man knew in his heart that it was the same craft he had seen so many years before.

The man had even spotted a Sasquatch before in the high sierra. There had been four of them in the car this time and they had all seen the creature. Their car had broken down in a snowstorm, and they had been stuck on the closed road. Eventually, they were the only car left on the mountain. It was many cold hours waiting for the tow truck. The man couldn't stand being confined in a car for such long periods with others. He had got out of the vehicle to stretch his legs and get some fresh air. It was then that the man saw the beast in the road up ahead. The snow had reflected just enough light from the night to make the Bigfoot a large, lurking shadow. The man called to the others, who all got out to see what all the fuss was about. They all saw the creature up ahead. At first it had just stood in the road, but when the man approached, the creature walked off the shoulder. It was then that the group knew exactly what they had seen.

Countless experiences like these had brought them to Roswell. There was something in and about this city that the man needed to find out. There were answers here. The UFO research center was very cool. Half of the museum was dedicated to the alien craft which crash landed in Roswell, and the other half was about random UFO and aliens. It was a bunch of things the man already knew, but it was fun to go to anyway. Seeing the original newspaper articles on the crash was very cool. The man knew something had happened here back in 1947. The greed had covered it well.

The man had planned on coming here to speak with a UFOlogist to explain what he had seen so many years before with his son. He was certain other people had seen the same thing. Surely it wasn't just him and his family. The man had a theory of the craft he had seen. After the second sighting, it had come to him. Maybe this craft traveled over the planet, nonstop, picking up the souls that were departing their flesh pods. Maybe it was a giant recycling plant for souls to be reborn or reassigned. His thoughts of speaking with someone about these things were thwarted. The people who worked there seemed to be college kids making a buck. The man didn't see anyone who worked there who seemed to give a shit about UFOs. This was just another tourist spot, feeding someone's pocket.

He began to doubt the authenticity of the museum. The greed was crafty. He had no doubts that they would perpetrate a scheme like this. Illusion was what kept the masses in fear.

The man noticed that one of the other people in the museum seemed out of place. He pointed the stranger out to the woman and girl and they both agreed. The lady didn't seem to walk normal like the other people. She seemed to shuffle along like she didn't really know how to walk. Her expression was more like you would have in a doctor's waiting room than a museum. She seemed uninterested in any of these exhibits. She was just waiting for something, rather impatiently. She was interested in a small boy. The lady sped across the space to encompass the child in her aura. The boy had a look of panic on his face. The lady whispered something in the child's ear. The boy's face seemed to change from one of terror to one of waiting. Passive was his expression. Just like the lady's face looked.

The man approached the lady and the boy. The lady turned sharply to see the man directly behind her. She cowered away from the presence, her face buried in the black wrinkles of her shawl. She reached her gnarled hand out as one last act of defiance. Her strange clothes fell away, slightly revealing a strange necklace the woman was wearing. The man thought it looked so familiar to him. He puffed up his energy to get a closer look and it was the breaking point. The man's energy was much too strong. The woman scurried out to the street in fear.

This was not the first time the man had experienced something like this. Traveling through south America, he had encountered some witches on occasions. These people had a fear of the man. The man had a serious distrust for them. They brought a darkness which most feared but the man pitied. They used this fear to get money from the weak. He had no time for their dark energies and fear mongering just for profit. They knew he could see right through them. These beings always steered very clear of the man. He found pleasure in putting himself directly in their path. The light was always stronger than the dark.

After the woman was gone, the man asked the boy if he was okay. The child had not turned and looked toward the man once. He finally turned and the man saw his eyes. They were solid black. The boy opened his mouth but did not speak. His words were in the man's head. They were calm but very stern. The words told the man one thing. "They know." It was repeated over and over. No one else around seemed to hear the boy. The man's grandson came up and caught his attention. He told his elder about some artifacts across the room. The man turned back around and the child was gone. He looked around the museum but could not find the boy anywhere. He knew now what he had come for. It was far more than talking to a self-proclaimed scientist.

The sun was very hot when they got back outside. It was early afternoon and time to get back on the road. The crow was sitting on the roof of the car awaiting its traveling companions. It flew to the south, same as they were headed. There was a commotion across the street that caught the family's attention. Normally not ones to watch other people's misery, there was no way they couldn't watch this. It was just too bizarre. The woman from the museum was there, and her arm was stuck in the mailbox, all the way to the armpit. Two men, dressed all in black with dark sunglasses, were on either side of her. They seemed like FBI or something. They were pulling on the woman very roughly. She seemed to be stretching like a piece of semi- hard chewing gum. Her arm would not come out of the box no matter how much they pulled. Finally, one of the men took a small tool from his pocket and went to work. The man didn't know what kind of tool it was but the base of that mailbox was off the ground in minutes. It hung from the woman's torso like an obscene arm. The three piled into the back of a large, square, white van and drove off. "Funny," said the girl, "only in Roswell".

It was time to get back on the road. When the others all got in the car, the man asked the boy if he had the box he had found in Bodie handy. "Of course!" the boy had proclaimed as he presented the object to his grandpa. "Who's got the key."

"It's here," said the girl. She flicked her fingers in the air and the key appeared in them. The boy and his grandma looked at each other with a strange wonder. The man laughed softly. The key flew into the lock and the box sprung open once again. The two objects inside seemed to emit a glow into the car. The metal cylinder they had found at the lava beds was now in its cutout spot.

"I knew it," the man said. "This stone with the sun symbol was the same one around that strange woman's neck in the museum. I knew I had seen it but, somehow, I couldn't remember exactly. It was as if the object had blocked my memories of it somehow. This object was not meant for us to possess. The beings who it belongs to know we have it and are watching us. They have been following us for many, many miles. We stopped here in Roswell to find this out and to let them know that we too know. We are not afraid."

The man took the silver cylinder out of the box. He pulled his phone from his pocket and brought up a picture he had taken in the museum. It was of a beam they had found at the alien wreckage site. There were markings on the beam, some form of hieroglyphics. The man knew as he felt the object in his hand. He needed not look at the picture on his phone but did anyway for confirmation. The markings were identical. The man had felt something strange about this object when the girl had first found it in Bishop. After losing it and finding at the SETI site, he had known the importance of it. The object went back in the box and the lid closed on its own accord. The boy stuffed the object back into his backpack and the family was off.

The talk on the road was filled with what the man had said. The boy wanted to believe what his grandpa was saying but it seemed so much like a movie. His grandpa had made grand productions on his behalf before and now the boy suspected this might just be one of those performances. All this talk about aliens and prophecies was too much to believe. He was seeing the same things, but his mind came up with different conclusions than his grandpa.

The woman saw her husband fall deeper and deeper into insanity. She had tried to go along with some of the things he had said so as not to disturb him. This, on the other hand, was pushing it a little too far: Beings following them for some stupid agenda: Sacred objects that looked like junk and rocks to the woman. The story was just getting to be too much. There were some strange things happening, she could see. But her husband's imagination had taken those things too far.

The next stopover would be the Carlsbad Caverns. The man had read on the internet the night before about the best times to go, and this was the time. It wasn't too much of a drive to get there, so the family was not so tired. Roswell had seemed to give them some rest anyway, and they were ready for adventure. They had always wanted to come to this place, and now wanted to be at their best. A large road runner ran across the road as they were approaching the entrance to the parking lot. They had been talking all day about seeing a roadrunner, and now they had, right at Carlsbad. It was almost like a guide to welcome the family to the park. The crow flew overhead. It and the roadrunner seemed to look at one another and understand. This was the coming.

Dropping the dogs in the kennel was a very hard thing for the group to do. Their dogs were princesses and would not be happy about this. There was just no way they could take them though and there was no way they could take turns. This was their only option. For the first time all week, the humans would be free from the leash.

There were many caves in the area where the man and woman lived. They had gone to them all countless times. The boy, however, would always balk about going into the cavern. Something about not having an exit was not good for him. This was the case at Carlsbad also. The boy decided not to go into the earth. He would wait for the others above ground.

The national park pass covered the entrance fee to the caves. The park ranger who vouched the tickets to the man gave him the whole lowdown. You could walk into the caves and take the elevator out or take the elevator in and walk out. She said the elevator wait down below was two hours. Pointing across the room to the elevator, she said "there is the line going down". There was no one in that line.

"That is the line for me," the man had said jokingly. The ranger told him he was making a smart decision. She made an odd gesture when she said it. It looked like a gesture warning the man to get ready, strangeness was about to happen.

A seven-hundred and fifty-foot elevator ride straight into the earth was very impressive. Two other tourists shared the glass car with the three. The rocks outside whizzed by like a blur. In minutes, they were at the bottom. The man and woman had been on an elevator this tall before in Sao Paulo, but that was to the top of a building blowing in the wind. This elevator was rigid and a pleasant ride into the Earth.

The first thing they noticed was the long line stretching out of sight. The wait going back up was indeed a long one. The cave in this part formed an auditorium of sorts. Vendors were sprinkled about. The three stopped at a stand to get some waters and were surprised that they were regular priced. The man told the vendor about the legitimacy of this. Most tourist places were out to gouge you. Make as much profit as possible. This place was the fairest they had been to yet.

If not for the elevator ride coming down, it would have been hard to believe they were this deep underground. Around a couple of corners and boom, they were in the main room.

The immensity of the cavern was staggering. This cave made the ones back home look like babies. It was the most beautiful cave any of them had ever been in. Its beauty, compared to that of the Grand Canyon. Every step brought a new wonder to the senses. There were formations they had never even seen before. The quantity of formations was also mind boggling. There was so much to take in.

Some parts of the cave almost seemed alive. The shadows would twist and turn with the placement of the lights. Some of the stalagmites seemed to be slow moving soldiers protecting their realm. It seemed like they had left the planet they were on, and now were here. It all seemed so foreign to them. They all spoke about how they could spend days at this place.

The other tourists all seemed to be respectful of each other. The ones stopping to look at a formation would get out of the way of groups passing by. Everyone seemed to be in a very good mood. This, the man thought, is how people should always treat each other.

The three would have spent so much more time but they couldn't stop thinking about the boy above ground by himself. The dogs too were of a concern. They walked through the main cavern rather quickly and headed for the exit. The ranger had told the man that the exit would take about forty-five minutes. They had already been underground for an hour and forty-five minutes so it was time to make their way back up top.

As with the other trails in the cavern, the lack of people made the experience more enjoyable. The hike up was vigorous but so very beautiful. They passed a guided tour which was slowly making their way up some steps. The group seemed perturbed when the family pressed to the left of them. When they had finally got past the group, the ranger/tour guide muttered something to the man. The man turned to ask the ranger what he had said. The rangers eye sockets were vacant. The man kept his mouth shut and kept on moving.

After passing the tour group, the other tourists became less and less. A few people coming the other way passed at first but after a bit, there was no one. They had the entire trail to themselves. This gave them ample time to take a break whenever they wanted. The walk up was very tiring. Finally, the three hikers could see light coming from up ahead. They were getting close. The sound of sparrows filled the air. There were millions of birds up ahead. The man thought he could hear another sound, outside the cave, that was very odd. It sounded like the roar of a large animal.

The last couple of hundred yards were terrible. The smell from the birds and bats at the entrance to the cave was almost unbearable. The strong smell of ammonia was everywhere. A couple of the birds lay dead on the path. The man stopped to look closer at the creatures. He had thought they were swallows but this looked like no bird he had ever seen. It looked sort of like a cross between and bat and a lizard. The feathers were more like scales than softness. The creature's bodies were not very big, with large heads almost the same size. They were black and looked kind of waxy. "You guys ever seen anything like this?" the man asked the others.

"Hell no," said the woman, "We need to get the hell out of here." Her words were echoed by millions of the birds coming out of their resting places in the cave and headed right their way.

The three bolted the last fifteen feet from the cave and spun to the right, next to some boulders, out of the bird's crazed path. Millions of the bat-birds flew within feet of the group. The man thought how they had been lucky that the hole to the cave hadn't been bigger. They would have been caught in the mayhem. He also thought it was odd that there were no handrails or paved trails coming up the steep incline. The rest of the cave had rails and pavement, but that last stretch was very natural. Even some bushes partially obscured the entrance.

The storm of birds didn't subside, it just ended. The family had hidden safely for at least the last fifteen minutes. The birds had never stopped coming until now. The family had seen nothing but black streaks the whole time. Now the terrain was visible. The sun was very low in the sky and cast a strange orange glow. The sky was filled with this color. The moon loomed large in the twilight sky, just over the horizon.

Scanning the view, everything seemed to have changed. There were no paved roads anymore, and no parking lot. No more guard rails, and mostly, no more people. The buildings had also disappeared. The man thought that maybe the exit just brought them out at a different place. He went in search of the buildings.

He came up on a bluff and scanned the area. This had all been desert before but now somehow it was a lush green forest. The group spotted some other people ahead and called out to them. The others looked over with shock and relief on their faces. The family made their way down some rocks, around some bushes and toward the others. They realized there were maybe twenty other people. "What's going on" the man asked the other group.

"We don't know any more than you do." spoke a woman of about sixty. We all just came out of that cave over there and found everything like this. Some strange sounds are coming from the forest over there."

The man heard the roar that he had heard underground. Now it was much closer and was a very dreadful sound. He had always kept his head. He knew danger was all around but he also knew panic would not help. He began to back towards the cave with the woman and girl following. He told the other tourists they should get back to the cave also. A few agreed and began to follow the group. The man never took his eyes from the forest. The family and few followers were quickly back up the rocks and getting further from the large group.

The other tourists said it was crazy for them to go back into the cave. Those bird things were going to come back, they had said. The man, woman, and girl had no time for this. They were ones to make their own decisions and never follow those of others. They watched as the forest began to come alive. First, some of the trees began to shake, and limbs were being snapped. By the time the first dinosaur emerged from the tree line, it was too late for those who stayed behind. Their pathetic shelter behind some rocks was quickly discovered. The man didn't know what kind of animal these were. They were about fifteen feet tall and walked on two legs. Their heads were large, and they had very large green eyes. Their teeth were about ten inches long. They were very hungry.

"Run!" yelled the man as the carnage unfolded. All those left behind were quickly torn to shreds and eaten by the ravenous breed of animal before them. There had been three others that had fled with the family. All six people ran for their lives toward the caves. Luckily, the other tourists had satisfied most of the creature's hunger. Only one of the beasts had spotted the others. It was the biggest of the herd and seemed to be very hungry. It chased the family and the others all the way to the cave. The man had fallen behind to make sure the woman and girl were safe, but the creature was on his back. One of the others, a young girl of sixteen or so, had been running right next to the man. She stumbled on some rocks and fell face first into the dirt. The dinosaur, forgetting the man, jumped on the easier prey.

The girl's mother and father, both a few steps ahead, stopped their running and turned to face the creature. As they were looking for a weapon, the dinosaur ripped the spinal cord out of their daughter and dropped it, still attached to her head, down its gullet. The girl's parents rushed the creature in a fit of rage. The animal roared at them as they approached, but they did not falter. The father had picked up a branch of some sort and went to stab the beast. The creature relieved the man of his head with one quick swoop, but not before the stick contacted the beast's mouth. Something flew toward the man and landed on the rock in front of him. The tourist's wife, in shock, stood silently as the dinosaur split her in two at the waist with its sharp talons.

The man had made it to the cave and watched the slaughter from behind some rocks. The creature had not seen him. He picked up the object which had landed in front of him and quickly but quietly made his way into the cave and the familiar energy of his people. "What was that?" asked the woman, still gasping for breath.

"I told you" said the man, "weird things are happening. You just didn't believe me." The man showed the others what he had found. It was a tooth from the dinosaur. The other man had knocked it out, and it had landed right by the man. The tooth was exactly like the one the boy had found in the box in Bodie; the one that had been missing for the last few days, seemingly taken by the crow.

The cacophony from outside had finally ended. First, the human's screams of anguish. Then the dinosaur's screams of orgiastic joy. It had been deafening, but now was silent.

The group made their way further into the cave before stopping and coming up with their plan. They for sure didn't want any of those things getting seconds. Finally, they decided to make their way to the bottom of the cave. There was plenty of food and water down there, and they could assess what their next plan would be. It was going to be dark soon and there would be nothing they could do on the surface, except maybe get eaten. It was best to once again descend.

"Wonder what happened to our grandson?" the woman thought aloud. This is what worried her the most. Their family always had a way of dealing with everything that came along, and this would be no different. She just wished the boy was with them. If only he would have stayed with the group. Something told the woman that they would need the boy if they were to get out of this alive.

As they got farther and farther into the cave, they began to hear voices. By the time they got to the elevator, everything was the same as when they had left this area, except the line for the elevator. There was no one queued up now. A ranger approached them and asked what they were doing. The man told the ranger that there was something odd on the surface. The ranger could sense the anxiety in the man and his companions. He told the group to calm down. They had just imagined this. The oxygen was different down here, and sometimes people had strange hallucinations. It was nothing to worry about. The ranger also told them they were going up on this elevator car waiting for them. It was one of the last of the day, and they were the last of the tourists in the cavern.

The family rode the elevator ride to the top. They talked about what had happened, and how they had lost so much time. Where had all the other tourists gone? They never once passed any on the way back in. "I don't care anymore," the woman said in defeat. "I just hope our grandson is okay."

The boy leaped into his family's arms as soon as the elevator door opened. He had been so worried about them. They said they would be about two hours but six had passed. At first, he was angry that they had taken so long, but that soon turned to worry. He had long ago gone back to pick up the dogs. The kennel closed at six, and he didn't want them to have to stay there all night. The dogs too were so happy to see their people. They were sniffing all over them. They could sense something was not quite right with their humans.

The boy asked the others what had happened. As they walked to the car, the man told the boy in detail about the events of the last hours. The story continued even as they were on the highway crossing into Texas. The boy was very skeptical about his grandpa's words, but his grandma and cousin verified everything. When the man pulled the tooth from his pocket and tossed it to his grandson, the younger knew the story was true. This tooth still had fresh blood on it.

The boy had deep regret now that he had not gone into the cave with the others. This sounded like another adventure out of a movie. The boy began to think that this whole trip was maybe a movie. The reality was really happening when they were sleeping.

The family all talked about all the strange things going on. The woman said that maybe they were all going insane. The man told the others about how people his whole life had said he was insane or crazy. Because he was different, the man had said, you don't fit in with the normal way of thinking. "It all comes down to conforming," he told the others. "Most humans are controlled by something or another. They are downright brainwashed for the agenda of the greed. If you are not one to conform to this control, then you are insane. If you know the truth, they call you a conspiracy nut."

The man told the others that the true insane were the ninety nine percent. These were the ones controlled by the greed with ease. They were the ones who would keep this planet going on its reckless collision course with disaster. They were too blind to see and too quick to point their fingers at those who could see.

The man could see. His family had always been of this type who could easily see right through the maze and control of the greed. The man and his family would be the ones to make changes, not conform. Their time had been coming for a very long time, and now it was here.

Time seemed to be passing very strangely the rest of this day. They covered over three hundred miles, but the sun remained in the same spot in the sky. It had seemed to be setting the whole time. The clock in the car was no help either. It kept shifting from one time to another. Sometimes the numbers would even seem to spin and stop as if were a slot machine. Every occurrence with the clock ended up with a different time displayed.

The other instruments in the car seemed out of whack, also. The speedometer didn't seem to accurately read their speed. The outside temperature was fluctuating by over fifty degrees, at times. "Maybe they were going through a magnetic field," the man had told the others. "This is the area of white sands, after all, where they tested the first nuclear weapons, and many more after. Maybe the destruction had damaged the earth's magnetic field in this area."

The man had remembered his dreams from this area the night before. Being in the museum, he realized that they were passing by this spot exactly sixty-nine years after the crash. It was to the day. Once again, the numbers always seemed to add up in the man's life. Toomey's words played in his mind. The being had spoken about the absurdity of the human's using nuclear weapons. It is why no other beings in the universe had contact with them. They did not trust the humans and their greed.

It had been many miles since they had seen any other cars, and even longer since they had seen any towns. Texas, the sixth state on the trip, had begun. The family agreed to stop at the next town they passed. That town ended up being Big Spring. It seemed like a quaint little town, but it had a hotel and a couple of diners. This place would be home for the night. The family had been following the maps closely and saw that it was many more hours before they got to the next town. They didn't have a couple more hours left in them.

The man asked the clerk at the hotel what time it was. The clerk said seven. That was impossible, thought the man. They had left the caverns at seven. He asked the clerk if there was a time change between the two places, but it was a negative. The man felt a bit queasy. This was very wrong. The time couldn't change like that. It reminded him of the dream after his brother had died; the one where he could turn back time. All night in that dream, like a mathematician, the man had turned back time in his sleep. He had figured it all out, until he had woken up. The key secrets had been hidden in his subconscious. His conscious mind would not be able to figure it out.

The man got into the car and drove to their room. The woman asked her husband what was wrong, he looked so pale. The man told her what time it was, and she didn't see anything wrong with the time. She said they had left the caves and drove all afternoon. She had booked this hotel two hours ago, soon after they had passed into Texas. She said she didn't know what the man was doing while she and the others were sleeping, but she could guarantee it wasn't time travel.

The other two laughed loudly. It did seem absurd now that his wife had said it like that. Things seemed to be happening that were so out of the ordinary, but then when the man tried to recall those events, he usually couldn't. Instead, he knew there were memories there, but he could not bring them into his consciousness. Some of the memories were not like he remembered them. It was almost like they were someone else's memories.

Unpacking the car, the humidity was heavy. The man told the boy that this was real Texas. He and the girl went out to the parking lot to smoke a cigar. The boy and his grandma prepared to go for a swim. Outside smoking, the two talked about the day's events and what was happening to them. They both agreed that some weird shit was going on, but the truth hadn't come to them yet. All the pieces were coming together and they were building the key.

The two did understand that they were on a path though. It was their destiny to be reborn and learn the truth. This path had been laid out for them so many centuries before.

The sun setting in the West made the sky look like an inferno was blazing. The colors of the sunset in Texas were impressive. Food and rest were on the minds of the two. It had been a very long day. So much had happened that they couldn't even remember all of it. "The story tonight is going to be a long one," the man told his niece.

A specter came out of the darkness and approached the two. The energy was very familiar to the man and his niece. When it got close enough, they could both see the shadow. It had no form but it was a form. They didn't need to see the face to know. It was the man's nephew. The girl's brother. He held out his hand toward the others as his face came into perfect clarity. His eyes were a fiery ember and he had his normal grin that he wore his whole life. The girl raised her hand toward her brother's outstretched arm. When she made contact, the apparition in front of them dissipated like smoke. Their homie was gone. His energy flowed between the two as it disappeared in the night breeze.

The crow flew in front of the two. It cawed three times in agreement to what they had just encountered.

The nephew's energy had become one with the others.

All three auras had merged into one.

CHAPTER 11

The morning was started with some fresh coffee the man had bought on the road, somewhere in New Mexico. The woman had prepared it the night before. All the man had to do was turn on the coffee maker, which was the first thing he did when getting out of bed. He had let the others sleep a little later today. He had been pushing the group hard this whole trip. The man was one for minimal sleep and lots of adventure. He had to remind himself that the others couldn't always keep up with his pace. The extra time they slept, the man used to his benefit anyhow. He wrote all night on this night. The book he was making was writing itself. He just put the pen to the paper, and it knew what to do.

He knew that he had slept a bit because of his dreams. Toomey had once again come to him and showed him a large brown lake. Inside the lake, there were creatures that people could not imagine. They were creatures that had been mutated by radiation and acquired a taste for flesh. They had not yet evolved beyond the water, but land was in their evolutionary future.

The man went to the lobby to see what breakfast the hotel offered. The heat was stifling. It was just six thirty in the morning but felt like mid-afternoon. The trip across Texas was going to be a long hot one. They had decided to go for it and make it across in one day. The sister's house was calling them. There was nothing in between that they wanted to see. The only stops today would be to eat some Texas barbecue and let the dogs wander around.

This hotel didn't offer breakfast, but they did have the local paper. The man saw the headlines and gasped. He asked the clerk if the papers were free and headed off to the room with one in his hand.

"Look at this," he said as soon as he entered the room. The girl was coming out of the bathroom, while the woman and grandson were just getting about. He thrust the newspaper in the girl's face, startling her for a moment. On the cover was a picture of a man. The headline said, "Man kills five members of family, still on the run."

"Oh my god," said the girl, "is that the guy who was in the room next to us in Gallup?" The woman blurted out her disbelief. The man took the paper to her and showed her the killer. She too gasped. The picture looked a lot like the guy. The family couldn't be certain but they were almost sure it was the same guy. He read the article to the others. It talked about how the man had killed his wife and four small children. He was believed to be in the Gallup area for at least twenty-four hours after the killing. They thought he was with another man and they were both in a work truck.

"You going to call the cops and report this, Grandpa?" the boy asked. He knew the answer as the words were coming from his mouth. His grandpa was not one to call the cops for anything. He always said that the cops would turn things around and make him into the guilty one.

The man did not trust the greed. He had never been a criminal. As soon as you talked to a cop, you were the suspect. The man saw exactly how it was. He saw the cops as a nationwide gang of thugs and criminals. They had their own set of laws that differed from the laws they upheld on everyone else. Even their families were immune to the laws. The man also felt as if the cops were stupid. He had seen the whole picture while in the military. There were different levels of the greed. They needed soldiers to uphold their agenda. The military served this purpose overseas, while the police upheld their agenda at home.

What these two groups didn't realize is that they were puppets to the system. They were the lowest on the chain of command. They were paid the lowest and made to work the most hours while in harm's way the whole time. They were the bitches of the greed. But the cops and military got thrown little perks to make them think they were better. They were put on a pedestal by the greed to make them think they were something they were not. The prosecutors and judges upheld all those narcissist beliefs in their rulings. Puppets were created using a form of superiority control over the weak. The guarantee of being illustrious was inviting to many humans. All the while, the greed laughed at how easy it was to manipulate the public mind and control the masses.

The news in the last months was filled with this. The cops would kill unarmed men. Sometimes it was justified, most of the time it was not. Every one of the shootings would create civil unrest. The shooters would never be prosecuted for their deeds. The media only focused on black people getting shot so the truth was never told.

It was always the same in the media. Tell the people only bits and pieces of the puzzle and let them imagine the rest. It was the way the greed kept all the people divided. It was easy to separate the people, they were the flock. If they were divided, they would never be united.

The man thought about these things often. He was always thinking up solutions to the problem but there was only the one solution. Get rid of the greed. That would be the only answer. It would take many years for anything to change no matter what changes came. Most likely, the only change would come with a cataclysmic event from the earth or space. It would take something epic to purge this planet of the dark.

People's minds could never be changed, though. The greed was very smart and controlled the masses like science. The flock envied the greed. It wanted to be just the same. Given any chance, ninety nine percent of the population would turn into the greed. The fools already emulated their idols every nuance.

The greed would never give up the power and wealth they had created on this planet. It was the darkness that consumed all. They had convinced the humans that they were the light, but the universe knew different. The greed was one of the darkest forces in the cosmos. It is where black holes originated, eating everything in its path.

After getting gas, it was back to the highway and the many miles across Texas. Going down the on ramp, deva vu struck the family again. On the embankment, rolled on its side, was a big rig truck. The driver must not have been paying attention. There was no other way the truck could have smashed through the guardrail and rolled down the grass. The driver was standing next to the truck. It was a distance away, but the man could have sworn it was the same driver who had crashed the logging truck on their first day. Impossible, he thought to himself. There was no way this could be the same guy.

The crow flew in between the car and the truck driver. The truck driver's sheepish expression changed to one of fear when he saw the bird. The flying motion directed his eyes further until they met the man's eyes, passing in their minivan. The man saw in the truck driver something familiar yet so strange. He had seen this look from others on the road. It was a look of familiarity and fear on the trucker's face. They knew the group was coming.

San Angelo was the first mid-size town to come to on the road. Texas was very spread out. The rolling hills and grassy terrain were a lot like the part of California they were originally from. The speed limit, being 75 on these back roads, was awesome. The family had heard legends of the barbecue in Texas. They were excited to try some. This food lived up to everything they had heard. It was off the charts. Even the fries were done to perfection.

They had found a food truck, kind of like the taco trucks at home, that served burgers. There was a little picnic spot set up and the family tore into it. It was just before lunch so the crowd did not exist. There was a line of fifteen people when they were finishing their brisket sandwiches. Again, they had come just before the crowds.

So far, everywhere they had stopped had been the right spot. All the food they had eaten, and the coffee they drank had been wonderful. It seemed to the boy as if these places were calling to the group. His grandpa explained that as you get older, you just learn more and more the right places to go. "When you get my age," he had told his grandson, "you will be very good at finding good food and other pleasures of life. These are things that come with your life experiences. It is almost like studying for a test. The more you study and practice, the better you get. Hopefully someday you will get an A." They all laughed at this as they piled back into the car.

The woman said she would drive the next stretch. Texas was going to be a long road ahead and they would both need to be at their best. After the drive all morning and those bomb ass brisket burgers, the man didn't argue. It was only a few miles back down the Texas highway, but the passengers were already fast asleep. The lack of sleep for the man had caught up with him. That, and the cookies and food, put him in the deepest of sleep.

He awoke to the sense of weightlessness. It felt as if the car had left the road and was floating through the air. The man sat up puzzled. He asked, "what happened," as he looked to his wife in the driver's seat. But there was no one in the driver's seat. The man wondered how he was still moving if nobody was driving. The terrain outside the window sped by so fast it was all just a blur. The car was moving so fast that everything looked almost completely white outside of it. The interior had a strong metallic smell to it. Also, the interior seemed to be aglow with a strange, dark orange light. The man could feel the luminosity, like a warm radiation of energy.

The man thought that, if he was dreaming, it was strange to be able to feel and smell also. This did not seem like a dream to him. It seemed like this was perfectly normal and had happened to him many times before. The music blaring on the radio was foreign to him. It seemed like a bunch of metal rubbing together. The man had taken hallucinogens many times in the past. This was almost the same as those trips. He thought that he was speeding through time and space. All the while, it felt as if his senses were all wide awake.

The man awoke somewhere on the road. He cocked his head towards the woman and she looked back with a smile, "hey there sleepy head. Thought you were going to sleep the whole way," she said.

"Where are we," he asked groggily. His dreams had been so vivid. It felt good to have dreams again. It had been too long. The two-year hiatus that his dreams had taken were not healthy for the man. He had always cherished his dreams and looked forward to them. No matter how strange they would be, they were still therapeutic.

"We're somewhere in Texas" his wife replied. "You've been asleep for over two hundred miles."

The man thought this to be impossible. He was never one to sleep in the car more than ten minutes, let alone hours, especially with his seat in the upright position. Surely, he would have woken up once. He reached in his pocket to retrieve his phone and found his shirt had a long tear up the side. His pants also had a tear on the knee. It looked almost like claw marks. His phone said it was three. But they had left the burger spot at ten thirty. How had he slept so long. "What happened to my clothes?" he asked.

"You were all restless and acting like you were fighting something. I looked down and your clothes were just ripped. We just figured you did it in your sleep." she said.

The boy was staring at the man with a very distant look. It was as if the boy was looking deep into his grandpa. "What's up?" the man asked his grandson.

The boy talked in a strange voice. It was like a whisper but commanding at the same time. He told his elder, "I know". The man could see the look in his grandson's eyes. He had awakened. The boy did truly know. The collective was growing stronger.

After a short break for the dogs and humans to run around, it was the man's turn behind the wheel. The highway was littered with dead turtles and armadillos. It seemed almost as if people tried to hit them. The man had seen so much chaos from humans. Whoever had called 'man' kind, was very mistaken.

The family crested hill after hill and passed over so many rivers. The lure of fishing was great, but they had to get to the sister's house. There they could fish and relax. After this day, there would be no more long drives for a few days. It was going to be time to rest.

The crow seemed to follow them the whole day. The man had gotten used to the creature on their daily path. The bird was part of their family. It seemed to know things that it wanted to share with the family. There was no doubt that it was the same bird that had begun the trip with them. The green eye told the man the whole story. They were connected. The bird also seemed to help navigate the map for the four. When they weren't exactly sure which way to turn at a certain intersection or which highway to take, the crow every time would fly in the direction, which would prove to be the right direction. The family decision to bypass all the cities would make map reading difficult at times. The large, brown bird was always there to assist at these times.

All the roads led to the cities. They sucked you in like giant magnets to pull your money from your pockets and the energy from your soul. The greed would like nothing better than to have all the people in their cities, just like they kept all the pigs in the pen. This way, control was the easiest. The man and woman had grown up in cities and had seen the dread. They had both moved to small towns, and then to the country after moving away from home.

It was easy for them to take the back road. They had taken this path their entire adult lives. It was one of the things that attracted the two in the first place. Neither of them had time nor patience for the cities, nor its masses.

The energy in the car was explosive. It almost felt like they were going to the Grand Canyon again. The man felt his sister's energy getting stronger and closer with every passing mile. It had been only a couple years since they had seen each other, but it had been thirty-five years since the man had been to his sister's house. They had always been very close spiritually. However, the distance and their careers had kept them apart far too long.

Outside of Houston, the woman contacted the brother in law. He told them of a way around Houston which would save hours of driving. The man was happy they had contacted his brother in law. They would have gone through Houston at rush hour and had a huge headache otherwise. The loop around the city was filled with toll gates, but all were electronic. Millions of dollars were collected on top of taxpayer dollars, daily, on these byways of the greed.

The man didn't know how the electronic tolls would work with the rental car, but figured they would deal with it later. This was a new concept integrated by the greed over the last few years. Replace human workers with computers to save money. Efficiently collecting tolls made more money. It was all profit for the greed, while the 'consumers' were sucked deeper into debt.

The directions from the brother in law were spot on. They took the family along the western side of Lake Conroe right to their house. The neighborhood seemed like a typical Texas suburban neighborhood. The yards were green and nicely maintained. Nice houses of all shapes and sizes and a lot of American flags. Everything swam in the humidity.

Reflections of the trips to his family's houses when he was a child came flooding back to the man. His sister's house reminded him of their earlier relatives. He almost expected his aunt or uncle to answer the door.

As soon as the brother in law opened the door, the man and his family knew they were home, at least for a few days. Much needed rest was awaiting them. The inside of the house was very cool and pleasant. The man worked with air conditioning, so his house was all set up. Decorations filled the house. It really felt like every other house the man had walked into that belonged to his family. They had all been collectors of random things, but in a tasteful way. Again, the man thought how funny DNA was and the connection people had to their relatives.

The brother in law was a great host until the sister arrived. The man had briefly met his sister's husband a couple of times, but this time would be different. They would be spending some days and get a chance to know each other. It would also give the others time to get acquainted with their uncle and brother in law.

The man had always liked his brother in law. He seemed like a genuine guy and had cool things to say. Six months before, he had a massive heart attack and almost died on numerous occasions. Being strong, he had pulled through. The man was surprised at how healthy his brother in law looked after such a short time had passed. He had been near death numerous times in his fight to keep his heart going.

It made the man think of his theory about death. Maybe his brother in law had died and now was just in another dimension where everything was almost the same. Maybe each time he had died on the table, he had been in a separate reality, if only for a short time before being thrust into a new dimension. Maybe, those thoughts that he would have in those dimensions is what people mistook for 'seeing their life flash before their eyes.'

Maybe they were just seeing other flashes of reality while they were crossing into their parallel life.

The reunion was awesome when the sister arrived. It was a reunion that was long overdue. It had been two years since they had met. The sister had come out for the funeral of one of their brothers. The brother's wife had major issues with the sister and man. They were not welcome at the funeral. So, the sister had spent three days with the man and his wife at the tattoo shop. It had been a nice time together. She also got to spend time with her nephew, whom she hadn't seen in almost twenty years. The time had been good. The man had even tattooed his sister. But that had been two years ago.

The man had always remained close to this sibling. Out of seven children, some strife is sure to occur. A couple of kids in their family had been ones to cause strife and had divided the clan. All over greed. These two were the ones who had been demonized. They were also the ones who never defended themselves nor talked bad about the others. They were the ones who could sleep well at night because of their actions.

With just four kids left in the family and both their parents gone, it was time to reconnect. After that, it would be easier to stay connected. The man repeated to the girl what he had said before. "Good things sometimes come from the bad. Maybe this is one of the good things that came from the bad. Maybe we wouldn't be here today if it wasn't for all the strife that we went through. Maybe the bad is what is driving us now towards the light. Bad energy only remains bad if you let it."

"You're a trip, Uncle," the girl said in a lighthearted way. "I understand your words. My dad used to speak the same talk, but I didn't understand then. I was too young. If only I could go back and talk to him one more time. If only I could go back and talk to them all one more time. I would be so enlightened."

"You are enlightened," the man told his niece. "All this happened as part of your awakening. Things are coming our way that most wouldn't understand. You will be a huge part of that. You are a huge part of it already happening. None of this would have happened without all the grief and heartache that we were forced to go through. I love you, Niece." The man spoke to his niece with genuine respect.

"I love you too, Uncle" the girl said with admiration.

The second round of the trip had begun. The moon was phasing into a new era. It was a half-moon this very hot Texas night. The family spent much time outside the first night. They had been in the car a lot the last week and would enjoy the fresh air. The sister had a screened porch in the back with furniture, so they had found their spot. The backyard was large, and the dogs were happy. They finally had a place to run around. Run around was exactly what they did. It was the happiest they had been all week. It was as if they too were home.

The family had been happy not to be in the car. They were looking at a chameleon on the screen. It was making a nice meal out of some fireflies. The whole family was enjoying looking at the different insects and creatures of Texas.

The sister had two wiener dogs. They were older and had to stay in the back yard. The family dogs did not get along so well with these two. The Yorkie especially would not put up with another dog thinking they had the dominance. The two groups barked at each other and ran around. They just seemed to be getting used to each other when one of the wieners let out a terrible howl. It stirred the humans out of their conversation to investigate.

The entire group left their screened enclosure to investigate the piercing howl. One wiener dog was lying lifeless in the middle of the yard, while its companion was giving off the unearthly howl. The group ran to the assistance of the fallen dog. It looked like something had ripped its throat open.

The family was very perplexed. There was no way one of the small dogs could have done this. They were both cowering on the back porch now anyway. Whatever it was, it had been strong. The dog had been killed in one swipe. "Do you have mountain lions here?" the man asked the others.

"No, but we have bears," the brother in law replied. "I've never seen one around here though, and surely wouldn't expect one in the neighborhood. There are just too many people for that. I don't know why we didn't hear anything. If it were a bear, the dogs would have been going crazy. They didn't even bark," he said in his southern drawl.

The man told the others that he thought it best they get back inside. He had looked to the porch and had seen a shadowy figure occupying one of the chairs they had been sitting in earlier. The figure wasn't paying any attention to the group; it was just looking at the door to the house. "What are we going to do about the dog?" the sister asked.

"Grab me a shovel and I will take care of it. You guys just get inside with the dogs," the man said to the women. He was always one to take charge in a quick minute. He looked to his sister. She was sobbing lightly as she listened to her brother's words. "Your husband will stay out here and keep an eye on things. Whatever killed your dog may still be lurking around. Grandson, bring me out my flashlight, it's in my backpack. Then you need to get inside, too, and take a shower. That way it will be my turn for that shower when we get done. I'm going to be more than ready for it."

Everyone muttered their agreement and went towards their duties. The dogs were clawing at the door to get inside. The shadow figure on the porch dissipated as the others got closer. Soon, they were inside and back to safety. The brother in law emerged from the side of the house at the same time the boy arrived with the flashlight. The boy wanted to stay, but his grandpa asked him nicely to just do as he was told. This was not going to be a cool task.

The man and his brother in law checked out the dead dog. It had been killed by something large with sharp claws or teeth. Its head was almost completely chopped off. When the two picked it up to carry it to the corner of the yard, the head hung grotesquely to the side. The dog didn't seem to weigh too much. The man thought for sure it would be much heavier. It only seemed to weigh maybe three pounds or less. This dog should weigh at least twenty to twenty-five pounds. Maybe the situation had fired up his adrenalin and he was stronger now, the man thought to himself. Like people who could lift a car off someone to save them. They would gain superhuman strength in a crisis.

The ground was soft and easy to dig. This area had been having massive rain storms lately, and it had loosened up the soil. The man got the dog in the ground as quick as possible, while his brother held the flashlight. The brother distracted the beam of the light so many times. The man asked him why he kept shining the light away and he said he kept hearing sounds. It didn't seem like they were alone. The man understood. As soon as they came into the yard to check on the dog, he had felt like there were others around them. The feeling only intensified the longer they remained out here.

The man spoke to his brother in law about what could have killed the dog. He asked him if he or his sister had seen anything unusual happening in the last few days. The brother told the man about an experience on the way home a few nights before. A mini-van with four people inside, had sped past him on the way home from work. A sheriff had pulled into the road to help a motorist and the van plowed into its side. All the people in the van and the cop were killed instantly. He said when he drove by, he didn't see anyone in the van. It was engulfed in flames but there was no one there. The accident happened right in front of the fire department. They were there to assist immediately. The brother in law spoke about the firemen's movements. They didn't seem to be human. They were more robotic, mixed with the actions of a serpent. Their shapes seemed to shift and warp.

The brother in law spoke also about his wife's experiences. He told the man that his sister was having premonitions of things of a cataclysmic event. Something huge was going to happen. Her dreams had been telling her. There was not a bit of doubt in her belief. The brother in law said there were other things that had happened, but they would have to wait until later. He wanted to get the hell out of this back yard and into the safety of the house.

The dog got chucked in the hole as soon as it was deep enough. The man quickly threw the dirt on the animal and backfilled the hole. There was barely enough dirt to fill the hole all the way in. The man took the flashlight from his brother and surveyed the area. He didn't think he had thrown the dirt all about and the light proved it. Why wasn't there enough dirt, he wondered. He tossed a couple nearby ornamental rocks on top of the grave and called it a burial.

The man had enough of this madness. He grabbed his brother in law by the shoulder and pulled the man out of the daze he had fallen into. The dog's grave had captured the brother in law's attention and wouldn't let go until the other man pulled him free. The two headed swiftly for the house. The man felt a terrible dread passing through the yard. The large tree seemed like the only bit of reality to remain. He felt light headed, almost like he may pass out. His brother grabbed him by the waist but he fell. Suddenly, another hand came from the porch and grabbed the man as he was falling backward. It was the large hand of his grandson. The boy pulled his grandpa onto the porch right before he lost consciousness. Once again, he had saved his elders from certain doom.

As soon as they crossed the doorway, the man felt better. He sat down for a moment on the porch to gather his strength. There was rustling in the bushes immediately outside the porch. The smell of burnt metal assaulted their senses. The two men were done, they went inside. The boy stayed outside for a few moments with the flashlight. There were sounds all around outside. It sounded to him like a jungle. Something large hitting the screen was all the boy could endure. He leaped the few feet to the door and was inside the house.

This would be the man's first real shower in a week. There was no way a dead dog was going to ruin that for him. He had been looking forward to this for many miles. The man stayed in the warm water much longer than he should have. He progressively was making the water warmer, creating a steam room in his sister's very air-conditioned house. It felt so good to the man to be clean. The miles of dirt flowed down the drain.

Blood in the water caught the man's attention. At first, he thought it was dirt but the color was more red. He was not unfamiliar to nose bleeds. He had them many times as a kid and a couple since being an adult. This was not the same. The blood seemed very thick. It hung in ropes floating through the water. Also, it was a very dark color, darker than any blood he had ever seen. The man wiped at his nose with the back of his hand but only water remained. He was not bleeding from his face.

He looked over his body but saw no wounds. Nor did he feel any pain from a wound that would have to be bad to be creating that much blood. The steady trickle of blood flowing down the back of his left thigh solved the mystery. He felt around on his back. Just above his belt line, in the kidney area, there was a small puncture wound that seemed to be healed, but had split open. He couldn't see the incision, but could feel it and its repair. The man had many stitches in the past and knew full well what they felt like. This was like no stitch he felt before, but it served the same purpose. It had been closing a wound before its abatement.

The man felt around the area. There was no pain, but the wound seemed relatively fresh. He could not remember how he had gotten it. Furthermore, he could not remember how he had gotten it repaired. He searched his memories of the last few days, trying to remember any kind of accident he had. There were no memories of this. There had been no accident and certainly no hospital.

It felt as if there were a ball or something under the stitch. He rolled it under the skin and thought it was an odd thing to have under his skin. Once, when he was a child, he had taken his brother's ten-speed bicycle without permission and crashed it coming out of the driveway. He had landed on his knee. Later that night, in the shower, he had felt something strange in his skin and squeezed it out. A small rock had popped out of his flesh and hit the shower floor. This felt like the exact same scenario. It was just slightly different, but the man seriously felt like he had been through this before.

He squeezed around the object embedded in his being. He was very displeased about this. It felt like someone was playing a game with him or something. After catching the object in the middle of his fingers, the man pulled while squeezing. The object popped out of his skin and hit the tub with a hollow, metallic sound. A stream of blood plasma came flowing out of the wound. It looked almost like a small garden hose was being opened in the man's side.

The man reached into the bottom of the tub to retrieve the object before it rolled down the drain. He grabbed the orb just as the first rush of his plasma hit the tub. The object looked like a small marble or ball bearing. It wasn't exactly circular. It seemed to have strange hard edges while being smooth at the same time. The globe was very familiar to the man. The shape was one like he had drawn before, pulled from his imagination. He rolled it in his fingers and straightened up. This is when the blood left his head and he lost consciousness.

The faucet broke the man's fall. It hit him square in the middle of his forehead. Another object popped out of his skin when he hit the faucet. It was a tooth. He had acquired this tooth back in sixth grade playing flag football. He and another class mate were going for the same kid's flags. The kid had ducked out, and the two had collided. The other kid's tooth had broken, and the man got sent home with a large lump on his head and a lot of blood. The tooth had been in his head ever since, without his knowledge. Now the tooth went directly down the drain, taking its dirty little secret with it.

The loud thump from the bathroom brought the others running. The woman was the first inside the door. She could barely see anything through all the steam. The dark figure standing in front of the mirror was much too tall and thin to be her husband. The figure twisted into the movement of the steam and dissipated through the door to the hallway.

The woman had to shake her head and blink rapidly to get that image out of her mind. Her mind had been playing many tricks on her. She was beginning to think her husband had orchestrated a grand production for their benefits. So many strange things had been happening. It really didn't seem like coincidence, nor reality.

Lying motionless in the bathtub was her husband. The entire shower enclosure was covered in thick, dark blood. The water was so hot it was difficult for the woman to reach her hand in and turn it off. Once the pound of the water was gone, the woman could assess the situation. The sister and her husband were first responders. That was their calling in life. They both sprang into action and came to the man's assistance.

The man had hit his head hard on the faucet. Blood had pooled in his eyes and was now dripping down his face like tears. The lump on his forehead looked like a baseball but miraculously, there was only a small slit in the middle. "He got lucky," the sister said to her husband. "I was expecting to come in here and find his head split in two with that blood all over."

The sister and her husband got the man out of the water and onto the floor. The woman had piled a bunch of towels there so they would have a makeshift gurney. The brother in law told his nephew to call 911 and the boy leaped into action. The head wound looked very bad. They were sure he was going to have a concussion. The man had not come to yet, which really worried the others.

It was about ten minutes before the paramedics showed up. The woman had gotten her husband partially clothed in this time, although he was still unconscious. The sister and her husband had looked him over well and saw no injuries except for the lump and slit on his forehead. They did not know where all the blood had come from in the shower. This wound did not look like it had produced that much.

The blood in his eyes told the two that he had a concussion. The ambulance drivers were very professional. They were in the house and conferring with the sister immediately upon arrival. They did their quick field tests and then loaded the man on the gurney.

Wheeling the man out of the house, the boy stopped the two briefly. "Excuse me," he said to one of the paramedics, "do I know you?" The boy had this feeling as soon as the two paramedics had walked in. One of them looked so familiar to the boy, but also it was a feeling deep within that told him he had met this older gentleman before. He just couldn't place the man or his voice. All the man's mannerisms were familiar to the boy. It was almost like they were distant relatives.

"I don't think that is possible," the older paramedic said. He seemed to shy away from the boy, like he was hiding a secret or something. The boy did not trust the paramedic. He told his grandma that she should go in the ambulance with her husband. Something was not right here. The uniform on the man had a name tag, but it was made of symbols the boy was not familiar with.

The driver argued with the woman. She insisted on going in the ambulance, and the two paramedics insisted against it. In the end, the woman had stronger reserve and the others agreed to let her ride with them. "Be careful," the boy called out to his grandma as she got in the back of the ambulance.

As soon as the vehicle pulled away, the dogs started howling. First the Chihuahua; then the Yorkie and the surviving wiener dog added to the ruckus. The sister and her husband had followed the ambulance, leaving the boy and his cousin behind. The racket created by the dogs was deafening. The two decided to go into the bathroom and clean it up some. Maybe there they could escape the howl of the dogs.

There was a lot of debris in the bathroom. The EMT crew had left so many pieces of plastic wrapper behind. The boy and girl went to work throwing the trash into large garbage bags. They talked about what had just happened. They also spoke of the paramedic who had come. The boy was telling the girl about this when she remembered. It was the same man they had met back at the Grand Canyon. Why hadn't she been able to remember before? The two spoke of the strange things that were happening. The boy asked his cousin if she thought his grandpa was crazy. She told the boy that his grandpa was probably one of the only sane people she had ever met. He was the only one she knew that truly knew.

While mopping some of the blood from the tub, the boy found something else. It was a small piece of metal about half the size of a marble. It wasn't quite round. It was very light, like it was hollow. The boy thought this would make a great memento of this experience and dropped it into his pocket. Almost immediately, the dogs stopped howling. They all three appeared at the bathroom door and looked inside to their humans.

All three dogs burst into their playful mood. The two older ones already had their toys and were ready to play fetch. The boy and girl looked at each other perplexed. Moments before, the dogs had been in a frantic state, and now they were happy as could be. They finished the cleaning and went to be with their canine homies.

As they came out of the bathroom, the boy and girl both saw a shadowy figure pass through the hallway. A faint light at the end of the hallway illuminated the shape. Now the light and the shape were fading. The girl grabbed the bags of garbage and headed out to the trash cans. The boy was momentarily in a frozen state of thought. He stared at the end of the hallway with a blank expression. All the madness that had been happening came rushing into his thoughts. The bathroom door slammed closed behind him on its own accord.

The lamp at the end of the hall began to glow again. It was too much for the boy. He burst into tears. The tears flowed all night and well into the morning. They had been building in his being his entire life. Now they flowed like the rivers they had passed on this trip. The tears washed all the bad energy away from his soul. The boy was cleansed.

The light rays from the front door brought the boy out of his reverie. How could it be morning he thought. Surely, he couldn't have been standing here all night. The door to the garage opened and in came his cousin. Her face was streaked with blood like she had been crying tears of crimson. The look on her face told the boy that she had been in a daze also.

"What happened to your face?" the girl asked her cousin. "And what happened all night? I just woke up standing next to the garbage can."

"I don't know," replied the boy, "but your face is covered in blood. Your clothes are all ripped up too"

"Your face is covered in blood too," the girl said to her cousin. The two hugged an embrace of survivors.

The memories of the night before came flooding back into the girl and boy's minds. The others were at the hospital. What had happened to them all night when the others were away? They both remembered cleaning the bathroom, but that is where the memories ended. Next thing they remembered was waking up standing, covered in tears of blood.

The girl grabbed her phone and called the woman. She had to find out what happened to her uncle and when they would be back. The ringing in the bedroom caught the boy's attention. It was his grandma's phone. Maybe in the commotion of things, she had left her phone behind. The boy went to the room and looked inside. There on the nightstand was his grandma's phone. It was ringing and flashing and vibrating all at the same time. The light from the phone illuminated the room. It cast just enough green glow for the boy to see the figures lying in bed. He crept closer. Who was in his grandparent's bed, he thought.

One of the sleepers rolled over slightly and the boy saw the face. It was the face of his grandma. Only now her hair was a dark color and there was something slightly different about her features. He crept out of the room as quietly as possible. He had to tell his cousin about this.

His cousin was already asleep, though. She was snoozing deeply on the couch, all wrapped up in her blankets. The boy wondered how she had gotten to bed so fast and into such a deep sleep in such a short time. He had only been gone for a minute. Or so he thought. It was too much; he laid on the cot which had been set up for him and thought of it all.

It wasn't but a minute before he was fast asleep.

CHAPTER 12

The deep slumber the first night at his sister's house was much needed. The bed was probably the softest the man had ever slept in. Almost like sleeping on a marshmallow. It was so good, it felt like being in a dream. The house was very quiet, and the drapes were blackout. Just like at home. The hotels on the road had been anything but quiet or dark. The family was not used to that. At their house and at their apartment, the noise was only from nature. The light was blocked from coming inside. The sister's house was the same.

The lack of sleep had caught up with the man and his senses. It had been getting harder for him to differentiate between reality and fantasy. His mind was working like crazy every mile of the road, thinking about the story that would be told that night. When the woman drove, he rested, but seldom got to that full sleep. Now he felt like he had been asleep for days and had made up for all those lost hours. Now he had truly rested.

He went to scratch his head and found a large bandage wrapped around it. He felt around the wraps. The bandages seemed to fill his whole cranium, but weren't on his face. He tried his best to remember what had happened, but everything was so hazy. The haze reminded him of the steam from the night before.

Suddenly, the memories came floating back as the haze cleared, just like steam through the bathroom vent. He remembered falling into the tub. He vaguely recalled a lot of blood and an object that had come from his body, but those were distant glimpses of memory. He felt around his forehead, remembering the impact. There was no pain under the bandage.

He turned his head to see the woman looking at the ceiling. "Hey there sleepy head," she said. The words brought a serious recollection to the man. She had said those exact words to him, and very recently. His wife was looking at something with joy in her eyes. That something seemed to captivate her attention. There was something slightly different about her face but the man thought it must be the morning shadows filling the room. "How are you feeling?"

"I guess I'm alright," replied the man. The sleep was fully clearing from his head now. "What happened?"

"You fell in the shower and hit your head. An ambulance came and took you to the hospital. By the time your sister and I arrived, you were already in the emergency room. You had a severe concussion. Somehow, you did not bust open the skin except for a small little slit. They kept you at the hospital for the night and next day after the surgery. Then your sister insisted she bring you home. There was an issue she had with one of the doctors and she would not let you stay there any longer. With her credentials in first response, the hospital had no choice. They released you into your sister's care."

The man looked around, expecting to see an IV or monitor or something, but there was nothing. He only saw the countless knickknacks that filled the room. "How did I get back here?" he asked his wife. "How long have I been in this bed?"

"Me and your sister brought you home in the minivan. We had followed the ambulance and waited with you all night and the next day. They had you in observation after the surgery. Our brother in law stayed behind with his niece and nephew. They were all so worried. We thought it best not to leave them home alone," the woman explained to the man. "The doctor said there would be memory loss and some disorientation. After all, you just had a four-inch plate put in your head."

The man felt sick to his stomach. How had he had surgery and not even been aware of it? Furthermore, how had he gotten released so soon after surgery on his skull?

The woman had still not made eye contact with the man. He thought this to be very odd. Normally, she would be all observant of his condition and caring about his status. But now she seemed so distant. Like the man was a footnote in a story that she had no time to read. He asked her why she wouldn't look at him. She said he was just being silly. He wasn't thinking straight.

The woman got out of the bed and walked to the dresser, opening the drapes a bit on the way. The man had seen the disparity as soon as the light hit his wife. They were not ones to wear clothes to bed. They both had full body suits of tattoos and needed no artificial covering. Today, the woman wore strange pants and shirt. It looked to be one piece like something a Genie would wear. The man could see through the material. Its greenish fabric was transparent.

On the woman's back was a large phoenix. Impossible was the thought that the man raked through his head. The sight made it feel like he had taken shrapnel to the head. His wife had a large Japanese dragon on her back, not a phoenix. Furthermore, when the sun ray poked through the drape just enough to settle on her head, the man got the real shock. Her hair was solid black. It was so black it almost had a blue tint in the sunlight. His wife's hair was gray. It was speckled with black, but it was gray. He had always loved her hair and immediately noticed the difference.

The woman dug through her suitcase for the day's attire. The man asked her when she had dyed her hair. She called him silly, and said it had always been that color. When he asked her about the tattoo, she spun around and asked, "Are you alright?"

It was then that the man saw her eyes. There was no longer any white left in them. The pupils had dilated to the point of taking over the entire eye. The woman saw the look of wonder in the man's eye and quickly turned away. "You need to just lay there and continue to rest," she said, facing the wall. "I'm going to go tell the others you are awake. They've been very worried about you and will be happy to hear the news. Are you hungry? You haven't eaten in three days."

"I'm starving," the man said excitedly. His stomach once again spun with the thought of being asleep for the past three days. The weird events with his wife and bad feelings in his gut were quickly superseded by the rumbling of hunger. Everything seemed so odd to the man. Had he really been here for three days? His wife and the room all seemed so much different than he remembered. Rest was probably what he needed. He was still trying to grasp the fact that he had a plate in his head.

It seemed like hours had passed, and the woman did not return. The shadows from outside played across the room like a sundial in the man's mind. He kept thinking he would do something and then think he did it, only to question his actions later. In his mind, he had already gone to the bathroom twice and gone for some water. But there was no water next to him, and he had to use the bathroom very bad. The sound of muted voices was a continuous play on the man's mental state. He figured it was his family speaking, but couldn't discern any one voice. None of them sounded familiar to the man, who prided himself on voice recognition. It sounded like a horror movie in his swollen mind.

He decided it was time to get out of this bed and get about some. His thirst and hunger were driving his will. It was very difficult to throw his legs over the side, but it was almost impossible to stand. His legs felt like wet noodles that wouldn't quite support his weight. His head spun with the threat of spiraling out of control. The man had been through a lot in his life. Pain and misery were a daily visitor to his being. He had learned how to adapt to this. This would be no different. He stayed steady for a few minutes, letting his body adjust to the standing position while hugging the bed. Once he was steady, he could take a step or two. Then he was at his suitcase getting some clothes.

It was a slow process, but the man made it to the bedroom door. The voices outside were a steady drone of darkness. He opened the door slowly and steadied himself into the hallway. The voices stopped as soon as the door peeked open. The only sound in the house came from the constant whir of air escaping the air conditioner vents. He walked the short distance to the living room and found his wife sleeping on the couch with a book propped up on her chest. She heard movement in the room and fluttered her eyes open.

The woman jumped to her feet and raced to the man's side. "You shouldn't be out of bed by yourself like this," she told him. "You took a nasty fall last night, and you should really be resting some more."

The woman's hair was back to its gray color. Her face was now the familiar one the man had loved all these years. "What happened?" asked the man.

"Oh man," she said as she steadied him toward the couch. "You were in the shower last night and took a terrible spill. You were knocked out for some time but came to in the car on the way to the hospital. Your sister and I had taken you there and waited for a few hours until they released you. We brought you home. It was about three in the morning when we got here. You went right to bed, as the doctor had suggested. Your sister stayed by the bed all morning until she had to go to work. She was so worried about you. Then your niece and grandson sat by your side until noon, and I had just come out here to read about thirty minutes ago. I must have fallen asleep, too."

"Did they put a plate in my head?" he asked his wife.

"No, silly, you had a pretty bad concussion, but there was no plate put in you. The doctor said the stress of the road and lack of sleep probably intensified the situation, and you might have some hallucinations and feelings of being light headed. You will be just fine; you just need to rest some more."

"How long have I been asleep?" the man asked. "Where are the girl and boy?"

"About twelve hours. I don't think you woke up once. The boy and girl went to see about renting a boat for tomorrow, and were talking about doing a little fishing. They went to the dock just down the way. They wanted to let you rest. I'm going to text them now though, and let them know that you are okay. I'll text your sister, too. They've all been very worried about you."

The man asked what all the bandages were about. There seemed to be an awful lot of bandages for such a simple wound. The woman told him to quit acting like a fool. He had hurt his head, and they had to bandage it. It wasn't like a conspiracy or something. The man thought it strange that the woman used this word to describe how he was feeling. He hadn't said anything about a conspiracy.

He decided to take the bandage off and see for himself. The woman said she would suggest he leave them on, but the man's mind was made up. The boy and girl arrived home just as the first gauze was unraveling. They were both very happy to see the man up and about. Last night, seeing the man lying on the bathroom floor with that huge lump on his head, they had been very worried about him. They both knew he was a tough old bastard, though, and would get through this.

The boy and girl were not surprised to find the man taking off his bandages. Once, when the boy was young, the man had cut his leg with a chainsaw. The thirty-six stitches needed to be taken out, and the boy's fingers were the perfect size. The man had enlisted his grandson to remove his stitches, and he had done it well. The man had told the boy then that you only went to the doctor for things you couldn't do yourself. Otherwise, you would just throw hard earned money away to the greed. The man felt the whole medical industry and its insurance brothers were a huge part of the greed and their plan to destroy Pachymama. All for the benefit of the self-proclaimed 'public servants'.

The bandages made a nice little pyramid at the man's feet. A convenient curio cabinet provided the mirror the man would need. The lump was not very big at all. About the size of a silver dollar. It was an angry shade of purple, and the man could see the small slit in the middle. It almost looked like some strange little creature might crawl out of the incision at any moment. The bump throbbed a couple of times, and the pain came. It felt like he had been hit with a baseball bat. For that matter, the man thought, he had.

He asked his wife why they had used such a large bandage, but she said she didn't know. She wasn't the doctor. The man then asked who had shaved his head. He wasn't completely bald. It was like someone had shaved crop circles on his cranium. The man often would let his family cut his hair in this fashion. He would let them cut his hair in any way they would want. Sometimes, it was way out there and crude. Other times, it was very refined. This time, it was more refined than ever. It looked like the patterns had been cut in his hair with a laser. They were very precise and seemed to have meaning.

The woman said that the boy had cut his hair back in New Mexico. She asked if he remembered or not, but the man could not remember that. "Where did you get these patterns from, and what do they mean?" the man asked his grandson.

"I got them at that gift shop in Marble Canyon," said the boy. "The lady said they were representatives of the solar system. I shaved them into your head at the hotel in Roswell. I can't believe you don't remember this. Lightning struck while I was cutting your hair."

The boy had been spinning a small metal object between his fingers. The man asked him what he had, and the boy showed him. It was a small disc shaped object of a shiny metal. The man asked him where he had gotten the object, and the boy said that he had found it in the shower after the man had gone to the hospital. They had been cleaning up the blood from the bathtub and he had found this orb.

The man held out his hand, and the boy dropped the object into his grandpa's palm. The metal spread a warmth throughout the man's being. He knew this object. They had once shared the same flesh pod. The man had a flash of the night before in the shower. He remembered a lot of blood and finding something like this orb he was holding now. Had it popped out of his side or something? The man felt to his back, in the kidney area. Sure enough, there was a small scar. The man had his wife look at the skin and she confirmed that the blemish was there. None of them knew how it had gotten there. The scar was about two inches long and very well healed. It was through the tattoos, leaving a tattoo of sorts on top of the tattoo.

The man was passed knowledge by the object. He told the boy to get the box he had found in Bodie. The boy was standing at the counter with the box as the words were still coming from the man's mouth. He had the same exact idea. As soon as the box was in front of him, the metal globe in the man's hand split in two. Each piece magnetically found their place on the corners of the box. The indentations that had been cut on top of the box were the perfect shape and size for the pieces. They locked into place and became one with the One. These pieces of metal had been on this box before. They were part of it. Each half of the sphere appeared to be a crescent moon in their respective slots.

The brother arrived home. He was very happy to see the man up and about. He was not so sure of his condition last night, and wasn't sure how long it would lay him up for. Soon after, the sister also arrived. She had taken off work early to get home to her family. This was the first time anyone in her family had come for a visit in such a very long time. Then this happened. Every time their family got together, something weird was going to happen. As soon as she was in the house, she was by his side. She was very happy to see her brother doing better.

The family was famished and ordered some pizza. The brother raved about a pizza place nearby that served an authentic New York style pizza. They had to try some. It was about forty-five minutes waiting for the food to arrive. It gave the sister and brother time to unwind from work and change clothes. The woman kept a watchful eye on the man the whole time. He said he was feeling better, but he was still a bit unsteady on his feet. Some of his words were slurred, too, and he was saying some things that were very absurd, even for him. She wished he would just sit on the couch and relax, but that was not his way.

At one point, the boy and girl went outside for a bit. The man asked his wife to see her back. She asked him why, and he said it was something that he had dreamed. It just kept nagging at his conscious. If he could see her back, the thoughts would go away. The woman stood and pulled her shirt up. There, on her back, was the large phoenix tattoo. The man said nothing. The woman saw the puzzlement in his face and said, "now you don't remember tattooing my back?"

"I remember just fine," the man said. He was very confused. The food arrived just after, and the man's mind was distracted for the time. Visions of the phoenix would linger in his mind all night. His wife had a dragon on her back.

The family enjoyed the fantastic pizza with some nice conversation. None of the group were drinkers, so the talk could stay on the truthful side. It had been so long since the man and his sister had time to catch up. The boy was very surprised to learn that this was the man's half-sister. It was his father's daughter from his first marriage. The man had never talked about this to the boy or others. To him, this was his sister. There was no way he would ever diminish who she was to him by calling her a half. His sister was whole to him.

The sister had come to live with the man's family when he was born. Before, she was living with her uncle and his wife and kids. The man didn't know all the details, as he was just a small child. When the man was about six years old, he came home from school one day to find his sister gone. His parents had said that she moved away and was living with her real mother. This had naturally torn the other children up. Their oldest sister was gone. The one who had nurtured them and played with them, had been taken away in a flash.

The man and sister spoke of all these things until about midnight. She told the man things that made the puzzle of his life more complete. He knew there had been strife back then. He had felt the animosity from his mother toward his sister his whole life. The oldest sister of his mother also made life very unpleasant for her half-sister. She was the oldest and was not about to give that up. Their relationship had never been a good one. Now the one sister was dead, and here they were.

The family had been brought up very strict Catholic. The mother had been a nun back in Kansas, along with her two sisters. The religion ran very deep in their German bloodline. The father had been an Okie, without religion. These were the people so easily grabbed into the greed.

The children were forced to go to the family church every Sunday. The man hated this day as a boy. It filled him with a sense of dread, starting Saturday afternoon every week. Church was the biggest waste of time to his young, creative mind. He would much rather be riding his bike or playing with his buddies. He also did not trust most of the people who were at the church. They had an aura about them that seemed very sinister to the boy. When they would shake hands, their hands would always be cold and clammy. The boy knew there was something very wrong with these people. They were the true evil. All the while, they pointed their fingers at an imaginary creature and said that was the evil. More control through fear. The greed was tricky alright.

At age eleven, scandal had rocked the man's church. Two of the priests were accused of molesting hundreds of children. Another priest had embezzled millions out of the parishioners' donations. The flock strayed. The man's parents decided that church wasn't for them anymore. The man was very fortunate, there would be no more spending his Sundays listening to some dry ass child molester. He never went to church another day in his life. The greed could keep their savior and their payments to heaven. He was one to distance himself from fear, not be in the middle of the hysteria.

The family all started to wander off to bed. Finally, just the man and his sister were left. He told her that he thought the church had an agenda, and they had controlled millions. They were involved with others who ran everything. It was all the greed. He asked his sister if she ever had strange premonitions or weird things happen to her. She laughed, and told her brother that he had always been a little crazy. He had always spoke of spirits and dreams, but she had never encountered any of it. She was laughing when she went into the house, leaving the man alone on the porch. The chameleon had been on the screen all night, listening silently to the conversation while eating its fireflies.

The man had seen the look in his sister's eye when he had asked her about spirits. Something was there that she wanted to tell him, but she had not. Was someone holding her back? The man knew that his sister held a key to their heritage. She had held it for a very long time. She had denied its existence for a very long time. Now, this trip was the time for truth.

Finally, the man went inside. He and his sister had been out on the porch together for hours. It was now after midnight. The girl had just lied on the couch after getting out of the shower. The boy was not on his cot. "What happened to the boy?" he asked his niece. The man had a very bad feeling.

"He decided to go fishing down by that dock," replied the girl. "I told him not to go but he did anyway. He said this is when you catch the big ones."

"Damn boy," said the man with irritation. He went into the bedroom, where his wife was lying in bed, reading. He asked her if she knew the boy went fishing, and she became very upset that the boy had left. She said she would never have let him go at this hour. Earlier, the boy had even had a hard time finding the dock. She didn't know how he was going to find it now, in the dark.

He told his wife that he was going to look for the boy. She said she would call him first. The boy's phone was on the coffee table. Its ring was like a dreadful scene in a bad movie. The woman pleaded with her husband not to go. The injury to his head needed to heal. The doctor had said to rest. She said she would go with him, as did the girl. The man declined their invitations, though. He said they were already dressed for bed, and he wasn't. The dock was only two blocks away, anyhow. He would be back in less than ten minutes.

The two women were almost begging the man to stay as he went out the door. He wasn't going to let anything happen to his grandson. He trusted the boy a great deal, but the boy didn't know Texas like he knew California. He wouldn't be thinking about this with his fourteen-year old brain. The two blocks distance was quickly overcome with the swift walk of the man. He felt a sense of urgency in his step.

The dock was vacant. He shined his police style flashlight around the platform and the adjacent woods. There was no sign of the boy or any of his gear. There was no sign of anyone at this hour. Only a couple of the houses even had lights on still. The man was getting very worried. The boy had spoken so much about catching turtles. "Maybe he had wandered off searching for some and got lost or something," the man thought. The girl had said he had left about two hours ago. He could be anywhere.

A bubbling sound drew the man's attention toward the water, just beyond the dock. With the only sound before being crickets and the night, this sound stood out. A strange greenish gray glow was coming from the water where the bubbles were. It cast the bottom of the dock in a strange glow. It reminded the man of his hot tub back home.

He rushed to the bubbling. The man stood on the edge of the dock, peering over the side. What he saw in the water turned his heart to ice. He felt as though he could literally drop over dead from the heart scare he got.

Floating about five feet under the water was a human figure. It was dressed in strange clothing the man hadn't seen before. Almost more like metal than fabric. The green glow seemed to be encompassing the creature. The light shined from within the figure. It seemed to be staring directly at the man. Their eyes met, and they shared a common bond.

Even through the water, the man could detect the facial features of the other being. It looked exactly like his brother. His heart, beating so strongly, couldn't take much more of this. His brother had died twenty-two months earlier. His death had been very hard on the man and the girl. They had been so very close. Now here his sibling was, at this very spot in East Texas.

"Bro," the man said to the being in the water. He knew in his mind that this was indeed his brother. Their energies had always been connected. They had always looked identical and they had also shared a mental connection.

His brother's form in the water began to increase in luminescence. Soon, the light got so bright it overtook the man and the forest behind him. The light continued to increase in brightness until it consumed the entire lake. The man was blinded for a moment. It felt as though his brother was all around him. Like their auras had become one. The light had a vibration to it, like it was being driven into his soul. The man had not felt this safe ever in his life.

The light was suddenly gone. It was once again dark outside, with the half-moon providing the light, along with a couple of street lamps. The man was standing in front of his sister's house. The other members of his family were all standing in the front yard in their pajamas. They all shook their heads when they saw the man standing there. The boy ran up and hugged his grandpa. "I went looking for you," he told the boy.

"Grandpa, where have you been? I never left the house. You went for a walk after you ate some pizza and never came back. Grandma has been so worried about you."

The man walked the few feet to the others. "Are you alright?" his wife asked. She knew the answer already. She could see the look of happiness on her husband's face. It had been years since she had seen this look on him. It made her very happy and relieved at the same time. Death had been hard on all of them.

She decided to let it go. The fact that the man had been gone for six hours didn't matter at this moment. All that mattered was that things were going to be good again.

The woman embraced her husband in a hug of relief and love.

In the darkness, she could not see the eye that had begun to peek out of the lump on the man's head.

Chapter 13

When the family got up in the morning, the sister and her husband had already gone off to work. A note on the table said to make themselves at home. They would be home around eight.

The man couldn't imagine sitting around his sister's house, watching television. The day before, he had used his time wisely. He had painted a page in his mask book. The reference had come from a mask he had seen at the UFO museum in Roswell. He had brought the book to keep up with the rhythm of the paintings. Yesterday had provided a perfect day to get it done. He was already a few days off schedule, being Tuesday and all. He didn't want to fall very far behind. He had never been that kind of person. Once something was in his thoughts, he was going to work on it until it was done.

This day, there was nothing more to do around the house. The man gathered up his niece and grandson and headed for adventure. The woman stayed behind with the dogs. Her dream of vacation included some rest, while the man's idea of vacation was to go nonstop. He was out of bed as soon as he had heard his sister and brother leave for work. He had written in his book all night anyway and had only rested for the last couple of hours. He didn't think he had gotten any sleep, but he had not heard his sister or her husband getting ready for work. Sleep must have visited him.

He had remembered a bit of his dream. He had been down by the docks and saw an alien in the water. The being had spoken to him in his mind. The feeling had been a comforting one when he was in its presence. His dream had seemed so vivid.

The woman had insisted on putting the bandage back on the night before. She said the doctor said to leave it on a day or two. The man had complained about being so tired after the pizza. The woman knew that he was nowhere near being healed. She had wrapped his head just after dinner and right before he had bedded down for the night.

The man threw his hat over the gauze to hide it the best as possible. He wore the same clothes as the day before. This was vacation. He had no one to impress. It was still very early when he emerged from the room.

His niece and grandson were already awake and dressed. They, too, seemed ready for some adventure. The man assessed the grocery situation at his sister's house, and away they went. Conroe was a cool town. It reminded the man a lot of the San Joaquin valley back home. Just with a giant lake in the middle. The people were very nice, and the things were not so hard to find. They had a list of things to get, and would have to go to multiple places. They had no problem with this, long as they weren't sitting around the house all day.

They stopped at a large box store to get some picnic supplies and hats. After the grueling sun of the last few days, the family decided they needed better hats to protect their heads. By the third store, they had managed to acquire the four items they needed. It was one of the things the man hated about corporate consumerism the most. When you went to get something, they were out. You would have to go to multiple places to get all the things you needed, all the while being tempted to buy more stuff.

The hope for hats was almost lost. The last store had three hats left that suited the family's needs. So many tourists were in the stores. The family talked about how this must be a serious tourist town, and it must be a very popular weekend. Many of the people were pushy. They seemed to be in a hurry to get back to their slow lives with their phones. The family spoke of humans losing their empathy and, along with it, their dignity.

While making sure the hats would fit, the girl asked the man who painted the eye on the middle of his bandage. He asked the girl what she was talking about, and she turned him toward the store mirror. He had thrown his hat on immediately this morning, and had it on when he brushed his teeth. This caused him not to see the eye painted directly in the middle of his forehead. The eye was very detailed. It looked almost real to the man. He quickly put his hat back on.

A small crowd of tourists had begun to gather around the three. They were watching the family intently. There was something very robotic about the people. They didn't seem to have emotion.

The three purchased their lids and were swiftly out the door. It was on to the grocery store, and then back to the safety of the house. The man, over the last years, had these experiences more and more. Everywhere he went, a group would gather around. If he was at a yard sale looking at something, seven more people would come. All of them would look at what he was looking at. Some would even push him out of the way to get access to his finds. He had seen this at every tourist spot they had stopped at on this road trip, also. People seemed to gravitate to the family. It sometimes made him somewhat angry. He didn't invite these people to invade his space. It was the accumulation of all these experiences that made the man cherish his alone time all that much more.

The man had decided to make Eggplant Parmesan. It was one of his specialties, and most of the ingredients were already at his sister's house. She had stocked up for the family visit. She need not have, her pantry and four freezers held more food for two people than the man had ever seen. First responders obviously understood the importance of being stocked up.

The people in the store looked very strangely at the family. The man did look a little disheveled. He had been wearing these same clothes for the last days and the bandage really made him stand out. The girl and boy were also stared at, though. This store was big, and it was early. There weren't many patrons besides themselves in the store. The man told the others that the workers were just curious about them. They were so different than what they normally would see. The man felt like he was being watched the entire time they were in the market. The feeling wouldn't pass until they got inside their minivan. They got their groceries in a hurry, and were out the door.

The drive back was chaotic. The man was not familiar with the area yet, and relied on the memory of the girl and boy. The cars on this stretch of road were very crazy. They sped by very fast, and did not wait for anybody. A large white truck almost hit the family car, and swerved off to the left. The man saw the pro-gun sticker plastered to the lower back window as the truck barely missed them. The truck hit a light pole and glass went flying. The gun sticker flew at the man's head, still holding the corner of the glass together. He swerved slightly and the glass flew to the right-hand lane. No one even stopped to help the driver. He was on his cell phone immediately. It seemed to be business as usual on this road.

The sister had told the man that someone died every day on this stretch of road. She had not been joking. The man was very careful. They almost got hit three separate times. After the first accident, he took it even slower. This was worse than driving on the freeways of Los Angeles, he thought. Cops were everywhere, but it did no good. They were there just to clean up the broken lives being wrecked by the careless drivers.

Finally, with good directions from the other two, the man pulled safely into the suburban driveway. The woman was still sleeping when they entered the house. Looking to the clock, the family realized that they had only been gone for forty-five minutes. They still had the whole day ahead of them.

He started in on the eggplant as soon as they arrived home. He was excited to show off his cooking skills to his sister. Cooking was such a huge part of the Creative agenda the man had taken on his path. Creating was everything to him, and his life revolved around creation. It was being one with God. It was almost like being God, he thought. God was the creator after all. If God made us in the same image, then we were creators too. Just like God.

The food went in the oven, and the man could take it no more. The eye drawn on his bandage had bothered him since he had seen it. The thoughts consumed his mind. His head had a terrible itch now where the bump was. He couldn't shake the feeling of being watched, either. It wasn't as profound as earlier at the store, but it was still there. It was a feeling he had grown accustomed to on this trip.

He stared at the drawn-on eye in the mirror for a few moments. The drawing was very well done. It really looked like his style. Could it be something like his book, writing itself with an unseen hand? Yet, in this case, he had drawn an eye onto his being while in the subconscious.

The man found the end and started unraveling the gauze. It spun off the top of his head and went right into the garbage. He wouldn't be wearing any more bandages for this wound.

His hair had seemed to grow a lot already. Over an inch of light brown growth was present where it had been bald before. The patterns in his hair were barely visible.

The man had to shake his head to clear his vision. The lump on his forehead had not gone down in size. Purple in color before, it was now almost black in the center around the slit. The other part of the lump was a very angry red. He looked closer in the mirror at the slit. It looked like a bite from a brown recluse, the man thought. He poked the center with his finger, and the slit seemed to clinch. He tried it again and got the same response. It looked like he could see something just behind the dying skin. It looked like his skull but he knew the wound wasn't deep enough for that. If only he could get a closer look at that angle, the reality could be seen.

When he came out of the bathroom, all the others were in the kitchen, eagerly waiting for lunch. The man's sister had come home early. "What did you do?" she asked her brother, "Your hair!" All the others were looking at the man with shocked wonder. His wife was looking at him like he had completely lost his mind.

The man rushed back into the bathroom to get the shock. Only moments before he was amazed at the hair growth from the last couple of days; now, the face staring back was framed with a very thick head of long black hair. It extended down past the man's shoulders. He shook the hair and couldn't believe the situation. The lump on his head came into view when he shook his manes. He saw the tattoo. It was of an eye, almost like the one on his bandage. It was in the same exact spot on his head, like it had bled through the bandage, permanently staining the man's head. The lump that had been there before was now no more than the size of a marble. The discoloration of the wound was gone. The small slit remained, but now that formed the pupil of the eye. The lump made it seem to protrude from the man's head. It almost looked like the eye was going to blink, it was so realistic.

The woman appeared at the man's side and steadied him. This was too much for the man's brain to take in. Just moments before, he had looked in the mirror. He had looked much different. His wife's voice sounded like it was at the other end of a tunnel. The bathroom had begun to spin out of control. The man's senses were all twisted into a ball of confusion. If it wasn't for his wife, he would have been falling in this bathroom for the second time in two days. Once again, the others would think he was crazy.

The woman laid the man down in the bed again. She knew it had been too early for him to be out and about. He must have really tired himself out with the injury and all. She had tried to get the man to relax some, but that was not in his nature. He was one to always be on the move, and getting something or another done. Half the time, she thought he was neurotic.

The sound of banging pans brought the man out of his sleep. The light was barely trickling through the blinds now. The man was fascinated with light rays, and today was no exception. He watched as creatures and shapes took form in the thin beams of light. He knew it must be getting late, the sun was showing the time to the man. He groggily got out of bed and headed towards the kitchen. The banging had only increased in tempo and decibels. It felt like it was going to split his head in two.

As soon as he opened the bedroom door, the banging stopped. The house was eerily silent, except for the soft conversation coming from the kitchen. The voices were so hushed he couldn't even discern who was talking. The man came around the corner of the kitchen, and there was his wife and niece. They were sitting at the breakfast counter, and acknowledged the man with concern as soon as they saw him.

"Are you okay?" the two asked in unison. "We've been very worried about you," finished his wife.

"I think I'm okay," the man replied. "What happened? I remember combing my hair and then I was almost passing out. Did someone drug me or something?"

"You were in the bathroom, and I heard you scream" the woman said to her husband. "It was the first time I had ever heard you scream, so we all came running. You were looking in the mirror, combing your hair, and you were looking at something behind you. You kept asking if we all saw it there, but no one else saw anything. You started to go into convulsions and were pointing at the mirror, making strange sounds. It sounded like you were talking in tongues. We got you to bed, but that was hours ago. Your eggplant Parmesan was awesome. We saved you some."

The man stared at the woman, but he didn't hear the last of her words. He had been inundated with the recollections of what had really happened. He had been looking in the mirror, and a dark shape had appeared behind him. He had turned to look at it, but it was not in the reality. It was only in the mirror. He focused his eyes, and could begin to make out the features. It was his nephew. He couldn't believe it. This is when he had screamed. It was the scream of joy. He had been so close with the young man throughout his life. Here they were, back in each other's presence. The boy was looking at his uncle with a look of serenity. The young man looked very happy. "We miss you so much Bro," the man had said to his nephew. "We need you. There is a hole in our existence that you opened when you died, and now we want it closed. We want you back."

The woman had come in then, and the boy began to fade away. By the time the rest of the group got to the door, the figure had completely faded. None of the others had seen his nephew. He looked at his niece, who was staring at the mirror. He saw the look of knowing in her face. Just because she wasn't seeing this for herself, she still believed what her uncle told her. Her brother also visited her occasionally. She was just hoping to see him this time. She did smell the faint aroma of her sibling's favorite cologne in the bathroom. Their bond had been strong. Bonds like this lasted lifetimes, both past and future.

"Where's our grandson and my sister?" the man asked his wife. "And where is that Parmesan?"

She was already getting the plate from the microwave as she answered his question. "They went to the emergency response training class tonight. Your sister is the teacher, and grandson will be her test victim. Remember, she told you about it last night." The man couldn't remember anything from last night. For that matter, he barely remembered even coming to this house. He remembered driving some, but didn't even remember how long they had been on the road. The only thing he knew now was that he was extremely hungry.

After macking down on the awesome grub, the man and his niece went out to smoke a cigar and let the dogs run around. The humidity was very heavy this evening. The man and girl talked about it being tolerable, the weather. Where they were from was very hot in its own way. They were ones to adapt to any situation that came along. You could go with the flow or let the flow ruin your good time, the family had always said.

After getting his thoughts together, the man suggested they take a little drive to the forest and see what they could get into. They had not come to Texas to be indoors. The three piled into the minivan and went in search of adventure. The brother had told them the night before of some good spots to go to. It was not much of a drive; within twenty minutes, they were parked at a trail winding into the forest.

The three went walking down the winding path. The man noticed that it was very quiet out here. The others agreed. There were no sounds of birds or even insects. With the humidity, the man thought there would be so many bugs that they wouldn't be able to handle it. There were none. They walked for about two miles and saw nothing but trees and bushes. The trail had a gravel covering, which made the walk pleasant. Around every turn, the three thought they would see water or animals or something, but there was nothing but green.

The sun seemed to stay in the same place in the sky the whole time they were walking. On the drive into the forest, they had been worried that daylight was going to be lost soon, and they would have to go on an abbreviated walk. It had not been the case. The daylight was their friend this day, and lit the way for the entire walk.

Finally, the three had enough and headed back to the car. The humidity was very bad. They dealt with it just fine, but the lack of wildlife made it unpleasant. The man and girl had even overturned decayed logs in hope of seeing salamanders or lizards, but they did not exist. They did not even see an ant.

The man couldn't get the heavy feeling of being watched out of his head. It seemed like the forest had sucked them in, and now didn't want them to leave. By the time the family got to the car, the man was feeling that familiar feeling of dread. He had picked up the pace, and had almost began to run when he saw the crow. It was sitting on the gate, leading off this trail and back to the car. It was looking directly at the three. The bird made some clicking sounds and flew away. The man knew everything was okay, once again. The dark shadows had passed, to be replaced with the light.

The family arrived back at the sister's house, but no one was there. The brother had told them where the extra key was, and the man retrieved it. After letting the woman in the house, the man and his niece decided to stay outside and have a smoke. The man had some things to tell the girl about the place they had just been. A lot had happened this day that needed discussion.

The brother in law arrived home before they had barely two drags each. He was wide eyed as he pulled into the driveway. His eyes were directed toward the man whose gaze was intense. The man could feel it on his skin. He jumped out of the truck and strode up to the man and girl. "Where is your bandage?" he said in his Texan drawl. "You was s'pose to wear it for three or four days."

"I couldn't take it anymore," the man said. "It was driving me a little crazy. It had to come off."

"Are you wearing a wig or something?" the brother asked. "What's that on your forehead?"

"Nah man, I took a nap after making lunch and I woke up with this bad-ass head of hair. I can tell you like it. Yesterday, I was rocking a cul-de-sac, and now I look like a rock star. I don't know what is up with the tattoo. I know I have all these tattoos but I have never tattooed my face, and I never will. Your face is your best tattoo. This eye was under the bandage and one was painted on top of the bandage as well. I honestly do not know how either one got there."

The brother said he needed to check the wound and make sure it was okay. The man trusted his sister's husband very much. He was not one to trust people, but he trusted his sister and this man.

The brother was amazed at how fast the wound was healing up. He told the man that the lump was almost all the way gone. He did say that it was strange how the slit seemed to be in the pupil of the eye tattoo. They both made a couple of jokes about this, but the man's tone changed the subject. It was very disconcerting to the man about the eye tattoo. It made him feel very uneasy and strange that something so intense could be done to him without his knowledge. What else had been done to him that he did not know about, he wondered.

After taking the American flag down for the night, the man, brother and niece all filed inside. The raising and lowering of the flag had been a tradition in the man's family since he was a small child. His father was a Navy man, and he bled Navy. He had installed a flagpole in the front yard when the man was such a small boy. His father had been so eaten up, he had even put an intercom system throughout the house, like the 1MC system on a Navy ship. This flag pole in Conroe was very familiar. The brother told the man it was because his uncle had made the pole for him. The uncle was the twin brother of the man's father. It all made sense to the man now. His father and uncle had been very close and similar. They were both true Americans.

The woman was happy that the others had come back in. Warm greetings between the family were a nice way to start the evening. The brother refused to eat eggplant, so had to settle for leftover pizza from the day before. It didn't seem to bother him, though. A loud knock at the door interrupted the third piece of pizza. The brother cursed about who would come to your house after dark, as he was ambling towards the door.

The man had seen this scenario so many times with his dad, when he was a boy. He was one to complain when someone would call or stop by at an inopportune moment. He would grumble all the way to the phone and answer it with genuine politeness.

The man really missed his father. The elder had died ten years before. The man and woman were building their house to be closer to his parents when his father succumbed to dementia. His mother had taken care of her husband for the last five years of his life. The man thought of his mother as a saint for this. It had taken its toll, wearing down her health both physically and mentally.

This is one of the reasons the man had fought to keep their mother out of a nursing home. She deserved much better than that, and had provided much more than that for their father. In the end, when their mother couldn't take care for herself any longer, the family relented. There had been no other option. The greed was adept at keeping people alive to very old ages, just to shuffle them away to the only care they could afford. All the while, their elders who did not know hard work, were treated like the royalty they were.

It was a decision that haunted the man's soul for the rest of his life. His mother lived three more years in the home. The man saw the unhappiness in her face every week when he went to see her. She had died almost one year before. It had been on the one-year anniversary of her son's death. Another of her sons had died earlier that same year, and her daughter six months after. A grandson and daughter in law passing at this same time had really taken its toll. The family had been struck down with tragedy.

The man thought of the death all the time. There were not many times in his life when he was free of the thoughts of his people and the dream of hanging out again someday. He missed them all so terribly much. He was happy to have his wife, son, niece and grandson. He also still had three sisters whom he cared deeply for. He also knew that he would be hanging out with his people again. He had seen it all, in his subconscious. There were no doubts in his mind.

"What the fuck," his brother shouted from the front door. His voice broke the man out of the daydream he was in. He often found himself thinking of these things and zoning out for some moments. He jumped up and rushed to his brother's side. There had been a cautious tone in the other man's voice that the man knew was not right.

Standing next to his brother, the man saw the intruders. He had seen this before and had heard others with similar accounts. His son had even had this happen to him. It did not scare the man. He knew. "Tell them to leave," he told his brother in law. The other man was silent. He couldn't take his eyes off the three children standing on the doorstep. Their faces were pale. There was no white to their eyes. No Iris, no pupil, just black. The man had seen this before. He called them the black eye kids. He knew that the little creatures' goal was to get inside.

The man really looked them over this time. The last times when he had encountered these beings, he was in a stupor or something. It was the same state his brother in law was in right now. He had not been able to discern any details about them those times. This time was different. He was fully aware of what was going on. It almost felt like his senses were heightened. He felt super human, glowing the aura of thousands.

The clothes on the children were plainer than plain could be. They wore the most basic pants and shirts. It reminded the man of when he was a child, and his mother would make the clothes for her children. Their shoes were black leather that looked like a very old school style to the man. The tallest boy appeared to be about twelve, the girl about eleven and the small boy maybe ten. They never once took their eyes from those of the brother in law. It was like they were connected, mentally, with a strange mental beam coming from their eyes.

The sister's headlights pulling into the driveway snapped her husband out of his trance. "What the," was all he could say as the children left the porch with a robotic movement. They were through the grass and down the road before the sister and grandson even got out of the truck. "What was that?" the brother in law asked the man. "Why did they want to come in the house so bad?"

"I don't exactly understand who they are, but I call them the black eye kids. You can see why. Whenever they come to your house, they capture you in their gaze, and then almost beg you to let them come inside, all with their minds. Believe me, you never want to let them come inside. I've heard stories about what can happen then. You do not want that."

The grandson and sister were coming up the walk by now. "Who was that?" the sister asked. The man said it was some kids looking for a lost cat. The sister looked at the man strangely, shrugged her shoulders, and went inside. It had been a very long day for her. The grandson hugged his grandpa and uncle and dragged his tiredness inside. The brother looked to the man with question in his eye.

The man spoke to his sister's husband. "I know I didn't tell them the truth. It is better this way. There is no need to get them going about something that we really don't know about. It's over now anyway. They won't come back tonight. Be warned though, usually when they come, they keep coming. At least two more times you will see those little demons. Just remember, don't let them in. If you don't answer, they know you are inside and will not leave until you answer. Be careful with these fuckers." The brother could see the serious look in the man's eyes and hear it in his voice. He would never forget this happening to him.

The rest of the night was filled with conversation. The man and his niece smoked much of the mountain tobacco they had acquired in Gallup. They found the smoke very pleasant. They were both occasional smokers. The smoking had increased on this trip. Tobacco was legal in these states. Marijuana was not. Tobacco would have to be a substitute on the whole road trip. The nicotine was much more harmful to their bodies, but that is how the greed rolled. It was not about health to them, it was about profit.

The man tried to talk to his sister about spiritual events and awakenings. She seemed to not want to talk about such things. He really needed to try to figure out things that had happened to their family in the past, and learn why they were the way they were. The man had realized long ago that all his brothers and sisters were not on the same path. Some were very spiritual and others were not. The man and his brother had always been very spiritual. The sister in between their ages was the other. These three understood things most people would shun. They were the ones who could see the future. They were also the ones who could see spirits, beings that most others could not see.

The man knew it was no use talking about these things with his sister. She had never believed in the spirits nor the clairvoyance. The conversation drifted into the past and reliving old ghosts. The man already knew all about his family history, at least he thought he did. He was the one who had kept track of it all these years. He was the one who always tried to keep the family together, usually with negative results.

The man knew his sister was holding out. He couldn't help but thinking it was because all the others were present. He was going to have to get some time alone with her to get the truth. He knew it was there. It was why he had come.

The conversation flowed into the deep night. Again, the family sat on the back porch, talking and watching the chameleons. Sounds from the back yard were normal again. After the death of their dog, things had been as usual, as far as they could tell.

The man couldn't stop thinking about the eye tattoo. It was such a weird thing to happen. Whenever anyone in the group would talk to the man, he could tell they were staring right at his forehead and his third eye. He kept wondering who had done this to him and why. After this tattoo, nobody would ever look at him the same. It wasn't as if they looked at him favorably anyway. The man had realized long ago that it didn't matter what you looked like, people were going to talk crap about you. People talked crap about others instead of looking in their inner beings and seeing their own faults. Everyone had fault, it was just easier to point out other peoples than to find your own.

The man saw his hat at the other end of the couch. Nothing had ever seemed like such a security blanket of safety until he saw that hat. He asked his wife to pass it and quickly put it on his head. Now the others could look at his face as they talked to him. He felt very ashamed of the new tattoo. It felt as if he had done something wrong and was now awaiting punishment. That full head of dark black hair was also quite disturbing.

"Is this my hat?" the man asked his wife. This hat was like a child's hat or something. It was much too small for the man's head. It felt like a mushroom poised on the top of his dome. He took the hat off and looked at it.

"I don't know who has a hat like yours," the woman answered. She was right. The hat was the same as the one he had come with. It was an old hat with the logo of their tattoo shop. No one else had this same hat in this same color. He fiddled with the rim a bit and tried the hat again. No luck. It was much too small.

"Maybe it's because of all that hair, Grandpa." the boy said. He had a smirk to his voice as he said it. The man had noticed since his sister and the boy had arrived home that something was not quite right about the two. They seemed to have a monotone sound to their voice. They had told the man about an accident they almost got into on the way home, but there was no emotion at all in their voices. The boy had told the man about coming within inches of his life, but he may have been telling him he was going to the store. There was no excitement.

"I don't think the hair is the problem," the man said. He went into the bathroom to investigate a bit further. He put the hat on and looked in the mirror. His head didn't seem to look any bigger. Yet that damn hat just wouldn't fit. He really felt like someone was messing with him. It seemed like someone was trying to drive him crazy. He pulled the hair back and got a closer look at his scalp. The skin seemed to be a weird color of orange, but the man chalked that up to the light in the bathroom. He saw no other abnormalities on his scalp.

The eye tattoo on the other hand, that was a different situation. The pigment seemed to have gotten darker in tone. The lump on his head was still in the same place. Everything looked pretty much the same as a couple of hours ago, except for the blood. The corners of the eye tattoo were caked with dried blood. A drop had even dripped down his forehead a bit, looking like a bloody tear. The tattoo almost looked like a real eye. If it was glossy, the man would not be able to notice the difference. He could swear that the eye would contract sometimes, almost like it was trying to blink.

The man knew that he was walking in a weird script. It all seemed so preordained. This was all meant to be.

When he came out of the bathroom, the boy was laying on his cot, fast asleep. The girl was on the couch, also snoozing soundly. The sister left many lights on in the house so he could easily see and navigate his way to the kitchen. Everyone must have gone to bed, he thought. He thought that he had only been in the bathroom for about five minutes, but with the way that time was twisting, he really couldn't be sure about anything.

He got some water and headed to the hallway and the bedroom. His sister was standing in the hallway, in between the bathroom door and their bedroom door. She was staring at the wall like she was reading something. She had a very distant look in her eye. The man had never known his sister to be a sleepwalker. That is what it looked like he was seeing now, though.

Once, when he and his brother were very small, they had looked out the window in the middle of the night and saw this sister walking down the street in her nightgown. Their sister was asleep in her bed, though, in the locked tight house. She had never left the house. The brothers had spoken their entire lives about how they had seen their sister's ghost.

"Are you okay?" the man asked his sister. There was a burning sensation in the middle of his forehead. It felt like when you get sweat in your eye. It was an odd feeling for the spot, and the man did not like it one bit. His sister looked slowly to the man and said that there was something she had to tell him. The look on her face told the man that she was at odds with herself, if she should tell her story or not.

The two went through the garage and sat on the porch swing. The sister told the man that she had promised never to tell this to anyone, but he had been so persistent. She also could tell that his family was on a mission, and this information was going to be crucial to them. She was torn between telling and not telling and had decided this was the best.

Her story began.

"You were born on the same night as your brother and sister. You all three shared the same womb. You were the last one born that night, sister was second and brother was first. You were all born exactly four minutes apart. Brother was large, sister was medium and you were small. Like the three little bears. The doctors told mom and dad that there were anomalies with their children. The church got involved. They brought me out from auntie and uncle's house in Arkansas to help with the children and the deception that was coming. Brother went to school at four, sister at five, and you went at six. It was easy for them to tell everyone that you were all one year apart. At home though, there was no keeping the three of you apart. It was apparent from the beginning that when you were together, you were connected. Things floated in the air and everyone who came over thought the house was haunted. It was just the three little triplets, letting their minds wander. The three of you could predict things and they always came true. You also made friends with all the animals you encountered. When you were seven, I threatened, out of a moment of anger, to tell the whole story. Mom and Dad sent me to a very strange place at the church with dark shadows and men in all black. I could only see their faces sometimes, and when I did, it was scary. They were twisted into a grin that consumed their entire faces. I fear these beings to this day. It is why I never told you. They said they would fill everyone around me with pain if I ever said anything. I was sworn to secrecy out of fear."

"You have nothing to worry about with these beings," the man told his sister, while giving her a big hug. He could feel her entire being shaking with relief of getting something so terrible off her mind. "Thank you so much for telling me this. It explains a lot. It also tells me who has been following us all these miles. I love you sister." The man hugged his sister as they went to their separate bedrooms. The man had thought before that crazy things were happening. Now, his sister had just dropped the atomic bomb of weird on his thoughts.

After getting some water to clear his extremely dry mouth, it was off to bed. Coming into the hallway from the kitchen, the man saw his wife standing in the same spot as his sister had been standing a few minutes earlier. She was looking at the same place on the wall that his sister had been gazing. A sharp stinging in the middle of his forehead made him wince with irritation. He knew what it was, but tried to make himself not believe it.

He told his wife that he would be right back, but her expression made it seem as if she hadn't heard him. He slipped into the bathroom and closed the door behind him. He knew better than to leave his wife in the hallway, but he had to see. Sure enough, his stress was realized. The eye tattoo was weeping a fresh drop of blood. It had welled up at the bottom of the tattoo until it had no place to go except down. The eye seemed even more alive now than it had moments before.

Stepping back into the hallway, the woman was not there. The man began to inch the door to the bedroom open when his sister came out of her room. She got a shock when she had seen the man. She had not expected anyone to be in the hallway, and he had scared her. The man's sister asked him what he was doing standing in the hallway, staring at the wall. He had no answer, and she had no time. She was off to work. She would see the family later.

The man crept into the room he shared with his wife. She was fast asleep in bed. The dog also was tucked up under her ribs in full slumber. It had been strange to see her in the hall. It seemed like the situation was completely out of place, like they were in a dream or something. The man picked up the book to write, and again It was filled for the day. The man hadn't read what was being written in this book for a few days. He had seriously focused on writing the Truth. This other book was a product of his imagination. The Truth was the product of a planet and a species spinning rapidly out of control. The words needed to be in print. The people needed to understand and know what to do. The time had come. The greed could be no more.

The story took so many turns and twists, the man could barely keep up with what was going on. Like before, the pages told the tale of the last couple of days at his sister's house. Again, the story was slightly askew as to what really happened. It was mostly true, but some things the pages said were skewed. Or, maybe the man thought, they weren't altogether true in this dimension, this reality. In another reality though, all these things might have happened just as they had been written. Maybe, even, he was living parallel lives and sharing experiences amongst them.

It was so much for the man to contemplate. He had always been one to think of the deepest thoughts possible. This existence was one of learning and enlightenment. All the other existences in the future and past relied on this existence; just as this existence relied on all those existences. It was a huge cycle, he knew. Just like the seasons.

Sometime in the hours of writing, an energy source came to the man. He was not meditating. Creating would sometimes put him more in tune with energy, just like meditation could. This was one of those times. This energy felt very comforting to the man. The man couldn't see the energy except for the faint disturbance of dust moving through the morning light, beaming through the blinds. The man felt this energy and was fully aware of it. It was an energy he knew oh so well. It was almost like hanging out with a good friend. This energy had been frequenting the man's presence on and off his whole life. It always brought the man knowledge and a sense of safety. This time was slightly different, though. It still made the man feel safe, but there was more. The energy told the man about an event that was about to happen. It had been coming for some time, but the end of the cycle was here. The energy told the man that he and his family were going to play a very big part in this cycle's end. They were going to be the end. After the end had come, the energy had communicated, the beginning would be upon the planet and the universe. The beginning was when the family would come into play. It would be something that people had waited a very long time for.

The thoughts from the energy dissipated with its aura. The being had gone. The man looked down at the book he had been writing. He had written over ten pages since he had come into the room. When the energy was communicating with him, he had been writing like it was with someone else's' hand. The words had flowed from his hand, not his head.

This is what he had planned. The message needed to get out there. The book was going to heal the masses. They would see the truth.

He read the last sentence on the page and felt a deep sense of connection. "Death is the beginning, life is the end," was what the words read. "Fear neither."

CHAPTER 14

The last day in Texas began early. Like almost every other day on the trip, the man was out of bed at sunrise. He would lie in bed all night after his writing sessions. He could feel when his niece would wake up. It was like a signal was sent when the girl entered consciousness. The man had always been aware of DNA, and the connection he had with his brothers and sisters. The connection with his son had always been the same. They could almost read each other's minds. It was the same kind of connection with his niece.

The man was becoming more and more enlightened in all aspects of life. The last two years had been a spiritual awakening for him. His thoughts had always been spiritual and deep, but this was far beyond that. Sometimes he thought that a bit of his brother's energy had flowed into his being. It sure felt like he was having different thoughts, sometimes. Since the death of his family, it seemed in his mind, that he had taken on more knowledge. His thoughts were there. He was more aware of people and the actions of them than ever before. Always one to read people well, now it was almost too easy. Looking at a stranger, the man could tell so much about the person. It was all about reading their aura. There was no faking your aura. It was your true color.

He dressed quietly as to not wake his wife. He felt bad that he woke them all up so early every day. He had tried to sleep, but it was impossible. He would write and meditate all night. The recharging of energy for his mind and body was still there. The minute he was fully conscious, his mind could not enter the rest state again. If he lay there, he would just toss and turn. He thought creeping out of the room was the better option. Of course, he would still wake up the woman and boy with his commotion, but at least now they could sleep a bit longer.

The niece was the only one awake when the man came out of the bedroom. She was sitting on the couch, already dressed, listening to soft music on her phone. The man gave the girl a head nod, which was returned. He was on his way to the kitchen to make some coffee. The girl followed the man into the other room. He heard the song. It was his dad's favorite song. It sung about a woman with the same name as his mother. There had been many covers of this tune over the years, and the man and niece had multiple variations. It was just another connection with their people.

It brought joy to the man's heart to hear this song, this morning, with his niece. He deeply missed both of his parents. They had been very good people. The man had remained close with them their entire lives. He had watched how his brothers and sisters interacted, or didn't, with their parents. The ones who truly cared did not want anything in return from their parents, except their love.

Some of the other children had done the man and his wife very dirty. These were the ones, like always, who demonized the man and woman to the rest of the family. The man had stayed true to his parents, and did not let the words change the way he was. Even when his parents helped the hateful with loans and support, the man stayed true. These were the same ones who only came around when they wanted something. To call their parents to say hello, or wish them happy birthday, was something that never entered their minds. It had strained the entire family's relationship. The once close tribe had become divided.

These times and actions taught the man a great deal about human nature. If his own brother would do him dirty, then anyone would. Seeing someone destroy their own family out of greed showed him how he would never be.

He was with both of his parents to the end. It was difficult to see them so lost mentally. He always thought that they were inside their heads still, with normal thoughts. They just couldn't talk or do things like before. Their brains were disconnected from their actions. All the while, they could truly understand everything going on around them. He saw it in their eyes.

The man and girl took their coffees and a cigar and headed on a walk through the neighborhood. The man kept having strange visions of that dock down the way and wanted to go see it one more time before they left. It was calling to him. Something very strange had happened there, but the man could not remember anything about the incident. It was a void in his memory. He knew it was there somewhere, he just couldn't grasp it. Maybe seeing the spot again would jog his memory.

The humidity was very thick, even at this hour. They took their time, coffee and smoke in hand. The two enjoyed these times when they could talk. They often talked about their people and the good times. The man would tell the girl things about them from before her birth. They had very many deep conversations on these walks. Theirs was a mutual understanding of minds. They believed in the collective thought. They believed in the ONE.

They found the dock and sat on the edge. The water was very brown here. The two both said that they had never seen water so dark brown before. There had been recent storms of record proportions. The rain had been here in the couple of weeks before they had arrived. It had been a massive storm and there was much flooding. The lake held the debris.

A fishing boat drifted by and the anglers gave a half kind of slight wave. They seemed out of place on the water. Their clothes looked like they were issued rather than bought. The boat seemed high-tech to the man. It was all black and looked more like a government vehicle than a fishing boat. Twin motors on the back turned up the dirty water. Something about the fishermen's faces made the man feel uncomfortable. Their poles were hanging off the sides, but the man couldn't tell if their lines were in the water. There was absolutely no sag to their poles. Nothing seemed right about the scene in front of the man and his niece.

The two men floated in their vicinity for quite some time. They sure seemed to have a staring problem. It didn't seem like they meant to leave. Finally, the man and girl decided they would go. They came here to get away for a few minutes, and now these goobers were ruining it. The fishermen had the whole lake and yet they had to come here. The girl was about to say something, but the man stopped her. "These are not folks to talk shit to," he told her.

On the walk back, the man told the girl some things about the fishing duo. He told her, "there had been no numbers on the side of the boat. The guys clothes were brand new, never washed. They were very stiff. Their clothes, shoes and sunglasses matched. One of them had a very small ear bud in. Their faces looked to have been made of plastic. There was a strange aura about them. They were watching us the whole time, fucking perps!" the man said.

"Yeah, they were definitely weird. I got a really bad vibe from them," the girl answered.

They got back to the house, but the brother in law's truck was gone. It saddened the man. He was hoping to hang out with the other man today. He liked his sister's husband and wanted to get to know him better. He had talked the night before about taking off this day. Obviously, that had not worked out.

The woman and boy were awake and ready when they man and girl came back in. The rush of cold air coming in from the heat was wonderful. They were both very sweaty. "Are you guys ready?" the man asked the others.

"We're just waiting on your sister to get up," the woman said. "Then we can all go run around some".

The sister came out within minutes of the conversation. She was ready to go. She asked the others what they wanted to do, and they said they didn't care either way. They had checked into renting a boat on Lake Conroe and could do that in the afternoon. Besides that, they were open to anything. She loaded the gang up in her bad ass ford truck and headed off to adventure. It was the last day, they were going to spend it together.

The man had wanted to ride in this truck all week. It was a beast. Every added feature was possible. It had been the dealer's car to drive around and show off in. The sister had bought it and was very proud. She drove many miles a day and deserved to have something nice to get around in.

The local thrift store was the first stop. The family enjoyed thrift stores. This is where they bought most of their clothes, crafts and whatever else they could find. On this trip, though, the man decided to stay in the car. One week into the trip was too early to start acquiring things. It was much too hot to leave the dogs in the car anyhow. The others went inside, while the man could enjoy his very rare alone time.

His brother in law had told him about the seven-hundred-watt stereo in this truck, and he was anxious to test it out. One of his favorite songs came on. It always reminded him of his dad and his son at the same time. The man turned up the music very loud. He was not one to normally listen to his music all that loud. However, the system in this truck sounded wonderful, and he could not help himself.

Without thinking, the man found himself singing along to the song. His brother and himself used to sing along to many songs together. Some the right words, most made up. After his death, the man sang no more. The song of happiness had left his heart. Just one year before, the man had sung with his niece one night. It was the night his mother had died. It was also the one-year anniversary of his brother and his family's death. The music had gone on all night long. The mourners sang their sad song. The full moon had smiled upon the two all night. They knew their mother/grandmother would be very happy the two were together, celebrating her beginning. Just like in life, the man would be with his parents in death also.

The woman and sister were in the thrift store a very long time. The boy came out after only minutes, and the girl was not far behind. The man and girl shared a cigar while watching the strange black birds. They looked like crows, but were much more thin and smaller. They made crazy sounds and acted very erratically. The family had always loved birds. Nature was the gifts on this planet that all living creatures got to enjoy. The man had often told others, very religious people usually, that maybe now, in this lifetime, on this planet, we were in heaven. It was a very special, magical place if you could just open your eyes and see through all the filters in place by the greed. Of course, you also had to live in harmony with all creatures to see the heaven in this existence.

By the time the two had come out of the store, the other three were ready to go. This was their last day, and they were ready for adventure.

The group headed to Huntsville for the next stop on their excursion. This was a very cool little town in Texas with a lot of history. The family walked around a massive statue of Sam Houston. It was an amazing thing to see. The family talked about the craftsmanship involved in building such a huge monument. The man knew all about creativity; the drive to make something. His creativity and imagination worked just fine. He was always creating something or another. This is when he felt most complete. This is when he felt he held the wisdom.

The crow on the statue's hand caught the boy's eye. They shared a welcoming glance. The crow made a soft whistle sound and flew away. The others had seen nothing. They had been too busy talking. It seemed strange to the boy to see something that only he had seen and not the others. It brought a feeling inside that was very unfamiliar to him. It felt almost like he had a secret.

The family was very impressed with the countryside. This part of Texas was very green and filled with rolling hills. The roads meandered through the countryside. The man was impressed when he saw a gasoline sign selling their product for $1.99. It had been a very long time since he had seen gas for such a low price. Just one year before, gas hovered around four to five dollars a gallon. The food prices had all doubled; because of it, everything else along with it. Now gas was much less. The man figured it was a plot by the greed to take down some oil producing country. It was their way of eliminating foes through financial means. The elite had only one concern: Themselves. Now that gas prices were cheaper, nothing else went down in price. People would forget that the food prices went up because of gas prices, and it would be business as usual for the money hungry. Nobody would stand up. They were all sheep. The greed knew it oh so well.

There was not a whole lot to do in Texas besides spend money. The family headed back to the lake. The man and girl had come here before to check out boats, and now they would rent one. The sister had told them that the lake was not so clean, but the woman and boy really wanted to go. They both enjoyed boats and water very much. The man had brought it up yesterday and couldn't go back on his words today. One hundred forty dollars later, and they were chugging across the very earthy lake.

None of the others wanted to jump in. The man couldn't see being on a lake without swimming a little. He took the plunge. The water was very warm, like a bathtub. It had a faint smell of diesel to it. It didn't take long for the man to get back in the boat. There was something about this water that he didn't like. It wasn't just the dirt, either. It was almost like the water had energy. This energy the man felt disconcerted by.

When he got out of the water, the woman commented on his hair. She said it looked even longer now, and blacker. The straight hair hung most of the way down the man's back. It felt good on his skin. He hadn't had long hair in years. He had cut it all off when the top of his head began to bald. He wasn't going to be one of those guys trying to retain a youth that had passed.

The man was seriously regretting his time in the water. His whole body was covered in grit. It felt like he had rolled around in a wet leaf pile. He rubbed the water off his body with his hands but much of the debris remained. There was a strange wound on his lower leg that he had not had before. He examined the lesion. It looked like something was moving beneath his tattooed skin. He squeezed around the puncture with force. He was not one to have anything in his skin like this. A small worm looking parasite popped out of his leg. It came out with a rush of blood. It was about an inch long and a quarter inch thick. The thing looked like a species of pupae. The parasite writhed on the carpet of the boat for a moment until the man smashed it with his flip flop. He could have sworn that he heard the thing scream.

"What the hell was that?" asked the woman.

"I don't know, but please check me over for more," he said back. She looked him over quickly, but the man was impatient to get the boat started. He hadn't even wanted to come out here and now he had some weird lake creature inside his body. He raced as fast back to the dock as he could. Unfortunately, he had rented the cheapest boat and it was very slow. The whole way back, the man watched as his leg pumped a stream of blood down his foot, onto the deck of the pontoon. The woman had made a makeshift bandage, but it had soaked right through. There wasn't pain, just lots of blood.

After docking the boat, the man and girl headed into the office to make sure they were squared up. They walked by a group of three others who were also finishing up a day on the lake. The man noticed the shirt that the woman in their group was wearing. It was a very strange shirt. The man had never seen anything like it. It almost looked like it was made of paper or some strange substance the man didn't know about. Her breasts spilled out the bottom of the fabric, whatever it was. Anyone looking could see her large boobs on display.

The two men in the woman's company shot the man and girl glares as they passed by. The men looked the man and niece over with a look of intimidation. The man was not one to be intimidated. He laughed slightly at the men. They both stopped in their tracks and loomed over the family. Their dark skin had a strange shine in the rays of the sun. They looked like they might attack the man and girl.

"Hey guys, everything okay?" the man said to the strangers. His way of dealing with intimidation was to be extra polite in return. He was not scared. He wanted to change a bad situation into a good one. This was always the way. It had worked hundreds of times in the man's life, especially on cops. They were the kings of intimidation. These two were not bad people. The man could see it in their auras. They were just confused. They were like the rest of the human sheep and did not know how to respect all living creatures. They were lost like the rest of the species.

The larger of the two men looked bewildered. As he had seen countless times before, the man saw the other's face change from anger to calm. There was no threat here. These were not their enemies. His companion too changed. His look was now one of regret and guilt. The man could read in his face and actions that he regretted invading these other people's space. They looked to the man like he could have been an old friend. In truth, the man thought, they just saw the truth. Briefly, they thought that the man and girl were just like them. Briefly, they forgot all about the prejudice that the greed had burned into their beings. For one moment, the two strangers understood.

The four beings shook hands in silence. Words didn't need to be spoken for what had just happened here. The man tried as best he could to make all those in his presence understand, but most didn't have enough care to understand. As the two men walked away, the man noticed a strange growth just above the smaller man's shorts. He was always on the lookout for natural, physical anomalies in people. It fascinated the man. He had never seen anything like this before though. It looked like the man had a small tail, maybe eight inches long and as thick as a broom stick. It seemed to move oddly as the man walked. The man and girl looked at each other. They kept each other's' gaze for about a full minute, standing silently in the parking lot. They didn't need to speak words. They both knew.

It was a very short drive back to the house. There was always a lot of traffic on this road but it moved extremely quick. Pulling up to the house, they noticed the brother's truck in the driveway. "I'm glad he's home," the man said with genuine excitement. All the others agreed.

The day together had been wonderful. The man and his sister had always remained close. Some people saw the ignorance of choosing sides in a conflict. She was one of them, as was he. Their relationship had always been a good one. They had always been very close, never doing each other dirty. Nor were they interested in getting something from one another. All either of the siblings wanted was companionship from the other. They were true family.

The group brought out the computers and chips. They all had their own libraries to show to get the others caught up on the last years. It had been too long since they had hung out together. The deaths in the family had not brought the survivors closer. They had remained distant as before. The man didn't want this to happen. He felt a strong desire to keep his remaining family together. It would be much easier to get over the extreme amounts of death if they were united. That is why they had come to his sister's house. That is why they had come on this trip.

Remembering old times also stirs up heartache. The family had a great time that last night, but there was an underlying edge of sadness. There was no telling how long before they would all see each other again. It had been a long time since the last visit, and there was no guarantee it would be different this time. Everyone would once again get caught up in their own lives. Also, as they got older, the man knew every visit could be the last one. Their father had always taught them this, 'never leave angry at each other'.

The others had all drifted off to bed. The man and his sister reluctantly parted their magnetism for the night. The man so wished he could stay some more days. At the same time, they were out for adventure, and that lay down the road. He was one who was always happy with whatever he got. This visit had been very nice. His favorite saying was "you can't have your cake and eat it too." Wanting more was what brought on the greed.

The man adjourned to his little corner in the bedroom he shared with his wife. His sister always had multiple lights on around the house. The one in the bedroom was in a perfect spot next to the chair. It provided the tranquil space needed to focus on his words. The words began to flow like a stream from his hand. It flew at a pace which was faster than his normal erratic scratching. The pen made its own line across the page. There was no pressure needed from the hand.

The man had been writing for about thirty minutes when the massive explosion of pain rocked his frontal lobe. The constant headache hadn't seemed so bad this day, and now it came back with a vengeance. When he had showered earlier, the brown muck from the lake flowed down the drain. A couple of sticks even had washed out of his hair. He was worried about getting a weird virus or something from the water. Now he was lying in bed, thinking maybe that was what had brought on the headache. He felt around the wound from earlier at the lake and was happy to find the bandage dry. The bleeding had stopped by the time they had gotten to the truck. When they had gotten home, his wife had put a bandage on for the night, just in case. She hadn't wanted to ruin the sister's sheets. By the time everyone had gone to bed, he had all but forgotten about the parasite, until now.

He had been drinking so much water, so he knew that was not the cause of the headache. The heat on the boat was bad, but they hadn't been out there too long. Maybe it was that damn eye tattoo, he thought. He felt around his forehead, tracing the lump with his middle finger. The slit in the middle seemed to be getting deeper. The whole tattoo never really started healing. It just looked like he had it for a couple of months or something, except for the fresh wound in the pupil. The brown pigment in the iris seemed to be lightening to a hazel color. Funny, the man had thought earlier while brushing his teeth, same color as his eyes.

Unconsciousness seemed like the only cure for this headache. Everyone else in the house was sound asleep. He was on his own in a house he did not know. He had found during the very stressful times of his life that meditating was the best thing to put you to sleep when it was difficult to leave your consciousness. It was a bit harder with headaches, but was better than lying there suffering. A few times, his meditation was broken with bursts of sharp pain. It felt like he was getting shot from the inside of his head.

These times would bring his eyes fully open. Many shadows danced around the room. The blinds were closed as well as the drapes. Just enough light must be peering in, the man thought. He had unplugged the night lights, and the moon was the only source of luminosity. There were so many shadows. It reminded him of when he and his brother had seen the cosmic serpents as children. This was similar, but different at the same time. Large swatches of shadows would move across entire walls then burst into smaller shadows like leaves on a tree. The room seemed to be alive with the movement.

The man got up for water once and saw the entire house was filled with these shadows. They moved not just on the walls and open space, but one was creeping around his grandson and another around his niece. The shadows did not make the man feel weary nor dreadful. They were just there, he had no feeling good or bad. They were putting on a very cool show, the man thought to himself. He saw that something very strange was happening, but could not get his head together enough to figure it out. Lightning was shooting through his brain.

A brief stopover in the bathroom provided nothing. He had hoped to find some aspirin or ibuprofen, but there was none. The medicine cabinet in the bathroom was filled with so many prescriptions. It would have taken him an hour to dig through them all. The man was not one to dig through other people's things. He would rather suffer through the pain than to invade his family's space.

The man had no choice but to wake his wife. She was half asleep as she dug through her purse looking for some headache relief. Luckily for the man, his wife was always well prepared. She had rescued him many times in the past from one thing or another. She produced her last two ibuprofens and was instantly back to sleep. The man had to grab her purse from her before it fell to the floor. She had fallen asleep before even setting her bag down. He was not one to take drugs, but there was no choice with this headache. He needed to sleep a little before the long drive the next day.

The sleep did not come easy. The headache had progressively gotten worse. Sleep came in short bursts, accompanied by very strange dreams. The man had been having strange dreams involving numbers since his brother's family died. They seemed to be telling him something in a binary code. Sometimes the numbers even turned back time. This night, the binary code was more pronounced than ever before. They consumed the man's thoughts when his thoughts should be resting. He felt that the answer was right there in front of him, but he could not quite understand.

He did not know why these numbers were coming to him in his subconscious. They, for sure, seemed to be telling him something. Maybe it was a premonition, or maybe it was a secret long ago hidden from humans. Maybe it was even a code that would communicate with other peoples from the dimensions humans were unaware of. Maybe they were the bridge between the parallels. The numbers meant something. He had started studying their correlation to each other, but could not fully figure out the pattern just yet.

The dreams connecting into his conscious were troubling to the man. It felt the same as when you have a concussion. It would be hard, upon waking, to determine if the dreams were actual reality.

In one dream, they were driving down a country road. The few cars ahead were slowly being waved through by some state troopers. Approaching the scene, the family saw a young teenage girl's body lying crumpled on the side of the road. Her legs were draped across the asphalt, while the rest of her body was in the dirt. A woman sobbing hysterically by the body was obviously the girl's mother.

The man sat upright in bed. The dream had been so vivid. He could clearly see what the woman and the dead girl both had been wearing. He could even remember smelling the faint smell of honeysuckle in the air. The dreams of carnage continued through the night. He had four dreams of disaster that night, all ending in death. They had all seemed so real. Each dream awoke the man from his short sleep. Whenever awake, he would see the shadows dancing their night time dance of long awaited freedom. In between the dreams of wreckage, it was all numbers in the man's head.

As every day, the man got up before anyone else. It felt as if he didn't sleep all night. He couldn't remember falling asleep once, just meditating. He knew that couldn't be true though, he had those strange dreams all night. The lingering memories of all that destruction was still very unnerving to him. They were getting back on the road today. His dreams had come true in the past. At least in these dreams, they were not the ones getting in the accidents. The completed details of the dreams had faded away, just the bad feelings survived.

While brushing his teeth, the man noticed that there was a drip of blood hanging on the corner of his eye tattoo again. He looked closer and wiped the blood away. It seemed to be protruding more than the night before. The whole tattoo was becoming very three dimensional. At least the headache went away, he thought with relief.

The man relished in the act of brushing his newly luxuriant hair. It seemed to have grown more since last night, even. His hair had been thinning for years, so he was very happy to have these thick locks. To his dismay, down the top of his dark black hair was now a white streak. It looked like a lightning bolt. He grabbed a small mirror and positioned it with the larger one to see the back of his head. He knew before he saw. The lightning bolt went from his forehead to the tip of his long hair. It followed the entire length.

He looked closer and saw a small wound in his temple area. It looked like a good size pimple or something, so he gave it a good squeeze. Something seemed to move under the skin, irritated from the pressure. The man squeezed with all his might, his actions almost frantic. Out popped one of the parasites from the lake. Whereas the one in his leg was an inch long, this thing was about two inches long and as thick as a pencil. It looked like a caterpillar as it hung halfway out of the man's head, writhing in the air. The man grabbed the creature and pulled it from his flesh. The thing seemed to make a faint squealing sound. The man threw it into the sink and smashed it with a shampoo bottle. Blood burst from the parasite, covering the inside of the sink.

Blood was running down the side of his face like a waterfall. He grabbed a bundle of toilet paper and applied it to the wound. The man searched the rest of his body for any other parasites, while applying pressure to the wound.

When the first tissues were saturated, the man already had a towel in hand. The tissue was not going to stop this heavy bleeding.

Dropping the paper into the sink, the man heard a hollow metallic sound. He saw a small metal sphere fall out of the toilet paper. The man went to grab the object, which was half the size of a marble. The orb uncurled like a potato bug and scurried down the sink drain. He tried to grab it before it went down the drain, but the creature was too fast.

He knew now where the headache had come from. Something had gotten into his brain.

The man, once again, thought he was losing his mind.

Chapter 15

It was a long, hard farewell for the sister and her family. The sadness was thick in the air, like the humidity. All the years in between visits, and now this one had ended. There was no guarantee of a return visit. Words were talked but not always came true. The sister knew better. When it came to action, years then decades might pass between visits. With the familiar tone of death always lurking, nothing could be certain.

The sister had felt alone out here in Texas for many years. Most of the other family was in California, and she rarely got to see them. She had come out here with her son forty years before. She had met her husband, and the two of them had made a life here. Her son lived within two hours driving. The man had told her that she should be happy with what she had. Being close to your children was the most important thing. She understood his words, but still longed for the family she had left behind so many years before.

Her husband came home for lunch just as the family was finishing packing the car. He too wanted to see the family off. He had showed the man, on a map the night before, of a different way to go. This route would take them through Houston, which the man was not excited about. This way would go through Galveston and onto a ferry. The man wanted to see as much of the gulf coast as possible, and this way would provide it. The girl and boy had never been on a ferry, so this was the chosen way.

Just like when they were kids, the brother and sister waved to each other until they were out of sight. It was with a heavy heart that the man was leaving. So much loss had engulfed his being in the last two years, and now this was another one. At least he could see his sister again. He swore in his mind that he would try his best to see her soon.

The drive through Houston was a cluster fuck. There were way too many cars on a neurotic freeway system. It added up to very unpleasant driving. It was the same problem as everywhere else. There were just too many humans, and they were multiplying way too fast. The family saw at least six different accidents through the city. A couple of them looked fatal.

The man knew that the answer to all this mayhem was simple. If everyone just went the speed limit, not faster or slower, then the traffic would move like water. It was never the case, though. Many people were always in a rush to get ahead of the next guy, while others were in their own world in the fast lane. It wasn't just the freeway either, it was all of life. If everyone just went the speed limit, life would be much better for all.

It took them a few hours to get through the tangle of freeways. This was the only traffic they had hit on the trip, and felt fortunate for that fact. Their planning had avoided this scenario from happening over and over. The talk was about the good times seeing their family. It made the drive much more fast and pleasant. With that and the air conditioning, it was not such a bad time after all. The passage through Houston was soon a distant memory.

The directions from the brother had proved to be spot on. They ended up directly at the ferry building. The man had not been to Galveston in thirty-five years. He briefly remembered the sea wall and the bridge, but not so much else. Nothing seemed familiar. Even the sky seemed different. He had only been fifteen years old the last time he was here with his sister. They had come on a day trip, and the gulf had been very active. Waves had almost been up to the bridge on that trip. Now, crossing the same place, the sea was calm.

The line at the ferry seemed to move fast. They were on one of the large ships within thirty minutes. The lack of sleep had been catching up with the man. He was hoping to find a nice place to take a nap, but it was so very humid. Sleep would be impossible without the air conditioning of the car. You had to stop your motors on the ferry, so there would be no rest for the man. He would just have to make the best of it, like he had grown accustomed to his whole life. Everything that came along, he would just flow with it. Sometimes he felt like a fish, swimming upstream, navigating the hazards of a world out of control.

The girl and boy's first ferry trip was pleasant. There was an aircraft carrier anchored in view next to a battleship. Being Navy families, the group was very impressed and interested. The man retrieved the binoculars out of the car to get a closer look. He went to the bow, but the others were no longer there. He looked through the binoculars. Both the ships looked to be very active. Being on an aircraft carrier himself, he was familiar with flight ops. Aircraft were all poised on the vessel, ready for launch. He could even detect some steam venting from the loaded catapult system.

The aircraft were of a world war two vintage. They seemed to the man to be loaded with some large fuel tanks or bombs. A few of the propellers were spinning on the planes. The battleship also looked to be active. Crewmembers were loading something at a rather frantic pace. The man thought that maybe there was a re-creation they were practicing for. The Fourth of July was just a couple weeks away, after all. The American flags flying from the ships seemed slightly different than the current ones. The star pattern looked different to the man. The wind did not cooperate, and he could never quite make it out.

The ships were only in his line of sight for a few minutes. The ferry had turned starboard, and the large vessels passed behind an island.

The man wandered around the ferry. The ride wasn't very long, but there was not much to look at after they had passed the Navy ships. He saw a crewman and asked the man about the ships and what they were preparing for. The crewman looked at the man very strangely, almost like he had seen a ghost. "Nobody has been on those ships in a very long time," the crewman said distantly, "they've been mothballed in that same spot for more than sixty years. Many say they carry the spirits of the sailors on board."

The heat was unbearable as the man stood with the crewman. They were in the sun. The sweat pouring out of the man's skin felt like it was carrying the toxins of all the miles. The air was so humid it provided no relief. The crewman's words seemed like they were coming from a very far distance. It was hard to focus on what he was saying. The man was very distracted by something inside his head. The thickness of the humidity had seemed to creep into his brain and cloud its thoughts.

A scream on the other side of the ferry drew everyone's attention. A group of passengers had quickly gathered around the alert. He was not one to gawk at someone else's bad fortune, so he stayed put while the crewman rushed off. Something kept pulling the man toward the crowd. Normally he would have minded his own business, but in this case, he could not fight the urge to go. He headed in the direction of the scream, around the ferry's island to the other side of the boat.

"There he is," someone screamed. The crowd retreated as the man approached. He was somewhat bewildered at this, but went forward anyway. At the end of the opening, he saw a child unconscious on the ground. The man noticed the clothes immediately. It was the same clothes the girl in his dream the night before had been wearing. The girl had turned a very dark shade of blue. A woman crouching next to the girl, holding her in her arms was also familiar. She, too, had been the same woman from his vision the night before. The mother was sobbing uncontrollably.

As the man approached, the crowd gathered saw a strange light coming from his being. The light moved with every movement of the man. None of them had ever seen an aura before. They did not know what they were seeing. The air had become very still and silent. Some of the very religious in the crowd began to pray. The man reached out to touch the girl's head, but stopped about an inch away. Electricity seemed to be pulsing through his hand. It felt like he could shoot lightning bolts from his finger-tips. The energy connected the two beings into one.

The girl's eyes fluttered open just as she took a deep breath. It seemed like she took in so much air that the others around gasped once. She had sucked all the oxygen out of the air. Her color came back almost immediately.

The girl looked around in confusion. All the people standing around made her feel very uncomfortable. The sky was so bright, but a lone figure was captivating her attention. "What happened," she asked her mother, almost in a whisper.

"You just fell down and stopped breathing," her mother said, pointing to the figure in front of the girl. "This man saved your life."

The man had already turned to walk away, even as the mother was trying to explain his actions. All eyes in the crowd were upon the man. Some of the passengers wondered who the man was, while the others thought he looked so familiar. Whoever he was, they all thought, something very special had just happened. They had all anticipated the arrival of the man before he even came. They knew he was coming. None of them were aware of how they knew, they just did.

The man made it back to the car just as the ferry was pulling into the dock. The others had all arrived and were standing around the vehicle, awaiting the man's return. His wife asked where he had been, and he told her he had just been walking around some. She saw something strange in his eye, like there was much more to the story. She saw their friend, the crow, fly off its perch, which was in the same direction her husband had just come from.

The horn from the ferry was blasting. It was time to get back on the road. The woman didn't know if she really wanted to know what had happened, anyway. She was tired and in no mood for a story. She just wanted to get out of this heat, like the rest of them.

The family crossed into Louisiana along the gulf coast. There were so many birds to see. The countryside was very beautiful, with ocean on one side and bayou on the other. They stopped once at a place on the beach and took a little stroll. Cars and trucks were lined up on the sands, and the people were all in preparation of partying. They looked at the strangers walking down the beach with distrust. The campers could not keep their eyes off the family. It was only about one hundred feet down the beach that the group had enough, and they all turned back. These were not their kind of people. They saw countless rebel flags and huge beer bellies. The man knew this crowd. It was one that liked to rumble. They had nothing against these people or any others. This family was ones to stick to their own. Their mission was much different than most.

Through the Louisiana back country, the family came upon another ferry. This one seemed to cross a small stream and only held two cars. The ferry was on the other side of the water, and the family was first in line on this side. The wait wouldn't be all that long, they thought. They were wrong. While waiting, the woman began her search for a hotel for the night. They were all getting very tired. The man could barely think straight, he was so exhausted. Lack of sleep was catching up to all of them. Having no food for the last five hours was also becoming a very big issue.

The woman found that there were no hotels up this road for hundreds of miles. Four cars had now filed in line behind the group. The family all decided to flip it. A few miles of back tracking might save them hours later when it was time to stop. They had really wanted to stay on the beach this night, but there was no way. This region was going to take extensive research if they wanted to stay on the beach. That would have to wait until the next trip to Louisiana. Tonight, they just needed some rest.

They thought that the Lake Charles area would be a good place to stay. It was a resort area and had many hotels. Unfortunately, it was Friday night and not a room was to be found anywhere. They drove around the area for almost an hour with no luck at all. Getting back on the highway, they noticed the other on ramp had been closed briefly. More than twenty police cars, with their lights on, were escorting a semi-truck with a strange cargo. The whole convoy was moving at about ten miles an hour, winding their way around the on ramp to the freeway.

The object being trucked was huge. It spilled out on either side of the trailer at least ten feet. The thing must have been twenty feet tall. The large tarp barely covered half of the monstrosity. The man wondered why the object was on a truck and not some other kind of transport. It was triangular with a large round top. It looked like some kind of aircraft but had no visible markings. The entire thing seemed to be made of a shiny metal. The family all said that it was very weird. There seemed to be something surreal about the whole scene. It was like it was out of a movie or dream or something. They were most curious why so many cops were escorting the device. It was obviously something of great value to someone.

It had been dark for quite some time. They had lost the rest of the daylight long before Lake Charles. Now it was almost getting urgent that they stop. The man was at the end of his strength. It felt almost like he could just sleep on the side of the road. Thirty miles south of the lake, they finally settled in Jennings, Louisiana. The family checked in and unloaded the car in a hurry. It was almost nine and they really needed to get some food and then some rest.

The woman had found a nice restaurant to eat at in this town, and they had all agreed. It was a seafood place serving Cajun food. The family was excited to try some real Louisiana cuisine. They had heard the stories, and now they were here.

The restaurant said it was open until Ten o'clock, but it looked closed. All the outside lights were turned off, but the inside was still buzzing with diners. The man got out and tried the door, but it was locked. There were over a hundred people inside eating. The man wondered why they had closed early when they were so busy. He was not one to push things though. He would never knock on a locked door expecting special treatment. It was not his way.

With sadness, the family went to the second choice for the night.

This place was a Mexican food diner. Being from California, they were very familiar with Mexican food. They just hoped it would be different than the food they got back home. They could eat California Mexican food any time back home. This town was very small and at this hour, there would not be much more open. Fast food was never even an option for the family. They liked food that tasted good and made you feel good after.

The place was big and had a lot of cars in the parking lot. All the outside lights were on, and people were both coming and going. This was a good sign for the group. Entering the restaurant, they were happy when a Mexican lady seated them. They all disliked going to a Mexican restaurant that was only staffed by white people. They liked to call this white people Mexican food. Unfortunately, they were seated next to a large group of cops. Of course, every one of their eyes were on the family as they sat down. A couple of the uniforms made comments about the group, but the man thought how stupid it made the cops sound. The man wasn't intimidated by cops, as were none of the others. Cops were just like every other gang they had encountered. Mind your own business and they generally left you alone.

This time, being in the company of cops was to their advantage. The gang members began to speak of their fellow cops in Lake Charles. They spoke of the strange cargo that they were escorting. Obviously, the cargo had passed through this region and these very cops were the ones that had been doing the escorting. They were trying to talk quietly but they could not control the awe in their voices. One of them asked the others if they had seen what he had seen. He was talking about the thing inside. "Was it alive?" he had asked the others.

Another one of the cops changed the subject quickly. He asked the others if they were aware that the One had passed through Texas and into Louisiana. He said a whole group of people had seen the being, but none could describe what he looked like. Some witnesses had said that the One was shifting shape. This made it difficult for them to really understand what they saw. The cop told the others how they would have to be on the lookout for the being and be ready to take him down. They would have to be ready all the time. There was an excited agitation to the cops' voices. You could tell they loved this. They seemed ready to go out and take charge. Maybe even kick some ass.

"I don't give a shit what this guy looks like," growled one of the cops. "We're gonna get this guy and show him who's the boss. We don't need some freak trying to change the Way."

"They say that the being is connected to the device that we were escorting somehow. Supposedly it has healing powers. It also has been uniting the masses into a collective.

You know how our bosses are not going to put up with that. Collectives spell trouble for those in charge."

Just then, all the radios on their belts went off at the same time. The words were garbled. It was a strange language coming over the speakers. It was like no other language that any of the family had ever heard. Maybe just some Cajun talk, the man had thought. All the cops jumped to their feet and headed for the door. They seemed to be in a very big rush. For a small town in Louisiana, the man thought, there sure is a lot going on. One of the last uniforms to leave looked to the man. His look seemed to say that he wanted the man to pay for all the food that they had just ran out on. The man chuckled to himself. The cop had seen the mockery and looked at the man with hatred. He was a cop after all. He was used to people kissing his ass. This family, however, were not like the rest. They were not in fear. The cop made his way to the counter and said something to the hostess. He cocked his head toward the man and his family, and the eyes of the employee followed. The cop shook his head in disgust as he was headed out the door.

The family could now enjoy the rest of their food in peace. Whenever in a cop's presence, they would try to force intimidation on you. It was part of their training or something. In the recent months, the media had been filled with cops killing black men. The man knew that cops killed all kinds of people, not just black ones. If they didn't like how you looked, you were fucked. The cops were so weary of everyone without any reason. The people were weary of the cops for very good reasons. Maybe if they were nicer and gentler to people, not bullies, people would treat them the same in return. Instead, the police liked to make criminals out of the citizens.

The food was very good. When they finished, the hostess approached the table and offered the family free dessert. She told them that the cop had complained that they would not pay for his and his gang's food. The girl thought it was very cool that the family had stood up to the bully. "Him and his cronies come in here all the time and do the same exact thing. Intimidate someone into paying for their food. You are the first in months not to go for it. I respect you folks."

Unlike the cops, the family settled their bill and headed off to the hotel. It was just a few blocks back. There were no cars on the road at this hour. Even passing the liquor store, there was a serious lack of people for a Friday night. "Must all be at that seafood place," the man had joked to the laughter of the others.

The hotel was next to the highway. The artificial glow from the road and huge merchant's signs made the man feel sad. Sadness was a feeling he was so familiar with in his life these last years. The trip had for sure made him happy for the first time in a very long time. This day had been filled with sadness again. It brought back all the bad times from the last years and wore heavy on the man's soul.

The hotel room was not very nice. It was far from being clean. The hour was late, though. After ten thirty already. They would just have to deal with it. At this point, the man thought he could sleep in the car if he absolutely had to. He was beyond the point of exhaustion.

The man and girl went for a walk around the grounds to have a smoke. This place seemed so familiar to the man, he had to explore it further. The boy went to the front of the hotel to call his other grandparents. The woman would stay inside alone and relax. The man and girl saw so many frogs. The bugs living in the grass made it alive. Every inch held hundreds of bugs, mostly crickets. The frogs had an endless supply. Obviously, the lights attracted the bugs, which attracted the frogs.

The scene reminded the man of his last house, when the mottled house spiders would build their traps under the halide lamps and feast all night, with the frogs on the ground taking leftovers.

A fence ran the perimeter of the hotel. Beyond the fence was a small airport whose runway ended at the lodge. Most of the lights on the runway were off, except for a few clear ones showing the ends. Next to one of these lights, the man and his niece saw a man's shadowy figure standing at the edge of luminosity. It was looking straight at them. The eyes seemed to glow like the ember at the end of a cigarette. The figure was only about one hundred feet away, but it was so hard to discern its features.

After a time, the shadowy figure turned and walked into the darkness, out of the soft glow from the runway light. The walk seemed fluid almost. The being seemed to melt into the darkness.

The man and girl looked at each other. They spoke about the energy that had been building on the way to the sister's house and the entire trip. How it had built up on the way, and then deflated when they had left east Texas. The man told his niece that the energy was just taking a small dip down for now. Just like the skip of radio waves, energy is the same. There are high points and low points. It was all a cycle, like everything else. "We have a few days here in the bayou to let our energy rest and get back in tune with each other. Soon we will be headed up the River and going to your other aunt's house. This energy, combined with the other from before is going to be explosive. The whole mission is going to become clear when that energy combines. We will truly know our path."

Thousands of bats began to come out of nowhere. They were swooping through the night air, catching their vast amounts of insects. There were hundreds of thousands of them. The sky turned into living flaps of their leathery wings. The thick air echoed the shrill cry coming from the masses. It was time to go inside. The man and girl were not afraid of bats, but this was not cool. They raced up the steps and got to the room at the same time as the boy. The boy was very excited. "Did you guys see all those frogs?" he asked.

"What about all those bats?" his cousin answered.

"What bats?" the boy said.

The three went back downstairs and around the corner. Sure enough, there was not a single bat flying in the sky. The man had to shake the thoughts from his head. Surely, they didn't imagine it.

The man felt like he was in a tunnel as his niece said something to him. In the field, beyond the fence, he could see two red embers glowing in the dark. An air horn from a lonely trucker permeated the humidity.

The boy caught the man just before he hit the ground.

CHAPTER 16

The man got some much-needed sleep this night, as did the rest of the family. After writing for less than an hour, his creativity was drained. He woke at six, according to the clock on the nightstand. His dreams, still so vivid in his mind, had been so very strange. He was dreaming that there were kids in the room next door, and they were coming into their room through some connecting doorway. The kids were just using this room as an extension of their space next door. One of the kids wore a Spiderman wrestling mask, like the one his grandson had back at his house.

He couldn't really remember what had happened the night before. He remembered the dinner and the cops. Had one of the cops dropped something when they rushed off? The man fleetingly remembered finding a small metal orb on the ground in between the tables. He had put it in his pocket without the others seeing. He remembered coming back to the hotel, but the rest was a blank. The last thing he remembered was the brightness of lights all around, and the feeling of dread. Two small red embers had glowed in the brightness. They had been very strange lights, but he could remember no more.

The man felt the conscious state of his niece. The girl was also awake. The man quietly got out of bed with a quick head nod to the other. In the bathroom for the morning business, don some clothes and the man was ready to go check some Louisiana shit out. The woman and grandson were also awakening as the girl was popping into the bathroom. The man opened the drapes and started the coffee maker.

Religiously, the woman had the coffee ready to go every morning. It was a little bit of home on their journey.

There on the floor by the bed were two separate piles of dog pooh. They didn't really look like the pooh from their dogs, though. This almost looked human, smaller, but still bigger than the dogs usually produced. This was very unlike the dogs. They had never used the inside like this. The man searched around and found a wet spot on the floor next to the television. There was a child's foot print in the wetness and another fainter one a half foot away. This is where the children were coming through the door in the man's dream. The man cleaned up the messes before the others got out of bed. He never told any of the others about the footprint or the dreams.

The humidity was so thick that morning. The man's glasses got fogged up as soon as he walked outside. The difference of the cold in the room, and the heat outside, made sight very difficult. The man noticed immediately the small airport next to the hotel. A small aircraft of vintage military design was taking off and buzzed right in front of the hotel. The pilot seemed to look directly at the man, as he made his flanking maneuver to the port side. His eyes were covered by dark aviator glasses that were pulled over his leather skull cap. The pilot's face looked to be very long and narrow. The man thought it strange that the pilot was looking at him instead of looking where he was going.

The family packed the car, a routine they were becoming very familiar with. They had brought just enough stuff to fully load the back of the car. Everything had to be put in just right, or it would not fit. Checking out of the hotels had also become a familiar routine. Then it was into the car and out of the maze of a parking lot.

"Oh shit, the back is open!" yelled the girl. The man had just pulled onto the road from the lot, and there was a small trail of their bags following them. The man and boy ran back to retrieve the lost items. A quick search of the parking lot for any more lost items, and again they were off, this time more secure. They were now truly on vacation, they had all agreed, while laughing off the absentminded event.

The Louisiana outback was everything the man had hoped for. So much greenery and wildlife abounded everywhere. The sky was open and clear. "This is God's country," the man said to the others. Some miles down the road, the family found a bait shop and went to get their fishing license. The lady behind the counter was about the man's age and very nice. She was happy to tell them all the lowdown on Louisiana fishing.

They were happy that a license was not expensive at all, and you could get it for a few days. California was the opposite on both counts. The lady asked where they were from, and they briefly told her about their trip. She told the family about a story that was coming out of Texas about a prophet that was changing the way of things. She said that the holy man was being called the resurrection of Jesus.

The man told her, "people are just searching for something but they do now know what that something is. They are blind. They grasp onto any words of the coming of Christ but do not truly believe even their own religions. Real prophets are not holy men. They are the speakers of the truth. They are the ones who carry and share the wisdom. Knowledge and enlightenment is available to everyone, you just need to open your mind. You just need to wake up."

The woman looked at the man in awe. Handing him the four licenses, she 'accidentally' touched his hand. The man saw it in her eyes. The clerk had indeed woken up. She had listened to the knowledge and accepted it. If every other human on this planet would do the same, the greed would crumble. The planet and humans alike would prosper. No more would the self-proclaimed one percent have it all. Everyone would be equal. Possessions would no longer matter, only happiness. They just had to wake up first and see the greed for what it was.

With licenses, worms, and snacks in hand, they headed off for some fishing. It was just a few miles before they found their spot. This part of country was teeming with fishing spots. You just had to pull over and claim one. There were very few cars out and absolutely no other fishermen. The lady at the store had told them to look for canals that met up with each other. "That'll be your spot," she had drawled. This place they had found was exactly what she had told them to look for.

As soon as they got out of the car, the boy yelled, "Alligator!". The man was used to the boy crying bear all the time back in California, but the excited look on his grandson's face told the truth. There, across the canal, up on the bank, was a four-foot alligator. The family was so excited. Their main goal coming to this state was to fish and see some alligators. Their first stop was successful. Now they were excited to get some lines in the water. All four were like little kids as they unpacked the equipment.

The travels, however, had made a mess of the fishing gear. The man got it all untangled and the poles put together. He had planned on doing this in Texas but had hesitated with the distance still in between. Two of the reels were completely tangled and would need to be restrung. Somehow, the others didn't know how to string a fishing reel, so the man went into action. This took all the patience and control he could muster. He had dreamed of fishing here this whole trip and now this frustration. He told himself he had waited this long, a few more minutes wouldn't matter. He would feel much better if everyone else could fish at the same time. He had been trying hard to work on his patience. Bad things always happened and if you just accepted them, it made it much easier to deal with.

The alligator had slithered into the water and was lurking on the family. The man told the others to keep a close eye on the dogs and the gator. He needn't have mentioned the dogs. They sensed the danger and were on point in the back of the car. The first cast from the man's pole landed in the middle of the canal. The gator swam at the bobber as if to check out this new intruder. The reptile gently took the floater in its mouth, like a dog putting something in its mouth it doesn't like. It seemed to curl its lip some and gingerly bite on the object to taste its worthiness. The man gently tugged his line. The alligator's mouth slid down the fishing line, and the man hooked its mouth. This was not expected by either of them. The man felt a connection to the creature. He seemed to understand the gator. Their energies seemed to be entwined through the thin filament.

The man lazily reeled the gator closer to shore. The beast twisted and turned in the water as it was pulled closer. After a few moments, the man began to wonder what he would do with the alligator if he was to reel it all the way up. He didn't really want to deal with that. He was happy he had only used six-pound test, and the hook was very small. The gator fought harder as it got closer to shore. It was creating quite a commotion in the water when the line snapped. The man was relieved. This was the best solution to the dilemma.

The family stayed at this spot for several more hours. The woman did not fish as much as the others, but all had a very good time. They each caught their share of alligator gar, a couple bass, and the girl caught a very large crappy. Once again, they would not be eating their fish this night. The alligator gar would bite through the lines before they got them to shore. The family was happy about this, they had sharp looking teeth. None of them were familiar with this fish, and all of them wanted to keep their fingers.

The alligator floated around the water the whole time. It kept a vigilant watch on the man and his every movement. The man continued to feel this connection with the creature. He seemed in tune to the reptile. Once, the man sat on a culvert. The water was only about one foot away from his leg. The alligator disappeared. Calm waters on the canal seemed surreal. The man quickly returned to his spot on the bank. He wasn't scared of the gator, but he had respect for it.

Just before noon, the fishing had dried up. The family was very hungry anyway and went in search of some food. The a.m. radio station provided the family with a constant barrage of bluegrass music. The man felt like this was very fitting for this region of America. Not to mention his love for this style of music. Passing through a small town, the man saw the poverty in these parts. It was a hard life here; the jobs had long ago gone away with international trade deals.

It was something the group was seeing all along the road; more and more poverty. While more and more Dollar Stores popped up. All the manufacturing jobs in this once proud nation had been shipped overseas by the greed. You could make a lot more money when you paid your employees peanuts. Throw in no worker rights and no environmental protections and the greed jumped all over trade deals with poor countries. Then they could ship their cheaply made goods back to America and sell them to the same people whose jobs had been stolen.

The man thought it was just another way for the greed to control the masses. If you were mass manufacturing things you were being productive, not creative. Imagination and creativity could easily be stifled when everyone worked at stores, factories, and restaurants. There was no creativity in these jobs. You just worked all day for peanuts. Then you would go home and watch your propaganda all night long and do exactly like you were told. This was the true American way.

Slavery had never ended in America. All the people were slaves to the greed. The masses just got enough thrown their way so they would put up with it. Like sheep getting thrown some alfalfa, they were content.

The family stopped at the only diner that they saw in this town. The man almost wrecked into the sign protruding from their building. The sign was held in place on a very sturdy metal frame, attached with zip ties. It was put in a very awkward place. They knew almost immediately that this place was not going to be the best. It seemed like the lunch room at a second-rate hospital. Out of hunger and lack of other choices, they settled for the diner. The food was mediocre at best, and the service no better. They hoped that all their eating choices in Louisiana were not going to be like this one.

Coming out of the diner, the crow was sitting on the monstrosity of the sign. The boy made a cawing sound. He too had learned the birds cry. The crow responded with some cawing of its own and jerked its head in the direction of the south east. The family had planned on going due east but the bird got the man thinking. He fetched the map out of the console just as the bird flew toward the direction it had indicated. The man saw that the only thing there was Palmetto Island, but it sounded intriguing. They would have to go onto a small peninsula, and it was at the tip. They had no other plans but to experience Louisiana. If the crow wanted them to go this way, it would be the way they went.

It was not far to the Island, maybe thirty minutes. The park was not all that big but the trails were very poorly marked. The family drove through the entire park twice before settling on an area they could walk around. A couple hundred feet down the road, they found the trail. They all commented on the lack of signs but thought maybe it would be a good thing. More signs meant more people. They were right, they would not encounter another human on this path through the bayou.

The trail wound around and next to a swampy canal. The green moss and trees were like pictures they had seen. Birds and lizards filled the forest. The family saw so many species of birds in a short time it was unbelievable. The trees and ivy were also very impressive, totally different than that in their native California. The air seemed so clean here. There was still some humidity but nothing like where they were before. It felt like they were in paradise, the woman had said.

The girl called the others over to some trees. It looked like she was looking at the air until they got closer. Webs were everywhere in the foliage. A large yellow, black and white spider species was everywhere. They ranged in size from a dime to a baseball. The man looked very closely at them. They were not aggressive. He took many pictures and was fascinated. He had never seen spiders like this before. So much reference was filling his mind and his camera.

The family walked for about two miles. The trail kept on going, but they figured it was time to get back. The dogs too seemed to be getting tired. Right before turning back, the girl started jumping about. She had walked through one of the webs by accident, and one of the spiders had gotten on her hat. It had dropped down in front of her face, and that is when she lost sight of it. Her hat flung to the ground, she began her spider dance. After a moment, she calmed enough for the man to tell her that surely the spider was gone. "I know you like spiders, uncle, but I do not like when they get on me" she said. "Make sure it is not on me." The woman came to assist and cleared the girl of any spider hikers.

Walking back to the car, the family found a little spot tucked between the trees. It was all muddy and led to the water. Foot prints and scraping in the mud told the family that this was an alligator hangout. They looked around carefully as they swooped the dogs into their arms. They would be too tempting of a meal for a gator. The man noticed so much trash mixed in among the small diameter trees. It was a dump forest of some sorts. The man felt bad that people would do this to their home planet. This was a place of beauty destroyed by an ugly people.

Movement in the water got the family moving. They had all been having a sense of danger and had been cautious of their surroundings. They knew how big the gators got here. The size of the scraping in the mud told them that it was not a small creature. As they were getting back on the main trail, they all saw the behemoth that had been lurking. This alligator must have been fifteen feet long and stood four feet off the ground. The family and the gator stood frozen on the path for over a minute, while each sized the other up. Finally, the gator knew it had no hope against four adults and retreated into its hidden den. The group knew it was time to go.

Getting back to the car, the family was getting tired and out of breath. They had brought water with them for the walk, but that had long ago been consumed. A late model van parked next to the minivan brought a mixed emotion from the man. He was not a trustful person. The parking lot was empty except for these two cars. The paved expanse was also very large, which brought suspicion from the man.

He opened the doors closest to them with remote. As they got closer, the man had a very bad feeling about the other vehicle. It had a very dark energy coming from it.

The others had filled their water and were drinking freely. The dogs had jumped in the car as soon as the door was open. It was customary behavior for the canines, not wanting to be left behind. The family was wandering around the vicinity of the car, but the man could not shake the feeling coming from the vehicle parked next to them. Flies were buzzing around the back window and it gave off a bad smell. There was a bumper sticker on the back window. It read in black letters on a yellow background, "UFOs exist, the government is not real". This bumper sticker seemed so familiar to him. He seemed so sure that at one time he had one of these stickers. This van, too, was very similar to a van he had about ten years before. He had traded it for tattoos and drove it for a few years before selling it to the scrap yard. They sure looked similar the man thought. Even the ladder on the back and the way the doors shut irregularly seemed eerily the same.

The man thought he saw movement in the bushes. He adjusted his eyes and could swear he saw a being looking back at him. The feeling of being watched was profound, along with the feeling of dread. The man trusted his instincts. They had gotten him and his family out of many near disasters.

The man had enough of this place. His mind could not take the impending feeling of doom any longer. He got the others in the car and headed off Palmetto Island. There were absolutely no other cars or people as they passed the entrance shack. The park had not been crowded before, but it also had not been deserted.

Just up the road, a tailgater had emerged from nowhere. There were no other cars on the road and now this black car with their tinted windows was going to tailgate. It was pulling right next to the van's bumper and then backing off. The man could not see through the windshield of the car behind them. It too was a dark tint. All he could see was the sun glinting off the solid black Cadillac.

As his eyes were leaving his side mirror, a very nice swamp came into view off to the left. The man would have stopped had it not been for the guy riding his ass. The car finally went to pass, and a large raccoon ran from the right of the road, directly into the path of the minivan. There was nowhere to go, as the tailgater was on the left of their vehicle. The man braked and the front wheels missed the animal. Briefly, the family thought that the raccoon had made it. The creature did not get so lucky with the back tires. The car bounced slightly as the wheels went over the large rodent. The man looked in the rear-view mirror to see the animal writhing in agony in the middle of the road. It was the largest raccoon he had ever seen. The boy and girl were also looking out the back window, with looks on their faces of sorrow.

The boy was cursing the car for passing at the same time, but the man told him it was just the way things were. All the numbers lined up and it was your time to go. That is what had just happened to that raccoon. The boy seemed to understand. He was agreeing with his grandpa when they saw a tortoise crossing the road. They had seen many dead ones, but this one was alive. A large four-wheel drive truck came barreling the other way and hit the turtle squarely with its' massive tire. The turtle's innards squirt fifteen feet in the air, spraying the forest on the other side of the road. The boy told his grandpa that he understood what he had just told him about death. The numbers had lined up for the tortoise as well as the raccoon.

The black sedan had slowed after passing the minivan. The windows seemed to be the same material and color as the rest of the vehicle. A strange antenna, almost like a satellite dish, was sticking out of the roof of the vehicle. The man had thought it was a Cadillac, but now saw that it was a model he had never seen before. It looked like a presidential car from the sixties, but much more aerodynamic. Its tires were very low profile.

After ten minutes of the car playing speed up and slow down, the man went to pass. He pulled alongside the sedan and looked to the passengers who were behind the darkness. The car sped off at an unbelievable speed. It was up the road and out of view in seconds, leaving the minivan alone on the Louisiana highway. The man and woman looked at each other. Neither of them needed to say anything. The strangeness of the events told the whole story.

Some miles down the road, the energy took a low turn. The family all fell asleep while the man drove. He felt like he would like to sleep too, but didn't mind being the driver. The girl was going to help drive too, but the rental car company had strict regulations on drivers under twenty-five years old. The woman was not getting much sleep, and the driving was hard on her. The man had been pushing this crazy ass schedule on all of them and had decided to do most of the driving himself. The car was comfortable anyway, and he could see the countryside. He was seriously thinking about stopping soon. The day had been long and filled with so much adventure. When the others woke, he would have them start looking for hotels.

Moaning from the back seat brought the man's attention back to the inside of the car. His niece was saying that her ear really hurt. Her voice told the man she was very distressed. The boy and woman had now begun to waken. "Pull over! Pull over!" the girl shouted frantically from the back seat. The man swerved to the side of the road and stopped. The girl was not one to panic. She ripped open the door of the van and fell to the shoulder of the road. "Get it out," she was wailing over and over while clutching the side of her head.

The man was beside her in an instant. "Calm down," he was telling the girl. He was crouching at her side and could already see the legs of the spider sticking out of her ear. He calmed her enough to snatch at the arachnid and give it a tug. It didn't seem to want to give up its grip on the girl's ear until she jerked, and it came free with a popping sound. It instantly clamped itself to the man's finger. He shook his hand free of the spider, but it ran up his arm. The man had always been fast, but he was no match for the speed of the arachnid. It was on his head in a flash, but stopped at the eye tattoo. He swatted at the arachnid, but it was already gone.

"Check my ears," he said, and the woman was right there. She checked the man out, and said the spider must have fallen and ran away. The man looked at the girl and asked if she was alright. She was very pale. He honestly did not know how that big ass spider had gotten itself into the girl's ear. "It must have been in her hat or something," he told the woman and boy.

Morgan City was the next place on the map that seemed like it would have adequate lodging and food. Many towns were so small throughout the south, the family realized. Many didn't even have a diner or hotel. All of them had a Dollar Store.

They were ready for a rest and maybe some more fishing later. The swimming pool was very dirty and full of debris. The recent storms had muddied up a lot of Louisiana and Texas. The family went to the pool anyway. They cleared the lawn chairs and the floating debris from the pool, and found it suitable for swimming. The water was so warm and refreshing.

Clouds filled the sky with the threat of more rain. The boy asked if maybe they should get out of the water, in case there was lightning. The man and his niece laughed. The hunger in the bellies was what cut the swimming session short.

Finding a Cajun restaurant was not difficult at all. This whole area was lakes, and this place was right on the water. Boats surrounded the diner lined up on their docks. The family was so hungry.

The awesome smell of the food was the first thing that hit them. The second was the feeling of not being wanted in this place. The man had experienced these kinds of prejudice so many times in his life. With tattoos and before tattoos, someone always showed prejudice. If you were not the same as some folks, they did not like you. This place was no different. The waitress reluctantly sat them at a table in the corner. The talk had been boisterous when they walked in the door, and now it was all hushed tones of disapproval. Some loud mouth women hollered back and forth about the strangers. She said something about the circus just coming to town. The man heard the alcohol effects in the voices. They continued their banter the whole time the family was there. Underlying their ignorance and arrogance, the man detected regret in the words they spoke. They only said these things thinking it made them cool. When they would get home, and look in the mirror tonight, they would cry their made-up faces into the sink.

The family did not fall into the rhetoric of hate. If these people wanted to be biased against them, then it was a bummer for them. They were just like the other ninety nine percent of the population who had no clue about the truth. The man also knew booze would make people say and do things they normally wouldn't. Just because he hadn't had a drink in a couple of years, he remembered what it was like.

One of the other women in the place had joined in with the other two mouths. She and her husband were sitting rather close, and the family could hear their words of hate. Even the young waitress seemed to be disgusted by the strangers.

It was meaningless to the man. He was so hungry. He and his grandson went to the salad bar to begin the meal. The girls lagged a bit and joined the others when they were halfway done. The boy asked his grandpa about pickled okra, and his grandpa gave the thumbs up. A lady serving herself at the salad bar said he should try it. The man agreed.

The woman's husband glared at the man. He was very large and obviously had a bit to drink. The guy was looking at the man with jealousy in his eyes. The man thought for a moment that he was going to have to fight this guy. He wasn't scared of this now or ever. His senses were alive. His eyes were wide open allowing for the true perception of events.

The man knew that he would be fighting everyone in the room along with this giant. He ignored the haters and returned to the table with his grandson. They waited for the women to get back before beginning their meal. This had always been customary in their family, and no matter how hungry they were, they would wait for the others when eating together at a table.

The third woman talking shit saw the fact that the men were waiting at that devil table for the women to arrive. The man saw the tone in her thinking change with the look in her eye. Suddenly, she understood. She said something softly to her husband and he nodded gently. The whole air at their table had changed from disgust to respect. The husband turned to the man and his grandson and gave a friendly nod of the head. His look was one of apology. The two returned the nod. The man told his grandson that it was the way. People were walking around like zombies. When they awoke, they would understand.

The waitress had a serious attitude toward the family, but the man did not care. She seemed to serve them fast, as if trying to get them out the door as soon as possible. The man saw the fake niceness she painted on her face. If it would have been up to her, this sort of people would go somewhere else. They certainly didn't belong here.

The food turned out to be top notch. Everything the group ate was fantastic. It was difficult to enjoy such fine food while people openly talked shit on you, but they seemed to manage. The man just imagined how black people here felt and it made him see the stupidity of the whole situation even more. These sheep knew nothing but hatred. This hatred, in truth, was them. It radiated out of their beings, engulfing everyone in their presence. Their hatred bounced off the family like they had a force field around them. Everyone else in the diner absorbed the darkness of prejudice while the family was oblivious to its grasp.

The bill came before they had finished their food. Even the management was ready for them to leave. The food was not cheap but well worth it. The man tipped the girl thirty dollars, a very hefty tip. He liked to show people like this that judging others was stupid. You never knew who you were judging, nor why. Good people came in all different pods. It was not what you looked like on the outside. It was all about your energy and your aura.

As they were getting up to leave, the angry man from the salad bar earlier leaped to his feet. "Here we go," the man said to his wife, fully preparing for the battle he was sure was coming. Instead, the man realized the other diner was choking. All the people in the restaurant had stopped eating and talking so they could stare at the man dying. They seemed almost happy to have something new to break up their monotonous lives. Some of them had their cell phones out and were recording the misery.

The man and woman jumped to the chokers aid. They both had CPR training and knew exactly what to do. The choking man was so big the man had to stand on a chair to perform the Heimlich maneuver. The alligator chunk came out with the first heave the man had given him. He had placed his hands well and heaved with all his might. He was not so worried about breaking a rib or two on the man. Having many broken bones himself in the past, the man knew that it was not as bad as losing your life.

The man started to breathe immediately after the obstruction left his throat. The woman was there with a glass of water, which the man eagerly took. The other patrons looked on in awe. The wife of the choker was at her husband's side, offering him help. She looked to the man and his wife with admiration and respect. They had just saved her husband's life, while everyone else just sat around and watched. One of the waitresses began to applaud. The other diners joined in until the room was filled with applause and catcalls. The man took off his hat and did a mock bow in jest.

That is when the others saw the tattoo on the man's forehead. The loud noise quickly turned to silence. Not a word was spoken by anyone in the room except for the man. He asked the choking man if he was alright, and the other man hugged him. He didn't care what was on the man's head. You were to always be in debt to a man who saved your life. Loyalty and respect were the first steps to repaying this kind of heroism, the choking man had thought to himself.

The boy and girl were there with the others. The girl looked green, almost like she might pass out. The boy said, "It's the spider, grandpa. I think it bit her or something." The man was trying to figure out how she could have gotten so sick so suddenly from a spider bite. These spiders were not poisonous, anyway. She had been eating shrimp. Maybe she was having an allergic reaction.

The boy told his grandpa to hold still. The youngster couldn't believe what he was seeing. The spider was sitting on the eye tattoo in the middle of his grandpa's forehead. It was the same spider that had come out of the ear of the girl earlier. He didn't know how it got there, but the boy wanted it gone. The spider took off with an anticipation of the boy's next move. It ran down the man's body onto the floor of the diner. It raced across the floor and ran up a man's leg that was in a wheelchair. "Let's get out of here," the man said urgently to the others.

"Quickly," the others all pitched in, as the man in the wheelchair was gently caressing the lump in his pant leg. His hand looked misshapen. It was long and had only two fingers and a thumb. When the wheelchair guy saw the man looking at him, he promptly shoved his hand into the pocket of his windbreaker. He had a vacant look in his eyes.

There was no white in them. His aura gave off a shadow of sadness and hopelessness. The man kept his eyes on the others for moments. A mutual thought came into each of their heads at the same moment. It was a thought of hope.

The girl had begun to get her color back. The others were pulling her towards the door and freedom from the strangeness of this diner. This experience could fuel a future story, the man had thought as they were headed out.

The choking man insisted on paying for the family's food. The man denied his gift, but there would be no refuting the gesture. His life had just been saved. He owed his life to the man. He gathered the man's money off the table and handed it back to him. "Please mister, let me do this for you". The man finally agreed and took his money back. When they turned to leave, he left a hundred-dollar bill on the table. He felt like they had disrupted this place enough. Money always seemed to appease the blind.

The silence had remained in the restaurant the entire time. All eyes in the place were on the strangers again, but now there was a genuine respect. Their minds had been opened here tonight and they would live their lives on a different path from this day forward. They had truly seen the light.

As they were passing out the front door, the family heard a loud exclamation from the dining room. "My legs, my god my legs" the voice said excitedly. "I can feel my legs by God". The man did not let the words impede his retreat. He was very ready to get out of this place. It was after sunset already, but not all the way dark. There was a little time left in the day for adventure.

The boy commented on the man in the wheelchair getting up as they were walking out the door. He said the others were looking at him with shock. One of the women talking trash earlier asked the others what had just happened. The other trash talker said she thought they had been blessed. The boy said everyone in the restaurant began to cry when she said this. He asked his grandpa why they were crying, and he said maybe they were just happy that their friend had been saved. He also told the boy that maybe the patrons had finally seen the light. They had woken up. Theirs had been tears of joy, mixed with shame.

A few fishing spots were checked out for the next morning. They were on the way to the room and the family really wanted to fish some more. There was a sea wall around this area, and the family was scoping that out. It seemed to go on for a very long way. They found a spot to enter and saw many boats and anglers in the parking area. They got out of the car and walked in search of a good place to fish. They thought about fishing now, but the mosquitoes were out of control. They settled instead for some dusk pictures and were swiftly to the safety of the minivan.

They had not thought to close the doors to the vehicle and now there was a colony of mosquito in the cabin. They were swarming almost as bad as outside. As soon as the man breached the levee, he opened all the windows and gave the minivan gas. The speed slammed the insects into oblivion on the back window. The threat was over. It was a peaceful trip back to the hotel. The family talked a lot about all that great food they had just ate. Nobody talked about the strange events nor the talk of the other patrons. They were happy just to have some fine Louisiana cuisine.

The woman stayed in the room while the others went on a walkabout. They needed a few items from the local corporate. Walking down the street, they passed two dark skin men who looked at the group with deep respect. One of the men dropped to his knees on the sidewalk, blocking the family's path. "God bless me," he said with desperation in his voice.

The man put his hand just over the kneeling man's head and said, "We are all blessed. God is inside all of us and all the things around us. We are all God. Be One with the One."

The two strangers began to weep. They praised the man and promised dedication to the way. They were still calling to the man and his family even after they had long been out of sight.

The guy at the pharmacy was a very nice Cajun man. The man thought that it was nice to meet some genuine southern hospitable people. They had made friends along the whole road and would continue to do the same the rest of the way. They had a message of peace and hope. True change was their message; a drawing away from the greed, into a new realm of existence. None of the rhetoric like the media spewed. 'Make America great again' pitches from the rich greed were ridiculous.

Make the Planet great again for the first time since civilization, when the greed had first taken over control of the planet. This was the true path. This was the destiny for the family.

The girl at the counter had Turrets syndrome. While taking his change, the man awkwardly touched the girl's hand. A strange energy passed from her fingers. She looked at the man very strangely and withdrew her hand, almost reluctantly.

While they were walking out the door, the cashier called out to the three, "Ya'll forgot something".

The man returned to the counter and the girl behind the counter dropped the object into his hand. It was a metal ball slightly smaller than a marble. The sense of deja vu almost made the man pass out. He looked to the cashier and realized she had no white in her eyes. They were solid black. "Have a nice night," she said to the man as he put the object in his pocket.

The Turrets symptoms had vanished.

CHAPTER 17

Fishing got the family out of bed early. The man had slept a couple of hours this night. He wrote in his book for hours until he nodded off. His book and pen were in bed with him. He had been having dreams where someone was chasing the family. They were doing everything they could to lose the tail but just could not. It was that familiar feeling of running but being in place. If only he could see who was chasing them. The boy in his dream was much older, as was his niece. His wife seemed younger. The dream faded as he thought about those fishing holes they had scoped out the day before.

A park on the outside of town seemed like the spot for the family. They arrived shortly after sunrise. There were multiple docks in the water, but no boats. A few other anglers dotted the area, but this place was big enough where everyone would have space. They were all excited to get some early morning fishing in. The group all split up and headed for their own dock. They had gotten more worms and had enough for each to take a container with them. Fishing was supposed to be fun, not stressful.

While walking to his spot, the man passed by a woman in a wheelchair. He made eye contact and greeted her with a "good day." The woman smiled broadly at the man. Her face seemed to be lit up by an illumination from deep within her being. She reached out her hand and grabbed the man's arm. Her touch spread a warm energy through his entire body. Briefly, their energy had become one. Smiling broadly back at the woman, he said, "I know". She smiled back warmly, like they were long lost friends, and slowly withdrew her hand. Her gaze never once left the man.

The end of the dock was where the man had decided to fish. The others were spread on their own platforms, a short distance away. The dogs were so very happy to have this run around time. They ran from one family member to the next and everywhere in between. They, too, were here to have fun. The morning on the lake was a beautiful one. Mist covered the water and gave the feel of a movie. The only sound was the water slowly lapping at the metal piers.

Unfortunately, there wasn't a single fish biting. After about forty-five minutes, the group decided to pack it in and find a different spot.

As they were leaving, the man could not spot the woman in the wheelchair. He was looking around all the docks and the cars, but she was nowhere to be seen. He hadn't seen the woman leave. "What are you looking for?" the woman asked him.

"The lady in the wheelchair," the man replied.

"You must be tripping," said the woman, "we were the only ones out here the whole time." The man was confused. He looked around again, and there were no other people. He was getting very used to this feeling of confusion. Maybe his active imagination had finally taken over his reality. His mind either wasn't working right or someone was really fucking with his head. He told himself that he would start to concentrate better.

Down the road a bit, they stopped at the next fishing spot. This was a levee filled with water plants. It would not be good for fishing. The family spotted an alligator floating among the plants. They were all happy to see another gator. A walk down the trail was only appropriate. They did not find much farther down and decided to get back to the hotel. They were really enjoying the outdoors and the wildlife, but they also knew that this state was large and they would have a lot of cool things to see. There was a lot of Louisiana to explore.

When checking out of the hotel, the clerk wouldn't look at the man. The guy kept his eyes on his computer the whole time. The man looked at the girl, and they exchanged odd looks. She would come in with her uncle each morning and settle the bill for the room the night before. It was important for the girl to help pay her way. She was an adult now and took it very seriously.

"Excuse me," the man said to the clerk after standing there for minutes being ignored. There was no response. The man left the keys on the counter and went to leave. They had already paid the day before anyhow. On the way out the door, the clerk finally spoke.

"Excuse me," he said in a muffled tone. The man looked at the receptionist and realized he had no eyes. There was a soft glow of green coming from the sockets where his eyes should have been. "We know who you are," finished the clerk as his gaze dropped back to his computer. The blue glow from the screen contrasted with the green coming from the being's eye sockets.

The man was going to say something, but he and the girl knew it would be of no use. There was no talking to the being they had just encountered. They slipped out the door into the air conditioning and safety of the minivan.

The woman and boy could tell something was wrong with the other two. They asked, but the man and girl said it was nothing. "Just some more bullshit," the man had said. "Let's get out of here."

The sea wall from the night before was the same road they took to the Northwest. The man had read good things about the bayou from this area all the way to Baton Rouge. The wall seemed to go on for over a hundred miles. The man wished he could see an aerial view of the area, but he was driving and never used his phone when he was driving. He would have to leave it to his imagination as to what was on the other side.

The man couldn't stop thinking about all the strange things that had been going on. Why did he keep encountering these people with their blank eyes? Why did his path keep crossing theirs? Who were these people, and why were their eyes missing? He knew something very odd was happening. Their path was so much more than what they had thought. When they had started on this trip, it was to heal the wounds left behind by so much death. Almost as soon as they had left their house, the man had realized that much more was going on than just healing.

All things as they had known them seemed to be changing. Reality seemed to be bending. He knew these things should worry him, but they did not. He liked change in life. He was a Pisces. He flowed with change like the water. 'Along for the ride' had always been his motto. He would just continue to go with the flow and see what happened. It was all part of the adventure.

Some miles had passed before they found their next fishing spot. They had crossed a draw bridge and watched as it opened to allow a barge to pass underneath. Neither the boy nor girl had ever seen a draw bridge. The man was happy he could give them both new experiences. One of the things he really wanted to accomplish on this trip was giving the youngsters new adventure. This was the idea of traveling to him, seeing as much as possible.

They stopped up river and threw the lines in the water. The woman decided to stay in the car, with all the doors open, and hang out with the dogs. The river was wide here, and there was a nice wooden dock about ten feet above the water. The spot was perfect for the three. A snake swam by. The three fishermen were overjoyed. They loved nature, all of it. The family believed that all creatures had God within them. In this regard, all creatures were God's too. The family showed respect to all beings. They were all related to each other, after all. All creatures on Earth were part of the planet. The planet and all its beings together, created the One.

The three kept getting snagged on the weeds close to shore. They had been fishing for a while and had each caught a small, fish but that was it. Once when the man was snagged, he had caught a fish while getting untangled. This was the only fish at this spot for him. They were not sad about the lack of catches. This was a beautiful spot, and the family was really enjoying some relax time.

They all knew that the next four days were going to be a lot of driving. They would take any rest they could get, now. Catching fish was always secondary for the family anyhow. The real enjoyment came from being outside and with your homies. This place was so serene and pleasant, the group felt as if they might just stay there all day.

The three were happy when a light rain had started. The man had decided not to change his shirt all the way to Minnesota, and now it would be getting washed. Being from the arid lands of California, the family welcomed the rain. They continued to fish for some time, but the rain just got harder and harder. Finally, it was getting too hard to even see their lines in the water, and they decided to pack it in. The three fishers were soaked. It seemed more like they had been swimming in the river, not fishing in it.

The temperature of the air had dropped almost fifteen degrees. It made their wet clothes feel like air conditioners on their skin. The humidity had dropped a bit also, giving the family a small reprieve from the heat.

Driving down the road, they got the full experience of Louisiana rain. It came down so hard that it made it almost impossible to see the road. The man had to slow down to about thirty-five and take his time. They were in no rush anyway. The rain lasted for about fifteen minutes. The man could tell they were headed away from the storm as the force of it decreased. They had caught the beginning of the cell while fishing, and now had come out the other side to fluffy clouds spotting the blue sky.

Passing through Plaquemine, Louisiana was the first thing after the storm. They were all hungry, and spotted a Cajun stand on the side of the road. The family knew all too well about these stands. Sometimes it was where you got the best food. They only sold a few items, but it did not matter. All the items on the list were foreign to the group anyhow. The lack of a menu made ordering much easier. They all settled on Boudin with crayfish and corn on the cob. They took their takeout and went in search of a nice place to eat lunch.

A local park provided just the spot they needed. The smell of the food in the car mixed with the hunger in their bellies made waiting impossible. The family tore into the food as soon as they found a place to sit. The sausage and corn both had a very strong spice to them. The woman, not one to enjoy overly spicy food, gave hers to the man. He put all that food down in minutes. It felt like he hadn't eaten in days. Even after all the good Boudin, he was still hungry for more. This was food he had always dreamed of eating.

The park turned out to be very nice. A large wooden pavilion was next to the river. Walkways of concrete on the earth and wood on the water made a network. A family was fishing off the pavilion and seemed like they were having a great time. The dogs enjoyed the freedom of being out of the car; as did their people.

The family walked around the park. It was not overly large, so it did not take all that long. The dogs were very happy to run around without rain. A huge lock was situated on the river, taking up one whole side of the park. This lock looked very old and reminded the man of ones he had seen in Amsterdam. It was made of concrete, which had grown moss over most of it. The operating shack was situated right on top of the structure. It too was made of concrete.

Walking out on some metal docks, they could see into the waterway. As a former sailor, the man was very impressed. The boy and girl had never seen a lock before, so it was another new experience for them. The family turned to walk back to the car, but the man remained. Something shiny had caught his eye up the river, in the middle of the lock. His view was blocked by the concrete walls. He walked as far out on the deck as possible and leaned over the water. He had his camera extended in his right hand, pointed into the lock, and snapped a picture.

He looked one more time to see a large metal object slip into the water. It was quickly gone under the calm river. The whole thing lasted maybe two seconds, and the water in the lock was not even disturbed. If the man would have blinked, he would have missed this strange shiny disc.

The man started analyzing the situation some. How had the object gone into the lock while it was open? Surely the water wouldn't be deep enough to conceal the shine of a large metal object. He looked up to the control room. There, atop the small concrete enclosure, sat a very large crow. When it turned its head, the sun reflected off a shiny object in the bird's beak. The crow was looking directly at the man. He knew this bird. It was their old friend. The animal gave a strange comfort to the man. The bird took flight and dropped the metal object out of its beak. The man watched as the object fell into the water in the same spot the larger object had been before. The water seemed to flash a green pulse when the object entered it and sent ripples outwards about fifteen feet.

The man stood looking to the water to see if there was going to be more happening. The crow swooped down to the place where the object had hit the water. Its black talons skimmed the ripples, causing water to trail behind its graceful flight. It flew off through the lock, its talons dripping water the whole way.

When the man got back to the car, the girl asked him what he had been taking pictures of. He turned on his camera and looked at the last picture. The screen was filled with a strange light. The man couldn't make out the features in the light, but it looked almost like a face. A face so close it filled the whole picture. Like if you held the camera a foot from away from your face and snapped it. The boy looked over his grandpa's shoulder and said the picture looked like an alien.

"Why do you say that?" the man asked his grandson. The boy just shrugged his shoulders. The girl and woman also looked, but they both said they saw nothing but light and shadows. The man thought to himself that he would for sure be looking at this picture blown up on his computer when they got home. Something very weird had happened at those locks. He and the crow had been part of something that he couldn't quite understand yet.

A short time up the road, the family passed into Mississippi. It was the seventh state on their journey. They had wanted to stay in Louisiana another night and fish some more, but had decided against it. As they got more and more north, everything was much more populated. They had enjoyed their stay in bayou country, but had opted to head north in search of different adventure. By the time they had gotten there, they regretted not staying south longer.

They had caught a tributary of the Mississippi river a hundred miles back. Now in Mississippi, they crossed the main river for the first time. The green countryside had spilled over from Louisiana. The family loved all the forest and open road. The lack of traffic was still making the entire trip very nice.

A sign for some Native American burial mounds caught the family's attention. The man and woman had always wanted to see these mounds, and now here they were. This trip had been so many firsts for the whole family.

Natchez was the place and they were introduced with a nice museum. The curators of the museum were very nice and were there to help in any way. They didn't allow dogs, though, so the group would be split in two. The man had read extensively about these mounds and was a good guide for his grandson as they learned the museum. They walked through the small museum, refreshing their minds and learning some new things along the way. It was very comprehensive and well laid out. The man was very impressed.

Outside, the place was beautiful. The woman and girl were coming back toward the building as the man and boy waited. The area of the mounds hadn't taken so long for the two to walk. The same time as the museum had taken for the other two. The man and boy took over the dogs, and the two groups again went in different directions.

This ancient place held an energy that seemed to flow through the family. This location was connected to them.

The man and his grandson really enjoyed walking around the mounds. They read every one of the placards telling about the spot. It was very interesting. They learned about the Son, or ruler who was in touch with the stars. They also read about a dance of the tattooed serpent. The man took a picture of this and promised himself to look it up later.

Midway through the hike, the two saw a nature trail tucked into the forest. A sign said how this had been a logging trail in the past. The man's imagination was running wild here. There was a very strong energy that had held onto this place. Or maybe, he thought, the energy was why these people had lived and held their ceremonies here. He could envision countless beings using this trail throughout the centuries.

The trail went downhill, led to a dry river, and then snaked back uphill. The whole walk had taken minutes. When they crested the last hill, back into the field of mounds, the two froze in their tracks. In between the three mounds, directly in the middle, a fire was burning. There were shelters of wood and mud that hadn't been there before. The boy asked the man if they had gotten lost and came into a different field. None of this seemed familiar. The man turned around and saw that there was no way they could have gotten lost, the trail was only about a hundred yards long.

The man and boy took some steps closer to the smoke. The buildings on top of the mounds intrigued them. They looked like temples built on the top of earthen pyramids.

Around the fire, there was a group of Natchez standing, performing a ceremony. They were standing around the fire but there were two open spots to make a complete circle. The man and boy got closer. The man wondered how he was even walking. It seemed like his whole being was on autopilot and levitating toward the ritual. Someone else was in control. He couldn't look at the boy, because he couldn't take his eyes off the scene in front of him.

The smoke from the fire seemed to be forming into strange shapes of animals and beings. The man thought the smoke looked alive to him. It reminded him briefly of the smoke in a room with the sun coming through the blinds.

On the other side of the fire, standing on an object of about the same height as himself, was the Son. The man had studied this culture for a long time, and the drawings inside the museum confirmed what he was seeing. He knew this was no re-enactment.

The man and boy ended their journey when their bodies filled the last pieces into the circle. They became one with the others, sharing their knowledge and their truth. The others did not look at the two newcomers, as they did not look at them. All eyes were upon the Son in his full regalia of clothes. All the beings were locked together in the circle. The ceremony had begun.

The Son had been looking to the heavens with a wooden chalice grasped between his hands. The man saw on the chalice a symbol of a sun that looked like the one on the rock that the crow had gifted him way back when. The deity shifted his eyes from the heavens to the newcomers. He lifted the chalice in the air, but in the direction of the man and boy, directly across the fire from his being. A ray of sun came pouring from the sky through the smallest of holes in the clouds. The beam fell directly on the holy man and concentrated on the opening of the sacred chalice. The object seemed to be dripping a liquid that the man thought looked like sunshine.

The Son held the chalice out, in front of him, as if offering it to the man and boy. There was a look of respect in the ruler's eye as he made eye contact with the man.

Just as the man extended his hands to accept the chalice, the entire scene before them was gone. It didn't fade, it just disappeared. The man and boy looked around. Minutes before, the mounds had been mostly earthen without any grass. Now they were covered in a sea of green. The buildings on top of the mounds, as with the ones on the ground, were no longer there. There seemed to be a small indentation in the earth at the man's feet. Seems like a fire pit, he thought. He crossed to the other side of the indentation and saw a shard of wood the size of his finger. He picked it up and saw some strange carvings on the wood. Someone had worked this piece of debris. He thought about leaving it behind, but the object went into his pocket. He felt like this might be some sort of piece to the whole puzzle they were building. He didn't realize it until later that night, in the hotel, that the markings on this splinter were the same ones he had taken pictures of back in Roswell at the UFO museum. It had been a shard of wood there, too, retrieved from a crashed spacecraft in 1947. The symbols, as were the shape of the wood splinter, were identical.

When the man and boy returned to the others, waiting by the car, the woman asked the man if he was okay.

"Sure, why?" he asked.

"Your hair has another white streak and it seems longer" she said to him. There was something else wrong with the man, but she just couldn't pinpoint it.

His reply was odd, like his life. He simply said, "Good energy has enclosed my being," and got in the car. The boy almost began to tell the others what they had seen, but he wasn't sure himself. When they had been walking back to the car, he had asked his grandpa what had happened. The man had simply said, "Wisdom".

Crossing over the Mississippi river for the second time that day, the family was back in Louisiana. They had decided on a little town called Tallulah for their stopping point. It was still relatively early, they still had a few hours of sunlight. They unpacked the bags at the hotel and went in search of some fishing spots. The areas of water here all had large southern homes built next to it. Their lawns went all the way to the banks. The man knew this would not be a kind spot to fish. He knew that people like this would be calling the cops on people like them quickly. The houses were big and impressive, but the man pitied these people and had no respect for them nor their mansions. They were part of the greed. If everyone had the same riches, there would be so much less problems.

Mixed in with the mansions was an occasional historic marker for some civil war something or another. The family stopped to read a few. They were all interested in history. It was obvious why the fighting had broken out here. It was clearly about money and these mansions.

The man told the boy and girl that greed was always what drove humans to war. The men making the weapons got rich, while the politicians got rich on them, and the elite supplied the whole campaign. The greed was all about war. It was very profitable to them. "Unfortunately," the man had finished, "while the greed profited and ate their fancy dinners served by butlers, the rest of the people suffered. They used humans as their puppets for their own profits. It didn't matter how many lives were ruined in the process. As long as they can eat their caviar and lobster every night and wallow in their knowledge of the misery they have created".

They drove around for quite some time before finding a spot under a bridge. Nobody's house was close to this overpass. The family made their way down the muddy slope, only to find a dump. There was so much garbage, it almost sickened them. The water had a strange sludge on the top. Greenish in color, splashed with purple swatches. The family debated not even fishing here, but they were not catching fish to eat them anyway. The man thought this might be the most polluted water he had ever seen in the world. They were tired of driving around, looking for a spot in the land of greed. This place would have to do.

As soon as the lines hit the water, the rain started. It didn't sprinkle or mist, it just started raining. Being under the concrete bridge, the family was sheltered from the water. It was coming down very hard, just like before. They fished for some time, thinking the rain might stop. It never did, the intensity staying the same. Water ran off the sides of the overpass like sheets of water. The family could barely see anything away from the forty-foot-wide strip of dryness provided by the bridge. Everything outside of their sanctuary was a blur of green.

The girl, on her third cast, caught a log floating by. She gave it a yank and something floated from under the wood, dislodged by the disturbance. "What is that?" she asked, but the others could not tell. It wasn't wood, but it could be so many things. There was a lot of garbage here. As it floated closer, the boy snagged it with a branch. They could now see that it looked like a small human body, maybe three feet tall. It had one arm and half a leg, but its head was intact, just very swollen. They all thought it looked like a human.

As it got closer to shore, they could smell it. This creature had been in the water a very long time. It had been eaten by some of the river creatures. The arm that was intact had only three fingers at the end of it, without a hand. It was as if the fingers just protruded from the arm. They were webbed. The creature rolled when it was close, and the group saw the spine. It looked like a rocky ridge from the alps. "Turn it over," the man said to the boy. He grabbed a sturdier stick and rolled the creature over. The body wasn't all that heavy to the surprise of the boy.

Its' eyes were gone, as was half the face and mouth. The nose was just two slits in its leathery skin. The man thought the skin looked more like that of a bat than a human. There was no lump where the nose should be. A small frog pulled itself from the eye socket of the corpse. It dislodged some debris on the creature's forehead, and they all saw it at the same time. The creature had the same eye tattoo as the man, directly in the center of its head. This one had a slight variation of pattern around it, but it was the same. The other three looked to the man. He didn't know what to say.

"What is it," the boy asked. The man did not reply; he took the stick from the boy and pushed the creature back into the depths of the water. The body sunk slowly back to its watery grave.

"Why did you do that?" the boy asked the man.

"All beings deserve their peace," the man said. A bubbling in the water told the group that the body was gone, deep below the surface once again.

The tattoo on the man's forehead had been pulsing since they got to this spot. Now it felt like it was trying to burst out of his skin. The pulse seemed to spread through the rest of the man's body when they had found the creature. It seemed to fill his whole being. A soft euphoria washed over him. He felt something new taking hold of his thoughts. The rain seemed to take on a soft greenish glow.

The bridge couldn't shelter the man's ears from the rain. It carried a message. It told the man that all the years of heartache had ended. Good things were coming their way. They had to go through all the bad for the good. The beginning was near, as was the end.

The dinner this night was only mediocre. The family knew that food in Louisiana was very good, last night had been a testament to that, but they were not staying anywhere near a good place tonight. The diner was like the one the day before where they had gone for lunch. A small cafeteria setting with little effort put into the food. The place was close to the hotel, though, which proved to be very convenient. They ate for nourishment only and headed back to the hotel. The rains had just begun to let up.

A swim after dinner called to the man. He and the girl and boy headed to the pool area. Lightning had been flashing, but the rain had calmed to a shower. "Perfect conditions for swimming," they all joked. The lightning, while in the pool, enhanced their experience. Fear of death was not something any of them held inside. How could you enjoy life if you were in fear of death? The man and girl believed they were already dead, just like they had been taught by their family.

Fear was not part of their beings. This was the main reason they did not participate in organized religion.

There was no fear involved when you were talking about God.

The lightning began to get closer. The thunder began to crash louder and longer. Just as the three exited the pool, a large bolt of lightning hit the water where they had just been. They all looked at each other and laughed. The man thought about this on their leisurely walk to the car. Maybe they hadn't gotten out of the water on time after all and had died. Maybe their bodies were buoyed in that pool right now as they walked off in another dimension. Three corpses, floating lifelessly, just like the creature they had seen at the river earlier.

His thoughts were shaken by a bolt of lightning even bigger than the last. It hit their car, parked on the other side of the small lot, right on the roof. It lit the vehicle with a bluish color. The man could have sworn that he saw someone in the car, illuminated by the blue flash. He looked in the car as he passed it on the way to the room. Nobody was inside the vehicle.

A very small bolt of lightning came off the antenna of the car and hit the man directly in the eye tattoo. The throbbing that had been going on for the last hours instantly stopped.

The man felt more alive than he had ever felt before.

Chapter 18

The third week of the trip started on the summer solstice. This was a true holiday for the family. They all knew the importance of this day. They had the knowledge of its significance just as the ancients had.

This solstice was to be extra special. Not only was it the longest day of the year, it was also a full moon. It was spiritual beyond what all religions could only dream of.

Just because the greed had destroyed the history of the planet, did not mean that none of the creatures held the knowledge. There was a blood lineage, which had been the keeper of the truth for the history of the planet and its creatures. This bloodline continued to this day. Its descendants held the wisdom.

As usual, it was very early in the morning when the man arose. He had such strange dreams the night before, once again. In the ones he could remember, the family had been running towards something while at the same time running away from something. The feelings were very intense when he awoke, but faded fast. Thoughts with lightning and the sky opening in front of them and a cold darkness behind lingered. It was all just a foggy haze. The man was just happy that his visions had returned to him. He had thought that insanity was invasive when you were not dreaming.

On this trip, the short times he slept were enough to fuel his subconscious. His mind was finally healing.

His forehead had a stinging to it like he was cut or something. He felt around and remembered the lump on his head. The eye in the center of his being seemed to be calling him to go outside. The pull toward the door was getting so strong he couldn't resist. He stood up and opened the door. The humidity spilled in the space. The room instantly became steamy.

There was a strange car parked in front of the family's room. It looked like something someone had made at home. There were multiple metals, and all the parts seemed to have been pressed together. Rivets held the other pieces on. The tires were not rubber; they looked more like an epoxy of sorts. The wheels were small and barely seen under the slender chassis. The man had never seen a vehicle like it. It almost looked like a large boomerang on wheels.

A very small man came out of the room next door but avoided eye contact with the man. The stranger seemed to be wearing weird workout clothes that were metallic in color. The man could see only the side of the stranger's head. It seemed misshapen to him. The stranger's eyes seemed very strange, also. The light of morning was just coming up, though, and the man couldn't really be certain. He had just been asleep and was still trying to shake the waking transition off his mind.

The stranger scurried down the walkway into the lobby, disappearing from sight. A glint of light from the strange vehicle caught the man's attention. The light seemed to come from what appeared to be a windshield made of some unknown element. The oily like substance was solid black, and now had a bright blue pinpoint of light coming from the interior. It looked almost like the light from a torch.

The sound of thunder made the man look to the sky. He noticed that it was very cloudy outside, and it for sure looked like rain. It was time to wake the others. The day had begun.

The family was experienced at traveling by now and did not take long to get ready in the morning. They were usually ready in about thirty minutes. This day was no different.

When they went outside to pack the car, the strange vehicle was no longer there. In its place was a motorcycle with a trailer. The biker was standing next to his bike with his coffee and cigarette. He began to tell the man and girl a very strange story.

The biker said he had been riding his motorcycle through Texas when a bright light had appeared. The light followed him and his three companions for maybe thirty miles, and then disappeared. When they got to the campground for the night, the place was deserted. They had enjoyed the solitude for the first time on the road. They had built a fire and drank a few beers and were out early. They had all slept better than they could ever remember under the Texas stars.

In the morning, they could barely remember anything from the night before. Their camp and gear looked foreign to them. It was like they were at a different campground than the one they had stopped at.

One in their group was missing. His motorcycle was there as were all his clothes. Even his tent was still standing. The sleeping bag looked like someone had just crawled out of it. They had searched the area all morning. Finally, one of them went to the nearest town eighty miles away, and got the sheriff. The search party the locals mounted was extensive. They had searched for four days. They had never found their missing friend. That had been two weeks ago. The others had waited around the spot for ten days after the locals had given up. The guy never returned. No one else had ever showed up at the campsite while they were there. They were alone the whole time.

Strange lights came in the sky every day and night. Lights that flew in ways that none of them thought possible. Finally, they had given up. Now they were headed home. They had seen things in the sky like space itself opening. There were many hours that they couldn't remember. Sometimes, they would wake up in different places and find their way back. This is what had kept them there. They knew that something weird was going on, but it had obviously happened to their buddy as well. They had all made it back, they had hopes he would, too.

The rugged features of the biker's face showed anger mixed with helplessness. The man saw the pain in his eyes. The older guy was maybe seventy-six, with a long white beard and white hair. His hands and neck had tattoos, but the rest of his person was covered in leathers. The man was intrigued by the story, as was his niece. The boy had joined the group and was listening intently to the story being told.

"Is it your relative that is missing?" the man asked the stranger.

"It's my brother. We are very close. We are the only two left in our family of nine. He was two years younger than me. I would still be out there but I couldn't take the barrage of punishment those alien bastards were throwing our way. We had to go. Those fuckers took my brother." The biker shed a tear as his words ended.

The man saw something in the older man's eyes that looked very familiar to him. The older man reminded him of his brother, only much older. He was the same size and stood the same, also. The older guy was much more wrinkled and spoke with a deep rasp. He felt a connection to the biker.

"Who took your brother?" the boy asked.

The biker threw his cigarette and walked away. The man and girl looked at each other and both said "Bummer". Their trip was a crazy one, but at least nothing like this had happened to them. Their family was still together. The biker had seemed shaken up. The man asked the girl where the man's friends were. There was only one bike parked here. She looked at him with a puzzled look. It was a very good question.

The parking lot was empty except for the crow sitting on the dumpster thirty feet away from the family car and the motorcycle. By the time the family had packed the car, the biker had returned, silently sat on his motorcycle, started it, and pulled out of the parking lot. He didn't once look the way of the family.

The crow's stare as it watched the biker depart was intense. It began to violently shake its head and caw at a loud decibel. The man had never heard a crow make this sound before. The bird seemed like it could fly into a rage. It cawed its insolence the whole time the family packed the car. It was telling them that today was one of those days when the dimensions would line up. Their parallels were going to cross at points, and many strange things would be happening. The numbers were all going to line up. This day was going to be full of surprises and madness.

Pulling out of the hotel onto the freeway, the man noticed the overturned diesel right away. The truck, carrying a large culvert, had rolled down the embankment maybe two hundred feet. The truck and trailer were a twisted heap of debris. The culvert had obviously come loose early and flipped down the hill, end over end. It came to rest up on its end on top of the truck's cab. It was like a giant exclamation mark on the whole scene.

One cop was on the scene. He was very young, and the man could see he wasn't handling the situation so well. The driver of the truck was surely dead, and it was making the officer sick. He was bent over at a strange angle with his back to the road. A few other people had stopped on the road to help or watch. A few of them were taking pictures and video of the carnage.

The man saw movement by the cab of the truck. It looked like a large shadow was enveloping the cockpit. The man looked to the sky, but the clouds were still thick. Looking back, he could see the shadow had encompassed the truck and now the cop. Something ran from the wreckage, but it was too fast to see. The creature was about a foot tall and seemed to run on its two legs. The man had never seen something run so fast.

Just then, three more cop cars and an ambulance showed up. The family's help was not needed here. It was time to get down the highway. As they were driving off, the man looked back and saw something very strange. The cop was now standing straight and looking right back at him. Next to him was a tall man in a black hat and black suit. He, too, was looking at the family. The crow was flying above the two figures, cawing its frustrations. The man got a very bad feeling from the vacant gaze of the two voyeurs. He swiftly went down the onramp and onto the highway.

The greenery in these parts was even denser than the last days. The family crossed from small town through small town. They were in search of a place to eat, but it was not coming easy. The lack of cars made driving very nice. They were in no rush to get anywhere.

The family slept a lot in the car, so it gave the man time to get his thoughts straight. It was at these times that his story was unraveling in his head. He would be thinking of all the things happening to them and putting it into words to be written later. The book of the trip was still writing itself anyway. Basically, when he was driving, he would think about it all, and at the end of the day it was on paper. It was like his brain was a computer and the paper was the screen. His brain told the story, and the computer did the rest.

After about two hours, they found a small diner in the middle of corporate greed country. They had crossed into Missouri a bit back. It was all farmland along this stretch of highway. A genetically modifying company used these parts for their testing grounds. Everything was lush and green and full of genetic mutations. "Another way of the greed controlling the people," the woman had told the others. "If they are changing our food, how is that changing us?"

An older gentleman was the only patron at the diner when they arrived. The lady behind the counter took the order while her husband made the food. By the time they had ordered, the lunch bell had obviously rung and the place was filled with farm workers.

The older gent stopped at the family's table on his way out the door. "Where y'all from in California?" he asked in his friendly southern drawl.

"Central," the man replied, with nods from the rest.

The stranger went on to tell the family how his son and daughter both lived in California and worked in agriculture. He went on to say how the way agriculture was done in California was about to drastically change. He said there was a new technology that was going to change the way of the world. He also said there would be a lot of people getting rich off this technology. He said it was the future, like it or not.

"This doesn't sound good for the environment or the people," the woman said. "Like always, a few will profit while the rest will suffer."

"That's about to change, too," the gentleman said, "Evolution is about to get a shot in the arm. This has been coming for a very long time, and now it is upon us. Y'all have a nice day now. God Bless," he ended as the door shut behind him. The family could tell this was a very important man around these parts. The way the others reacted to him told that whole tale. They hadn't talked to the man, but every one of the workers in the diner had looked at the gentleman with respect.

The older man's words stuck with the man throughout lunch. The food was very good and hit the spot. The family talked some about what the gent had said, but the man changed the subject. He had known about some things going on with agriculture in the last years, and now they were getting confirmed. The San Joaquin valley was about to get a huge agriculture experiment dropped on it. It was going to be tested in a place that was an ecological waste site. Its goal was going to be able to change the weather and the entire dynamics of this region. Basically, they were going to drop an agritomic bomb on the farms of the valley. In doing so, they would be dropping that bomb on the people at the same time. No one really knew what the outcome would be.

The man thought about this well down the road. He was all too familiar with the elite and their way of wanting it all. Power and money were the way of greed; both dark forces. They didn't even strive for the light, but they would portray themselves as being one with God through church and state. Concepts they had created along with their self-titled 'civilization'.

With no light in your life, destruction of others was imminent. This is what had happened to the humans and the planet. Greed! The masses had wanted to be just like their masters.

The man's goal was always to speak wisdom to his family and teach them the things that he knew and observed. His whole life was observing and being on the path to acquire knowledge. He saw things others didn't, but wanted to open their eyes to what was really happening.

He told the others as he navigated the green Agri-highway, "This guy that we met is what I like to call a speculator. These are guys who use their money to make more money without doing any work. What that means is that these jerks use their money to invest in things that other people manufacture, farm, or mine. They buy up property and commodities and get rich sitting behind their desks, while the common folk are working their asses off. These same workers look up to the elite and want a piece of the same. The elite are wealthy demons who ruin people and families by their addiction to having more. Sadly, the father of our country, George Washington was a speculator. There has been a shit river of them before that butt nugget and after. Most of the richest families in the world got their treasure from this dirty deed. Once they become rich enough, then they are bankers. Then, they buy and inflate even more until they are swimming in money. Others want to be the same. Medical Marijuana clubs in California are one of the biggest examples. Most people call these guys the middle man, but in truth they are lazy assholes who want a lot of money without any hard work. There are many guys who have gotten rich off the locals by speculating and ripping folks off. Then, this same guy self-proclaims himself the community leader or mayor to look like he really cares about the community. He will be the first to have a fundraiser for this or that, but he does not do any of the real work. When the project is finished, this guy will be the one to cut the ribbon like he was the one who got the task done. He was the one to collect the money and take all the glory. All I can say is, I feel sorry for these people. They point their fingers at everyone else their whole lives so they don't have to see the disease which permeates their souls. That disease is greed!"

The man had solutions for the problems on the planet. He knew that nothing would ever be an overnight fix, and any kind of change would take many trials and tribulations. However, doing nothing out of fear of change was for sure not the way. That is what ninety nine percent of the people really wanted. The greed gave the masses just enough to pacify them, and the sheep were happy with what they got. It could not go on like this forever. The home for all animals was being destroyed by the greed. It would have to end. They were destroying our true god, Earth.

Making a true democracy would be the first step. As long as the elite voted for the greed to get benefits and more money, it would be very lopsided. As soon as the true majority voted daily, or weekly, we could get rid of the politicians, the lobbyists, and all the special interest groups. Then everything could be about the people.

This would be fully possible with the internet. Everyone could vote daily. The people could debate with their co-workers and family over issues. Political ads and endorsements by fellow elite would come to a screaming halt. The issues would be put out there by the people, for the people. Decisions on matters could be made free from of the influence of money.

Of course, the greed would make it seem like it would be easy to hack this system. They would not want to give up their power nor their riches.

Safeguards would certainly have to be put in place. Anything online would always be somewhat vulnerable. However, the amount of deceit would be a fraction of what was being perpetrated by the greed already. The best hackers could be hired, by the people, to eliminate any threats.

America could bring its military home and put them to work on rebuilding our infrastructure. Voting in diplomats for relations with other countries would make the world full of friends, not enemies. Everyone could then truly be equal. The media would change, because they could report the facts. The lies handed them every day by the propaganda machine would end up in the trash.

After democracy was truly in place, the people could audit the work that politicians had been doing with their constituents' money. Appropriate actions could be held against any criminal. Accountability would be imparted for all the crimes that had been committed against the people of Earth. Vindication would finally come to all who had lost their lives to the greed.

Then, everything could be reset. The economy could restart in a healthy manner, without the last two hundred fifty-year greed shadowing its progress. All prejudice would be put behind in the awakening country. Taxes could go to fund education, medical, and many other programs for the people. The ones who profited off people's misery would be imprisoned. True crime was one against other people, violent or economic. America and the rest of the world could be great for the first time ever. Free of the greed that had repressed the humans for thousands of years.

The family hugged the Mississippi river throughout the day. They crossed the bridges that spanned the river and drove along its banks. Occasionally, they would stray from the water, following the road inland a bit before heading back. They passed briefly into Arkansas and drove a bit through its beautiful country. The man thought about going into Conway. He had old family there and would like to reconnect. The more he thought about it made him change his mind. He hadn't seen his cousins since he was a small child. They had always been much older than he was anyway. With his tattoos and attitude of difference, the man didn't want to chance a bad reunion.

They had continued up the road, passing over another bridge, back into Missouri. There were many burial mounds in this area, and the family decided to check out another one. This museum allowed dogs, so the family could stay together this time. They decided to walk around the field with the mounds first this time, and then read about them. This site was much bigger than the previous one. The sun was trying to come through the clouds but wasn't succeeding. Shadows played across the whole encampment.

Some archaeologists were digging in a corner of the area, in front of a mid-sized mound. All the mounds were covered in grass. Anyone walking by wouldn't even know there were many centuries of humans buried in the temples. The people here had hidden their treasures well.

The family had made their way toward the archaeologists. The dog with the workers was not too happy about the intrusion. The girl stayed behind with the dogs as the others approached the tent. They had to check this out. "Find anything good?" the boy asked the team. Four archaeologists made up the crew. There were tables and sifters dotting the small tent. A very dirty ice chest was open and had pottery sticking out.

"We find things all the time," the youngest of the group answered. "Some things seem more valuable than others, but to us, every small piece is important. This place is telling us a story about the past. People lived here over a thousand years ago and are the ancestors of many Americans. We are telling their story."

"We are part of the local university," another archaeologist said. "This is our professor, his assistant. The girl and I are students trying to get our doctorate." The others waved with an awkwardness reserved for the true intellect. The socially awkward some would call them. The family found the group to be very cool. These were the people they liked to spend time with. The ones who would hold a lot of knowledge were the ones this group got along with.

"Would you like to shake a little?" the professor asked the boy as he held out the screen. He had plopped a scoop of dirt in the middle and it was ready.

"Of course, I want to shake," the boy said. He had the screen in his hand as he was finishing his words. He seemed to be a natural. The boy had watched the others on the walk over and knew to shake the screen over a barrel that would catch the processed dirt. The rest was treasure. He had loved this since he was little. Treasure hunting had always been a part of his life.

The boy shook for less than a minute when he exclaimed, "Found something!" All the others under the tent gathered around to look at the object. The boy had pulled something from the dirt and was now holding it in his right hand, between his thumb and forefinger. He was examining it closely. The object was about a half inch square and a quarter inch thick. It seemed to be metal and had a wire sticking out of it. The edges were rounded. It looked like something out of a transistor radio. "What is it?" the boy asked.

"It looks like something modern," the head archaeologist said. He looked at his three companions with a look of shock. They looked like they had seen a ghost. The man saw the look and thought it very odd. The vibe under the tent suddenly got thick to match the humidity. The man suddenly felt unwelcome. That familiar feeling of dread was once again upon him. This was something different though. They had stumbled upon something out here in the forest that they hadn't been expected to find. They had just opened a door into something they wouldn't understand for another twenty-two years. The feeling of being overwhelmed was the only way the man could ever explain the feelings he had that day.

The boy asked if he could keep the object, but the assistant archaeologist scolded him for asking. The boy's grandma told the woman that she didn't have to talk to her grandson like that. The assistant shot her a very angry look. She began to say something infused with hate when the professor put his hand on her arm, as if to quiet the woman. "It is lunch time for us, maybe you should go now," he said to the family. They didn't have to be told twice. They were more than ready to get away from these people who had been so nice and then shape shifted into anger and darkness.

As they walked up to the door to the museum, the curator hung the closed sign on the door. He looked at the family blankly. Absolutely nothing showed on the man's face. One to read everyone he met, the man determined that this man was a robot of some kind. 'Programmed to receive' popped into the man's mind. The thought made him think of the archaeologists in the field. They had acted the same after the boy had found the metal object.

Just before leaving, the man looked to the tent the archaeologists had been using. It was not very far from the parking lot. Theirs was the only car there. The tent was now vacant of people and treasures. All that remained under the blue tarp was a couple of tables. The wind had begun to blow harder. It carried a strange tune as it passed between the mounds. Once again, the man understood.

As the group was getting back into the car, the boy said, "I'll be right back." He ran the short distance back to the digging site before bending down by the table. After picking something up, he ran back to the others

"What was that all about?" his cousin asked.

"I had to go back to get what I found. I saw it drop from the main dude's pocket when he bent to pick up some papers. It had landed parallel with the leg of the table. They had not seen it. I did." The boy held the object in his hand while the others looked. It was a strange device. The wires nor the object looked anything but ancient to the family. There was no corrosion, but it had obviously been here a very long time.

Cars arriving in the parking lot got the family moving down the road. The first was a black SUV with solid black, oily windows. It reminded the man, somehow, of the strange vehicle that had been parked outside the hotel room that morning. The SUV parked very close to the minivan. Its occupants did not get out of the car, but the entire family could feel the stare of the strangers. By the time the third black SUV arrived, they were tearing out of the drive and back onto the highway.

As the family was leaving the parking lot, the occupants of the first vehicle were getting out. There were four of them, and they were all dressed in black with black sunglasses. They were all staring at the van and pointing their fingers in the direction of the family. The other two SUV spun around and went in the direction of the minivan. Their tires seemed to get stuck in thick mud. They were at the entrance, spinning their tires frantically, as the man raced out onto the highway. He watched for at least thirty miles for the vehicles to come up behind them, but it never happened. They had escaped the darkness.

The road snaked next to and across the Mississippi river for miles. The country was beautiful. The family was very impressed with the big river. They wanted to spend some more time and explore, but it was not in the cards for this trip. They would have to settle for the awesome countryside that they passed through and only dream of the adventure in these parts later.

Another bridge brought the family into Tennessee. There was a crop duster on the far side of the crossing. It captured the man's attention as he drove across the long span. The others had been asleep in the car for a bit. The man had become accustomed to driving while the others slept. It was at these times his imagination ran wild. This was one of those times.

The crop duster seemed to be flying oddly and very close to the ground. It wasn't making rows of passes on the field like they did at home. This one was flying around in circles, like it was looking for something. Its flight pattern was like no other crop duster the man had ever seen.

The man decided to stop on the far side of the bridge and walk around a bit. He was becoming a bit drowsy and needed a bit of air. He hadn't been in Tennessee since he was eighteen, fresh out of boot camp and stationed in Millington. That had been so many years before. It is where his son had been born. It was also where he first became aware of the greed.

The man was happy to put his feet on this state's soil once again.

As soon as he walked to the guard rail and looked at the field of brown, he saw the circles. Now he understood what the aircraft had been looking at. There, in the middle of the field, was a series of three circles inside one another. Many smaller circles geometrically decorated the first. Another large circle was a hundred feet away, connected to the others with a perfectly straight line. The man was seeing his first crop circle. It was just another strange sight to behold in his life, the man had thought.

The aircraft seemed to be getting a good look at the pattern. He flew very close to some power lines, and the man felt dread for the pilot. He had seen an aircraft crash at an air show once, and this felt the same. The pilot had been flying an SNJ3 Texan. He was doing barrel rolls and got closer and closer to the ground. The man and his co-worker were there waiting to taxi the aircraft after landing. They had both just commented on the pilot's arrogance when the aircraft had hit the ground, flipped over, and exploded. The pilot died instantly in front of his wife and kids and one hundred thousand spectators.

This was almost like deja vu for the man. There were no crowds, but the pilot was making the same mistake. After a few more flyovers, the pilot's wing clipped one of the electric lines stringing the large towers together. The aircraft fell the one hundred feet to the ground and landed with a thud. The silence had only been interrupted for that moment, and now it returned. Ten seconds later, the aircraft burst into flames. The explosion caught the entire field on fire, destroying the cryptic message hidden in its grain.

Fire trucks were on the scene within five minutes. The man knew there was no need for him to scurry down the hill to fight an inferno. Just like all those years ago, there was absolutely nothing anyone could do. The pilot's time had come. All the numbers lined up, and this time he wouldn't be walking away. Or would he be in another dimension, the man thought. Maybe the pilot was still flying around, looking at something, just not in this place. His wife would still be home waiting for him after the day of flight. Only in this dimension, had this tragedy occurred.

Six fire trucks had arrived. They were down the embankment, but the man could see them clearly. One of the trucks was different than the other five. It was rounder than the others and not as big. It looked almost like a cylinder. The crewmembers from that truck were not with the other fire fighters. They were all standing around smoking a strange object. The man saw no smoke coming from their mouths, but that is what it looked like they were doing. These firefighters also moved very oddly. They seemed to have very stiff movement. It seemed to the man that they weren't of their free will. Something was controlling the actions of these firemen. One of them was staring at the man the whole time. The stranger never once took his eyes off the guardrail and its voyeur standing behind it.

The woman brought the man back from his daydream. "What's going on?" she asked him. She had appeared at his side. The man looked around, a bit bewildered. He didn't know at first why he was standing on the side of the road. The smoke made him remember the fire, but nothing else. He had stopped to walk around a bit and had seen the fire immediately. It was burning about two acres and spreading.

"That field is on fire," the man replied. "The fire department just got here."

"How did it start?" the woman asked.

"I don't know," the man replied, "it was burning when we got here". He looked to the fire crew before getting back to the car. The three trucks were all amass with activity.

All the firemen were busy working as one to get the blaze under control. Miraculously, the man had thought, no one else had even stopped to see what was happening.

Driving away, the boy swore that he saw a face in the smoke. The woman said she had seen wreckage in the field right in the middle of the blaze. Again, she asked the man if he was sure that he had seen nothing. The man did not reply. His mind was already locked away again in insanity. It was all so much for his mind to sort through. All the events from the last two years coupled with the strange things happening to them now were making him lose his grip on reality. He was beginning to think that he might not be returning from this trip.

A pass, through Kentucky, was very nice. The farms dotted the countryside. The man thought that he had never seen so many shades of green. The roads were vacant. They didn't even see people out and about. The stops at the small towns sometimes looked like nobody even lived there. It was like they had built these nice little towns, put in a majestic park, and then moved away. The family was still stopping every couple of hours, and sometimes more. The long drive up the Mississippi was taking its toll on them. Illinois was the next state to check off, and then it was back to Missouri.

The miles passed by in a sea of green.

Six times they crossed the Mississippi that day. Every time had been memorable for the man and any of the family who had been awake.

The drive had been long this day, and the sun was beginning to get low in the sky. The woman had lined up a hotel in Cape Gerardeu for the night, and that would be the end to this day. A swim and some relaxing were in the plans for this evening. A few more miles, some check in to the hotel, and they were ready for some relaxing.

The family found the swimming pool. It was indoors and nice. Another couple was swimming, but that was all. The swimmer was from Arkansas and liked to talk big. The man thought that the stranger and his wife were a bit drunk or on drugs. Having family from Arkansas, he knew it was a different culture. This was different though, the stranger and his wife had a bad energy to them. The girl asked the man if he saw this, and he confirmed her vision. These two were not to be trusted.

The man apologized to the others but headed to the room. The water was a bit chilly, and with no sun to dry off, he had found the experience not so nice. Added in was the mouth at the other end of the pool and the man had enough. The others were behind him by about ten minutes.

The family settled on a chain restaurant. It was close and they could walk there. It would be the first chain restaurant to eat at on this trip, and the last. This was not a choice normally for the family. They preferred to eat at locally owned places. Mom and Pop places as they were called. Just like their tattoo shop was. This is where the people took the most pride in their work. The man and woman knew. This is where you got the best quality.

At dinner, the waitress dropped a glass of water on the boy. She was serving the table and the glass had gone tumbling. She was very embarrassed. She told the family how it was her first day and she could not believe this had happened to her. The family all reassured the girl that they understood about accidents. Everyone had them at times and people were not right if they judged you for this.

The waitress was about to cry when the boy asked her awkwardly if they had a condom machine in the bathroom. The waitress looked shocked at his question and then began to laugh. She hugged the boy and said thank you so much. When she brought the boy his water again, she slipped a piece of paper and a small packet into the boy's hand. She had just given the boy her phone number and a condom.

The family did not stay for long. They just ate the corporate food, filled the void, and got back to the hotel for some much-needed rest. It had been a very long day.

The man and girl walked to the store, across the highway. Traffic was light. There were not many people in this small town. It was a quick jaunt to the convenience store and back. The full moon was coming over the horizon when they were walking back. It was very bright and large. The whole scene seemed so surreal to the two.

The man and girl talked about it being the summer solstice. This was their true holiday for our planet. Religions based their holidays on this day. The two talked about how the moon and the solstice together in this little place in Missouri were very special. The people who had built the mounds they had visited knew all about the sun, moon, and Earth. This was a special day for all creatures. It had been since the beginning.

When the two were crossing the second side of the highway, a large diesel truck came out of nowhere and was headed right for the two. The man had not seen where the truck came from. It just appeared. "Watch out!" the girl yelled. It was too late. The truck was upon them. Its lights blinded the two until all they could see was the bright light. It encompassed their beings. There was a loud sound and the smell of burning metal. Then, there was no more.

Walking past the last highway sign, back onto the sidewalk, the girl and man looked at each other oddly. "What just happened?" the girl asked her uncle.

"We were crossing the road and then there was a light" he replied, "I guess it was the moon. Fuck man, my mind is really playing tricks on me."

"Me too," the girl answered.

The two talked about the strange events happening to them as they walked through the parking lot of the hotel. It was completely dark now. The man wasn't even tired. It felt as if he had just woken up. He knew it hadn't been the moon that they saw. It was a truck. He was beginning to recall the things that happened. It's like his memory banks had been broken and were slowly coming back online. He knew the truth. The truck had run them over. And now, once again, everything was slightly different.

The room smelled of saffron when they entered it. The woman wasn't there, and the boy was asleep. It would be two hours before the woman returned. She wouldn't remember where she had been. The man had worried about her the whole time.

The man and his niece had gone searching for the woman, but she was nowhere near the hotel. Her purse and phone were on the dresser of the room, which was the most puzzling. When she got back, she seemed to be in a daze. She said something about a dream where she was running, but like a zombie. She was completely out of it. The man got his wife to bed for some much-needed rest.

The man's writing in his book had told the whole story for the day. As he read it, he felt a strange feeling. The fire he had seen earlier was different in the story. In it, the man had seen an alien spacecraft crash into the field, starting the inferno. A piece of shrapnel had exploded from the wreckage and impaled the man in the head. He had died instantly.

The rest of the story too seemed twisted and distorted from the actual events of the day. The story had just left out the woman getting back. Now the writings were complete. The story for the day had been written. The group was together as one. Now the family could rest and get ready for the next long day of driving.

The man slept none this night. After the others went to sleep, he wrote in his book until daybreak. It seemed like he had just poured his inner being onto the paper. When the others began to stir, he put the paper and pen aside and went outside. He needed to clear his mind. The eye on his forehead had been pounding all night.

When he got outside, the sun was just peeking over the horizon. A motorcycle was parked in front of their room. It looked just like the one from the day before. It even had a trailer.

The clean air made the man feel good. The humidity had lessened as they got farther north. It was a welcome change from the thickness of the south.

The man went to the front to get some coffee. Walking into the lobby, there was a man sitting in one of the chairs, dressed all in black. He was looking at the newspaper but had his sunglasses on. He seemed to be very large. The stranger did not even look at the man as he walked in. The man was perplexed, this stranger had no aura. The man could not detect any energy coming from the being.

The stranger made the man feel very uneasy. He didn't want to be anywhere near this being. The man quickly went outside and back to the room. It was completely dark outside again when he left the lobby. The man could have sworn that the sun was out. Their minivan was the only vehicle in the parking lot. The motorcycle was no longer there.

When he got back to the room, all the lights were off and the entire family was sleeping still. He looked at the clock on the nightstand and it said two. The man knew he was losing his mind. This had to be the worse, knowing you were going insane.

The man went in the bathroom with his book to write. Opening the page, he read the long, deep passage that he had written the night before, just one hour before. How had the time gone back and how had he wrote all these twenty-five pages in just one hour? It was impossible.

Time was no longer working correctly. For that matter, the man thought, nothing was working correctly.

The man fell asleep sitting on the lid of the toilet. He had made it to page twelve in his reading the writing from the night before. Exhaustion had finally consumed his conscious.

It was time to cross back into the subconscious.

It was time to dream.

CHAPTER 19

A loud knock at the door woke the family. The man jumped from bed and yanked the door open. Nobody was there. He looked down the corridor, but it was empty. The sun was just coming up. The lack of humidity was noticed by the man immediately. It was a very nice morning. The parking lot was mostly full. The man didn't remember so many cars the night before.

While brushing his teeth, the man tried to remember as much about his dreams as possible. Every day, the dreams would come, but he wouldn't be able to remember them for a very long. At some time throughout the day, something would happen that would flash back to the man's vision the night before. Daily, he was having a strange premonition.

In his dream this night, he had wandered around the town, looking for his niece. He had lost her somehow when they went to the store together. He stopped to ask people along the way if they had seen the girl, but none of them would pay any attention to the man. It was like he didn't exist. He had stopped at a corner to ask a woman standing alone.

A tall figure stepped out of the shadows. The being was cloaked in black and seemed to move like smoke. The man spoke to the being in his dreams, and it looked directly into his eyes. It was the face of his niece. She began to laugh. That is when the man had woken up to the pounding on the door.

The rest of the family was still very tired. The last days of travel had been exhaustive. The family did not know where the man's energy was coming from. He seemed to need minimal rest and was always ready to go. The niece, too, seemed to have found a new energy, but not as intense as her uncle's. As the others became more and more tired, the man seemed to absorb their energy.

The man told the others that he would go down to breakfast by himself. That way, the others could rest some and he could watch the dogs when they went to eat. They were all thankful for the extra thirty minutes of rest.

The breakfast was a buffet and looked surprisingly good. The man was the only person there at this early hour. He was not one to normally eat buffet. He found the idea of people picking through the food and coughing on it disgusting. He had seen far too many examples of things happening that kept him away from this kind of sheep trough dining.

This buffet was not so bad, though. It looked like he was the first one. The food did look very greasy, but at least it was hot. It was the first hot breakfast since Arizona.

The man made the mistake of being polite to the worker. The woman, around his age, took this as a welcome sign to begin speaking to the man. Even as he sat to eat, the woman continued her talk. She asked the man so many questions. For the first time in three weeks, he was alone. Now this lady was going to take that away from him. The man tried to be polite, but she would not stop asking him questions. He wished that she would go do something else. He tried, successfully, with all his might not to offend the woman. She was nice and meant no harm. After speaking to a good listener, the woman had somehow come to trust the man.

The worker began to tell the man about strange things that had happened the night before. Strange lights had been seen in the sky. The local Catholic Church had burned down in the early morning hours. People said they saw a dark figure walking calmly away from the inferno, only after the structure was fully engulfed. The arsonist had watched his handiwork.

The woman looked in the man's face and asked if he was alright. He said he was fine and asked the woman why she had asked him that. "Because you look very pale," the woman replied.

The man thought with all his thoughts for the woman to leave. She began to choke on something. Probably her tongue, the man had thought. She was gasping and then started to cough uncontrollably. She was spewing her spit all over the place. Holding both her hands over her mouth, the red-faced woman coughed out an apology and stiff-legged it away. The man waved nonchalantly, dismissing the worker. He looked at his food. There was no longer an appetite.

It was still early and the car was packed. The others had gone down for a quick meal and were back swiftly. Better food was always to be found away from these hotels.

It was going to be a lot of driving this morning, so every moment counted.

There was a problem checking out of the hotel. The clerk charged the man's credit card, but he had paid cash the night before. Just like every night before on this trip and every other trip, he paid cash for his room. When you paid cash, you paid upon check-in. They said that the man and girl did not pay the night before. The man went to the car to get his niece. The smell of burnt metal assaulted their senses. She came inside and confirmed that they had paid the night before. The manager was called and the security tapes were reviewed. The tapes showed the man had not paid when they checked in. He swore that he had paid. The man saw that the manager and clerk were honest. He could see it in their faces and their auras. He admitted to having made a mistake. He paid the bill.

The man noticed someone standing in a corner of the lobby. He had not seen the figure before. It was a tall man and very large in stature. He was wearing black garments that looked like a robe, or wrap, to the man. The stranger was watching the entire scene in front of him. The man felt a sense of being violated. He could see the aura around the creature, filling the corner of the lobby. Its aura was a dark gray color. Its energy appeared to be moving like serpents. The man got a very bad vibe from this newcomer. He looked to the girl and her face confirmed what he was feeling.

The man apologized to the manager and clerk for his mistake, and headed toward the door. The stranger was blocking their exit. The man wondered how the being had crossed the entire room in the time it took them to take a few steps. The figure loomed in front of the man and girl, casting a menacing shadow on the whole room. A loud coughing from the corner caught the man's gaze. There in the corner was the woman from the breakfast room. She was still coughing loudly. Her aura was the same exact as the man had seen on the figure standing in the same spot only moments before. This same figure was now blocking their path. Turning back to the exit, there was a soda delivery man coming through the door. The dark figure was gone. The man held the door for the deliveries to come through and headed out of this twilight zone. Their early start had been delayed by an hour, and now it was time to make some of it up.

When they were on the highway, the woman asked the man and girl what had happened in the hotel lobby. The man told her that it was all weird. He told her when the manager looked at the tape, her face had changed from pleasant to one of shock. Something she had seen on the monitor had troubled her. She had not let the man or girl see the footage. He also told her about the lady from the dining room earlier and once again about seeing her in the lobby. "She's going to die today," the man had said idly to the others.

"What a terrible thing to say," the woman said back. Her husband made no response to her words. He was always saying some nutty stuff like this. The others were all used to his cryptic words.

The road through Missouri was a very long one. They had decided to try and make it to Wisconsin tonight. The man had a friend who lived there, and they would be passing right by his city. The man had called his friend a couple nights before and they had made plans to meet up. They could arrive in the morning, but that was the only day they had to hang out. The decision had been made, they would arrive tonight. They wanted as much time as possible to hang out with the third friend on the trip.

Bypassing the cities in this instance bit the family in the ass. They were trying to make up time but ended up getting lost. The back roads around St. Louis were a mess of suburb after suburb. Farms were mixed in throughout. The road system was set up on an alphabet grid. Sometimes the roads merged. Sometimes there were multiple roads with the same letter. Either way, the foreign road system cost them an hour and a half. At the end of the day, they would be paying for this time.

Finally, they were back on their path. They had come back to the river with a bridge and knew exactly where they were. The friend lived right on the old man river. They would just have to follow it north.

Weaving in and out of the small towns was a dream for the man. It reminded him of the times when his family had traveled when he was a child. Then, as now, he felt a strange fascination with the towns and the people who had lived there. He had always been one to buy old books with photos documenting people of the past. Traveling was going to those places and seeing them in person.

The family had met so many nice people on the road. Today was no different. Every place they stopped, they were greeted warmly. They spoke about how people of Missouri were very friendly. The girl said that she wished people in California were nice like out here. The man said that the problem there was that there were too many people. The region people lived made their lives very unhappy. If your life was unhappy, you could never truly be nice to other people. "It was why there were so many assholes in the city," he had told the others.

The farmland began as soon as the family rolled into Iowa. The family talked about how agriculture was different out here. They were very familiar with farming. The San Joaquin Valley was the 'breadbasket of the world', so it was called.

The fields rolled through the hillsides as they passed down the highway. Silos and barns dotted the countryside. The man and woman were very impressed with these buildings. There were silos and barns in California, but these in Iowa were much older. They had a different feel than the ones back home. They had been in the same family for a couple of centuries.

They stopped at a convenience store for gas and a stretch. Some coffee was needed by the man to continue the trek. Paying for the items, the man began a strange conversation with the clerk. She was deaf but her speech was very good and audible. She asked the man when his birthday was as she was handing him his coins. The change was one dollar and eleven cents. He asked the young woman why she wanted to know his birthday and she said, "Because we share the same birthday."

"How do you know my birthday?" the man asked with wonder in his voice. He had heard of people guessing your age or weight but this was strange.

"It is because we are connected. Our paths have crossed before in another time and place. Once again, our paths are crossing." the cashier said. "Your birthday is April twelfth, as is mine."

The man stared at the cashier in disbelief. Maybe his wife had told her his birthday. He looked to his niece, who was standing right next to the man. She was staring back with wide eyes. "I know you too," the clerk said, pointing to the girl. "We've crossed paths before too, and not so long ago. You and I will someday walk the same path together, if only briefly."

The clerk's words were comforting to the man and girl. They were always ready for something to happen that was out of the ordinary and this was no exception. They listened closely to what the woman had to say. They understood. The familiarity was felt by both the family members toward the other woman. Their bond was a mutual one. Their DNA was connected.

"May I hug you?" the clerk asked. Before they could answer, the woman had hung over the counter and swooped the man and girl into her arms, pulling them close into a tight three-way hug. A deep warmth spread through the man's body. It felt like he had absorbed the energy from the other woman and his niece for the briefest of moments. For just a flash, the three beings had become one. The man felt alive once again. The exhaustion that had crept back into his being down the road had been replaced with renewed energy. It felt like he was wide awake. His senses were in overdrive.

When they broke their embrace, it felt like a magnet being pulled apart. The three stumbled, a step or two back, to release the hold of energy from their beings. The clerk looked at the two and said, "This is what awaits you on your path. Now you have a little sample of the way things are going to be. They know you are coming, but it will not matter. We are the One. It is our time."

The man didn't want to leave this woman's presence, but they had no choice. It was time to get back on the road. On the way out the door, the man told the clerk to have a nice day. "I already have," was her response. He wondered how the woman had understood what he had said. He wasn't facing her when he had spoken.

Iowa seemed to stretch on for a very long way. It seemed like it would never end. The countryside was still fresh and beautiful to the group so it made the journey tolerable. They still stopped every couple of hours for the dogs and their legs to stretch. They did not want to come to hate the car. At one stop, a crow flew onto an electric pole right above where the man and his niece were standing. The bird began to make its call of clicks and knockings. The man mimicked the bird. Suddenly, they were talking back and forth in the crow's language, like old friends. The girl was amazed by this. Her uncle was always doing something weird, and this was one of them.

"He says we are okay," the man said. Just then, the large bird swooped down and landed on the girl's shoulder. The man was impressed with the girl's attitude. She had not become startled when the creature had flown down on her, its wings feathering its descent. It made one more call to the man, this time almost in a more frantic note. It plucked a small bit of the girl's hair out and flew away, out of sight. The other black birds in the area all took off at the same time. With a terrible racket, the creatures all took a frenzied flight and flew in the direction of the large crow.

"It's going to protect you," the man said to his niece. "It needed your hair to know who you really are. The bird is on our same path. Its energy has been connected to ours. It is not the first time our paths have met. We have traveled with this crow throughout time. We are all One."

"I know uncle, I too am awakening," the girl replied. Both looked to each other and smiled the smile of knowledge.

On a back road in Northeast Iowa, the family had been napping, and the man was once again in his own imagination. He was thinking about all these silos, and thinking maybe some had nuclear missiles under them. The greed was an angry bunch, somehow with the intention of world destruction. The man did not doubt that it could be true.

A large man, wearing black clothing, was standing by a mailbox in front of one of the farms. The stranger made eye contact with the man as he drove by. It was the look old enemies would share.

The man thought this guy looked almost exactly like the man he had seen in the hotel lobby that very morning. Even the garments looked the same. The man saw the being was wearing a long necklace. Its pendant looked like the stone they had been given at the beginning of the trip. The man got a very bad feeling about the being. It seemed to silently call the man to stop, but he did not want to. It took all the man's strength to keep the car headed down the road. He never once looked in the mirrors to see the being behind them.

Just before crossing into Wisconsin, the family stopped at a scenic spot overlooking the Mississippi river. It was a large area, and the scene was beautiful. They had taken some pictures and walked for a bit, but ultimately, it was time to get on the road. Their friend's house was calling them. Wisconsin was on the other side of the bridge, just up ahead. Iowa was ending.

Up the road hugging the Mississippi was awesome. The full moon had crested and now was following the family like a searchlight. It loomed on the right side of the car the rest of the trip. The girl said the moon was like their tour guide, illuminating the details of the things they were seeing. The family was beginning to get excited to get out of the car. They spoke of all the things they had seen this day and how these experiences were combining with the others to make an epic journey.

A large buck jumped right into the road in front of them. Where they were from in California, there were many deer. The man and woman both knew all about driving around these creatures. In this case though, the man had been distracted by some fireflies and didn't see the animal until it was too late. The man's eyes met the beast's eyes, illuminated in the headlights, briefly. The creature's eyes looked very unusual to the man as he pulled the wheel hard to the right, toward the shoulder.

The car and buck collided. The animal flew into the middle of the road and landed with a crack. When it hit the ground, the buck burst into many smaller pieces. Each of these pieces had a life of its own and scurried off the road. They all seemed to go to the right shoulder and disappear into the bushes. The family, all asleep, had seen none of this happen.

The man's mind was spinning out of control.

The car spun three times on the deserted road and came to a halt. The man asked if the others were alright. There were two answers in the car but the niece was silent. "Oh my god," the boy exclaimed loudly. Turn on the light. The man turned the interior lights on and was shocked to see what the boy was looking at. The girl was sitting in her seat looking straight ahead. Sticking into the side of her head was the antler from the deer. It had somehow burst through the passenger window and struck the girl at the right angle. Her eyes were still open. She looked like she might say something. Consciousness went spinning into darkness for the man. This was too much. His brain simply shut down.

When he came to, they were at a rest stop. The woman was giving the dogs some water. "Where are we," the man asked his wife.

"Somewhere in Wisconsin," she replied. "You've been sleeping for a while. You drove such a long way today. You were saying some crazy shit in your dreams, but I couldn't make out your words. It sounded like you were talking in a language that I never heard before."

"Where are the others," the man asked cautiously, the memories of the dream still fresh in his mind. He looked in the mirror to see his condition and was surprised to see his long head of hair completely gone. His hair was the same as it had been for the last ten years once again. He shook his head to clear his mind. It was then that the boy and girl appeared from the shadows of the bathrooms. Fireflies danced around the two cousins' heads. They bounced up to the car and asked the man if he had a good sleep. He was very happy to see the two. The girl was wearing a strange jacket that almost looked metallic. It seemed like it fit her like a balloon. "Where did you get that jacket" the man asked.

"Silly, you bought me this jacket back in Roswell at that thrift store," the girl replied, "don't you remember?"

The man did not remember. In fact, he did not even remember how they had gotten here. The last he could recall, they were just leaving Kenab and headed to the Grand Canyon. Everything else was a blank.

"I will drive from here," the man stated. The woman was happy to hand the keys and control of the vehicle over to her husband. It was getting very late and they still had a bit to go. It would be her time to rest. The man thought it would be his time to think. There was a lot going on that he needed to process.

When they went to pull out of the rest area, the woman asked the man where he was going. "I don't know," was his answer and she pointed him in the opposite direction.

"We're never going to get to our friend's house if you go back the way we just came."

The man saw a sign as they were leaving the rest stop. It said La Crosse, 100 miles. The man suddenly knew where they were going. His friend lived in La Crosse. This strange day was soon to be over.

The man and woman used the last miles to tell the younger ones about the friendship they shared with the guy in La Crosse. They had met him many years before from the tattoo shop. The guy had been a youngster from Wisconsin, in the Navy, looking for some tattoo work. The man had worked on the guy a few different times, and then he had got stationed somewhere else. He didn't see him for three years after that.

One night, the guy just popped back in. A friend from Brazil had just arrived that day. He and the man were both tattooing. The friend was a Japanese tattoo specialist. The guy said he wanted to get a back piece done, and the rest was history. That night, after work, the two began the man's dragon back piece and a lifelong friendship. By the time the man's tattoo friend had gone back to Brazil, they had simultaneously finished the guy's entire back. It had made the two legendary among their peers.

Over the next years, the man and three of his friends worked on the guy religiously. It was not long for the bodysuit to be complete. The guy had reached his goal through perseverance and a whole lot of pain. He was a man who did what he said he would do.

One week after the last session, the guy was working on an oil pipeline in Socorro, New Mexico. Many native people had been protesting. Armed guards had to escort the workers to and from every job they did. They were in constant contact with the armed forces of the greed.

One night, he had to go to a remote place in the desert and was sent with one other worker and a guard. Soon after they had arrived, the radio began going crazy. There were some problems back at the base. They would have to return. The guy persuaded the guard to let him and his co-worker stay. No one was out here anyway, and they had at least five hours of work. The guard could go back, take care of business, and come back for the other two in the morning.

Not long after the guard had left, a bright light had appeared in the sky. According to the co-worker, the guy was sucked up into the light. He had said the light was a beam and the guy was slowly drawn up into it. There was no craft or ship at the end of the light. It just seemed to be a ring in the sky, and this light came from it.

When the guard had come back in the morning, he wanted some answers from the man. The remaining worker was visibly shaken up. His hair had been black the night before, but now it was white as snow. The two searched the area some but found no trace of the guy. Where the man had said the light hit the earth, there were strange crystals embedded in the sand. They looked like a cross between glass and stone. The guard picked one of these crystals up and put it in his pocket. That night, asleep in the barracks, the man would unexpectedly die of a massive heart attack. He was twenty-five years old.

The guy had not been found for three days. Some miners in Roswell, fifty miles away, had found the man in one of their pits, naked and burned over his entire body. The company had put him in a hospital for ten months, all the while in a coma while his body healed. The burns had been caused by radiation, and it had removed all the man's skin, while cauterizing his flesh at the same time. The scarring miraculously healed over time, but the tattoos were no longer there. It was like some being had stolen his tattooed skin.

Many scientists and military men had come to see the guy while he was unconscious. They had many questions to ask the guy. Even when he came to, he had no answers for the others. He only remembered working in the desert and nothing else. After so many years, they had finally left him alone. He knew the greed were still watching him as were other species, but it did not matter to him. At least they left him alone.

The man and his friend had kept in contact. The man had started a new body suit on the guy, replacing the one which had been taken. It was a project that was going to take some years, but it was something the two of them were excited about doing. Their energies were strongly connected. Their paths had been planned to cross way back when.

They were finally rolling into La Crosse at eleven. They had driven six hundred and fifty miles this day. Fifteen hours on the road. The friend met them at a large parking lot, and they followed him back to his house. His place was very rural and would be hard to find at this hour.

The family felt good to get out of the car knowing they had no driving to do the next day. The friend was very happy to see them there and safe. Introductions were made with the grandson and niece, and it was time to relax. The friend had prepared some barbecue, and the family had brought conversation. Although exhausted, the family stayed up very late talking. They needed the time to unwind and catch up with an excellent friend.

The food and talk were worth the sleep they would be losing.

Finally, the man had enough. The friend's house was under construction on the inside, so it would be a bit different. The family did not care one bit. They were happy to be here with such a cool guy. After the shower, the man found all the others already in bed. It didn't seem like he had been in the water so long, but obviously he had. There was some blood coming from some phantom wound on the man's body, but he felt no pain from it. He saw it on the towel as he was drying off. Probably that damn eye tattoo, he thought.

The man climbed the stairs to the loft he and his wife would be sharing. The friend had graciously given up his bed and it was very comfortable. The woman was sound asleep with a content look on her face. Seeing this made the man feel good. Seeing his wife relaxed and happy to be in a restful place was joyous to the man. It was especially comforting knowing they would be here for the next two nights.

The man could barely keep his eyes open but felt like he had to write a little bit at least. The story needed to be told. He also felt that if he lagged one day, it would get easier and easier to lag until the story was shelved on the memories of life.

He was just drifting off to sleep, pen in hand, when he felt as though he was being watched. He fluttered the pages and put the pen back in its case. He read the last sentence he had written and there was gibberish. It wasn't even in English, he thought. It didn't even look like his handwriting. It seemed to be a foreign language. He just didn't know which one.

Movement at the window caught his eye. He couldn't shake the feeling of being watched and now knew why. There was a large dark shape outside the window. The man tried to act as if he did not see the creature and readied himself for bed. He acted like he was going to turn off the bedside lamp, but instead shone it right at the window. He just caught a brief glimpse of the creature as it was frightened back to the forest.

The being was very hairy. Its head looked huge, almost filling the entire window. On the creature's face was a very broad grin, like its face was frozen in a grotesque mask. Its face was lopsided, one eye higher than the other. The corners of the mouth and nose were the same. It reminded the man of a false face mask from Native American stories.

The man took a blanket from the closet and draped it over the window. He was not going to have this big ass creature looking at him and his wife all night. Sleep would never come under those circumstances.

The man wasn't scared of the being. Its aura had not been a bad one. It was the opposite. The being had an aura that radiated in tune with the moonlight. The two seemed to be one.

Peeking out before covering the window, the man could see the being making its way down the river. The moonlight illuminated the creature. There was no denying what the man had seen. He had seen one so many years before on Donner Pass. For sure no one was going to believe this one in the morning. Nevertheless, it had happened. He had just seen a Sasquatch.

By the time the man had gotten to the other side of the bed, he was done. He had turned off the light and climbed into bed in the same motion. He was sound asleep as his head folded into the pillow.

CHAPTER 20

The sun beamed through the small crack in the blankets that covered the window. The light pierced the man's skull, shining directly on the eye tattoo.

He had been dreaming of levitating. It had been a dream that recurred to the man since he was younger. It had not come in a very long time. He had thought that in his subconscious mind he had forgotten how to fly. The dream this morning proved him wrong. He would just float, inside or outside, upon his will. In his dreams, it was perfectly normal for him to hover above his house and look at his brothers and sisters playing below. This night, he was levitating above a river, and he was looking at something large and shiny in the water. When he woke up, the secret of levitating would be lost. It was like there was just one little part that he couldn't bring back into reality. Unfortunately, that was the part that kept him on the ground in his conscious state.

Today would be the midway part of the trip. The time hadn't seemed to pass too fast just yet. Recalling previous travels, he knew the next part was going to fly by. It was the way it always was when they traveled.

He heard the stirrings on the bottom floor. This was always his cue to get up at anyone's house that they stayed at. If he just got up when he woke up, he would be outside trying not to disturb the others. This friend was ex-Navy. He got up early. The man's wife was awake too. He knew his wife would like to sleep more but this was a good friend. There would only be one day to visit. They would need every bit of the day to make it a good one.

The house was gutted on the inside. The friend had been in the Construction Battalion when he was in the Navy. He had a penchant for construction. He apologized for the lack of furniture or fixtures. The painting, cabinets and carpet were all getting done in the next two weeks. This was just how it was for now.

The family told their friend that it did not matter. The house was going to be wonderful. The night before, they had hung out exclusively on the deck. It overlooked the Black River, a tributary of the Mississippi. The friend explained his intentions for the house as he was cooking the family breakfast. He made his own venison sausage and bologna. That mixed with some eggs, fresh salsa and jelly from his aunt, and it was on. It was by far the best meal the family had in the last three weeks. The friend was a wonderful host.

After breakfast, the family went exploring the yard and river. The friend had three acres and it was sparsely wooded. He had made a trail down to the riverbank and they followed it down. Some logs he had erected for a bridge had slightly shifted due to the recent storms. Animal tracks abounded in the area. They talked about fishing and the nature of the place. The friend showed them the plants and trees and gave them a guided botanical tour of the Wisconsin forest. The family was grateful. This is what they traveled for, knowledge.

The entire time they were by the river, the man was looking for larger tracks than the ones they were seeing. He was certain of what he saw the night before and knew there had to be some footprints. The search was unsuccessful.

As soon as he had gone outside this morning, the man had gone around the side of the house to look at the window to their bedroom. It was twenty feet off the ground. The man wondered if the dream of levitating was somewhat connected to the sighting of the Sasquatch at such a height.

The friend had built a large fort/tree house, complete with three swing sets. The family walked over the top of the structure, admiring the view. The man told his friend how impressed he was. This was very nicely built. He explained how his wife and grandson had just worked with him to build their tree house back in California. It had taken them just over a year and was nowhere near as nice as this one. This beauty did not diminish the love he felt for his tree house back home. It had been a lot of work and he was looking so forward to getting home and being back in it. There was a lot of creating to do on that platform in the future.

The boy and girl had gravitated to the swing sets. The man joined in. It had been a very long time since he was on a swing. It felt good to feel young again. He had retained his youth for so much of his life. The last two years had taken that away from him. He knew the child was still inside of him, it was just more buried than before. He just had to find ways like this to release that hidden energy.

On the walk back to the house, the family came across some turtle eggshells. They had already hatched. While checking them out, the man asked his friend if there were ever Bigfoot encounters in these parts. The friend looked at the man blankly. All the color seemed to leave his face. "There are stories of many things around these parts. It's all about what you want to believe. It's also about what you want to share, in fears of being ridiculed. For me, I just don't talk about such things."

The girl was looking at her uncle, wondering what he had going on now in his head. She loved to hang out with the man. Strange things always came up. She remembered when she was very little, how her dad and uncle would always hang out. Their motto was that 'whenever they got together, strange things were going to happen'. After her family's death, the two had retained their strong bond. It had grown much stronger with the trauma that they had to endure together. Now, whenever they were together, strange things happened. Just like it had been before. The two just figured it was the odd connection that their family had with one another and all the energy around them. They were magnets for this sort of madness.

The family unloaded the minivan so they could go explore the town a bit. The friend had a girlfriend who had three kids. She was at work, but the kids had summer out of school. Town was not very far away. They went to the apartment and picked up the children. The youngest boy was eight, the girl was twelve and the oldest boy was sixteen. The youngest took an instant liking to the man. Their energy connected like gears turning. The twelve-year-old was the same with the niece. The two of them became instant friends. The oldest boy and grandson, close in age, were indifferent to each other at first; as two teenage boys will be. Within an hour, that had completely changed.

The expanded group went to a local diner in La Crosse. The young boy held the man's hand every time they crossed the street. He had the biggest eyes the man had ever seen on a human. He felt that this boy was a very old soul. It seemed like they had been friends before, in another time, in another place. The youngster once called the man by the man's father's name. He looked at the boy in shock. How had he known his father's name? The boy just smiled up at the man. His big eyes, almost solid black, seemed to hold a truth deep within.

The diner was very nice. The family loved eating in places like this, small town America. There were pictures all over the walls of the town from the years past. It was also a bar. The people in the place were very friendly and minded their own business. Nobody even cared about the strangers that had come into their place. The man was thinking how he liked Wisconsin so far. The people all seemed so nice, and the countryside was beautiful. It was a place he would like to come back to some day and spend more time.

The diner specialized in Walnut burgers and homemade potato chips. The family was not hungry after breakfast, barely two hours before. They could not pass up on this rare treat though. They ordered a couple of plates and would share. The Mississippi river was visible out the large picture windows. The family needed this down time. It gave them a chance to relax, and replenish the lost calories from the road. It also gave them the flavor of Wisconsin. They only had one day to relax before hitting the road again. They were going to use it to the fullest.

When they were finishing, the friend pointed out a large barge getting ready to go into the lock system on the river. The family really wanted to see this. They quickly paid and headed to the river, just one block away. The barge was just beginning the approach, so they got to see the whole process. A lookout area, some thirty feet high, provided a great vantage point of the barge and the Mississippi. The family and friends all watched. Some signs told of the amount of cargo each barge held. The man was shocked to see how much they carried. The capacity was much more than what a train could load. He had seen barges before, but nothing like this.

The barge passed through the lock. A worker sitting idly on the bow jumped into action. His job was to wrap a very large rope around a tie off point on the dock. He swung the ten-inch diameter rope around the metal fitting and wrapped it around a couple of times. As the barge got closer, he wrapped the rope more and more until it had a great tension on it. The popping sounds coming from the tie down sounded like gunshots. The man wondered to himself if the rope ever broke.

Then he saw the crow. It was sitting on top of one of the hatches used to fill the barge. It was looking right at the man. It was moving its head in an up and down fashion, like it was laughing. Just then, the rope began to make a louder creaking and popping sound. The man thought it didn't sound good. Everyone on the observation deck looked just in time to see the rope snap with a loud bang that hurled the worker into the water. The man must have flown fifty feet into the swirling waters of the river.

A loud horn started to blast, and the crew came running from hidden places. One man, in a button up shirt with sweat stains around the armpits and a pocket protector full of pens, raced up the steps to the tourists. "I'm sorry, but y'all gotta get going now. We're closing this whole area down," the authority said.

The family was not ones to argue. This was not the way for any of them. They really didn't want to expose the little kids to any more carnage. They left swiftly, making their way down the concrete steps and back to the parking lot.

"Do you think the guy is okay?" the youngest boy asked while on the man's back. He had jumped aboard for a piggy back at the last step and now was enjoying the free ride.

"I don't know," the man replied to his passenger, "it didn't look good." Nothing more was ever said about the accident amongst the group. It was almost like it never happened.

The next stop for adventure was some sandstone cliffs. This whole area was interconnected with waterways, and this was one of them. The group hiked around some cliffs and crossed small streams. The forest was beautiful. The family had never been in this part of the country. They were happy to experience its awesome nature.

Half the group took off and headed down a trail that had a closed sign. They followed it anyway and ended up at the river. Small waterfalls dotted the flow. The smell of popcorn had been hanging heavy in the air. Now they could see why. There was a silo at the edge of the water used for drying corn. Propane from the bottom heated the corn, giving off the smell of popcorn.

The friend and grandson headed back to find the others. They had thought that the rest of the group would be following, but they never came. The closed sign must have sent them back. The man said he wanted to stay for a bit and take some pictures. The group split once more. The man had no intention of taking pictures. He had seen movement in the forest earlier and now was getting that feeling of being watched again. He walked as far out on the embankment as possible to get a better look, but almost fell. While catching his balance, he saw a figure floating in the water. There were a lot of strange foam here, and at first that is what it he thought it was. When his angle had changed, however, he could see it was a body floating in the river, its long black hair fanning out across the top of the water. The current had a hold on the figure and pulled it over one of the water falls. Over the second waterfall, the man lost sight of the corpse.

He looked back to the forest just in time to see a large, shadowy figure sliding back into the greenery. The man could not make out any features, but he could tell it was on two feet. Besides that, its movements were just a blur. The man could feel the intense stare of the creature even when it wasn't in sight. It did not scare the man nor give him a bad vibe. Once again, it was the opposite. The man felt an excitement in seeing the being. It seemed like the creature had something to tell the man but was waiting for the right time. The man knew in his heart that it was the same being that he had seen the night before, outside the window. He also knew that they were somehow very old friends.

The friend was an excellent tour guide. He showed the family around the older parts of town and explored a bit more of the wilderness at the same time. Everyone's spirits were high.

The family stopped for some cheese and jerky. The friend had often sent packages of these to the man and his family in California. It was in a class all its own. There was good cheese and beef in California too, this was just different. Being half German, this German style food was very appealing to the man. Again, the people here were very nice.

The man started to think that the people were almost too nice. It almost seemed like something was wrong, but he couldn't put his finger on it. He wasn't complaining, though. It was awesome having everyone be nice to you for a change.

The family had met many good people on the trip. Everywhere they had gone, people had been nice to them. The man understood this and spoke to the others of it often. If you were nice to people, they were usually nice back to you. Some called this Karma, but the man disagreed. Good energy attracted good energy, and bad energy attracted bad times. The man thought that overall, people in America were very nice humans. The people had never been the source of the problem anyhow. Out of their blindness they were just a byproduct of the real issues. The greed was the parasite on this planet.

The friend took them to a park where the Mississippi river met the Missouri river. It was a winding road to the place, but worth the time. The overlook here was very nice. Flowers had been planted all along the trail leading to the lookout spot. The view was panoramic. Off to another side, the group had an awesome view of La Crosse. It really told the story of the waterways that they had been on earlier.

The trail around this hill top was lengthy. It felt good for the family to walk around and get movement flowing through their bodies. The dogs were in their own little heaven. The car was wearing on their nerves, too. Nature made all their minds better.

The last two days had been spent mostly in the car. This would get them ready for the road tomorrow. The next stretch wouldn't be long as the last, but it was still driving.

It was time for the family to call it a day. They dropped the other family back at home and headed for the friend's house. He had planned a barbecue, and they were all ready for a little relax time. The menu consisted of venison sausage and an array of barbecue vegetables. The friend ate exactly like the family, healthy. It was a nice treat. This and last night were the only barbecue they had on the road at someone's house. This might even be the last. They were going to enjoy it with the utmost appreciation.

The conversation this night was filled with catching up on each other's lives. The woman started telling the friend about all the death that they had incurred. The man joined in the conversation. It wasn't often they talked about these times nor the black cloud that had hung out around them for so long. It felt good to talk to someone about this. It was a difficult thing to do, but the man needed to get the thoughts out of his head. They had hung on to his being for way too long. It was time to move on.

The friend also had his trials of life happenings in the last years. As life is for everyone, there could not just be good times. Bad times are always one step behind you. There was no avoiding it. Sometimes, the bad times would run into you. It was going to happen. You just had to be prepared for the worst to happen. If you were prepared, there would be no pieces to pick up after a tragedy. There would just be healing of the soul, the one. When you went to pieces, it was over for you.

"Have you heard of the secret?" the boy asked the others.

"You mean the movie about knowing the secret?" the man asked.

"Yeah, I haven't seen it but my friend told me about it. What do you know about it grandpa?"

"I started watching it and realized the 'secret' is a lot of bullshit. It is a polluted message sent out by the greed to try and trick the humans who think they are smarter than the others. It tells of always thinking positive. Every wish you have will come true if you just think hard enough about it. 'Never think the worst', was its grand secret."

"I think it is all bullshit. No matter how much you think about something, thoughts do not make it come true. The only way you get what you want in life is to work very hard for it. Just like my tattoos and paintings. People say I am talented but in truth it is just hard work like any other profession. The people who sit around and talk about how good they are will never be. It is like thinking up an idea and miraculously getting your rewards. It is missing the main step involved in it all. That step is working towards your goals."

"Furthermore," the man said to his grandson, "if you only think good things are going to happen, then you are not prepared for the bad times. If you think the worst, and then the best happens, you are sitting in happiness. You were prepared."

The mosquitoes in Wisconsin, next to the river, were mind boggling. Spray and repellent torches helped, but the family was getting eaten up. They decided, around midnight, that they had enough. It was time to go inside. Although the friend had to work in the morning, he graciously gave up his bed to the couple once again. Again, they would not complain. Sleeping in a nice comfortable bed was only known when they were visiting someone. The rest of the time, it was hit or miss in a hotel room bed. It was usually miss.

As everyone was getting ready for bed, the man stayed outside to finish his smoke. He pondered the fact that this was the start of the second half of the trip. The moon too was in its next cycle. It had been full last night. The celestial body was giving good vibes to the man. The moon and sun were all connected, as was everything else. The man knew his connection to the cycle. He, too, was part of it. Everything was part of the cycle.

The man thought that this moon phase was slightly different. He felt like this was the cycle of' enlightenment. He felt like he was on the verge of figuring it all out. The whole reason for everything was in his grasp. He felt like the knowledge was flooding into his being. He felt like he understood his path. He was a seeker. Knowledge of creating was the whole focus of his life. It was his destiny.

His niece was on this same path. She too was a seeker. It was the way of their family. It was the way to the 'ONE': The collective: The true higher being.

There were just a few more barriers that had been imbedded in them and everyone else, that needed to be broken. A couple more threads torn through, and all the knowledge and secrets so long hidden by the greed would come forward. They would again be connected to the cosmos fully. The end would finally be here. Once again, they could begin.

As the man got out of the shower, he thought that he saw something run down the drain in the tub. He looked closer, but without his glasses, saw only blurs. A strange smell like a wild animal seemed to be coming from the hole. The man felt the stinging glare of a watchful eye. Someone or something was watching him. He looked to the small window in the corner of the bathroom, but it was dark. He quickly dried, got dressed, and left. His body and mind were done. It was time for bed.

The exhaustion did not stop the man from writing in his book. There was a lot to say. He had many feelings about the things that had happened today. Some nights, he wished he could just write down the day's events, like a diary. But every day it was the same. That story had already been written. The day's events had already been documented by an unseen force using the man's handwriting. So, he was left to write about the truth instead.

The man felt like this was his true calling, anyway. He had been seeing the wisdom for so very long. He used to think that many others saw the truth also, just like him. He didn't think he was different than anyone else. Over the years, though, he saw that most people didn't know nor care about the truth. If they did know, they didn't care. Small comforts were what most people really wanted. They were content with the bones thrown to them by the greed, while the elite enjoyed the luxuries of it all.

The shadows played on the walls in the room. The man felt energy in the room besides himself and his wife. It wasn't a menacing energy, it was just there. He thought that his mind was so tired that it was playing tricks on him. He rolled over to turn off the light and saw movement in the window, just like last night. Turning off the light, he pretended to lie down to sleep. In reality, he was looking directly out the window. The same hairy figure was outside the glass, wearing its large misshapen smile. Thousands of fireflies flew all around the creature, illuminating its features just enough for the man to see.

The creature knew that the man was looking at it. Their eyes were connected over the distance. The vision of the visitor needed no light. He looked through the darkness into the man's soul. Their gaze was one of friendship. The man held the being's gentle gaze until he could keep his eyes open no longer. He had become hypnotized by the gaze of the stranger outside the window. He drifted into a deep sleep. Almost immediately, the dreams began.

In his dream, he was dressed in animal skins. His long black hair hung freely down his shoulders. He was in the forest, and the ground was covered in snow. He came upon an encampment of creatures that were not human. These creatures were large and covered in hair. There were maybe twenty-five of the beings, ranging in size from three feet to over nine feet. Some were obviously female and others were young. In his dream, these were a familiar being to the man. They shared a relationship built on respect. They had the same goal. Take what you need, leave what you don't.

The man felt at home with these beings. It was a peaceful atmosphere. The sound of crashing trees brought the creatures out of their divinity. The forest was suddenly alive with intruders. They meant no good to any animal who called this place home.

In his dream, the man stood still and silent as the other beings all raced into the forest and to safety. This was a being that could blend into its environment and be unseen. It was its defense. Some large machines rolled into the clearing that the man stood in.

These machines were not on wheels; they seemed to float above the ground. They destroyed everything in their paths. Trees became splinters; boulders became pebbles, as the hundreds of machines floated through the forest. The man held his ground as one of the machines followed its path directly in line with his. The behemoth stopped barely one yard from the man. It pulsed and shook, as if impatient to get on with its destruction. All the other machines came to a halt also. They all turned to the direction of the man and began to vibrate like the first one. A bright light hit the area, like the light from a bomb. The man could only see white for a moment. When his sight returned, the machines were gone. The smoke from the destruction had cleared, leaving behind a burnt metallic smell. The man could see the extent of it. Behind him was all green forest, before him was nothing. Just brown earth stripped clean of any organic material. The planet had been eaten alive.

The man was woken in the middle of the night by a loud banging on the window. He thought at first it was a dream, but the second, lighter tapping made him look toward the glass. There, outside, was the creature from earlier. He wondered if the being had been out there all along, watching the man and his wife sleep. The Sasquatch was beckoning the man to come outside. He looked to his wife, but she was sound asleep, as was their dog. He didn't know how the two had slept through the racket, it had woken him right up.

Almost on auto-pilot, the man made his way down the steps to the front door. He pulled his shirt on and was fastening his shoes when he heard the soft tapping on the door. The creature was impatient. The man opened the door to see the Sasquatch walking down the five steps of the deck, into the forest. At the edge of the foliage, the being stopped and turned back toward the man. The Sasquatch waved to the man to come closer as it folded itself into the darkness of the trees.

The man's eyes were becoming accustomed to the dim moon light. He could see the shadow of the Sasquatch making its way down the path they had taken to the river the day before. The path was familiar to the man. It seemed to him that he knew it much too well for only having been down its trail the day before.

The man followed the being. It seemed like it wanted to show him something.

It seemed to the man like he had followed the Sasquatch for a very long time. The being did not put off a very good scent. It was very musky, the worst the man had ever smelled. It smelled exactly like what he had smelled in the bathroom earlier. At times, the odor almost became nauseating, but then a small wind would blow it away.

After five or six turns in the river, the man found himself in a clearing. The Sasquatch was close, but the man could not see it. He could smell it, though. When he got to the center of the clearing, a bright light came from the sky and landed directly on the man. It felt exactly like the time when he was seventeen. This was the same light.

The light filled the man's being with energy. Knowledge and truth were passed to him by some unseen creature, through its powerful ray of light. The man was aware that he was floating, just like in his dreams. He was about twenty feet off the ground.

The Sasquatch had returned and was now accompanied by the rest of its clan. There were over twenty of the beings gathered around the circle of light. They were holding hands, multiplying the energy being produced by thousands.

The man knew that something very spiritual was happening. This was part of the path.

The whole destiny of their way was now known to the man. This trip was way more than about them. Everything that they had been through in the last years was preparing them for now, this path. Things were about to change, and they were going to be a huge part of it.

Light was about to return. The greed had their turn with their dark ways. Now was the 'time of the goddess' to return. It was how the cycle had always been.

The man felt good. An inner strength had built inside him that would not be broken down. The family was on the path of the righteous.

The light was upon them.

CHAPTER 21

The man awoke expecting to see the sunlight beaming through the window. Instead, it was just barely getting to be dawn, another hour before sunrise. In his dream, he had been blinded by a very bright light. It was so bright, he remembered thinking that it should burn him, but it didn't. Instead, the radiation from the light produced euphoric warmth in the man. He could even smell the light, organic and very pure. Darkness upon awakening had taken over the light from his dream. The pure smell turned to one of burnt metal. It was time to leave this place.

The friend was stirring when he came downstairs. The man had been worried that his friend would get up late. Being in a different room of the house surely put a strain on the quality of sleep, the man had thought.

Coffee was ready when they came down. The friend was already dressed in his professional clothes and was ready to head out. The two men took a couple quick pictures together and it was off to work for the friend. He reminded the others to turn off the coffee pot. Their farewell was never a sad one. They knew they would be seeing each other again soon.

This was just one more stone they had stepped together, on their separate paths across the river of life.

The girl and boy hadn't awoken yet. They would miss saying farewell this time.

As the others got ready, the man grew impatient. His sister's house was just up the road. The pull had been strong since leaving Texas, but now it was getting so strong the man could not restrain it any more. He had thrown his things together earlier while the rest were just waking up. His sharpie marker and stickers would keep him entertained. Like all other times in his life, good or bad, creating things just made everything better.

He had made this sticker project over the last couple of years. His brother, niece and himself had gone to an estate sale in Stockton on a Sunday after visiting their mom/grandma. The man had found two rolls of wine labels for five bucks. He had started making designs on some of them and got it into his head to get them done by the end of the year. Then the tragedies had begun. Life as the family knew it was put on hold for some time. Everything they had all known, had changed.

The rolls of stickers ended up being two thousand five hundred. The man had made about half the first run. A few months before the trip, the man had decided to resume the sticker project. He wanted to see how many he could get done before their departure. He ended up finishing the whole project in three months. There was one week to spare when the madness was over. All the other painting, tattoos, stickers, writing and the rest of his creations was the therapy the man had needed. If he was thinking about creating, he wasn't thinking about darker times. As a bonus, he felt, you had all this stuff to look at that you made.

The stickers got stuck wherever there was an available spot in the house. Being under construction, most surfaces were dirty. The labels only stuck on a very smooth surface like glass or plastic. The markers were the solution. The man was happy to leave behind, inside the wall, a little thank you to the friend. He had been the best of hosts. The hospitality was top notch.

The family was sad to see the house vanish from sight. They had liked it here very much. The man and woman knew they would be coming back here in the future. The other two were not the same. They were on their own paths in their lives. Their travels were going to take them in different directions. They would be making their own friends along the way.

More adventure was on the way. It was time to get on the road again. Stopping for gas and some road coffee in La Crosse, the lady at the counter was very nice to the man and his niece. She asked where the two were going and where they were from. The girl spoke in words that sounded almost poetic to the man. "We're coming from many miles behind to get to the many miles of the next."

"What are you, some kind of smart as….." her words trailed off as she looked up, into the girl's eyes. Her face changed to one of enlightenment. It looked like a light was shining on the woman's face, but the man knew it came from within her. "I'm sorry, I didn't know. I've been hearing about you all. I didn't think it could be true, but now I see. God bless you," the clerk finished with soft tears.

"Now you can understand," the girl said, "you are God, as we all are. So, God bless you, too." The woman reached out to touch the girl's hand, but the man had already pulled her toward the door by her shoulder. They had many miles to go and no time for this. Not to mention it was only six thirty in the morning. It was way too early for the normal madness to begin.

The friend had told them about a pie place/general merchandise store up the road about eighty miles. The family would be stopping there. Pie seemed like exactly what they needed for breakfast. After getting gas and filling up the water cooler, it was up the Mississippi river once again.

This part of the waterway was very beautiful. More wooded than the south. The family passed by nice houses for sale with prices that were very inexpensive. The man and woman floated the idea of moving out of California someday. They loved where they lived, but things had changed. The laws and taxes in their home state had always been silly, but now they were completely out of control. The greed had taken over everything and benefited from their slaves. The People!

After their family had passed, there was no one else in their area that they knew. Their whole reason for moving there had been taken away. On this trip, they would see if they liked some place well enough to consider moving some day. It was just an idea they talked about sometimes, not a plan. Marihuana cultivation in their county had been legalized and the man foresaw a boom in property values in the next few years. If they could turn a nice profit by selling their house, they would be out of there.

The crow was around every bend. The man felt the pull to his sister's house getting stronger with every mile that they passed. He sensed that the girl felt it too. It was her blood. Somehow the crow felt it also. The man sensed that his wife could tell that he was very amped up. It had been some years since he had seen his sister, and much longer since they had hung out. The woman understood this about her husband.

The man still set the cruise control. He was ready to get there, but he was still not in a rush. They were driving through beautiful countryside that none of them had ever been to before nor may ever come back to again.

The family stopped at the little town the friend had told them about. The gray skies cast a very peaceful glow on everything. The lack of people and traffic all morning did not go unnoticed by the family.

The store was closed. The man even turned around and drove back by in hopes that maybe they had not opened all the doors yet. He was wrong. The sign on the door told the entire horrifying story. There would be no pie for breakfast.

The family was starting to get very hungry. They had already traveled many miles and were starting to get a little irritable. They stopped at another town and the same scenario was in store. It was just too early for any restaurants to be open. Checking in at a pizza place that was closed, there was a little closet of a room with two late eighties style arcade games.

One of them was the man's all-time favorite. When his son was young and it was just the two of them, he had bought the boy a video game and they had played this game together. They played a few games and beat them together, but this was their favorite. The man had to play. He had the boy take his picture as he was finishing up with level one. Level two was getting long and hard on his wrists. He lost his players and hit the road. It was fun, but not the same as if his son had been there. That is where the enjoyment of the video game had come from. The act of being together with your boy was the fun of it all.

After a few more miles of frustration and no hope of a diner being open, the man remembered the beef jerky they had bought the day before. The pieces were long and the family tore into them. It was delicious. The family all agreed that it was the best jerky any of them had ever had. It would hold them over until they could find a place to eat. Now they could take their time, their choices would be much more appropriate.

Level heads had returned to the car with the hunger fulfilled.

Not so urgent, the family enjoyed the sights of the Mississippi. At times, they strayed farther from its waters and then twisted back to the banks. Small towns dotted the highway. This is what they had come to see in this region. Once again, this was true America.

They stopped at a Diner at about eleven. They figured everything should be serving by then. The first place they stopped at was open and that was all they would need. They walked into the bar area and waited to be seated. A table of twelve burly men all turned in their seats to get a good stare at the newcomers. The exchange lasted a couple minutes. The boy said something about the men staring but the man told him to bite his tongue. This was not the place to run your mouth.

When the waitress arrived, the rest of the family followed, but the man lagged. He gave a head nod toward the table of locals, who had not once taken their eyes off the man. They all at once nodded to the man in return, most of them smiling broadly. They had a look of awe on their faces. The man thought that these gents had very nice auras as he followed the rest of the crew into the dining room. The stranger's table was one the man felt comfortable enough to sit down at and join the conversation.

The building seemed to be at least one hundred fifty years old and was furnished very nicely. It was a mom and pop place that had been in business for three family generations. The food was a grilled onion soup with cheddar cheese, bacon and croutons. Roast beef sandwiches finished off the goodness. The cuisine was delicious. The family was very glad they had held out and come to this place. It had been well worth the wait. The waitress was excellent at her job, and it added to the warmth of the home cooking. The family enjoyed the Wisconsin hospitality.

While waiting for the bill, an older couple sat at a table behind the family. The man began to tell the boy why he told him to bite his tongue earlier. He said first off, he didn't want to get beat up because someone was running their mouths. If he was going to get beat up because of someone's mouth, it would be his. "Second," he said to the boy, "those guys were all nice guys. They were just here on their lunch break. They probably come here every day. Today we walk in, we look like the circus. They have never seen anyone like us before. They're just intrigued by what they are seeing; a bunch of tattooed people with piercings. They meant us no harm, trust me."

The boy nodded in agreement. He told his grandpa with sincerity that he understood. When the check still hadn't arrived, the family got up to go out front to pay. The food and atmosphere were great here, but it was time to go. Walking back toward the front, the man had made eye contact with the older gent and his wife. The man gave a nod to the couple and the gent nodded back. His wife got a smile on her face as it lit up like a flashlight. The man felt a warm energy spread from the older couple.

The man finally found the waitress and asked how much they owed. She said their bill had been taken care of by the older couple who had been there. The man went back into the other room but the couple was gone. He didn't know how they had left so fast. They had just been here moments before. They had also just arrived.

The man gave the waitress a twenty-dollar tip. She was very appreciative. The man thought this might be the biggest tip she had ever got, but he felt as if she had deserved every bit of it. Not having to pay the bill had been an awesome gesture. They wanted to make one in return. They rushed outside and looked around but the couple had vanished. An older model light blue Chevy was turning the corner a block away. The man thought this would for sure be the older pair.

As before, there were very few people out. They had no more time for this. The group found a community park for the dogs to run off some steam and the humans to walk off some food. It was back on the road. Minnesota was pulling them. The crow flew overhead, voicing its readiness and its impatience.

A full belly of food was what the family needed. The excited mood from earlier had returned and they were up the road. The family all took a little nap. The man, driving, couldn't see how they could sleep. He was very amped up and ready to get to his sister's house. The connection was pulling harder and harder as they got closer. It felt like he was a magnet, and a like magnet was pulling at his core. He couldn't have wasted time if he wanted to.

The man had been on the interstate for a bit. There was no way around it here. The interstates in these parts were like the highways had been in the rest of the country. They were wide open without a bunch of corporate stores everywhere. Small towns were everywhere, as were lakes. There were not too many cars, and the man was making good time.

Flashing lights ahead broke the man's good reverie. Traffic slowed to a crawl as the people had to drive by slowly to see the victim's misery. There were only a few cars ahead of the man. The accident had just happened. Two police cruisers were present. One officer was directing traffic while the others seemed to be helping at the crash. Movement from the left caught the man's attention. He was just coming up on the accident and had been trying to keep his eyes straight ahead. He thought maybe it was one of the officers waving over people for help and looked.

After trying to avoid it, the man was looking right into the inferno that was engulfing both cars. One of the vehicles was completely in flames, while the other was just the engine and passenger area. The car had the same look as the one they had seen when leaving the restaurant, a light blue Chevy. The man didn't see anyone in the car, but the flames were intense. The other car was once a minivan. The man couldn't tell what had happened, but there were certainly no survivors.

Movement drew his attention to the minivan. A shadow seemed to be dancing around the vehicle, playing a sick kind of tag with the flames. The man saw four figures in the van. It looked like they were in a movie. They looked like they were still driving. The man could swear that it looked like they were singing and having a good time. It seemed like the flames were just another reality that beings in this dimension didn't understand, but the passengers of the van did. A quick glance back to the car and the man saw two figures in the seats. It too was covered in flames. These folks though, seemed like they were not on fire yet. It seemed as if they were oblivious to the flames. The driver even seemed to take a drag off a cigarette.

A sharp rap on the window brought the man's attention back to the road. It also woke the rest of the family. The man looked directly at the cop. Both men were wearing sunglasses. The officer looked at the man with a knowing but distrusting look. The man thought that he would probably be getting harassed right now if it wasn't for the accident. As he was passing by, the cop waved to the man to stop but it was too late. The man had seen the movement but wanted nothing to do with these beings. He knew what was behind the glasses of the traffic cop. Looking in his rear-view mirror, he could see the cop muttering something into his radio and looking directly in the family's direction. A large dark shadow had cast itself on the entire scene. The entire area was completely cast in an eerie darkness; a contrast between the bright red flames and the gray sky. The man got a very unpleasant feeling.

"What's going on?" asked the woman groggily. "Where are we," she asked, as she was looking around.

"We just passed into Minnesota. There was an accident back there, but you guys were sleeping and I knew you wouldn't want to see that. So, I just kept going and here we are. We are much closer to my sister's house. I can feel the energy," the man said to the others.

"Was anyone hurt?" the girl asked her uncle.

"I'm not sure," he answered, "I was trying not to look." The girl could hear the lie in his voice. She had been paying close attention to the actions of the man. She had seen what most would call erratic behavior, but what she saw as a person on the road to truth. Strange things had been happening to her all along, too. She had talked some with her uncle about some of the events, but had kept many to herself. She too was waking up.

The man had told her things too, but she knew he was holding out also. The truth was coming to them, the girl knew it. Wisdom was in their reach. The four of them were on a path to righteousness. When the time came, all their knowledge would be one anyway. Her father had spoken of this for many years and so had her uncle. They need not have spoken about it to the girl. She knew all about the ONE. She too had the visions.

The man needed to stop for a bit. His nerves needed to be calmed after such a horrendous sight he had just seen. He was sure that the car belonged to the man and woman from the diner. It all seemed so surreal, walking into that restaurant. The guys staring, the man and woman and the whole scene was just so odd; even the awesome quality of the food. It had felt so scripted to the man, like they were in a strange movie. That movie had ended on the highway.

The family found a small park that the dogs could run around in and got out to stretch some themselves. The man took off in a direction of his own. He couldn't forget the sight of the passengers in the minivan looking like they were singing. It had been so bizarre. A lot of strange things had happened, but this was very weird. The man couldn't help but think that the minivan looked a lot like theirs. There had been fishing poles scattered around the road also. He had to get it off his mind.

"Are you okay?" the girl asked while handing her uncle a smoke. "You look pale. What really happened back there?"

"You know, some people got all fucked up back there. I just didn't want to ruin it for everyone. I could see the look in your eye when you woke up. You instantly knew what was going on. You even looked immediately to the Chevy and then to the minivan. You were dreaming about this when you were sleeping, weren't you?"

The girl looked at the man with very large eyes. "How did you know that?" she asked.

"Because the dreams are part of it, don't you see? They follow us everywhere we go. It is our portal to move on from dimension to dimension. It's our bridge between the conscious and subconscious. We are harnessing our dreams. Learn what they will teach you. Life after life comes to each of us and we don't even know it. You, I, and our group know it. We are beginning to understand that this today is just here in this place at this moment. It is in between then and tomorrow. We live a completely different life in our subconscious. We live a completely different life in each dimension. Sometimes they interconnect. Those are the days that everything seems surreal. These are the days that everything odd that could happen does happen. This is the day that all the stars seem to line up in your life, for good or bad." The man preached to the girl in a very soft voice.

The two began to walk back. The dogs were having a grand time so they were in no rush. The girl had a way of taking the man's mind off bad thoughts, and this time was no different. They talked about how excited they were to see the sister. Some of their family had always had a strong bond and were drawn to each other. When they got in each other's presence, their energy would be strong as lightning. The man reminded the girl of the time of her eighteenth birthday. She had come to the man's tattoo shop with her mom. It had been a most wonderful time. The man had been so excited that the girl asked her mom if her uncle was okay. She had told her daughter that her uncle was just very happy to see them. It had been true. They stayed at the apartment that night and had some beers and smoked some very good weed. It would be the last time the man ever hung out for the night and partied with his sister in law. Just four months later, it had all changed.

The man talked to his niece about the connection family members had with each other. How when you met family members, you could see the same traits in them as you had. How they seemed like good friends as soon as you met them. DNA was a strong thing, they often talked. But there were other opposites in every DNA. That is why every family had good people and bad people. It was the cycle like everything else. Every positive had a negative. It was the way.

The man pondered these issues all the way to his sister's house. Another hour up the road, at least ten police cruisers, lights and sirens blaring, went screaming by in the opposing lane. They were followed by five ambulances. The man was happy they were headed in the other direction.

The crow had been following them the whole day. It too was happy to be back with its people. Soon, their entire clan would be united. At times, the bird purposely made a shadow on the car below it. The creature knew the power of the shadow you created. It too was a part of your being. The family saw the shadow every time they were cast in it. It made their connection with the crow that much stronger.

"Where do you think those cops were going?" the boy asked.

"My guess is they are going to that place where we had those bomb ass roast beef sandwiches and cheddar onion soup." The man replied with normal conversation. The woman looked at him for a sign. She wondered why he had just said that. Did something happen back at that restaurant that she was unaware of? Either way, it was a very odd thing to say.

The man thought the rest of the drive. He played through his play list, randomly shuffling its entire content. He wondered why strange things had always happened to him. What most people would say was crazy was normal in all ways to the man. Since he was little, he understood that he was different. He was not one to ever be bullied, nor to bully anyone. He had always kept to himself. Drawing and creating had been what he was into his whole life. He got along fine with other people, but he also liked to have his time alone.

The man's sister and brother had always been the same. Strange things had always happened to them. They were the two people in the man's life that had done as much craziness in their lives as he had. They had all traveled many places. They had also lived on a different side of society. Not outlaws. Workers who did their jobs better than the rest, but played harder than the rest when not at work. The three of them, by far, were the craziest people the man had ever met. And none of them had ever been in serious trouble. They were also the only others the man had met that truly knew the truth. The wisdom had been in the three siblings since an early age.

Now there were only two left. A huge part of their being had been taken from them. The ONE is strong, but it can be wounded. However, the brother had been replaced. The niece had taken the wisdom of her family and used it for the light. All the best traits of her parents and brother, the man saw in the girl. He thought many times how it was so awesome; all the best traits of your loved ones in one person, without their dark side. She was the truth. She was the ONE. And now, the three would be united once again.

The Minnesota countryside stretched on. They knew it wasn't so far away, but it seemed to be taking forever. The friend had told them about six or seven hours, and he had been right. The man and woman told the other two stories about the sister. The two women had met even before the man and woman had met. They had been brief friends when the sister lived in the San Joaquin valley. The man's girlfriend met the woman through the sister. The man met the woman through the other two, and a friendship started that lasted three years. Love followed behind.

They had not seen the sister much in the last fifteen years. The rift in the family from the youngest brother and his wife had deeply divided the entire family. The man and his sister's relationship weren't divided, but the man had decided to stay away from it all. He had just moved closer to his parents and older brother and focused on his life with his wife, son, and parents. The younger brother had killed himself two years before. The wife was no longer welcome among the man's siblings. They had only put up with her because of their brother. With the darkness removed, the family could begin to mend.

The family had to stop for a drawbridge. They were all happy to have to stop on the bridge and watch the barge go through. The crow sat atop the shack where the bridge operator sat. It looked in the man's mind like the bird was the one operating the pulley and chains that were moving the bridge. It seemed to be having a great time, whatever it was doing. When the bridge was closing, the bird flew to the East, toward Hoyt Lakes and his sister's house. The sign for their destination said fifteen miles. They were right there.

Driving through the last small towns, the man kept getting a strange feeling about things. Everything seemed so perfect. Almost like the twilight zone. The houses were perfect along with their manicured lawns. The parking lots for the stores were simple rectangle shapes with easy entry and exit. They were nothing like the maze of corporate parking lots back home which kept you from leaving.

There was no trash anywhere. Even a policeman driving by waved to the family. It all seemed so strange to the man here. The last neighborhood they drove through before the sister's house confirmed the man's feeling. The houses and the streets were perfect.

The man understood why his sister had moved here. It was paradise. Like all light though, there was a dark side. The man had it in his head to figure it all out before they left here. He would understand why it 'looked' so perfect. It would just take him a day or two to do it.

The family, at last, rolled up to the sister's house. The four practically ran out of the car to the front door. The sister was there waiting. The family's dogs mixed with the sister's American bulldog and mayhem happened at the front door. It was all the man could do to get a quick hug from his sister, drop a few things on the ground and calm the dogs. Being cooped up in the car had wound them up, and now there was another dog to unwind them.

After restoring order, the family could properly greet each other with hugs. They all felt a gracious joy at their reunion. It had been too long. Their energy was once again whole.

Introductions were made. The boy had never met his aunt, and it had been a long time for the girl. She had met her relative before, but it had been many years. The girl had been very young the last time she had met her aunt.

The sister's boyfriend was a new acquaintance to the family. The two had a temporary boarder. It was a guy of about thirty.

The group picked up like they had never been separated. The tour of the house was next. The man liked his sister's home very much. The siblings had all gotten an inheritance from their parents earlier in the year. The sister had used hers to buy a house here in Minnesota. The family was impressed with her choice. It was a three-bedroom house with a basement. The kitchen had a glassed area leading to the back yard. It was a perfect place for two people.

The boyfriend offered the man a cigar. He said he had purchased an entire box just for their arrival. The man was happy to smoke a good stogie. The cigars they had been smoking on the road had been hit or miss. Mostly miss. It was good to enjoy a nice one. The two sat on the back patio and smoked their tobacco. The boarder came out to listen in on the conversation.

The others would come around, stay for a chat, and move on to the next conversation. It was nice to be here, getting rekindled with family. Knowing they didn't have to be back on the road for some days made it even better. The family was happy to be here and ready for adventure and fishing. It was the land of ten thousand lakes, after all.

The cigar was enjoyable, but the man did not trust the boarder. He was the type who had done everything you had done, but even better. The man and his son called these people the 'one uppers'. Whenever the man was talking to someone, the boarder would interrupt and tell his own story. According to him, he had done just about everything. This guy also did not have a job. This did not sit well with the man. He understood some people could not work, but he also understood that a lot of people just did not want to work. He could tell that this guy was one of the latter. The guy was young and seemed to be in good health.

Not working and sucking up off the system upset the man. He had been paying taxes since he was thirteen years old. He had supported guys like this one his whole life. Almost forty years. Never once did he take a break from paying taxes. It had been every month, every year, since he was thirteen. There was no excuse not to work unless you were seriously disabled. The only thing disabled about this guy was his personality.

The man instantly recognized that this guy was an implant on his sister's life. He, too, had been thrown a few of them before, but had luckily been able to see it. His years of tattooing and the intimate connection it gave with people had made it easier to read these vampires. They were in our lives to suck our energy slowly. Their main purpose though was just to keep your spirituality and creativity at bay. If you were in doubt of your thoughts, you were no threat to the greed. If you were confident and sure of yourself, their implants could have no effect on you.

The man did everything he could to get away from this guy and finally succeeded. He had to finish the whole cigar to do it, but the man took off to hang out with his sister. They had a lot to catch up on. They also had a lot to talk about. Things were happening. Most people would never be able to see it. The man saw it coming like a slow pitch softball. His eyes were wide open. Life as they knew it was about to change very drastically. Humans had talked about change for a very long time, but now was the time. The age of Aquarius had arrived.

The man and sister understood the power. They were fully aware of the cosmic trinity that they had with their brother. Their talks had always been the talk of shamans. Deep conversations came naturally to the three. Nothing was taboo in their conversation. Everything that mattered to humans and the earth and universe was discussed by the three. They were Seekers who were looking for the Truth. Now, joining the man and his sister was the niece's spot in the circle. She had filled in the vacant spot her dad had left open. The circle was once again ONE.

Some barbecue burgers finished off the evening. The boyfriend was cooking, but he let the man take over. He was a perfectionist at barbecuing. This was the second home barbecue in three weeks, and he was excited to be part of it.

The man had always been one to take charge and get things done. TCB had been the motto of their family for a very long time. All the brothers and sisters had been the same. They were leaders, not followers. When the family had died, the man's wife, son, niece and sister all came together and got everything done. This had been their saying this time, 'Taking care of Business', just like Elvis.

The man and sister talked about how they had always been different than others. The girl also spoke about her ways that most would see as odd but were perfectly normal to her. The other people were the ones who had odd ways, the girl had said. Her aunt and uncle agreed. They spoke of how they could see certain things that were there for all to see.

The sister said that there were strange things happening in her house. The man and girl both told her that they had already felt this and were on top of it. There were energy forms in this house and they abounded. She also told the other two about the odd things happening around town. She had been hearing odd noises. She said she could not talk about this too much. Her boarder did not like her to speak of such things. The man and girl understood. There was going to be a lot to talk about it in the next few days.

After burgers and baked beans, the family adjourned to the living room for some relaxing. The drive had taken them seven hours this day. The day before was a little restful but they had not really rested since Texas. The man had continued to wear his shirt the whole drive and was going to retire it to the dirty clothes bag tonight. After a shower, it would be a night of writing and relaxing and getting ready for the next day. They were all excited to check out northern Minnesota and hang out with the family.

The sister took the first shower. The man saw her reflection in the front window of the living room, walking toward the kitchen, signaling to him that she was out of the bathroom. He got off the couch and went to the bedroom to get his clothes. He was just coming out of the spare bedroom, and was reaching for the bathroom door, when his sister pulled the door open. The door flung open just as his hand was touching the doorknob. The man looked at her oddly. He knew for certain that he had seen her reflection in the front window. He asked her if she had gone back into the bathroom, but she said she had never come out. The man knew. He looked at his sister and she knew that he knew. "You've seen them, haven't you?" she asked her brother. "I knew you would, it was just a matter of time."

"I felt it as soon as we came to your house, even outside." the man told her. "I've been seeing shadows throughout your house all day. Your house is like a magnet for spirits. Energy gets sucked into it and it remains. All that iron here is making a magnetic field pulling all kinds of things into it. It is what you are hearing. I know what to do."

The man went out to the car and retrieved the gong that he had brought along. He had rung it a couple of places on the way, but he knew he had brought it for this reason.

It was one of two gongs that the family now possessed. The brother had a thirty-two-inch Gamelan gong that he had acquired. The man had purchased this twenty-inch tool a year before. They were very spiritual instruments to the family. They played them at the house in the mountains when the time was right. The day they had buried all the ashes, the time had been right. The gong got rung all night long. They had sung their song.

He rang the gong throughout the entire house, including the basement which had darkness to it that the man could feel. It wasn't a menacing feeling, it just wasn't the light. The man spoke to the spirits in his mind. He could feel the energy all around him. There was much energy in this house. It would come up to the man and timidly touch him, like testing the water before jumping in. Most of the energy was benign, but some of it cast off bad vibes. The man understood. It was like everything else: Dark and light.

His mind was all he needed to communicate with this energy. The music from the gong bridged the gap and made the two dimensions flow together instead of crashing into each other. "All the spirits in this house would sleep very well tonight," the man thought.

While in the shower, the man thought about the crow. He had not seen it since they had arrived at his sister's house. He had seen it at the last place they stopped for the dogs but didn't remember if he had seen it since.

The water made his imagination flow like its eddy into the drain. He was a Pisces. When he was around water, he was at his most creative. So many times, at home, he would be in the shower and come up with the next painting or drawing or story or whatever else. The water opened his mind. They both flowed as one. He didn't feel any energy in the bathroom. Could it have been so easy to cleanse this house? He didn't think so. There was far more going on in this area than such a simple cleansing would cure.

When he came out of the shower, all the others were already in bed. The girl met him in the hallway and they gave each other a fist bump. They did not need to speak. It was happening. They both knew it. Words could not speak what was in their hearts. The One was strong.

The man's wife was already asleep when he got to bed. He tried to be as quiet as possible but it would not have mattered either way. The woman was sound asleep. The road had been hard on her. The man was happy to see her so deep in sleep. His love for her was strong. He knew he was not an easy person to be around all the time. The intensity of his personality was upsetting for some. His wife, however, accepted him for who he was and encouraged his creativity. Their bond was one of love and mutual respect. Most of all, they were friends.

He picked up his travel book and opened it to the pages for the day. Again, they had already been written. The man could not understand this. It was almost a feeling of dread now every time he picked up the book. He could not shake the feeling. It was so very weird. This night, he decided to read the last couple of paragraphs. If it was like the other days, the last paragraphs would have happened just before he came to the room. His day was being written out as he lived it.

The man closed the book with such a fluster that it made the woman stir. He threw the book back into his backpack where it belonged. He didn't know who was writing these things, but not all of it was so true. Some of the things just didn't happen the way they were told in the story.

He went to the kitchen to get a glass of water. He needed to calm his nerves. The light above the stove was the only light in the house. It cast a bluish color on the kitchen, which spilled into the hallway. The man felt so surreal as he walked down the short hallway into the kitchen. His sister was standing by the stove, staring at something in the corner where it met the ceiling. Her entire being was coated in the blue glow. He asked if she was okay but she didn't take her eyes off her target, nor did she even acknowledge the man's presence. The man looked to the spot which held his sister's gaze and it looked like the corner of the kitchen was moving like smoke. It looked like a portal had opened in the space that was absorbing the blue light.

The man could not believe how thirsty he was. It felt like he was going to pass out if he didn't get some water immediately. He got his drink and turned to leave, but his sister was standing in the doorway. She asked him what he was doing and he said getting some water. He asked what she was doing and she said smoking a cigarette. The whole scene had changed since the man had opened and closed the refrigerator. The blue glow now was more of a soft yellow, normal light coming from an incandescent light bulb.

The man asked his sister, "Is your boarder okay?"

"Yeah, why do you ask? We were just watching a movie together downstairs, and I came up here to smoke a cigarette."

"Because I've been writing this book but I'm not writing it. It is in my hand, but I do not remember penning it. Every day since we started this trip, it is the same. At the end of the day, the events have already been written down when I open the book. Tonight, in my story," the man said with a twisted exuberance in his voice, "I just killed that lazy fucker."

The man and his sister stared at each other for about thirty seconds. Then, at the same moment, they both broke out in a very maniacal laughter. The man was still chuckling to himself as he made his way back to his bedroom and shut the door behind him. Like always, when the siblings got together, sanity was something they could do without.

The man went to sleep as soon as his head was down. Sometime in the night, he had a terrible dream that had rattled his soul. In it, the family was pulling out of the pub where they had the sandwiches and soup the day before. As they exited the parking lot, onto the main road, an old Chevy took a turn too fast and couldn't stop in time. It had plowed into the van. Both vehicles had burst into flames. The family had died instantly. The man was aware of their death, but somehow, he was not only conscious of what was going on but he could also still function, even though they were consumed in flames. They were all singing to some song that was on the radio, but it was so garbled that the man couldn't discern it. It sounded like music playing underwater, slowed down. But somehow, the family sang through the whole thing. Somebody drove by in a minivan that looked just like theirs. The man turned his head and looked directly at the driver of the other minivan. The driver looked exactly like him. It was his doppleganger.

The dream had shaken the man awake. There was no clock in the room. It was still dark outside. Some lights at the window drew his attention. The room was dark but the window had some light coming through. He squinted his eyes but could not see well without his glasses. As he was fishing around for them, the lights kept moving around. He realized it must be fire flies outside the window.

Suddenly he smelled it. It was the same smell that he had smelled back in Wisconsin for the last two nights. He knew what was outside. He had no need to find his glasses anymore.

Tonight, he was not going outside to play with the creature. He was staying put and getting some rest. He didn't care if the being watched him sleep all night. It did not make the man feel uncomfortable. It was the opposite, the being made the man feel a very strong kindness inside his being. The Sasquatch was there to teach him something. He was ready to learn.

His thoughts quickly faded back to the subconscious. Sleep overtook his mind. All night he would dream about running with the Sasquatch. They had let the man into their group. He was at one now with the most spiritual beings on the planet.

They were going to form an alliance. The creatures had been getting the man prepared for the integration. In his subconscious, he was Sasquatch. In his conscious, he was the piece that was going to connect all the beings together to stop the greed.

The ONE was coming. The final unity was already underway.

In the morning, the sister asked the man how he had got all that mud into the house the night before. She asked him if he had been running around the forest all night and the man just laughed. The sister looked at him with a common bond. She understood.

He hadn't gone out of the house the night before. Not in his conscious state at least. The sister sat in her chair and looked at the mud trailing throughout the house and even down the stairs. She knew what she was seeing.

It had begun.

CHAPTER 22

The man did not sleep so well the night before. His dreams had been very strange again. Before, he had wished his dreams would return. Now they had with a vengeance. He thought about the old saying, 'Be careful what you wish for'. He felt this statement was true. In this case with the dreams, though, it was not a bad thing at all. The wilder his dreams were, the more he liked it. He couldn't remember the dreams from the night before. He thought that they had to do with someone outside the window. Some other time that night, it sounded like someone knocked on the door. That was about all he could remember.

The man had a very restless sleep pattern anyhow. This house had many spirits, and they were fidgety. It did not make it easy to stay in the subconscious. The man had felt a strange magnetic energy as they were driving north. He knew the energies in the house were tied to the energy in this entire region. He felt like he was on the verge of figuring it all out. It was just barely out of his grasp.

These feelings of spirits were not foreign. Many places that the man had visited held strange energy. He had been in touch since he was a child growing up in the house of ghosts. There were many spirits here, congregating in an eternal party at his sister's house.

The house they had grown up in had multiple spirits too, maybe three or four. The energy had been different there. It had been much more heavy and oppressive. Its purpose seemed to be to scare you. Maybe it was because he had been a child and got scared easier, but the man didn't think so. He had never encountered another energy like that one had been. The energies in his sister's house were not menacing in the least. They were just hanging out; vying for their own space in the dimensions surrounding the dimension that most humans knew.

The man and girl spoke of these things often. Their belief was that there were spirits among them all the time. They were not necessarily conscious of us just as we were not always conscious of them. But sometimes, humans could see to the other dimension and crossover into the other worlds which abound all around them. Sometimes the parallels met, allowing windows to open into the other worlds. Most people could not see them. There were too many distractions around them. Fear had blinded the masses of their real sight. It did not mean the spirits did not exist.

The man's family had never rolled over to fear. They had distrusted technology for generations. Their ancestry was a simple one. Their people had been more interested in spiritual enlightenment and wisdom than greed and power. Distractions were a thing for the other people in society. They were for the ones who had been blinded: The ones who would never see: The true ninety nine percent.

The man's father had a gift. He could see into the future. He could predict a few minutes before someone was going to call or knock on the door and sure enough, it would happen. Many times, the man had witnessed this gift in his dad as a young child. One time when they were children, the mother and father had planned a trip to a southern California theme park. The kids had been very excited. The night before however, the father had told their children that they were not going. He had a bad feeling about the trip, and they would have to go another time. The children were crushed. The next morning, a huge 7.8 earthquake hit southern California. They would have been on the highway where the most damage occurred. Many people had died. The kids' father went from being the villain to being the hero. The legends began that day.

The man's mother had a connection with the spirits. She had been deeply involved in the church when she was a child. As a teenager and young woman, she had lived at the convent. It had been in the days of the depression. The families had no choice but to send their daughters to the system. This is where she had noticed her gift. She had told the family so many stories about when she and her two sisters lived at the convent. Many strange things had happened. They had continued throughout her entire life. Even at the end, the woman had possessed her gift.

She had told the man about being approached by a man made of ashes one week after her son had died. The Ash Man, as she called him, had come the day after her son's cremation. He had been coming for the last three days and was sitting with them now, outside on the patio. The man had looked at his mother with awe. She had not spoken coherently to him for over two years. Now she was talking like her normal self, before the dementia had took her mind. It only lasted a few minutes, but it had made the man feel such a deep connection to his family. Once again, his mom had been the communicator. For just a brief instant, the three of them were sitting there like old times. Everything had been okay for just those brief moments. This was one of the man's most cherished moments of his entire life.

The man had inherited each of his parents' gifts. His older brother and sister had also acquired this knowledge. Some of the children of the three also had the insight.

Somehow, the family seemed to complement each other which made the powers stronger. It made them see all the things that were happening for what they were. They did not walk through life with their eyes closed. The man believed that his parents did not use their gifts for all they could. They were from a different time and talk like this brought odd looks and cold shoulders.

The nineteen fifties, sixties and seventies were a time to fit in with your neighbors. It was the time to be like everyone else. The humans became robots living in house after house of non-creativity. It was the beginning of suburbia; the rise of modern submissiveness.

The man also saw that some with the gift could not handle it. He saw the gift in his brother and knew it was very strong. The man also knew that this was a big part which had driven him to his untimely death.

Pressures of seeing the truth did not come lightly. They were a very heavy symptom of being able to see. Being filled with the knowledge could also drive you mad if you didn't know how to keep it in check. Some would think that it was inner demons who were attacking them. It would be true, their own mind being their own demons. The man knew that all demons came from our minds. There were good and bad, light and dark, but demons in your head controlling you was not how the man saw things.

Many of the Earth's prophets would have had to fight these thoughts. When you can see the absurdity of some and pass it on, it will take its toll on your being. The things you see to have that passion would have to be more than the average person could take. When your voice is heard by many, your energy goes out to them at the same time. If you didn't know how to recharge that energy from those same people, then you were going to lose your mind. You had to learn to take back the same amount that you gave out.

The people thinking these prophets were God only made the stress of their knowing minds the more fragile. They were not Gods. They were humans with a message. Prophets had lived among humans long as humans had lived on Earth. They had always dealt with the same issues. Because of their confidence, they were perceived as arrogant. Because of their convictions, they were considered dangerous. Because of their wisdom, they were looked upon as Gods.

The man got up before anyone else so he could work in his mask book. The project was moving along. He had just brushed his teeth and was wiping the sleep out of his eyes, when he wandered into the kitchen. His sister was there making coffee. She had a percolator, which was a treat for the man. She asked if they slept well, and the man said yes except for all the activity. The sister looked at him and said, "I knew I wasn't going crazy." She was off down the hallway in a flash of red robe. The bedroom door shut behind her.

The sun had just begun to come up behind the trees. The man seldom saw this time of day back home. He usually slept in a bit more back home in his routine. Now they were on vacation. Just because they were at the sister's house didn't mean he could do nothing.

He had already started the drawing for this page back in Missouri or one of the states before. Now he just had to add the color. He had brought a watercolor kit that he had found at a thrift-store, years earlier. It had turned out to be good paint and was perfect for taking along on this trip. If he could get this done before everyone else got up, he would be feeling ahead of schedule all day.

The man's niece was there about the time the coffee was finished. The man knew that the girl was going to be up shortly after him and welcomed her company. He cherished their time together. He had a son who understood the bond. The girl was like a daughter to the man. She too understood. The time you spent was now. Later may never happen. They took advantage of any chance they could to hang out.

The girl asked the man how his writing book had been going. He said it was good. He told her he had kept up on it every night since they had been gone. He told her about the knowledge that the book would tell. Some people would not take kindly to these words and might retaliate. The man told the girl that he didn't care anymore. He had kept the truth to himself for so very long, and now it was time to speak.

After the death of their family, they realized there was a calling. Something much bigger than they understood had been happening. This trip had been unveiling it all to them, piece by piece. The destiny was unfolding daily.

They talked about how humans weren't the most intelligent beings on this planet. There were multiple other species of beings that were all around but not known to the arrogant humans. Some other beings were controlling things. They were setting things in motion and seeing how the humans would fuck it up. It was a large experiment, and the humans were the rats. It was the reason they never had contact with the other beings. The scientist does not communicate with the rats.

They also talked about how much control of the media there was. Even the UFO information that had been denied and debunked was all part of their ploy to hide the truth. Hiding the truth was the job of the greed. It was their way to get the humans to do anything they wanted. They were the masters of the manipulation. Their technology was far more advanced than anyone ever could have imagined. They kept it hidden well, behind their media curtain.

The conversation even got around to the election of a reality show star. Humans were completely lost. Again, they would believe anything. Their way was grasping at false Gods and following their every whim.

Getting change from the greed, who were the problem, was a joke. However, people would vote for it because this guy said so. Although his track record didn't stand behind his words, maybe he will change. The people had been completely disconnected from the cosmos. They were now one hundred percent slaves to the greed.

Another pot of coffee had to be made by the time the others got up. The man had finished the page in his book as he and his niece had a great conversation. It was only eight in the morning. The sister made the family a nice breakfast of eggs and toast. They caught up on old times, but mostly talked about the now and future. They had never been ones to talk about old times. It was better to live the times now. There were many things to talk about with the deaths in the family, but that did not have to consume all the talk. The energy in the kitchen was explosive. It was great for them all to see each other again.

The group all talked about the strange things that had happened the night before. The boy spoke about someone coming downstairs in the middle of the night, but never going back up. The boy had slept in the basement.

The girl spoke about someone coming into her room the night before, but it had not frightened her. It had more been an irritation she had said, like they were invading her space.

The woman spoke of her clothes being scattered all over the floor this morning. They had been pulled from her suitcase, and it looked like someone had tried them on. She, too, said it wasn't scary, just irritating.

The man and his sister looked at each other and passed the look. They had been passing this look since they were small children. It was the look that they were thinking the same exact thing. The niece recognized the glance between her elders.

After breakfast, the sister showed the man a rock she had found. It was a white stone that was irregularly oval shaped. It had two chips on the front and one on the bottom. It looked just like a miniature alien head.

The man examined it very closely. He knew all about this stone. It had been coming to him in his dreams off and on throughout the trip. It had been a guide of sorts in the man's visions.

The rock seemed to have a strong energy flowing through it. It seemed to hold knowledge and some form of thought. The sister told her brother that he could keep the stone. She also told him that its name was 'Toomey'. They both said the name at the exact same time. Again, the two shared the look.

The fossil swiftly went in the man's pocket, where it traveled for the rest of the trip across the states.

The family unloaded the minivan to make room for the sister, boyfriend, and boarder. They had decided to go on a short sightseeing journey around the Minnesota backcountry. It was a beautiful day. Puffy clouds dotted the sky, casting shadows on the perfect houses. Not just were the buildings perfect, so were the lawns and sidewalks. There was not a single tree that wasn't pruned. Although it was summer, there were no children out playing. The neighborhood looked deserted.

The boarder sat in the front seat, with the excuse of being the navigator. He would not relinquish this spot the rest of the stay. Anywhere they would go, he would automatically take the front seat. The man had issues with the men sitting in the front seat while the women and the rest sat in the back. He had never let that happen, as his father never let that happen. His mother had always ridden up front, just like his wife did now. The man was becoming more and more distrustful of this outsider. He could put up with the talk, but there was a dark side to this human that the man did not like. He knew that the guy was an implant. His actions and words left no doubt to the man. He was blocking his sister and her boyfriend's aura and creativity.

The first spot they stopped was at a bridge covering the river. Wildflowers abounded in the area. The family was happy to get back to nature. The last week had been mostly driving, and now it was time to reconnect with Pachymama. Away from the highway, they could finally relax. The lack of vehicles made the place even better.

A beaver swimming in the water intrigued the family. There were beaver where they lived, but you would seldom see them. The group just liked animals. Even a squirrel's antics would catch the attention of the group. They took many pictures of flowers and each other before getting onward to adventure.

The next stop was to find some yard sales. There were a few, and the sister knew exactly where to go. The navigator proved to be a dud, a tell-tale sign of more to come.

The first yard sale had a bunch of fishing gear. The family had brought gear with them, but 'you could never have too much', was their motto. Their reels had taken a beating on the trip. They could use some fresh gear. The homeowner, his brother, and wife were tending the business. The man and woman, like they often would, struck up a conversation with the people. At first, they had been slightly standoffish toward the tattooed people, but when the family began to talk to them, they were instant friends.

The homeowner walked with a serious limp, assisted by a cane. The fishing gear he was selling was brand new. He had worked for a corporate sporting goods store that went out of business. The head office refused to pay the employees with cash, but said they could take merchandise instead. That had been over ten years before.

A few years back, the homeowner told the family, he was fishing on Lake Superior, and a large monolith appeared out of the water. It did not ascend from the water, it was just there. It was about five hundred feet away, but it blocked the man's vision almost to his peripherals. It seemed to be hundreds of feet tall. His boat had been going at a decent rate of speed when the object appeared. It took all his boating skills not to slam into the behemoth. When he turned away from the huge stone-like object, he could not proceed. His boat was at full speed, and the water was splashing around the bow, but the object got no further away. After what seemed like an eternity, the man could not power the boat and watch the monolith at the same time. He had stopped the motor. The next thing he remembered was the coast guard pulling him from his watercraft, on a stretcher. He had been afloat for three days. When they got him to the hospital, they found him to be fully nourished and hydrated. He had no abrasions or scratches on his entire body. He seemed perfectly healthy except for the terrible limp in his left leg that he did not have before. The x-ray showed that the bone in his leg had been cut just above the knee. A four-inch section of bone had been taken out to be replaced by a rod of metal. The metal was secured to the bone with small screws. The doctors nor the man had any idea how he had gotten this rod in his leg. The wound seemed to be over twenty years old by the way it was completely healed. There was nothing in his medical record to support this operation ever happening to him. He had been disabled since, and just stayed at home. The doctors had said there was nothing they could do for him.

The family loaded the new reels and rods into the minivan. The owner had given them a good deal on a package purchase. There was enough for two full setups and a whole bunch of sinkers. It was the kind of yard sale the man and boy dreamed of hitting together; all fishing gear and a cool story to boot.

The man thought hard about the homeowner's words. It was not the first yard sale that he had been at where the proprietor told him about their UFO story. It happened to the man and his wife quite often. People felt free to talk to the couple, and they were correct; they could say anything.

As they were saying goodbye to their new friends, the homeowner and his people drank from their beers. They spoke softly about the encounter they had just had. They knew there was something special about the group that had just been here. They shined a light that had touched them all. The woman told her husband that she thought these people shined a light on many people. They spoke of hope, something they had not had in so very long, coming back into their lives. The man laughed at this in a happy kind of way. It was the first time he had laughed like this since he had lost his job ten years before. He headed into the house to get the next round of beers, his limp was gone.

The second yard sale consisted of more good people. This was a woman in her fifties and her granddaughter. They had mostly kid stuff but the man did find a book on the paranormal. The woman asked the man if he believed in these things, and he said of course he did. It was normal as the sun rising every morning, he told the vendor. She told him about a strange creature that they had seen behind their house some nights. She said the creature walks upright and seemed to be about eight feet tall. It had a terrible smell to it. No matter what they did, they could not get a picture of the creature. Even installing trail cameras was of no success. It almost seemed like the creature didn't show up on photos.

Two weeks before, the vendor's two-year old grandson had come up missing one evening. The locals all came together to help find the boy, but were unsuccessful. They had searched all night around the woods. The next afternoon, a group of campers found a boy sitting in the forest by himself. He was not dirty or hurt in the slightest. They had wondered where the boy had come from and how he had gotten into the middle of the woods unhurt. They contacted the family, and they retrieved the missing relative. It was fifty miles from where he had originally vanished. The woman finished her story by telling the man that her grandson didn't seem the same since the ordeal. She said there was a different look in the boy's eyes. She said that it seemed like the same person.

Her eyes became distant in thought. It was the perfect time for the family to make their escape. They had liked this lady, but they had come here to see the sister and fish. Fishing was calling to them. They stopped to get some licenses and bait. It was a small store selling fishing and hunting gear. The man got a license for everyone in the group. He had no problem paying for a license. It was not so expensive out here to fish. Compared to just about anything else you did, fishing was about the least expensive. Catching fish was a bonus. Hanging out, outside with your homies, was the real enjoyment. These times were priceless to the family.

Some barbecue was just what they needed to finish the running around. The boyfriend cooked up outside while the sister took care of preparations inside. A jug of root beer from the local burger spot was the icing. They enjoyed their meal and were ready for some adventure. The boy, girl, and grandpa went to load the fishing gear. These three would be fishing a lot in the next days. Everywhere they went, there was water. Minnesota was going to be their fishing dream come true.

After rolling up to a campground and traversing the campers, the family had finally arrived at a dock and were ready to fish. There was a boat at the landing and a couple of families. They had many kids running around. The man thought with all the lakes, that they would go someplace where there were less people and more fish.

The dock was a nice place, and there did seem to be many fish. It protruded out into the water and formed a T shape. It easily held all the anglers and could have fit more. The family was catching many fish. The man caught a couple of northern pike and a small mouth bass, but mostly it was all bluegills and sunfish. It was action from the minute their line would hit the water. The whole family was faring very well. A couple of very large pike swam right in front of the dock. The man had been to Canada fishing for pike before and guessed these were about fifteen pounds each. Every fisher person on the dock headed to their side for a shot. The fish swam away free, awaiting another day to play the fisherman's game.

A couple of the kids had come over with their parents and were fishing right next to the family. The children did not swim off when the pikes did. The man's pole fell over, and his hook went right into a small girl's hair. Hook and worm entangled in the blonde locks. At first, the man thought that it had caught the girl's scalp. That was how his luck always went, but luckily it was just hair. He told the girl to hold still and slowly removed the hook. When he was pulling it free of the last strands, the man noticed a shiny object under the girl's hair. It looked like the object was implanted in the girl's scalp. He was trying to get a better look at the thing when her parents noticed what he was doing. They grabbed the girl and quickly left the dock. In their haste, the family had left behind one of their fishing poles.

The man ran after the family, pole in hand. He would have liked to give the man back his pole. The man had raced up behind the family, but they had vanished. They were nowhere to be seen. He didn't know how he had missed the family. They had left the dock less than one minute before him, with three kids and their stuff.

A tall stranger, dressed in dark clothes walked past the man. The man asked him if he had just seen a family walk by, but the stranger did not acknowledge him. His blank eyes, covered in black sunglasses, had been held forward.

When he returned to the dock, the boy asked the man what they were going to do with the pole. The man told him that they would just leave it here. Surely the stranger would come back for it later. It was a nice pole. They were not thieves. It was bad luck. If one of the other fishers on the dock took the setup, it was fine with the man. That wouldn't be on his conscience.

Loons were shrieking in the distance. The sun was beginning to fade. Mosquitoes were coming out in battalions. It was time to go.

Driving back to the house, the man realized something. He had still not seen the crow since they had arrived. He had seen every other kind of bird imaginable, just not their large, brown friend.

When they got back from fishing, it was getting dark. The man went straight to the rock his sister had given him earlier. He had left it on the dresser in the room when they went fishing. He did not want to lose it at the fishing spot. The stone seemed to speak to the man. He could not stop thinking about it the whole time he was on the lake. It made him feel at ease; a feeling that did not come to him often anymore.

This stone was not new to the man. It had come into his life many years before when he was about two years old. He had held onto this stone for many years, but it had gone missing along with the memory of it. His sister had found it for him, at Lake Superior. Here it was again. It had made the circle back into the man's life. In his dreams, it had never left. This stone was a piece of the overall puzzle. One more clue had been dropped. The family was one step closer to the truth.

The sister and boyfriend went to bed, as did the man's wife. The other three retired to the basement to watch a movie the sister had gotten to give to the man. It was about a guy who put on some glasses he had found, and he would see aliens walking around as humans. He could see another race of people pretending to be regular folks. But they weren't regular. It was the rich people, the media, and the police. It was the politicians and the religions. It was the greed.

They had made a movie about the truth and everyone had thought it was fiction.

The sister had a theory that movies were made by the greed to get us ready for new technology or disease or war or something. This movie seemed to confirm her idea.

The man opened his book, expecting the pages to be scrawled in. Instead, the pages were blank. Strange, the man thought; the book stopped writing itself on this day of all days. The story flowed like water this night. The man had very much to say. The rock sat on his lap the whole time. He felt a strong vibration from the stone. It seemed to flow through his entire body, concentrate, and flow out his hand in the form of words.

The girl ended first, then the boy, then the movie. All had moved into the subconscious. The man would have to finish watching it the next night. The day had been very long. It was time for bed.

Climbing the stairs out of the basement, a strong force stopped the man about midway up. It was like a magnetic force, opposite of his, was in the stairwell. He could not pass around the energy. The force field irritated him but caused no fear.

"Enough" he said firmly. The energy was gone as suddenly as it had been there. His passage was once again unimpeded. Getting to the top of the stairs, he saw a shadow moving through the back door as it swung closed. There was the smell of burnt metal in the house. He could feel spirits all around him. It was like they wanted the man to hang out with them and not go to sleep. They called to him to forget about the subconscious, it was much better in the conscious.

The man fought through the thoughts and ran to the back door. His flashlight was right there in his backpack and swiftly in his hand. He got through the glass doors just steps behind the shadow that had just exited. He shined the light throughout the yard but did not want to hit the houses. It was two in the morning. They didn't need the cops coming out.

As he was going back into the house, movement in the bushes, outside his window, drew his attention. He shined the light in the direction to see something very large, on two legs, run around the side of the house and into the forest. It was gone before the man could discern any features of the behemoth. He did not need to see. The faint smell of the beast, fifty feet away, told the man exactly what the creature was.

The beast had been following the family for the last few nights. How it had gotten so far north in the same time as they had drove puzzled the man. Obviously, these beings had gifts that were not known by humans.

Lying in bed, the man listened to all the sounds of the house and its inhabitants. There were six beings in the house now, and countless more that could not be seen. When the man rolled over to turn off the lamp, he saw movement out the window, followed by thousands of dragonflies. He told himself he would go outside tomorrow night and find out what was going on. When the creature came back, he would try to contact it. Tonight though, he was just too tired. He felt like there was nothing left in him.

The man picked up Toomey after turning off the lamp and wrapped his hand around the object. He felt like this stone had been a part of his being at one time. Like a long-lost limb, miraculously given back.

A grayish green light softly emanated from the stone's eyes when the overhead light was shut off. It lit up the room like night vision goggles. The man could clearly see everything in the darkened space. The light coming from the small stone seemed to be way too strong compared to its source. The stone was barely glowing, but the whole room was lit up.

The light from the stone also lit up the window. The man could clearly see what he had been suspecting. Outside the window was a large, humanoid creature, covered in hair. It was a Sasquatch. It was not alone, though. There were two other fellow creatures with this one. They were all three looking at the man with rapt attention. They seemed to be very interested in the stone and what he was doing with it.

The light coming from the rock began to lessen. Within minutes, the luminosity had stopped altogether. In his head, the man heard the word, "Soon."

The man knew the Sasquatch had communicated this message to his mind. He too felt the connection. He knew what the message had meant. A time was coming.

The man and these beings were part of it. Many of their kind had died before, all for the name of survival of their species. Now there were just a few who survived the ways of the greed. Just like the man's people.

Their energies were going to have to be united if they thought they would ever be spiritually strong enough to pull off this cosmic task. Defeating the greed and sending them away once and for all.

They were going to have to be stronger than ever before.

They were going to have to become the ONE.

CHAPTER 23

A vibrating sound on the end table, next to the bed, brought the man out of his dream. In it, he had been hanging out with his older sister, who had died in the springtime. The house they occupied in the vision was the house they had grown up in. The older sister didn't say much. She didn't need to. The man could tell what she was saying by her expressions. Her look told the man all he needed to know. It was a look of peace and serenity. It was a look that made the man 'sense' that his sister's soul was well.

It had been the same when he had dreams of the rest of his family after they had died. Going back to his father ten years before, the dreams had always been similar. The man would be so happy to see his family member, alive one more time in his subconscious. The relative in the dream would never talk, just give that look which the man read so well. It was the look of wisdom. They would come to his dreams one to three times, soon after their deaths, and then never return.

This was the first time his sister had come to him in his subconscious. He was happy for the visit. He had been waiting.

The man believed that these dreams were of a prophecy of the afterlife. He felt like the energy of the dead would hang on until their mission was complete. Then, their energy would go on to the next place, forever leaving their loved ones behind in this dimension. After his brother had died, this had become very apparent to him.

His brother had come to the man's dreams three times. Each time, it had to do with getting something done. There was a sense of urgency in these dreams. The last dream that the man had of his brother, they were in a car. The brother told the man, in the same manner of speech without words, that this would be his last time. He was on his way. There would be no more hanging out.

The man would have to finish the mission for them both. The brother was truly moving on.

The man had thought of these dreams every day since having them. He knew it told of what really happened when we die. The knowledge was mostly there, but there were a few more pieces to the puzzle. He also knew that the distance between all realities was getting narrower in his existence. Soon, the knowledge would be in his grasp. Then, his mission could be complete.

The persistent vibrating on the table pulled the man from his thoughts. He thought it was his cell phone at first, but upon looking, noticed it was the rock his sister had given him. It was vibrating like crazy. It almost fell off the table a couple of times, but would change its course every time it got to the edge. The man grabbed the rock. The vibration stopped, but the warmth from the object spread through his being. This stone was very special. It was possibly a bridge over a gap of realities and dimensions; or even a passageway through the universe.

The man threw his clothes on quickly and headed for the bathroom. The rock was clutched tight in his fist. His niece was already up and ready to go. While brushing his teeth, the man looked at the stone again. In the light, he could see that the rock had changed color slightly. Yesterday, it had been solid white. The missing chips were a bluish gray. Now, the whole stone was bluish gray. The missing chips had turned an odd color of brown, almost like the color of dried blood. The man dropped the stone in his pocket. It would not be leaving his side on this fishing trip. He had made a new friend.

The boy was in the living room talking to his cousin when the man came out of the bathroom. After the fishing excursion the night before, the three were more than ready. The woman decided not to go. It was barely daybreak, and she wanted to sleep in a bit. The man had no problem with this. He was happy that he wasn't dragging her out of bed. There had already been enough of that on this trip.

The sister met the three before they were leaving. Her sleep was erratic. Sleep came when it did, no routine involved. She looked wide awake to the man. They invited her to go along, but she declined. Her health was not at full strength, and she would like the time to rest. They invited her boyfriend also, but she said he wasn't feeling so well. On the way out the door, the sister called out to them, "be careful". The man had thought these words were odd. They would haunt his thoughts the rest of the day.

The first stop on the way to the spot was the convenience store to get some more worms and coffee. The boarder had told the group not to go to this store, as the people were very rude. The man did not care about any of this and went anyway. There were only two stores in town, and this was the only one that sold worms. The family had no time for silly quarrels. The clerk proved to be very nice. She was a woman of about fifty and talked politely to the family. She did not, however, try to make small talk with the family. The man was happy. He was here to be with his niece and grandson. There was no time for small talk. They were not small people.

The boy asked the lady where the sugar was, and she came over and practically put it in his coffee for him. The boy looked at the woman strangely. Something seemed wrong about the lady to the boy. When they were leaving, the clerk told the group, "God bless". The man returned the gesture. He was not a religious person. God bless was just one of the nicest things you could say to a person. Everyone wanted to be blessed, even if you didn't believe in God or religion. He believed it was like praising Earth. That was their true God, after all.

When they got into the car, the girl asked her uncle if he had seen that woman's aura. He confirmed to the girl that indeed he had seen it. It had been very bright. The man told the girl that the woman was there. She understood. The boy piped in and said that the lady looked familiar to him. He also said that her eyes were strange. They were a shade of greenish blue that the boy had never seen. He said that they seemed like the eyes of a goddess.

The man and girl both laughed at the boy as the man said, "you just had a crush on her. She sweetened your coffee and your ego at the same time." The boy joined in the laughter. They were all in a very nice mood. Today was going to be an adventure.

The fishing turned out to be fantastic. The man and girl caught many fish in a short time. Unfortunately, they also caught a lot of turtles, so their bait would only last so long. The man had gotten some leeches the day before and convinced the others to try putting them on their hooks. The boy jumped right into the task, but the girl hesitated. The man told her that leeches were a part of nature and that we shouldn't be afraid of them. Movies had given them a bad rap.

The girl understood what her uncle told her. He had told her to never let fear control you. She picked up the leech and put it on its hook. It was not so bad. The man looked to his niece with respect. She truly was one of their clan.

A bald eagle swooped over the group, maybe ten feet above their heads. It seemed like the bird was giving its approval to the girl for facing her fears. The man had studied these birds. This one was a juvenile. The spotted colors told the story. It flew into the top of a tree, maybe fifty feet away and watched the family.

The boy had not been catching any fish. He had been getting very frustrated. His grandpa and cousin were reeling them in. They had caught bass, sunfish, and bluegill, while he stood idly by, watching with envy.

Finally, the boy had enough. The fishing pole was discarded, and he settled for just the line and a hook. Dropping the filament next to the dock, he immediately caught a fish. After the fifth or sixth fish, the boy caught in ten minutes, the man and girl took notice. They were very happy the boy was finally catching something. The man remembered the boy's dad, around the same age, fishing in the same fashion. It gave the man a knowing feeling. DNA was a very strange thing. The boy had never once fished with his father, but his technique was the same.

The storm began to brew in the distance. It brought back memories of a dream the man had the night before. In it, they were all fishing on the dock, and it suddenly began to thunder and lightning. Toomey had appeared and pointed toward the parking lot. Its motions became frantic, as the others looked on while still fishing. This spot was one not to give up at any cost, was his thoughts in the dream. The bolts ripped around them, almost like they were aiming for the family. Finally, they dropped the gear and ran for the car. A solid bolt of energy came from the heavens and struck Toomey in the top of its head. The lightning had shot out of the eye sockets and converged on the fishers. All three of them had been hit by a single bolt, which had been transmitted through Toomey. The dream now made the man very uneasy. This was a lot like his premonition.

The man looked to his phone. He had a satellite program on it and could track the weather. With the app, they needed no weather forecaster.

A stranger came out of the bushes, down the steps, and onto the dock. He was an older gent and looked very familiar to the man. He kept his face turned slightly, so the man never got a good look at the fellow. The stranger came right up to the man and asked how the fishing was going. The man told him "great", and they began to talk like old friends. Fishing was the main topic, but more was thrown into the mix. The man thought that people in Minnesota were very friendly folks. The stranger talked about the impending storm and told the man to be careful.

The words from his sister echoed in his mind.

The stranger, while walking away, told the man that they were awfully nice people for being from California. The man didn't quite know how to take this statement. He didn't realize people from California had such a bad rap here. "Our family speaks the word of peace," the man said to the stranger, as he was ambling up the boat dock. The man waved but did not turn around. He disappeared into the thick Minnesota brush, with the stormy gusts covering his path.

The clouds had begun to get very close. The winds had picked up to the point where the three had to take off their hats or risk losing them. The man and girl had slowly begun to pack up the gear, all the while with a line in the water. They didn't want to stop fishing, but the rain was coming. The satellite confirmed the intensity of this storm. It also confirmed the nearness. Thunder had begun to crack in the near distance. When a bolt of lightning was immediately followed by thunder, the man and girl ran toward the car.

The boy said he was going to fish just a bit longer. The girl turned and yelled for him to get his shit together and get to the car. The boy nor the man had ever seen the girl like that. She had just taken charge, and she was very good at it. By the time they got to the edge of the trees, the large drops of rain had begun. By the time they got to the car, thirty feet away, the downpour was starting. The boy still had not arrived after they had all the gear loaded. The girl said she would go gather him up. She disappeared less than ten steps into her trek in a shower of wetness. The rain had begun with force.

The man couldn't see anything through the rain. He was very concerned about the girl and boy. He had not even got into the shelter of the minivan. He stood in the heavy rain, dripping wet, looking in the abyss. A dark shadow appeared from the torrent, and the man was thankful. It turned out not to be his niece and grandson, though.

It was the man he had met on the dock earlier. He stepped out of the wall of water, right up to the man. The man recognized the stranger now. Earlier, the stranger's face was covered by his hat and the angle of his head. Also, the man had been focused on fishing, and the guy had been a distraction. Now he realized who the stranger was. It was the same man he had met at the Grand Canyon and befriended there. This same guy, or someone who looked just like him, seemed to keep popping up on their trip.

The stranger seemed taller to the man and was now wearing dark glasses. He spoke with a strange accent that seemed to originate from these parts, but the man could not be sure. It was an accent that seemed to incorporate many different dialects, thick and guttural, but flowing at the same time. The stranger had not spoken with this accent down on the dock. He said to the man, "some folks get hit by lightning around these parts."

"Are these people alright?" The man asked, while waving toward the campground full of campers.

"I don't think so," replied the stranger, as he faded back into the downpour. His shadow trailed for a few feet, but then his presence was gone. The water had absorbed the being.

The man had a very bad feeling. He had these feelings before, and this one was a whopper. He knew that something terrible had happened. He raced back to the dock but could see nothing in the rain. If not for the guardrails, he would have been lost. He felt along the rails while calling their names. He was getting very worried about the others.

He went to both ends of the dock but there were no signs of the boy or girl. The boy's fishing gear was still in a corner, but there were no people. The man looked in the water next to the dock. This is the exact spot that the boy had been fishing.

He saw a shadow in the water and got down on his hands and knees to investigate. He had to hang his head through the railing of the dock to get close enough to see through the deluge of rain.

In the water, about five feet from the surface, was the boy. The girl was by his side. They were only about three feet from the side of the wood structure. The two seemed to be standing on the bottom of the lake and were looking skyward. Their eyes were wide open, and it looked like they were staring directly at the man. There was a look on their faces of serenity and contentedness. They looked both at peace and happy at the same time. It was the same look his sister had in his dream the night before.

His heart filled with heaviness. This could not be happening. They were both excellent swimmers.

The man leaped into action. He had never been one to panic and was always ready in an emergency. He jumped onto the rail of the dock, barely touching the wood as he leaped toward the water below. Just as his feet hit the water, a large lightning bolt tore out of the sky. The stone in the man's pocket, Toomey, acted like a lightning rod, which attracted the electricity. It absorbed the strength of the lightning and acted as a superconductor. The energy threw the man, already in motion, deep into the water. After the turbulence of the water had settled, the man was next to the boy and girl. His resting spot would be where it was supposed to be, with his people. He too was looking skyward.

The last thought that went through his mind was one of peace. He had accomplished his mission. This was the way things were meant to be.

The sound of the garage door opening woke the man. "What happened to us?" the boy asked from the back seat, just coming out of sleep.

"Yeah," said the girl, "I was having the weirdest dream right now. How did we get back to aunties house?"

The man was wondering the same thing as the girl was speaking. "How had they gotten back to the house?" The rain was still coming down at a furious pace. The last thing he remembered was running to the van. There was a faint recollection of stopping to get gas, but something had happened. They had not been able to fuel up and had come home instead. He couldn't remember if that had been a dream or not. His clothes were damp, but it was obvious that he had not been out in this rain for long. His clothes were not nearly wet enough for that.

"I think we must have just fallen asleep or something," the man said to the other two. They did not believe him. At the same time, he did not believe himself. Something very weird had just happened to them. He looked at his phone and saw that it was eight. They hadn't been here very long.

He had to do a double take on the picture on his phone. It was a picture of his niece holding a very large northern pike. He would guess it was a twenty-pound monster. She was wearing the same clothes as now. The man couldn't remember the girl catching a pike. They had not caught anything over one pound.

He looked to the girl to show her the picture and noticed something different about her. Her skin seemed to be darker than normal and one of her eyes seemed to twitch, ever so slightly. The man asked if she was alright, and she said of course she was. She returned with an "are you all right" back at her uncle with a made-up voice. The three of them laughed at this. They needed some laughter with all the strange things happening.

They left the gear and headed into the house, through the garage. The house was silent on entering. The man thought that someone must have been watching for them and opened the garage door. He had been mistaken. The door leading into the kitchen was open, too. "How had that door been open?" They wondered. They took off their shoes and headed into different directions of the house. The boy went downstairs, while the man and girl went back down the hall to their bedrooms. Shadows seemed to part ways as the two of them walked down the passageway. The spirits ran rampant when the two weren't there. When they were present, the shadows gave them space.

The man was concerned about the happenings in this house. He wasn't worried about his well-being. It was all about his sister. He could see in the last two days that something was affecting her in this house. Spirits and energy affected us all in a different way. Shadows permeated this house. The man felt a darkness lurking somewhere here, hidden but right in the open at the same time. The other energies stayed away from this one. It was different. This energy was bad.

The woman and their dog were just waking up. She was very happy to see her husband home safely. She said she had been having terrible dreams since they had left that morning. Her dreams had something to do with lightning. She was so worried about them. She had heard the storm coming and was hoping that they were on their way back. She hopped out of bed and gave the man a big hug. The dog jumped on her naked butt, tail wagging. The canine wanted in on that hugging, too. The man left his wife to get dressed and went into the kitchen to make some coffee. His sister had just beat him to that task.

"What's up," was the greeting they had shared since they were small. It was the same as they shared today. The niece came into the room and shared the same greeting. The man couldn't get over how much the family was alike. Their traits were so similar in many ways. The man could always see the traits in his niece that she had inherited from her parents, but on this trip, his understanding of this had been tripled.

The three talked about the strange things in the house. They could all feel the energies. The man and girl told the sister about all the weird things happening already this day. She understood what they meant about all the dimensions lining up, creating a twilight zone of a day to follow. She too had days like this. This was to be one of those days. She had felt the numbers coincide since waking up.

Just like before, whenever their family got together, strange things were going to happen.

"Who opened the garage door for us?" the man asked his sister.

"Nobody opened it. I was wondering how you guys got inside," the sister answered.

Over coffee, the man asked his sibling where her boyfriend was. She said he was still in bed. He was sad that he had not been able to go fishing with them.

He then asked his sister where the boarder was and how he had come to live in her house. She looked blankly at the man and gave an unsure answer. She said something about trying to help the son of a close friend. The man knew where the darkness in the house was coming from. It was from this guy. He hid his darkness well, but the man could see right through it. The girl also could see the darkness surrounding this guy. Of all the energies in the house, this one was foreign.

The live-in seemed like he was a fill in actor being placed in a sitcom, whose cast were long time regulars. But that fill-in was just inserted to destroy the harmony of the cast and bring an end to the play. That is how it felt this guy was. It seemed like someone had sent him, or inserted him, into his sister's life. However, he did not fit in. His stories did not add up. He was an implant.

There was no way this guy could end the harmony in this family. They had been through way too much for that to ever happen. His ways were going to create problems, for himself. The man had seen these kinds of souls many times in his life. Half the people he met had the same kind of energy. They were the balance. He wasn't scared of the darkness. He embraced it. The light was always stronger.

The sister whipped up some breakfast burritos, and the family grubbed down to stories of fishing, turtles stealing bait, loons, and bald eagles. It was an awesome morning to be with the sister. The boyfriend had joined the others and carried on with his jovial way. His way was of genuine friendliness. The man still seemed a bit under the weather and was unable to eat any of the breakfast his girlfriend had prepared. The boarder took care of the leftovers.

The man told his sister that they should go to Duluth and stomp around a bit. He had been telling her about an inversion table for her back and wanted to go and buy one for her. The boyfriend was just not up to it and went back to bed. The boarder happily said he would take the vacant seat to Duluth.

The man said anyone who wanted to stay was welcome to. He was going to Duluth to buy a table for his sister. He wanted to help her end her years of back pain. The best gift he could ever give his sibling.

The man had learned about the inversion table from a holistic doctor whom he used to go to. He had gone specifically for back pain. It was not the first doctor whom he would go to for this problem, but he would be the last. The doctor told him about the inversion, allowing blood to flow back into your cartilage inside your spine. This would make it soft again and your back pains would be alleviated. It was the only good advice a doctor had ever given him regarding his back. He had gone initially to get his medical marijuana card, but ended up finding the cure. The doctor told him that most doctors told you to get surgery or take a bunch of pills, or both. They were just out for your money. There were big profits in keeping you in their care. It was the only honest doctor the man had ever met.

The inversion table was the only thing proven to cure you. The doctor made no money from this prescription. It was something seldom talked about. Money was the concern of most doctors and the health care conglomerate. Healing the patients was the concern of few.

The man had continued to go to this doctor for three more years. One day, three men in dark suits and sunglasses came into the office and gunned down everyone there. The receptionist, billing lady, and all the patients were killed in a hail of gunfire. Even the janitor had been shot thirty-eight times. There had never been a single suspect. All the surveillance tapes had been erased in the entire building. All the witnesses had been killed.

The family was all on board for the day trip to Duluth. The sister said she too was going, which prompted the boarder to repeat his reservation. This was the kind of guy who could not miss out being around the others. Thinking he was going to miss out on something, he had to go. The kind of person who never did a thing, just waited for others to act and then jump on board.

Again, the stranger sat in the front seat. The man now knew for sure that he was indeed an implant by some strange agency to keep an eye on his sister. She was too wise. She held the knowledge, and that was always something to worry the greed. Their spies would keep the woman in check.

A few miles down the road, there was a house on fire. The man thought it strange; he had not seen any smoke. The house was set down a driveway, which was lined with trees. The man saw the flash as they approached, and looked right at the inferno. All that remained were the chimney and a few boards, which had been the frame. The house had completely burned to the ground. The fire department was standing there with the homeowners. Obviously, there was absolutely nothing they could do. It was just a flaming skeleton of the once proud home.

The man could have sworn that he saw a large figure of a man standing in the middle of the fire. A large bird was on his shoulder. The image was gone before he could focus and be sure. It had been a small opening in which to see the inferno, and now it had passed. He excitedly asked the others if they had seen that, and his sister said she had. All the others hadn't seen a thing. The man didn't know how that was possible. The man asked his sister if she had seen 'it', and she said she did. The boy asked what 'it' was, and they said it was nothing. Just some game they had played since they were kids.

Some more miles down the road, they passed an old elementary school with signs out front advertising a yard sale. The family couldn't pass this up. They loved second hand shopping. The boy agreed to stay behind with the dogs. It was humid this day, in between storms. The windows would have to be left down. Somebody would have to stay behind. The man told his grandson that he would get him something good for being a team player. He was proud of the boy.

The family split up in different directions when they entered the doors. A sporting goods sale straight ahead caught the attention of the man and his wife. The girl always hung with her uncle at yard sales. Today was no different. These three were close. Their bond was tight, and they kept their energy close.

The sister took a right and headed to the other section. The other guy who was tagging along went in a completely opposite direction than any of the others. There was not even a sale in the direction he went.

It was a gold mine of sporting goods where the man, woman, and niece had decided to go. The man bought the boy a bow. The grandson was very much into archery and would love this. There were many fishing reels, too, and the man bought six. The prices were so inexpensive that the man thought for a moment that he was dreaming. These were the kind of sales that he hoped for every time he walked up to a yard sale or thrift store.

He had been talking to the woman running the sale, and she said it was mostly her husband's stuff. He rebuilt every one of these reels. The sales lady was standing in front of the green chalkboard. The man could see the aura of the woman. It was very bright and almost pinkish. The man felt a very good vibe from this person. He could tell that she felt the same toward their group. She told them that her husband would be there in a couple of days, and they should come by and meet him. He was an avid fisherman and liked to talk fishing.

Down the hall to the next sale, the man felt like he was in school. It reminded him of movies of old schools, but not like the one he had gone to. His school had been more modern, nineteen sixties, and more open. This one was early nineteen-hundreds and all one building. It was expansive and had a lot of character. The man could see shadows running through every part of its halls. Children had left much energy behind in these shadowed hallways.

The second sale was a compendium of items that had no fit with each other. The man and girl dug through the books for sale. They were mostly school books, but the two were happy to find a couple that interested them. The best find was the book on electromagnetism. It was very basic and made for kids, but it was exactly what the man needed to know. He would figure out the rest. Since coming to the north, electromagnetism had been weighing in on his thoughts very much. Now, coincidentally, he had found a book on that very subject.

While digging through the rest of the store, a radio broadcast came on warning of an impending tornado. The store was going to close. The family would like to have dug through the stuff a little more, but it was not meant to be. The sister had seen a bicycle for sale, but there was no room in the minivan for it.

The man promised his sister that he would bring her back in a couple of days to pick up the bike. He wanted to come back to this store anyway. Everyone agreed. As they were headed out the school doors, the boarder came out of one of the classroom doors with a look of guilt on his face. The others asked him what he was doing, but he said he had gotten lost. The man was getting fed up with this person.

It was back on the road to Duluth, with the storm threatening the whole way. The boy was in the back seat with the biggest grin. He couldn't believe his grandpa had got him a bow. The reels, too, made the boy's mind race with adventure. He and his grandpa always fished together, since the boy was a very small child.

Thanks to the woman and niece using GPS, the family found the corporate chain store quickly. It was in a shopping mall, like they usually were. The man and his group went in search of the table. His sister walked a little slower, and her friend even slower.

The man heard some other patrons talking shit about them, and it could have made him angry. He was above petty words, though, and would ignore what he heard. He was here for his sister, and that is what mattered. He wanted to heal her aching body, just like his had been healed years before. Finally, they found their treasure, using the team effort that they were so used to. The purchase went smoothly, like it always did with cash. Soon the boy was carrying the table out to the car on his shoulders. The family had only had to endure seven minutes in the corporate trap.

The clouds had become very dark when they were in the store. The man told the others that perhaps today, was the day, they saw a tornado. The boarder tried to scold the man for saying this, but he just laughed as a reply. This guy knew nothing about their family. The man had seen a tornado before and was ready for the next. He was not stupid and was not going to get close to one for a picture or some dumb shit. He was just going to look at its awesome power from a distance.

Downtown Duluth was the next place to wander around. This would be the biggest city to visit on the trip. It was a nice enough town. However, the man could easily see the hardships the greed had brought to this area. There were so many homeless people. The man had seen the homeless population in America rise throughout his lifetime. He knew full well why that had happened. It was the greed. The elite sat in their penthouses and laughed at the hardships of the masses, which they created.

The family went into a store that they had seen advertised for hundreds of miles on the highway. They sold clothes and other merchandise. The man wanted to check out some of their self-proclaimed world class underwear. The man was quickly back out the door when he found out that the underwear was thirty-five dollars a pair. There was no way he was going to pay that kind of money. He was not a stingy guy. He was a sensible guy. This was all part of the greed. He wanted nothing to do with it.

Behind downtown Duluth is Lake Superior. The man hadn't seen the lake since he was in boot camp so many years before. Now they were walking on a foot path looking at the broad expanse of the grand waterway. The storm had been increasing when they were in the store. Now the wind was really beginning to get blustery. The sky had turned dark, and there was a faint rumble of thunder in the distance. You could feel the drop in the barometric pressure. The tempest was approaching quickly.

There were very cool bronze statues in the park and the man took pictures. They were of an abstract nature that seemed familiar to the man, but he could not exactly place them. The artist's name, too, seemed so common to the man, but it was just out of the grasp of his memory.

The boy and girl couldn't believe the size of the lake. It looked like an ocean, the boy had said. An object far out on the lake caught their attention. It looked to be a large monolith. It was very far in the distance, so it was hard to discern what it might be. It looked huge to the group. It was much taller than a ship. The man asked his sister if there were oil rigs on the lake. She said she didn't think so. Even if there were, this one would have to be over a thousand feet tall, judging by the height and distance. Others along the walk were stopping to look at the strange object in the lake. Most of them were filming with their cameras. The boarder spoke up and said that it was an optical illusion. He said they happened on the lake all the time. All the spectators looked to the guy with disgust, like he had told a very racist joke. They all looked back to the lake with wonder.

The weather was getting worse and worse. It was time to get back to Hoyt Lake.

As soon as they got in the car, there was an emergency broadcast system alert on the radio. There was a tornado spotted nearby this area. The man felt a rush of excitement. He knew it was a little crazy to want to see a tornado, but he couldn't help himself. He loved seeing and feeling different things. He felt that seeing as much as possible was what fueled your imagination. If you weren't feeding your brain imagery, then you could never come up with new ideas for creating.

The drive back was a stormy one. The winds had begun to really throw the car around. Lightning and large drops of rain pelted the car. A couple of times, they hit some intense hail, but no tornado. It kept looking like the clouds could swirl, but it never happened. The woman and boy were happy about that. They thought the man crazy for wanting to put them and their whole trip in jeopardy. They knew the man was a little nutty, but this was a little too much involvement with the others.

The niece, on the other hand, was all in to spot a twister.

When they were about halfway home, the man missed the turnoff. The self-proclaimed navigator scolded him and complained that they would have to go all the way to the next exit and then turn around. The man ignored the brash voice that was thrown at him. He was one with patience and did not lose his mind over small things like this.

He went to the next exit, barely two miles away, and flipped it. The whole ordeal had taken an extra five minutes. A small gas station on the road back to the highway filled up the very empty minivan. "All is well," was all the man said when they were back on the highway. The boarder growled softly, so as only the man could hear, not the others. The man broke out in laughter.

The man had been paying attention to the countryside the whole way. He had been to central Canada before, and this looked similar. The man noticed that this was iron land. His sister told him that a whole lot of the metal was pulled from the earth here. The man thought about this a lot. His tattoo machines ran off electromagnetism and the key metal was iron. So, maybe this area was the core on the planet that the electrons raced around, creating magnetism. Gravity might just originate from this spot on the earth.

The man had read about how an ancient meteor had hit this region billions of years ago. It had hit when the Earth was still soft. The celestial body had sunk into the planet, leaving behind its large iron deposit. It covered thousands of square miles in this area and had been mined for the last couple of centuries.

The man was beginning to figure out this area. It was very different, geologically, and the people. They almost seemed like robots. These people were affected from this iron in the ground. It was affecting their polarity to the planet and to themselves. They were truly living in a magnetic field.

The rain was coming down when they got back home. Minnesota was a place of rain cells passing through, spreading its drops only to move to the next suburb, leaving the sun behind in its tail. The man said he would cook dinner for the group and did just that. He could tell that his sister had become a little worn out from all the running around and wanted to give her a rest. He knew that their visit was creating a stress on her and her boyfriend's peacefulness. He wanted to be the least burden as possible. This is how their parents had taught them, and the way he and his sister lived their lives.

The sister's daughter arrived after dinner. She lived six hours away with her three kids and ex-husband. The man had been watching out the window for their arrival. His niece had come out to California three months earlier for the funeral of her aunt. She had brought her kids and come up to the man and woman's house for the day. It had been seventeen years since the man had seen his niece. They had picked up right where they left the conversation at the last meeting. The two had always been close, and that bonding was passed on to her kids.

The kids ran up the walk and hugged the man tightly. The older daughter was not there. The two youngest were four and six. The older sister had remained at her cousin's house and were coming the next day. She was ten. The hugs passed quickly as the kids ran into the house to make their presence known. They were cool little kids, and the man looked forward to hanging out with them some more. The niece shared a big hug with the man and introduced her ex-husband, who had his arms full of luggage and toys. He told the man he would shake hands in a moment. The man liked this guy instantly. He could see a genuine kindness in him that made him want to get to know him better.

The house was full of talk after their arrival. Pods of conversation were scattered throughout the dwelling. There was so much to talk about. Being around your family always makes conversations flow like creamy paint. There is never a lack of things to say. You are all so much the same from your DNA. Even the kids fit right into the equation. You all flow as one.

It had been a long day and the family began to fade. The sister and her boyfriend went to lay down. The man gathered up the rest and headed into the basement. The niece had brought some weed, and they were looking forward to the first smoke in two weeks. They still had their cookies, which they sampled daily, but a nice smoke was always wonderful. The end of the movie was waiting for them, and they all took their seats.

Something was wrong with the movie. It was the same movie, but now the quality was kind of fuzzy. There were subtitles on the bottom in a language they had never seen. The movie didn't start from where they stopped it the night before. It started about twenty minutes before the spot. The sound seemed to be riddled with a strange noise that seemed to be making a pattern. "Funny," the man said, "all this happens with this movie about the greed; a movie about exposing their true kind. Maybe they know and are watching us." the man said jokingly. The power going off punctuated his words. It was only briefly before it flickered back, but it was enough for the whole group to look oddly at each other.

They watched the rest of the flick while smoking it up. The boarder came out of his little closet of a room in the corner of the basement. He tried to sit in on the smoke session, but the niece who had just arrived shut that down. She obviously did not like this stranger any more than the rest of them. The family passed the smoke as the guy looked on with anger.

The man said he was tired of this movie and was going to bed. He planned on getting up at the crack of dawn and fishing if anyone else wanted to go. The boy and girl said they would be there, as did his sister's daughter. She asked the others to wake her up, but they told her their policy. If you didn't get up, you didn't go. They were not alarm clocks.

Fishing was set for the morning. Now they needed to get some rest.

Walking up the steps, the man felt the presence from the night before that had halted his progress. This time, he knew this energy and passed right through it. He felt a sense of familiarity as his being united with the other for that moment. It felt as though the spirit was an old acquaintance of the man. They understood each other.

The hallway had a mirror at the end. As the man was fumbling for his door handle, movement in the mirror, just two feet to his left, made him spin in that direction. It was his shadow looking back at him, but it was not standing in the same position. His reflection was facing forward while he was standing sideways. His reflection seemed to be signaling something to him with its hands, but the man didn't understand. The gesture was of a large circle with a point in the upper left side. The reflection faded immediately when the bedroom door opened. The suddenness of the situation startled the man. It had made him jump slightly. His sister was there. "What are you doing?" she asked.

"I honestly don't know," the man answered. "There is a lot of weird shit happening in your house."

"That's what I've been saying all along," she said. "Everyone thinks I'm crazy. I'm glad you are here. I knew you would see it also. I know I'm not just imagining these things. Now, everyone maybe will get off my back."

"See you in the morning," was exchanged as the two went in their separate doors. The woman was fast asleep, their dog cuddled by her side. The man was very tired, but was not going to be left behind on his story. Many things had happened this day, and they needed to be written down. He took up a chair at the end of the bed and began his tale of the day. He was relieved to find the page blank when he opened the journal.

The man had written a few pages and was nodding in and out of sleep. He didn't even know how he was writing. Once he started, it was like his soul took over from his brain and poured the words onto the paper. He was just about finished for the night when the woman sat straight up in bed.

"What's wrong?" he asked his wife.

"Did you just sit on the bed?" she asked with wide eyes. She seemed kind of pale to the man.

"No, why?" the man asked the startled woman.

"Something just sat right there on the edge of the bed," she said, pointing to a spot at the bottom by her feet. The man, barely four feet away, looked at the spot where she was pointing. There did seem to be an indentation in the mattress. He felt the presence of the energy, even as the being began to materialize. At first, it was just a little shift in the air, like heat over the barbecue. Then it began to take on a foggy outline of a form. The spirit continued to gain sustenance, until the man could tell it was a human shape. It was looking in the direction of the woman, and she was looking back with her mouth open. She was in shock by what she was seeing.

The spirit slowly turned its entire form toward the man. It looked directly at the man and closed the distance between them until it was only a foot away. The spirit was looking right into the man's eyes. The feeling of oneness within the man was very strong.

He knew this spirit well. The energy, floating in front of him, looked exactly like he did. Consciousness left him.

The man woke in the middle of the night, very stiff. He had fallen asleep in the chair. His book and pen were lying on the ground. Someone had shut off the light on the dresser. He crawled into bed. It felt warm, like he had just got up. Looking at the clock, it read 3:33. It was always the same time when he looked at the clock. The numbers always matched up when it came to time.

It felt like there was someone else in the room, but he was too tired to think about it. The smell of Sulfur stung his sinuses.

The bed moved slightly, but the energy was gone. He closed his eyes again, sleep overcame him.

CHAPTER 24

The story was unfolding. The man had always thought he saw the truth but now things were clearer than ever. After each family member had died, his insight became more and more clear. Each time, following death, a different kind of truth would surface to mingle with the others. It was as if the man absorbed some of the wisdom from his family as they passed into their next dimension. He felt the path to true enlightenment was on its way. He was a patient man, though.

First the story would have to be told. The clearer things got, the easier the words came. With the story came the enlightenment.

The man and girl had talked about a dark cloud hanging over their family. This shadow had followed them for two years. They had made the decision to leave this cloud behind for good on this trip. It was time to move on from the tragedies that had gripped their lives like a vise. The sun had come out again. A new day had opened in their existences. The Gods were once again shining, sending the darkness back to their shadows.

The energy the man had felt the first days in his sister's house had diminished. The man thought that maybe it was because of all the family that had gathered. The other niece arriving with her kids had amplified the energy. That much aura in the house had made it too crowded for the normal spirits. They had gone elsewhere for a bit, a little vacation of their own. The dark forces had been quieted completely. Harmony had returned a balance to the energy in the house.

The man, girl and boy once again got up at the crack of dawn to go fishing. The fishing here was too good to pass up. With the hole being so close to the house, they knew that they would never forgive themselves if they didn't fish as much as possible. The older niece had told them to wake her up, but the man had told her his policy. She was not up and ready.

His sister was up already, coffee brewing. The man enjoyed a cup with his sibling and niece as the boy got ready. He and his niece and sister stood around the kitchen talking the familiar talk of family. The man once again asked his sister if she wanted to go fishing, but she declined.

The three were loyal to their word and to each other. The man spoke of this on the drive to the dock. If you said you were going to do something, then you had to do it. Otherwise you were just a talker. This family was not talkers. They would not say anything about their future activities until they were certain that it would happen. They were people who spoke their words with respect.

The three already knew this spot and did well in its waters. There was no need to spend precious fishing time looking for another spot. This time, there wasn't even a boat on the dock. The family didn't really know what day it was nor did they care. They were on vacation and it felt great. The boy had his pole-less line in the water long before the other two. He caught three fish before his grandpa and cousin even had their line in. He had caught ten by the time they caught one. By the time they went home that day, the boy would catch more than fifty fish.

The fishing wasn't as good this day, except for the small bluegill that the boy was raking in. The niece caught a nice largemouth bass and a few bluegills. The man fared the same, but his was a small mouth bass. His stomach started to rumble, and he knew he was going to have to go back to the house for a toilet break. He had felt bad for bailing on the other niece and her kids anyhow. They did not get to see each other very often, and the man wanted to take advantage of their time.

The man and his niece rolled up to the house. The older girl and her ex were there wanting an explanation. They said they were sorry, but they couldn't wait. It would have taken them an hour to get ready and in that time, they had been fishing. The man excused himself. On the toilet, he got on his phone. He hadn't used the device much on this trip, except for directions or the weather, but there were no magazines.

The entire trip he had been having strange things happen to his phone. Reception was sporadic at best. Texts would sometimes go through and other times not. Even the time on the screen didn't always seem right. He felt it best to leave the phone alone. He really didn't like the device anyway. Everything made by the greed was bad. This little device was much more than a phone, he thought. It told the entire world anything they wanted to know about a person. It was also a tracking device and could easily be used to control people. He did not put anything past the greed. Their ways were completely evil, while wearing the mask of good.

The man checked the satellite, and it looked like clear weather for the next few hours. There was plenty of time to get some more fishing in. He checked the messages, but there were none. He had only received messages from the others in the group the entire way. He had called his son in California a few times while on the road. His son had said that he also sent text and pictures to the man, but they had never arrived. He also said that only some pictures from the Grand Canyon and then one from Minnesota had come through. But that had been back in Wisconsin when they had talked. He had asked him what the picture was, and he told his dad that it looked like him and his sister standing together. It was all blurry, almost like it was underwater.

The photo was another strange occurrence that the man perceived. When he had talked to his son from Wisconsin, he had not even been to his sister's house yet. It was impossible that he could have sent this picture out to California. He had looked on his own phone for the picture, but it was not there. His son had tried to send the picture back, but it never arrived. The phones were part of the oddities of the trip. Strangeness had encompassed their entire journey.

The man's wife was more than happy that all the others were going fishing. She and the dog would have some nice time to relax. They were going to be back on the road in a couple of days, and she was going to need to get some rest. The sister, too, said to have a good time, she didn't feel like fishing. The boyfriend came out to say hello but the man could see his condition had not improved in the slightest. He would be staying behind once again.

The boarder came from the basement and asked the others if he could come along. The older niece asked if he had any fishing gear, and the other guy said no. "That is your answer then," the niece had said flatly. There was no emotion in her voice, because she held no emotion for this guy mooching off her mom.

The expanded group, excitedly, jumped into the minivan and headed back to the fishing hole.

The man saw the gift in the small children. They had a way of seeing things that the man recognized. The two siblings fought over just about anything, but the care and love were apparent. They reminded the man so much of him and his sister when they were young. The man so wished that their older sister could have come with them, too. At ten, she was the one in charge of the others. The man thought oversaw everything. The man really wanted to get to know these kids and see if they, too, like his brother and sister, held the trinity. The torch was to be passed. The man felt it burning. He wanted to see who would be the next bearer.

The man had seen the gift in others of his family. Theirs had been a big clan. Many of them had not seen the gift, while others ignored it. Many of the family abused drugs and alcohol, clouding the gift and their better judgment. The man had been through it all. He had seen all aspects of the gift and how not to abuse it. It was a gift, after all. Only fools stomped on gifts. The mind was the greatest gift of all. You just had to be awake.

Creativity was the conscious, and imagination was the subconscious. Both intertwined right in the middle.

The boy was happy to see the others return. The man and girl went ahead, as the niece and her family got their things together. The boy had been looking for them and waved as soon as they came out of the bushes. The girl waved back, distracting her attention from the three-foot garter snake on the path. The lazy snake slowly slithered into the greenery, just as the man called out to the girl. It was the exact same kind of snake that he and his nephew had seen nineteen months before, when moving bricks. The boy came over and told them about all the fish that he had caught. He had stopped counting quite some fish ago. Excitement was pouring from the boy's being.

After dropping their gear and the worms, the man and girl went back up to help the others. The little kids were good, but they were little. They got to the clearing, and the ex-husband shouted out that they had it all. Arms full of gear, they made their approach. The man and girl turned around to see the garter snake again, sunning itself on the warm dock. This time, the girl saw it in all its beauty. The creature seemed to share a moment with the two before slithering away. The two looked at each other and smiled. Pachymama had once again showed them the beauty.

A symphony of voices approached. The rest of the family had arrived.

The fishing still had not improved. The wind had strengthened, but not the bites. It was good times for the family. The man and niece caught up on old times, while all three cousins became homies. The ex-husband was well liked by the man. Conversation between the two flowed very easily. The man had respect for the ex, he was a great father. He was the one who got the kids ready and got their poles in the water. The man always had a deep respect for a good parent. There were many bad parents. It made the good ones, shine. The future of the children lay in the hands of their elders.

The loons had been calling loudly this morning. The sun flickered off the water, which was choppy from the wind. The man was staring at the speckles of light dancing across the top of the water. He started to get very sleepy. Someone behind him said something, but it sounded like he was in a tunnel. A loud roaring buzz zipped by, like the sky had been cut in two. Moments after the sound, the man saw the flash of silver whiz across the sky, from horizon to horizon. The water began to boil and the dock seemed to shake like they were in an earthquake. The sun was the last thing the man saw as his head hit the dock.

The man woke up back at the house. He was lying in bed, and his wife was in the chair at the foot of it. She jumped to his side as she saw him stirring. She took his hand and looked to his eyes to see his condition. The pair had been married a long time. The woman knew her husband would not like a bunch of questions right off.

The man squeezed her hand and blinked out the haze. Coming back to consciousness had been very difficult. He had been in a very deep place of sleep, like he was in a third or fourth layer of dream. Like his dream was in the basement of his mind. A bright light was all he could remember. "What happened?" he asked his wife.

"You were fishing and just fell down. You had told the girl that you were not feeling good earlier, before you came home. Then you said you were feeling bad again, but kept on fishing. Next thing they knew, you were on the planks of the dock."

The man felt around the back of his head. There didn't seem to be any kind of lump there. There was a terrible pain in his head, but it wasn't from the back, it was from the front. His hand went to his forehead and was alarmed at what he felt. The tattoo in the center of his head was now much more than a tattoo. It was raised like an eye would be. The lids were sealed shut, but the man could feel a seam and even small eyelashes. He pulled his hand away. He had been wearing his hat for the last three days, except when in bed. He didn't want anyone asking questions about the eye. He was still somewhat embarrassed. It made him look like a robotic fortune teller in a wood display, asking for your quarter in exchange for your fortune; Voltar the Magnificent or something.

"How did I get back home?" he asked.

"Our niece drove you home. They had spoken about it and the boy said the girl should drive, and they all agreed. They had put you in the back and brought you right home. The boy and ex-husband carried you in. That was about an hour ago. You must have been exhausted or something. It's not like you to pass out like that."

"I didn't pass out," he said. "Something flew by and stole my energy. It sent some weird wind our way. The water reflections increased into a binary pattern. It almost hypnotized me. I felt the energy getting stolen from my being. I fought the thieves with my mind and all the willpower I could muster. Who knows what would have happened to me otherwise. It was like that time I told you that I was touched by the hand of God. This was similar, but a completely different kind of energy. This one was not so good."

The sister came in and said she was happy he was alright. The man was getting out of bed and putting on his hat when she entered. She told him that he didn't have to wear the hat anymore. They had all seen the eye. They didn't exactly know what it meant, but they were accepting of it. Tonight, when the time was right, there would be talks that had been coming for a very long time. She told her brother that she had saved him some breakfast, but with the kids around, it wasn't going to last long.

The man was eating his plate when his niece came in. He was out on the patio and welcomed her conversation. "That was weird what happened out there," the girl said. "I saw that thing zip by. I don't know why the others didn't see, but it was there. The light had got all bright and the air grew very still. Next thing we all knew, you were on the ground. I swear uncle, for a split second when the craft flew by, you disappeared. I was looking right at you. Something was calling to me in my mind to look your way. I know it was your subconscious. You needed me to see what happened."

The man told the girl that he knew that she knew. He knew the girl was the strongest with the gift. The family had all been strong, but their energy was focused on the girl. She was the one who was to enlighten many.

The man had made it a goal of his to help his niece on her path. The death of her family had been very hard on the eighteen-year old. It had crushed her soul, as it had his. The man had seen it and would do anything to help the girl. She was chosen, though. This had all been predestined long before by unseen numbers. The years since the deaths had brought an awakening in the girl. She saw things the right way. The way most could never even imagine. It brought joy to the man and woman to see their niece doing well. She was on the right path. She was going to fulfill her calling. She was going to make a change.

The man and girl spoke about the spirituality that their family possessed. They were ones who stood for the way of righteousness: The common-sense way to live with your-self, your neighbors, and every living thing around you: The deep belief in the spirituality of the mind and Earth, not one of false religion. This made them outcasts among the Masses.

Their vision used all their senses together, which formed the sixth sense. The sense of wisdom!

The two spoke again of dimensions. How they could be coming in and out of dimensions all the time; passing freely from one realm of existence to another. The man said that the dimensions converged here, at this spot. That is why there were so many spirits about. They always congregated around the seams of the dimensions. It was almost like a waiting area for souls in transit.

The man's wife came in and joined in the end of the conversation. She was always accepted in the talks and would join in when ready. She had always known there were odd things about the family, but she just went with it. She, too, had experienced strange phe-nomena, some before they had met, some after. Since she had met the man, many things had often happened that could be in the category of bizarre. She saw that her husband was fascinated by such things and very in tune to them.

The man knew his wife also had vision. She could see things sometimes that most others couldn't. Each time, the man was surprised that someone else saw the strange-ness besides himself. He could see that his wife thought he was crazy most of the time, but at the same time, he also knew that she believed. Her spirit was going to be a huge part of the things to come. When the energy was going to come together, hers would be strong. The whole picture was coming clear to the man. His eyes were seeing, his mind understood. He felt like he had finally awoken.

The sister joined the others on the patio. The kids, grandson, and boyfriend were all downstairs. It gave the four a great chance to talk. There were many things to say, and time was running out for this trip. The man knew this time was important. He had a feeling he would never see his sister again. Theirs had always been a tight bond, but the physical aspect of it in this dimension was coming to an end. When he saw his sister again, it would be in a different realm.

The man and his sister spoke about their father's family. They had known the German bloodline on their mother's side, but the fathers were cloaked in mystery. Stories their father had told them were not consistent with photos and other info the man had dug up while packing up his mother's house. Their father had told them that his mother had died when they were nine or ten, but there were pictures of their mother and the twins when they were sixteen. The man had never met his grandparents on this side, and his father seldom spoke of them. He often wondered who his ancestors really were, and why their story was so secretive.

Something had always told the man that things were not quite right in their family tree. The gift had begun long before. It had been shunned. The man knew now why others had always looked at him with a slanted eye. People had always looked at their family the same, since the beginning. It was because they were different. They shared a similar DNA with other humans, but it was not the same. It is why other people fell into the distractions handed to them by the greed, while the family stayed far away from it all. They could not be influenced by the madness of the masses. They were their own species.

The sister and niece agreed the whole time. They knew the looks people gave them when they went places. Since they had both been young, the siblings knew they were different. All the people that had come and gone in their lives had proven that. They had never been ones to keep friends for very long. The relationships would get played out, and contact would be lost. It had happened time and time again. For the entire group, this is how it had been. That is why the friendship, the true friendship, was right here with your family. That is why they had never done each other dirty.

The family went into town. There was a dime store there, and the family wanted to go. The man's mother had been a big fan of the dime store back in the day, dragging her kids with her whenever she spotted the bargain spot.

It had been threatening rain all day. The clouds floated through the sky like groups of puffy helium balloons. The family all split into different directions like they normally did in a store. The man quickly realized that this was just a condensed version of a corporate pharmacy. They sold all the same crap, just packed tighter in the small space.

The man found the aisle with the little kids' toys. He had remembered playing with some of these same toys when he was little and on vacation. He wanted to bring a little of that joy to his great niece and nephew, while reliving some of those awesome memories. The children brought the man right back to the time when he was their age. They reminded him so much of his youth with his sister. The children were special. The man could see it in their auras. They had a pure energy. They were the next generation of this family. They would be the next seers.

The lady at the counter was very rude to the man. She was about his age and seemed to have a grudge on the family as soon as they had walked in the door. There had been no one else in the store. The man thought they would be happy to have some customers, but obviously not. The woman and girl had carried in the dogs and it seemed to be a major issue. They held the dogs the whole time. The lady said nothing until after the man paid. Then she spun and barked at the others for bringing in their animals. The man had always tried to be fair and see everything from all points of view. He didn't know what this lady had already been through today. He said very nicely that the clerk could have just told them not to bring the dogs, and they wouldn't have.

The clerk scowled at the man and told him he to go, before she called the cops. He laughed and told her that it was going to seem odd to the officers that he had just spent eighty dollars in this store on toys for kids, now he was going to get arrested because he spoke up for his people. She looked back at him blankly. The man told her that if she had thought with kindness in her heart instead of anger, they wouldn't be in this position right now. "I know who you are," the woman screeched at the man. Her voice reminded him of the Chupacabra sound he used to hear in the San Joaquin valley. "Now get out and never come back."

The man ripped the smelliest fart he could muster as the family left the store. The boy said something about going back in and smacking the lady for talking to his grandpa like that. The man just told the boy to calm down. The woman's life was already in misery. It is why she was acting like that. His fart was her just reward. A younger girl came running out to apologize to the family. The man told the lady that she had nothing to apologize for. She had been perfectly nice; it was the other woman who needed to work on her people skills. He told the lady that good came to the good. The lady's eyes lit up on the man. "I've heard all about you and your group. I didn't know you were around these parts," she said to the man as she looked to him, like he was the answer to all her prayers.

"God bless," the man said to the girl, and they walked off through the parking lot.

The girl was laughing when they piled into the minivan. The man joined in. "You fucking ripped the loudest fart, uncle," the girl choked out. Tears had begun to run down her cheeks, she was laughing so hard.

The man told the others that this was his point. "No matter how good you are to people, no matter how much good energy you project, there would still be darkness all around. When you encountered this kind of negativity, how you react is how your day will follow. A positive reaction to negativity usually brought very positive situations. React negatively, and your day is ruined. All day will be stuck in the thought of how you could have dealt with that better. That is why negativity is best dealt with a fart." The man punctuated his words with a loud fart. Everyone in the car understood. They all laughed loudly and rolled down the windows as fast as possible.

Down the road into Bagley, the sister needed groceries. There wasn't much around this town to do, but the man thought he would walk around anyway. Everyone else asked where he was going, and he said that there was something in this town that they had come for, and he was going to find it. Something was calling to him, pulling him toward a very bright light. It knew his name.

It was just one block away, and the man saw what he had come for. Standing on the sidewalk in front of a quaint little building, was a cutout of a gnome. The man had seen it the day before when they drove by here, but he wasn't sure of what he had seen. Now he was so very sure. His niece and wife had joined him. They knew that when he was on a mission, the man was the one to follow.

The creaky door and small bells welcomed the three visitors. A lady of about fifty greeted the family and made them feel instantly at home. As she was making them some coffee, the man thought how it had just felt like they had gone to an aunt's house, or even grandma's. This lady was so nice and welcoming. It felt as though they had a connection that went deep into their DNA.

The lady's husband came out of the back to meet the newcomers. He, too, was very kind and welcoming. The husband and wife told the others to look around some while they got the coffee ready. The man told his niece that this was what he had just been talking about. Just minutes before, they had met some dark negative energy, they had responded with positive insight, and now they were here, meeting people who shared the light.

The man knew immediately that this husband and wife team could see the way. They, too, looked to the visitors and could see that they knew. The two groups became instant friends.

The husband would make all the repairs and build things for his wife to paint on. It was a very nice setup. This was their gallery. The man could tell right away that the lady painted for the love of it. She did not paint for the love of the money. It was so easy to tell the difference. These two entities had found their creativity and were using the gift every day. They were one with the wisdom.

The man knew that few people would ever find their creativity. It had been blocked by the greed for thousands of years. The man had heard it over and over how people would say they were not creative at all. They had just never tried. The man pitied people like this. His imagination was what got him through the hardest times of his life. When your world seemed like it was crumbling around you, creativity would keep it all in place. This is where happiness and solitude came from. This is when the man was truly at one with the universe.

The others had all come in search of their missing members. The man could tell everyone was impatient to go and said he was coming. All the others left except for the girl. Her life of creativity was just beginning, but she already knew the spirituality of the imagination. Listening to her uncle talk to this woman was enlightening. She, too, was on the path of imagination.

As soon as the others left, the woman's tone took on a more serious note. She asked the man and girl if they felt it. The man asked if she meant the change that was coming. The woman looked at him with a kind of relief. "Then you do know. I thought I was going crazy or something."

"You are not going crazy," the man replied. "We feel it too. Our family is on this road trip right now to find the path to the knowledge. The time will be here soon and people like us are going to be needed to shine the way. Most people are not going to be able to handle the change, but that is okay. It is time for Pachymama to heal and this is the first step. The greed is about to end."

"I had a dream that you two were going to be here today," the woman said. "My husband thought I was crazy, but now I see the recognition in his eyes. Your path has crossed ours today for a reason. Our energy is going to be with you all the way to the Pacific Ocean. Go now, be with your people. You have a mission that is going to shine a light on this planet. Things are going to be beautiful again, like they used to be, thousands of years ago, before the greed. God be in you." The lady hugged the man and his niece and ushered them out the door. She knew it was not right to keep the two. Every minute of their trip was important. She was happy to have spent a couple of those minutes with them. She truly felt enlightened by the visit. When they had gone, the woman locked the door to their gallery. She and her husband hugged. They both began to laugh. They felt optimism. True hope, not the kind fed to you by the media to pacify your mind. Now that they had felt true faith, they realized something. They hadn't truly felt hope in their entire lives, until this moment.

As the man and his niece walked to the car, they spoke about the good energy that they had just received from the gallery owners. The girl told her uncle that he was right about the bad energy turning into good. Everything was on a cycle. Without both, balance could not be had. All things in life would be lopsided.

Knowing these things had always made the man's life much easier. It put the bad times in perspective and kept the good times in check. They would both be right behind the other.

The family returned home to playtime. The man unloaded all the toys and went in the backyard with the kids. They were fully entertained for about two hours. The man observed how the boy and girl played with each other. Competition was strong between these two. Everything was about who could out-do the other. The man told the two over and over that fighting was not making their lives any easier. He could see the understanding in their eyes, and they would try at times, but for the most part, fighting was their way.

The man was tired of this game after getting toys out of the trees a hundred times. He had come on vacation for adventure, not sitting around. He gathered up some of the others and off on a fishing excursion they went. The sister's boyfriend was not going with them again. His health, if anything, had gotten worse.

The niece gathered up her kids and ex-husband. The grandson and niece were already outside and ready to go. The man's wife decided to stay behind. She wanted to spend a little time with the sister while they had the chance. They all piled in the car and headed for the dock. Light was not going to be around very long. They had no time to hesitate.

A large storm had been blowing in for quite some time. The storm had been coming and going all day, but now it was on its way. The group had caught a few fish each, but it was time to go. The others had already packed their gear and were headed for the dock. His grandson and niece took their time, savoring the last of Minnesota fishing. The three all waited for each other. Their group stuck together.

The man threw his line out one more time, just as the sprinkles started. A large northern pike jumped out of the water and hit his bait, tugging the line to the depths. This felt like the fish he had caught up in Canada, fifteen years before. As he was slowly reeling the fish up, the rain had really begun. He yelled to the boy and girl to go up to the car and let the others in. He flicked the girl the keys and said he would be right up. There was no way he was going to lose this whopper.

The pikes were always a slow one to reel up. The man was taking his time but was getting impatient and tired. The rain had already soaked him, so that was not a problem. The thunder was. It sounded like it was directly over the top of the man. He could see the fish now, so close to the dock. The rain had obliterated his sight past fifteen feet.

He looked up the dock toward the path and saw a large dark shadow standing there. He thought it might just be the trees, but there was a red glow softly coming from the eye area. The figure did not move. The man, temporarily distracted by the shadow, was jerked back to the fish at hand. The pike had moved into some weeds and was trying to shake loose. The man knew this was the crucial moment. He had to be patient for a few more minutes. The pike had worn itself out.

Reeling the fish to the dock was like reeling up a log. There was no movement left in the pike. Its strength had been exhausted. Just as the man was reaching over the railing to get his catch, a large bolt of lightning hit the water, traveled through the fish, up the fishing line and through the man's body. He couldn't see it, but the lightning had passed all the way through him and went back into the water behind the dock.

The force of the electricity threw the man ten feet up the dock. His arms were smoking. It did not knock him out, but the man could not move. He knew he had been hit by lightning. His mind was clearing. He could see through the wall of rain like he had special goggles. The shadow at the end of the dock was now running toward him. The force of the steps made the dock shake. The man knew it, he had just died, and this was the grim reaper coming for him.

"Are you alright?" it was his wife's voice. "You just got hit by lightning." The boy was now by their side. "Can you walk?" the woman asked.

"I think I'm okay," he said, and got to his feet with the help of the others. His legs were very wobbly. He would not be able to walk without the assistance of his wife and grandson. "What happened to my fish?"

"I can't believe you are worried about your fish. You could have just died," his wife said.

"It was the biggest fish I ever caught," he said. "How did you get here? You didn't come fishing with us. You stayed at my sister's house."

"You're being silly," the woman said, as she shot her grandson a look of worry, "I came with you. I ran up to let our niece in the car and put away some of the gear. Me and the boy were coming back to help you get the gear together and saw you get blasted by that bolt of lightning. I can't believe you are alive, let alone conscious."

The woman drove back to the sister's house. It was only a five-minute drive, but it seemed to take an hour. The children were no longer with them. It was just the group of four travelers. "What happened to the others? Did they go back already?" the man asked.

"Are you okay?" the woman asked, "They stayed behind to give the kids a bath. Don't you remember? Just the four of us came. I think you need to get back and get some rest."

The man could not remember anything on the way to the house. A water tower that he remembered was nowhere to be seen. The gas station where he bought the worms before was there, but there were three stores around it. Pulling into the sister's driveway, the brick house struck the man as odd. He could have sworn that this was a wood house.

The four crept into the house. The television was on, but it was only on blue screen. It cast an eerie blue glow across the room and spilled into the kitchen. There was not a sound in the house. The family tried to be as quiet as possible. Something seemed so strange. This house seemed like a stranger's house to the man. It felt like a crime scene. Everything seemed so surreal. Walking down the hallway, the man expected to see a body lying on the carpet. There was nothing but the soft glow of blue filling the house.

A quick shower was what he needed to clear his head. His arm felt like it was still filled with electricity. It almost felt like he could shoot a lightning bolt out of his hand if he wanted to. The water made his mind relax and his imagination kick in. Why hadn't he felt any shadows since they had gotten home? Something seemed so different about this house.

The man smelled a strange smell, like burning metal. The smell of ozone had clung to his nostrils since the lake, but this was different. This was a smell that seemed so familiar, but he could not place it.

The water crackled as it hit the man's skin. Small pockets of steam would float into the air. His skin was electrified.

Coming out of the bathroom, the house was completely dark. Not a single light cast its illumination. The television had been turned off, and the boy was softly snoring on the couch. The man felt his way to their bedroom and quietly slipped in. His wife was sound asleep. It seemed like she had been asleep for quite some time. She had left the light by the chair on to navigate his way. He would use that light to light the way to his book. He had a lot to say tonight. So many strange things had happened. Now it was time to try and make sense of it all.

The man couldn't help but notice that it was very cold in the house. He could see his breath. He grabbed a blanket off the shelf and cuddled up in his chair. The words felt like they were fighting to get out of his head. The pen seemed to fly into his hand. Just as the pen was touching the paper, his phone rang with a text message. He picked up his phone and saw the time was two a.m. That was impossible. They had come back home at eight. There was no way that he could have been in the shower for six hours.

He clicked on the text message and saw it was from his niece. The screen had already begun to fog over because of the cold.

It was crystal clear what the message said though. It had made the cold room even colder. Ice ran through the man's blood into his heart. He looked to his wife, who was lying in bed, and realized it was just a bunch of pillows filling the blankets.

The man read the message, on his phone, one more time with disbelief. On the screen, the message simply asked, "Where are you?"

Chapter 25

The man didn't remember going to bed. He had just awoken with the softest of gray light filtering through the window. His dreams had been odd. In them, he had gone on a walk in the woods, just to come upon a stranger. The newcomer had looked at the man, but the eyes were just orbs of haze. The creature spoke to the man in a voice that was much louder than expected. As the words left its mouth, the stranger held out a gnarled hand to give something to the man. It said "now", in a thunderous voice, and dropped the stone. It was the same one that his sister had given him. Looking closer at the stranger, the man realized it was his sister. She had just aged so many years and was so weathered, he had not recognized her. She reminded the man of a crow. Her appearance seemed to be in the distant future. In his dream, he was just a small child.

He tried to remember what had happened the night before, but the dream consumed his thoughts. It had been such a strange dream. He had felt a strong knowledge wrapped up in his vision. He had been one with the wisdom. Everything about the dream seemed so common to the man. He felt as if he had been thru this experience before. As he lay in bed, he tried to recall why it was so familiar. In his conscious or subconscious, something was stirring his memory.

He knew the stone that his sister had given him had power. The dream had confirmed what he had already known. This stone had been in their family a very long time. His sister had found it when they were small children. They had been on one of their family vacations and were passing through New Mexico. They had stopped at a gas station and the two brothers and sister had wandered away from the others. They were ones to explore. A small hill behind the building was all they needed for adventure. The sister had found this fossil on that small hill. Her younger sibling begged the girl, until she had relented and given the object up.

The man rolled, reaching out to the nightstand to grab Toomie. The stone was not there. This really baffled him. Now the mystery of the night before deepened. He had put the rock in the same place, each night before sleep, since his sister had given it to him.

He looked around the floor but the object was nowhere to be found. He grabbed his pants, lying by the bed, and checked the pockets; nothing but lint and a couple of pennies in there. He was perplexed, what could have happened to the stone?

The man got into his clothes and was ready to begin the day. He had plans for fishing, but one look outside told him that it was not going to happen. The sky was gray and the wind was blustery. He would, instead, use his time to work in a page of the book. The project had moved along nicely. If he could get this page done, he was right on schedule.

The book meant a lot to the man. His main drive was getting things done. He felt that so many people would start things but never follow through. He was not one of those. When he started something, it was going to get finished. He felt there were three things to creativity. Come up with the idea. Implement the idea and see it through until it was done. The outcome was the finished product. Then it would be time to begin once again. Creativity was a cycle just like everything else.

The mask book was calling him this morning. The love of painting was strong in the man. It was his way of being in tune with things. It helped him to figure out all the events that happened around him. It taught him the way.

Painting and using the imagination had enlightened the man. This project had helped get him through the worst times of his life. It had been a therapy that was deeper than he would ever be able to pay for. There was no need for an explanation. This book was made solely for himself. Few others would ever see the contents, let alone understand its deep roots.

A statue that he had seen was the inspiration for the next page. Half the pages in this book were either borrowed from inspiration seen in a book or in person. The other half of the pages had come straight from the man's imagination. The whole book made up the One. There was a collective energy emanating from the book that the man had begun to feel after the first few pages. Many times, he had felt energy emanating from the paintings he was creating. That is one of the things that had driven him to paint so much. This was similar but all the energies from each painting made the collective. It gave the book an overall vitality that the man had never encountered.

He understood that when you created, the energy between yourself and the project became one. All the energy around the One would also be absorbed. The aura would glow like a beacon. That is why people were always attracted to anyone creating. They wanted to see what they were making. In truth, their primal senses had been blocked by the greed. These instincts were drawing them toward creation. Like moths to the light, the masses would flock to the aura of creation. The souls yearned for creating, but their brains wouldn't let it happen.

Both the nieces were up early and ready for the day. The man had already made coffee and had the page drawn and outlined in pen. It was the other sister's birthday back in California. The family had all got together the day before and made a happy birthday video for her. Her birthday was one day after the older sister's, who had died. They had been very close. The family knew that this first year would be hard on their kin so they had sung her a song. They had hoped that this sister could also be here, but it just wasn't possible. Although close in spirit, the sibling's lives were all on different paths.

The family had always made it a goal to be the first one to call on someone's birthday. The man had told the niece to get up early before someone else wished her aunt happy birthday first. She had done just that, but it was too late. Making coffee, while working in his book, he also sent his sister the first text of the day. He knew it would be four a.m. in California, but it did not matter. He was the first.

The niece laughed so hard when the man told her what he had done. They both couldn't help but to laugh at this silly joke. The two of them were connected. Their DNA was the same. They saw humor in the same things. They saw many things the same. Most of all, they both saw the whole picture.

The man finished the page as the rest of the family awoke and began running around. The little ones were very much ready for adventure with their favorite uncle, aunt and cousins, but they would have to wait. Their grandma was making breakfast, and the man needed to finish his painting. It took patience to get the watercolor just right on this paper. It was not made for watercolor. The man had that patience. He tattooed for a living. He was used to a lot of things happening around him when he was creating. He preferred the solitude to create, but had adapted to multitude instead.

The talk this morning was about everything and about nothing. The older niece had grown up around the man when she was little. Up until she was eighteen, they had been very close. The rift in the family had changed so very much. The niece moved to the Midwest when she was a young adult. That had been the last times they had hung out.

The two had always been close and now were the same. They had seen each other back in March, but that was not enough. There was a lot of catching up to do. There was a lot of family business that needed to be discussed.

The two cousins hadn't seen each other in a very long time, either. The older girl had lived with her grandparents for a while when she was in high school. The man's brother and their family had lived just down the road. The niece would go to her aunt and uncle's house in the forest every weekend and party it up some. A small pond out front provided hours of fishing fun. Everyone was safe. The byproduct of the visits was that the two nieces got to hang out. The youngest at the time was a very small girl, two to four years old, but a bond is a bond.

All day the two were best of friends. The man cherished this morning. He thought that he would remember it for a very long time. Their energies were becoming one, once again.

The conversation ended when the book was closed. Some great grub went down smoothly and it was off to the thrift store. The sister had bought the bicycle there a few days before when they went, and the man said he would take her back.

The man really wanted to check out that fishing gear some more, anyhow. He was more than happy to go back to the old school house and look at more junk. This time they wouldn't be pressed for time, either. They could browse through the store and talk with the owners some more. The boy could come in this time, also, as the dogs had stayed behind with the woman. She had been happy to stay behind with the kids and their dad. The dogs, too, needed this solitude before the madness to come. It was back on the road soon, and rest was welcome.

The boyfriend, too, stayed behind. His health was getting progressively worse. He couldn't even muster enough strength to get out of bed and join the others for breakfast this morning. The whole family was worried about the guy. Having only met a few days before, they had all grown fond of the man and his joking ways.

Unfortunately, the boarder had talked the others into letting him ride along. He said there were things that he needed to get from the sale that he had no money for on the last visit. The man was going to ask him where he got the money now, but decided to let it go. He really wanted to have zero interaction with this guy. It was bad enough that he had to sit next to the guy for the next thirty minutes.

The man and boy headed straight for the sporting goods side, while the others went to the other direction. The schoolhouse had a lot of leftover energy in it. The man had felt it when they were here before. Once again, it was very strong. The shadows that the gray skies cast inside the building intensified the shadows. Places like this confirmed the man's theory about spirits. It was just leftover energy. Trapped for however long until it dissipated back into the giant energy pool, which was our universe.

People were mistaken to think that spirits were only from death. Some spirits could be left behind by the living. The dimensions would line up and a spirit would be born.

This time, the man who repaired the reels was at the store. The guy wore a fishing vest and hat. He really looked like he was from a sporting goods catalog. The man and boy spoke freely with the sportsman. They told him that they had met his wife the day before, and she was very nice. The salesman said that she had talked about the man and his family. He was happy to meet them. The man felt good energy from this guy, and he could see in his eyes that he felt the same. The man noticed the aura around the other guy. It was very bright. It contrasted with the green from the chalkboard, creating a deja vu in the man's mind. He had seen the same exact aura on the man's wife the day before. It was odd, the man thought, he had never met two people who had the same aura, and here were two that were married.

As he and his grandson were looking at reels, something on the table made the man's head spin. It was the stone that his sister had given him. He had searched the bedroom extensively this morning and throughout the house. He had not been able to find it anywhere. Now he knew why, the stone was sitting on this table in this old schoolhouse. He wondered if the same thing had happened to Toomey when he was a small child, but he had never found it.

The man picked it up and held it tight in his hand. The stone merged with his energy. They were meant to be together. The man would hold the rock in his hand for the rest of the day. Later that night, when he would relinquish his grip on the object, its imprint would remain on the man's palm. The scar would never go away. It would be on the man's hand for the rest of his life.

The man bought a few more reels from the salesman. The guy told the man which ones he thought were the best bargains and which were his favorites. By the time they had left, combined with the last visit, the man ended up buying eight reels from this thrift store. They cost him the same as one reel would have cost him in California. He told the salesman this, and he said that he was happy that they had come in. The man felt like they would be catching many fish with these reels in the future. They had very good energy in them.

The man and boy made their way to the room of random things, with a stopover at the books. Their time had been cut short on the first visit and now they had the time to really explore the knowledge. A book about heat and radiation, and another on light and rays were the good finds of the day. These two books, combined with the one from before on electromagnetism, seemed to call out to the man and his niece.

They had talked about doing experiments when they got home to try to harness the electromagnetic currents of the earth. The man at the Coral Castle in Florida had done it, and they thought that they could, too. They just needed some basic principle to go off from.

The man thought it was ironic that he found these books now. Just like everything else on this trip, things just fell into place. If they thought of something, it would happen. It really felt like the entire trip was scripted.

The man showed the book to his niece. She understood. She, too, felt the energy that had been created on the road, culminating in the visit here. She had awakened.

The man bought some jewelry for the kids and his wife. They had stayed behind, and the man wanted to bring back gifts for them all. The kids were leaving later today. It would be a six-hour drive for them in the night. The family was leaving in the morning. They would like to stay a day or two longer but the Fourth of July weekend was coming up, and they would need to try and miss being in any kind of tourist area for that. Besides, they were all ready to point the car west and start the long trip home. The west coast was calling them back.

The ride back to the house was filled with laughter and good times. The oldest niece tried saying things about how she had it so bad when she was little, and the man had to tell her to stop. He had been there. The things she was saying were what she told others who didn't know any better. The man told her that they knew the truth.

His sister thanked the man so much. She told him how her daughter was always blaming her for her bad ways. The girl was lost. The man could see it. At thirty-six years old, she had done nothing with her life except have kids. The kids were cool for sure, but there was more to life than just this. Every living being had a purpose; it was up to them to find out what it was.

Earlier in the morning, the niece had told the man that the solution to the world's problems was love. The man had laughed in her face. She had told him many things of this nature throughout the morning, and he had rebuffed her every time. The man lived his life. He saw the truth, not the falsities of the greed. He had told her that life was not the internet. She needed to start coming up with her own words and thoughts and stop being like everyone else who wanted to be like everyone else on the internet. The youngest niece seconded this thought with conviction. She, too, saw the stupidity of it all. Internet prophets who never left their couches, thinking they were changing the planet with their words of knowledge. In truth, their words added up to a pile of shit.

The man stopped at a restaurant on the way back to check the business hours. A big sign proclaimed that Walleye was their specialty and the man was ready for that. He told the others that he would buy for the whole family this night.

Once again, the boarder had sat up front. His directions had already got them turned around three times, and it had just been thirty miles away. The guy wouldn't even get out of the car to check the sign on the door.

The man ran up to the entrance, in the misty rain, to find that the place was closed on Monday. This just happened to be Monday. The man thought it was just his luck. Getting back into the car, the stranger said something silly about the man. He was not one to get offended from a joke, but this was different. This was downright disrespect. He had enough. The man calmly walked to the other side of the car, opened the door and yanked the tall, large man out. He fell to his knees to the ground, a look of anger mixed with fear. He opened his mouth to say something, but saw the look in the man's eyes. His friend's brother was a lunatic. He saw the look of insanity in his eye. The guy knew it best not to say something to the man.

The man slammed the car door and got in the driver seat. "Now we can enjoy the rest of our day," he told the others. His grandson was quick to hop into the vacant seat. The man looked to the boy and smiled a smile of connection. They both knew exactly what the other was thinking. It was all they could do not to laugh. The man spun out of the parking lot, kicking a cloud of dust and rocks onto the pathetic being. He heard the man yell out to his sister as they sped away. Looking in the mirror, he could see the guy was openly crying, on his knees, in the middle of the restaurant parking lot. The man laughed a small laugh of satisfaction and sped off toward the house.

On this day, the man started to figure out this region. There was a strange kind of magnetic energy here that created a vortex of some kind. Everything looked so perfect, but there had been something lying beneath. The man had been feeling it since arriving in Minnesota, and now he knew. The magnetism was drawing energy to this place. It was energy of many different sorts, but all energy. Something or someone was creating a giant magnetic reactor and drawing off the energy of the humans and the planet. The pillage took from both the physical and metaphysical. It was enervating their beings.

A water tower on the edge of town had seemed like it was in an odd spot before, and now the man understood. There had been a water tower in every town here. Why would there be a need for these towers in the land of ten thousand lakes? These were not water towers at all. They were something entirely different. The man thought for sure they were made of an iron core with copper on the outside. He stopped at the gravel lot next to the behemoth and looked up. Sure enough, the bottom of the water tank, at the top of the ladder, was peeling its paint. Underneath, there was the sure colorization of copper.

This explained a lot to the man. The others asked him what was going on, but he said it was just something that he was thinking, but he had been wrong. He got in the car and drove the last two blocks to his sister's house.

His sister and niece looked at him oddly the rest of the drive. They knew he had just made a crazy ass discovery. It was written all over his face. When they got home, the boy and older niece went inside. The niece asked her uncle what he had seen back at the water tower. He told the girl and his sister a story that would seem so unbelievable, it had to be true.

He told them that when he was in the Navy, he was sent on a detachment once in the desert. There had been strange looking water towers like these. One day he had a watch on a holiday. It consisted of walking around the aircraft for whatever reason. These strange towers were at the corners of the tarmac. There were three of them in a triangular formation. Everyone else from his command had gone into town to party it up, leaving the man alone on the small base. A strange hum had begun to come from the towers. After a few minutes, all of them began to hum in sync with each other. The airplanes on the airfield began to pull at their tie down chains. Some firefighting equipment and a truck, which weren't tied down, began to levitate before the man's eyes. An unseen force had lifted the vehicles. The man had watched all this from the safety of the hangar. When he stepped outside the hangar doors, he felt a force which seemed to zap all his energy. It took all his willpower to pull himself the half step back into the safety of the hangar bay. He had never told anyone of this, until now.

"My theory is that those are coils, just like on my tattoo machines, but much larger. They are probably arranged in a near perfect circle with a large iron deposit between them. When they get power hooked up, they omit a strong magnetic pull toward anything in between those towers. Their pull might even extend beyond the circle; guaranteeing that they are in a perfect sync. The sounds that people are hearing up here are coming from those towers and the electromagnetic pull they are creating. The iron under the ground is getting pulled to the surface and jostled around from the magnetism. It is what people are hearing under the earth, crashing together. Whoever owns those towers, is creating a strong magnetic field for whatever purpose they have. I am sure it is not for the good of the locals nor the environment."

"It is why there are so many spirits here. We are all animated with electromagnetism. Its pull here is out of control. I saw how the magnetism here is affecting the people. It is dissolving their beings, like the iron underground."

The other two readily agreed with the man. "It sure seems like that is what is going on," the sister replied. "I hear weird sounds, like ringing that turns to a melody, sometimes. Other times, I hear a rumbling under the earth, like rocks are colliding. Humming in the air is a constant. Whatever is happening up here, it is some weird shit."

"It's just weird to us. If you talk about things like this, then everyone says you are crazy; a conspiracy nut. In truth, conspiracy nuts are considered anyone who thinks outside of what the media feeds us. The free thinkers, the truth seekers, and the ones who question, are all labeled as crazy. The normal people might have some doubts about things, but they would rather rationalize their thinking so as not to look different. In truth, they are truly blind. They start looking to religion and false gods; walking blindly through this existence looking for something to grab onto. They will never find out who they truly are," the man said.

"Sister, you are only hearing these things because they actually exist. The electromagnetic waves create sound in some people's hearing. You are not going crazy."

He could feel the dire times that the humans were in. Bad things were on their way. He had sensed it for so very long. This trip had made him realize how fast that clock was ticking. His sister had told him that she had a plan for saving the human population. The man and niece had talked against this. The humans were the reason why the planet was in the state it was in. The greed had not cared about Pachymama one bit, and the flock had obligingly gone along.

Now the greed would be purged with most of the other people. It was the natural cycle of things. A great awakening was coming for all living creatures on the planet. Dimensions that had been lost to the humans so long ago were going to come back into everyday living. Blocks that had been in people's minds were about to crumble.

He really felt like the greed was accelerating the pace of the destruction. They obviously had a back-up plan to fall back on when they had turned this planet into a wasteland. It seemed like they were in a competition against a force unknown to the ordinary man. Whatever it was, it was going to be winner take all. The greed, of course, wanted it all. The losers, like always, would be the common folk.

The woman was just waking up from a nap when the others got home. The man gave her the thrift store necklace he had gotten her. The children ran from the basement to greet the great uncle. He gave them their jewelry and helped them put it on. The kids were beaming, and for a quick minute, did not fight. The house seemed peaceful to the man. There seemed to be an eye of the storm that they had been riding out since being here. It was time to relax.

The woman asked her husband where the boarder was. The man turned away without an answer. The sister interjected and said that he had argued with the others all day. Finally, they had left him down the road. "He could walk home," she had said. The woman did not really believe this story. There was something in the way her husband had turned away that was very odd. She was going to say something, but decided not to. She, too, did not care for the guy, and found it no big deal that they had left him behind. When she had been home the day before, the sister and boarder had not realized she was in the bedroom. The guy had ripped into the sister's energy, telling her hateful things about the visit of the family. The woman had heard it all, quietly trying to stay out of it all. She had seen the dominance that the guy had tried to interject into the sister's life. Her husband was right, this guy was an implant.

This was an afternoon that the family could relax. The older niece said she was going to go fishing and invited the rest along. The man declined. It was back on the road the next day, and he was going to need to get some rest. The girl convinced her cousins to go, and the three were off. The ex-husband stayed behind with the kids. Everyone, like always, did their own thing.

The man had gotten a couple of wood pieces from the thrift store. In the last two years, he had mostly just painted on wood. It was not a new thing to him, but the degree that he had produced in the last twenty months was incredible. These two pieces would look great in his sister's house. He set to making the first and was done in forty-five minutes. The young children were very interested in what their uncle was doing. They, too, were drawn to creation.

The dogs were very stressed by the kids and stayed away. That meant they stayed tucked on either side of the man the whole time he was painting. The kids were relentlessly ruthless in poking at the dogs and trying to get them to play. It was trying on the man's nerves, but there was no way he could let frustration turn to anger at these two little homies.

On the second board, the man began to doze out some. He had been dreaming that he was in the mountains and there was a gong playing in the distance. A strange, golden light engulfed everything around him in his dream. A creature had walked out of the glow and stood in front of the man. It was a woman whom he recognized. It was the woman from the gnome place. She was holding a bird in her hand. When the man reached for it, the woman and bird dissipated. The dream was lost. The kids had awakened him up trying to pet the dogs.

Soon after finishing the second painting, the cousins arrived home. The boy had found a stick that would be the perfect one for his walking stick. He ran right to his grandma to show her his prize. The woman was impressed as was the rest of the family. The boy had found a good one.

The brother and sister's thoughts had been very similar their whole lives. They were united in a relationship of blood but also one of connective thought. When they were young, many mistook them for twins. They, too, had often thought they were twins. The bond with the older brother had been the same. This family, had it remained intact, would have been very powerful. It was still very strong, but parts had been amputated like an infected finger. The wholeness of the One now was concentrated in the surviving members of the family.

Since the restaurant was closed, the man asked if there was a place to buy pizza. The town neighboring this one provided a very nice Chicago style pizza. Being from California, the family knew they were in for a treat. The man had been to Chicago before and sampled the pizza, he told the others what they could expect. Their mouths watered with the prospects.

The family was so busy hanging out this last day that it seemed like the pizza guy got there in minutes. In reality, it was one hour. The man had been in the backyard with the kids and nieces when his wife had come and got him. When the man met the delivery guy on the front porch, he was shocked. The guy looked almost like the guy he had met at the Grand Canyon. This guy was maybe twenty years younger, but he looked identical. The two took care of business quickly. The man thanked the guy for the prompt delivery. The place was almost thirty miles away and the family was thankful for any kind of delivery. The guy counted the money a few times. The man thought it odd but everything in these parts was odd to him. As the guy walked away, the man noticed a familiarity in his step. He wondered why he kept encountering this stranger. He wondered if the guy was a stranger after all.

The pizza was fantastic. Everyone, by this time, was very hungry. That, nor the pizza, lasted long. After, the man went to the backyard to enjoy more time with the kids and their plastic toys. The sister also came out, and the two played with the little ones. It felt real nice to be with his sister again. Playing with the kids reminded him of when they were the same age, playing with the same toys. His imagination propelled them back to that time. The only difference being, they did not fight often. Their parents would never have put up with that. The sister told the man how happy she was that he had come. It had been the happiest she had been in a very long time. The man agreed with her. Life had been hard on the two for a very long time. The last couple of years had been times of deep depression. Happiness was a thing that had been a distant memory, not a reality.

The man and sister began the talk that had brought them back together in the first place. Just as things got deep, the man's wife came into the back yard with her phone in her hand. She said the pizza guy was on the phone and wanted to talk to him. The man looked to his sister with the same insight. Every time they began to talk privately, something or someone would interrupt them. This time it was a stranger who wasn't such an unknown. Someone did not want them talking about what they knew.

The man took the phone and made his greeting. The pizza guy explained that he was ninety percent sure that the man had given him twenty dollars too much for the pizza. The man said that he did not think so. His business was a cash only one. He counted money all the time; sometimes large amounts. He was not one to miscount, ever.

The pizza guy said he was sure, though, and said he would bring the money back on the next delivery. The family went about their evening. About dusk, the delivery guy showed up. The man had completely forgotten about the whole situation and was done with it. He told the guy that either way, he got an extra twenty bucks today. It was another awesome tip to add to the one the man had already given him. The pizza man was very happy. The man told him that honesty and integrity go so far in life, and most people were missing these basic traits. The two shook hands. Their eyes locked when their hands met. The man felt a strong energy flow from the guy's hand. His handshake, like everything else about the guy, was very familiar.

As the pizza guy drove off, the man thought he saw a large man dressed in black on the street corner. The car honking its farewell pulled the man's eyes away for a second. When they returned, the man on the corner was gone. The man knew he better get some rest before they got on the road the next day. His mind was playing some serious tricks on him. He wondered why the pizza guy had honked on his departure. This place was getting odder by the moment.

The niece and her family packed the car and hit the road. The man was sad to see them leaving, but he felt in his heart that they would see each other again soon. Big hugs were passed around. It's always a bummer to say goodbye to your family, but they always left on a happy note. The man called her by the nickname that her brother and cousin had given her, and they both laughed a laugh of friendship. The little ones were weeping softly as they said goodbye to their people. Even at their young age, the two felt the bond with their family. The niece was off.

There were many chores to get done to be ready for the travels ahead. The woman set about doing the laundry. It would be a long drive across the next couple thousand miles. Clean clothes made things so much better. The boy and girl retired to the basement to cut the walking stick he had found. It was much too long to fit in the car. The man had told him it would make two sticks. The sanding followed the cutting.

The man and sister had a time to talk. Their talk had always involved spirituality. Since they were little children, the two had been enlightened. They had all chosen not to go to church when given the option at an early age. Their spirituality did not lie inside a building with expensive stuff, paid for by people who were struggling to put food on their tables. Outside is where God lived. Inside of all of us is where God lived. They had understood this since they could remember. God was everywhere. They had always been in tune with the truth. Giving your money to buy a place into an imaginary heaven was a silly idea to them. What if they were already in heaven, they thought. Nobody really knew, so why not.

This trip, they spoke of the change. Something was coming. Life as they and their fellow humans knew it was about to be completely different than ever before. There was a presidential election coming up, and it proved to be disastrous. Just like every election. Politicians were into the game for their own benefit. Profit and control was their way. They were the greed. Their debates and bickering were showmanship for the masses. They were all friends, their only enemies being the people. Either way it turned out, we would have another puppet of the greed in the white house. Everything had blown up and then blown up again. Now, like an overfilled colon, it was going to explode. The greed was about to see their last days. They had finally gone too far.

So much was happening in the world and so fast. Technology was exploding at a rapid pace, and the humans could not keep up with it. They were going to destroy their own existence with their technology. The man and sister laughed at this concept. Humans were very good at one thing. Making species go extinct. Now they were going to do it to themselves, with greed. Their arrogance would prove to be their final downfall. The people were not going to stop them. They were more than happy to have their electronic devices and make-believe worlds. They were being molded right into the technology. Give them all a voice that they could follow, and it was hook, reel and slaughter. Most humans were too blind to see it.

They knew where the technology came from. There had been a couple of spurts of human enlightenment throughout history: The Sumerians, and then Egyptians, suddenly began to make elaborate monuments and art: The rise of Christianity and the abandonment of the Goddess cultures. The Renaissance: Finally, the twentieth century. All these times had been visited by beings from another dimension that we did not understand. They could go back and forth between dimensions at will. Their influence had been minor at times and major at others. Their craft were of a sort not known to humans. In the early years, they had been called angels. They had come from the light. They had brought the technology with them and given it to the humans when they felt the time was right. Then, in 1947, something went wrong with a couple of their craft.

In Roswell, New Mexico, a space craft crashed landed on a ranch in the middle of nowhere. Two days later, another craft crash landed in Socorro. Both their craft and beings had been confiscated by the greed. They were held in secret facilities so the scientists could study them and recreate the technology found inside their ships. It had been a treasure trove of information. Suddenly, technology began advancing thousands of times ahead of its natural course. The greed found profit in the knowledge. They exploited every bit of everything they had found in New Mexico. After they had figured out how to build the computers that would run it all, the other stuff blew up. Just a few years after computers, artificial intelligence appeared. Fiber optics, cell phones, cameras, drones, all of it came from these two crashes.

That was the false information that the greed had fed to the media in trickles. They wanted the humans to believe that they were getting this technology from space craft from outer space, but leave serious doubts in their minds all along. This way, the humans would never be sure of what really happened. The truth was easy to hide from the masses. They would latch onto anything that the greed fed them, and follow like ducklings. The kings of disinformation were the greed. The humans were the arrogant suckers who fell for it all.

What really happened in Roswell was much deeper. A species of beings from space had tried to contact Earth. The blue planet held many riches for their species. When they had come into the Earth's atmosphere, the greed had immediately spotted them. They let the newcomers scout the planet for a week or so and then shot them down. It was not the first time this species had come to this planet. This was the first time they had been shot down, though. The greed did take some of the technology from the other beings, but it was crude compared with their superior ways. They had been around for billions of years, absorbing every bit of knowledge that they came upon. It was what enabled them to so easily take over entire solar systems.

The beings from this other solar system tried to reach out to the leaders of this planet but were shunned and threatened. The greed was experts at intimidation toward any species in the universe.

The greed, after this incident, made the people believe that they were coming up with technology from these crashes. They had wanted to blanket their technology over the planet for a very long time. They had just been worried about how the humans would perceive this sudden flux of knowledge. They made up this conspiracy, and the humans believed it.

If the information came too quick, the species could not keep up with the implications of the technology and would all perish. Slowly, they could become accustomed to it and get used to it before progressing on to the next. That is the way it had been before, but now the greed was tired of playing with the humans. They were ready to accelerate their existence, as the acceleration of technology exploded.

The brother and sister talked about how, if all the humans could gather their masses and make a collective of all their energy, then they might be able to fight the greed. Unfortunately, the people were afraid of the greed and of change. "It would be impossible to amass enough people to make that kind of change," the sister told the man.

"Maybe so," the man said, "but what if there is a collective force that is strong enough because of the great energy it possesses? This force, in its collective, could bring together the other collectives and make a collective that could possibly take down the greed. This collective has already begun. We are part of it. The One is coming. When we understand the One and how to tap into that energy, the greed will fall like houses made of ashes. It is not going to be long now. The One is coming. I'm sure you can feel it."

"The One is already here," the sister said, looking at the man with a look of deep respect.

The man told his sister about all the strange things that he read about happening up here in the North. He told her about monoliths that had been appearing around the area of Lake Superior; strange shapes and lights that would appear and disappear. He also told her about the many things in the sky that had been appearing. Lights and craft were showing up all around the planet. Other species, too, seemed like they were tired of the greed.

The sister told the man about something that had happened to her when she was little and had recently occurred again. The man knew before she said her next words what they would be. He felt very light headed.

She told him that when she was young, lying in bed, there would be the vision of a small weight which would turn into a very large weight. The vision would bring a feeling of being sick of sorts. It was a very uneasy feeling, almost one of dread. The man was finishing every sentence his sister started. The same exact things had happened to him as a child and recently, it had recurred. He said for him it was like a pebble that turned to a boulder; a smooth transition from wee to mammoth. "Yeah, yeah, yeah," she had agreed. The man said that when it happened to him a few months before, he had learned how to control it. When the pebble appeared, the man forced his mind not to let it grow into the boulder. This time, it did not leave that 'ugly' feeling inside. The sister said her experience recently had been the exact same.

The man got a blinding pain in his forehead. He crumpled to his knees while knocking the hat from his head. He was grasping his forehead. A trickle of fluid ran over his fingers. The pain subsided quickly. The sister had not even gotten out of her chair. She was staring at the man. She knew. He slowly stood back on shaky legs and rubbed his forehead clean. The burning sensation in his forehead was piercing. He shook his head slightly to regain his vision but everything looked different. He could see through his eyes like normal, but there was now another vision along with the vision from his eyes. This vision was a bit blurry and was coming from a few feet above and behind the man. He could see the top of his head and everything else. He looked to his sister and could see the look in her eyes. His third eye had opened.

The man could see the monolith blocking his sister's mind. He knew now what had happened to them. When they were children, they had been implanted with a device that would create a barrier in their brains. This barrier would make it easy to influence and control them. It would also squash their creativity. A lot of the humans had this implanted in them. This had been going on for a very long time. The church was a part of it. The parents trusted the church and would let them do whatever they pleased to their children; long as they were going to heaven.

The man had been reading about the monolith of the mind for the last year. He had not really understood until now. Now all the pieces of the puzzle fell into their perfect spots. Now he truly understood. The greed had controlled the people for thousands of years with their little devices. They had made slaves out of every human who walked the Earth. Now, his monolith had exploded into the confines of his memories. His mind was, for the first time, working at its full capacity.

The man said to his sister, "Do it". She fell back in her seat, clutching her forehead. Moments later, her eyes were clearer than the man had ever seen them. A small metal orb came out of the corner of her eye and rolled down her cheek. The sphere made its way into her shirt and down the sleeve before falling out and hitting the carpet below. It seemed to melt into the carpet, becoming one with the weave. The man could not detect the monolith in his sister at all. She, too, had purged the greed from her body. Now it was going to be their goal to tell everyone else and get the people on the road of thinking for themselves.

The man told his sister that now she could see. Now she would understand what he was about to say. He told her about the journey they were on. They had been chosen many years ago, and now the destiny was coming true. Their path was to begin again the next day. When they got to the coast, they would be reborn. This is when the truth would begin. Everything was about to happen. He also told her how distractions had been sent their way to try and divert their path. There were monoliths all around them. They would not fall into this trap. They had the end sight in their minds. Distractions were to be ignored.

The man also told his sister how people had been implanted into our lives since we were young. They were watching us our whole lives. They were the ones who would convince you not to follow up on your convictions. They were the ones who would try and destroy the creative mind. Imagination, to them, was something to laugh about. He said that he believed the boarder was one of these people, sent to keep her and her boyfriend from fulfilling their true calling. "Now you are lost here and can't find your way out," he had told her.

Just then, there was a creak on the floor in the kitchen. The man instantly stopped and listened. Shadows floated through the hallway, but the man knew these spirits were not the ones creating the creaking. The man had only heard a spirit make the floor creak once ever. It had been a year earlier. There had been a devastating fire in their county which burned many homes. It had started just after the man's mom died. The day that the man, woman, and niece had gone to her cremation, the fire had surrounded the family's house. The man had a feeling that their house would burn this day. As he was looking at his mother's smoke coming from the chimney, a butterfly landed on his shirt. He knew then that their house was going to be fine. When the evacuation was over, the man and woman had returned home to a dwelling unscathed. The first night, when they went to bed, there was a creak in the living room that only happened when someone stepped on it. Their dog leapt from bed and began to run around the living room, playing fetch. The man knew that it was his mother, coming for one last visit to let them know all was well, and to play one more time. After about ten minutes, the feeling passed, and the dog came back to bed, exhausted.

The creak in the kitchen caused the man to get up and walk the ten steps, around a corner and into the kitchen. The man got a bit startled. There opening the refrigerator, was the boarder. He was dressed in his house coat. He looked like he had just woken up. "I must have taken a nap or something after we got home," he said, "I don't remember a damn thing. I don't even remember coming home." He reached into the fridge and got a soda and shuffled back down the steps.

"Was that my boarder?" the sister asked.

"Yeah," replied the man, "that was really weird."

The sister got up and told the man she was going to bed. It had been a long day. He, too, was ready for some writing and then some rest. He went downstairs to check the progress of the others, but they were not there. He looked throughout the basement, but there was no sign of the others, just the boarder in his corner room. He searched the whole house but could not find them. What was going on, he wondered with a deep concern. The boarder had miraculously showed up like nothing had happened, and now the others were missing. Everything in this house was getting odder and odder.

The man sat on the couch and began to write. Maybe the others had just gone out for some ice cream or something. He surely thought that he would have seen them leave, but nothing was certain these days. His mind began to get heavy, and he felt like sleep would come very quickly. He could not rest well, though, and fought the sleep, until he was sure the others were safe.

The man thought of the talk he had with his sister. Their talk had always been enlightening, but now it was at another level. Now they were figuring out some cosmic secrets. The man could always see, but now things were opening at a rapid pace. The truth was coming.

Loud thumping brought the man out of his rest. He opened his eyes and saw his wife carrying the laundry basket up the stairs. Had he just dreamed about going down looking for them? She told him that the others were cleaning up. She was going to bed. The man agreed. It had been a very long day.

He went to close his book, and there was a familiar symbol on the page, in the middle of the writing. It was a symbol that his brother had marked up his entire house with. It was the symbol for the One. The man didn't remember drawing this. He flipped through the pages and was startled. There were over twenty pages written in his handwriting this night. He didn't remember writing one word. Each of the pages contained the symbol.

The girl and boy came upstairs with the walking sticks. The girl showed the man the one she had been sanding and pointed out some markings. They looked exactly like the stone the sister had given her brother.

The boy gave the man the stick as a gift. The man held it and thought it was one of the best gifts ever. He noticed a natural slot at the top of the stick and put the rock, still in his hand, into the slot. It was a perfect fit. The stone was meant to be in this spot.

An electric current sparked through the rod. A green light pulsed from the eyes in the stone. The two had been reunited. The being was whole once again.

Strong Energy coursed through the three family members.

It was Energy of happiness.

CHAPTER 26

The dreams this night were very vivid. The man dreamed that he was in the house alone. It was late, and he was looking for the others. The whole scene seemed like a crime scene. Things were knocked over and misplaced. The coffee table was lying askew across the sofa. There was a strange blue light emanating from the television screen, coating the entire house in its blue glow. In his dream, the light had changed to that of flashing lights, like a police car. The man had peered outside the window and saw more than ten cop cars outside. All of them had their flashing lights on. The police were positioned around the vehicles with their guns drawn, pointed right at this house.

The feeling of others waking up also woke the man. His dream had been so odd. He was happy to wake to the feel of the others' presence. He realized he was very in tune to this. As soon as someone else in the house would wake up, he would feel their conscious energy and wake up. He had felt this his entire life, but was really noticing it on this trip. His parents had always been early to rise. When the man was small, he was always the first out of bed, he would get up as soon as his parents were awake. Other people waking in the same house acted as an alarm clock to the man.

The man and sister had some time in the morning with the niece. Again, the man thought about their DNA connection. Their family all got up early and stayed up late. The man observed the fact that his wife and grandson slept later, arising at the same time also. Their blood line dictated this to them. Over a nice cup of coffee, the final conversation began. The family knew that this was the purpose of the trip here to the north. Things had to be talked about. Changes were coming.

The girl was the conduit to the energy. The man had seen it for years. Since the girl was very small, she had possessed the knowledge. She had already realized that she was different than others. She could see things the way they really were, the truth, without all the distractions of the greed. She had blocked all the diversions that her friends had sunk into. The man spoke often to the girl about what was to be; she was one of the few to ever understand. He knew that this person was going to be the One who brought a positive to the planet. She was the One who would make a huge difference in the survival of their species and their planet.

The brother and sister spoke to the niece about the conversation the night before. They told her the revelations about the monoliths in their minds. The girl told her elders about the way that it happened to her. She spoke about her 'ugly feeling' that came from one brick and would increase to millions, completely blocking out the sky. She was having the same experience. The family all agreed. The only way to describe the feeling was one of feeling ugly inside.

The man told the others about the monolith of the mind and what he had been reading about that. Now they all understood. The subconscious of the human species was being obstructed. Their dreams, creativity and imagination had all been blocked. But who was doing the blocking? How long had the humans been manipulated? Everything in a person's life could be manipulated through their subconscious. Breaking those barriers would be impossible for most. They were not even aware of the control they were under. The man decided then that he would ask others about their experiences with this and spread the word. The humans had a right to know. If they knew, the barriers could come down.

So many questions came into the conversation. The three had found out why the truth was so hard to come by. It had been barred from their minds. They talked about how they were getting so much closer to the light. The key had opened the lock. The man told the others that they were not the only ones. Others across the planet were also waking up. The obstacles put in their minds were slowly becoming obsolete. A new way of thinking was coming, and the ones who understood would be the righteous.

The energy this morning had been beyond words. The man could see that his aura had combined with that of his sister's and niece's. Their energy had become one. If they could shed these flesh pods, their being would become one with the Gods. It was not the time for this yet. Their pods were going to get them to the next level of enlightenment. These receptacles were the vehicles to transport their souls to the next level of consciousness: One where the subconscious and the conscious would be in perfect harmony with each other: An enlightenment that hadn't existed in humans for thousands of years.

The woman had come into the kitchen to join the talk. The family had always welcomed the woman in their conversations and activities. She had been with this family for a very long time. Her energy was linked with theirs through their auras. They all flowed together. The man told the woman about the talks they were having about the monoliths in their brains. The woman's eyes got very wide and she told her version of it. For her, it was a small light which grew in intensity until it was all around her being. The light was all that she could see. It was the same impediment that the others had been experiencing.

The man wondered what they had stumbled upon. Who was doing this to the humans? Whatever and whoever it was, it was huge and covert.

The sister gave the man a piece of diamond wood. It looked just like a magic wand. The man knew right away that this object was like the others that he had been acquiring. Greater powers were at work. All these objects would be important to their mission somehow. The man felt a connection to everything that had come to him. It was like they had all fallen into place, at the right exact moment.

Things always seemed to fall into place in his life, for better or worse. The man understood how things would line up, and changes would come. This was different, though. This almost felt like a treasure hunt where the prize was the truth. All these objects coming to him were part of that hunt; pieces to the great overall puzzle of existence.

The sister cut the man's hair before they got on the road. He often had his people cut his hair in any fashion that they wanted. He had walked around with some very strange haircuts in the last twenty years. The sister shaved a large number four on the back of his head. They understood the numbers. They were in everything and entwined with every bit of life. The codes were there, they just needed to be read. Today, the siblings could begin to decipher these codes of digits. They had broken down the monoliths that had been thwarting their thoughts.

The man understood the importance of the four. His sister knew the mission they were on, and she had seen the light. She told the man as she was buzzing away to look on a map. Her house, his house, and the sister's house in Texas formed a perfect triangle on the map. She said to check it out. It was all a part of the whole picture. The three were connected by far more than just DNA.

The sister gave the man a strange kind of hat. It looked like something an Arab guy might wear. The man liked it and put it on. The feeling of the material was odd as soon as it touched the skin. It felt almost like he had just put on another head of hair. The hat did not feel like cloth on his scalp. It felt more like a wig.

The eye in the middle of his head was closed. It had a life of its own. It would open its lids when the time was right and needed. The rest of the time, it stayed idly closed. This morning, when they had been talking around the table, the eye had fluttered open when they were speaking about the barriers in their minds. The eye had seen the auras of the others like the energy of its own entity. The flesh pods could not contain the vitality that the beings possessed. The man's mind understood everything that the third eye saw. It was not just an organ for seeing it was a tool for perceiving.

The boyfriend came out of his room to say goodbye to the others, but was in terrible condition. He was yellow, sweaty, and looked like he was going to die. The family all told him that he needed to go to the hospital, but he was stubborn. The others stayed their distance from the man as he said his goodbye from the hallway. After, he faded back into the shadows of the bedroom.

The boarder appeared from the basement with a large grin on his normally robotic face. The man felt as though the guy was very happy. He was glad the intruders were leaving his house. The man tried to wrap his thoughts around what had happened yesterday. He could have sworn that they left the man on the road, but he was here last night. Now he was saying goodbye while herding the man and his family toward the door. The man felt a serious threat from this guy toward the harmony of his sibling. He worried that this guy was destroying his sister slowly. His goal was to take her soul. It was his mission. The guy had seen the threat and insight from the others and now wanted them to leave.

The car was packed. The sister gave each of the four travelers something special to take them down the road. The energy was very high. There was a message to speak. Maybe a few would believe. No tears were to be shed this day. The family was ONE and would always remain. The occupants of the van drove away and waved to the sister until she was out of sight. The man watched in the mirror the whole time. His sister was on the porch waving her goodbye.

The man knew it would be the last time he ever saw his sibling. The thought made his heart heavy with sadness.

Driving through the neighborhood and then the town for the last time, the epiphany came to the man. This place looked perfect, but it had hidden problems that were masked well. The man had been thinking hard about it since the day before, when one of the neighbors painted his garage in a rainstorm. He had realized then that it was indeed the twilight zone in these parts. The bars were the key in the man's mind. Each small town had at least eight bars lining its street. Wisconsin had been the same. The places here were very nice and looked so perfect, but, the people were not truly happy. Alcoholism was rampant in these parts, you could see it in the bar count of every little burg.

The first stop on the trip home was for water and ice. Although the first half of the trip had passed, time wise, this was the second half of the trip in miles. It was going to be a long drive back to the Pacific Ocean. The man felt like everything was surreal this morning. Walking through the store felt like walking through a movie set.

After paying, the man helped an elderly lady to her car with her groceries. She had been in line in front of them and needed assistance, but the store employees were all busy. It was still very early in the morning. The store had just opened. The man didn't even think twice. After loading her car, the woman was very appreciative. She offered the man money, but he refused. Instead, he said as payment he would take a handshake.

The woman's hand was soft and delicate. As soon as their skin touched, energy flowed. The man felt a very warm zest coming from this person. She was a very gentle soul. The woman looked at the man with a kind of awe. She spoke, still gently holding the man's hand in front of her. "I've been waiting my whole life for this moment. I had a vision when I was a small child that I would meet you. That vision was almost eighty years ago. I have been anticipating this moment since. Thank you." She dropped her hand as her words ended. Tears were streaking down her face. Her aura glowed like that of an angel.

The man and woman silently parted ways. She headed into another store while he rejoined his group. They were all curious about what had just happened. The man told them that she was just thankful that the man had helped her. She was so happy to see that human kindness still existed that it had made her cry. The man told the others that everyone should be nice to each other. It made every day a lot better. He also told them how most humans had lost any sense of kindness. Electronic devices had taken that from most. They lived their lives caught up in the internet. When they would meet people in real life, they wouldn't know how to treat them.

"The internet is the Antichrist," the man told the others. "I do not believe in religion, but it exists. If there is a good and evil, the evil is the internet. It is the dark side of the planet. It was put in play by the greed to further control the masses. It was one more crime committed by them to take every resource and turn it into theirs. Social media was the end of the spirituality in the humans. Now, they are all part of a machine: Both consciously and spiritually."

Some construction got the family turned around. One of the workers in the median was working by herself. She had long blonde hair and a small build. No other workers seemed to be around. The man joked that the worker looked like the girl, and they all laughed. As they drove past, the man caught a glimpse of the side of the woman's face. She was a woman of about forty. The road work had toughened her skin a bit. The man looked in the side view mirror after they passed to get a better look at the crew member's face. Just as he suspected, the woman looked a lot like his niece. Although older, the worker still had the same features as the girl in the back seat. They could have been mother and daughter, they looked so similar. The man looked in the rear-view mirror and saw that his niece was looking at him. She knew that he knew. He knew that she knew. The madness had begun once again.

The crow flew overhead. It cawed three times, signaling that it had returned as the guide for the family.

A few miles down the road, the family saw a large rainbow around the sun. It was the largest solar rainbow the man had ever seen. He knew it had something to do with the strange magnetism in these parts. The iron and the electromagnetic fields it was creating were warping everything in this region. It almost looked like the northern lights had wrapped themselves around the celestial body.

The energy from the sister's house began to ebb as they got further down the road. The last days seemed almost like a dream. So much energy had come together. It felt like they had all hung out together in a different dimension. Everything had been so right except for the outsider: The implant. Now, as the energy faded, things seemed like they would go back to the normal craziness. Reality was just around the next bend in the road.

Many miles and lakes later, the family was out of Minnesota. The man had held the wand the whole time. There was a special power inside the stick. It was of great importance somehow.

The family talked about not seeing the bird the whole time they were at the sister's house. Now it was back. It had not been needed at the sister's house. It was their guide. That familiar green eye was once again showing the family the way. Many other crows had joined this one. It was like this creature was also visiting its family and now they had all come along to guide the group the rest of the way.

The family saw many roadrunners in these parts. They were much larger than their kin in Arizona. The man contemplated things this whole day. There was a lot that had happened, and his mind needed to sort it all out. He wondered why no one really spoke about the eye forming on his head. He always wore a hat in public, so that wasn't a problem. But his family surely could see it and its progression. They never mentioned it. It was a perfectly normal thing to them, it seemed. He knew that he had always been weird and the others knew it too, but this was a little bit over the edge.

North Dakota did not have much to offer in way of adventure. There were a lot of farmland and open prairies. Everything was set up on a grid. It was a lot like home in the central valley of California. The lands stretched on for a very long way. Silos and barns littered the countryside. The family spoke about the harsh conditions out here in the winter. This was unforgiving land. It had taken a lot of human endurance to be able to live on it.

As they were driving, the man thought about how everything seemed so perfect in Minnesota. Now, in this state, it seemed more normal. The man had never been anywhere else on the planet where everything seemed so perfect.

The lack of cars this day was rewarding. They could focus on the driving and getting to their next destination. They passed a large building that was entirely made of metal. "It looks like a rocket ship," the boy had said. Indeed, it did. It was large, maybe twenty stories tall and cylindrical in shape. It looked like a giant metal cigar. The man pulled to the side of the road to get a better look at the strange object. His wife had just pulled her camera out to take a picture when their peace was shattered.

Two black SUVs came out of nowhere and flanked the minivan. The windows were completely black. Large men in camouflage jumped out of the vehicle. All eight of them were wearing dark sunglasses and carrying M'16's. They were on the family in a moment, knocking on the window with the barrels of their guns pointed at their faces. "What are you doing out here?" the leader asked in a commanding voice. "This is a restricted area."

"I just pulled over because I was having a sneezing attack," said the man with calmness in his voice. As soon as he had seen the vehicles pull up, he knew they were in for a confrontation with the greed. He had said the first thing that he could think of. "We are back on the road right now."

"Forget what you saw out here today," the soldier barked. "If you know what is good for you. And don't ever stop here again."

"You got it," the man replied. He put the car in gear and peeled out. Dirt and rocks peppered the eight military guys. They looked on with steady eyes until the car was out of sight.

"What was all that about?" asked the woman.

"I don't know," replied her husband. "Obviously they didn't take kindly to us looking at their devices. Something was very wrong with those guys. They didn't seem human. I couldn't see their auras."

The group all agreed that it had been an unusual thing to happen like so many other events on the road. By the time they would stop this night these events would be lost from their memories. The military guys had a way of erasing memories and it is exactly what they did to these four. They didn't want people talking about what they were really doing.

The family was running low on energy. The trip across Minnesota and North Dakota had been long and tiring. They had rested at the sister's house, and it had been good rest, but not enough. Now the miles had caught up to them. They pulled into a hotel in southern North Dakota for much needed rest.

The man and his niece went into the office to get a room for the night. The desk clerk was a young guy whom the two instantly liked. His aura was a strong one. He was one who could be trusted. The rooms were all rented out already. They did have some trailers out back that they also rented, and they had one of those vacant.

The family was too tired. They took the mobile home. The two talked about how it would be nice to stay in a place that was more like a house, not a hotel. It had two bedrooms, so they could spread out and have a little privacy. Privacy was something that did not exist on this trip.

The building was very warm inside. The man immediately turned on the window air conditioner and commenced to unload the car. After unloading, they were off to adventure. It was much too hot to stick around so they decided to go get some food. The trailer should be cooled down when they got back, was their thinking.

Dinner was satisfying. It was hard to be in a good mood after driving all day. The family needed rest. Tempers would be short after so many miles. It put a hurting on the mind and on the body. Some dinners they had on the road were just for sustenance, while a few were for relaxing and enjoying. This was the former. There was no energy left to stay at this place for an extended time. It was just for nourishment and then back to the place of rest.

The family went right back to the trailer after dinner. They were too tired to even think about doing anything different. The room had cooled off nicely while they were gone. A quick smoke outside ended with the swarming of mosquitoes. Sunset was here, as were the insects. Relaxing in this place was nice. It almost felt like being home. The family all kicked it in the living room and enjoyed a talk. The others drifted off to sleep rather early.

Just like every day of his life, the man woke up as soon as the sun went down. He had a sudden burst of energy and began writing.

The man seldom went to sleep early. He had never been one to require a lot of sleep, anyway. He always was the last one to bed and the first one up. His sister was the same.

He was happy that not only did his dreams return, but also the deep sleep. Earlier in his life, years had passed when he could not sleep an entire night. Every night was filled with waking up, and then fighting to go back to sleep.

After his brother's family had died, his sleep had returned, but the dreams were gone. For the last two years, he truly felt like he was rested when he awoke in the morning. Before the deaths, it had been over a decade that he had not slept well. The dreams during this time were crazy, just the lack of sleep made everyday living hard. He had talked to his sister about this, and she said it was the same for her. Their lives were equidistant.

Around midnight, the man suddenly put down his pen in mid-sentence. He felt that something was different in the energy surrounding their abode. Another entity had permeated their sanctity. The man had been writing like a demon. The words had been flying from his fingertips. The story was unfolding now like the man could never have anticipated. He had a story to tell and it was getting told. He knew all about the creative process. He knew that these writings were just an outline of what was to come. Just like when he made a painting, the sketch was the first thing.

The writing was teaching the man a lot about the similarities of creation. The creation of whatever you were doing was the most important. Just getting off your ass and using your mind for what it was made for was step one. Most people never got to this step. Most would never use the gift of creativity.

The man knew that when he got home the story would unfold further. He was just keeping track of things now. He would never be able to remember all their experiences or thoughts if he did not keep some form of journal on the road. The real writing was going to take months, maybe even years. He did not know. He had never written such an extensive story before. Most of his writing had been short stories and poetry. This was a whole new playing field for the man. It was something he had thought about on and off since he was seven years old. He had often fantasized about writing a book. Now he had begun.

His awakening had begun when he was seven. Before this, his mind had been clouded by other forces. Remembering details of his whole life made it easier to analyze his existence. Before he was seven, the man was just like any other child in school. He was average in school and in everything else in life. Then, at seven, he had a dream that he was possessed. In his dream, he had somehow exorcised the demon from his being. The dream had remained with the man, vividly, the rest of his life. It was at then that he became very good in school. He took a class in summer school that taught him how to draw. His creative writing began in this era, too. Basically, all the man's creativity that he still had to this day began during this time of his life. Everything he had become within the universe revolved around getting rid of the demons; the barriers.

The man had often heard talk about these demons. He had heard this throughout his whole life. People would throw this word around as an excuse. Anything bad they did, it was their demons. It was all bullshit. Growing up Catholic, demon was not an unfamiliar word to him. Most of his family had used this word their entire lives, it was always easier to blame an imaginary creature than live up to your imperfections. The man thought that they were not so wrong. They were not demons like in the biblical sense, though. That religion had been created by the greed to control the masses and mask what was really happening. Implants, mind manipulation and the media were all factors in the demon. People had been controlled by the greed for so very long. They were the true evil on this planet. You just had to be stronger than their control.

The man had somehow broken free of this control when he was seven. Somehow in his subconscious, he had fought the outsiders. He had gained complete control over his creativity and his mind. He would be able to see the other side for the rest of his life. He was not one to believe such bullshit that the greed fed to the people. It had been in his destiny to break away from this and become a true free spirit.

That same year, he began to write his first book. He began to draw and make things in the yard and garage. He became the one that the mother and father would call when they needed help or guidance at times. It was also during this period that the man saw through the falseness of the church that they attended every Sunday. Suddenly, he understood many things. When he shook the other parishioners' hands at the end of mass, and their hands were a cold sweat, he knew not to trust these people. They had darkness in their souls.

He had become enlightened. Not from seeing God or the light. He had simply evicted the greed from his being. This was when his mind cleared. This was when he went on the search for the wisdom. It was a path that continued his whole life.

It was also during this time that the man had become capable of seeing other people's auras. Some that he had seen in the church were worse than the scariest horror movies that he and his older brother would watch on Bob Wilken's Theater every Saturday at midnight. The aura of the priest and its bishops looked like dark serpents. These visions gave the man a serious distrust of the church from an early age.

The pen fell from the man's hand. These thoughts, about so long ago, had come flooding into his brain. He had been looking at the front door, maybe eight feet away, the whole time. A soft knock came from the portal. It was barely perceptible over the clank of the air conditioning unit. The man had been almost waiting for the knock, though. He knew it was coming. He would have heard it even if it made no sound.

He looked over to his grandson, but the boy was sound asleep on the sofa. The man felt a strong pull toward the door. He wouldn't have been able to not open it even if he tried. He slowly turned the knob and clicked on the outside light at the same time. The creak of the door made the situation so much better for the man. He liked to have different experiences. Everything that happened with those occurrences was duly-noted. They were all scenes in the cinema of his life.

The door opened into another dimension. The porch and night were all the same, but standing on the porch were three small children. The man guessed them to be about six, eight, and ten. The older two were girls, while the youngest was a boy. They were wearing strange clothes that seemed like their mothers had made the garments for them. Their hair was mostly covered with a shiny looking cloth which matched the clothing. The hair that was hanging out of the hats seemed to be very stringy and dirty. They held their heads down, as if something on the ground intrigued them.

The man saw that the biggest child was holding something in her hand. It was by her side, so he could not tell what it was. "Can we come in?" the girl asked. Her voice was monotone and sounded much older than a child. She continued to look at the ground. None of the children moved at all. The voice almost seemed to come from the night.

The man held out his hand slightly and said, "Look at me." The three children all lifted their heads at the same time. It was like one brain controlled all three beings. The man noticed that the three children looked exactly like his nieces and nephew he had just been hanging out with. The older one had not been at his sister's house, but she was here now. Their faces were very blank and somewhat pale in the glow from the porch light. Their eyes were very large and wide open. There was no white. Their eyes were solid black.

The man reached his hand a bit higher and the oldest girl extended hers at the same time. Her hand only had three fingers and a small thumb. The object it was holding looked exactly like the stone they had been given way back when. It was roundish and had a sun in the middle. The sun seemed to go all the way through the stone.

Her twisted hand reached right into the man's and dropped the object into it. As soon as it touched his skin, a blinding light filled his being. All his senses were touched by this light, as was the eye in his head. It suddenly popped open. As before, the man could see from a spot above and slightly behind himself. Everything was blurry again. The aura coming from the three beings on the porch was intense. The man had never seen anything so beautiful. It was pure energy. Thousands of shades of green and gray permeated from its existence.

The man felt more comfortable and happy than ever in his life. He felt as if he were reunited with long lost parts of himself that had been gone for so very long.

The small boy spoke this time, "may we come in?" His voice sounded exactly like the girls but had a slight accent that the man did not recognize. The child's mouth barely moved as the child spoke. The words from his tight lips just formed in the space on the porch.

The whole situation was so strange to the man but comforting at the same time. He had dreamed of this moment many times before. The recollections of those visions raced through his head as he stood in the doorway.

There were no doubts in his mind. This had all been foretold.

The man stepped aside. He let the children in.

CHAPTER 27

It said three thirty-three on the digital clock sitting by the television. Its green glow cast a strange aura about the room. The man had woken from a dream. He had been sitting in this same room with his sister from Minnesota and his sister from California. Their brother was also there. His siblings were all young, but he was his current age. They spoke of things to come. The new beginning was coming, and they would all be together again. Soon, their childhood games would be re-lived. The end was near.

The dream seemed to go on throughout the night. The man somewhat remembered some strangers coming to the door the night before, but it was vague and fading, like the dream he had just woken from. It had all seemed so real in his vision. He fully expected to see his siblings sitting in the other chairs. Their relationship had always taken on a mental connection. The man's subconscious had brought them all into reality.

The boy was snoring loudly when the man awoke. Somehow, the light had gotten turned off. Tightly gripped in his left hand was the stone his sister had given him. His pen and book were both on the floor, dropped when consciousness had left his being. He picked both up and put the pen in its case. His backpack was on the table, and he stopped long enough to put the book and the pen case away. The stone went in the case with the other devices. He looked around the darkened room once more, thinking for sure that his siblings would be there. Only emptiness and snoring remained.

The man stumbled into the bedroom and fell immediately asleep.

The beds in this trailer were grimy. There were no blankets, only sleeping bags. He felt very itchy the rest of the day. It was a familiar itch, like the one he had gotten in the Virgin Islands when he was in the Navy. He had hung out on the beach for three days, getting sunburned on top of sunburn. The sand fleas added to the mix and it was a terrible experience for the next three weeks. This felt almost the same. The man hoped that the itching would not last long like that other time.

There was a lot of wildlife driving through South Dakota. The family saw bighorn sheep, pronghorn sheep, coyotes, buffalo, prairie dogs, and numerous species of birds.

The land had been flat and straight, but the family enjoyed the sights nevertheless. The lack of cars reminded the family of their wise decision to take back roads. Here, they were seeing true America. Corporate America and the greed were miles away on the interstate.

Once again, they passed a construction zone. The family was very familiar with road work in their native California. It was abundant in the summer months. The woman spoke about the lack of construction that they had seen on the road. They had seen some delays caused by workers, but after all the miles they had traveled, it was minimal. The family spoke of the reasoning behind this. It was because the way was calling them. The man would just glance at the map in the morning over coffee, and the way would become clear. The crow would appear when they were in doubt and set them back on the way. Their path would then be filled with good energy and good adventure. It was all meant to be. Everything was flowing like water through their cosmic journey.

It was only minutes before the family passed the flagman. He had a distant look on his face. There were only three or four cars ahead of the minivan, but the flag guy had ignored them all. The man had never seen a flagman who didn't wave to the cars. When they got next to the worker, the man looked to the side to get a good look at the signaler. He was tall, maybe six-foot-ten. His clothes were of a normal worker, and he had on the customary orange vest. Everything seemed normal except for his blank stare. It was focused down the road to the left, behind the approaching cars. It seemed like he was looking for something that was coming their way.

The flagman wore cop style aviator sunglasses. The man caught a quick glimpse of the man's eyes from the side, just behind his frames. His eyes were not there. There were only blank sockets. As he got face to face with him, the flagman looked directly into the man's eyes. The sun reflected off his glasses, temporarily blinding the man. The car passed before the man could focus his eyes again.

"What was up with that guy," the grandson said from the back. "He was looking at us like he wanted to abduct us and do bad things to our family, like in the movies."

"It looked to me like he was a creeper." the girl said.

"I was blinded by his glasses," the woman finished. Silence overtook the car. Everyone in it had just had some kind of different experience back there and they were all trying to figure it out in their heads. They passed some large machinery that the man had never seen before. It looked like a mushroom shaped behemoth. It didn't seem to be sitting solid, more like it was hovering slightly above the ground. The whole thing was as big as four train cars laid out next to each other. It was of a shiny metal and very smooth, almost polished.

The machine was kicking up a cloud of debris as the family passed. It was a strange dust, bluish in color. The particles didn't seem to get close to the cars as they passed. A large vacuum on top of the machine was sucking up the dust from the air. It looked like it was mining the side of the road. It was the only machine in the construction zone, which stretched on for three miles. The family passed a few workers, who all stopped to look at the passengers of the minivan. They all had the same blank stare as the first guy. They seemed like robots.

All the other cars had driven very much ahead. It was as if the family was on this stretch of highway, alone with the construction crew. The group was in no hurry, though. They were intrigued by the strange machinery and the odd behavior of the crew. They took their time and took in the knowledge.

As they were coming up to the second flagman, the family noticed that he, too, was standing very still, facing the traffic coming into the work zone. The worker slowly turned to face the family as they approached. He looked identical to the other worker. Everything about him was the same, including how he was looking inside the car at the family. The man said, "Look away," as they approached the orange cones signaling the exit.

Everyone in the car looked in any direction except at the flagman. The man could feel the gaze from the guy. The worker was angry, he wanted them to look his way. They had not played into his game, and he was powerless against them. As the family cleared the oncoming cars, they all laughed.

These beings were part of the greed. They were here to stop the family from their mission. They were powerless towards the four, long as the family stayed true to the path. The man could feel the gaze of the flagman until the small dot of orange was completely out of sight.

The greed knew all about the family. Their deeds were upsetting to the greed. This did not happen to them. They were in control of everything and anything. To have any species get over on them was unheard of, let alone their human slaves. Their think tanks around the globe were coming up with their next plan of attack. The four must be stopped before getting back to Mountain Ranch.

The woman had been driving for some time as the man relaxed and thought. His mind kept going back to the conversations he had with his sister and niece. Their connection was very tightly woven into something grand that was coming. He was thinking about when he was seventeen. He had some polyps removed from his sinuses. He had been having problems breathing and smelling for at least five years before that. He remembered just before he went to the hospital. He had been working his job painting houses commercially. It was summertime. Their crew was painting the interior and exterior of a very nice country home. Halfway through the day, the man had gotten light headed and almost passed out. He could not breathe out of his nose at all. His sinuses had finally sealed themselves shut. It was time to go to the doctor.

The day of the operation, his dad had taken him. It was very early in the morning. The nurses had given the man a shot of Demerol but it did not fully knock him out. He was conscious the whole time the doctor dug in his sinuses. It was by far the most excruciating thing he had ever felt in his life. He remembered the doctor cutting out the first one and it was large. The second was much more painful, but slightly smaller. The man could not believe that these things were coming out of his sinuses. They looked like giant dried cartilage boogers. They were kind of clear and had some veins running through them. After the third one came out, the doctor exclaimed, "Oh my god! There's another one." The man didn't know if he could take this. This one felt like it was pulling his eye out of its socket. The nurse had long ago abandoned holding his hand, instead placing it on the railing surrounding the table.

There was no way to stop. The man felt like these were an alien being inside him. He wanted them out. The doctor also told him that he would be able to breathe again, and he was looking forward to that. He could endure the pain. Snip and pull and the fourth one was out. This one was slightly smaller, the size of a small Cheetos. It was much redder and bulging with veins. It looked almost alive, the man had thought. He was on the brink of unconsciousness. That one had felt like it was ripping a part of his brain out. The man wondered what kind of parasite this really was. Why was it attached to his brain? His grip remained tight on the rail, but not as intense. His mind was an explosion of pain, dissipating like a bomb blast.

"I can't believe this," the doctor had shouted. The man knew what he meant. He had almost been in the sweet embrace of subconscious but the words had pulled him back to reality. That reality was that there was another one of these fuckers inside his sinus. His teeth were gritted. The doctor looked right in his eyes and asked if he was going to be able to take this. The man just nodded his head. He thought he had told the doctor to rip it out but he was not sure. He wasn't sure of anything. All his mind could think was of the pain he knew was coming.

The long tube looking device, with a metal wire blade at the end, entered his nose once again. The doctor was a bit gentler this time. It was way deeper in his nasal cavity. Very close to the brain. He told the man when he was ready and pulled quickly and with pressure. The pain was blinding. The man would later learn that he bent the rail surrounding the operating table while simultaneously crushing the hollow metal bar.

The doctor grabbed the last polyp and pulled with a different instrument. This one was long forceps with wide jaws. It gave a sharp pain like the dentist hitting a raw nerve, only in your sinus. The doctor yanked harder the second time and out popped the growth. It looked like a miniature brain but longer. The man could see where it had been attached to his flesh. It was squirting blood from the wound. The doctor held the polyp briefly, right in the middle of both their line of sight. Their faces were maybe eighteen inches apart, with the object in the middle. The doctor turned the light slightly and they both saw it at the same time. Their eyes confirmed to each other that they were both seeing the same thing. There were two small pieces of metal sticking out of the polyp. The doctor swiftly dropped the flesh into the tray beside the table. It made a squishy sound mixed with a slight metallic ding.

The doctor had finished the procedure by breaking the man's nose. His cartilage had gotten misplaced by the pressure from the growths on the other side. There were no polyps on this side, but the nasal passage was distorted. The man had almost felt relief at this. He could not have gone through having another alien pulled from his brain.

This doctor had called him throughout the weekend and for the next few days, checking his progress. The man had never had another doctor do this for him. He asked the doctor during one of these calls if he could get the growths. The doctor said it was impossible, as they had been destroyed. The man asked the professional what had been in the last polyp. There had been hesitation in the doctor's voice before telling the man that he did not know what he was talking about. He said that the man must have been out of it. He must have imagined the devices being inside his head. Before hanging up, the doctor cryptically told the man, "Some things are best never to talk about."

The man wondered if maybe everyone had implants in their heads. Most people would never know it. Some people would surely reject it. Maybe he was one of them. His body had rejected the implants all those years ago. Maybe it is why he never got sick. Maybe it is why he used his creativity and imagination. There were many others like him. He had met some of them. Maybe they had also rejected their implants and were living with the wisdom.

He wondered why he had felt the power of the monolith in his mind, but realized it was before the surgery. After the operation, the only time that the feeling of the rock and pebble came on, it was easily controlled. All the knowledge was coming back to the man. He knew. When he had gotten rid of his implants, he had also gotten rid of the control of the greed over his existence. The few years in the military showed him the inner workings of their evil ways. Ever since, he had stayed as far away from the corporate takeover as possible.

A flock of pheasants woke the man from his daydreaming. The music was always mellow when the woman drove. The man looked over at her and thought how much he respected her. Her life had been hard, too, yet she had always remained true to her people. In the end, this is all that we had; our people. Staying true was just the way it was. She looked over at the man and saw him looking at her. "See those pheasants?" She asked. He nodded dreamily and smiled. The two were very close. Their bond was one of balance, friendship and the truth. They both understood the truth. They were on the same path. The woman smiled back with warmth in her eyes.

This trip was meant to cleanse their souls from all the bad that had happened. So far, that was exactly what it had been doing. The family felt closeness: A bond that was getting them through the long miles back to the coast. The distance it took to get here happened with unity. They had all endured so much in the last two years, and now they were being reborn. They spoke often of their son back home, running the tattoo shop. They spoke about how it would have been very cool if he were with them, too.

The son being at home was a huge help for the whole family. They could have closed the tattoo shop for thirty or forty days, but with so many other tattoo shops in the area in the last years, it was better not to. That is what made a strong family. Everybody does their own part without the need for greed. Every member understands that a family works together like a machine. If something gets out of whack, things get whacked. A family and a team were synonymous.

The man and woman talked about the amount of wildlife in the Dakotas. There were so many pheasant. The man had not seen a flock of pheasant since he was a child in California. He maybe had seen these birds two or three times since. Out here, they were everywhere.

The family all spoke about how the animals in California had been hunted almost to extinction. When the miners had arrived, it was too many of one species thrown into the ecosystem. The balance got toppled. The hungry miners hunted so many animals to extinction. Throw in the cities and all those hungry mouths, and it wasn't long before most of the animals in that state were gone.

The family spoke about how the humans were destroying the Earth. The elite acted like spoiled children who thought that they could do anything they wanted. They had no regard for others or the planet, all they cared about was getting more.

The man had met many people who, when asked why they did something, would say, "Everyone else does it, I may as well too". Or even better, "if I don't do it, then somebody else will." These words were excuses. They would give up their dignity and respect but use these phrases and everything would be alright. But it wasn't alright. Excuses were what was ruining everything. People would rather blame everything else than take responsibility for their actions. It was the root of all the problems.

If everyone began to think of the overall humans, the collective, and forget about focusing on the individual profit, then the planet would be a much better place.

The family stopped for breakfast. They spoke about how fast time passed when everyone was talking. They were all very hungry. The food turned out to be very good.

The man noticed that the people were changing as they went west. The people out here seemed to be on a different time. Everybody was very laid back. Nobody even looked twice their way. The people here were caught up in their own lives. They had no time to judge others. They were happy with who they were.

The energy acquired at his sisters was changing, too. Everything seemed to be going back to a slower pace. The magnetic pull was getting thinner and thinner. The man hoped that the connection would not snap with the distance they traveled. Their lives were getting back to the normal climate of the West. The pull of the coast was not as strong as the North had been. It was different. This pull was one of a more homeward pull. The urgency was not the same as before, when they had been going to the sister's house. This pull was gentle and accepting. The ocean awaited them. Its peaceful embrace was just a few more days away. First, there were things to do on the way.

The waitress had looked very familiar to the man when they had arrived. A connection was made with the energy of her and the man. He could feel it. It took them until they were done with breakfast to figure it out. As the waitress brought the check, the man remembered why she looked so familiar. She looked exactly like the gnome lady they had met in Minnesota. The man was dumbfounded. She even had the same mannerisms as the artist they had met.

The man looked to the kitchen. A small window separated the two rooms. The man was expecting to see the artist's husband in the kitchen cooking, but he was wrong. In the kitchen cooking was a very tall man wearing work clothes, like a road worker. He had cop sunglasses on. The man recognized this guy, too. He was the flagman back at that construction site they had passed.

He couldn't take any more of this. His family was all looking at him very strangely. The man dropped the money on the table to cover the food and promptly moved away from the table. All the other people in the restaurant were looking down at their plates. They didn't pay any attention to anything going on around them. One man had been reading the paper the whole time that they had been there, but the man had never once seen him turn the page. The man also noticed that nobody in the place had spoken except the waitress. The place felt like the twilight zone. The man's head was beginning to get that familiar feeling that it was time to leave. Things were beginning to spin. He felt very light headed.

The man was outside in a moment, but the others said they had to use the bathroom. He told them all to hurry and be careful. They all looked to him like he was crazy. Another day of playing into the man's imagination, they had all thought.

The man thought it would be a good time to catch up on the news if there was cell phone reception. He was one to keep up on the events of the world. Nothing was ever going to change if people were not up to date on current events. He felt that knowing was also keeping connected to the planet and all the madness that happened here. He didn't read many of the stories. It was all bad stuff anyway. Mostly, he just read the headlines and anything that seemed interesting. It was five minutes a day that could easily be given up to this greed. He liked to see what they were up to. If you kept up on the news, you could even predict what they would be doing next.

The man noticed, in the news, that there had been a lot of accidents involving trains and autos in the last weeks. There were also many fires around the southwest and Midwest. The names of the towns were all so familiar. Every cataclysm that the man read about was in a town they had either passed through or stayed the night. Whole families were dying in the wake of their travels. The man thought about the guy killing his family back in Gallup. They were leaving weird energy behind, and it was affecting the flow of things. They were leaving a ripple through this dimension, opening it just a bit. Other dimensions were flowing through the rift they created, bringing destruction with it.

The others seemed like they had remained in the diner for a very long time. The man had read the news from two different sources, and they still had not returned. When he had come out to the car, the clock had said ten. Now it was saying eleven. Had they been in there a full hour? It didn't seem like he had been reading the news for that long.

The man thought he was going to have to go inside again. Just as he was leaving the car, the front door of the restaurant opened and the other three came bouncing out. They all had a solemn look on their face. The man asked what had taken them so long. They were all climbing in the car, and the woman said that they had just used the bathroom and come out. There had been a segment on the television news about a train crash in North Dakota that killed a lot of people in a construction zone. The boy had said that it looked like where they had come through, and the others had all watched the coverage. It had only been a minute or two, she told her husband. He looked at the clock. It said ten oh five. Time had just turned itself backwards.

The man had been driving for a while. The others had fallen asleep after breakfast. This morning, like the others, had begun early. The friend in Wisconsin had told the group about a reptile house in southern South Dakota, and that was going to be the stop for the next morning. The friend had also told them about a town called Wall that was kind of cool. They thought that would be a great resting place for the day. It would not be too many miles this day if they stayed in Wall. The family could use a little bit of a break from the grind of the road. It had been many miles since the sister's house and would be many more to the coast.

The man couldn't shake the feeling that they were being followed. They were few vehicles on this highway, yet one seemed to always be in the distance. The man could not make out the car, as it was too far away. But it was there. It seemed to have been there since they left the sister's house. When they stopped, the man would look for the vehicle but see no sign of it. As soon as they got on the road though, there it was; always following at its safe distance.

They made it to Wall in the early afternoon. It seemed like a small town, and there were many tourists. The friend had told them about the large store in this town, and the family wanted to check it out. It was very easy to find a hotel during this time of day. The prices were right, and the group unpacked the car. They left the dogs in the room and went on the adventure through the Wall drug store.

There were so many tourists buying the normal tourist wares. The man did not like these kinds of stores, and this one was no different. The only difference was that this one was very large.

Soon after entering the first store, the man and girl were looking at the cheap items for sale. They would not stay long in this tourist trap and went in search of the others. They passed a short bald man in long shorts, a Hawaiian shirt, and sandals with his white socks pulled up to his knees. The tourist smelled like he had shit his pants. It was one of the worst smells either of the others had ever smelled.

The man and his niece passed the older guy, and he looked to them with hatred in his gaze. The man said to the other, "God bless you". The other guy cringed away like they had attacked him. He scurried into a corner of the store and disappeared into a section of coats. The man and girl quickly made their exit. Their sense of smell had just been raped.

The man found some books that would be good for his business. The woman had wanted to find her mother a nice Cameo broach, and this was the place to find just that. The family made no other purchases in this town. It was all the stuff that they saw at thrift stores all the time anyhow. If they were to buy tourist items, they would be much cheaper second hand. They would only be used in an art project, anyway. This family would not be throwing their money to the greed on this day.

They had returned to the hotel within the hour. They did not want to leave the dogs behind for very long. The day was still young. The man had seen a sign for the Badlands National Park, and they talked about going there. The man and niece were smoking on the second-floor balcony when they saw a large man, dressed in black, standing on the edge of the hotel parking lot. He was in the far corner of the lot where nobody was parked yet. There was not another soul to be seen.

The man decided to go and talk to the figure. The niece was not to be left out on this endeavor. The two walked right up to the large figure and immediately realized that they had been wrong. It wasn't a man dressed in black at all. It was the trunk of a large palm tree that had been chopped down. The shadows had made the trunk look much different. On top of the tree, perched with a solid stare, was the crow.

The man shook his head in disbelief. He had known there was a man there, but now it had changed into this. The man looked at his niece and saw the confusion on her face also. The bird cawed at the two three times while bobbing its head towards the East. It flew off in the same direction, looking back once, calling for the two to follow. The next decision was obvious for the two. The crow had flown into the Badlands. They were going to follow it.

The wait to get into the park was very minimal. The man thought that they had seen more cars and people in Wall than here in the Badlands. "Tourists were silly," he thought to himself.

Prairie dogs were everywhere, chirping their warnings to the rest of the gang. Heavy dark clouds had begun to accumulate on the horizon. The weather looked like it was going to get bad. The family was very happy. For the past two mornings, the man had been telling the others that they would be storm chasing. He had followed his satellite on the cell phone, but all the storms were in the complete opposite direction. This storm is what he had been waiting for.

The family had stopped at the visitor center to ask some questions about agates. They were very interested in finding some of the beautiful stones. After the artifact situation at the sister's house, agates were on everyone's mind. The park ranger was a very odd lady. She was about the man and woman's age. She seemed to ignore the family at first. Another guy came in, and she was very nice to him.

The man was used to this kind of behavior. He knew what was going on. She didn't trust the family. The tattoos gave the lady the wrong ideas. After the other guy had asked his fiftieth question and left, the man approached the ranger lady. He asked her where they could find agates to take home, and she showed him on a map the spot that was okay to pick through. It seemed like a very long drive. It also seemed very confusing. It was like the lady was giving them directions to a place that she had never been to before.

The Badlands were a beautiful place. The rocks looked like nothing they had ever seen before. It looked more like an alien landscape than something on Earth. The first stop was breathtaking. They were surprised at the lack of visitors. The canyons and cliffs here were impressive. Wildlife was scattered about the terrain in every direction.

The family hiked around a bit and soaked in the sights. The wind began to whip up along with a chill in the air. The storm had begun to come closer with the wind, and now it was upon them. Lightning lit up the dark sky.

As soon as they got into the car, the rain began. It was large drops, but not too heavy. They still had a great view of the scenery. They continued to get out and walk around some, but the dogs would have none of that. They stayed in the car the whole time. The rain was starting and stopping. The lightning bolts were followed by strong claps of thunder. The clouds, for a bit, almost looked like tornado weather. The family was hopeful, but it did not materialize. The man told them it was probably for the best, anyway. Out here, there was no place to take cover. They had seen what tornado weather looked like without the twister materializing.

They had to pass out of the other entrance of the park to get to the spot set aside for treasure hunting. There was nobody in line at this gate. The family realized their mistake after passing the agate spot twice. The man saw the spot and pulled in. There had been a small opening in the fence, and the man had driven through. Instantly, he could tell that the mud was very slick from the rain that was still coming down. He did not stop. He did not want to get stuck out here in the middle of the Badlands in a rain storm. He kept the vehicle moving and slid around the enclosure until he was skidding out of the fence opening. Safely back on the asphalt, the man put the car in park. The family got out to retrieve rocks.

The woman, niece, and dogs were back in the car in seconds. The mud here was a form of white clay that stuck to their shoes and embedded the rocks. It was like having concrete shoes. The man and boy did not care. They loved rocks and had hunted them together many times in the past. They each found so many nice specimens. The better ones were shared with the other. They talked about finding arrow heads or dinosaur fossils, but mostly they just talked about the good time they were having on this trip.

The boy exclaimed, "What's this Grandpa?" In his hand was a small stone that looked like a human skull. Whatever it was, it looked to be fossilized. There was a depression on the bottom of the stone that looked like an inscription. This stone held a story. The boy said to his grandpa that he was ready to go. He had found what he had come for. Being soaked to the socks, the man agreed. After ten minutes of digging white mud off their shoes, they were heading back into the park.

The drive out of the national park was just as amazing as the rest had been. The storm had passed to the South, leaving a very bright rainbow in its wake. The rainbow seemed to light the way for the family. It was a different kind of light than anyone in the car had ever seen. It appeared more like solid beams of light pressed together to melt into endless hues. Its color range encompassed colors that the family had never seen before. It was like their eyes, seeing only three before, could now see multitudes of spectrum. The rainbow seemed to be coming from the ground. As they passed by the light spectacle, the crow morphed from the colors and swooped in front of the car. Briefly, the man saw the bird; he could see all the colors of the rainbow in its feathers. The crow was the rainbow, the two were one.

It was about forty-five minutes back to Wall and the hotel. The family was getting very hungry. It was time to get back. Some ladies at the tourist shops told the man and boy about two different restaurants in town that were very good. The family made their choice and packed up the car. They had decided to bring the dogs with them. There was something about this hotel room that they didn't care so much for. The canines would be much happier waiting in the familiar car.

Buffalo burgers were a must for everyone. The restaurant was very busy when they got there, but there was no wait for a table. The food was very good but overpriced. It was a typical tourist town. Everything was about how much more money could be made. It was all about the greed.

While waiting for the waitress to bring the check, some local farmers, who were standing at the register, decided to talk some trash on the family. The man pitied people like this. Their lives must be very bad if they had to talk about others who they knew nothing about. This was one of the reasons why the man was sick of humans. They were all just concerned with themselves instead of thinking about the whole picture.

The man kept his gaze on the four farmers. They had been laughing and pointing at first, but stopped when the man did not look away. The waitress had still not come to take their money, so they were forced to stand under the watchful eye of the man. The awkwardness of the actions the older men made told the man everything. The farmers were regretful of their words. They would not look away from their shoes. After paying, all four farmers finally returned the man's gaze and gave him a nod of the head. The man returned the nod with genuine empathy before looking away. The rest of the restaurant was unaware of the spiritual bond that had just been made.

Many had talked about saving humanity. The man thought this was hopeless. No matter what happened, if there were many humans, they would be fucking things up. The humans who were meant to carry on the species through their enlightenment were the One. The chosen. They were the ones who did not fall into the tactics of the greed. They were the ones that had lived their lives by the truth. They were the ones with the true wisdom.

Rolling into the hotel parking lot after dinner, a large lightning bolt flashed in the distance. A blue light, like a digital clock, flashed in the top of the trees after the light had passed. It was like an aftershock of lightning. The woman asked what the blue light had been and the man was relieved she had seen it. They both agreed that it was like a digital clock that was searching for its time. The man said maybe they were just in a game and it was a glitch. Maybe they were just characters in some video controlled by a joystick. This glitch was something that some technician would have to work out tomorrow after the family had moved on to the next level.

The rest of the group looked oddly at the man. His words were always a little nutty, but being part of a video game was a little over the top. They all wondered where he came up with his ideas.

The family was done. The day had worn them out, and the food had been the last straw to break their tired backs. The girl's back had been hurting her all day, as had the boy's head. The tolls of the road were starting to take their dire effects. They were all tired in the mind and bodies. Rest was here, and very much deserved.

The man had been writing for a while when there was a knock at the door. The entire family had been snoring, and the sound did not awaken any of them, even the dogs. Another soft knock and the man stared at the door. He had a bad feeling. He suddenly was very sweaty and felt kind of ill. There was a terrible smell in the room. It smelled like the guy at the tourist shop earlier.

This time the knock was a bit bolder. It seemed to fill the man's head with dread. The others were still snoring. "Go away," the man said quietly. He knew it would be a very bad idea to open that door. It all seemed so familiar to the man, but he did not quite know how to react. He just knew that he wasn't going near the entrance.

Strange sounds squished down the hallway. The sound and the feeling were gone in minutes. The smell had also completely dissipated. The man did not like this hotel. This room, and the entire premises, had a very bad energy to them. Odd things happened here in the past, and the man thought that odd things still happened all the time. The man wondered how many people came up missing in places like this: Right in the middle of America: Right where all the interstates connected: Right where all the tourists flock to.

He had been asleep for some time when water sprinkling on his face woke him up. He thought that it was his grandson playing a game with him, but he was wrong. He was standing in the parking lot, looking up to the sky. The rain had returned and was gently peppering his face. "How had he gotten out here?" he wondered. He was not one to ever sleepwalk. He was wearing the same clothes as he had worn to bed, but now they were soaked from the showers.

A bright bolt of blue lightning lit up the night sky. The blue light in the tree was once again present, but now it was much brighter. It reminded the man of the dream he had where he could reverse time. This felt almost the exact same as that dream. This time, he was going to remember how to turn it back and return to the way things used to be. This time, he would be able to bring his people back.

Another bolt of lightning, and the light in the tree dissipated. The third bolt was so bright that the whole parking lot lit up with a strange light. It had looked like an x-ray. The light had illuminated a large figure standing in the corner of the lot. It was only about fifteen feet from the man. A red glow and the smell of tobacco told the man that the stranger was close.

Tonight, the man was going to contact the being that had been following them the whole trip. The man sensed that this was the driver of the car that had always been there, but not ever there. He took another two steps, but the figure did not move.

The glow of the cigarette cast a subtle red luminosity on the stranger's face. The man saw a glimpse of familiarity. It couldn't be. The man's heart began to race. He took the last two steps, until he was a foot from the stranger. There seemed to be an icy cold coming from the being. It hit its cigarette one more time, fully illuminating its face.

The man was not shocked. He had realized moments before that this was his brother, and now it was confirmed. How he had gotten here, the man did not know. The man opened his mouth to ask his brother just that when a bolt of lightning tore from the clouds, ripped through the air, and struck the man in the center of his forehead. The energy hit the man directly in the third eye.

Everything got real bright in the man's mind. The purest of light raced through his being. He did not know it at the time, but the lightning completely reset his inner sight. Nothing would ever look the same to the man again. The last of the barriers had been removed from his being. Now everything would be crystal clear to his sight and perception. Now, he was whole again.

He could sense that he was laying on something, but the light precluded any of his other senses from functioning. A familiar voice said, "Wake up".

The brightness began to fade. Reality was cast in a different light now. Everything was soaked in the radiance that had permeated the man's mind. He had a hard time making out objects at first. The command to wake up was repeated. He looked to the voice and the shadow behind it. The light did not allow the man to completely see the being, but he knew who it was. He could feel it and hear it in the shadow's voice.

This was his brother.

The sibling spoke once more with urgency.

"We've got to get going!"

CHAPTER 28

The man awoke in what he thought was a cold sweat. The bed sheets were soaking wet around his skin. They had molded themselves to his body. He felt like a sausage. The room had no clock, but it was still dark outside. His mind was stuck on the dream he had been having. It had seemed so real. Had he possibly been outside for real? The man got out of bed and went into the bathroom to dry off. His towel from the night before was still damp, but it provided more than enough to dry the wetness from his body. He was soaked.

After getting sufficiently dry, the man passed the mirror going into the other room. He had to stop and look again. In the mirror, there were multiple people in the room with him. They were all milling about doing their own business. The man could make out three women, two men, and about five children.

One of the children in the mirror saw the man looking at her. She stood very still, unsure of what she was seeing. In her dimension, the man looked just as she looked in his dimension. Neither were startled. They were not like the rest. The two beings separated by the parallel looked familiar to the other. An unknown message was sent between the two. It was a message of understanding.

The man stood looking at the mirror and its inhabitants for a full minute before heading back to bed. He had felt the energy in this room as soon as they had entered. The dogs had felt it, too. The man had seen it in their actions. Now, he had seen the other entities that called this place home. Their presence had been strong before, but now that the man had seen the actual beings, he could easily detect their whereabouts throughout the room. He could even distinguish each of the beings' energy and place it with the visual he had of the entity. He had crossed into their dimension.

It didn't seem like he slept, but he remembered having dreams. Slumber must have visited him sometime in the early morning hours. He was alone in his dream in a room that was empty, except for the medical bed he laid on. A bright light obscured any detail of the room. It absorbed the man's being. He heard the others calling his name, looking for him. He could not remember anything else from his vision except for the feeling of dread.

The man was first out of bed, like every day. The boy had wanted to go to the reptile house outside of Rapid City. He had not asked to go to any specific place this whole trip, except this one. The others had all agreed to take the boy and check it out. The man had researched this place and found out that dogs were allowed. They would all be able to go together. He also found out that it got crowded fast. It was best to get there early and leave early.

The girl was up and ready next, and then the woman and boy got going. The woman had once again made the coffee the night before. It was brewed up in minutes. The bags were packed as the family got ready. They had gotten into their routine many states ago, and now it was just like autopilot. The man couldn't find his flip flops. He had them the day before, going outside in them to smoke on occasion. They were nowhere to be found.

The family packed the car, followed by the custom of searching the room for any left behind items. The man and woman would both perform this ritual every day. The woman said, "Here are your flip flops, they're all wet."

The man looked to where the woman was kneeling beside the bed. It was her side of the mattress. He did not know why his sandals were on her half and not his own. He crouched down and saw that the carpet was very wet all around the shoes. At least an eighteen-inch circle of water dotted the ground. The dream from the night before came flooding back into the man's mind. He felt light headed a bit, and sat back onto the bed.

The woman stayed with the man until he felt better. He had told her that he just got a head rush from standing up too fast, but the look in her eye told him she knew better. She had asked him how his flip flops had gotten wet. He had answered with a slight grin. The woman knew her husband had lost his mind. She just hoped he could hold it all together to get them back to the Pacific Ocean. She felt in her heart that when they arrived there, everything would be alright again.

Driving through Rapid City was a construction zone disaster. The man wondered why municipalities made such a mess of the roads when they were repairing them. It seemed not too hard to plan the work around the traffic, and the traffic around the work. If everything flowed together, everything worked out just right. This was not how it worked with those in charge. Nothing flowed in the government, except a bunch of bullshit and greed. Money that the common folk would spend wisely was just thrown around like monopoly money by the corporate leaders. A game piece was all that money meant to the elite anyhow. They had created it as another way to control the humans. It was all part of their game. They had no use for currency. They had absolute control.

The man was becoming frustrated. The morning had already begun on a negative note. It was zone after zone of construction. Everything just seemed to get worse. The man recognized this. He was a first- hand account of bad things happening in succession. Things would get worse and worse until some light would come in and make things all better again.

The tank was empty. Gas stations lined the construction area, but most were not easily accessible. At last they couldn't wait any longer. They had passed more than ten gas stations, but this was the one the man had chosen. He followed his heart. It told him the way. He heard the faint call of the crow as he got out of the minivan.

When the man and girl walked into the convenience store, they both realized why they had come this way. It had seemed to take them so long to go such a short distance, but now the truth was obvious. They had come here to meet the clerk at this store. He was a man of about fifty-five, slight of build; just an average guy. But his kindness was genuine and immediate when the two walked into the store. There was sincerity in the clerk's voice as he told the two about the coffee, the construction, and whatever else he could think of. The man and girl poured their coffee while gladly listening to what the clerk said. They, too, had joined the conversation and had a new friend by the time they were ready to pay for the coffee and gas. The man said he would use the bathroom, and the girl said she would pay.

The man recognized the cleanliness of the bathroom. They were ones to keep their business back in California clean and he was happy when he found similar businesses. He thought this must be a mom and pop gas station.

When he came out, he sensed something was wrong before his eyes saw. His vision had shifted into another realm. The third eye had opened once again. It's like the scene had shown itself inside his head, like he was wired into the security camera. What he saw made him freeze in his tracks and duck behind some shelves.

Two large bearded men, wearing flannel shirts, had entered the store and were in the process of robbing it. One of them had a shotgun pointed at the clerk. The other assailant had the niece in a choke hold, using his large tree like forearm like a vise. His grip around the girl was so tight she had started to turn red. This assailant was holding a pistol that was not pointed at anyone. It was like a prop in a movie, hanging by the side, ready for action.

The man was never one to hesitate. He saw his quick plan and began his creep toward the robbers. The store clerk saw what the man was doing but remained very calm. He reached into the drawer to give the gunmen some cash. He told the robbers that the timed vault opened in ten minutes. He waved a handful of fives and tens in the direction of the vault he was speaking of. Both the robbers looked toward the lure of the green. They were for the briefest of moments distracted by the clerk's words and actions. They were here for greed.

This was when the man made his move. He had carried the same knife on his belt for the last ten years. His friend had made it for him out of Damascus steel. Folded, it was barely three and a half inches long with a very smooth action. Now, the quiet lock of the blade made the stealth move deadly. The man slowly pushed the tip of the blade into the bottom of the large robber's skull, right where his spine met his brain. The man stiffened, twitched twice, and fell sideways dead. His grip on the niece was instantly released, and the girl was freed.

The shotgun guy spun around and fumbled to take a shot at the man. The man pushed the girl aside just in time. The clerk had pulled his own pistol out of the drawer and blown the robbers brains all over the spot where the girl had just been standing. She had narrowly missed being covered in death.

Silence filled the convenience store for minutes that seemed like hours. The clerk looked to the man and told him that they should go. They had saved his life, and he was grateful, but the police would be coming soon, and he didn't want to get them involved. He said that the cops around here were very racist and did not know how they would feel about a couple of heavily tattooed people killing a couple of their local good ole boys.

The man asked the clerk what would happen to him. He was a black man, and there did not seem to be many black people around here. "It's okay," the cashier told the man and the girl. "I know my way around the folks here. This is the tenth time this year that my store has been robbed, and now I finally got a couple of them fuckers. They killed my brother earlier this year. We had made a promise when we opened this store together to see it through, no matter how bad things got. Well, I'm still here. Thanks to you, mister. Now go. I see you are good people. I see that you have a destiny that you are fulfilling. Just like me." The clerk threw the man some hand wipes as he was finishing his speech.

"Sir, I see you will make it fine." the man said, "God bless you". He finished the cleaning of his hands and knife with the wipes the clerk had given him. There had not been a lot of blood. The blade was thin and hit the sweet spot right into the robber's brain. Nevertheless, there was some blood on the knife and hand. Washing death from his hand was the best cleansing that he had ever had.

The man and girl kept a knowing eye on the clerk as they walked out the store. The cashier was already pulling the DVR out of the recording device, erasing any evidence of the family being there. The man asked the girl if she had paid for the gas, but the clerk said just go. The boy had already pumped gas, and there was no need to pay.

He urged the family to go. The police would be coming soon.

The man held onto the hand wipes as he came out the door of the convenience store. He had a baggie in the car that would be perfect for this garbage. He would have liked to rid himself of it here, but DNA testing had come too far for that. You could never be too careful when it came to the greed.

The man and girl, walking to the car, decided not to tell the others about this. The boy had been looking forward to the reptile house for eight hundred miles and they didn't want to ruin his experience. The man knew he would tell the others eventually, but for now, this was the best way.

When they got to the car, the woman asked what had happened inside the store. They thought they heard shots, and the boy said the place lit up once. The man and girl assured them that all was well. They had just gotten into friendly conversation with the clerk and got caught up in time.

"What's up with the bloody hand wipes then?" asked the woman.

"I got a bloody nose, and the clerk gave them to me. I didn't want to leave them behind in case the government is trying to get my DNA." They all laughed at the man's comments. He put the bloody tissues in the zip lock bag that he had stashed in the door panel. The bag went back to the same spot. His wife knowingly handed him some fresh wipes and they, too, went in the bag after their purpose had been fulfilled.

Once clear of all the construction, the family could begin to breathe again and get their thoughts together. A stop at the grocery store was a daily must. A supermarket was never a hard thing to find in any state, and South Dakota was the same. The boy stayed in the car with the woman. He was amped up and ready to go. The grocery store could easily have been postponed until after the reptile house.

The man needed to get out of the car. He had looked in the rear-view mirror and seen the look on his niece's face. It was one of shock. It was the same look he felt on his being. Stopping for groceries would give them a chance to unwind.

On the walk to the store entrance, the man asked the girl if she was alright. He said that what happened back at the store had been a little crazy. She told her uncle that she was fine. The madness that had happened to their family in the last couple of years had made her pretty oblivious to most things. Where she lived in California, too, made things out here seem mild. She had known that crazy things were going to happen on this trip, and they had. It was all part of it.

"Yeah, but that was out of control back there," the man said. "That guy had taken you hostage, and I just straight up killed that fucker. I've gotta tell you, I don't feel bad about it, either. Actually, I feel pretty damn juiced up right now."

The two laughed. A woman walking by looked at the uncle and niece and thought in her head that the two were insane. She had never heard a laugh like that come from any human. It seemed more like the sound that an animal would make.

The people of this grocery store were very nice. Almost as nice as the clerk they had met earlier. They gathered up their food, water, and ice for the day. They regretted not getting a cart, nor even a basket. They were used to having the boy there to help carry things, but with just four hands, they were stretched. They piled their purchases on the shelf checkout island and began to fight with the machine. The man knew it was coming; this was the first years of automated checkout, and so far, he had found not a single machine that worked smoothly or properly. This would be the same.

As the young clerk was punching her secret codes, she looked at the man and girl like they must be dumb. 'These machines were so simple,' was what her look told the others. An older gentleman who was the only live cashier told the two to slip into his line. It was still very early in the morning. The store had only a few patrons at this hour.

The cashier spoke about how the automation of things and increased technology were ruining everything. He said he was glad he was old and didn't have to live to see what was coming next. He just knew that whatever was coming, it was not good. The man and cashier talked for a bit about this subject. The girl interjected that someday we would not even talk face to face with another human. All our talk will be through computers. All three agreed that it would be a sad day when that happened. Humanity had been a dream that had become forgotten.

On the way to the car, the man and girl spoke about how nice people in South Dakota were. They both said that they could live in this area. The man reminded the girl about the robbery just thirty minutes before, and she reminded him where she lived now; the same city that he had grown up. She was just like her uncle. She went along with the way things were, adapting to the changes as they flooded her being. Death had taught the family well.

Again, the man told the girl that he had felt an intensity killing the other being. He had never killed someone before. He was on an adrenaline rush, like when they had gone skydiving together. They both laughed at this and headed to the car.

It was going to be a long day. They needed to get to the reptile house before it got to be tourist hell. They also needed to get far away from this city and the deeds they had committed. They were not the criminals, but they knew how cops were. They would make anyone a criminal if that's what they wanted to do. They just didn't have to like you and would commence to ruining your life.

Only three cars in the parking lot told the family that they had arrived in time. Using the internet, the research had once again paid. The man thought it so silly that most used the internet to keep connected with people. This was the last thing he wanted. He didn't want anyone to know about his life. He didn't want to know about theirs either. If they were your true friend, they would call or send you a message, or go old school and write a letter. He used the internet as his tool. Anything he was to buy or anywhere they were going, the internet and his research were the solution to wise decisions. The man wasn't going to be sucked into technology like most, but he wasn't going to ignore it either.

The man could not stop thinking about the dirty little secret in the bottom of the car door the entire way. The thoughts lingered until they got to the reptile house. As soon as they parked, he emptied the bag into the garbage in the parking lot. The bag would go in a different garbage bin. Again, he could never be too careful. Like the garbage, the incident was discarded from the man's mind.

The reptile garden was a place the man could have bypassed. The enclosures for the animals seemed small. They were nicely made, and the animals seemed healthy. They all seemed to be well taken care of.

The man had always disliked zoos and the like. He felt bad for the animals to be enclosed in cages. There was nature all around outside, but most people didn't have a moment of their day to stop and appreciate it. They would rather bring their families to places like this, along with all the other sheep. Look at nature, crammed in one day, in one place, and then get on with their drone lives.

There was a dome in the middle of the place that held orchids and birds. The boy and man went first, as there were no dogs allowed. The flowers were beautiful and provided some nice pictures. The tropical birds, however, did not seem happy. They followed every movement that the two made.

A young girl who worked there approached the two. They were the only ones in the dome at the time, and the girl seemed bored. She asked them if they had any questions, but the man said no. He was never one to have a tour guide. If there was a choice, his was no guide.

He could see clearly what was going on here. The birds looked to the two as they walked through. Their eyes pleaded with the man and boy to open the doors and release them. The man thought how horrible humans were. He thought they deserved any fate that came their way. The arrogance to keep other animals locked up in cages was terrible. Again, these creatures seemed to be taken care of, but there was sadness in their eyes. Their auras, too, were bleak and drab. Their only pleasure was to play with the very species that imprisoned them, day after day, year after year. The humans!

The woman and niece took their turn inside as the man and boy walked around. There was a circular hallway around the dome that had enclosures for many different reptiles. A very large alligator was in a room behind glass. The beast was enormous. The man felt a strange connection to the reptile. He looked around for a way to free the gator but came to his senses. What had he been thinking? Releasing the alligator. He had never had thoughts like this before. It was as if the gator was telling the man to release it. Briefly, they shared their thoughts. The reptile was filled with misery and pain.

The man walked away, unable to help the creature on this day. He assured the beast, though, that its time was coming, and it would be free to roam. The man had told the gator which direction to go when it was released, and what part of the year to go. If it followed his words, the man had said, it would survive and be free.

The four family members met up in the middle of the hall and checked out the rest of the exhibits together. The woman and niece agreed with the man about the animals. It was sad for humans to treat any creature with less thought than themselves. They spoke about how humans did not even show respect toward each other, let alone 'lesser' beings. Mankind was a word made up by the greed. Man had never been kind and never would be. Man was anything but kind.

The last of the cages came not soon enough for the man. He was ready to go outside. The energy inside the reptile zoo was a very dark one. The animals were very depressed. The man could see that their auras were flat and lifeless. They existed just because they were not allowed to desist. It was almost like they were being kept alive on artificial life support. They were fed by an entity and could not leave their small enclosure. Their natural ways were taken from them and locked into a tiny box with their energy. All the people sticking their faces to the windows made it all the worse for the creatures.

Outside, the clean Midwest air was a welcome relief to the family. The boy wanted to go see an alligator show and a couple of other performances. The man, woman and niece went in search of other things to do. They were not into these kinds of productions. The man told the others, as they were walking away, that the thing he didn't like most about these shows was how the guy with the microphone would talk nonsense. Even as a child, the man had seen right through these guys and stayed away from any entertainment with an MC guy. He felt like they were usually foolish and for little kids.

The woman and girl both laughed and said they felt the exact same. The girl said maybe they should go watch just to see if the guy lost a body part to the alligator. The man said if they all were over there, then for sure something like that would happen. They all laughed and walked through the grounds. It was better to stay away from the alligator show.

The woman had seen some giant tortoises and wandered in their direction. The man and niece saw an enclosure in fake stone and went to investigate. There was a large owl inside the pen which stood about thirty inches high. The bird immediately honed its keen eyes in on the teacup Yorkie. The bird fluffed its wings. Its pupils seemed to pulse as they got bigger, then smaller. It shot off its feet like a rocket, propelled by the promise of that tasty treat in front of it. The girl pulled back in shock. The owl hit the glass with a terrible impact. The hunter came at the dog again, and hit the glass with such force, the window cracked. From its base to the very top, where it met the fake stone, the fissure was deep.

The bird perched on the ground and caught its collective. The Yorkie was no longer in its sight. The owl had seen the crack it had formed. Now the man read in the bird's eyes a story of escape and freedom. This was a mighty bird. It was ready to fly free once again.

"Now," the man softly said, while looking in the predator's eyes. The owl fluffed its wings, as if gathering all its energy in the center of its being. Its pupils exploded with intensity. The bird leaped to the window. One great flap of its mighty wings, and a push with strong legs was the only propellant it needed. It smashed into the window with the force of a tree trunk. The glass exploded outward, landing in a scatter of broken shards some fifteen feet away. The shards littered the asphalt walkway.

The owl landed on top of this glass. Its eyes, moments before mighty, were now dazed and confused. The bird tried to regain its footing, but the glass was making it impossible to get its claws securely on the ground. The bird screeched once in its frustration. "Here, hold the dog," the niece said, handing the Yorkie to the man as she passed rapidly by.

The girl raced the fifteen feet to the bird and bent to assess the situation. She held out her hand and the owl leaped onto her forearm with confidence. The girl stood up, proudly displaying the giant horned owl sitting on her arm. The man couldn't believe what he was seeing. His wife had heard the glass break and now was running toward them. She, too, saw the girl with the owl on her forearm.

The owl seemed to regain its strength and its wits as it fluttered its wings on the girl's arm. The bird was searching the grounds for its next action. The man could see in the creature that it knew it was free. Its aura was one of sweeping shades of gray. The girl's aura seemed to mix with that of the bird that perched on her arm. The brightness of her being seemed to mix with the dull aura of the large bird. The aura of the predator changed to a color of dark red as the bird gained its strength and new freedom. The girl had given it some of her energy.

As fast as it had happened, it was over. The owl flew into a tree on the other side of the perimeter. It paused there only a moment before spreading its wings once again and flying off into the distance. The girl would later swear that the owl had looked right at her when it took its final flight. The man and woman would later confirm her story. The man told his niece that she was now connected to the bird for the rest of their lives. They had shared their energy. The girl had rescued her friend.

The man began to wonder where all the employees were. He couldn't believe none of them had accosted them on this situation. He scanned the entire yards for as far as he could see. The three of them were the only people out there. The man heard the voice of the alligator wrestler in the distance, talking his nonsense. He figured the other employees must be over there with all the other tourists.

The man looked for cameras but did not see any. He felt fortunate that they were the only ones to witness this strange event. With the internet and everyone having cell phones, they would surely be all over the news and the internet tonight. It would take about ten days for something on the internet, no matter how benign, to ruin your life. The internet was indeed the antichrist.

The gift shop at the gardens was the best part of the experience. It was not your normal tourist shop. This store offered items that were difficult to find in other places. The man saw a necklace with a pendant that bore the same symbol his brother had used. He had put it on everything in his house. It was the symbol for the One. His brother had known all about it, and now here it was, in a little gift store in South Dakota. The man bought the necklace with the intention of giving it to his wife. He liked to buy gifts for people and then leave them in the bag with the other purchases. When they got home and were looking at the things they had got, it was always the best surprise. These were the true gifts that you gave in life. Not because you had to because of a special day, but because you wanted to.

The girl came over and excitedly told the man that there were singing bowls for sale here. The two were very in tune with the singing bowls. They had taken an astral trip at the mountain house about a year before. The friend of the family had loaned them a singing bowl to try out, and the family had become very enchanted. They had been looking for their own singing bowls since that time. Their search had ended.

The man and his niece tried every brass porringer that the place had. There were over forty, but they wanted to make sure they got the perfect one. There were various sizes, but finally they both decided on the bowl that fit their energy best. Some tourists, a couple of about sixty, came up and asked the two what these bowls were. The girl told them all about the musical device, in a very professional manner. The guy picked one up and immediately began to make it sing.

The man looked at the guy oddly, he was sure it was the same guy that they had first met at the Grand Canyon and many times after. He was playing the bowl well. It brought the man back to the night at the house when his niece had played a bowl similar to this one. It had been the night his mother had died. It had made the man go into a trance then. It was happening again.

The guy's aura danced around his flesh pod and the bowl, like they had become one. The man could faintly hear the girl giving the woman instructions on how to play it. As her husband was playing such beautiful melodies, his wife was silent.

The man's wife brought him back to consciousness. He had been floating in that space in between parallels. That place where all of life's answers resided. You just had to get to that point and embrace it.

She told the man that it was time to go. The boy was feeling sick suddenly. The man and girl brought their purchases to the desk. The lady was very nice and was proud of her collection of singing bowls. The man and girl praised the clerk on the variety of the store. They told her that it was the best part of the reptile house, and she blushed with pride. She was the one who purchased the items for sale.

As they were leaving, the clerk called out to the man and girl, "God bless". The two turned and repeated the greeting back to the woman. They both felt good vibes from this lady and were happy to get these bowls and necklace from her. They believed that when you bought something from someone with a good presence, a bit of their energy would be retained in the purchase.

The singing bowl from the tourist lady filled the store as the two were leaving. The man looked to the girl and smiled. They both knew that the girl had just taught the lady how to use the bowl. She had opened the older woman's eyes. They also both knew that the tourists they had just encountered looked very familiar.

As they walked out the door, five of the zoo workers went running by, toward the outside enclosure. They seemed to be in a panic as they raced through the lobby, crowded with tourists waiting in line. The memories of the owl came flooding back to the mind of the man and his niece. They had been hypnotized somewhat by the singing bowls and had forgotten about the incident. Now it came rushing back to them as they hurried out the front door.

Crossing the short distance to the car was rapid. Halfway there, the crow swooped within fifteen feet of them and dropped a wooden dowel looking object into the parking lot. The girl picked it up. It was one of the tools used to play the singing bowl. "How had the crow got it from the store?" the girl asked her uncle. He asked her how she knew the bird had gotten the stick from inside. He asked her if she had checked her bag.

The girl was surprised but not shocked to see that her stick was not in the bag with her singing bowl. She had seen the lady put it in the bag all wrapped up. The wrapping was still there, but the stick was in her other hand, dropped from the talons of the crow. She asked her uncle how the bird had gotten the stick and how he knew that it had happened. The man told her that crows were tricky, mischievous creatures that liked to play games. He had seen the stick, it looked like hers, and he had just figured out the rest. "This bird has adopted us as part of its flock," he told his niece. "That's their game amongst their kind. A kind of hide and seek."

The girl tucked the stick into her bag and tied the top. That mischievous crow wasn't going to get anything from her this time.

As soon as they had exited the doors, the man noticed that the parking lot was full. There were over five hundred cars here now. There had only been three when they arrived. The family all agreed that they had not seen many people inside. Who did all these cars belong to they wondered. Then they saw the line. It stretched down the sidewalk and into oblivion.

The family all thanked the man as they buckled up. They asked the boy how he was feeling, and he said that he was feeling kind of sick but would be alright in a bit. He just needed to get some sleep. The woman took over driving for a bit. The reptile house was a thing of the past.

As they were driving away, unbeknownst to the family, the park employees came rushing out to look for the perpetrators in the attack to free the owl. There had been one witness who told the others that the rescuers had been three men and a woman. It was a young girl of about ten who was the one to behold the events. She said they had thrown a rock at the window.

In truth, the girl was lying to protect the family. They were her family. This was the niece who had not come to visit with her siblings in Minnesota. This was the oldest of the three. She had kept her identity hidden when she saw the others because of what she had seen at the owl enclosure. She had made up her scheme and it had worked. The workers were none the wiser.

The family stopped somewhere on the road to let the dogs run. The humans also needed to stretch. The group had passed into Wyoming. The country was turning more forest like. The family was enjoying the new scenery, but the miles were wearing on them. They had a mission to get through today and were right on schedule. Fourth of July weekend was only a few days away. They knew there would be countless more tourists on this popular weekend. They wanted to be far away from it all.

Driving through Mount Rushmore, the family grubbed on some cherries. They had been missing the fruits of California the whole trip. Now their bodies were craving fruits and vegetables. That was seventy five percent of their diet back home. They had purchased the cherries at the grocery store earlier in the day. They turned out to be delicious. The family could tell they were getting farther west with the quality of the produce. They were getting closer.

Mount Rushmore was a nice place to see. The traffic was not too terrible, but it was also not great. They could see the monument from different angles as they were driving towards it. The man stopped a couple of times so that they could get a grip on the magnitude of the carvings. They were enormous. The family was very impressed. They drove to get to the main trails but found it to be a mess of cars and tourists. It looked like a professional football game was cracking. The fee to park was eleven dollars. The family decided to not stop at this spot for walking around. They could go anywhere up the road, pull over, and get a great view of the Presidents. The family did a drive by of the main part while looking for their own personal spot.

It didn't take long to find. A spot about a half mile up the road provided the view that they were looking for. The lack of people made the experience that much better. The boy had begun to feel better, so the group got out and hiked around some. The mountains and plants were awesome. The stone effigies only enhanced the scene that nature had graciously provided. The family was impressed to see up the former President's noses. The sculptures were amazingly done. They all had a deep respect for the work which went into this project. It was truly a National gem.

It was sad that it had been stolen land from the natives, but it was still impressive.

Down the road more, the family saw a marmot, deer, bighorn sheep, and lots of tourists. They stopped at a secluded area, and the woman and boy did some rock climbing.

The man and niece combed the area for rocks and other things that they could make into stuff when they got back home.

They stayed at this spot for some time.

After the woman had been back for thirty minutes, the boy had still not come back. His grandma finally had to go and find him. She, too, was gone for about ten minutes. When she returned, the boy had already gotten back and was asleep in the back seat of the car. He had told his grandpa that he wasn't feeling well again and needed to rest. The woman asked the man how the boy had gotten back without her seeing him. The man said he did not know. The boy had just wandered down the same path that the woman had been on.

The boy was groggy and out of it. His color was grayish, and he had a cold sweat going on. The others all promised to check on the boy regularly. They might be making a trip to the hospital this day.

The family drove through a fifty-foot tunnel. It seemed like they were in a movie. Emerging from the other side, straight ahead about two miles, was a beautiful view of the Monument, framed by miles of trees. The man stopped and took pictures. This view was his favorite. The faces looked fainter from here because of the distance. This increased the power of the Monument to the man. Its impact from every angle had been amazing.

It still did not compare to the beauty of the land which had been raped to create this monument to the greed.

The family continued through the Mount Rushmore loop. They were tempted to see the Crazy Horse Monument in work but would have to come back another time for that. The family was sick of all the cars and motor homes. They were ready to get back on their back roads and enjoy the freedom the countryside brought. Clouds had begun to form in the West. This day was far from over.

Driving through the Big Sheep mountains was a test of patience for the man. The rain was very hard and relentless. The road held the water, which caused terrible hydroplaning. He had driven through a lot of bad weather in his life; this ranked among the worst. The man was a very experienced driver. He accepted the challenge. He turned up the music some and got the playlist rocking. With both hands on the wheel, he navigated through the deluge and the other cars.

The gas light flashed on the instrument panel. Things could not get any worse.

The man did not tell the others about the fuel warning. He figured there was no need to worry them further. The lightning had begun and now was almost nonstop. Once, it even seemed to fill the car. The man felt the electricity flowing all around. He knew the others must be feeling it, too, but he had to concentrate on the road.

They were in a life or death situation.

Thunder shook the car. The man could hear the claps even over the stereo, although it was turned very loud. It's beat mixed with the thunder, truly rocking the car.

In one of the flashes of lightning, the man saw a strange shape filling the sky. It looked like it was part of the clouds, but something was different. It was a giant airship. It was all gray and blended in with the clouds so well. The image was gone as soon as the illumination from the lightning ended. The man thought he had imagined it.

The next bolt of lightning came from the same spot that the man had seen the craft. The blue flash, like a digital clock, that he had seen the night before, was once again there. This time it was large and filled most of the sky. The man got an uneasy feeling in his stomach. He was familiar with this feeling. It was the same one he had as a child; the feeling of ugliness inside. He shook off these feelings like he had months before, the last time it had happened. He had a duty. It was time to get the family to safety. It was time to get off the road for the day.

After thirty miles and an hour of driving, they were free of the tempest and all its madness. It had been thirty miles an hour for the entire time, and at times that was too fast. The lightning had continued the entire time, but the man kept his eyes on the road. He had no control over what was happening in the sky. All he could control was the steering wheel.

The rain finally stopped. It was time to make up miles. Getting gas at a small market was the first stop. Filling up and stretching were very necessary after the ordeal the family had just gone through. It had been harrowing. Like all tragedy in their lives, though, they had made it. Their will and energy were strong. They took care of business.

Wyoming was a beautiful state. The countryside was very green, and there were animals everywhere. The lack of cars made things all the better. The music got turned down, and it was back to conversation. The family spoke about Mount Rushmore and the miles in between. The rain storm had been intense, but they had safely made it through. Now they all had a good energy flowing. They had once again cheated death. It felt like a celebration inside the minivan.

The family ended up in a small town called Thermopolis. The family really liked this little burg. There were natural hot springs all around the city. The river running through town had discolored the rocks with its minerals. Here at this place, a hand of nature had been playing artist. The family had seen this art the entire trip. Art abounded on this planet. Nature was the most gifted artist of all time. Our planet truly was God. The Creator!

Sunset was approaching, and the family was tired. They headed for a hotel to drop off the dogs. A small hotel in town was perfect for the night, and there was a grocery store across the street. The guy behind the hotel desk was a young guy, maybe seventeen. He had an Army veteran hat on. The man inquired about the hat, and he said that his dad had served in the Army, and he was the one who ran the place. He had many medical problems, so the son would fill in. The clerk wore his hat because he was proud of his dad, a disabled veteran and bronze star winner.

The family went into the room and the girl instantly to the bathroom. The look on her face when she came out immediately told the others the whole story. This toilet was backed up. They would be moving to another room. The man went in search of the clerk, but he had somehow disappeared. It was fifteen minutes before the guy came out of the office. By now, there were three other people waiting to rent rooms. The man could not wait for this nonsense. He grabbed the youngster and replaced his key. They headed to their new room. It had been one more hotel ordeal. The family had become accustomed to it. Something always seemed to go wrong with the lodging every night.

The family would not be leaving the dogs here alone. They would be much happier in the car than in this corner of this old hotel on the side of the highway. They also wanted to explore this quaint little town a bit. There were hot springs all around, and natural baths. The smell of sulfur hung heavy in the air, permeating the sense of smell. The terrain was very beautiful; another signature masterpiece from Pachymama.

The four went walking around some paths and next to a river that mixed with the hot springs. The dogs were in paradise to be able to run around and be free for a moment. The long days on the road were hard on the little travelers, too.

They walked around a large monument that had been formed by a single drip of water. The calcium content in the water had accumulated from the single drip into a monolith of twenty-five feet high and twenty feet across. It looked like a giant wax beehive. The family was impressed and walked all around. A cloud came from nowhere and produced one bolt of lightning that hit the deposit directly in the center of the top. The mound became translucent for a moment. The family saw it all. It was like they had seen an x-ray of the monolith.

None of them talked about it, but they had all seen the same thing. Inside the calcium deposit was a large stone about five feet across. It looked exactly like the stone the sister had given the man, Toomey. All of them had the same thought, 'the others had seen it too. There was no reason to talk about it.'

It had begun to get dark. The air here was very nice here. It was cool and fresh from the minerals. The four were worn out, though. As much as they would like to stay here longer and explore, it was time to go.

The family went in search of a place to eat. They found a Mexican restaurant, which was across the street from a Masonic Lodge. They sat upstairs to eat and had a great view of the entire street. On the way up the stairs, the bartender hollered to the man that they did not allow hats to be worn in this place. The man had been afraid of this happening in the Midwest. It was one of their quirky traditions. His dad had taught him all about it.

The man had been planning in his mind the whole time what he would do when this situation arose. Now it was here. He had simply taken off his hat and headed into the upstairs dining.

Luckily, there was no one else in the room. The waitress had been busy getting the table ready and had not noticed the man's forehead. Maybe, he thought, she would not see it at all. He sat with his back to the door to lessen his chances of being seen. Where he had grown up in California, you would never sit with your back to the door. It was a quick way to lose your life. In this case, though, in this small town, he wanted to become invisible to as many people as possible.

It was not the first time the desire of invisibility had come to the man.

He knew that this situation could start a serious uproar. There were a lot of conservative, religious folks in these parts. They were not hard to offend.

His plans did not work out so well. The waitress had walked to the other side of the table to take the man's order. There was no way she could have missed the eye on his head. Just as she was stepping around the table, the eye opened. The man had a new view of the woman now. He could see through her eyes. He was looking at himself. The waitress's eyes got very large. She opened her mouth and made a sound like throat singing. The man thought that maybe she was going to pass out. He jumped to his feet, seeing his actions from two separate aspects, one from his point of view, and one from hers. The man was there to catch the waitress. He steadied her as she fought off his touch. She leaped back about five feet, fear filling her face.

The waitress stood frozen with terror. She could not move. The man reached out his hand gently, as one would to a foreign dog. He touched the woman's arm, just below the elbow. Her face went from fear to enlightenment. She had just been saved. She knew the truth. She looked to the man and said with sincerity, "thank you". The waitress disappeared without taking the man's order. The man told the others that they should leave. He knew that there was going to be gifts involved now and wanted no part of it. He would rather go to another place.

The woman said that she was too hungry for that. She was sure the waitress was coming back with their food soon. "You just need to be patient," she had told her husband.

The niece and grandson had never heard of the Masonic Temples. The man gave them a brief oversight into this secret society. The boy pressed the man more but the man told him he did not know much about them. He had told them everything that he knew. He had not given them his opinions, though. He did not believe in these secret societies. There were too many secrets already on this planet perpetrated by the greed. The man believed anyone who kept secrets from all humans was a part of the greed. The man had no time for any of it. He was one who understood the power of one. The power of a few was not the natural way. One was everything.

The waitress brought a bonanza of food. There was a little sampling of everything. It was some of the best Mexican food any of them had ever eaten. They grubbed like they had not eaten since leaving California. After thirty minutes of feasting, all at once, the family pushed themselves away from the table. They were done.

The waitress had somehow sensed when they were done. She came upstairs with the bartender. She told the family that the man was her husband, and she had wanted him to meet them. She said it was the first time in fifteen years of business that she had done this.

The man stood to shake the hand of the bartender. He was one to always stand to shake hands. His Navy upbringing had taught him this, and it was something he would always respect. The bartender's eyes lit up, and the two shook hands. "My wife told me there was something special about you, I had to see for myself. God bless you, sir," the bartender said to the man.

"God bless you," the man said in return. The two men shared a look of mutual respect and broke their connection. The man asked if he could have the check, but the owners both refused to take their money. They shared warm handshakes with the rest of the family and headed back downstairs.

The man tucked a hundred-dollar bill under one of the plates, and the family made their way downstairs. Opposite of upstairs, the downstairs was full of people. Everyone in the place stopped eating, some with their forks in mid-air, and stared at the family as they made their way out the door. One of the ladies that they walked by was crying. Her tears were tears of hope and gratitude. The man quickly led the others out the door and immediately put his hat back on.

Back at the hotel, the family all split into different directions. Some made phone calls while others just got away. The man went across the highway to the grocery store for provisions. The store did not open until nine in the morning, and he planned on being long gone by then.

He realized that people of Wyoming were very nice. He found that most people were nice to you wherever you were, long as you were nice to them. Put off good energy, good energy came back to you. Some called it karma, he called it the cycle.

The man's hands were full of plastic bags and groceries as he made his way back across the highway. There was not much traffic at all. The sun was almost gone for the day. This town had a strange feel to it, the man thought to himself. It had an underlying layer of darkness that was only perceptible because of his heightened state of consciousness. Sometimes the man thought that he had absorbed some of his family's consciousness, increasing his own. Other times he thought back to being a child and having the same kind of weird thoughts even then as he did now.

On the far side of the highway, the man saw a figure standing. He thought maybe it was the boy, waiting for his grandpa to get back safely. It was difficult to see if it was his grandson in the light of dusk and at the distance. A car zipping by halted the man's progress. As he got closer, the man realized it was not his grandson. It was the figure in black that he had seen so many times on the road. The scene was so familiar to the man, but so foreign at the same time. He thought that tonight was the night that he contacted the being.

When he got a few steps away, he slowly came to a stop. The creature's face was twisted into a very large grin. The mouth seemed to take up most of the face, leaving small bits of features poking out here and there. Teeth that did not seem like any animal the man had ever seen filled the creature's head. There was row after row of teeth. All were of various sizes.

"Who are you?" the man asked the creature.

Words did not come from its mouth, but the man understood. The creature said, "You know". It raised its hand, and the man took a half step backwards.

The white light was the last thing that went through his head. It had just appeared out of nowhere. The brief recollection of the lightning earlier made a strange bridge of thought in the man's mind. The smell of burnt metal filled his nostrils.

The bags of groceries scattered over the highway. The man had been barely two feet on the asphalt and was dragged over three hundred feet in a trail of blood, before the big rig could stop.

The driver had been past his deadline and was making up for lost time by hauling ass through Thermopolis. Now he had run someone over. He had looked straight on at the man just before he had hit him. The pedestrian seemed to have just appeared in front of his truck. He had not even had time to swerve away. The man's face had seemed so strange to the driver. It looked like he was oblivious to everything around him. He would never forget that expression for the rest of his life. He would never forget this moment, either. It would haunt the driver's dreams, both conscious and unconscious alike, for the rest of his life.

A large crow flew over the truck as the driver was getting out. The bird dropped something on the pavement right below the truck steps. The trucker bent to pick the object up. It was a stone. The guy had never seen anything like it. It looked like a small fossilized alien head. Two small chips were missing, giving the impression of eyes. The whole thing was maybe one inch across. It was red, the inside black. The trucker thought it strange and dropped it into his pocket. The bird had temporarily taken his mind off what he had just done. He did not know how, but it had.

The distraction of the bird quickly passed. There was no more time for this nonsense now. The trucker had much more serious things to think about than a stone.

CHAPTER 29

The man woke up with pains throughout his entire body. His dreams had been very strange, as usual on this trip. This night, though, they had been the strangest he had in years. He dreamed he was being operated on, and he was fully awake. He did not feel pain. His limbs were being replaced with robotic devices. The doctors had strange masks on, covering artificial looking faces. Their instruments seemed to be alive, moving independently in an intelligent manner.

The man couldn't make out anything beyond the light that enveloped him and his surgeons. The rest of the room was completely dark. Figures in masks faded in and out of the shadows. Each of them had their own organic instrument, ready for use. The man was not scared in his dream. This seemed like a familiar thing to him. It's like he had dreamed the same thing over and over but it just kept getting more intense every time. It was as if his dreams were advancing to different levels, like a video game. Every dream prepared him for the next. Somehow, in his vision, he knew that everything was going to be alright. He was going to make it to the final level.

The sleep the night before had been restless. The hotel room wasn't very nice. After the ordeal with the first room's toilet, they should have known not to stay in this place. If the family was to get bed bugs, this would be the hotel. The air was hard to control, leaving the temperature in the room uncomfortable. Then there were the dreams. All of it combined to make a lack of sleep.

The man knew what was going on. His dreams were so real and prophetic. Throughout each day, things were coming true that he had envisioned in his subconscious. Sometimes they even seemed like he had lived the same events more than once. Enlightenment was coming continuously, but it seemed like every time he grasped something, he had already gained that knowledge before.

Somehow, the knowledge he was gaining on the road was getting erased, only to be learned again and again. He thought that maybe they were just crossing into different dimensions and didn't know it. Each dimension had a knowledge to be gained before that life could be complete. When it was over, the soul would bounce into a parallel and be life as usual. Mostly usual, that is.

On the drive to Yellowstone, the man kept to himself. He had so much to think about. His head needed to clear, but it was getting more and more difficult. He knew that his mind could not take much more. Too many things had been happening in the last years and on this trip. They were all coming into perspective now, at the same time. It was almost overload for the man's brain. An avalanche of information dropped on his being all at once.

On the stretch of highway to Yellowstone, the man noticed the top of a mountain ahead that looked like a profile of an old man's face. The top of the mountain brought back memories from deep within his mind. When he was much younger in the Navy, his brother had bought a painting and left it at his house for some time. His wife at the time and himself had noticed a face at the top of the peaks. This one was the same exact mountain. He remembered it so clearly. There was no mistaking it. He had looked at that painting every day for six months.

While he was looking on with wonder, the mountain opened in front of the man. It looked like the face in the mountain opened its mouth and emitted its toxins. A reddish smoke came out of the large crater that was forming. Lightning struck from within the caldera. A strange craft appeared briefly but was gone in an instant. Cars all along the highway came to a halt. People jumped out of their cars to take pictures. Tourists were running up the hill to get a better look. The man saw his opportunity and pulled into a tunnel. It reminded him briefly of when he was a child and his father had pulled under an overpass to save the family from a tornado.

Rocks began to rain down on the entrances to the tunnel. The Earth was shaking with a vengeance. People were screaming and running for their lives. They were all getting bombarded by red hot boulders. None of the fools were worried about their precious pictures now. Nobody on social media wanted to share pictures of their doom.

A landslide buried the family in their shelter. There was no escape. Another car had barely made it into the tunnel, too. They were the only two cars that had made it.

When the ground stopped shaking, the passengers of both cars got out to figure out what was going on. The two groups merged. The family had been asleep, so they had no idea what was going on. The man could only guess it was a volcano or something. They were close to Yellowstone. There was a lot of seismic activity in these parts.

The two groups assessed the damage inside the cave with the illumination from the headlights. The family decided to head to the far end of the tunnel and see if they could dig out. The trembling of the Earth had stopped, and they hoped that the cataclysm was over.

The boy helped the man fish the flashlights out of the back of the car. They were going to need more light than the headlights provided. The tunnel was eighty feet long. They began their journey to the far side when the other car blasted their horn. The family approached the other car at the insistence of its passengers.

The other group of survivors decided it would be best if they stayed put in their car. Help would surely be on its way. Digging would be a waste of time, they had said. The man tried to tell them that it would be better if they all helped, but the other tourists would have nothing to do with it. The family began the eighty-foot walk to the far side of the tunnel.

Less than ten feet in, the rumbling began again in earnest. This time it had seemed to get worse. A large rock came free from the top of the tunnel and came crashing down, right onto the other car and its passengers. The whole group was instantly killed by the boulder that was twice the size of their car. They had not even known what had hit them.

The man tried to figure out why this was happening. Surely there would have been indications a volcano was going to erupt. He stood looking silently at the smashed car in front of him. So many emotions went through his head. The woman, standing next to her husband, silently held his hand. They both were trying to wrap their minds around this strange turn of events.

The boy and girl had begun to dig some rocks away on the far side. Some light filtered in through gaps in the stones, providing the smallest amount of light. It was a light they were thankful for. The man and woman went to help the others. The boy had dislodged a large rock and it tumbled down the pile. More light filtered in.

The family all saw the smoke in the light rays dancing their dance. They seemed to be alive in their movements. The family smelled the smoke after they had seen it. It smelled like pure sulfur. They knew they were in trouble. The air seemed to be getting very thick with the toxic gas. The family was having a hard time breathing. They all tried to make it back to the minivan and the safety of the interior. They only made it about halfway there. They had to stop and take a break. They huddled together. Sleep was impossible to ignore. It was the sleep they had been ready for their entire lives.

A loud sound brought the man out of his slumber. 'Where am I,' he wondered. He was in the car, but the others were not. He looked around and saw steam all over the place. They must be at Yellowstone. "How had they got here?" He wondered. He didn't even remember leaving the hotel this morning.

The dream he had been having was fading, but he remembered being stuck in a tunnel or something. Had he been operated on, also? He could not recall. His dreams were so vivid again. They all seemed to mix together somehow. Sometimes, lately, he couldn't remember if his memories were real or if he had just dreamed them. He knew he was losing his mind.

The man got out of the car. His old friend, the crow, made a pass around the car, telling the man that all was well. He spotted the others on a wood walkway that snaked around some geysers. The dogs saw him before the others and came running. The geysers were amazing, as was the terrain of this park.

The man made his way to joining the others. They were all in a great mood. The woman asked her husband if everything was okay, and he said yes. He asked when they got here and she told him, "you drove all the way here this morning. As soon as you parked, you laid back the seat and instantly fell asleep. The rest of us have been exploring this place for over an hour."

Walking amongst the geysers, the man tried to remember the events of the morning. The last thing he remembered was walking back from the grocery store the night before.

The woman told the others that someone had fallen into one of the boiling cesspools a week before. They all asked how he had done that, and she said that he was trying to get a selfie next to one of the steam vents, lost his footing and tumbled in. He had died instantly. They had never found his body. The stupidity and vanity of humans never ceased to amaze the group.

As they walked along, one of the geysers erupted. Some erupted almost continuously, while others not at all. One of the geysers was a rolling boil of water that came up about ten feet. The entire family saw the skeleton float through the water, then disappear back into the fissure in the ground. They all looked at each other with a knowing look. The family never spoke of what they saw. There was no need to. Their faces said it all.

Like many beautiful places on Earth, tourists will straight fuck it up. Yellowstone was no exception. The crowds for old Faithful turned the family away. It had been the same at Mount Rushmore. They got away from the main attractions and enjoyed a more peaceful time. They had traveled a lot and knew how to get away from tourists. Usually, the tourists congregated around the main attractions. There were equally beautiful places away from the flock.

They stopped by a bridge, devoid of tourists, that spanned a pond filled with lotus. The man climbed down the small hill with his camera and began to take pictures. By the time he had taken five or six, ten cars had seen their minivan parked there and thought it would be their stop, too. If someone else was there, then it must be a good spot. The man disliked this kind of sheep behavior so much. It is why he had such a dislike of the humans. They could not think for themselves. They were always looking to follow. It was because they did not use their creativity. They relied on others for that.

The man could not deal with the sudden influx of people. He climbed the hill back to the road, passing by at least fifteen others. When he got to the top, his niece was ten feet away. People were all around, staining the secluded spot the family had found just moments before. The man shouted and pointed into the forest. He yelled excitedly, "look, there's one right over there. I knew we would see one."

The girl went along with the joke, instantly knowing what her uncle was up to. She pointed to the same spot and said, "Oh my god. I can't believe we are seeing this."

All the other tourists who had just pulled into this spot came running. Most of them had their cameras at the ready. They were all looking in the direction the two had pointed. One guy even ran into the forest in search of the mythical being the others had pointed to, with absolutely no regard for anything but himself and his selfie.

The man and his niece got into the car. The woman and boy were already inside. They laughed so hard at the joke they had just made as they were driving off. They had tricked those fools, and good. It had been like spreading wheat hay for the cattle.

The family found a nice secluded spot on the lake and stopped for a picnic. The clouds had begun to form. They made sandwiches and filled their bellies. While they filled theirs, the mosquitoes also filled their bellies with the family's blood. They wanted to see wildlife something terrible. The man had never even seen a bear in the wild. So far, they had only seen buffalo in this park. It wasn't for the lack of trying. The family had kept their eyes on the forest the entire time. The most prominent animal they were seeing walked on two legs and took many pictures of themselves.

While grubbing his sandwich, the man noticed movement in the tree line. He looked to where the movement was but only saw shadows. He focused his eyes to the darkness and spotted something strange. It looked like a very large human standing next to a conifer. The creature seemed to be very hairy and stood with a bend to its shoulders. The man could barely see the figure and wondered if his eyes were playing a trick on him. It wasn't moving at all. The man blinked. The trees blew in the wind, as did the shadows. The figure was no longer there.

A large crow flew from the forest out over the lake. It looked back to the man with a knowing glance.

The family stopped at a few more wooden paths to check out the geysers some more. They had overheard a couple of groups of tourists talking. They all seemed to be talking about the same thing, like it was front page news across the country. They spoke of the Messiah. They were saying how the Messiah had been born and now they were all going to be saved. There was a strong hope in the people's voices.

Propaganda was what the man thought of all their words. A true Messiah need not be spoken about. Maybe these people should try to save themselves, he had thought, instead of looking for false gods.

After a few hours, the family could not deal with the tourists any longer. An Elk in the trees had spurned hundreds of tourists to stop on the road and get as close to the animal as possible. They were all looking for the best camera shot. This was the final straw. It was time to get out of Yellowstone.

Passing through the village, the family saw irony at its best. There were Elk everywhere in this part of the park. They were walking among the humans, and even seemed to become members of a couple families who were having lunch. A couple of the animals seemed like they were having a picnic with their new, two legged friends. The family laughed at the other people, in the other parts of the park, running to take pictures of elk. Surely, they would feel like fools when they saw what was going on over here.

It was still early afternoon. The family decided to try to make it to Butte, Montana this day. It would be a few more hours on the road but the man said he was up for it. The countryside was beautiful anyway. The man had not minded driving once. He had seen so much of America behind the wheel of this minivan. While the others were sleeping, he was soaking up nature's beauty. The driving would get him tired out, but he did not need much sleep. He would sleep when they got home.

His mind was creating the story the entire time anyhow. He never once got drowsy while driving, because his imagination was working in overtime. All the sights he was seeing added to the creativity being created. The man felt at one with everything.

They heard a newscast about Yellowstone on the radio. A helicopter had crashed in the park. All on board had died. The family, upon entering the park, had spoken briefly about going on a helicopter ride. They had not wanted to spend that kind of money, though. It had been a lot. They were happy now that they had decided against it. It could have been them on the craft. The radio got shut off after that. The family did not need this kind of news, nor most other. It was back to music from the IPOD for them on the road to Butte.

Butte had grown since the last time the man and woman had been here. More than thirty years before, they had spent some time here. Now talking about it in the car, they could not remember what they had done in this city. They knew that they had been here and even remembered certain buildings, but could not remember anything else. It was like all their memories of Butte had vanished.

Settling into the hotel was a relief for the woman and boy. They were very worn out from the drive, the adventure, and the lack of sleep the night before. They fell into the separate beds.

The man was too wound up from driving all day. He looked in the phone book and found a couple of thrift stores. He and the girl went in search of some treasures. They were ready to get out and stretch. The confines of the car wore on them, too, but in different ways. It did not tire them like the others, it made them wound up with energy that would need to be expelled before any rest was possible.

The stores ended up not being far away, but they still had a difficult time getting to them. There were a lot of one-way streets in this city.

They both sensed that somebody was following them around the town. It was not a good feeling, either. It felt like dread was on their heels. The shadows had caught up to them.

The first thrift store was like dumpster diving. The lady was very rude to the two, so it was an easy decision to go looking for more friendly shops. The lady said something under her breath to the other clerk as the man and girl walked out. The girl turned around and said in the nicest voice she could muster, "God bless." The woman looked at the girl with wide eyes. It looked like she had just seen the light. The two laughed as they passed through the parking lot to the minivan.

Just a few blocks away, they had found what they had been looking for. The second thrift store was large, clean, and the clerks were very nice. The man and girl dug through the store for over an hour. They both found a few things, but the enjoyment came mostly from looking at all the stuff and talking crap about it at the same time. The clerks kept to themselves after giving their warm greetings. The two were the only ones in the large building. They felt very comfortable.

Some old pictures on the wall caught the attention of the two. They seemed to be from the eighteen-hundreds. The man was shocked at one of them. It was a picture of an old building he had seen in town on the way over. But in the picture, it was not old. It was brand new, and a man in a suit was cutting the ribbon in front of the door. Standing to one side, wearing clothes from the era, were the man and his wife. He had to look twice and then looked even closer. There was no mistaking it. It was them. Somehow, they had lookalikes from an era long ago. Maybe it was a past life, the girl said to her uncle. "Yeah," he had said, "and it was the two of us together then like now. The guy cutting the ribbon sure looked a lot like the guy we met at the Grand Canyon. Did you notice that?"

"I did," she replied. She was looking at the man with intensity, trying to see his reaction. His face was blank. It was almost like he was disinterested in the picture and its inhabitants.

The girl was surprised when her uncle did not buy the picture. She thought for sure he would spend the twenty dollars for something so unique. She asked him on the way to the car why he didn't. He told her that too much was happening, and they didn't need to throw more fuel onto that fire. "Our plate is already full. The picture was not a piece to this puzzle. It was just one of those things that are around us all the time, reminding us of the multiple dimensions which exist along our journeys. For all we know," he had told her, "that picture could have been taken tomorrow, and we were here yesterday. It is the way things work."

The two found a coffee shop and headed back to the hotel. The feeling of being followed persisted. They pulled into the parking lot of the lodge. It had gotten much more crowded than when they had left. They pulled into the spot nearest the road and went next door to get a stogie. Walking in the store, the man was struck with a sense of strong déjà vu. He had been in this store many times in the past. A bank of photos on one wall showed all the employees since this place had opened in 1970. The man expected to see his or his wife's face on the wall, but they were not there. The man almost felt relieved. They got their tobacco and headed back to the hotel.

The man asked the girl if she ever thought about why we made some of the decisions that we did. He asked her why she thought they had come to Butte. He told her that something had called him to this place. He had to come here to remember something from his past that was going to be very important for the future. Destiny had truly called him back to this place.

Walking up to the hotel parking lot, the crow was sitting on the top of the minivan. It watched the man and girl walk by, only fifteen feet away. They also stared back at the bird. The two felt a strong connection to this creature. They had been seeing it off and on for the entire trip. They were sure it was the same bird. It seemed impossible, but lately, that was a word that they did not really use. All kinds of oddness had happened on this trip that they would never have dreamed possible before they had started out on the road.

The family went to dinner, but the man stayed behind with the dogs. He was ready for the first time he had been alone in the last month. Alone time was not a thing common in his life anyway. Somebody always seemed to be around him. The man could deal with that, though, it was how his life was. However, he wasn't normally in a car with others and then in the hotel at night, too. The time alone would give him time to draw and write. He was keeping up on the mask book and did not want to fall behind. The journal of the trip was also going well, as was the book of the truth. He knew he was neurotic. He could not sit still and do nothing. He was always creating. When others were not around, his imagination was all he needed. The creations at these times were his best.

The others were gone for hours. The man had fallen asleep for a while. He had been dreaming that he and his wife were scientists, but much younger. They were wearing lab coats and were in a field surrounded by mountains. They were probing the earth with long rods. A short distance away, there were eight or nine more scientists all dressed the same as they were. They were prodding a large metal object that was sticking halfway out of the ground. The part that was sticking out was thirty feet tall and cylindrical in shape. It seemed to have portals lining its side. The man, in his dream, had struck something with his rod and called to the others. An older scientist came over and took over where the man had been. He pulled an object out of his pocket that looked like the rock the crow had gifted them. He held it over the ground, and the dirt seemed to shimmy back and forth. When It settled, there was a glass cylinder, maybe sixteen inches long and twelve inches diameter, lying half buried in the ground. The man could see the eyes and large head of the extraterrestrial. It seemed to be aware of the others around. The man looked to the older scientist and saw that the man was the same one whom he had met at the Grand Canyon. That is when he woke up.

It was nighttime when the family got back to the hotel. When the others came through the door, the commotion had woken the man from his visions. He was so relieved that they were back. He noticed immediately that their hair was completely different. They were now all sporting full heads of long black hair. It was so black, it almost looked blue. They all had a strange blankness in their eyes.

The man asked them if they were alright. His voice seemed to awaken them. The woman said they were fine and asked why he wanted to know. It was then that the man realized that other things had also changed. The boy was now the tallest and the woman the shortest. They had reversed their heights. The girl seemed to be the same height, but something about her legs and arms seemed odd. They seemed longer than they did before. The arm that the man had tattooed was now blank. The man looked to the woman's arms and saw that she, too, had blank skin. What had happened to their tattoos, he wondered. The man asked the boy what he had eaten at dinner and he replied, in a monotone voice, that he did not remember. They all seemed to have changed since they had left the night before.

It seemed like they had crossed into a different dimension while they were gone. These people were not the exact same as when they had left. Maybe they had gone through a portal or something.

The others had all laid down on the beds almost as soon as they had come inside. They were fast asleep in minutes. Even their breathing seemed odd to the man. He had gotten in tune with these people and now they were different. He looked to the other beds and saw his family, but not his family.

The man decided to go for a little walk and clear his head. This was a lot to take in. So much had happened in the last month, but he didn't know how he would deal with the others changing. As soon as he left the parking lot, he saw the flashing lights down the road. Obviously, there had been a huge accident and the fire trucks were finishing the last of their cleanup. The accident was a stoplight away, and the man could not tell what had happened. Not that he cared. He was not one to get amusement from people's misery.

He walked down the highway in the early hours just before sunrise. Not many cars were out, and there were no other pedestrians. The man stopped at a convenience store to get a coffee. The guy behind the counter was very friendly. Being the only customer in the store, the man got sucked into the clerk's conversation.

As the man poured his coffee, the clerk spoke about the upcoming presidential election. They both spoke about how two-party politics were a joke. There were always two shit bags to select from and the outcome would be the same either way. The greed ran everything and it was all for the elite. The rest of the humans were just slaves to the greed. It didn't matter how they voted or what their opinions were. They were meaningless to the elite. Most humans could not see it, but it was true.

As the clerk talked about a pipeline that was to go in nearby, destroying the water supply, the man walked about the store enjoying his coffee. A wall of photos drew his attention. He was always one to look at old photos wherever he was. There were many pictures of Butte in its heyday as a mining town. Most of the pictures were over a hundred years old. The most recent was one taken in the eighties or so. It was a picture of a shiny metal cylinder sticking out of the Earth about twenty feet in the air. It looked like a large metallic cigar. Standing around the object were about ten scientists dressed in official looking coats. None of them were smiling. The man looked closely and saw exactly what he was looking for. The two figures standing on the far-right side of the group was himself and his wife. They were both much younger, as this picture had been taken thirty years before.

It was exactly like the dream he had just a few hours before. The man now remembered why he and his wife had been here so many years before. But how could he have forgotten something like that. This had been one of the craziest things he had ever been involved with.

The man shouted to the clerk and asked if this picture had been taken nearby. The clerk was no longer behind the counter. Now he was standing directly behind the man, looking over his shoulder at the pictures he had seen many times before. The man smelled an odd odor of mold on this guy. He laughed to himself at the thought that maybe the guy was a mushroom.

"That picture there was taken right here on this spot. This store was built about a year after that photo was taken. Over the years, all kinds of reporters and UFO nuts have been coming around asking questions. I tell them all the same thing. I know nothing about some UFO here except in that photo. I remember being a boy and all the hoopla over the Martians crashing here in Butte. I never saw the craft. There were a bunch of guys running around here for a while with black suits and black sunglasses. There were also a bunch of scientists running around. It was probably the most exciting thing that ever happened in these parts. When it was all done, the newspapers said that it had been a top-secret spy balloon that had crashed landed. Of course, there's always been talk to the contrary, but with no evidence it is just all a conspiracy."

"Is there a place I can get a copy of this picture?" the man asked the clerk.

"As far as I know, it is the only one in existence." the clerk replied. "The government confiscated all the film from the local developers that had been taken before the craft was secured. The owner of this place developed his own film and that had been the one picture he had taken. He always talked about the friendship he had struck up with the different scientists who had come. It was what had inspired him to build this station all those years ago. God rest his soul. You can just have that coffee on the house, mister. It was worth it to have someone to talk to this morning."

The man made his way out the store and back up the street. The sun was fully up now and the heat was soon to follow. The man thought that maybe he could get a little rest before hitting the road but he knew that it was a big maybe. He was wide awake and ready to go.

The crow seemed to follow the steps of the man. It was flying around at first and then came up and hopped along in cadence with the man. The two were communicating in a tongue only known to them. The man had figured out many miles before how to communicate with the animal. Now they were walking down the highway in Butte, Montana chumming it up like old friends. The man understood the bird, and the crow understood the man.

They spoke of the coming. They spoke of change and how things were going to be good again. They spoke about happiness returning to their lives. The man knew who this bird was. They had been related in many lives before. Their path was the same in every life, in every dimension. The crow and the man were one.

Entering the room, the blue glow from the television lit up the small room. The man could see the others sleeping soundly and crept in as quiet as possible. When he went to turn off the television, an electric jolt ran up his arm and into his heart. The pulse had made his heart beat one strong thump. All the blood from the man's body seemed to get drawn into his heart in the brief-moment, only to be expelled again in a rush throughout his entire being.

The man lost consciousness as his heart stopped beating. He fell backward, right onto the bed and next to his wife.

Sleep had come after all.

CHAPTER 30

The man and girl were the first to awaken, as was the case every day. The girl had been having strange dreams this whole trip. Her dreams, unlike her uncle's, had never stopped after the tragedy. They had remained in full force. She had always been one to have odd visions throughout her life. Her mother had thought about getting her counseling at one time. She had been having a difficult time understanding the difference between her dreams and reality. Her dad had stepped in and said that the child just had an active imagination. He had told his wife that his brother had been the same when they were children, and now look at the things he created. "They just have creativity in their souls," he had told her.

The dreams this night were very real to the girl. She had visions that her uncle had gone outside to investigate a bright light and had come back hours later. He had come in the room silently as to not disturb the others, but the girl was lying awake, in her dream, watching the whole scenario. The man wasn't alone when he came back. There were two other beings accompanying him. They were much smaller with large heads. The strangers sensed the girl looking at them and raised their fingers in her direction. She had felt an intense pulse of pain go through her skull, and then she woke up.

It was now morning and her uncle had already gotten dressed and was ready to go. It looked like he had never gone to bed. The girl told him to wait a moment and she would be ready to go, too.

The man went outside to wait as his niece got ready. He wasn't sure if he was dreaming or awake, but he was sure he had wandered around this town all night long. He had seen things in his subconscious that showed him that they were not alone on their journey. Others had been on their tail watching them all along. He had encountered some of those beings the night before, but he could barely remember any details of this meeting. Everything was so clear, but hazy at the same time. It made the man uneasy to have this feeling. It was like he was losing control of his existence. Something was trying to make him go insane.

By the time the girl got outside, the man had completely forgotten about the night before and was ready to go. "Why are you in the same clothes as last night?" the girl asked.

"I don't know," the man replied.

"I saw you come in early this morning. I thought I was dreaming, but I can't shake off the vision. You looked like you were making two shadows at the same time, but there was no light in the room. I thought it was a dream at first, but when I just now went in the bathroom, the truth came to me. You were not alone, and I was wide awake."

The man and his niece looked at each other for a moment while standing in the parking lot. Simultaneously, they began to laugh loudly. It was laughter of madness. A murder of crows flew over at the siren the two produced. The birds mimicked the sound that they were hearing.

The two were very close. It wasn't just the blood that ran through their beings. The girl had so many similarities to her uncle in spiritual ways. They talked often how every family in their clan had always had the One; the creative soul that stood out from the others. The man was the One in his family as his niece was the One in hers. It was almost like they were the Shaman to their peoples. They could see things the way they really were. They understood about decisions and how important they were to the future. They were the ones who had always tried to keep relationships with the others, even when they were thwarted. The two had also worked very hard from an early age.

The man's father had been the One in their family, just as his mother had been in hers. Their relationship had always been a strong one, too. They understood each other. Their energy flowed together.

They spoke about this before, but this morning everything was very clear. They, too, understood that the woman was the One in her clan, as the grandson was the One in his family. They were together for a reason. Their other friends were also the One. That is the one attraction they had all had together. With so little in common, it had been the strong thread that tied them together. They were all the leaders in their families.

The two walked down the highway in Butte, searching for some coffee. Eventually, they settled for a convenience store and their brew. When they walked in, the clerk was very friendly. "Hello there, back already I see," he said to the two. The man and girl looked at each other blankly. They had known he was going to say that as they walked in. The clerk asked if they were leaving this morning. He seemed to be an old friend to the man and girl, but they had never been in this store, nor this town. While they were pouring coffee, the two saw a picture on the wall of a young couple standing next to this gas station. There were no other pictures on the wall.

"Looks just like you and auntie," the girl exclaimed as she was studying the picture. The man leaned in for a closer look when the clerk appeared just over his shoulder.

"I thought you got enough of that picture yesterday morning mister" the clerk said. "You stood there looking at it for over an hour."

The man suddenly got that old familiar feeling of dread. He knew it was time to get out of here. They poured their coffee, paid and headed for the door. As soon as they stepped outside, the man felt better. His mind spun with the image that he had seen. It indeed did look like him and his wife when they were younger. The car parked next to them in the lot looked just like a car that they had when they had first got together. He had never been to Butte, though. His wife had lived here, but it was his first time. What the clerk had said was the final straw. He had said that the man had been there yesterday morning for over an hour. They hadn't arrived in Butte until yesterday afternoon.

The two walked around a bit, drinking their coffee and smoking a stogie. They spent many mornings on this trip the same exact way. Walking around, talking about this and that. Much of the talk had to do with the truth. There was the Way to live. They both saw it. We all made our own choices in life that would ultimately lead us to the destiny for the rest of our lives. Every decision we made now mattered so much to the future. That is why you always had to be a good person. Even when the rest of the world looked at you like you were bad, the right way would be to stay on the path of good. Others did not know about you anyhow, they just wanted something to talk about, right or wrong.

They also spoke much about their family and the things that had happened. The two were healing their souls. They could both feel it. Their energy together created the One. They were bound by tragedy, but more importantly, they were bound by friendship. The family that still lived meant everything to them. They always had. The ones who stood for something different went their ways, but the ones who saw the light remained very close. Their family was tighter now than it ever had been before. They spoke about the other two with them, asleep in their beds, and how much their energy was integral to theirs. Together they all made the One. The man told the girl not to forget this. When they got to the coast, the One would be united again. Things were going to be changed.

This area of Butte did not have much to offer for the two. It was all corporate stores and greed. The two did not like these kinds of stores. It was still very early, the sun barely over the mountains. They decided to go back for the car and go in search of the real Butte. The man knew that this town had much more to offer. When his wife was younger, she had lived here with her infant son for a winter. She had told the man about the experience many times. Every time they saw pictures of Butte, the woman was familiar with them.

A farmer's market was setting up in downtown. They had found the real town of Butte. They drove through the old buildings and were surprised at the number of them. This place had a very good feel to it. It all seemed so familiar to the two. The crow was swooping through the brick buildings. The creature seemed especially happy this morning. It had something in the way that it flew that was different he thought. It was more carefree and playful.

Coming around a corner into a residential area, the crow was sitting atop a small house. It was cawing and making strong gestures with its head. The man knew this was the house that his wife had lived in all those years ago. He looked to the porch and could swear he saw the woman standing there with a baby in her arms. The image faded quickly.

The man had a very good vibe about the morning and the events so far. They drove back to the farmer's market. Only a few booths were set up, but they thought that it would be enough. They parked and went to walk around, but the man realized that he had not brought his wallet. The girl checked and she, too, had brought no money. They had purchased coffee earlier and had their wallets. They did not understand what had happened to them.

The two laughed as they got back in the car and headed back to the hotel. This had been the final sign. It was time to get out of the Midwest and back to their beloved West Coast.

The traffic was thick on that Fourth of July weekend. They knew that it was just going to get worse. They were on the highway early. There were a lot of miles ahead of them, and they knew there would be so many tourists. The rest stops were full of people. The family was not used to this. After the trip across the states with not many cars, this was a shock to the nerves. People were being rude to each other and driving any which way they wanted. They were all thinking of themselves.

"It is sad," the man had said to the others, "these people have no patience for the other man because they are just concerned with themselves. We have learned patience on this trip and will wait through whatever we have to with dignity."

"Most of them are on their cell phones," the girl pointed out. "They can't even pay attention to what is around them. Probably they are posting pictures of their miserable lives, stuck in traffic, on their social media sites. They are truly pathetic."

The family all agreed. Whenever they had almost been in any kind of accident on this trip, it was because of the other drivers being on cell phones. They had noticed this trend in the last ten years. Ever since cell phones became popular. The man had many theories about the cell phone also. He had spoken with his family and friends many times about the dangers of the technology happening during this time. It was moving too fast. The humans couldn't evolve or grasp its consequences. The planet had become a technology hell. The greed had created it all. Their experiment had moved along very nicely. They sat back and laughed while being served in their mansions.

After some hours on the road, the family was getting tired of the traffic. The rest stops were littered with people with places to go. The man just wanted to be away from it all. Being around all these people made his head throb. So much tension had been put on him in the last years. He had tried his best to not be stressed anymore, but sometimes he couldn't help himself. He tried to be nice to all people and portray an aura of peace, but sometimes humans made it very difficult. He just wanted to get home to California and back to his normal, relaxed life.

The man saw a strange object on the side of the road. It looked like a hubcap, but was taller than most. It was maybe twelve inches high. The man had never seen a hubcap like this one. It looked like a flying saucer from the old science fiction movies that he loved so very much. The object was shiny and had small perforations around the rings, which looked like windows. It seemed to have three levels, which formed the complete saucer.

The man was going to stop and check it out, but he thought better of it. Too many strange things had already happened. There was no telling what that object would bring the family.

A few miles down the road, the boy asked the man why he had not stopped to pick up that strange looking thing. The man told his grandson it was because there was too much traffic. "It would not have been safe to stop", he had told the boy. This, too, had been the truth.

The man stopped many times this day. The miles had caught up with him. The stress with the miles had completely worn him out. They stopped at a bakery and the family had some very nice sandwiches. They were just what they needed.

The group found a nice spot in the forest and decided to have lunch there. The absence of any other people made the place very inviting and unusual.

It was a bit cold in these woods. The sun could not get through the dense growth of forest. A slight mist blowing through the breeze gave the place a magical feel. "This was a very special place," the girl said. The others all agreed there was something very cool about this spot. Energy converged here. Spirits resided amongst and within the trees.

The sandwiches were devoured in minutes. The long drive depleted their energy, and food was what would bring it back.

The dogs were also happy to have a place to run around in the forest freely. They, too, had enjoyed the sandwiches that the humans had provided for them. After macking down on the food, the family went in search of some adventure. They were going to enjoy these few moments away from the rest of humanity. They were going to have some alone time with nature.

The family was far from alone. There were strange creatures in the forest that they could only see out of the corner of their eye. They were like shadows but would go away as soon as you looked directly at them.

The man told the others about what he saw and they, too, said that they were seeing things happening in their peripheral vision. They could not get a grasp on what they were seeing, but there was something there. They could also sense the presence of the other beings. It wasn't only their sight-seeing them, but their sight from within. These creatures lived in this forest, and these humans were the trespassers.

Toomey began to violently vibrate in the man's pocket. A warm energy spread through his being, telling him what to do.

The man slowly took off his hat. He had known it was the thing to do. The eye in his forehead was wide open and ready to see.

Instantly the man saw what he had expected to see. It was what he had felt was happening but now was confirmed. The shadows they were seeing were Sasquatch. There were about six of them, and they were blended in with the forest. They were completely cloaked by a strange power they possessed.

The man was surprised but also fascinated with what he was seeing. He had always been interested in the Sasquatch, and now there was a family of the creatures frolicking in front of him. They could see the humans, but were playing games with the group's vision. They were careful to be very quiet.

One of the smaller Sasquatch noticed that the man could see them. He alerted the others with a sound that the man had heard before many times but had just thought it to be a bird. The others all looked at the man in astonishment. He was the first human to have ever seen the creatures. Their cloak was defenseless against this being. The man looked back at the creatures and there was an impasse. Finally, the man said, "I know that you know. You know that I know. I know that you know that I know that you know. We are the One. This is our destiny. We were sent to meet your family here, today, in this very spot. It has been preordained for a very long time. We will soon unite and help with the change. But the change is here."

The Sasquatch made a strange guttural sound like it was talking out of its nose but its mouth was moving. The creature spoke in a series of clicks, grunts and whistles with a lack of body language. He held perfectly still as he spoke to the man. "We have heard of your coming and welcome your presence. You are the first human to have ever seen one of our kind. This is our first meeting but not our last. We have been friends many times before, but this time is the one that matters the most. This is the meeting that will end the greed. This is the meeting that will begin to heal the wounds your people have inflicted upon Pachymama."

"Soon," the man answered back. He knew his place with the Sasquatch. This was all part of it. He had been having dreams about all of this, and now it was coming true. He put his hat back on, and the creatures faded back into shadows.

"Who were you talking to?" the woman asked her husband. She had been watching him very closely after all the strange behavior. Coincidences were happening right and left, but that did not excuse the man's behavior. He was really beginning to worry her.

"Nobody, just singing a song stuck in my head," he said in reply. The woman knew right away that the man was lying to her. After twenty years of marriage, she could just tell certain things about the man and his ways. Some other cars pulling up to their seclusion made them make the decision to get back on the road with all the other travelers. At least they had just had this one little place to walk around and get good vibes from. It had been the smallest of turnouts on the highway, but something had called to the man. It had been so much more than food and relaxing. They had made new friends and allies here today.

Up the road a bit, the man saw another one of the hubcaps. It was just the same as the one he had seen earlier. This one had a faint glow coming from it. The asphalt around it looked to be liquid, not solid anymore, like it had been melted from the heat on top of it. The boy asked the man again if he was going to check it out, but the man said there was no place to stop.

The woman looked at her husband strangely. She knew why he didn't want to stop. He had the notion that the hubcaps were UFOs or something. The woman sensed that her husband was worried about what he may find. She knew her husband very well. He was not one to pass up on some treasure hunting unless he had one of his bad feelings.

A few more miles up the road, on the shoulder, there was a man with an old Mustang. The trunk was open. The man slowed down to see if the guy needed help, but what he saw made him feel complete dread. The mustang guy was throwing the lifeless body of a young woman into the trunk of the car. The man saw that the girl was bruised badly. He slowed further to get a better look. He wanted to have a couple seconds more to plan his next move. This was something that could not go unnoticed. The mustang guy looked up as they passed. Those eyes met those of the man and girl, sitting behind her uncle. The guy's eyes were blank sockets. His sight was coming from something other than eyeballs.

The man saw from this angle that the body was not a body at all. The guy was throwing a tire into the trunk of his car. Moments before, it had looked like a body, but now the man and girl could clearly see the truth. Also, the man noticed that the guy was wearing dark sunglasses. Perhaps he had been mistaken all around, was a thought that crossed his mind, but was quickly deleted. He knew what he had seen.

The girl asked the man if he had seen what she did. He said he did. The guy was for sure throwing a body in, and he had somehow made it morph into looking like a tire. The man told the girl about how they had been seeing more and more people like this: Strange people who made odd movements, like they didn't belong: Beings who could twist your thoughts to make you see what they wanted you to see.

The man told the others that our real sight was always being twisted into the reality that the greed wanted us to know. On this trip, they had been seeing a 'behind the scenes' vision of the trickery.

These beings were the opposition. The greed and their cronies who would do anything they wanted towards humans and just laugh at the misery they created. The final battle was going to be a whole lot of creatures just like the one they had just seen on the side of the road. These creatures had been sent to combat the One.

The woman told the man to stop ahead so that she could drive. She was worried about these visions that he and the girl were having. She, too, saw that there were some seriously odd things going on, but sometimes the others were taking it a bit too far. She knew that the miles and the lack of sleep had taken a toll on all of them. The miles had stretched on, but now they were almost back to the West Coast. They were almost back home. Rest was not far away.

Just after the woman had taken over the wheel, there was another diesel accident. This one looked like there were casualties. The big rig had flipped over in the median somehow. It looked like maybe it had swerved to miss something and had toppled from the weight and speed. Whatever it was, the truck and its cargo flipped two or three times and came to rest hundreds of feet away. Pieces of truck and strange metal objects littered the highway and the median. The lack of police told the man that the accident had just happened. Already, there were five other trucks and numerous cars stopped. They were there trying to see if they could rescue the driver. The man knew the answer to that question.

The woman had to go slow to miss the debris in the road and the people running. The man told her to not stop. There were enough people on the scene. They would just be adding to the mayhem. As they passed the cab of the truck, a large man in a black denim jacket and a black trucker's hat was there in the shadows. On his shoulder was a large vulture that seemed to be acting as his eyes. The stranger's eye sockets were blank. He kept his face pointed straight ahead. As they passed, the man thought that the trucker resembled the guy with the Mustang, whom they had seen throwing something in the trunk. He could not be sure because of the shadows, but the resemblance was there.

The woman cursed for almost hitting some debris, drawing the man's attention. When he looked back to the cab, the trucker was gone. He had simply vanished.

The man changed the music and the crash was quickly out of their minds. He reclined his seat slightly and pondered what had been happening. Why had there been so many diesel truck accidents? All the people they had seen and the similarities amongst them. They all seemed to be signs that were thrown into their path. The man did not believe in signs to guide his life. He believed signs were something that people would reach out to tell them the path. Signs would pop up here and there giving you some direction maybe, but they did not dictate your future. The path was there. There were no signs along the way that would change it nor guide it. There were no directions. There was only the destiny of the way things to be and the way you chose to make them. If you were on the right path, signs would come up along the way, like billboards. You could read them however you wanted.

All these things happening to them were a part of that destiny. They were happening for reasons that were cosmic. The family was on the path to understanding it all. Their decisions would decide their fate, like it had from the beginning.

The visions had also begun to get stronger. Each of the family had begun to have strong premonitions of the next day's events. The boy had never remembered his dreams before this trip, and now he was watching movies in his subconscious and remembering every little detail. The woman was the same. Her dreams, too, had become vivid, and a few times when she was awake, she had thought of something happening. The exact event would happen within an hour.

The man and girl knew. Their premonitions had always been strong, but now they were becoming epic. They had talked just that morning about the change. It was here. They were having dreams, both asleep and awake, that were showing them in the middle of a battle for the planet. They were somehow a key to the survival of the humans and the planet. There were others who were the dark. They did not want the group's progress to keep on moving, but they were powerless to stop the family. The four were the One. They were to bring balance back to a planet that had been tilted toward the greed for far too long.

The man dozed off with his thoughts. He dreamed that they stopped and picked up one of the hubcaps that they had seen. There was a terrible feeling coming from the object when the man bent to pick it up. It was the same feeling he had so many times in the past; the feeling of dread and being sick. The object was very dark. He had backed away and the object began to emit a strong greenish gray glow. He had seen this glow somewhere before but could not remember where. The glow grew around the man, but darkness enveloped him.

He woke with a start, like when you fall off a cliff in the dream state. He looked about and saw the same country as when he had dozed off. He looked at the clock and was surprised to see that almost three hours had passed since they had seen the accident back on the road. All the others in the car except the woman were also asleep. She looked to be very tired and weary. The man asked if she was alright. She just nodded and said she needed to rest.

She did not tell the man, but she had seen something strange on the highway herself. Her husband had been telling her about a large man in a black suit and empty eye sockets. The woman had thought that her husband had been making up stories to enhance the experience. Then she had seen the being. It had looked directly at her, and she had gotten the worst feeling of dread. It had shaken her up pretty good. As they had gotten away from all the tourists and traffic, she had also noticed that there was indeed a car following them from a distance. It was too far away to tell what kind it was, but it was back there for a very long time.

A turnout ahead was pointed out by the man, and the woman took the small drive into a rest stop. There were no bathrooms, just a table on the side of the road. It would work out perfect for the family. They just needed to change drivers and stretch anyhow. After she parked, the man and boy simultaneously spotted a silvery object at the other end of the parking lot. They both looked at each other and strode off in that direction.

A few feet away from the object, the man stopped. The boy became weary when his grandpa had stopped, and looked to his elder. The man was very pale. "Are you alright Grandpa? You don't look too well," the boy said with concern.

The man did not feel alright. Memories of his dream only moments before were rushing through his thoughts. When he got close enough, he first felt the dread and the sickness. Then he saw the object. It was exactly like the hubcaps they had seen twice before on this day. They were a very strange shape for a hubcap. The man thought it unlikely the same driver lost all his caps. This one had obviously been run over. Half of the circular disk shape was flattened to about three inches, while the remainder was about twelve inches. The tire had not distorted the part that it had not touched. It was only flat on one side, like it had collapsed to preserve the rest of the object.

"I'm okay," the man said to his grandson, "that thing has some bad energy to it." The man was finishing his words as the boy was slowly shortening his distance to the object. The man removed his hat. The eye in his head showed him the truth. The object on the ground was an alien spacecraft that was being used to watch things. There were multiple ones in this region. The owners of these drone like craft had an agenda. Their agenda was control. They had been achieving their goal for thousands of years.

The man also saw clearly that the boy had a different kind of control over the craft. It did not make him sick nor did it affect him like his grandpa. He bent and picked up the object. The man could see the rage emitting from the silver disc in the boy's hand. The beings who owned it were not happy to see that these humans had seen it for what it was and were even playing with it. They were taunting the beings who were helpless. These were no ordinary humans. These devices had been watching the group for a very long time.

The boy held out the object to the man and said, "Look grandpa, it's like a space-ship or something. It has these weird lights or something all around it, and it looks like little windows. I wonder if there are little creatures inside of it." He was looking closely through the small slits in the object as he spoke. He was truly looking for little creatures.

The sense of dread was intense in the man. Suddenly, he made the connection. The conversation with his sister back in Minnesota had just popped back into thought. This was the same feeling as the one they had when they were children, with the pebble turn-ing to a boulder. He had blocked that feeling just months before and was now going to block this one. As soon as he told himself this, he felt a power inside that he had never felt before. The dread was instantly gone. He no longer felt inferior to these beings. Now he was in control, along with his grandson who was about to smash the saucer into smithereens with a rock.

"Wait," the man yelled. The boy stopped his arm motion inches from the rock hit-ting the silver object, which he had wedged on a rock. He looked to the man, who said to him, "Let me see that thing before you smash it. I want to check it out really quick." The man's grandson handed him the object. It felt warm to the man, but not in a natural way from the sun. This warmth radiated from inside the craft. The man turned the object in many directions and spotted some lettering on the bottom of the saucer. It was strange symbols that he had never seen before. The man took his phone out of his pocket and took a picture. He understood how cameras could see things the naked eye could not. The man shook the object but it was solid. The whole thing weighed maybe one pound, much lighter than one would think for the size of the disc.

The man dropped the flying saucer back to the ground. There was no doubt that the creatures who owned this craft were watching every movement that the family made. He could sense being watched the whole time. He had seen, through his third eye, a com-puter type being who was all observing through its devices. This was the being oversee-ing this device. Its drones were its eyes. And now it was scared. The man could sense the being through its craft. This was an actual piece of the entities being.

"Smash that fucker," the man said with a strong voice studded with conquest. He knew that this was to be the beginning of the end. There was no going back now. He also knew that they were ready.

"You killed my family," the boy shouted as he swung the rock down, cleanly smash-ing the complete side of the saucer into crumpled tinfoil. A pulse of energy came from the craft and hit the man's being with its hatred. The energy bounced pitifully off his energy. This was an act of war among species. The boy repeated the words over and over as he stomped, beat, and destroyed the device. The craft seemed to give its last breath and it was done. The boy's tirade was over.

The man had not known why the boy had always said this statement. Since he was young, the man would let him destroy things. The very first time he was about two years old. He had shouted, "you killed my family," just before and during his destruction of a bookcase. The man and woman had laughed so hard trying to figure out where the boy had learned it. He had continued to say it whenever he destroyed something. Now the man knew why he said these words. It was his destiny. He was the Destroyer. These beings had destroyed his family over and over for thousands of years, and this boy was the revenge for his entire bloodline. He was going to be the enforcer of the new rule on the planet. The rule of no greed!

The women were waiting for them when they got back to the car. The woman asked what that had been about over there. The boy said that some aliens had gotten in their way, and they had destroyed them. He was laughing when he said it. The boy told the others how the central being was watching them from the mother ship, or somewhere else, and they had just spit in its face. "Me and Grandpa were not scared," he told them. "You should not be scared either. They are the ones who should be filled with fear."

"You guys need to quit joking around about this nonsense," the woman said.

The girl looked to the two men with animosity. She too wanted to be in on killing some aliens.

The man told the others that it was best if they got down the road. It was just a few more miles until they passed into Idaho, and the West was approaching. Montana had been nice, but it was time to get on.

Idaho was only about eighty miles across at this point, so their experience with the twentieth state was short. The others had slept most of the miles while the man watched the beautiful countryside pass by.

They were swiftly in Washington. Marijuana had been legalized here a couple of years before, and the adults were ready to partake.

The billboards for recreational pot started as soon as they got into Washington. Spokane was the first city they came to and GPS on cell phones provided directions to some nice buds. They had to drive through the city for about twenty minutes to get to their pot destination, but it was well worth the wait.

Walking into the store, it was more like a cell phone store. The employees all stood behind a counter, and their product was behind them. The man and his niece were the only two people in the entire place. They each walked up to a representative and told them their needs. One ounce was the limit for each visit. The man thought that should last the three of them all night. He laughed at this thought. It would probably last them all week.

The smoke looked great and the prices were right. Walking back to the car, the man asked the girl where her sack was. She said that you had to be twenty-one to purchase the weed. She wouldn't be this age for another month. The man said it did not matter anyhow. They had enough and it was time to get on the road anyway. Washington was a big state to drive through, and the holiday weekend was quickly approaching.

The family drove through a large section of Washington. They were very tired and ready to stop, but the highway provided no hotels. The back roads had once again made it difficult to find lodging. They were not complaining though. There were very many beautiful sights in this state. The scenery made up for the lack of hotels. They would find a place eventually, like they always did.

The woman had been checking on her phone for miles, looking for a motel. The possibilities were looking grimmer as the miles passed by. The map said that the next city was Everett, a full two hours away. The man did not want to drive that far, but was prepared to do whatever they needed to do.

Just past Menachee, the girl shouted, "there's one!" The man looked to the right and saw the sign as they were passing the driveway. His heart leapt with hope. He was so ready to get out of this car. This had been a lot of miles traveled today, and he was ready for it to be over. He found a place to turn around and headed back to the hotel.

The family instantly fell in love with the place. A river was next to the small individual cabins. The place looked very clean. It also looked very vacant. The man and his niece went to the office expecting the worse. It was all changed when the owner came to the desk. The two instantly knew why they had not found a place earlier. They were supposed to stay here and meet this lady. She was a very nice person. The man and girl both felt a warm aura from her that was very inviting. The man told her about the dogs, and the owner hesitated just a moment before handing them the keys. She pleaded with the two not to let the dogs run amok. They assured her that their dogs were good dogs.

The lady told the two that everyone said the same thing about their dogs but it was seldom true. The man and girl nodded their heads in agreement and promised all would be well. They were off to some much-needed rest. With their honesty they understood, most people were not.

The family immediately unloaded the car while they still had the energy. All the family went in different directions of exploration and dog walking. The man took advantage of the alone time and rolled some joints out of the recreational pot he had purchased earlier. Being the first time in a state where weed was legal made the man very happy. He had never thought he would see this his entire life, and now here they were. Since he was a kid, he and his buddies had always talked about how cool it would be if the herb was legalized. Now it was time to enjoy some legal weed.

The man looked for his wife and niece but did not see them anywhere. He could not wait any longer. He walked the one hundred fifty feet to the river and lit up. The river was a rushing mass of water and the buzz was a rushing mass of relaxation. The two went so well together after the long day in the car. He was sitting on a car barrier looking at the water when he saw a body floating in the water. It had wedged itself into some tree limbs that were hanging in the current. The water was whipping it around but it was not getting dislodged. His mind flashed on the oddness of this situation. Hadn't he already found one dead body on this trip? Maybe two, he thought, but he couldn't think so clearly about all the details. He had this to deal with right now.

He found a long stick and poked at the corpse. It looked like it was wearing a black denim jacket and jeans. The head and feet were under the water. The third or fourth poke dislodged the body and it rolled over to face the man before getting caught in the rapid flow and floating downstream. The man had realized in that moment that it was not a body at all but a large log that had moss all over it.

"Why were his eyes playing tricks on him like this all day?" He wondered. Or were his eyes really playing tricks on him? Maybe these things that he was seeing were happening in another dimension that was parallel to this one. In that dimension, it was a body. In this dimension, it was a log. The man knew that the dimensions were fusing. Things that had been happening were occurring over and over. Other things were coming together from the past and the future to converge on this very time. He had been feeling it for a while, but the trip had intensified the feeling. The last couple of days had made the dimensions almost become one at times.

When the women returned, the group went in search of their smoking pit. They found it under a nice shade tree in the middle of the cabins with some benches. It was exactly the spot that the family needed to unwind. The boy had gone to explore the river, and the adults stayed behind to smoke some pot. It was a time the three desperately needed, to unwind and get rid of the stress and energy that being so close together for long periods of time creates. They smoked until they had no more rolled and went to the room to clean up a bit. The boy arrived shortly after with stories about a cave he had found next to the river. He tried to get the others to go along on his search, but they were much too tired.

The woman and boy had seen a restaurant and decided to go. The man and girl had bought some fresh fruit and veggies earlier. That and some sandwich materials and they were good to go. They were sick of eating out. They were back on the West Coast; back to their beloved fruit stands. It was time to eat healthy again.

The woman and her grandson were not gone very long. It was still barely light when they got back, and the boy went straight back to the river and the cave that he had found. He had said it was full of bones, like an animal den. The man had told him to be very careful. There were wolves and bears here.

Hours passed before the boy returned. The family had been very worried. Twice, they had gone in search of the boy with their flashlights, with no success. They thought that maybe he had just gone farther than he expected. Finally, the woman had reached him by text and learned that he was okay. He was on his way back.

When the boy got back, it had only been five minutes since his grandma texted him. He told the others a crazy story. He said he had gone back to the cave and went inside. There was something shiny in the back corner, and he crawled in to retrieve the object. He just got his hand on the metal sphere when the ground collapsed under his feet. He had fallen on his side and quickly jumped to his feet. He was standing in a small room that was all white with nothing in it. It was just four white walls, a white floor, and a white ceiling with a dirt door hanging down.

A door led to a long blank corridor. As he walked the seventy-five steps to the end of the hall, the boy counted his steps to keep his mind off the eerie feeling that he was being watched. It was a feeling of dread, like he had fallen into a hornet's nest. When he got to the end, the hall broke into a new hallway that was so long that he couldn't see either outlet. Some lettering on the wall to the right said, 'Aladdin', and had an arrow pointing in that direction. The boy had followed it for what seemed like fifteen minutes when a door suddenly opened in the blank wall, right next to him. A large, eyeless being in all black garments was a stark contrast to the white oblivion. The being pointed to the boy and a siren came from its mouth like an alert. The boy had turned and run. All along the corridor, doorways opened and more of the exact same beings were there, waiting for their chance to grab him. He was frightened at first, but quickly realized that the beings were afraid of him and the device he had found.

The boy had slowed his pace from a frantic run to a normal walk now that he knew that he was not the one in fear. These beings feared him, and they had reason to. He had been listening to his grandpa and cousin. He knew that they were on a journey of truth. They were bringing about a change.

When the boy had gotten back to the original room, the other beings had congregated at its entrance. There were thousands of the dark creatures filling the long passageway. The boy began to shimmy up the doors back into the cave when the others tried to follow. They were trying to come back into this reality with the boy. He dropped the device into the void and the creatures scattered. He used a stick to grab the large doors and pulled them closed.

That is when his phone rang. His grandma said that they were worried about him but he said he was coming back. He said he had only been gone for about thirty minutes.

"Look what I found," the boy said to the others as he fished around in his pocket. He became frustrated. His search became frantic, like the object meant life or death. Dejectedly, the boy said that he must have lost the object. "You should have seen it, Grandpa. It was a stone about this big," the boy said as he lifted his hands and held his fingers to indicate something that was about four inches long and about three inches high. "The stone had an eye in the middle of it made of a shiny metal like the one we found earlier. Exactly like the eye on your forehead."

The boy wanted to go back with the flashlights to find the object, but the family talked him out of it. He had already lost three hours earlier. He had also lost the memory of dropping the device on the other creatures. When he had closed the doors, he had closed reality. Time that he would never be able to account for was gone.

There was no way the family was going to let him explore this place alone again. They told the boy to get cleaned up and they were going to enjoy one more smoke before going to bed. It was getting late. A strange glow came from the West. It was as if the sun had never fully gone down and they were in a perpetual dust. The man had experienced this in the North before. He just didn't think they were that far north.

The glow grew stronger and more intense. There was no way it was still the sun at this intensity, the man had thought. A flash of green changed the tone of the glow to one of an olive yellow hue. The glow remained like it was a permanent fixture in the sky.

The boy couldn't stop talking about his strange experience in the cave and the object he had found. The others finally got the boy calmed down enough to go and take a shower. As soon as he was gone, the others talked about his wild story. They had no doubts about what the boy said, he was not one to make up stories. It had just been such an odd tale. What was a room of white doing in a cave, next to the river in Washington?

A bald eagle flew over the hotel with a fish in its talons. It took their minds off the things that had been happening. The family all talked about how this was Pachymama at its best. They had seen so many cool things in nature on this trip. They were looking forward to seeing so much more.

Unfortunately, the parking lot had begun to get more cars. It was filling up fast. Their solitude was going away. They decided to finish their smoke by walking around the premises a bit. Flowers planted all around the place would occupy their minds, while the other tenants made their way to the rooms.

Just past the main office, the family saw a small shed with a bumper sticking out the back. They were already going in that direction and decided to check it out. They were all fans of older cars and knew there were treasures all around small town America. They saw that it was a Mustang as they got closer. They also saw that it was blue. It looked exactly like the one they had seen on the road earlier. The three got a little closer look and noticed blood on the back bumper and back of the trunk lid.

The door of the house burst open. A large man who looked very familiar strode angrily toward the family. He stopped when his face was just inches from the man. The women both were in a worry. This guy did not seem happy. He spoke to the man, "Time to go home, son!" His tone was a whisper but it felt like it echoed through the man's being. The stranger's voice made the man feel at ease. This man was a friend. The man recognized him. He was the guy from the Grand Canyon, just twenty years younger.

The man reached out his hand to shake that of the stranger's. The large guy extended his arm but a hand did not appear from his denim jacket. Instead, it was a talon. Inside the talon was an object that appeared to be metal. It looked to be the same size as the boy had found earlier. Instead of taking the man's hand, the talon dropped the object and the man caught it. It shot electromagnetic currents through the man's body. He looked at the object. It had strange symbols carved into the bottom of it. They were like the ones the man had seen on the disc him and his grandson had found earlier. He flipped it over and was not surprised to find the eye the boy had described to him. It was just like he had said, a shiny metal forming the eye that was on his forehead. It looked the same. The device gave off warmth that made the man feel good.

He looked to the creature in front of him and saw the answer in its eye. This was an ally. It was a being who understood the wrongs that had been committed on this planet. The two were friends and had been for a very long time.

The beings were to unite in power very soon and the truth was going to be freed. The two entities held their gaze for over a minute. Finally, the large man spoke. This time, his voice sounded like thunder.

It said, "Go home!"

Chapter 31

A high-pitched whistling sound woke the man out of his dreams. It was piercing to his ears. He had been in the middle of a dream, but all memories of it were erased with the loud tone invading his ears. His niece, in the other bed, was sitting straight up. She was holding her hands over her ears in pain. The man looked to his wife and grandson. They were both sound asleep. The dogs were also still sleeping, safely tucked next to the woman. The man did not understand how the dogs were not awake. Their ears were way more sensitive than the humans, yet they were impervious to the noise.

The sound stopped after a seemingly long time. The man had never heard a sound like that before. It was a solid piercing tone that cut like a needle through his brain. The girl was obviously feeling the same. She looked at her uncle and asked him what that had been. He told her that he did not know. He said that it seemed to come from inside their heads. That had to be the only reason that the others did not hear it. Whatever it was, the two were happy that it was over.

It was barely light outside when the two emerged from the cabin. They were both on the same program as far as sleep went. The man had rolled a couple of joints while the girl was in the bathroom, and now they shared one of them. The first smoke was always a most pleasant one for the two. Even at this early hour, the creativity needed to be woken up. The herb also would help ease the anxiety caused by the rude alarm this morning.

The owner of the hotel was about, watering the plants on his plot of land. The girl asked her uncle what he had spoken about to the man the night before. She said that she had seen him and the other man talking together by that old car. "You had walked away from the other man in kind of a daze or something. We asked what was wrong, but you just walked past us without even a sideways glance. You walked right back to the cabin and went straight to bed."

The man was looking at the girl with a memory that was not there. He remembered looking at the car they had seen earlier, but that was all he could remember. They walked to the buildings to get a closer look. The man's head was spinning. He was losing huge chunks of his memory. It worried him. Both of his parents had died with Alzheimer's disease. He was now beginning to understand what they had gone through.

The man looked under the shed for the Mustang, but the car was no longer there. The open spot was all that remained. "What time was it when you saw me talking to that guy?" he asked the girl.

She told him, "It had been about ten thirty. After the boy had returned from his outing, we had all been exhausted. It had been a very long day. We just all thought that you were exhausted and were done being around people."

They jumped in the minivan and went in search of adventure. In central Washington, at five a.m. there is not much human activity. They were happy to find a coffee place that was open. It was what the two needed, more than anything. While making the coffee, the barista began to talk to the two. Being early and the only souls present, the man and niece had opened themselves up to friendly prattle. It had been anything but.

The coffee guy told the two that a major explosion had happened the night before at a huge computer complex outside of town. They still didn't know what happened, but the fire was burning all night, and the fire department just got it out thirty minutes before. "All the firemen came in to buy coffee on the way home," the clerk said proudly.

"Was it to the North?" the man asked the other.

"Yeah, it was. The fire gave off a weird green glow. A couple of the firemen said that they had never seen anything like it. Electricity was flying everywhere. There were strange fields of energy that they had never seen. One of them even told me that whatever they were doing there at that facility, it was not approved of by God. The entire place was destroyed. Aladdin is no more."

The two looked at the clerk incredibly, as his words hit home. They looked to each other, quickly paid and were out the door. The clerk called out to them for their change, but the door had already closed.

As soon as they got in the minivan and down the highway, the man asked his niece, "does that name seem familiar to you, too, or am I just going crazy?"

"Yeah uncle, you heard right. It was the same name that my cousin saw written on the wall. I looked Aladdin up last night and found out that it is a giant computer warehouse here in Menachee that is basically the brain of all computers. This is where they predict the future. All computer knowledge comes from here and all knowledge comes back here. This computer is the evil. Their symbol is the eye, like the one on your forehead. Like the one that cousin found last night emblazoned on the piece of metal in the cave. As I was looking at the facts, my phone flashed brightly three times and then started to strobe. I remembered what you always told me about phones and immediately put it down away from me. This morning, the battery was dead, but I haven't charged it yet. I truthfully don't want to."

"You shouldn't charge it. Let's not say anything about this to your aunt. Let's see how the boy reacts today and see what he says. Last night, he couldn't remember. Let's see what he says today. It looks like to me, he straight up took out the brain of the greed last night."

They both burst out laughing and were on the way. The mood was light, but the mission was becoming more serious.

They talked a bit more about the night before and the meeting with the owner of the hotel. The man was perplexed how he did not remember anything. In his drinking days, this would not be so rare; but he had not had a drink in a couple of years and was not accustomed to blacking out.

They both talked about how they were having serious lapses in their memory.

They saw some yard sale signs, but it was much too early. The sun had just barely begun to come out. The town was also vacant. The two made the decision to go back to the hotel. There was plenty of wilderness there that they could enjoy, while also enjoying some legal recreational weed.

The marijuana laws in America were silly to the man. He saw how the greed made the laws to benefit themselves. Their laws did not benefit the people. They were supposed to represent the people, and instead they took advantage of them. All for their greed.

The government, by keeping marijuana illegal, paved the way for Opioids to take over the drug market. If people smoked pot for their pain, then no one would take pills. Also, the government would seize property from arrested persons affiliated with pot. The police departments around America got rich and heavily armed from stealing. Stealing from law abiding citizens who saw the benefits of marijuana and the insanity of prescription drugs. The more powerful the police got from buying weapons and helicopters from seized property, the more their gang was unstoppable. There was not a police station in the country that would do anything but slam the progressive movement to legalize pot. If it were legal, their robbery scheme would come to an end.

The man and girl saw the benefits of marijuana. The depression that had set in after the death of their family was helped greatly by the herb. It was a gift from nature that was healthy for the body and soul. The pains that the man endured from sitting hunched over were greatly alleviated by the smoke. Sleep came easy every night after eating an infused cookie. The plant was perfect for the family. The only ones who weren't for it were cops and people who had never tried it.

The main benefit of smoking marijuana was the creativity that it opened in your mind. As an artist and philanthropist, creativity and imagination was what the man used all the time. He believed by controlling the imagination in humans, the greed controlled their very souls. It was the main reason marijuana was illegal. Humans were given the gift of creativity; the greed took it away. Most were too blind to see it and would follow what everyone else did instead of thinking up their own ideas.

Other medicinal plants had also been criminalized over the years. The coca plant was one of them. That and the hemp plant were the two most important plants to humans, yet they were both illegal. Illegal to the common man, that was. They both held all the amino acids that the human body needed for healthy survival. If people were to eat a plant that grew in their backyard, then supplements and vitamins would go away. Somebody would lose a lot of money.

The greed just did not work that way. They were the true evil ones. They called themselves the one percent, but they were wrong. The man knew who they were, and he also knew that they were going to fall. Their time had come. It was long overdue. The true one percent, the ones who saw the truth, were the strong. They were the ones who could see through the greed, and distanced themselves as much as possible from it. They were the Ones.

The man and his niece had been talking about all of this while puffing their fat one. The owner of the hotel had approached, but the two did not see him until he was standing next to them. The man thought that the owner was about to say something, but he just stuck out his hand and took the half smoked joint from the man. He lifted it to his lips and took a huge puff. Then another.

The owner told the two about the laws and how they were benefiting the people of Washington. They used to jail people for smoking weed and now it was legal. "The citizens are happy," he told the others. The owner told the two about something he had heard on the radio. "They spoke about a ray of light that was heading this way. The radio spoke of the light changing things as we knew it. It also said that government officials from every branch were coming to Washington to stop the light. They said stay away if you see it. It is dangerous."

The man told the hotel owner that he had sensed change coming and knew it was on its way. He told the other guy that the change was going to be a slap in the face for most humans. "The evil is going to be expelled from the planet and only the righteous will remain. The greed is at its end, and a new beginning is coming. There are many things happening on this earth that most people have no clue about. Things are on a much bigger scale than anyone could have imagined. Even if they knew, these same people could never understand. They have been completely brainwashed by the greed."

The path was becoming clearer and clearer to the man.

The owner, suddenly, burst into tears. He hugged the man in his large bear like arms. "Thank you," he said with admiration. "I knew there was something special about you folks." The man remembered the conversation with the hotel owner the night before. It all came back to him. They had spoken about the truth. The owner had been in a kind of daze last night, much different than his confidence this morning. He had come running when they looked at the Mustang. The two had spoken of the planets aligning for the first time in over five thousand five hundred years. They had talked about going home.

The man had remembered going to the room and laying down. He also remembered getting up in the middle of the night to sit on the front step and write. Shadows had danced through the trees surrounding the hotel and bordering the river. More than once, the owners of the shadows got too close and the man could see their physical being. They were small human looking things with big eyes and small mouths. They had no ears but their heads were large. The man knew exactly what they were and what they wanted with him. They were not to get it. His energy was his and he was going to keep it that way.

The owner of the hotel pointed to the West. He looked at the man, finger still raised, and said "Go. Your path has crossed my path and I will be forever thankful. My whole life is complete at this very moment. You two take care of yourselves and the others. You will be with my energy also. Now go, it is time." The crow cawed three times as it flew overhead. It, too, agreed that it was time to go.

After waking the others, it was back on the road. It was now seven in the morning and traffic was going to get rough. The early start would pay off well in the long run. The man and girl had already got gas earlier on their outing. They all enjoyed some fresh coffee that the woman had brewed, packed the car and were off.

Just before driving away, the man jumped from the car and rummaged in the back. He emerged with a paper of some sorts in his hand and ran to the door of the office. The owner was nowhere to be found, so the man left the painting on the screen door. He had made it the night before while sitting on the porch. The painting was of an Earth in the shape of an apple. Spirits in gray fluttered all around the object. Across the bottom, written in a scroll was the word, 'wisdom'.

"What was that all about?" the woman asked as her husband got back in the car.

"I liked it here so much that I made them a painting last night," he had replied. Everyone in the car agreed that their stay had been very nice. It had been the nicest hotel that they had stayed in for the entire month. Their theory once again was proven. Mom and Pop places cared about their hotel, while corporate hotels cared about your money.

After a couple of hours, the man spotted a sign for a deli. It was just before ten and the family knew that every place was going to be crowded in about an hour. This place was a convenience store, gas station, and deli. The man normally would have driven on, but it was different than most. The place looked clean. The women running the place were very nice, and there were no other people in the store. It was the spot they would be getting their grub.

After ordering, the man and girl went outside, while the woman and boy went inside to order. The dogs were a tag team affair whenever the situation arose. A man selling fresh produce pulled the two to his truck like it had a hidden magnet inside it. He was selling peaches and apricots. The two were ready to indulge in some fresh golden fruit. The fruit guy was a very nice older gentleman. He was a little stand offish to the two at first, but quickly warmed to their pleasant auras.

The peach man's eyes reminded the man of his father. They looked very much the same. He was also from Oklahoma, just like the man's father had been.

The three became instant friends. The man told the vendor about their habit of buying fruit and vegetables from the farmer himself. They never bought produce from the grocery store. Paying good money for bad fruit and vegetables was not in their destiny. It was all part of the greed. Buying a tomato that came from Mexico instead of one that was grown down the road was the stupidest thing ever to the man. Everything you needed to eat grew in your area. If it didn't, then maybe you didn't need it.

The man told the vendor how his wife went to the farmer's market every week to get produce. This is what they had eaten for over twenty-five years. They would find the good fruit stands, where the fields were right there, to supplement the farmer's market.

When the man went into the store to get the food, it had become packed with people. They were all standing in line like sheep. The man almost felt sorry for them but knew it was their own fault. We all made our own decisions. He went to the far end of the counter, as much distance from the strangers as possible. They were all watching the man with lameness. The man could see by their auras that these people did not know who they were. They were searching, and like most, would never find. None of them understood, they were just lined up at the feeding trough.

The man went back to the fruit guy. A table of college age guys had filled up about twenty feet away, and they all thought it to be funny to laugh at the old guy. The man did not like this kind of behavior. These guys were lost souls. The man had no time for their stupidity; he had to have some more of those peaches. The man and girl began to eat peaches in front of the vendor. There was no doubt they were greatly enjoying the fruit by the sounds that slurped from their mouths. They proclaimed how delicious the fruit truly was.

The older gent began to weep. He said, "You two don't know how happy you are making me right now. Eating those peaches with such delight makes my heart sing. I have heard about your path and now here you are, standing in front of me, eating my peaches. Thank you and God bless." He was holding the man's hand the whole time. Now, he slowly released it to gather more fruit for the family to take. The vendor would not take money for this new batch of fruit. The man tucked it into the fruit sellers vest pocket when he wasn't looking. They were not ones to take things for free. The fair price was the right price. It was what made everything work so smoothly.

The vendor asked the man and girl what they thought about the politics happening. It had been a circus with the first woman candidate fighting the first reality show host. The man did not like either of them, but he never liked anyone who was running for president. For that matter, he did not like politicians in general. He did not trust them. They were all part of the greed and would continue with their greedy practices as normal. They were, in truth, puppets to the elite.

The vendor said, "I must tell you something very important. I have never told anyone this in my eighty-six years. Now, I see why. I've been holding on to this story until I met you two. It started when I was a boy in Oklahoma. When I was about fourteen, a new kid showed up in our neighborhood from Germany. At our school, there was a lot of animosity towards this newcomer. German sentiment in the country at the time was obviously not good. I had befriended him, as I was an outcast too. Over the next few years, we became best of friends. At first, he would not speak of his time in Germany and what had brought his family to America. Then, one day, he was mad at his parents and told me the entire story. He had told me that his dad was a banker back in Germany and had fled when the war was not going their way. All the elite had fled Germany, along with many of the top military officials and scientists. They all moved to separate areas of the globe to make detection not so easy. The Jews hunted down the war criminals, and the governments split the scientists between them. The elite, however, the ones who had financed the war and begun it with their rhetoric, safely took their money and carried on their agenda. In secret, of course. He had told me that they would be strong again and one day would even have their own party back on top. Eventually, they were going to get one of their people in the White House, and then the Nazi agenda would be refueled like never before. All the mayhem in the world would build up in the people until they were fed up and then go for anything. This is what had happened. Their party, over the last seventy years, had become strong once again. Their boy is now headed to the White House. It should not be a surprise that he has blond hair and blue eyes. All you must to do is watch and it will unfold before your eyes. There is going to be waves of racism, sexism and the destruction of the environment. But all will be well in the people, they will have jobs. Just like it happened in Germany. This time, they have learned from their mistakes."

"That is a very interesting story," the man told the vendor. "I believe every word of it." He turned with his niece and went to the car.

"It's crazy what that guy just said," the girl said to her uncle as they walked to the car. He looked at her, in full agreement with the vendor.

The boy ate a couple of peaches and went to thank the man for growing such wonderful fruit. The parking lot had filled with cars. The line for sandwiches was outside the door. The man noticed that there were still no people in line for the fruit. Humans had it all wrong, he had thought to himself.

He had noticed, once again, that a place they had come to had filled with people not long after they had arrived. This happened to the family a lot. It seemed like they had a tourist magnet attached to the back of the minivan.

The table full of guys was looking at the family and cracking some jokes. They were the same ones who had been talking trash on the fruit vendor earlier. One of their group broke away from their traditions and walked up to the peach guy. He purchased a few and began eating them on the way back to the table. His friends all teased him for being a sissy and buying fruit from an old guy. The man could see that the vendor was getting very angry at the words being spoken about him. The girl ended the tension with just a few words. She said, "those guys over there are trying to be something that they are not. The only cool one is the one who bought peaches."

The young men all bowed their heads when they heard this blond girl, of their same age, tell them how it really was. The only one with his head held high was the one who had defied them. He was looking at the girl, smiling a smile of gratitude. All the other people in the parking lot were staring at the family now. The man said it was time to go, and now. He was feeling a threat from a couple of the beings. Most were sheep, but there were two energies in the crowd that were very powerful. These were not ordinary humans. "They were probably the ones following them," he had thought.

The drive through the Cascades was amazing. The family had seen many mountains, but this was quite an experience. A low mist had crept into the green forest and enveloped the hillsides. Shadows danced around the car and the road. The crow was swooping in and out of view this whole day. The man thought back to his sister's house, and wondered why they had never seen the crow there. It had stayed away. The man knew that the answer to this and all his questions were soon to be answered.

Along the road, the family found a small turnout that would be a perfect spot to stop for the dogs. When they got out, they noticed a trail that wound through the forest. The family was compelled to follow this concrete path winding through the trees. As they were hiking, berries dotted the trail. There were blackberries, boysenberries and salmonberries. The family grazed as they walked and filled their bellies with some mother Earth.

The trail snaked around an old, abandoned train trestle which had been used for logging. They had walked for over a mile when they heard a scream from a train whistle blowing close by. The sound instantly made the man and girl feel uneasy. It was the same exact sound that they had woke up to earlier this day. This time, all the group heard it, especially the dogs.

The four-legged homies began to run around like they were in pain. The family all looked around for the source of the sound but could see nothing. Like this morning, the tone just ended, leaving the forest once again in silence. It was a relief to all the beings.

"I think we should get out of here," the girl said, "I'm getting very bad vibes about this place."

The rest agreed and headed back to the car. Berries were the last thing on their mind now. They just wanted to get back to the safety of the minivan. When they got there, they were surprised to see ten other cars parked around theirs. About six people were standing around while the others were looking at a caboose parked a distance away.

The man once again felt the presence of the same beings they had encountered earlier. These were the same beings creating the sense of dread in the family. This time, the man spotted the others. They were by the caboose, but looking at the family. Their clothes and faces looked like everyone else, but their mannerisms did not. They carried themselves like an animal that was using this pod to fool people. It was the same as riding a bicycle that you were not familiar with. They were awkward.

As they were getting back into the minivan, the two strangers took off running toward their own car. This vehicle looked like a presidential motorcade kind of car. It looked very distinguished. The man noticed suicide doors on the auto, but there were no markings of the maker. The two were climbing in as the family drove by. The man had told the boy something earlier and said, "Now". The boy lit one of the mortar fireworks they had gotten back in Missouri and tossed it into the open door of the vehicle, as the others were climbing into it. The look on the stranger's faces was passive. Their mission was to follow this family and nothing else.

As the family drove away, a loud explosion rocked the minivan. The man stopped to watch the entire scene. The car that had been following them exploded in a manner that was not expected. It looked like a bomb hit it. The entire vehicle exploded into a fiery ball of flames which shot into the air and were sucked back into a vortex around the dark car. When the smoke cleared, seconds later, the car was no longer there. "Let's get the hell out of here," the woman had excitedly said as the man was already pulling back onto the highway.

The family was happy when they got to the Puget Sound. They had finally made it to the Pacific Ocean. The salty air told them that they were home. The man spotted a Fireworks stand just before entering the line for the ferry. He still had many fireworks from Missouri, but wanted to have some for New Year's Eve and the Fourth of July. Fireworks were not easy to come by in California. He wanted to be prepared.

The ferry said that it was a two hour wait, but the family was patient. They were in no rush this day. They would be spending the next few days here. The wait gave them time to eat their sandwiches and relax a bit. The wait turned out to be not so long and the family was happily on the boat. The winds had kicked up but it was very sunny with fluffy white clouds in the sky.

The four decided to stay inside the enclosure instead of braving the winds. The man loved being on ships. Even a ferry satisfied his need to be on the water sometimes. His father's boat on the San Joaquin Delta, and then his subsequent days in the Navy, made his love of the water great.

The ferry ride was pleasant and short. After only twenty minutes, they were driving their car off the ship onto Whidbey Island. This day of driving was almost over. They made a stop at a park for the dogs to run around. They also needed to unwind a bit before getting to their friend's house. They were not ones to arrive and line up for the toilet while the dogs were going crazy. They could get all that out of their systems before, at this grassy haven.

A guy playing basketball was the only other person in the park. He had his convertible parked next to the courts with the music on full. He was listening to hip hop and trying to impress the niece. His technique of impressing needed a lot of work. After a quick smoke and bathroom break, they were off to the last house on their visit.

It had been almost ten years since they had seen their friend. She had worked at the tattoo shop when she was barely eighteen. It was a summer that friends from Europe were visiting. It was a very magical season. They had made a bond over a four-month time. The bond had never broken. The man and woman had seen their friend off and on for years, but since she had moved to Washington, they had not seen each other. When they had met her husband was the last time they had seen her, but that was the last time in ten years.

When the family rolled up the driveway, the young son was playing in the front yard. His long blond hair was tied in a braid hanging to his waist. The whole scene seemed like a movie to the man. They were all the actors. As soon as the boy saw the family, there was a mutual bond. They were instant friends, as they had been friends in the past. The boy's aura told the man that he was One. This boy understood.

The eight-year old greeted the family warmly. He did not speak much more than a hello and to tell them that his mom was in the garden. He did not need to speak words. He was in tune with the others. The reunion was wonderful. The man was shocked to see that the lady looked the same. Maybe a wrinkle or two more under the eyes, but this woman was thirty-six years old. She had barely aged. The man had always seen the bright aura from the lady, even when she was a young adult. It had not diminished in all these years. He had always known that she was special. She held the knowledge. She knew.

The husband got home shortly after their arrival. His job was as an arborist. His days were long ones, even on holiday weekends. The two men picked up right where they had left off. The man expected none less from their friend's husband. Special people befriended like souls. She had chosen very well. He too was there.

The house was very impressive. It was just the right size for the three in the family. The place was just far enough away from the neighbors to be secluded. The lady had worked the garden extensively. They had their own little piece of paradise on Earth. The house merged wonderfully with the energy of its residents.

The woman realized that she had lost her phone. They searched the car and the surrounding areas. It was nowhere to be found. The man and his niece went back to the park. They figured the woman must have dropped it when she used the bathroom. It was only about five miles away.

When they got there, a woman went into the bathroom at the same time as the girl entered to look for the phone. The girl came out and told her uncle that they would have to wait. It was a twenty-minute wait. The two smoked one of their cigars while waiting but were becoming very impatient.

At long last, the woman came out of the bathroom. She was fidgety and kept her eyes nervously on the ground. The man saw something odd about her face but could not make it out. Shadows enveloped the woman. Her presence was a very dark one. The man noticed that they were the only people in the entire park. It seemed odd for a fourth of July weekend. He thought for sure there would be many more people.

The girl had gone into the bathroom and back out while the other woman still milled about outside the structure. Immediately, the man saw the phone in the girl's hand when she emerged. It was dripping wet, but she had retrieved it. When she got outside the pavilion area, the phone in the girl's hand began to make a high-pitched whistle. It was piercing their brains. The man recognized the sound as the same one that had woke him up this morning. The same they had heard in the forest. It made his mind unable to think for just a moment. Like someone else was trying to take control over his thoughts and actions. Surely, he had thought, this sound could not be coming from the tiny speaker in the phone.

Luckily, the sound lasted only seconds until the girl threw it to the ground. It stopped before hitting the pavement. The woman from the bathroom had emerged into the sunlight. The man could now see the being. She was dressed in all black that had a shimmer of gold, like light on oil. She was hunched over and her hands were twisted into gnarls that looked like tree burls. Her eyes were gone. Sockets vacant like her aura. This woman was pure dark.

Storm clouds had begun to blow in. The sky got very dark in a short time. It had gone from sunny to stormy in just a matter of minutes. The wind began to get very harsh and cold. Being summer, they were not ready for this. They began to make their way back to the minivan.

At first a walk turned into a trot. The man felt the eyes from the dark woman on his back the whole time. If felt like she was trying to curse him. He had felt this before and fought it off. Dark forces like this were a joke to him. The light was way stronger than the dark had ever been. You just had to believe. It was easy to believe if you knew the truth.

Large raindrops had begun to pelt the two by the time they got to the parking lot. The man and girl both turned back one more time to check on the whereabouts of the woman. She was still there in the distance, looking right in their direction. The two both saw that her eyes were glowing red.

The clouds had begun to turn an ugly shade of purple and orange. The sky looked angry. The wind whipped the formations into infernos of cumulus in front of their eyes. To the right, in the openness of the park, a bright light came from the clouds. It lit up the manicured park in front of the two. It was so bright, the flash blinded the man briefly. He turned his head away instinctively. When he looked back to the sky, the light was gone and the clouds were normal again. They were just puffy clouds lingering in the blue atmosphere, like they had been moments before.

He looked to his niece but she was no longer standing next to him. He was no longer in a parking lot overlooking the park. For that matter, he wasn't even in the forest of Washington state anymore. Sand and brush were around. Cactus and rocks were the new terrain, and a sweltering heat. The man was in a desert. Ahead of him was a huge building made of stone. It seemed to be an octagon shape of about fifty thousand square feet. The top was in the shape of a dome, also made of stone. It was covered in material that resembled gold. The whole thing stood about one hundred feet tall. He had seen pictures of structures like this before, but they had been ruins. This one looked like it had just been completed. It reminded the man of a Ziggurat that he had seen in a Sumerian photo book of ancient ruins.

On top of the octagon was the girl. She was waving to the man to come up. He heard his niece's voice in his head, even from this distance. He couldn't see the way, but he knew the way.

Suddenly, he was standing next to the girl on top of the monolith. "Look," she said while scanning the horizon with a wave of her hand. The entire view was covered with a lake of red. It went on as far as the eye could see. It was like they were standing in an ocean, atop their monolith, surveying the entire planet, which was covered in a molten sea.

Movement to the side caught the man and girl's attention. Two other beings were approaching from the side of the structure. It was the woman and boy. They were there. They too understood. This was the way it was going to go down. This was the One. This is where it had all begun, and this is where it would end. Then it would all begin once again. It was the way of the cycle. It was the way of all things, because all things were alive.

A loud metallic on glass sound awoke the man. He was startled to find himself in the minivan, fast asleep with his niece in the passenger seat. There was a cop at the window. He was making a gesture to roll down the window. The policeman asked the man if everything was alright. The man told the officer that they had driven a long distance this day. It must have caught up with them, they had taken a nap. The cop could tell that the man was legitimate, as was the girl. He wished the two a fine day and jumped back on his motorcycle. The cop had seemed familiar to the man. Could it have been the guy from the Grand Canyon, just much younger? The similarities were there, but he could not be sure. They had no time to think about that now anyway. The others were surely worried about them.

When they got to the house, the others acted like they had just left. The man looked at the clock and saw that four hours had passed. It was eight in the evening. He knew that they couldn't have been asleep that whole time. The other's words made it seem like the man and girl were gone for only fifteen minutes. The woman was happy to get her phone back. It did not work, but she could deal with that in the next few days. At least someone else didn't have all her information.

It was time to prepare dinner and catch up on old times. The friend cooked up a very healthy, good meal. The family was very appreciative. It was by far the best healthy dinner they had on this trip. Eating vegetables again was what their bodies craved. They were happy to be here.

The energy was very nice at the friend's house, as was the food. The two families meshed together very smoothly. The conversations took them all over the planet, and a few places beyond. There was much to talk about. They were all very happy to have a few days to do just that.

The families were all getting very tired. It was time to part ways for the night and get some rest. The friends had a trailer behind their house, which would be home for the next two nights. The boy got voted to stay inside to keep him from the smoke out that was about to occur. It had been a long wait to smoke pot again, and the three were going to toke that trailer up. Influencing the boy was not their intention. He was a sportsman, and they wanted it to stay that way. Everyone had their own calling, and clouding the judgments would not be conductive of the path.

The three made their way to their sleeping quarters and swiftly fell into bed. They lounged in their respective beds and talked, while the man rolled some doobies.

As they were passing the joints, the family carried on with their tradition of talking about everything but nothing. They spoke of their friends and how happy they were that they had come. They spoke of how happy they were that the friend's family was so happy. The bond between the two families was strong. It was in their energy that they were connected. Maybe they all shared a common thread of DNA.

The friend's son was of a special type. For being only eight, the family knew that the boy knew. His schooling system was one the man often talked about. It was the only way for education. The boys school taught the children that there was no wrong or right. Their purpose was to figure out things and state how they came to their conclusions. They were hands on with nature in the forest. They were learning about the environment and nature first. Reading, writing and arithmetic came naturally if your brain was already working in a creative way.

The family also talked about how school just taught the kids to be robots. To teach all the kids, who are not the same, the same thing, was a criminal act by the greed. They controlled our kids from an early age by taking away their imaginations and creativity. If they just taught the kids what they were interested in and focus on what they were the best at, the other things would be learned to the degree that the child needed. It would eliminate crime and every other pitfall of society. If everyone was educated in their true callings, the planet could truly be a Utopia. There would be no failures. The greed fully knew this and had never let it happen. Their ideas of Utopia only included themselves.

The family spoke about how the rebirth had begun. The ocean was near. This was the beginning of a new era of their lives. They spoke with confidence of a future written about in legends. This was the new moon cycle. Exactly one whole moon cycle had passed on their journey. This moon was to be the one. This one would see the end.

The man and girl told the woman what had happened at the park and the loss of time for the others. The woman told them that she had read events like this in books. It had been written about repeatedly in legends and science fiction. She said it was the time of things ending. A new beginning could then take place. These things happening were not what she thought earlier. She had been thinking about these events and about the stories she had read. She told her husband and niece that she was sorry for doubting them.

The two told the woman all the other odd things that had happened on the trip. The woman looked at the others shocked. So much had happened that they had kept inside. She knew after the death of their family the man and girl had shut down for a long time. They had got caught in the dark shadows of their minds where only depression lives. She had thought, on this trip, that this was a way for them to forget by creating this imaginary scenario. She knew now that it was all tied together. The deaths, the trip, the mission. It was all part of the same journey. It had begun very long ago and was now almost ending. The woman was ready for the change. She was ready to be a part of it.

After the fourth joint and a lot of deep conversation, the man and girl began to play their singing bowls. They spoke briefly about their good fortune of finding the bowls at the reptile house. As the notes began to filter through, the family began to understand the importance and spirituality of these instruments. They held a magic that the right set of hands could provoke.

A candle in the corner was casting shadows through the dense smoke. The minimal air movement made the inside of the camper crawl with shadows. They danced throughout the small enclosure. A wisp of smoke began to come from the girls singing bowl. It was lighter in color than the smoke around it. It had a slight bluish glow to it, emanating from inside the bowl.

The smoke from the bowl began to take on a shape. At first it seemed to linger in front of the girl's face. It created a circle with the three beings in the cabin. The smoke morphed into the form of a cloaked figure. It seemed to materialize but only slightly. You could begin to see features of the shape but it was still smoky. A face became more and more clear. It would fade into existence, in the middle of the cloak, and then fade into a blur again. This went on about seven times. The face became more and more recognizable each time.

The fifth time, the man realized that the face was that of his nephew. He faded out twice more before coming back the last time. It was almost like the young man was there. He was so real looking. It was no longer smoke. The beloved brother/nephew was here. The young man addressed his people. He was looking right at his sister. He said in a voice sounding like it was in a tunnel, "it's time to go," and faded away.

The family looked at each other shocked. They were all close to tears but knew this was not the time to lose their strength. All those deaths had prepared them for anything. They had a momentum going, and they could not stop now. Their family would not have wanted that. It was not the purpose of the visit from the brother/nephew. His visit was of one to give the others strength. It was a visit of solidarity.

The boy had always stood strongly by his family's side. The four had been very close. His death had hit them all hard. Now his strength was once again with them. They all laughed. His strength of energy had never left them.

The women were quickly fading into the subconscious. The man thought that maybe he could get a couple of pages written in his book before sleep overtook him too. It was sprinkling outside. Fireworks were going off in the distance. The island had become an artillery range.

When the man opened his book, he was shocked. Someone had gone through the entire book with a black marker and edited out words, sentences and sometimes entire paragraphs. One page only had two sentences which weren't blacked out. It looked like the way the government did documents before they got released to the freedom of information act. Redacted.

The last written page was the only one without big black retraction marks. Its words were written across the whole page in a scribble like the man's brother used to make. Every time the man got his brother to write something or draw something, he used this same scribble. It was his way of creating.

On this page was a message. The words, written repeatedly, were simple; "It's time to go."

The man fell asleep with the book in his arms.

CHAPTER 32

Fourth of July weekend had once been a favorite of the man's. When he was young, his family had been very patriotic. His father being ex-Navy was a huge factor. Through his young adult years, the man felt the same sense of patriotism. Then he began to travel extensively throughout the world with his wife. He paid attention to the news and the propaganda it spread. He concluded that patriotism was a word created by the greed to influence Americans. If they made a war, it was patriotic to go fight for them in it. If you didn't believe in their wars or their propaganda against other countries, then you were unpatriotic.

The man saw right through this. The greed took other countries for their resources. To sell the wars, they would bring hatred toward a country and its people. More racism and division created all the time. This is what the greed fed on. National pride was what the man had encountered in other countries. People were proud of their heritage but not always proud of their government. These countrymen were not going to be tricked into war anytime soon. Patriotism was not a word used in these countries. It was a word only used in America. The war machine for the greed. While so many died, they dined.

This year, at least the family had fireworks. After hearing all the thunder throughout the night, provided by pyrotechnics, the man was eager to see what would be happening tonight. Either way, they would be lighting off their own mortars.

The air was clean when the man emerged from the trailer. He liked Washington very much. It was a misty morning, and he was ready for some adventure. The girl had snuck into the bathroom before anyone else could get to it. The man had passed her on his way out of the toilet, sharing a knowing glance with the girl. They had both come from large families. They knew the importance of getting to the bathroom early. He was already done with all that and dressed. He was ready to go.

The boy was up when he saw his cousin. Sleep would have been nice, but adventure called to the boy. He loved the outdoors. He knew that his grandpa and cousin were going on adventures in the mornings. Today, he was not going to be left out. The woman decided to stay and catch up on some sleep. There would be much adventure this day anyway, and so much visiting.

Their first stop of the morning was to get gas. The people of the store were very nice and wanted to know about the family. The clerk was an older woman. She had an assistant who could have been her grandson. It was obvious that the woman owned the store. They talked about the fireworks the night before and all the noise. The younger clerk said "a bunch of people reported seeing a flying saucer last night. It was all over the radio today. The officials were saying that it was reflections from the fireworks. I don't believe that for a moment. Something happened last night that I will never forget. Something came in my room in the middle of the night. There were shadows all around my bed. I felt a serious sense of dread. I felt very sick. I must have passed out or something. I woke to a bright light but remembered nothing more. I was once again unconscious. I woke this morning thinking it was a dream but then I saw this. I didn't have it before."

The young man pulled down the front of his shirt and the family saw immediately. He had a seven or eight-inch incision going from the bottom of his neck to his sternum. It looked like it was a scar of maybe ten years. If he had got it the night before, it had healed up fast. The boy asked him if it hurt but the clerk said it did not.

The man's mind had been clouded at first when they entered this store. Something had blocked his thoughts. He had not seen. The words of the clerk make it all crystal clear. He decided against the gas and got out of the store. He grabbed the others on the way, making an excuse of being in a hurry. The owner's face changed from light to dark. She had worn a false face, and the man had not detected it at first. He was usually very good at detecting this deception, but today she had gotten past him. He had not sensed her aura at first, but now could see it in all its glory. This lady was part of the greed.

They quickly got in the car and sped off. The man could see the clerks looking through the front window. They watched the family until they could not see them again. "What was that about?" the grandson asked.

"Didn't you see?" his cousin asked incredibly.

"Those people were part of something that has been sent our way. They have been here a very long time and they are watching us. They have been watching us since we began our trip. Now things are happening that are making them scared. They are in fear of us. Our energy is getting very strong and they know it. We are a great threat to the threat. They have created fear on this planet for a very long time, and now the fear is being returned to them. By us, the One." The man explained to the boy.

"But what if those people had been abducted or something last night?" the boy asked his grandpa.

His cousin answered. "They may have been abducted or not, but one thing is for sure. They had the others inside them. They tried to hide it with niceness, but we caught them in their lie's. These are shape shifters that can look like anything they want. They pull it off well. But their auras tell a different story, as do their actions. They can manipulate them for a short time, but as soon as they begin to speak, they cannot hide their true being. It is like walking and chewing gum at the same time."

The man continued, "Didn't you think it was odd that they jumped in talking about UFOs and abduction? It was an instant indicator of their true-identity. The greed has always made up stories about the stories. They twist little bits of reality into bigger bits of false information and then deny it all ever happened. This was for sure one of their stories."

"How do you guys know all this?" the boy asked. There was not a note of doubt in his voice. He believed everything that his cousin and grandpa had just told him. It sounded crazy, but so many crazy things had happened on this trip. Maybe they had all been tied together.

"Because we are the One," the girl answered. You too are the One. We all are. Soon, we will show the others and the greed. Their fear is growing. Our strength gets stronger and stronger. As it grows, the answers are coming to us. Mostly in our subconscious, but also in our conscious."

"The biggest reason that they are afraid of us is because of our strength as individuals. Most humans do not have individual strength and count on others around them to make them complete. The greed misleads people into starting movements. The masses really believe their bullshit. The humans are now believing that if they all pull together their collective will, then they will be able to get things done. When, in reality, they are missing one step. To pull a collective together, everyone must be their own collective of thought and enlightenment. Otherwise, you will just have a bunch of people together forming a weapon. Weapons destroy. Knowledge illuminates. We each are the carrier of wisdom. That is our planet, the wisdom. God. Our group is the most powerful of true collectives. We don't need to pull energy together but it is our destinies. Our individual strength is so strong in the four of us that, when we come together, we will be able to defeat the parasite of this planet. It is what makes them scared of us. It is why we keep encountering more and more of their kind. Long as we keep strong though, and follow the way of the light, they will never be able to touch us. They will only fear us.

The family was pulling into another gas station as the girl finished. This time, the man went in and paid without talking to the people. A coffee shop next door caught his eye. As he was pumping gas, the girl and boy came out of the store drinking coffees. The man told them that they were crazy, this was Washington state. Some of the best java in the world was here.

The family went next door to the coffee shop. The girl and boy both said that their coffee was excellent. Even convenience store coffee here was good. The owner of the shop was a friendly guy. The place was full for only being seven in the morning. The family spoke with the man as he prepared their coffee. He spoke some of the island and of the coffee. He took pride in the brew that he made. This was a guy who loved his work, not the money. The whole coffee shop was abuzz in the same conversation by the time the coffee was ready. Everyone else in the place, feeling the energy between the family and the owner, had joined in the conversation. It was about peace and kindness and the new way. It was about a new beginning. The three felt at home in this coffee shop.

The owner told the man that it was cash only. He explained, "the entire internet and its grid is down. It was wiped out by that fire at the Aladdin plant a couple of days before. No one knows for sure what was going on there, but it was obviously the brain of the internet."

As they drove away, the three talked about all the people they had met on this trip. Somehow, they were coming across all the right people. It was like their paths were destined to cross at the exact moment it did. So many places that they had been were hidden gems. Each of those gems was occupied by chosen souls. They were the good. The true one percent. It was odd how they kept coming across these people. They were drawn like magnets to the bright energy. They had met the dark too, but repelled that with ease, like opposite magnets.

Most of the masses fit into neither of these two classes. This was only two percent of the population. The other ninety eight percent were drones basically. They were flesh pods with a soul, but a very young soul. It would take many lifetimes before these beings even began to feel enlightened, if they ever did. It was easy for the greed to repress these folks and make them their slaves. They did not use their creativity. Everything they were told, they took as God's words. Even in their spiritualism, they were on the completely wrong path. They were on the path of the lies perpetrated by their false gods.

Looking for fun, the three explored the island a bit. They saw some yard sale signs and went to investigate. They drove around a bit but did not find any of the sales. They did find the beach. They were quickly on the sand, coffee in hand. This spot was an inlet of some sorts. It was low tide and the beach spread way out. It was not such a long beach, but there was only one other couple combing the sands for treasure. There was room for all without crowding.

The family had always loved the beach. Many treasures could be found lurking in the sand. It just took a patient, careful eye. It didn't take them long to fill one of the coffee cups with rocks, sea glass and seashells. Many tiny crabs were running around. They were small, pinky nail size. The family was happy to see the creatures. They had made new friends with the sea creatures and the other beachcombers.

The air was cool and clean, and they were at the beach. This fourth of July has started out wonderfully.

The man found an old rusty piece of metal. It looked like a large prehistoric shark tooth fabricated from a corrosive metal. The object seemed very odd to him. When he picked it up, the piece had a strange vibration to it. The metal seemed to be warm, although it had been in the cold sand. The man turned it over and realized how light it was. The thing was bigger than his hand and seemed to be of solid metal. However, it weighed maybe a half pound. He thought that maybe it was foam or something. He dug his fingers in each side but it was solid metal.

By now, the others had gathered around the man. The object seemed very odd to them also. The man bent down and cracked the artifact on a large rock which was covered in mussels. When the object met the rock, it cracked slightly right in the center. A green smoke came out of the middle of the treasure. A light seemed to be illuminating the smoke. The smoke wafted up into the air in front of the family and began to take a shape. It took a minute or two for the smoke to begin to materialize. The man thought that this surely couldn't be what he was thinking it was. It seemed like he had just released a magic Genie. Crazy things had happened, but this was just insane. He did not believe in magic Genies.

The man's anxiety over the Genie was gone swiftly. The smoke did not form a human shape, nor any other shape. It simply floated around the air for a minute and dissipated in the first strong gust that came along. He imagined that the creature had been freed and had no time for old wives' tales. It had floated away with the wind. The man laughed to himself. He thought that it had been a great idea for a story later. His imagination was working on overtime. His mind was making up stories one after another. His mind was healing.

The boy picked up the metal device and it fell in half. Inside one half, tucked inside its own little niche, was a large tooth. This was no ordinary tooth, though. It looked to be prehistoric, and it also looked very familiar.

The boy asked the others if they remembered the tooth that had been in the box he found in Bodie. The others said they did. He asked them if they thought this was similar, and they said it was exact. The boy told the others that he had not seen the tooth since the first time when the box was opened. It had disappeared, only to be found in this old piece of metal on the beach. It had come back to him.

Walking back to the car, the man saw the sign pointing up a driveway to the yard sale. It had been here all along. "Funny how things work," he told the other two. No one was present when they walked up, but they decided to browse anyway. It didn't look like much of what they wanted; but, being the only yard sale that they had found, they decided to look around some.

An older gentleman of about seventy came out of the house. He began to talk to the family and tell them his story. The man thought to himself that a lot of people they were running into liked to tell the family their story. It did not upset him though. He wanted to know about anyone that had something cool to say.

The gent told the family that he and his wife had lived in this house for seventeen years. Now the owner was going to sell it. It had been on rent control so remained affordable. As the years had passed, all other rentals on the island had doubled. Now, the owner of this house, too, wanted his piece of the pie. They could not afford to move anywhere else on the inlet. He and his wife were on a fixed income, and now they had to go back to Missouri where they could afford to live.

The man sympathized with the gent. He had heard the same story across America. He had been hearing this same story his entire life. Between 2008 and 2014, many people had lost their homes and everything else. Many had even lost their lives over all the worries. The greed didn't care about these properties nor these people. By taking the homes, they took their dignity. They took their pride and laughed about it. It didn't matter if you were a veteran who fought their wars, children, or disabled. They took from everyone. It was all about the greed and nothing about the people.

The man thought about these things often. So many regular people were in awe of the greed. They would sacrifice anything to be in the same class as the elite. Most people were full of the same spirit as the rich, take what you can and fuck the rest. It is what they had been taught by the media their entire lives. Empathy had gone away a long time ago. Most people didn't even remember what the word meant. Sacrificing your time and life was the way of living for the common man. That was the only way you could get by. The people who thought they could get more were fools. Dreamers. The greed did not want to share.

The gentleman's wife came out to talk to the strangers. She had heard voices from inside and brought out coffee. The family was very happy about this. Their coffee had long ago been consumed on the beach. These people had very good energy. The two families were instant friends. Again, the family had met the people that they were supposed to meet. The woman was in a very good mood. You could almost say she was ecstatic. She had heard of a being that was going to change it all. She said the family should look it up, it was all over the internet. The woman said that the being was supposed to be in the Pacific Northwest now. "Last night, many on this island say they saw a flying disc, full of lights. Maybe that was the being." She stated how it would be awesome if she met the holy man.

The man told the woman that instead of looking for prophets, we should all see the prophet in us. "We all have a vision. We all possess a creativity that is far greater than any war ever fought. We all have God inside of us. Everybody is looking for more, but it is already inside of us. Most people either don't know or refuse to use it."

The woman looked at the man with love in her eyes. She began to tell her story and the story of her husband. The man had known that the gentleman was a veteran, he always could tell. Once in the military, it changed you. It left a brand on your soul that could never be hidden. The woman told the family about her sister. She lived in the same town as the man and his wife, in the sierra foothills. Mountain Ranch. The town was only eighteen-hundred people so this coincidence was profound. The gent was from Festus, Missouri. Another coincidence, the family had passed through Festus on their trip. They had stopped and ate lunch there. The connection was complete.

After an hour, the family had to tear themselves away from the pull of conversation. The woman had offered lunch to the family, but they had declined. It was already mid-morning, and they needed to get back to the others. The family waved all the way down the driveway. The man saw a deep sadness in the couple. They were happy on the outside, but on the inside, they were losing it. Depression gripped their beings. Another product of the greed.

The man had seen it so many times. Once again, the greed had won. It had destroyed another American family. All over something so silly as money. The landlords could be happy now. Their lobster would taste that much better tonight when served by their butler. The man shed a tear as he got to the end of the driveway. It broke his heart to see the same thing happening repeatedly. Always to people who had worked their entire lives just to be done dirty by a system that was leaning against them.

The man knew that all our destinies were preordained somehow. It had something to do with numbers. Countless times, numbers had coincided in his life. Some were just too close to be coincident. His address now was one number off his brother's phone number. The numbers also, mixed up, was the same as the man's last phone number. Addresses, phone numbers, and other numbers had been like this his whole life. Numbers were the key factor in everyday life that kept everything running so smoothly.

They were happy to get back to the friend's house. The son was waiting outside for them when they drove up the long driveway. He was very happy the three were back. The boy had formed a bond with the family. Once again, the man saw the DNA and the effect it had on family members. They were close with the boy's mom, of course they would be close to the boy, too. They were the same genetics.

The friend was up and about also. The woman had joined the others in the kitchen. There was much to talk about this morning. The friend brought out a book that she had painted. The man looked through it closely, while the others looked on. The man had always been impressed with the lady's art. She was a true free spirit. It was easy to see it. She had created her own style of art and had kept toward her path of creativity. Most people copied others in everything of life. They thought that would be what made them fit in. It was so many people's goals to be like the rest. They did not use their imagination.

The friend had been like a daughter to the man and woman. They had become very close in that short summer, but the energy ties had remained strong. She still had the free spirit which originally drew the three into friendship. They had all been on the same path of enlightenment. They still were. Now there were two more in the couple's group and two more in the friend's group. The number was seven. A very special number indeed. The friend spoke about how seven was her lucky number. The man told her that he made his own luck and they all laughed.

The friend took the family to the thrift store. Her son came along with the group as the leader. The boy was special. The entire family saw it and respected it. The store was a very nice one. The family was surprised that it was open on the Fourth of July, but they were happy it was. The girl and man stayed side by side, and the grandson tagged along. Their interests were paralleled. The child on this day walked with them. The boy had become attached to the family. There was a knowledge between the child and the group. They were One.

They found many treasures in this store. Mostly, they just liked to walk around and see what the thrift store had to offer. They were not looking for many purchases, just items they perceived as treasures. A great find to them usually meant junk to others. They were just looking for items to make things out of. The man started up a conversation with the cashiers. They were slightly older than the man. He had felt a very good vibe from them as soon as they had come into the store. Now they were all standing there talking like old friends. The man commented on some jewelry, and it began an entire conversation. The woman had to remind the man that the friend had an appointment. It got the family out of the store. The woman had once again saved the situation.

The friend went off to her appointment with her son. The family went back to her house. On the way, the man pointed out something very odd to the others. Six or seven large birds were diving through the air. They would lift themselves and then dive bomb down. They looked like hawks to the man at first, by their actions, but they were much too large for that. When he focused his eyes, he could see. They were gray herons, acting like predator birds. The family all agreed that they had never seen cranes behaving like this before. The cranes continued their dance, just above the tree line, until the family was out of range.

Back at the house, the friend's husband had returned from work. He was talking with his friend when the man and girl walked in. Warm welcomes abounded. This new friend was also a familiar soul to the man. The man felt like they had been friends for many years. His name was an unusual one, the man had only heard it once before. That guy, who shared the same name, was the man's first client when he was to return home after this trip. The coincidence of this did not go unnoticed by anyone in the room.

When the man shook hands with this new friend, he said, "shake hands with a good man." The guy looked at the man strangely. Recollection was deep in his thoughts. The guy told the man that his father had said the same exact thing to him when they shook hands. Another piece of the puzzle had been fit into place. Everything was lining up now in a positive way. The people they were meeting were all energies who were meant to contribute to the family. Each of them were blocks, building the fortitude of the One.

After some smoke time and relaxing, it was time to get some food. The friend had arrived home, and the families were ready. They went to a nice restaurant, but there was no space large enough for seven. As they walked through the diner, the other patrons looked at them with contempt. They were not wanted here. There was a strange energy coming from the waitress, the patrons, and the restaurant overall. A dark aura in the corner of the room made the man turn away and head for the door. He told the others that if they were not wanted here, he did not want to stay.

In truth, he had to get away from that darkness. It did not frighten him. It just made him feel sick to his stomach and very light headed. He knew it was his subconscious protecting him from the dark when he felt like this. His inner eye was wide awake.

The man suggested that they leave. He said they could go buy groceries and go back to the house. He told the others that he would love to cook for them. He just wanted to get out of the place. He was beginning to feel ill from the bad energy permeating the walls of this restaurant. The others agreed. They could buy great groceries next door and cook better than eating out. They were all anxious to try a sampling of the man's pacific salmon entree.

Everything seemed to be different in the Pacific Northwest. The people were of course different. They were different everywhere you went. Towns that were just miles away from each other would be inhabited by people who had their own little culture.

It was more than that here. The man had felt a humming in his head since they had arrived on the coast. It had begun as soon as they crossed into Washington and had gotten stronger and stronger. Now it felt like he had a beehive in his head. Cooking dinner, he realized that the water boiled different. It boiled in small bubbles, no matter how high he turned the gas. The water looked like it was carbonated when it boiled. Other oddities had been striking the man all day. Just like the birds. Just like the coincidence with the names and the people from the yard sale. Today was a day that the numbers had all lined up for the positive.

The man was noticing that everything was changing. He no longer thought that he was just imagining things. Odd stuff was going on all around. There was a quickening. The awakening was near. They were very close. He could feel it coming with the humming in his head.

Dinner was a success. The friend's husband had helped the man cook. As was the case so many times, the man and the other male in the house cooked together. This was probably the sixth friend the man had cooked with, to the delight of the diners. The friend put on some disco at the man's request, and it was all one big family. It was one of the best dinner experiences of the trip. Good food and good friends made for an unbeatable time.

Fireworks followed dinner. The fireworks that the family had purchased before coming onto the ferry were shot off in less than thirty minutes. They had gone to a parking lot that was next to a church, just down the hill from the house. It was a great time to shoot off some pyrotechnics again. It had been many years since the man had shot off fireworks that went into the air. The laws in California were very strict on this. They sold fireworks there only in the summer when everything was super dry and a fire hazard. Only selling pyrotechnics that stayed on the ground was the answer to the fire problem. The greed worked in ways that seemed stupid to most but was clear. They wanted to bring about mayhem at any cost.

The real fireworks show was after they had launched off theirs. The two families went up to a housing area and found a spot on a secluded hill. The man saw all kinds of lights flying around in the sky and asked the others what they were. The friend and her husband both said they were drones. This island had a lot of people with money, and they liked their expensive toys.

The fireworks display they witnessed for the next hour proved their statement. The family had never seen so many fireworks lit off at the same time. The sky had been filled with a constant light the whole time they were there. The fireworks did not slow down nor diminish. The family went home, because they got tired of the display. There was only so much you could see before it got boring.

The man had been watching the sky the whole time for lights that were out of the ordinary. The fireworks were cool, but he was looking for so much more. He could have sworn that the light display was creating a pattern. He knew Morse code and it was something like that, only with pyrotechnics. They seemed to be spelling out a message in the sky. The man wished he had his camera with him. It had died earlier along with his phone.

All his electronic devices seemed to be working oddly in the last couple of days. They would not keep a charge and were basically worthless. He had tried to play his IPOD in the car earlier and it was the same result. He told the others about this on the way back to the house and one by one, they all agreed that the same thing had been happening to them. All their electronics had also gone haywire.

When they got home, the man and his friend had to get busy. It was already midnight and the man had promised to help with a project that had to be done by the next morning. The friend was going to teach a nature class to her son's school. It was an outdoor science camp that was all hands on.

The two had to make some flashcards of marine animals of the Pacific Northwest. They jumped to the project as soon as they got in the door. There were thirty-two cards to make, and it was going to take some time.

As the two got on the project, the woman made reservations for the Port Townsend ferry the next day. There was going to be a mass exodus of people, and they wanted to ensure that they would get off the island before too late in the day. The first opening was at two in the afternoon, but they said they could be on standby and get on earlier possibly. The family decided to book the reservation. They would see in the morning what they wanted to do. The friend had to leave early, and so would they. They just were not sure if they wanted to stay on Whidbey island until the afternoon, waiting for the ferry. They liked this island, but they really wanted to be on the beach by afternoon.

The man felt very happy to make the cards with his friend. Hanging out had been a great thing, but creating together was something even more.

Most people would never understand the connection you make with someone when you create with them. The energy you create is incredible. The two spoke of many things while they drew. The niece had stayed up most of the time, as had the woman. The two had slowly drifted off to the trailer as the morning hours passed. The friend's husband had long ago gone to bed. Work came early for him.

The man was very curious about people and how they interacted with everything and everyone around them. He really liked to pay attention to people's genetics and their ties to their bloodlines. It was a thing he paid close attention to. The man and friend talked about this, amongst other things. Her life too had been filled with turmoil and hardships. Truth came after many years of trials and tribulations. Fulfillment was something that had to be worked on for a whole lifetime. Nothing came easy. Just creating. The friend was there, she understood what the man said. He understood what she said. This is how true knowledge was formed.

The friend told the man a story about a wolf eating a sun. It was a story of rebirth, and a new beginning. The man was interested and amazed. He had not told his friend about the true destiny of their path. He had not told her about their mission. Yet, she had just told him a story that pretty much summed up their thoughts and their goal. To leave all the bad behind and start anew. To get to the end, so they could get to the beginning.

The man broke down in tears of happiness. The friend truly saw: Their bond was One. The two hugged. Tears streamed down the face of the friend, too. Her young features were soiled by the sobbing. The two hugged for a full minute. They both knew that the beginning was here. They both knew that everything was going to be so much different. Silently, they broke their embrace. They wiped the tears from their faces with their sleeves. Wordlessly, the girl went into her bedroom while the man went outside to navigate his way to the trailer.

It had begun to mist outside. The trail leading from the house was very dark and slippery. The man lost his footing and slipped on one of the steps. He fell face first, right into a stump which had been placed there as a seat. The man's head exploded with light as he lost consciousness. He had a vision in his subconscious that he was not alone. He was laying on a stone altar or something. He was surrounded by dark shadowy figures. It looked like a bunch of people wearing dark robes with hoods. The sensation of being in good company was strong. The group all peeled back their hoods at the same time, revealing their faces. It was the dead members of the man's family. All the ones who had died in the last two years were standing silently around the altar.

One of the figures had not taken off his hood. It was the seventh figure. Now, silently and with slow intention, the creature peeled back his hood. All the other robed figures shifted their attention away from the man and toward the other. When the face was revealed, the man was not so shocked.

The hooded figure was him. He was standing with his people, looking directly at himself. Now the others all looked at him again. They all raised their hands, including his cloaked figure. An electric charge ran through all their hands, making a circle of lightning around the man and the altar that he occupied. It focused its energy in the middle, maybe ten feet above their heads. The electricity seemed to gather strength at its apex, and then shot straight down into the man's forehead. It went directly into the eye that was wide open in the center of his head.

The man sat up with a start. His senses came rushing back into his being. His vision in the dark had now adjusted and he could see just fine. It almost seemed like there was a full moon, he could see so well. The rain told him that it could not be the case. He realized that there was a large figure hovering over him. It was the man in black that he had been seeing on the entire trip. Its face was distorted into a big grin. The remainder of the face was wrinkles created from such a broad, toothless smile.

The creature extended its hand. The man slowly reached out to touch it, but briefly hesitated. "Now!" commanded the stranger. The man hesitated no more. His hand contacted the grinning creature. There was no fear in his being. It was the opposite, he had never felt more comfortable in his life.

As soon as their hands came into contact, the man felt like he was being shot through space. Millions of galaxies and stars were whizzing past. The man thought it must be like traveling at the speed of light. Something in his head corrected him. He was traveling much faster than the speed of light. He was shooting into the cosmos. There was a light up ahead. It seemed very familiar. There seemed to be some shadows in the light. As he got closer, he recognized the shadows. He had come to the light, but the cosmos was still zipping by. The light was guiding the way.

The figures were there like they always had been since the beginning of the end. They were the ones who had been with the man all along, on every journey, since the beginning. Now the end was near, it was only natural that the three would be reunited.

The three of them were the key.

The figures in front of the man held out their hands, and the three made the contact. Energy flowed from all directions, shooting into the cosmos to flow throughout its ancient web.

This energy was strong. It was an ancient power that had been dormant for very long. A bond that had been formed at the beginning of the last end between these entities.

The man had been reunited with his brother and sister.

The end was here.

CHAPTER 33

It was a cold and rainy morning. The friend and her family had an early start. They all had business to attend to this day. The family felt the same. The trip had been long. The ocean was calling them. This island had been nice, but now they were ready for the wide-open Pacific. It was time to get back on the road and to their destination. The beginning was near.

After big hugs all around, the man and woman took a picture with their friend. It was a solemn morning. So much time had passed since they had seen each other last. They did not know when they would see each other again. The friend's son was also sad, but happy at the same time. He was going to an outdoor science camp and was going to have so much fun. No tears were shed as the two families parted ways. Theirs was a friendship that had grown to the niece and grandson. Their circle had grown. It was a time, in the misty rain, to be joyful of the energy they had all shared.

The family stopped at a small coffee shop on the side of the road. They had decided to take the Clinton ferry instead. It would be a bit of a wait also, but they would be well on their way to the coast by mid-morning. Waiting until two was not in their cards for this day.

The coffee place was a small drive up building. The Barista was a voluptuous blonde woman in a very small bikini. This was the first bikini coffee place the man had ever been to. They waited for the coffee while the boy got an eyeful from the back seat. He was not a pervert. He was not rude to the woman, but he was fourteen. This was not something that he got to see every day.

The line for the ferry began about two miles before the boat. It was only seven in the morning but the line had formed early. This was the biggest weekend on this island and many had to get back to work on the mainland. The wait was not bad. The island was beautiful, and the music flowed from the speakers. The weather was still a bit rainy and cool, but the coffee was hot. Being from the central valley of California, they were enjoying this weather. Soon enough, they would be back to one hundred degrees plus temperatures and no chance of rain.

The family spoke of many things on their wait. The woman asked her husband what time they had finished their project the night before. The man scratched his chin of whiskers and said, "I honestly don't know. I don't even know how I got to bed last night. I remember making the cards, and I somewhat remember being almost done. That is all, though. For all I know, I didn't even get to bed last night."

"I woke up once around four, and you were writing in your book. We smoked a joint together, but you said absolutely nothing. You wrote the whole time that we smoked." The girl had interjected from the backseat.

"I guess it is just another mystery, like the rest on this trip," the man said, still slowly scratching his chin.

The boy and girl both spoke of how much they liked the friend and her family. The man knew they would all get along very well. Free spirits stuck together. They were drawn like magnets. The man told the others about the sad feelings when they had to leave. "It is always sad to go, but the next adventure lies just ahead. Just like the boy earlier being sad, but excited at the same time, to be going to camp. That is what life is all about. New adventures always begin when old adventures end. There is no need to be upset when good times end. You just need to make more good times."

The wait this morning lasted only an hour. They were on the ferry, crossing the peninsula, in a timely manner. These guys were professional. Shortly after getting in the line earlier, the family noticed how many cars arrived after them. Within fifteen minutes, the line of cars stretched as far as the eye could see. Many others had gone this route, also. They had the same intentions as the family, to get off this island. The man was very happy they had left so early. He was not impatient, but waiting for hours would surely become stressful. He did have his limits.

The ride on the ferry was smooth and pleasant. The family all went in different directions after parking the car. They had been around each other for many days now, and were ready for a little time to themselves. The man went to the bow of the ship. The wind was blustery, but the rain was minimal. Being a sailor for so many years, he longed for this kind of experience. Anything to do with the ocean, he was ready for.

The man saw many shadows on this boat. He was just finishing up his coffee he had gotten earlier and saw the dark figures in every part of the ferry. He stood with his back to the railing, looking to the interior of the boat. There were not many people on this ferry. It seemed like maybe only one hundred. It seemed odd to the man, just days before, there had not even been a place to sit down. Now, there were barely any seats taken. There had been so many cars in line back on the shore, it did not add up.

The man was very used to the oddities happening now. The shadows were just something that were around all the time. He had seen them before in the past, but this was different. Shadows seemed to follow the family everywhere they went. They all saw spirits and shadows almost everywhere they went.

The lack of people made the trip all that much stranger. The man turned back to the railing and the approaching land. They were still about a quarter mile from their landing. Suddenly there was a bright flash of green light. It temporarily blinded the man. He was looking at the water when he regained his senses. Floating all around the ferry were what seemed like bodies. They were clogging up the waterway, making the passage of the ferry slower. The man focused his eyes more and thought that maybe they were just logs. Surely, he thought to himself, they could not be bodies floating in the channel.

He looked to the sky, but it had changed. Now it was glowing a greenish color, replacing the gray from earlier. The rain had stopped. Out of nowhere came a sea of helicopters. Most of them were all black, with tinted windows. They barely looked big enough for one person. Others were for sure military, and a few seemed to be rescue. They were all headed in the direction they had just come from.

The woman, wrapping her arms around her husband's waist, brought the man out of his daydream. The sky was gray again, and the light mist continued. The water was free of debris, and the ferry was pulling up to the dock. The man felt like he had crossed into another dimension there for a moment. Everything in that dimension was almost the same as this one, but devastatingly different. They were for sure parallel to each other and for one brief-moment, they had crossed together.

Taking the Clinton ferry meant that they would be going through Seattle. They had wanted to avoid the cities, but there was no way around this one. The family had planned to go all the way up the coast from the northern ferry, into Olympic state park. The crowds and wait had deterred them. Now they would be going wherever the road took them. They were only on the interstate for a bit and found a highway going straight to the ocean, passing through Everett. This was the road they would be taking.

Seeing the sky needle in the Seattle skyline was a nice sight. The family were all happy that they would not be going into the city, though. They had all had their experiences with cities. They preferred to stay on the small roads with the small towns. That is where they had found all the adventure so far on this trip. The cities only had one thing to offer. Lots of people. The family chose lots of nature instead. The cities could keep their skyscrapers, pollution, and humans.

Outside Seattle, there was another diesel truck overturned. This one was in the center of the highway. The family was just about to take the road to Everett when they came across this catastrophe. It was the worst crash they had seen on the road. This one had collided with a van full of people. Both vehicles lay twisted in the middle of the highway. It had obviously happened sometime in the early morning hours. The wreckage was all piled into the center of the median. Only police remained on the scene, with their distance meters and pads of paper. Many people had died here this morning. Once again, the family had been a late witness to it.

The sky had begun to take on a strange hue again. The others in the car had all started to doze off. It had been an early morning, and they all needed a bit more sleep. The man saw the changes coming in the sky. Just after passing the accident, they had taken a smaller road. This is when things began to change. The gray skies began to swirl and move with an intensity the man thought artificial. They seemed to be producing a light behind them. Like lightning that was building its strength in layers to cascade upon the ground, only to be denied release from the clouds.

There was a larger black cloud in the middle of the sky. It seemed to be above the car. A strange phosphorous green was coming from the formation. The man saw movement inside the cloud that looked like a beast trying to get released. The darkness grew and grew, until it was taking over the other overcast.

Another light flashed in the sky. It was the same kind of digital clock like light he had seen elsewhere on the trip. The light flashed through the clouds, almost in a straight line, for minutes. It seemed to be sending the man code that he could not understand. His head began to pulse. It felt like something was trying to get out the front of his head. He pulled off his hat and light flooded his inner being. It was not a light that flooded his vision, just his thoughts. His third eye read the digital lights with no problem. They were a binary code being sent from a being whom the man had always wondered about. Now the secrets were being shown to him. Now he would truly know the truth.

The smell of saltwater was strong in the air.

As he drove down the highway, the man deciphered the codes that were sent to him. There was not much to figure out as far as what they said. These numbers had been like reading English to him. They were clear in what they said, but their meanings had to be figured out. It was deep. It was the codes that had been since the beginning of the universe. It was the story of everything. It was the story of nothing. It was the true wisdom.

The man stopped for the dogs and a stretch. The drive had been enlightening this morning. The woman noticed something strange about her husband. There was a glow to him this morning that had been missing in his being for so very long. It looked like he had finally gotten away from the dark cloud that had been following him for the last two years. He was becoming himself again.

The sun had begun to peek out of the overcast. The dark clouds had cleared after Everett, and had been thinning since heading West. The woman commented to her husband that it looked like it was going to be a beautiful day. He agreed. He told her that some dark clouds had formed earlier, but they had dumped buckets of rain on them in a short time.

The clouds had lightened with the expulsion of their heavy load. The man felt the same thing happening in his heart. It was like it had lost a heavy load with the rains, cleansing it of its invasion. The ocean was here. It was time for the beginning. All the weight had been left behind.

First it was the end. They had waited a very long time for this moment. The numbers had told him.

Looking at the map, the family found where they would like to end up for the day. They dreamed of getting out of the car and enjoying the beach and the surf. There was a cleansing that needed to be done, and the ocean was the place for it.

They found a small peninsula parallel to the coast, and decided that is where they would find their place for the night. The drive up the small road was beautiful. It was only about fifteen miles long, but it provided much pleasantries to the eyes. The lack of cars was a definite bonus. Obviously, the people who had stayed in this area had also left early in the morning. The entire peninsula was mostly deserted.

They found a small town to get some food. The family were all very hungry. It had been a long day of driving, and they needed to replenish their energy. An afternoon snack was just what they needed. The food was very good. Coastal food was always pleasant to the man and woman. Seafood was a favorite of the entire family. The atmosphere was a pleasant one, also. The people all seemed to be enjoying themselves and were focused on their own parties, not on everyone else.

The family ate it up and got on the road. The man was very tired and needed to rest some. It was easy to get grumpy when you got so tired. The food had helped, but it was time to kick up the feet and think of nothing. They had made it to the coast, now it was time to enjoy it. Now it was the time for rebirth.

There were many hotels on this peninsula. One had caught the man's eye when they passed earlier, looking for a restaurant. Out of the twenty or more hotels, this one had drawn him back. When they went into the office/gift shop, there was nobody present. The man and niece walked around the store a bit, waiting for someone to arrive. Normally, they would have left and headed down the road. Something about this place had made that thought nonexistent in their minds. They knew when they pulled into the drive that they would be staying here tonight.

A lady of about fifty-five came out of the back office looking a bit embarrassed. She apologized for the lack of service but the others waved off her apology. They instantly saw the connection to this lady and her aura. The owner could see the same in them. She told the two the price, and the man readily agreed. The quality of the rooms and the price were more than fair. The two promised to return later to check out the gift shop as they made their way to the room. Key in hand, they grabbed the others and unloaded the car.

This room was by far the nicest they had stayed in on their entire trip. It was an upstairs room that you accessed through a sliding glass door, which overlooked the ocean. An extra bedroom and a trundle bed meant that the boy would have his own bed this night. The man and woman would also have their own room. The place also had a kitchen and a balcony large enough for the entire family. The lack of any other guests made the place a paradise which was much needed.

Walking down the beach helped clear the man's head. This was the final chapter in a healing that had begun two and a half years ago. Sadness had enveloped his being in the last years and now the healing was almost complete. Dealing with death was always a difficult thing. Dealing with so many deaths in a short time had been a test like no other the man nor his family had ever gone through. Most families would have disintegrated from such chaos. This family had just become that much stronger. They had turned the negative energies around into a positive. Their light was about to shine brighter than any light had shined in a very long time. It was all in their destiny.

The family walked down the sands together at times and alone at others. They relied on each other. They are what got each other through the hard times thrust upon them. The girl walked with her uncle much of the time. They understood each other. They both understood what the other had gone through. They had both lost so much of their bloodline. They had lost pieces of themselves. Now they talked about the new times. Now they talked about being over grief and moving on into the next chapters of their lives. Now they talked about being happy again.

The dogs were ecstatic to be on the sands again. They both loved the beach as much as their bigger homies. While the silly two-legged creatures picked things up and walked leisurely, the four-legged ones terrorized the beach with their combined fourteen pounds.

The group returned to the hotel with their pockets full of their beach treasures. They unloaded them into the room. The man, woman and niece went to the gift shop to see what they had to offer. Mostly, the three wanted to talk to the lady once again. Her energy had been a strong one. They wanted to be a little part of it. The boy stayed behind with the dogs. He had a headache all day and needed to try and ease the pains some. He also said that he would like some time alone. Being together all this time was hard on him, too. All living creatures needed their time alone.

The hotel lady was very nice. She was certainly one of the owners. The family could tell by the pride she took in the place. They walked around the store, not thinking to buy anything, carrying on a conversation with the lady. She was from Thailand and had many stories of enlightenment to share. She was a positive soul with hope.

The family thought highly of this lady. She was truly one of the true one percent.

Back at the room, everyone had some relax time. The boy's headache had increased. The others all sat on the balcony and smoked some of their fine recreational marijuana. The weather had turned nice, a bit humid even. The man painted some in his book. This was his way of unwinding. The niece played the singing bowl and the woman wrote. The three were making a trinity of creativity. The man became almost hypnotized by the sound of the bowl combined with the scratching of the woman's pen.

He could hear the different waves that flowed through the melody. The music coming from the bowl truly was singing. Its different waves seemed to be different levels of consciousness. The man closed his eyes and focused on the sound of the singing bowl and the rapid writing of the woman's hand. They seemed to take him to another world in his meditation.

He was flying through space briefly before landing on a nearby planet. It shared the same sun as the Earth's. This one was also full of water and was buzzing with life. From space, it was green and looked much like Earth. The man could see that nature here was different than on his planet. All creatures seemed to be in harmony with each other and their habitat. He met some humanoid looking creatures who said, through telepathy, that they would be his guide. They were much taller than ordinary humans. Their heads were much larger, but their noses and mouths were very small. Their eyes were very large and oval. Their faces were framed by dark, straight black hair. Their long arms held large hands with six fingers and an oversize thumb. They were very dark in color and wore strange clothes. Their demeanor was inviting and welcoming.

The beings said that this planet was called Krakatoa. It was formed many billions of years before the Earth. This planet was the origin of a species of human on Earth. They had seeded the blue planet many thousands of years before. Unfortunately, others had seeded the planet also.

Krakatoa knew about the turmoil that had happened and were going to try and salvage what they could of a once proud planet Earth. They would try again to stop something that had happened to their bloodline so long ago. The enslaving of the human masses.

Everything became blurry, and then faded in the vision. The music had stopped and the air was filled with sounds of the surf. The man came out of his astral projection. He looked to the book in front of him. There he saw a portrait of one of the beings who had been his guide on the distant world he just traveled to. It had been drawn, lined and painted. This page had been finished. The page had been blank when he sat down. He asked the others how long they had been there and they said only about ten minutes. How could he have painted this page so fast? Had he even painted it at all?

This was the moment that the man had been waiting for the whole trip. He had seen the truth all along, and in the last days even more. But now there was more. Now he knew where they had come from. He understood so much more than that. The sky earlier had opened and told him. The secrets to every question he had ever pondered had been answered in his mind. Now he was going to pass the knowledge to others.

Just a month before, the family had the cloud hanging over them. When death was around you, death consumed you. This was the philosophy thrust into their minds by some cosmic gag. Since that time, the light had returned to their lives. The path had been made. Now it was time to begin again. True spirituality was theirs.

Another walk on the beach with the woman was what the two needed. Their alone time this whole trip was minimal and this solitude was treasured. The two had spent many times on the beach together. Their married years had involved many travels and good times. The last two years had been hard on them and their relationship. They both had been through a lot of hardship in the past. They were not weak. They were fighters. They would fight to fend off the dark and bring light back into their marriage.

A loud sound from down the beach drew the couple's attention. It went a second and then a third time. It sounded like a whale calling out a signal for help. "Maybe a foghorn" the two said aloud. It was not discernible. They walked in the direction of the sound. It didn't happen again until they had been walking for over thirty minutes. Then, the sound seemed to be around them. It came from all directions. It sounded like a deep horn inside of a long tunnel. It was like nothing the two had ever heard before. The sound lasted over a minute. The man and woman were crippled with the pain pounding through their heads. The sound felt like metal coursing through their bodies. They could even taste and smell the sound. It was one of burnt metal. It had a feel of warm darkness.

The sound ended just as quickly as it had begun. There was not even the slightest echo from the cliffs to the East. The man and woman looked at each other for reassurance. They took the step to close the distance and realized that they were no longer standing on sand. The entire beach was covered in little balls of glass. The biggest was about six inches long and tubular. Most were roundish in shape and black. The man picked one up and held it to the sun. The object was transparent. The sun cast a strange reddish glow on the ground where it exited the glass from his hand.

He looked to the spot where he had picked up the glass and saw green underneath it. He reached down and scattered some of the glass off the top. It was not sharp. As the pieces moved together, they made a strange kind of music. Almost like the singing bowl earlier, but higher pitched. He dropped a couple of pieces in his pocket. They played a harmony the entire time they were in his pants. The green was also glass. This was of a clearer density and very light green. It kind of reminded the man of Emeralds.

The man and woman both knew what this substance was. They both knew their stones well. The green glass was Moldavite, the black glass was Tektite. They were both caused from a meteor strike. The earth would get super-heated, blow up into the sky and return as tektites. The two were perplexed at how these minerals had gotten all around them.

The man told the woman then what he had been thinking. He told her that a group of beings were using whatever means they could to stop them. They had just used one of their strongest weapons, to no avail. The One was strong. The One was the bringer of the fear, not the fearful.

The woman looked to her husband and said with a smile, "I knew you were going to say that."

The two filled their pockets with the Moldavite and Tektites. They felt that there was going to be a great need for it in the future. The weapons had not hurt them, but the others were alone back at the room. The boy already had a headache. They had been weakened. The man and woman made haste to get back to the room and to the safety of the group. This was not a time to be separated. Now was the time to unite and be ready for anything that got thrown their way. Just like this madness had been thrown their way.

The tektites covered the beach for over a half mile. When they got out of the ring of glass, back to the sand, there were dead fish and crabs all over the sands. Starfish, sea jellies, and clams were everywhere. The beach had become a graveyard since they had passed by just thirty minutes before. Every step was met with the crunch of dead sea animals.

As soon as they got to the room, the couple could see something was wrong. The girl was frantically trying to get the boy to wake up. She had ice from the machine downstairs covering the boy's body and forehead. He was a dark shade of red and sweating profusely, even covered in ice. The woman ran to his side while the man asked the girl what had happened.

She said, "We heard a noise that sounded like a foghorn or something. We heard it three times. Every time it sounded, the boy got more and more ill. He said it felt like something in his head was trying to get out. I had finally got him calmed down but he was so hot. I went to get some ice, came back and covered him. I had just finished when the sound happened again. This time it was loud. It made me feel a very strong sense of dread. It felt like it passed pain through all my senses. The boy passed out when it had sounded. He turned so red and I was worried that he had stopped breathing a few times."

The man knew what to do. He removed his hat. His vision had been working perfectly since they had gotten to the ocean. He had fully awakened on the trip this morning.

Now he could see what was going on. The dark had invaded this space and had the boy in its grip. The man could see the shadows filling the room. There were many spirits here. They had been sent. It was a way to put fear into the family, but just like the other weapons being used on them, this one was not going to work. He could see right through their evil ways. Fear was something the man did not have. He had died long ago. Without the fear of death, there was no fear left. After he had died, he was truly liberated. It was then that he began to live his life to the fullest. Most had called him crazy ever since.

These creatures, in this room, were not the same as the ones that attacked them on the beach. The man felt that there were a few different energies coming into this game. This was an old planet. There was a lot of history and time for many different species of beings to come and leave their marks. Some had stayed, while others had moved on to other worlds. The ones who had stayed had been here a very long time. They were not going to give up their conquests so easily.

The man took the singing bowl from his niece and began to play a harmony. He had pulled out the Moldavite and placed it in the bowl. The tektite pieces were longer. They made the perfect tool to play the bowl. His third eye kept a watch on the shadows. They did not like this kind of sound. It made them feel like the sound on the beach had made the family feel. The sound got louder and louder. The man and his being became one with the brass bowl and its tektite stick. The family had never heard sounds like the ones coming from the bowl. They all thought to themselves that it was the most beautiful sound they had ever heard. The sweet sounds filled the room.

The shadows began to gravitate toward the singing bowl. It was like the sounds coming from the object had suddenly become magnetic toward the dark energy in the room. The man saw the shapes fighting for existence even as they dissipated like smoke, into the bowl. The melody became so strong that the glass door began to vibrate. With the vibration of the entire area, the shadows could not take any more. The last of them entered the bowl.

The man had watched it all with his third eye. The girl also could see what was going on and sent all the energy she had toward the bowl in her uncle's hand. She had felt as if she were tied to the bowl through some unseen thread, although she was three feet away from her uncle. The woman had stayed by the boy's bed and had been giving positive updates the whole time. As the music had gotten louder, the boy had gotten better. His color had returned to normal, and he was no longer burning hot. With the last of the shadows entering the bowl, the boy woke up.

The man flipped up his shirt and spun the bowl around in one swift motion. The object contacted his flesh with a metallic clink. The man clutched the bowl to his stomach with pressure. He had trapped the negative energy inside the Moldavite.

He felt the energy from the brass bowl burning into his being. The metal was so hot to the touch that it felt like it had been in the fire. The man held it tight. He saw the light come from his forehead with his two eyes. It shot out across the room in a beam of bright green light. He felt like he was in a trance. It felt like he wasn't in control of his actions, but was in complete control at the same time. He felt all the negative energy flow through his being and emerge as the light.

The man walked slowly out of the room and down the steps. The girl followed behind her uncle. The woman stayed behind with the boy. He was just beginning to fully come out of whatever he was in. Whatever it had been, it had not been good.

The man made his way to the ocean with the bowl clutched tightly. Not once did it pull away from his skin. It was sealed tight. It felt like a suction had begun under the bowl. The man's intestines felt like they were being pulled to the surface. He thought in his head that it was not as bad as getting his stomach and ribs tattooed. The thought brought a slight laugh from him.

At the edge of the water, the girl called to the man. "What are you doing? The water is freezing." The man looked at her with the familiar look that they both knew so well. She understood that he understood. All was well. The man turned back to the water and began walking. When the waves got waist high, he dove in the cold Pacific Ocean. The water instantly revitalized the man's tired brain.

The bowl steamed when it hit the surf and broke free from his being. Steam bubbled to the surface with an explosion. The man could see the brass bowl floating down to the bottom for about fifteen feet before the object disappeared.

He looked to the shore but it was some distance away. He could see his niece standing there but she was barely a dot. He did not know how he had gotten this far out in the surf. He had just walked off the beach and now he was here. He saw a buoy a short distance away and knew he was in trouble. This was far out in the ocean. He decided it would be easier to make it to the buoy than the shore. Maybe the tide would shift after a bit and he would be able to get back to shore easier. The buoy at least would provide temporary safety.

The current cooperated with the man, and he was at the flotation in minutes. He thought that maybe he had been caught up in a riptide or something. It must be the reason he had been pulled out to sea so far. As he was climbing up onto the buoy, something pulled at his foot. He yanked, but the pressure was constant. It didn't feel like something was holding his foot, it felt like it was caught in suction. A memory of something he had read about many times in the last years flashed through the man's head. The reports were about people in the Pacific Northwest finding shoes on the beaches. The shoes were always a sports shoe and always contained a human foot. It had happened more than twelve times in the last years.

The man tried pulling himself onto the buoy but his foot was held tight. It felt like a clamp of water had a hold on him and wouldn't let go. Whatever it was, it began to suck him underwater. The breath was escaping his body. He popped to the surface once or twice more, but each time he got sucked harder into the water. His lungs began to burn. A strange light appeared under his feet. It seemed to originate from deep. He popped up once more, but knew it was almost over. He hoped that the others would be okay and not so sad. He was happy to save his grandson's life, even if it meant his own. He had a good life. He was not sad for this moment. He embraced it. In his mind, he had died all those years ago. All the ones since had been bonus.

The last breath escaped his body. His third eye did not go blank. His other vision began to get clouded with the lack of oxygen. The third eye was not the same. It got stronger as the man lost consciousness. This eye was not of the conscious, it was the subconscious. It was seeing clearer than ever before.

A shadow appeared in the water in front of the man. The glow from deep within the waters had made his last conscious moments surreal. Now this shadow of a figure was silhouetted against that glow. It seemed to be floating in the water, suspended in the light. The man reached out his hand to take hold of the other being. It all seemed so familiar to him. The other reached out his hand and made contact with the man's outstretched hand. Their faces floated to within a few feet. The man saw who the other being was. It was himself.

The man woke up on the beach. He was covered in sand and had crabs crawling on him. The sun beat into his naked skin like a laser beam. His head felt like twice its normal size. "How had he gotten here?" he wondered. These kinds of things may have happened to him when he drank, but he had not been drinking. His head felt like he had been though. He had a terrible taste in his mouth too, like he had been drinking seawater.

He crawled into a standing position. He was trying to remember what had happened to him. He remembered being at the hotel with his family, and next thing from the memory was waking up on the beach. Seaweed hung from his body, along with other debris from the ocean. He looked around the beach, but it was empty. There was a strange stone, a couple hundred feet down the beach, that had not been there before. The man could not spot the hotel and wondered if he was even on the same beach.

There was an odd smell in the air. It smelled metallic, kind of like when he ground iron in his workshop back home. The ocean looked strange, too. The water was a crimson shade. It reflected the many colors coming from the sky and clouds. The man had never seen so many colors in the sky. The moon was huge, bigger than he had ever seen it. The craters seemed different than he remembered.

The other direction, up the beach, looked foreign to the man, too. Even the trees in the distance looked different than before. When he was turning back to head down the beach, he saw what he had suspected. He didn't know why he knew it would be there, but he did. There was another moon in the sky. This one was smaller, but there it was. This one had craters different than the ones the man had known his whole life. At the same time, these moons seemed so familiar to him. Like he had dreamed about this place before. Or maybe he had been here before.

The man stumbled down the beach toward the monolith. The object called to him. It appeared to be about three hundred feet tall to the man. It looked to be a couple hundred feet across. The material seemed to be a shiny substance. The soft rays that the sun cast shined off the object's side. There seemed to be no shadow from the monolith. The light engulfed this object from all directions.

The man's progress was slow. His body was tired. It felt like he had been tossed around in the surf for the last few days. He was still covered in sand. His naked form was beaten and bruised. He could even see the black and blue marks through his tattoos.

About halfway to the monolith, a storm came out of nowhere. It was like he had walked into a wall of bad weather. The wind was the first to pick up followed by a heavy rain. The downpour was so severe, the man could not see in front of himself. He did not need to see, though. He thought that this was just another trick to stop his path. There was no stopping his way. This might slow him, but that was all it would achieve.

His third eye knew the way. The monolith was like a lighthouse in the dark to the man's inner being.

Suddenly he was there. He did not know how he had arrived so quickly. The storm was behind him, blowing its blustery gales. Before him was a stone, hundreds of feet tall. It was as tall as his eyes could see. Looking from side to side, it was immense. The man could not see the edges. The material seemed to be a kind of stone that he had never seen before. It looked sort of like obsidian mixed with quartz. Whatever it was, it was very smooth and highly polished.

Strangely, the stone was hovering about three feet off the ground. It seemed like the space between the monolith and the ground were one. They were part of the same entity. A strong green glow was coming from the space. The man thought the sight was beautiful. For as far as his eye could see, there was this stone with its light emanating from below. It was calling to him. He could not resist himself.

The man got on his belly and crawled under the monolith. As soon as the green light hit him, he felt at one with the entity. It seemed like his mind and all around it rocketed off through space together. They were passing through the cosmos as one being. It all felt so natural.

This was a familiar being. Its wisdom was beyond descriptions. It was everything but nothing. This was the man's true kin. It had been their origins and now would be the end.

The others would be here soon. For now, he would reacquaint himself with the One. For now, he would truly know God.

Chapter 34

The sound of the rain woke the man. He looked to the clock and was surprised to see that it was eight. This was the latest he had slept the entire trip. He tried to relax and sleep a little longer, but something was pulling him. This was one of those days where everything lined up. All the parallel dimensions would be crossing paths this day. The truth had come to him in his subconscious, and again as soon as he awoke.

He'd had these days before. Many things would happen this day that were so unusual. He knew, like he knew his name, that today was the day of alignment. Not only were things going to line up, it would be far greater than it had ever been before. The man thought that all the other times it had happened were preparing him for this day. He clearly remembered each of those days and their events. Today would truly be an epic one in his and his family's lives. Today was the end.

These were the first thoughts that went through his head when he woke up. His mind had been working oddly the entire trip, until yesterday. When they had gotten to the coast, his thoughts had cleared, and he understood. He was not going crazy. He was being shown. His dreams the night before had been an odd sort. He had died in his dreams, drowned in the surf. He had clearly remembered dying and the pain of being starved of oxygen. He remembered leaving his flesh pod and shooting through the cosmos. He did not feel alone. His people had seemed to be near him, but it was a faint recollection in his conscious.

The bridge had not yet been completed, connecting the subconscious to the conscious. Today felt like it was the day. Even his being was going to cross its parallel, merging his consciousness.

While stirring about, the man woke his niece. He had prepared coffee, but was somewhat disoriented. The room was slightly different this day. The kitchen had been facing the ocean before, but now it faced the back of the building. There seemed to be many more windows, too. The whole wall was a window and another sliding door was on the south wall. The whole room was encased in windows to the outside. He had only remembered one window the day before, the sliding door.

The man heard the faint rhythm of a gong in the distance, mingled with the sounds of the surf. Its melody was beautiful to the man. It made his heart feel complete.

The man thought of the energy that was coming from the day. Already the rain, the song, and the changes in the room. The day was only five minutes in. Today was the twilight zone, the man thought with happiness. He loved the strangest of the strange. The man went to make some coffee and saw a large pot on the stove. It was a stainless soup pot with the lid on. The gas stove under it was fired up and the man could hear a boiling inside the metal.

The man needed his coffee and was not to be stopped by a mystery. The dogs had awakened and were walking around in a relaxed state. The man had never seen the two dogs act like this in the morning. They seemed to be ready to go outside like usual, but were not their normal frantic selves. The man hurried and got the coffee ready. The dogs had been sitting patiently by the sliding door the whole time. They were in no rush at all. They too seemed to be in a kind of daze this morning.

The man opened the sliding door, and the dogs wandered out onto the porch. They made their way down the steps while the man kept an eye on them. Dogs this size were easy prey for large birds, small animals and humans. The dogs found some grass to do their business. A man and woman walked by with their two small dogs. At first, the family dogs did not see the intruders. The man was already hopping down the stairs as they turned their heads to face the newcomers.

The man need not have worried. The two small dogs ran happily right back to their homie. They had completely ignored the other humans and their pets. He had never seen them act like this before. They were aggressive little alpha dogs. They liked to let others know they were around. The dogs playfully chased each other, as the man looked on with amazement. They bounded up the steps and into the partially open door. The man pictured them running into their bedroom and jumping on the bed with the woman. It was their favorite place.

Walking back to the steps, the man noticed that there were differences on the outside of the building as well as the inside. The steps had been a darker wood stain in his memories of yesterday. Now they were a tan color, imitation wood. The patio, too, had seemed to be much bigger the day before. The chairs that had been there the night before had dwindled to one. The man knew that they had jumped into a new dimension. He had felt it since waking. Things were happening fast. Time seemed to be different. As he opened the sliding door, the smell hit him. Meat or something was cooking on the stove.

Time had changed. From the time that he had awoke, it seemed like a whole day had passed already. So many things were happening around the man at one time. The girl had started a song, 'Hurdy Gurdy Man'. It was the song that the man had likened to his brother. The song meant a lot to the man and girl. The song was their kin.

The man looked in the drawers for some hot pads. By the sixth pullout, he had found a sufficient set.

He slowly picked up the lid to the pan. "What are you doing!" startled him into dropping the metal disc back in place. His wife was standing in the entryway of the kitchen. "I told you guys last night not to mess with that. It's a surprise."

The smell had hit the man like a pit of death. There was something in that pot that was not so good. He looked to his wife, but there was no sign in her eyes. He could see her aura. It had always been a strong one, full of empathy. Today it was glowing like the sun. "Can't I just have a little peak?" the man asked. He knew the answer from the look his wife was giving him. Even being stern and holding to her convictions, she was unable to hide the spark in her eye that she still had for the man. He could see it and it always made him feel good. This was his partner for life. He just wished that the woman would let him see in the pot.

The sun had emerged from the clouds just as the others had awakened. Now, the clouds were wispy slivers of gray in the sky. The wind was mellow. It was going to be an awesome day.

The man took the dogs to the beach while the others got up and about. The dogs were very obedient on this morning and stayed right by his side. The sand seemed to have a red tint to it that reminded him of rust. It was cool to the touch on his bare feet.

There was nobody else on the beach this morning. The man looked up and down and saw no one. What he did see up the beach made the visions of his dream the night before come flooding back. There seemed to be a large object in the water, close to shore. It was maybe two hundred feet up the beach. The object looked like a four-story building with a large antenna coming from the top. It seemed to be square but only about ten feet on each side.

Red rays of transmission were zigzagging off the top of the antenna. The man couldn't stop himself from getting closer. The dogs stayed by his side the whole time. It seemed as if they too were being drawn to the object. This all seemed like his dream. He was remembering it clearly like he was reliving it in his conscious.

Suddenly he was there at the monolith. The dogs were by his side but he did not remember passing the distance. They had been down the beach moments before, and now they were standing in front of the large object.

The dogs sat on their haunches facing the metal object. Its material seemed to be a cross between gold and platinum or titanium. Whatever it was, it was cold to the touch. The man's hand could not be taken away after making contact. Energy from the craft flowed through his being. He knew things. It was like the monolith was telling him knowledge while his mind absorbed it all. The craft was from Krakatoa. It had been sent to assist the man and make things good again on the earth. It told the man that he would need to know the truth about Krakatoa before his journey could be complete.

They were a species almost like the humans. They had shared the same DNA when their planet had been seeded. The man saw the workings of the planet Krakatoa and its inhabitants. The people were very much like on Earth. Many different hues of skin and different sizes made their people interesting and creative.

These beings were the allies of the Earth. Another ally was a race of creatures that inhabited the inside of the moon. This was a species called the Lunark. They were a scientific breed of humanoid that had spread their DNA throughout this solar system. They had been watching their experiments on each of the planets and their moons ever since. They had much control over things.

The greed had been here for so very long. They had destroyed the solar system in a very short cosmic time. Now, the Lunark and all the other creatures of our sun were to rid themselves of the greed. Now, they were all going to ban together and create the One. The message was for the man to spread the word to the humans. He was to be their prophet. The messenger of the truth.

The visitor did not stay for long. What seemed like months to the man, were merely minutes. The information was passed and then the experience was over. The craft simply vanished.

The dogs barking and running around broke the man from his daydream. His hand was raised and he was standing with his mouth open. He looked down to the dogs and up and down the beach. He was still alone. His jaw was somehow sore. It felt like it was made of stone or something. He had a hard time closing his jaw until the pieces lined up and it closed. Instantly he felt something in his mouth. His jaw worked painlessly and efficiently when he spat the stone out. It was the stone that his sister had given him. Toomey. His jaw seemed to work normal now, but it felt different. It felt like his bones were different.

The man took his first step and his thoughts were confirmed. His legs and his arms both felt like they were made of stone, but covered in flesh. His fragile bones felt like they had been replaced with strong granite. When he used each body part for the first time, it would be stiff and painful. As he worked it the second and third time, it had worked out its kinks.

He began to make his way back down the beach. He shouldn't have left the others, but had felt very safe this morning. The energy was very strong.

He could feel the difference as he walked down the sand. Within thirty feet of where he had been standing, he was doing leaps in the air ten feet high. He did a couple of flips while walking and had broad jumped over a small river at least twenty feet across, with the dogs in his arms. His strength had grown by leaps on his walk. He understood it all. The truth had been told to him more than once on this trip. There was a reason for him to have this strength in his physical being. There was a purpose for everything that was happening.

The thoughts of the visitor were fresh in his head. He was not a prophet to the people and believed that most could not be saved. Let alone trusted. Being a Messiah for an intergalactic war was not to be in his near future.

He also had serious doubts about forming a collective with strangers. He had seen this happen on Earth many times where people thought that the collective was the answer to everything. He did not feel this way. He felt creativity and imagination were the way. Put together some humans that were creating, not debating, and there could be change.

Nature was the true decider of it all anyway. The universe was the true wisdom and ruler of the numbers. The strong would survive and the weak would falter. When things were destroyed, it seeded the new growth. It was the same cycle as everything else.

The man's mind had felt very clear after the encounter. He had rejected the words of the ambassador and knew it was not their path. They were on their journey. Getting off the trail now would not be a wise thing to do for them nor the planet.

The others were sitting on the patio when the man approached. They could tell that something was not the same with him. He was walking strongly. His body was normally wracked with pain from his work. Driving all these miles had not helped. Today though, he was strong. He also had a flash in his step, almost like his soul was in rhythm with everything around him.

"Mmmmmmm, what's that cooking?" the man had asked when they got inside. Whatever the smell was before, it was not the same now. It smelled like the woman had a roast cooking or something.

"I told you, it's a surprise," the woman answered. "Besides, we bought that smoked salmon, tortillas and eggs last night and you were going to make us breakfast."

The man remembered vaguely going to the store. It may as well have been a dream for as strong as the recollection was. He set to cooking up some potatoes. Fried onions on the side would do the man and his niece proper. Some blueberry cheddar cheese from Wisconsin and it was a feast that the family would never forget. There were no leftovers.

The family was not in a rush. They did not have to checkout until noon and planned to take advantage of the time. After breakfast, the boy went to the beach to have his own time. The other three smoked it up while enjoying coffee. Their talk this morning was of a spirituality not spoken by humans in a very long time. The day was pleasant. Waking up on the beach was what the family had been planning for the entire trip. Being there with the knowledge made it better.

The man liked to read the news with his coffee in the morning. Most of the news was nonsense, but at least he kept up a bit on what was going on. He did not trust the media one bit. Honest journalism had long been absent in corporate news. It had been part of the greed since the beginning. News was the tool to get all the mind control to the masses. Nevertheless, it kept the man up to date on a planet out of control.

The first thing he read was about a terrorist attack here in Washington. It had been on Whidbey Island. The Port Townsend ferry had been bombed yesterday afternoon. All persons on board had been killed. The man hollered for the woman to come outside. He started the article over but this time out loud. The woman and his niece were his audience. He narrated the tragic news as he read it.

"There was a bomb on the ferry yesterday at two thirty. Four square miles around the ferry buildings was demolished. Including Whidbey Island naval base. Thousands had perished. The rest of the island had been badly damaged and casualties were expected to grow. The news said that they still did not know what had happened. There was no radiation present so it was not a nuclear attack. They did not know what else could cause that much damage. Some speculated a meteor or something. They are saying it is connected to the fire at Aladdin."

The woman said that she hoped that their friends were okay. The man assured her that they were. They had a calling. This was not the way they were to end this existence.

The girl said, "our ferry would have been crossing at two thirty." She shot a look to her uncle.

The man had already known this fact. As soon as he read the story the first time, he made the connection with their reservation. Once again, something had tried to stop them on their path. Something very strong but not strong enough. The man felt even stronger than ever. If the greed were scared before, they should be terrified now. Everything they threw at the group was useless.

The man began to think of all the mayhem that had followed them on their path. It was following them like a dark cloud. It could never quite catch up though. It felt the same as the dark cloud that had followed the family for the last two years. This one felt more menacing but the man could not be sure that it was not the same thing. Maybe it had never gone away, just lurked in the background, waiting for a weakness. Then, it could pounce once again with its vicious attack.

The three went down to the beach to find the boy. The dogs, still mellow, tagged along. The women were amazed at how the dogs were behaving. The girl said that they seemed like different animals. The family picked up artifacts of the planet while talking about life. The boy had joined the others and was on the quest to find the coolest object.

And he did. The boy found a gold object that the others thought was a coin at first. Looking closer, it looked like a small disc, about two inches across and a quarter inch thick. It was oval and had inscriptions that had been worn in the surf.

The boy was shocked that he had found something so cool. He held it in his hand as the family made their way back to the hotel.

After getting back to the room, the man and girl went to the office to fetch some coffee. They had seen the sign the night before and remembered to come back this morning. The lady from the office was also the coffee brewer. The three spoke about the way. The man saw that this lady was One. Her Thai descent proved to the man and girl that it did not matter where you were from or what you looked like. If you knew the truth, you were the truth. The man and girl spoke to the woman about the division that had been created to make the people hate each other. This had been the main plan of the greed since the beginning. They had been very good at it. Dividing the people.

The woman spoke about how she felt guilty to charge people this price for a room. She wished she could make things much cheaper. The man told her that it was all part of the plan by the greed. They did whatever they wanted to get their billions, while making us feel bad for working hard, paying our bills and buying a new car. The man told the woman she had nothing to feel guilty about. Thinking about that made her unlike the other ninety nine percent. The woman gave the two the coffees for free. She thanked them for the conversation and went back into her office. It was the last time they would see the woman, they had taken and given energy. Their interchange was over.

Walking up the steps to the room, the smell once again hit them. "Does Auntie have some kind of sea creature in that pot? It stinks like hell one minute and the next it smells great. I sure hope she's ready to show us." The man shrugged his shoulders in response to his niece's question.

The woman was waiting by the door as the two walked up. She made a dramatic show of opening the door and ushering the two in. The pot was upside down in the sink, it's lid off to the side. On the counter was a large metal bowl covered with a kitchen towel. Under the cover was a sizable lump in the middle, making the whole thing a mystery.

"Come on, I can't take it anymore," said the boy. With his words, the woman whisked the towel off the bowl like a magician. The family was stunned. Laying in the bowl, looking straight at them, was the head of an alien. Its eyes had dissolved in the boiling water, leaving empty sockets. Its skin had been boiled away leaving a kind of biomechanical tissue under its surface. The small mouth was open slightly and the man could see rows of teeth in the creature's mouth where the tongue would be on a human.

"Where did you get this thing and why did you boil it?" the man asked his wife.

"These little fuckers have been following us this whole trip. They've been hounding me my entire life, since I was about three. When we were at your sister's house in

Minnesota, I realized the truth. I've been abducted by these little goblins for a very long time. Last night, you had been out late. I knew you had been acting weird and a part of it was these aliens. They have been stealing our time. I woke up in the middle of the night and surprised one of them. It was bent over our grandson, like it was going to take him or implant him or something. You had left that butcher knife on the counter earlier, and with one swoop from behind, his big ass head was bouncing on the kitchen tiles. Thump, Thump was the sound it made. The body seemed to turn to dust like in a vampire movie, but the head stayed alive. It was pissed. It was trying to talk in my head, but I remembered what we had talked about in Minnesota. I was no longer afraid of it. It no longer had any power over me. I boiled it all night. If that wouldn't kill it, nothing would. Now we're going to send those aliens a little message. That's why I boiled this bastard alive." She sounded very calm in her crazed dialogue.

The woman took the bowl to the balcony. As she headed down the stairs, the others all followed. The crow flew overhead, cawing its acceptance. When she got to the bottom of the steps, she headed a few feet to the left and into some overgrowth. A large steel pole was sticking out of the ground. She stopped, put the bowl onto some weeds and removed the head of the alien. With a squishy thud, she impaled it on the pole. When she gave it one final pull downward, the family all heard the metallic clang, like two metal pipes hitting.

The ground shook slightly and the air took on a metal taste. The foreign energy could not gain enough strength to harm the group. The beings had no power over the family. They had just spit into the face of the visitors and were not worried at all about repercussions. The visitors were the ones who were worried. The family knew exactly who they were.

The head began to make a long shrill sound. It was coming from its half open mouth and was deafening the family. The boy knew exactly what to do. He fished around in his pocket for the gold disc that he had found earlier. With dramatic movement, he stuffed the object into the alien's mouth. The mouth snapped shut like a spring had been inside it all along, waiting to be triggered. The sound stopped immediately. "Now, I too can say that I was a part of that alien's death." the boy said triumphantly.

The family packed the car and headed south. They had spoken earlier about staying another night. The alien head outside the hotel made that decision easy. The road called to them anyhow. They were on the coast and were ready to see some sights. The day was a bit overcast, but the air was nice. The family had a destination. They didn't know exactly what that destination was, but they would know when they found it.

They stopped at small places along the way for beachcombing and meeting people. They were successful in both regards. They stopped in a town called South Bend and went to an oyster museum. Oysters in this town were world famous. So famous, they even had a bad ass museum. The family checked out the museum and the bathrooms. The two women in the visitor center/museum were very nice and helpful in making their decision to stay and eat some world famous South Bend oysters.

On down the coast they went. They had passed so many small towns as they went. They had arrived in Oregon just before getting to South Bend. It was the twenty third state on this trip. The family had seen most of the country from the states just to the east of the Mississippi River to the Pacific Ocean. They had one more state to roll into. That one was home.

They were looking for a place on the beach, but kept finding small bays and inlets. The family was running out of energy. They were getting desperate to get out of the car for the day. They came across a town of over twenty thousand and thought it would be a good place to find a hotel for the night. They found a corporate hotel, which they decided to settle on. The employees were a fake nice to the man to get them to stay. The beach was a few blocks down the road. It would have to do.

Nothing seemed right at this hotel. It was like being in a B-movie as the lead roles. All eyes were upon them.

Their room was on the third floor. The garbage on the side of the hotel was piled up almost to the balcony. As the family unloaded the car, the manager came and decided to inspect what the family was unloading. She had looked at the man in the office with an evil eye. She had not liked him one bit. Now, she was sitting just ten feet from the car, watching every move that the family made. The man did not trust this woman. She was looking to control the family and take charge. The man did not like this kind of behavior towards him. When she made a comment about having two dogs instead of one, the man decided to leave. This was not the hotel for them.

The man got his money back. The clerk had tried to give him a hard time, but he did not care. He did not trust this place and was not going to stay. The room was far from the beach anyhow and was not right for them. The manager, who had been staring at them before, came in and approved the cash returned to the man. He laughed at their reluctance and walked out.

When the daylight hit him, so did the flash from the camera. Some tourist had his camera pointed right at the man's face and was getting ready to take his second shot. The man slapped the camera away, knocking it from the man's grip. The digital camera smashed to the ground. "Hey," the tourist yelled to the man, but his wife stopped him before he could say anything else. "Remember," is what she said to her husband while pointing to the news stand, just outside the office.

The man turned and looked at the paper in the window of the pay box. There, staring back at him, was a composite sketch of a man who looked just like him. The headline above it read, "Tattooed man wanted in terrorist attack." The man stuffed his money into his pocket and made his way to the car. The others were already inside, ready to go. The man did not hesitate. More tourists were gathered outside the hotel. They were all looking in his direction, some of them pointing. He hastily got in the car and drove away.

Looking at the map on the drive, the family saw that Rockaway Beach was only about another hour and a half down the road. Their son had stayed there a couple of years before and had really liked it. When they got into the town, they could see why their son had recommended it. It was a small town all on one street, the highway. They found a place right on the beach. The balcony was on the sand. The man could sense that his son had stayed here before. His energy was still here, waiting for the man and family to come and join it.

He had left on his dark sunglasses and wore a hoodie to hide his features. He knew just about everyone in these parts were looking for a guy that looked just like him. It didn't matter anyway, the guy in the office never even had time to look at the two.

The clerk was something to behold. The man did not understand why he met so many people who thought that they were better than others. This guy was one of them. He was tethered to his device like a junkie to his needle. This guy was another slut to the system. The man and girl dealt with the clerk long enough to get a room. It seemed like too much time to spend with the guy. When they walked out with their key, the girl told the man that now the clerk could go back to his video game life. It was more important to him than reality.

The beach was a very nice one. The stress from the driving and lack of sleep had taxed the family. It was time to get rid of the tensions. It was time for the family to re-build their thoughts together. Their son had stayed in this exact room. They could all feel it. The son had gotten food poisoning somewhere down the road and had almost died in this room. He had left a lot of energy behind. They were there to collect it and bring it back into their circle. They needed all their family energy they could get. That was their true collective.

The woman and girl went down the road into town and got some pizzas. The man had told the two that he would stay with the boy. He hadn't told them about the paper yet, but the rest of the world knew.

While waiting to pay, the woman saw the headlines in the newspaper and the composite sketch of her husband. She paid the dollar in coins and pulled the paper from the metal box. Just as she began to read it, the pizza was done. Her head was spinning as she paid for the pie. How had her husband's picture been put on the paper and why was he wanted for questioning? They had been nowhere near the Port Townsend ferry yesterday.

The two stopped for some coconut water and headed back. They did not want to be away from the others. Time now was crucial. On the way back, the woman handed her niece the paper. Just as the two began to talk worriedly about the headlines, a woman dressed in black stepped right in front of the minivan. The woman locked up the tires and swerved, barely missing the pedestrian. She looked around to see where the woman had gone but could not see her. The girl was also perplexed at the disappearance of the pedestrian. She had just appeared in the road and after they had swerved, she had disappeared just as quick. The two had seen some videos of teleportation and agreed that it looked a lot like that.

Another mile up the highway, the woman saw the stranger in black on the side of the road. It looked like she was going to jump into the middle of the road again. She slowed this time, but realized as she got closer that it wasn't a woman after all. It was a very large bird. Its proportions were more normal now, but back a hundred feet, the bird had looked like a small woman. The bird took flight as the van passed by. It looked directly at the woman and girl. They could both tell right away, this was not the same crow that had been following them for the last month. This bird was not a friend at all. It was large and grey. It's head and size looked more like a vulture than a crow. Neither of them had ever seen an animal of this species.

When the family pulled into the parking lot, the hotel clerk was standing outside the office. He looked flustered. The clerk spotted the van and waved them over. The guy looked very nervous. "I don't want you to think I have anything to do with this," the clerk said to the woman and girl, "but, the FBI called and said not to let you go anywhere. They've been watching you and your family and want you to stay here. They said you blew up something in Washington. They even told me to tell you these things."

"They only wanted you to tell us these things to scare us. But really, they couldn't keep us here if they tried. Luckily for you, we want to stay anyway and enjoy the nice beach. When you see the FBI arrive, since they like sending messages, tell them I said to fuck off. The only thing the FBI is going to do is create more fear in the humans so the greed can prosper more." the girl answered.

The woman and girl walked away with a confidence and closeness that had built among them for the last years. Their bond was a strong one. The whole family was strong. Their bond was one that was meant to last. Their bond was true. They were the One.

When they got to the room, the woman and niece both told the story of the clerk while handing the man the paper. He laughed when he saw the likeness. He told the others that the greed were fools. This was more lies. It had been one of their secret weapons that had taken out Whidbey Island. No ordinary man could do something like that. They would make up a scenario and tell the public and then they would be able to do whatever they wanted. They had done it countless times and used a patsy in every case.

The man told the others that it was not going to matter anyway. They all knew that they had been followed the entire trip. They had seen the creatures along the miles and had rejected giving them any of their attention. It had made the power of the darkness obsolete in controlling even one little bit of their journey.

The man spoke to the family of the approaching night. This would be the one. It was a new moon. This was the cycle they had been waiting for. It had been so very long and now they were here. The man explained about the One. "When the greed come, the One will be protected by Pachymama. The way things are going to happen, people have no idea. It is going to hit them fast and hard. God has made reckoning upon these lands. The Earth is about to cleanse itself of all its parasites. Our planet will be whole again."

The tide brought in the sound of hope. They had known when it was high tide and made their way to the water's edge. Buried halfway in the sand, the girl found a stone that looked like a head. The family had been searching for this stone since leaving the sister's house. It was the twin of the stone that the man's sister had given them. His name was also Toomey. They had all known that they would find this stone. They hadn't known where, but they knew they would find it. Of all days to find the last piece for the boy's treasure box. On the last day of the planet as they knew it.

The boy was the one to hold onto the treasures that the family had found. It was his duty to keep guard of these objects. Their purpose was to be a very important one. They would need to be kept safe until they were needed. He was the one to determine when they would be used and how. He took his job seriously.

The girl was the one to look for things. Objects or wisdom were always on the horizon of the girl's sights. She was looking for the objects that had called to her. The artifacts that would be used in the turbulent times that were on the way. Most of all, she was seeking the truth.

The woman was the one who had kept the family together after all the death. She had kept the man and his niece out of the insane asylum. She was also the one who was going to be a huge part in healing the Earth. She had always showed empathy towards others and towards nature. She cared, so she would.

The man was the one who could read all the pieces of the puzzle. He was the one who could see into the future and know what was coming their way. He was also the one who could read the people. Their auras were clear to the man. Most of all, he was the one who saw how things really were. He saw the absurdity of the humans and the greed. He also saw that the humans were not, by far, the most intelligent beings on this planet.

The energy flowed among the four, like directions on a map. They had always been close, but now they made a connection of energy that had not been seen on the planet in a very long time. Beings had been cut off from the heavens. Their connection to the cosmos had been severed a long time before. Now they were just wandering, soulless beings, praying to their imaginary gods. Slaves to their false idols. There were not many who knew. These four did. Their energy was of solar proportions.

The family had found an abandoned bonfire on the beach. There were few people on this beach earlier, and now they had all left. This stretch of coast was solely for the family. Darkness slowly overtook the sands. The family all saw shadows dancing around the dusk, but they were not scared. A few times, as the darkness enveloped them, the shadows crept right to the edge of the fire glow. The family could feel the cold, dreary energy coming from these shadows. The shadows were of a greasy species. Their energy was like oil.

The man was feeling stronger than ever this day. After what happened earlier, he had been feeling a strange kind of superhuman strength. He remembered the vision earlier of his bones turning to stone. If that had been imagined, the man's mind must be playing some serious tricks on him. His mind must have made his bones feel solid, because they sure as hell did feel that way still. He felt like he could jump to the top of cliffs if he wanted. He also knew that he should not be wasting his energy on playing with his new strengths. He had a feeling that he was going to need all his strength very soon.

The boy said he was going to go back to the hotel but his grandparents would not let him. They told the boy that it was very important for the group to stay together right now. A loud, shrill cry from the darkness made the boy change his mind. He would be staying with the others after all. The woman pulled a small pearl from her pocket, handing it to the boy. "I found it earlier when we stopped and ate oysters. I saved it for you." The boy smiled warmly to his grandma.

The four talked, sang and danced around the fire. They were celebrating. The man had got the others worked up thinking of the things to come. They sung at the top of their lungs. Songs that had meaning for their family. Other songs that were of an origin that none of them had remembered until this night. The girl was speaking in tongues that were unfamiliar just hours before. The family perfectly understood everything the girl was saying.

The dance, too, took on an unusual flow. They flung their arms and kicked their knees in the air, floating around the fire. An observer in the distance could have said that they were not even touching the ground. Their dance and song reminded them of Kokopelli.

The man kept feeling like there were watchers in the darkness. They knew the shadows were there and had been watching them all along. The beings that had been following them the whole trip were also present, but not seen. The man could also feel the agents of the greed, out there in the darkness somewhere, watching the family with their electronic devices.

The man told the others about the watchers through his song. His words were now of a language which had not been spoken in a very long time on this planet. The others felt for the first time in their lives that the language was pure. It was a language very natural to the family. This was the true tongue of their ancestors. This was the original language of the human.

The boy, in the same tongue, asked why all the beings were watching them. He wondered why they had all gathered here on Rockaway Beach, just to watch the family singing and dancing like lunatics. The man told the boy that it was what these beings did. They watched and made notes to go in files. Their whole existence was this. They loved to watch the creators more than anyone else. The people who used their minds for what they were used for. They knew that the family knew that they were there. It scared them. They had always kept their fear tactics secret and hidden. Now some beings were seeing right through it.

Around midnight, the man and his wife both brought out the twin stones that they each had acquired. They knew these stones were old friends who had walked the cosmos on their path before. The Toomey had always been with the family, and they always would be.

As soon as they were in view, the stones shot a beam of green light between themselves, and then straight into space. The eyes in the fossils had pulsed for a moment and filled with energy. They expelled it in one quick burst. The whole light show lasted about three seconds.

A familiar sound broke the family out of their revelry. They had been dancing and singing nonstop for three full hours. The sound came with the smell of burnt metal. It too was familiar to the man. He knew that the greed had been signaled. It was his purpose. Today, this new moon, was the night. This is where it all went down. It had been written so long ago.

The sound was the same as the singing bowl. The man and girl both looked to the other but their hands were empty. The song persisted. It sounded like it was coming from the fire. It was louder than any of the singing bowl sessions the two had previously had. The sound built in intensity until the sand around the fire began to vibrate and then levitate about an inch off the ground.

Suddenly, the boy shouted, "Look, up in the sky!" The others looked to see a huge red orb coming out of the heavens. It looked like it was headed right for them. The orb seemed huge and had a strange kind of green fire coming off it. It looked almost fluorescent, as it glowed against the backdrop of the stars. The object was quickly approaching.

The man looked to his side and saw someone else standing there. He looked to the right and another had joined the group on this side also. He looked to the others and saw each of them now was flanked by a being standing on either side of them. Their faces were dark and they stood still. Their forms seemed to be shadows but were solid. The man could clearly see the other eight beings with the family. He was not in fear. They were there to protect them. They were their people who held the same genetics. They had passed through time for many thousands of years together and now they were here again. For the first time in a very long time, the family was truly together again.

As the orb got closer, the man could feel the heat coming from the speeding object. He took the hands of the beings on either side of him and watched as the others did the same. The beings took the hands of the other beings and the circle was formed. The twelve beings had been brought back together for this very epic event.

The man started to chant in the tongues of his people. The others all joined in. The air felt like an electric current and the chanting seemed to combine with the charges in the air. The meteor made no sound. It was just hurtling toward them and their circle. None of the beings were looking at the space orb. They all kept their eyes on one another.

Just before the meteor hit, the man said, "here we go". The faces of all the beings in the circle lit up with a joy they had never seen in each other. Their joy was of Wisdom. The new beginning was here.

The meteor, two miles across, crashed to the earth in a green explosion. The equator of the rock had hit directly on the bonfire and the twelve souls standing around it. The beings had absorbed the impact and the energy from the debris, crushing their flesh pods into oblivion.

Everything had just ended.

Now they could begin.

Chapter 35

The One woke up. Dreams had come in layers of four all during the sleep. Its eye was fully open. The collective could now completely understand. The being felt more awake than ever in its existence. There was an understanding of the future and the past. The mission was completely clear now. The planet was at the end and needed some assistance. The ancients had once again come together.

The One emerged from the beach. It's stone reinforced flesh pod had been encased in a tomb of granite and sand and was now emerging from the cocoon. Upon waking, there had been no confusion. The being knew exactly where it was and why it was there. As it emerged from the small enclosure, the salt air was pure and felt good on the skin. There was no hesitation in its step. As soon as the One was free of its sleeping pod, it knew exactly which direction to go.

It was a very rainy and cold day, but the being did not need artificial warmth. The One had enough energy within its body to keep the shell warm. It had taken the pod of the man, prepared days in advance of the collective. The shell had been made strong with stone and microbes that could fight off any disease or infection. Wounds were repaired quickly with genes from extraterrestrial beings. Its strength was like no other animal on the planet. Mentally and physically. The One held genes of all animals. It was truly part of Earth. It had been one of the first humanoids on this planet, and now it was to begin all over again. Just like so very long ago.

As the One walked down the decrepit highway, it was struck with the destruction of the place. It came upon the place where the family had stayed before the cataclysm. It was not so discernible, but the being knew this was the spot. A dump truck was overturned in the parking lot, laying on top of another car. Skeletons were sitting in the cab of the dump truck upside down, still buckled in. There was litter and debris scattered across the overgrown pavement all the way to the highway, two hundred feet away. The highway was no better. Skeletons of cars were strewn down the road. The whole area looked like a bomb had hit it, but a long time ago. There were buildings standing but none were fully intact. Most were piles of rubble. The One saw nobody.

The only car not destroyed looked like a hovercraft more than a car. The One walked to the vehicle which was parked in front of what used to be the office of the hotel. The being remembered walking by this place and the clerk saying something about the FBI. The brick office building seemed to be partly intact, but the vines growing outside had completely engulfed the building. There was no getting in or out of that structure.

As the One walked to the vehicle, the doors swung open with a circular elliptical movement toward the front of the car. The cockpit was open and ready for the being. There was a slight recollection of this vehicle somewhere in the memories, but it could not remember exactly. Many thoughts and memories were going through its collective mind. Way too many memories to focus on every little detail. The vehicle did not have wheels, it hovered over the ground by about two feet. It was large inside, although it did not look like it from the outside. It looked to hold about six or seven people.

All the while he was checking out the car, the One felt eyes on his being. It was alert. The being held powers that could tell him exactly where the eyes were coming from. It looked to that direction. The being could not see anyone with its two eyes, but it could see the human with its third eye and mind. He read the voyeur's thoughts and took his knowledge. This was the man who had built this vehicle for the One. When the One was changing, this guy was getting its car ready for the final journey. He had been told by God to do this for the One. It had been his divine mission. The being gave the man a silent blessing that was graciously accepted.

The voyeur had been very religious his whole life and now saw his mistakes. It had all hit him with a blinding light originating from the being in the lot. God was not a religion. God was everything.

The one looked closely at the vehicle. It looked a lot like the minivan that they had taken so many moons ago. This looked like somebody had modified it into a modern traveling luxury. The One instinctively climbed into the vehicle. The door closed immediately and the craft swept away on its own accord. The vehicle swooped to about ten feet off the ground and followed the highway south. The one had to do nothing. The vehicle knew exactly where it was going.

The vehicle traveled down the Oregon coast. There was wreckage all around. The forests had grown back since the cataclysm, but the towns had not. The One saw few places with signs of humans, but there were some. It could see recent activity. The humans had never been a subtle species. They left footprints wherever they went.

There was also a serious lack of animals. Even birds were not prevalent.

The One stopped at the ruins of a small town. Smoke had been seen on the horizon, and the being thought that it was meant to be. This was the stop that had been calling.

The being walked around a small area of houses that had been slightly rebuilt. They were older homes with green all around. People had surely been here. The lawn was manicured. The smoke was coming from a peat moss fire on the corner of the property.

The One saw movement through one of the windows. It walked up the small porch and entered the building. It was greeted warmly with hello and hugs from two older women. They were the proprietors of a re-use store. They told the being that it was more just a way to collect what was left behind after the cataclysm. Sometimes, someone would come in and need something. Those were the times that they stayed here for. It had been their calling. They invited the One to browse and take whatever was needed. There was no need for money. That had been done away with long ago during the change.

The One looked through the store. There was something the being needed and this was to be the place to find it. The being knew, while it was on the road, that this was the first stop of the day. The women had come to him in a vision up the road a bit. It found a few items and went to the counter to talk to the ladies. They were surprised at what the being had gotten. It was simple things. A spool of copper wire and some four-foot metal rods. There was a small metal plate on the counter and the entity grabbed that, too. while talking to the women. The plate was like a trivet, made of iron. In its center was a fully open eye with rays coming off it. These were the only things the One needed. This and some conversation. It had been far too long since it had spoken with some humans.

One of the clerks spoke about how it was her first day to help at the store. She had been traveling and came across this gem of a place. Her and the proprietor hit it off very well, and now had become best friends. They had only known each other for one week, but it seemed like they knew each other a lifetime. She had chosen to help her friend out at the place just for something to do. It gave her a good excuse to be around her pal all the time.

The One saw a strength in the woman who operated this place. This other newcomer had arrived for a reason. She was to take over this thrift store, providing necessities to weary travelers. The other was to go with the One. It had been in her destiny. The One had known all along that he would find this woman in this exact spot. The being called the woman 'the provider'.

The two spoke of how the change had arrived. The greed that had been gripping the planet and the solar system was done with them. It was time for all the spiritual beings to bond with their surroundings. It was time to use the creative energy across the globe.

The woman spoke to the One about the stories telling of its arrival. Many years now, there had been talk of a creature, ancient on this planet, which was going to be coming this way. This creature was the final change. This being was the One. The woman had said that she recognized its energy as soon as it had come into her store. She felt light in her life at that moment more than at any other time. The light had not diminished since arriving. If anything, it had grown with hers.

The new proprietor was not sad in the least to see the others go. She was happy that the One had crossed her path. It had made her realize the calling that she had heard for most of her life. Every event that had happened in her life had led her to this place. She was to greet the needy traveler now. She was to take over for the woman who was needed by the One. There was no time for sadness. The light had entered her life. She waved until the strange vehicle was out of sight. Her week-long friend waved the whole time. They were true.

The two traveled down the coast and spoke about times to come. They stopped at another small town about a hundred miles down the road. The two got out of the vehicle and walked right up to a small store front. All the other buildings had been destroyed or were in collapse. This building had stood perfectly strong. The door was open, and the two went inside. Again, the One was greeted by two cheerful women. It thought fondly of the pleasantries presented so far from the humans. Before, humans had not been so nice to other beings.

They were ecstatic when the being turned to face them. So far, it had spoken to the two, but kept its back turned. When they saw the eye in its head, both the women knew. They, too, had heard the stories. In fact, there was not a single person who had not heard the stories. Everyone was anticipating the arrival of the One. It was what they truly had to look forward to. Everyone was awaiting the arrival of the truth.

The women of this store already had some items picked out for the being. She said that she knew that they were coming. One object was a quartz crystal orb the size of a bowling ball. It was a fine specimen of quartz. The stone was almost as clear as glass. The other item was a singing bowl made of Moldavite. The being was impressed with their choices. It was exactly why it had stopped, to get these two items.

One of the proprietors told the others that it was her first day helping at this store. She had met the other and become friends. The being was not surprised to hear these things. The mind was knowing. It understood. All things were on a cycle. Even events that happened throughout a lifetime. All of this was meant to be.

The One invited the holder of this store to also go with them. Her energy was one that the being could not leave behind. She was the Protector. The being had known that it was going to pick up this woman along with the other items. Everything was clear in the entities head before it happened. The mind of the One was its own destiny, seeing and correcting anything that might come along. The being could see numbers in everything and now could clearly decipher those numbers.

Numbers were what made the planets go around. From the overall universes floating through a numerical cosmos, to the smallest of amoebae inhabiting that realm. It was all about numbers. They are what kept the balance in everything. The being had understood numbers before, but nothing like this. Before the collective, the family had all seen the patterns in things and learned how to read them. When you could read the patterns, you could read life.

The three beings were back in the vehicle and down the coast once again. The newcomer felt as if she had been on this trip all along. The energy of the two was very familiar. The circle had begun to close once again. The One understood the role these women played in the overall mission. They, in turn, had no clue what was coming their way. They had visions of meeting the One and going on this journey. It was all they needed for peace of mind. Anyway, the One was not going to use them or abuse them, it was simply going to borrow their energy for the better of the planet.

All four directions had come together with the collective. The personalities of the four travelers, along with their thoughts, united in the middle of the being. Their collective memories had merged and become vague. Memories of the past on this journey would just cloud the future. Now was a time to focus on the road ahead, not the road behind. The past road was worn and tired. The future road was bathed in light from the heavens. The truth about the history would come forward, but that was on a grand scale. Memories of each being and their life time was small compared to the overall picture.

The crow had flown above the vehicle ever since the One had gotten into it for the first time. The being did remember the crow well. This bird had been its friend for a very long time and many miles. It had protected the family and showed them the path to the collective. Now it was continuing to be the trusted friend. They were both on the path to righteousness. The crow was the Navigator.

The thoughts flew through the being's head as they traveled down the road. It was like lightning going off in its head. All was so clear this time. The being knew that it had slept, but did not know for how long. The third eye had felt lethargic, like it was drowsy. Or maybe it had been closed for a long time and had awoke. Whatever it was, the eye was wide open now. The being felt wonderful. It was happy for the feelings.

Alone, the family had lost touch with what it was to be happy. Now, as the collective, elation filled its being.

The rain was bad at times and sometimes not. The One just relaxed and spoke with the others, when not in deep thought. There were many things to think about as the vehicle passed the miles. The being was also very happy to see the forest and wilderness regrown. The lack of animals still worried the One, but those answers, too, would come soon enough. This forest looked fresh like all the others they had seen this day. It was obvious that people hadn't been around in a very long time. Everything was too nice for humans to be living there.

It had been many miles of thinking before the One asked the two women what had happened. They said in unison, as if they had rehearsed this speech many times before, "Twenty-two years ago, a meteor hit in Kanab, Utah. Most of the middle of America had been wiped out. The impact had set off the super volcano in Yellowstone, and the cataclysm gouged a watery divide between the West and East coasts of America. The entire Rockies is now a twenty-mile channel. It went from the Arctic all the way to the Gulf of Mexico. Maps, if we had them, would never look the same. A strange virus was attached to the meteor. Its spores of death spread very fast in the consumer society."

"After the dust settled, many millions died. Other countries came to the rescue of America, but that, too, helped in the global downfall. The virus that had come with the meteor wiped out way more than the impact. Ninety nine percent of all people died within one month. The one percent who survived must have been immune. The sun was not seen for over three years, that was the next struggle. When it emerged, a fraction of the one percent was still alive. They had foraged and hunted in harmony with their fellow humans. There was not a single fight in this whole time among the species. The remainder of their people worked well together, as a unit. It was the key to their survival. Peace had truly arrived."

"The one percent who had survived were the ones who could see the truth. They were the ones who did not fall into the greed and their evil ways. Their simple, creative lives had spared them. They continued to exist on this planet, but in a different way than the greed had taught. They lived at peace with each other and with nature. It had been their way even before the cataclysm. They were in harmony with everything around them. These people were the only reason the human species has survived to this day. The planet has already begun to recuperate, but the human numbers haven't. No humans had been born since the meteor strike."

"Many tales of magic travel through the land. Creativity has been awakened again in the people of this planet. Imagination is the new ruler."

"There was no crime because there was no greed. Government was a silly notion now that there was no more elite. Now, the true sentinels take care of the planet. Nobody is in charge. We are all responsible. There are no rules, because the people have empathy for each other, and a strong sense of right and wrong. There is no poverty for the same reason. The planet has become a Utopia." The women finished. Throughout their entire dialogue, they had not missed a syllable of their synchronicity. They spoke like a robot with one mind but two pods.

"That is what I have been waiting for. It has been thousands of years that I have been waiting to hear these words from your species. A race who was so full of hatred and destruction. To be now living in harmony is the sweetest thing I have ever heard. Your species is not quite what you think. Your one percent, you are of the human species, but not exactly human. You were the higher intelligence on this planet, no matter what the tests of the greed determined. You, by being the righteous, have saved your species," the man spoke to the others. "I know by your ages that you were a part of the change. You helped to save this planet. It is still going through the change. I know that there has not been a baby born since the meteor strike. I also know that the two of you will be the first mothers of the new era."

"Where are you from?" asked the provider with wonder in her voice.

"I am where you are from, but come from far away from where you come from. I know this is hard to understand now, but it will all be clear later. Time and space are different where my being came from. In my realm, they are something that we create in our minds to suit our own personal needs. It has been a long journey to get here. The collective thought made it. Now the lives of the past and future can truly be celebrated."

"None of it matters anymore. Where we are from is meaningless. We are all connected. Origins, color, sex, thought, it was all ways to divide the beings. It is time to be united. The humans have begun. They have finally become one with themselves. That was the first step. Now that they know themselves, they can form their own paradise, free of any bias toward one another." The One finished.

"Where are we going?" the protector asked.

"We will be going back to California. There is a small town in the Sierra Nevada foothills that we must get back to. It is where we started. The beginning cannot come without the end. That is where the truth is going to come out. That is where we will make the final stand, in this cycle, for this planet. Tonight though, we will be staying in a small town that used to be called Yachats. There is something that we need to find there on the beach. We will also need some rest. The final part of the journey will be long. When we get back to California, we will be very busy." the being told the others.

The car was stopping as the One finished his words to the others. It was pulling into an old motel at the edge of the beach. Someone had taken care of this place. There was a small community of humans occupying its grounds. As soon as the vehicle stopped, the One was greeted warmly by the elder of the commune. The others followed closely. They all wanted to see the being that everyone was talking about. There was instant friendship among the two groups.

A lone figure approached the reunion from one of the hotel rooms. As soon as the woman stepped into the parking lot, the One felt her presence. It knew this person. She was the friend that the family had gone to see in Washington. She looked the same as the last time they had seen her except for one detail. Her face showed the look of loss. The One knew. The friend had lost her people. The One opened its arms, and the two beings gravitated together. An energy was created when their auras touched that made the rest of the people around take a few steps back.

The One knew why Yachats had been so important. It had just found what it had come for. The Leader was here. When the being hugged the woman, she said, "I knew you were coming. I've waited a very long time. Thank the Gods we are together again." The two beings wept tears of joy.

The people of the commune all knew what was going on. Their numbers consisted of about forty souls. Each of the survivors had made their way here on their journeys. Each had stayed for their own reason. The elder had been the original owner of the place before the change. After, he had opened it to anyone who needed a place to stay and a conversation to share. There had been so much heartache and loss those first years. Everyone had lost people. Usually, all their people.

The community members were a mix of all knowledge. The collective they made was a utopia. Everyone taught each other what they knew. Nothing was held back out of fear of someone getting better. In the collective, everyone benefited as more people gained knowledge; each person was a creator, and together they were One.

They had noticed that the animals had begun to die off in alarming rates. They had learned to live with the animals and learned their ways. When the animals realized that the humans were no longer a threat, and their extinction was imminent, they formed a bond with the two-legged creatures. It was the first time in over fourteen thousand years that the humans and animals lived as one, with trust for each other.

The animal's numbers had stopped declining but had not been increasing. Like the humans, they were slow to reproduce, if at all. Their population had been holding steady with the occasional birth of offspring. All the creatures on Pachymama had been reduced by over ninety nine percent. Over fifty percent of the Earth's animals had become extinct after the meteor strike. The plants and trees had not fared any better. Ninety percent of the world's forests had died off with the absence of the sun. After nineteen years, they were now just beginning to fully grow back.

The elder led the One and companions to a small open field. The natural grass was about a foot tall. Wildflowers dotted the scene. The elder spoke about the coming. The Earth had purged itself of the bad, and now good was to return. The man pointed out over the expanse of green with pride. They had worked hard and learned to become one with nature.

The One looked at the elder with admiration and disgust. "Do you really think that you have to learn to be with nature. Your species was with nature for hundreds of thousands of years. You all fell into the greed so easily. I do respect that you have gotten back to nature, but do not ask for praise. Being one with all creatures is the right thing to do. You should never look for praise when doing the right thing. Also, you are mistaken about your utopia. It was always the problem with the one percenters. You always thought you were the higher intelligence. You were wrong. And you are still wrong about that. Many species live on this planet. Do not think it is paradise yet. If it does ever become utopia, fight with all your means to keep it that way."

The One took the hand of the Leader and the elder, forming a small circle. The provider and the protector joined the circle and the flow of energy. The One felt the change of energy as each of the beings were admitted to the circle. It could feel the vitality that they offered. One by one, the rest of the community joined hands with the others. Soon, more than forty people had joined the circle. The One felt every one of their energies. They all held a very positive aura. One feeling was stronger than all the other thoughts of the group.

It was the feeling of Hope.

The One focused its mind to the center of the circle. It sent waves of thought through its being, into the hands being clasped. The elder and the leader were very strong. They were conduits of the energy the One sent out, focusing it and then amplifying it to the others. Everyone in the group felt it and knew it. They all at once focused their thoughts into the center of the circle.

A pattern began to materialize in the middle of the group. There was no dust or blades of grass flying. There were simply lines being made in the foot-tall grass and flowers. The One could see the pattern easily. I's eye was connected to the crow, flying above. What the bird saw, the being also saw. It was a pattern very familiar to the One. It was a symbol that its family had used for a very long time. It was a symbol telling the One that they would all be reunited again, very soon.

The One looked to the face of every soul in the circle. They were all crying in a way that made their auras dance throughout the circle. It looked like musical notes weaving in and out of the bodies. The notes ended at the leader. Her aura was attached to the One. The being could see and feel the connection being stronger, tighter than that of the rest of the crowd. The elder on the other side of the being was connected to the aura of his people. The One could feel the different paths the two were on.

The sun was blocked out by the craft. The One had seen this before. Some recollections of its past-memories were so strong, while others weak. This one was very strong. It had seen this all those years ago with the son. This was the same craft. The One could feel, through the collective, that a few others in the crowd had seen it before also. The One sent the collective thought not to break the circle. It was too late. One of them, a young girl of about twenty-four, panicked and broke away from the group. A ray of bright light came from the center of the craft and struck the woman. Her body froze in time and vanished.

The collective was strong. The individual, full of fear, was vulnerable.

The people from the commune had all been watching the entire scene. They had not taken their eyes off the vessel once. The One thought of how the humans had changed in some ways but still had a long way to go. They still loved to see death and destruction. The One did not have to look. The symbol that had formed in front of the group told the being everything it needed to know. The leader, by the side, was looking straight ahead. She had learned long ago to trust the family. Now, as the collective, there was not a doubt in her mind.

The craft opened a section on the bottom in the shape of a triangle. The provider and the protector were also looking at the crop circle. It held the secret to what was going on. The crop circle in front of the group turned from green to red. It began to glow with an unseen intensity. The pattern, at first, had withstood the heat at the bottom, but it too quickly succumbed. The heat from the fire became very hot. The humans all scattered in different directions, breaking the circle.

The One stood tall. The leader, holding its hand, was joined flawlessly by the other two women in their circle. They had appeared the moment that the circle was broken. Their hands met with the other two sets, never letting the circle be broken. The fire from within the circle had gone back to its green color immediately. There had been no fire. It had been a trick on the minds.

Now, the humans ran in all directions. The beam of light from the triangle lit up the sky, like twenty suns rising. All the humans and the animals they had been nurturing were gone in a flash. They had frozen for a moment and then were gone. There was no hiding place. The beam had taken them all.

The eyes from the craft on the One and its circle was intense. It felt like a whole world of people were all watching what the being would do next. The light from the triangle was pointing at the circle, but its powers were useless against the beings. The circle was stronger.

The One broke the grasp with the other three beings by throwing their hands away. Instantly, they were on far sides of the field. The four beings stood at exact points to the North, South, East and West. The crop circle in the middle had once again come back. Now, they stood on the four points of the symbol. Now, they were the symbol.

The One raised its hands in a pulling up motion. In front of the being, in the middle of the circle, unearthed the three metal rods it had acquired earlier in the day. They lifted out of the soil like they were on hydraulic pistons. When they got to their ultimate height, they stopped in a triangle shape. The rods were wrapped with the copper wire that had also been taken. The One had wrapped these copper coils while they were on the road. Now, they were going to get tested.

The metal plate that was found had been placed in the middle of the triangle, on the ground. The light from the spacecraft shot out and struck the triangle, but its beam was only like a flashlight on the object. The One bent down to pick up the key. It was the large quartz orb that the protector had given him earlier. It vibrated in the One's hands, and began to glow a blue light from the inside. Every vein inside the ball was visible, a map of the origins of so many things. The being held the orb high above its head and let the light flow out to the others. Soon, all the beings were enveloped by the blue light.

The craft, at first silent, now begun to make a strange sound. It sounded like the noise a pipe organ would make, a very low tone. It repeated the tone over and over, like a warning. The craft began to pull away. The triangular door was slowly closing as the behemoth, clumsily and noisy, tried to make its getaway.

The One had been waiting for this moment for a very long time. It rolled the orb into the center of the circle. The blue light from the ball cast strong shadows throughout the night as it rolled along. The object stopped on top of the trivet that had been placed in the field by telepathic partners. The light from the orb was intensified by thousands. Its energy shot upward, wrapping around each of the three coils. At the top of the coils, there was a slight hesitation as the coils built up the energy at top, dancing around the union. Then, a blue light shot from the tips of the coils, straight up to the ship above them. The light infected the entire bottom of the spacecraft. The object was visible briefly, illuminated by its destruction. It was organic looking, but metallic and stone at the same time. The light enveloped the entire craft in seconds. Then it was gone. Only stars remained.

The slight smell of burnt metal lingered in the air.

The One felt the energy immediately and saw. The circle had been returned. All the humans that had been abducted had come back to the circle. The One felt their energy, but something was different than before. It looked in the eyes of the humans to read their faces, also. With that and their thoughts, humans could be so easy to read.

All the people had the same look on their faces. The One had walked away from the circle. It had enough of the humans.

The leader insisted that the One and the other two women stay with her in her room. They all agreed without a thought. There would be a serious need for rest this night. There would be many days to catch up with the friend in the next days on the road.

The One was told good night by all in the commune. Each of them, warmly, took the being's hand and gave a small praise for the future. Kindness and respect filled their auras. There were so many things the One liked about humans. It understood that they were a relatively young species, but it didn't always help with the frustration. The One had been helping these humans for a very long time. Sometimes they understood, but mostly they didn't.

As each of the commune came to the being, it saw in each of them something that was not in them before they were abducted. They all had a common look in their eyes.

It was knowledge. Knowledge that had been kept from them for a very long time by ones who wanted nothing more than control.

Tonight, these humans had truly seen the light. Tonight, they had learned the truth. Now, with a new day tomorrow, it would be the time to spread the word.

CHAPTER 36

The One played the brass singing bowls all night long. It switched between the two every hour. The bowls did not need a hand to hold them. They held tightly to the being's legs with a common bond. It took only the left hand to make the melody, freeing up the right for writing. Neither appendage tired once throughout the entire night.

Now, more than ever, the words had to be spoken. There was a lot of knowledge future species would need to know. The wisdom, once again, needed to be set free. The One was the being to record this truth.

The One had documented the truth before in its existence. Millions of years ago, in a language now forgotten on this planet, the being had written the story of the Earth. It was the story of the last hundreds of millions of years. Before that, the One had no knowledge of what had happened on Pachymama. There had been artifacts from a species before, but they were mysteries. The story that the One had told was the way for the creatures of this planet. The path to living in harmony with all the other creatures of the planet and the universe. It was the way of the light and the dark.

The greed had other ideas. They did not want the humans nor any other being to have this awareness. They were on a different path. Their way was to spread enmity among the creatures. Theirs was the way of control. Knowledge for the masses created fear in the greed. They had destroyed all the history of the planet, or stored it in their private vaults. Much of the world's history was stashed safely away there. In these places, the knowledge could be contained, and the humans controlled. In the greed's mind, this was the only way.

The story by the One had been destroyed. It was the biggest threat to the greed of all. The greed was afraid of the One and the truth. The being was strong and getting stronger. It had brought fear to the elite and their lies.

The provider and the protector awoke at the same time. Although they had never met before yesterday, they were in unison in all their actions and words. The leader had been up for hours. She was not going to waste such a magical time with sleep. There would be plenty of time for that later. An hour or two of sleep was all her busy mind could handle. The woman stayed by the side of the One most of the night. Their bond had always been strong, but now it was solid as granite. While her friend played the singing bowls and wrote, she, too, wrote and drew.

The creativity the two beings made created an aura of its own. An entity of bright light had formed from their imagination and taken up residence with the four. Its glow lit the room, so they no longer needed lights. The luminous rays would even permeate to the outside, creating a small gathering of humans curious of the sight and feel of the energy. They could all feel that something very important was happening inside.

In this night, the woman would write and illustrate a book that would inspire generations of children. For the next thousands of years, the woman's book would teach kids the way, the path to enlightenment. It simply taught them respect. For yourself, and for others. The writings focused on using your imagination and creativity for your entire life. It taught the kids the art of kindness and empathy. The teachings centered around this book was the knowledge for all to live in harmony. It would make this species healthy again and strong. Wisdom began from birth, and this book was its guide.

The One had absorbed the energy coming from the friend in their creative bubble, just as she absorbed its energy. The being told the girl how proud she had made many. She had been a true wife and mother. She was a true friend. She nurtured so many in their times of need, sacrificing so much on the way. Now, she was to teach the next generations of kids. Now, she would spread her light.

The other women were ready quickly. Makeup and looking pretty were a thing long of the past. Natural beauty was the true beauty. Your outside reflected your inside that way. We are all what we are.

The group piled into the vessel and began their descent down the Oregon coast. The protector was surprised that the commune people didn't come out to say goodbye. The One told the woman, "they all left in the middle of the night. They had words to speak, and people to pass those words to. They had learned the truth. Now, they are spreading it."

The woman was surprised that the whole group could leave and not be heard. The One told of the group leaving on foot. None of them had gone the way of the highway. They had all headed overland, their animal friends guiding them, nurturing them. The humans knew now that they were not helping the animals. The One had showed them the truth. It was the other way around. All species on Earth helped each other by living in harmony. Everything had its purpose.

The distance on this day was not going to be far. They were going to the Port of Florence. The women asked what was so special about the place. The One said, "there is someone we need to meet there." The being said no more about it. It did tell the others that there were more items that they needed to pick up on the way. The re-use stores would be the place to find these items, while a few would be found on the beach.

The re-use stores were all run by citizens for citizens. There was no greed. Anything you wanted, you could have. If you wanted to leave something in return, you could. If you didn't, nobody would judge you. People brought all kinds of salvaged items to these stores. Some had made it their mission to find things that people needed. Without the greed, there was no theft or any other crime. Guns had long ago been done away with, except for hunting. Food was plentiful, too. After the sun had come back, so did the gardens and the pastures.

The being had visions along the road of a contraption that needed to be built. It had studied the Coral Castle in Florida and understood the ways of its creator. There were pieces to the device that were going to be difficult to find. They might find all the pieces at one place, or maybe it would take days. Whatever the circumstance, the One was going to take whatever time was needed. Rushing and settling for things that would not work one hundred percent was not the way. Time was crucial, but in the cosmic array of time, it was not everything. Attention to detail and perfection was everything.

The group traveled about fifty miles before stopping at the first re-use store. The women did not need anything so they stayed out in the car. These places were not for browsing and wasting time. They were for people who needed something.

The One was greeted warmly by the two women in the store. Everywhere the being would go this day and the rest of the journey, there were warm greetings. There was an excitement that seemed to be in the air. The people were happy about the truth. They were happy to see the One. They knew that change had fully come now. Their twenty-two years of limbo were coming to an end.

The group went to three more re-use stores as they traveled the miles. The provider was questioning why the One had picked some of the items that were now in the car. The being had got at least one item from each store. At one store, the man had come out with large spools of copper wire. The women did not know how it would fit, but the being made it happen. It also got metal rods and a radio like device. A telescope and some binoculars finished the treasure hunt at the re-use stores for this day.

"A stop on the beach is needed to stretch and get some air", the One had said. As they came to a stop only twenty feet from the water, the women ran into the surf. They had taken off their shoes and pants with the sight of the ocean and now were frolicking in its cold splash. The One stood outside the vessel and looked to the right, then to the left, surveying the beach in all directions. It took three steps to the left, bent down and began to dig with its hands. Six inches below the sand was what the being had come for. It was an agate the size of his hand. The stone was white on the outside, with chips missing. Overall, it looked like a skull from an unearthly being. The stone began to pulse and glow when the One held it out. The women all stopped their antics and looked to the agate. The stone seemed to speak to each of them in turn, yet all at the same time.

The three women all gathered around the One. They all outstretched their hands and placed them on the object. All four beings now combined their energy with that of the agate. Their position formed a symbol. It was their symbol. It was the symbol of the universe. The stone held special powers to the group as well as this symbol. This stone had belonged to the One long ago. This symbol had been used by the One long ago, also. Everything had come back around.

A beam of white light shot from the stone straight up into the heavens. Thunder roared in the cloudless sky. The heavens lit up briefly like a flash from an x-ray. The One took the rock away from the touch of the others. "Now we are ready," the being said to the three. It turned back to the vessel. The craft had been shifting shapes for the last couple of hundred miles. They had stopped on a beach earlier and picked up agates. This is when the craft began to change. It now resembled a large spacecraft more than a car.

The One told the others that their vessel was changing because of the agates. Each agate they collected made the craft more complete. This agate they had just found was the last piece of the vehicle. This agate was a fossil of an old friend. Toomey was now with them once again. Now they were complete. They had acquired what they were looking for. Now, they could finish their mission.

The group arrived in Florence mid-afternoon. There was a very warm welcome waiting for them. Many survivors had settled in this town, more than three hundred. More people had settled here than any other place in Oregon. In the last days, many more people had come. Word from the commune in Yachats was spreading. People were learning the truth and wanted to see it first-hand. Over a thousand-people lined the street as the group hovered into town.

An older woman of about seventy was standing in the street by herself. She was the elder in this town and would be giving the formal greeting. The woman greeted the other women first and warmly. When she got to the One, the woman became flushed with emotions. She had never thought in all her imaginings that she would be standing here today, face to face with the One. She warmly took the being into her embrace and fed her energy into the other. The two became stronger with the unity of spirits.

The elder stepped back and let the people come forward. They all wanted to touch the One. A little piece of its energy is what they had come for. The elder spoke to the One the entire time. It was just twenty minutes before all the souls had shared with the One. A large man came forward and said the feast was ready. The sound of feast had the stomach of the group rumbling. The being had been asleep for twenty-two years, and now it was time to get nourishment. The last miles had been so full of the mission, it had not even thought about food.

The waitress had a name that was very familiar to the One. It had been the name of one of its ancestors; a birth mother. The woman had the gift. The being embraced the server warmly. She was the one who was to nourish the group on this night. It was only appropriate that she had that name. The woman began to serve the family. There were many waitresses who had volunteered to feed this hungry mass, but this one had been cosmically paired with the guests of honor.

The food was fantastic. It replenished more than the body, it set the mind into the optimum working mode. Without fuel, the machine did not work proper. There was salmon, halibut, and cod. Fried clams, squid, and shrimp. Crab cakes and Oysters on the half shell and an abundance of fresh produce rounded out the feast. The celebration lasted hours. After the first round of food, the One and companions were very tired. They needed to take a small nap.

The group headed to their vessel. They were the most comfortable in their own quarters. They also did not want to be a burden on their hosts. The craft was nothing like before anyhow. The inside was like a small house, while the outside had barely grown. There seemed to be another dimension that they would step into as soon as they entered the craft. There was ample room for all to sleep in a corner that was so plush, it was like sleeping on a cloud. The four went to the corner and fell instantly into the subconscious.

The One awoke covered in a strange sweat. It was slimy and felt like a film all over its skin. The dreams which it had been having were of past lives and familiar faces. The one understood it all. We traveled through time walking with the same souls over and over. Our closest people now were also the closest in our past lives. They would be our closest friends in our future lives just as well. We truly never lost our loved ones. They are living in a parallel life with us in a different dimension. We never died in this regard, but we never really lived either.

More food was needed by the group. The nourishment earlier was just a warmup for the real feast which was about to begin. They made their way back to the tables, but only a few people remained. Most had gone off in search of other humans to tell the story.

The only ones' eating were the waitresses from earlier. The elder was with the women, and they were enjoying a story filled meal. They were all happy to see the One and companions return. The elder served them the food, while the others ate. This was a much better setting for the being. It had never liked crowds, as individuals; and now the collective did not like them either.

The being also did not like being treated like a God. It was not God, just another being like themselves that had ended up on Pachymama.

The group sat with the others for the next couple of hours. Their time together was one of good energy and a sharing of the aura. The One did not speak most of this time. It was listening to the stories of the women. There was a lot being said. The One felt it important to hear what they were saying. Their words were ones of hope and the path to enlightenment.

Finally, the group could take no more food. They were in dire need of some rest. They had things to talk about. Things that could not be said around others. The four bid their goodnight and headed for the safety of their craft.

On the way, the One encountered an energy in the forest that was out of place. It told the women to go on by themselves. When alone, the aura that the being had been feeling came forward. It was an old friend. It was a Sasquatch. The creature and the One raised their forearms and rubbed them against the others. It was a strange kind of handshake that hadn't been used on this planet for thousands of years. It was the shake between the One and its ally. Two old friends now reunited.

The Sasquatch gave a sort of whistle which originated in its throat. The One made a similar whistle with its mouth. The two beings were happy to be in each other's presence. It had been a very long time. This creature had followed the One around his whole life. Now that they had regained the collective, it was time to get reacquainted. The two spoke with their minds. The elation they felt was shadowed by the impending dark energy. It was heavy and looming in the very near future. The future of the Sasquatch, the humans, and the entire planet was soon to be determined. There was not time to celebrate. That would have to come later.

The One reassured the Sasquatch. It told the being to have confidence. There could be no doubt. This purging of the planet had been coming for a very long time. It had begun twenty-two years ago and now it was going to end. Then, everything could begin once again. This time, like so long ago, it would be a paradise.

The One told the creature that it had walked with his ancestors. They had looked up to the One as an equal. The One had looked at them the same. The One looked at every living creature as it's equal. It's being was no better than even the smallest ant. Everything had its own purpose, which made up the overall.

The Sasquatch slowly melted back into the forest. The beast had one intention, to let the One know that they were together. Their union would be at one again very soon in California. The Sasquatch had assured the One that they were ready. The One waited until the creature faded into the forest. It watched the aura of the Bigfoot for as long as sight would allow.

The Sasquatch had a different aura than the other species that the One had encountered. The aura of the Sasquatch was like ripples of energy pulsing from their beings. Their auras pulsed because of the energy waves that their species created. These energy patterns enabled them to fade in and out of sight, a cloaking device of sorts. They would use these pulses to shift shapes at times when in danger. They also could use this gift to move between dimensions. The Sasquatch were truly awesome creatures.

The One entered the vessel to find the women naked. They were all lounging in the large area of pillows and fabrics. There was no need for modesty. The collective was both man and woman. It was not a predator. It respected every being in every form. Beauty was in everything, including the bodies of the three women. One was thin and lanky, another was short and chunkier, while the third was medium height and full figured. The One liked the combination the group created. The women were all different skin colors and ages. Two of them had multiple tattoos.

The One saw the beauty in the creatures. It had always seen a being as how they were, not what they looked like. The outside was just how strangers perceived you. It was no more than a wrapper, keeping your aura inside. The inside is where your family and allies came from. It was where your true appearance resided. You just had to look past the shell of the pod.

The being remembered in the past when so many people were consumed with their looks and appearances. Color of your skin dictated what kind of person you were. It was so important for much of the population to show the rest of the world what they were doing, and let everyone else judge them, as they were judging those people back. Social media had taken over so many people's lives. It had all been such a waste of energy. All the narcissism only fueled the fear and insecurity. The One had laughed at people who became something they were not just to fit in with people they knew nothing about. The greed had brainwashed every one of them through their internet. They had controlled an entire planet. Only a few had seen it coming and were prepared. These were the ones who survived.

The One was happy to be beyond those days. These were the days of the greed.

The One did not wear clothes. It's being had evolved beyond this. The perception of other species varied from species to species. Humans looking at the being would see a tight-fitting space suit looking clothing; a bird would see the being as wearing feathers. The snake would see scales. In this way, the One was truly part of the other species. It did not shape shift, it did not need to. It dictated the perception in all beings that was a witness to the collective. It held familiar DNA with all creatures, who looked to the being as a part of their species. In this way, it was one of them.

The One lounged into the bed with the three women. Their flesh pods formed the symbol of the One. The women's energy was strong in the circle. The One felt a closeness with the others. They were the circle. They had begun this trip with four pods in the car, and now they would finish with four pods. The symbol produced an overall energy that made the entire interior of the vessel glow a strong, green light. It was so bright, the forest outside lit up with luminosity, when it passed out of the vehicle's windows.

The group didn't know nor would they care about the light that they produced. The One knew about the light that followed whenever a few beings would get together and join creative energies. Light of a very good nature would always come about. All imaginative creatures had a strong aura, when they were combined with those of others, they would sometimes give off a light that could be seen by all.

The group was happy to be in a world where people did not judge you. It had been getting crazy on Earth before the meteor strike. Most people had been so into themselves, that they thought it was okay to judge everyone else. Everything that people said or did was judged by someone. It began with social media and spread into reality. Censorship had been alive and well in everyday life. Almost everyone around you was a self-appointed censor, ready to point out their politically correct views. The One told the others that it could never happen again. When humans began to think of themselves as being better than others, they would be wiped from this planet. They were getting a second chance, this one time, after the change.

Now, free of judges, the group could do what they wanted. Every being on the planet had the right to do what they wanted. There was no more people looking down upon you. Everyone now was more concerned about making things work, with teamwork. The narcissistic ways of before had gone away.

The One took the hands of the women, creating the circle. The energy from the being was shockingly strong to the women. The green light coming from the entity had begun to swirl above their heads. The inside of the vessel seemed now the size of a large cavern. The light lit up the walls, which were filled with monitors and metallic gadgets. The light gained intensity until it looked like a tornado. Everything in the enclosure became a blur. The energy flowed through the four beings without resistance. It, too, became the circle, as well as the symbol.

The light became so fast that a watcher would not have been able to see the other beings. They looked like they were in warp speed, becoming the light. They, too, flowed in the particles of light, becoming one with the electromagnetic waves. On the inside of the circle, the four beings sat like before, holding hands and oblivious to the spectacle they were making outside the ring. Nothing mattered now except the halo their beings created.

The women were all making sounds of song. At first, when the light had started, their singing had started as a low hum. As the light sped up, so did the tones. Now the music was racing through their beings, only in opposite directions of the light. It had picked up the momentum until it's pace matched that of the light. The two forces, sound and light, were crossing paths in the middle of the circle. They were intersecting in the One.

The One lifted its head and received the music and light into its soul. The being felt a power that had been asleep for a very long time. Toomey was lying on the bed next to the collective. It raised the fossil with its mind until the agate was at about eye level.

The stone pulsed in the air and seemed to become larger. It changed hues from its white to every shade imaginable. The color changes flowed through Toomey as the light and sound pulsed around it.

The agate became a blur, with the lights spinning in the middle. The sounds seemed to be reverberating off its hard surface, while absorbing its sounds at the same time. The entire stone seemed to be pulsating in time with the music. The light, music, agate, and all four beings became one. Their energy all was tied together for a bit, connecting on a level that went back millions of years. It was an ancient energy they created, not one seen on Earth for a very long time.

The One pulled its hands away from the others, breaking the circle. The light and song funneled into the agate. Within seconds, the two forces were no longer present. The stone fell to the pillows below, now containing the power of light and sound. Its color was normal once again. It looked like an ordinary rock.

The women all fell backward into the cushions. They were all passed out in exhaustion. They had just gone through something that was not familiar to them. The experience was not familiar to any human that had ever walked this planet. The group had just cosmically mated. The women were pregnant.

Many hours passed before the One emerged from its craft. All the people were once again outside, awaiting the return of the One. They looked in awe at the being. The being stood naked in front of the large crowd. They looked in awe at the being's tattoos. They were of a binary sort, created by numbers to be read. The tattoos seemed to change and shift at times. The entire body suit seemed to have a life of its own.

The One raised its hands and the crowd stood silent. The large crow seemed to form from the hands of the being and take flight. It swooped into the vessel and disappeared in its confines.

The One spoke, "I am not a God nor am I your savior, I am merely a speaker of the truth. I have been to multiple dimensions. I have seen and learned the knowledge. Now I want to share that knowledge with your species. You all had the knowledge given to you, but it was destroyed by a few. Now, you humans are going to get a second chance."

The crowd began to cheer and chant for the One. The being forcefully thrust its hands forward and the large group fell silent. The One had always liked humans, but disliked them at the same time. They always had to cheer someone on. The being finished his words, "I am not one to worship. Follow me and you will see and know the truth. There is a story to be told, and we are all going to tell it together. We all know this story, but it has been blocked. You have all woken up. We are all Gods. Feel the truth."

This time, the crowd understood. They heard the words from the One, but also felt its energies. They all silently watched the being go back into its vessel. Its women were inside. It was where it belonged.

When the One entered the craft, the leader was the only one awake. She had not bothered to put clothes on, she was at one with the being. It told the woman about the end. It said that the meteor had not been a meteor at all. It had been a bomb.

"There were many different species of animal on this planet, and they all had their origins from the universe. Everything was connected. Earth was like an island, getting seeded from the rest of the stars. Some creatures had come here many eons ago and had changed things. They had altered the beings throughout the solar system and created humanoid creatures. Every planet and most moons in this solar system had their own species of humanoid, but they had all come from these faraway scientists. They had used the moon as their planetary traveler and home base. They had built this craft millions of years before and used it to conduct their experiments. They had come from a distant galaxy using black holes. They had resided inside the moon for millions of years."

"Another species had come from another galaxy, and theirs was an intent to control. They had many devices of destruction and mind warping. They had destroyed countless worlds with their weapons. Their whole pleasure was destroying planets and taking what they wanted. They would enslave the inhabitants and then wipe them out when they had gotten everything that they wanted."

"These beings had been the greed." The One told the woman, "Do not think the darkness has gone away. It was foolish for the humans to think that they would be gone so easily. These beings had been here a very long time and they were very strong. They had taken over many star systems and never once been defeated. They were not going to give up this planet so easily. The bomb had been sent to destroy the greed. The creatures of the moon, the Lunarks had sent it. They had been working on this weapon for a very long time. It had been aimed at the greed's main bases in Antarctica, but had been deflected by superior technologies. It had hit Kanab, Utah instead. Instead of taking out ninety nine percent of the greed, it had taken out the humans. They had aimed for Antarctica hoping the cold would prevent the spread of the disease to the rest of the planet, but the plan had failed. The virus, developed for the greed only, had instead taken out the humans. The Lunarks had once again been fooled by the greed. They had tricked them into killing off their own offspring."

"The bomb had been deflected as soon as it hit the Earth's atmosphere and began the web of destroying life. It was not like any bomb humans were familiar with. This was more like certain metals put together that would interact with the atmosphere and create a huge cataclysm. The bacteria were added to ensure the destruction of a complete target species. This bomb was sent by the Lunarks to rid the planet of the parasites. The moon men have been here for millions of years and were tired of the greed. Unfortunately, nothing went right. They had failed in their attempts to get rid of the scourge, and now the planet is being destroyed. The moon creatures had been neutral to the planets in the solar system until the greed had arrived. They had come to all the celestial bodies, not just Earth. Before the arrival of the greed, the Lunarks had allowed each planet to evolve in its own way to fulfill their experiments. They would observe and collect information on these beings, but tried to avoid contact at all costs. The humans had called these beings the grays."

"Now the greed has regrouped and are getting ready to confront the light. They had scoffed at the attempt by the Lunarks to destroy their species. In turn, they have all but wiped the moon dwellers out of the history of the universe. Now they are preparing to do the same to the light. They knew of the strength it had been gathering and it brought fear amongst their kind. They are strong creatures, though, who do not lose fights. They are the eaters of planets and souls. They are the darkness. The true evil. They will now try to wipe the rest of the light from the Earth once and for all."

"The remaining humans are going to be stronger this time than ever before. This time, it is going to be a collective that has never been achieved on the planet. Many beings will be united, the way it was in the long ago. The greed has split up everything on the planet for their benefit. Now the people are reunited. The elite know this. They are very afraid. Their control has led to wisdom in the masses. The minds of the people are now truly free."

The One finished its story and settled into the cushions for a small rest. Sleep was no longer necessary, but it still felt good for the being to enter the subconscious. It picked up a book and wrote hundreds of pages throughout the early morning hours. The leader had stayed awake for as long as possible, playing a singing bowl in rhythm with the writings of the One. The two sung a wordless song of unity and emancipation. The creativity once again created another entity of its own.

The leader finally succumbed to exhaustion. She was, after all, human and needed to get some sleep.

The One was retelling a story in the book that had been told so long ago but completely forgotten on this planet. The ancient histories of the Earth had been here, only to be destroyed by the greed. They had used the cover of religion or technology, but in truth, ignorance was their main tool of control.

Enslaving the people was easy for them, and it was their entire goal. They could get them to do anything they wanted by just telling a few lies. Anything major that would happen, they could just shift everyone's attention to another less critical issue. Their whole world of darkness was created with smoke screens.

Now, the One thought, the greed would pay for what they had done to this planet and its inhabitants. Once and for all, they were going to get rid of this species. Once and for all, the animals on this planet would be truly free.

The Earth could truly begin to heal.

The end was coming. The beginning would follow.

CHAPTER 37

The rain and cold were endless as the group of four headed south. The One had risen early, departing their parking spot before the others had even stirred.

It had been a long night for the women. Their human bodies needed much rest after all that had been happening. It was over one hundred miles before they regained consciousness. They had asked where they were and where they were going. The One told the others that they were still on the Oregon coast. They were going to make a stopover in Crescent City. There was someone they needed to meet there who would be important to their mission. This was the last person they needed to meet on their journey.

Many words were spoken along the way. As the four beings traveled through the rain, it was a time to reconnect. They had all walked familiar paths before. Their energy coexisted in different times and in different dimensions. The One explained this to the women. It spoke of days where our lives end and we are continuously reborn. It was the End and it was the Beginning all in one sun cycle. The cycle was in everything. It was all determined numbers.

"What about the billions of other people who have walked on this planet?" the Provider asked. "Are they reborn over and over too?"

"They are just filler. Kind of like robots in a way. They never found their truth, they were too caught up in the filler around them. Their souls were there, just never developed. They were all part of the same thing. Part of the greed. Few humans ever had the true knowledge. The path was not seen by most. They did not care to see it. The light was there for all to see, but most were blinded by the drapes the greed had pulled over their eyes. They were not searching for enlightenment, they were searching for more. The one percent were different. They saw the foolishness of the rest and decided to live their way. A creative way where fantasy and imagination were not a social crime. These are the ones who survived the sickness from the meteor. They were the offspring from a different bloodline of humans. They were chosen to be the caregivers of this planet.

They have done that in a very proficient manner for the last twenty-two years, and before. They have kept evil at bay the entire time."

"Who is the Evil?" asked the protector.

"It is the ones who spread fear among the people. They could make the masses believe anything. Government, organized religion, and the media were the true evil. They created a global economy. Creating an economy in the first place was evil. It was all for profit for the few who chose to be in control. At the same time, so many people did not care to be in charge. They were happy to live a simple life. So, the economy got bigger and bigger and absorbed all these people until it was a giant machine. The corporate machine. This machine ate the planet. The people were its slaves. The greed controlled the people with fear. Fear of going to prison. Fear of going to hell. Fear of terrorists. Fear of not having enough. Fear of not fitting in. It was all their schemes. They were rich beyond belief already. They just loved the power of complete control. They were the true evil. All the while saying that others were evil. They even called their people the flock. Most people were the flock, or the consumers. Like the sheep they were, these people would line up at their feeding troughs and eat up anything thrown in front of them."

"Why did they let it happen?" the women asked in unison. The One had been passing so much knowledge to the three. Their minds were completely waking up. They had been asleep for so very long. They listened closely to everything the being in front of them said.

The One answered, "Because they were too weak to think for themselves. Their creativity and imagination had been blocked by the greed. They didn't understand the true task of their souls. They wasted their existence. These kinds of souls represent the majority. They wander through the cosmos for eons before ending up in a flesh pod. Then they are reset and easily reprogrammed as a slave. They are filler, like I said earlier."

"However," the being continued, "those who have found the true path are the 'chosen'. Their lives flow through time like a river. Sometimes they are the same people in multiple lives. In one life they die, but their existence went on endlessly. Maybe some things are different, from life to life, as the dimensions intersect. These beings remained with their true soulmates for eternity. Their family is the same. Lives could snap into another time or place but they all flow together. Throughout the universe. Not just on this planet. All our souls are energy. That energy is connected to the cosmos. We are all One."

"How do you know so much about things?" the provider and protector asked in unison.

"There were four of us chosen ones sent on the path, twenty-two years ago," it began. "Many events had happened to all of us in the few years before the journey that had prepared us for the strange things which we encountered. Our group had been tested well. We traveled many miles, setting into motion a chain of events that would change human civilization and begin to heal the planet. We had been chosen from a long-ago destiny. Numbers which had come up hundreds of thousands of years ago lined up once again, like a lottery. The four of us had brought a storm with us which had followed behind us the entire journey. A storm that had brought unrest amongst the masses. Our presence stirred an awakening in the humans like this planet had never seen. Death and riots were in our shadows. The dark would always follow the light. Then we got to the coast and awoke. Our eyes had been shielded for so long. We met our shadows and broke all the blockades from our minds. Our drapes were fully open. On Rockaway beach, our souls fused into the collective. Our shadows were with us as we passed into the wisdom. We were in a type of spiritual hibernation for twenty-two years. In this subconscious state, all the knowledge of this planet which had been destroyed by the greed was given to us. Knowledge which was billions of years old was passed to us in a spiritual trance. Even knowledge of the future was passed along. It was all spelled out in numbers in our subconscious. We awoke as the being you see in front of you now. The One. The pod from the man had gone through transformation in the previous years, mentally and physically. His being had been prepared for the collective. This is who we are. Our mission is clear now. The numbers have told us. We can read the numbers now and we are going to teach all the rest of the creatures. The answers are spelled out and obvious. The path is clear. Now, we spread the word. It is time for all to see and understand."

"Where are we ultimately going?" asked the leader.

"We are going to a small town in California called Mountain Ranch. It is a place where the triangles begin and grow from there. Energy lines of this planet intersect there and make it a very spiritual place. A house is there that all four of our souls connected in. We are going back to that magical place. When we get there, we are going to build a device that will allow us to once again connect with the heavens. There is a message that we need to send and it needs to be done soon. The numbers have told us. The cycle is here. It is our destiny."

The group sat in silence for some time. It was a lot of information for the women to take in. They had stared at the eye in the center of the being's forehead the entire time. The organ seemed to be changing color as the One spoke. It looked to each of the others in the vessel with an analytical glance. This eye operated completely on its own from the other two in the being. This portal saw and perceived in a part of the brain that the One had not used in a very long time.

The entity was more than happy not to speak for some time. The being truly was still waking up. The nourishment and energy from the night before had been wonderful, but it was a twenty-two year sleep the being was coming out of. It had seemed like years since they had begun the journey. It had only been two days. The road stretched on. The lack of people and traffic were welcome. The being remembered the past and how people were so inconsiderate of each other. Cars that would drive slow, only to speed up during the passing zones. It had seemed like some got enjoyment out of causing mayhem on the roads. It was a time the One did not miss.

The One put these thoughts out of its mind. Recollections of past lives had been coming back, but the being was living for now and the future. This was a life in parallel to that one. Those four creatures had perished on the beach and their energies had merged. There was so much to remember about its history on the planet. The knowledge was there, it had to digest it all. The collective thought was strong. The One knew that others would understand and would want to be a part of it all. The humans were already the chosen. They had been here a long time on this planet. Now they were going to be enlightened.

The rest of the trip to Crescent City was spent deep in thought. The women used the time to meditate and prepare for what was to come. They all felt a glow inside their bodies. They knew they were pregnant. They had just been in the presence of the One, and somehow the three had been impregnated with a spiritual force. It was the first three pregnancies since the change. Even the older women knew that this was the most natural thing ever. They both had passed menopause but now were miraculously pregnant. These events are what religions are written from, the three women thought as one. The numbers that the One had spoken of were coming true. They had been changed so much in the last few days. Less than forty-eight hours. Now they could see the path clearly. Now they could rest their minds.

The women were awakened by a sudden stop. The vessel had stopped next to a beach. It had seemed like a random place, but the One had a mission. It got out of the vehicle and climbed to the top of a sand dune. It looked to the sea and began waving. The being spun back and beckoned the women to join in. The One slid down the dune like on a surfboard. At the bottom was a boy of maybe fifteen. The boy was dressed in a black garment that did not have seams. His hair was white. He was running toward the One. The two embraced tightly for a very long time. When they broke, the boy said to the One, "I've been waiting for you for so very long. It's been twenty-four years since we last saw each other. I am ready."

The two walked, side by side down the beach. The One understood that this was all part of the journey. Just as their collective had been formed using the pod of the man, this being had also formed its collective with its four souls. It had chosen the pod of this boy. The One was very familiar with this being. They were brothers. They had traveled together for eternity and now their travels were to resume.

Further down the beach, the two saw a figure approaching. It was an older woman of about seventy. Her looks were deceiving, though. The woman looked older, but her walk spoke of a much younger person. The One and its brother knew as soon as they saw the figure. This was their sister. Her collective had united and formed its entity. The three beings had now come together as One, once again. The two brothers and sister were back at the beginning. The way things had originally begun. It was a sure sign that the end was near.

The two brothers glided effortlessly to the sister. Their legs did not need to take steps. Their beings were in tune with the magnetism coming from the center of the planet and had adapted to it long ago. Their electromagnetism was at a similar polarity, but slightly off. In this regard, they could float a few inches off the ground. The energy to move came from the mind. Its electromagnetic pulses were what guided the flesh pod. The two levitated to the other.

The three beings embraced warmly. It had been many years since the three of them had been together at the same time. They all knew the reasons for their reunion. This time had been coming for a very long time. It had all been predestined hundreds of thousands of years ago. The prophecies would be common knowledge if that knowledge hadn't been destroyed by the greed. The three knew that this was going to be an epic time in the history of Earth. They also knew that it was a time of unity. Their energies were strong together. Their powers had been on this planet a very long time.

The One spoke to the other two about the collective thought. They already knew. They too had gathered their beings into the One. Enlightenment had spread to all three entities at the same time. They, too, had been in a slumber for twenty-two years and were now with the knowledge. Now the triangle could once again be truly completed. Now was the time for the three beings to use their energies and bring everything together again.

The leader, provider, and protector had caught up with the others. The One introduced its siblings to the women. The beach began to come alive with activity. As soon as the three beings had united, crabs began to come out of their holes. Otters were coming up on the beach to see the light. Birds and every other living creature were gathering around to see the Family. All the creatures were in tune with these beings, as they were in tune with the creatures.

Humans began to come onto the beach, out of the brush and caves. Soon, the entire beach was filling with living souls. They all made their way to the three entities and the light that they emitted. The circle formed around the three beings. They drew the energies from the people and the animals. For a moment, the entire circle felt like a giant machine. Each part was important to the overall function of the device. The One stood motionless in the middle of the circle with its brother and sister. The energy that was coming off the three beings was atomic in its strength. The light from this energy engulfed all the creatures around them. They all became One.

The three beings began to make their way out of the circle. The provider and protector began to follow, but the leader stopped them. She told the others that they were to stay here for a bit and nourish their babies and their minds. The people of this area were friends and they would help them. These were their people, they needed to be with them. They would know when to join the One and the others. The sign would be clear.

Miraculously, since they had gotten to this beach, the leader had noticed that she and the others looked to be about four months pregnant. It seemed impossible, but the women knew. Things that were impossible before were only because of the suppression. The magic of this planet had been taken away and replaced with technology. Things that were happening for hundreds of thousands of years had been robbed from the people. All to create control through fear. Now, all that was gone. Now, once again, anything was possible.

As the three floated out of the circle, they were impressed with how far the humans had come along. They were in unity with the animals, like the beings had never seen before. Crabs and birds sat and stood next to their human counterparts. Otters were like family pets with the way they interacted. All the animals had come together. It was a sight that the One thought it would never see.

As the three beings left the circle, the other creatures formed a small corridor for their exit. As they passed by, the aura from the others swam in and out of the three. The energy from the crowd was like tendrils of energy which permeated the other beings. The three accepted this energy and fed off it. It told the beings what they needed to know about these creatures. All the creatures. Their energy told the three that they were tired of the greed. All creatures on this planet were tired of a few destroying it for everyone else. They were all ready to get on with the end. Then, the planet could truly begin.

Many of the humans wanted to stop and talk to the One, but there was no time. It told the group that all their questions would be answered soon. The women they were leaving behind knew much of the truth, and the rest would come to them when they got to California. Their journey, too, was about to begin, the One had told them.

The three beings packed up the vessel with their pods and headed down the road. It would be a long way to get back to Mountain Ranch, but they had it in their minds to do it. There was much to do when they arrived. If they didn't get going, the people would once again delay their progress with feasts and festivities. There would be plenty of time for that later, though. Now was the time to get to their final-destination. Now was the time to get busy.

The three beings spoke the rest of the journey. There was much to talk about. They all had the knowledge and now were happy to have the others to share it with. Their thoughts were once again reunited as one. There was a much deeper truth coming that had been hidden for so long. Soon, that truth would be common again.

The three knew that the times ahead were going to be filled with enlightenment. They were to fulfill a destiny that had been set in motion so long before. There was no time for fear or doubt. These were senseless emotions that had been created by the greed.

The three arrived at midnight. The One noticed the lack of people on the last leg of the journey. It had remembered a lot of lost souls. There had been many righteous also. This had been the center. The place of the gold. Many humans back in the day had moved here because they too felt the energy. It had attracted many like souls. Unfortunately, the light also had attracted dark forces. The greed had infiltrated this small area also, searching for its riches.

This place, Mountain Ranch, would be where the beginning would take place. Humans would once again be on the same level as their true God. The wealth of the gold was not a concern. The gold was the conductor that the beings needed to get their devices up and running. The gold was the electromagnetic catalyst that they needed. It was going to be used by the three to bring total enlightenment to the creatures of this planet. The gold was going to light the true path.

The One knew what had to be done. The plans were all in its head. Now, the other two beings were here to make it happen. The knowledge would be greater than it had been in tens of thousands of years. The other creatures of the planet were uniting. Their energy would be combined with the energy of the All, and the planet would go back to the way it was so long ago. Before the dark had invaded. It was time for the light to be stronger than the dark, once again. It was the way of nature, and now it was to return.

The One was surprised when they pulled in front of the wooden structure. It looked exactly like they had left it. It was obvious that someone had been taking care of this house. The weeds were all cut back, and the house had fresh paint. There was not a single sign of deterioration. Even some hibiscus in the front yard were covered in white and purple blooms. Nothing here had changed in twenty-two years.

The three entered the house formerly owned by the One's collective. It had been a time when humans thought they owned things. In reality, they just used them in their lifetimes. When they were done with their 'possessions', they would go back to the Earth. The ultimate in recycling. No creature owned anything, not even the flesh pod they were borrowing during this existence.

The house was a modest house filled with paintings. The One had painted and created in its singular state. The souls had realized that creating was being one with God and had made a life out of it. Imagination had been encouraged and pushed. The three walked through the house, looking at the tributes to their people. The man had painted tributes to their entire family throughout his years of life in this house. It was a memorial to their ancestors.

In the back room, the Collective had painted a large wall. Its image was that of a distant planetary system. There were two suns' and fifteen planets in this solar system. The planets miraculously seemed to move and rotate around the suns. The wall was alive. In the foreground stood three large cone looking devices. Energy was coming off the top of the towers, depicted in paint. The energy was snaking through the planets, creating its own aura. This energy, too, seemed to be alive and wispy, as it drifted around the planets.

The One spoke to the others, "I am sure you remember this place well. I can see the recognition in your faces. It is where we come from. The three of us came to this planet a very long time ago. Now, I have figured out how to use the knowledge of our home to defeat the greed. I have acquired all the pieces necessary. After all these years, our time has finally come."

The brother spoke, "It has been a very long day, and we must get some rest. Soon, people will be arriving. We will need to be ready for them. They have been hearing about this story for a very long time, and they will be excited. There were many chosen souls here in Mountain Ranch before, tomorrow we will be connecting with them."

Each of the beings had their own rooms. It had been the same as when they had been young together, so many lives ago. The One remembered the different dimensions and lives that they had all gone through together. It remembered the energy that they all three shared. Their existence was an ancient one. They were some of the first on this planet. They had been part of it all.

Sleep came easy for the beings. It was not a sleep like they had enjoyed before. This was a meditation that put them directly into their subconscious. Each of their visions were interconnected with the others. They all shared the same dreams. Their flesh pods rested while their minds worked out details. Every living being lived two lives simultaneously. Each creature had a conscious mind and a subconscious mind. They lived as parallels. Humans had lost this knowledge with the takeover by the greed. They had convinced the humans that they were simply dreaming for no reason. They had taken the truth from them and ripped half of their existence from their souls at the same time. They had been left only with the conscious. The bridge to the subconscious had been destroyed.

The dreams were about the future. All the plans for the next journey were plotted out in the collective subconscious of the three beings. Their minds set in motion a series of events that would cleanse this planet once and for all. They knew the prophecy. They could read the numbers.

The meeting went on throughout the sleep. Their minds never once slowed in the visions that were flowing between the three minds.

Just before dawn, the three shut their minds down from the interactions with the others. The plans had been made. The three were close to their destiny. There was much more to talk about but there would be much time for that later.

The three beings knew that they would need to rest. The next rest might not be for weeks or even longer. There was much to do. It was the beginning. First, though, they would have to bring about the end. It had been coming for a long time.

The end had been started.

There would be no turning back.

Chapter 38

Darkness faded into light. The Three achieved full consciousness at the same moment. They had no use for time. It was made up by the humans. All that mattered to the three energies was the cycles. The Earth, Sun, and Moon were on a cycle which enabled the inhabitants of the solar system to be on the same cycle. This was the time of the solar system. On a greater scale, the Milky Way was the Mother to our solar system. It was all on a cycle. Deep into the far reaches of space, everything was interconnected with a cycle. This was how all things were one.

As the sun rose, the brother had begun to beat the gong. It's being had acquired this gong many years before. It had been waiting here, at this house, ever since. It had been awaiting the return of its striker.

The One was impressed with the condition of the house. The neighbors had kept good care of the place, with the knowledge that the One was returning. They had been friends with the family. Theirs was a mutual respect. They knew the significance of the place, and the reason why the beings had returned to it. They, too, had moved here as if called by some unseen force. Mountain Ranch had a strong energy that was conducive to many chosen ones.

The ringing of the gong echoed through the forest. The One and sister climbed into the tree house.

Before the trip had begun, the collective had built this tree house together. They built it to have something to do together at the time. The weight of death had been heavy, and they needed things to take their minds off it. Now, the true purpose of the platform was coming into light.

The neighbors had taken very good care of the tree house, as they had the land and the house. It was just as the One had left it. The two beings could see for a distance from the higher perch. They had brought their singing bowls and were chiming in their own music with that of the gong being played by their brother. The sounds together became hypnotic. They rang through the land with a gentle tune which embraced every living thing. The sound made everything connected.

The One and sister were elated to see chosen and other creatures emerge from the forest. At first, their numbers were few, but soon they numbered in the hundreds. The One saw many familiar faces from its recollections of this area. Many humans that the being had encountered in the town had survived and remained at this magical spot. All its neighbors were present. The One had realized long ago that the neighbors here were chosen, but it had no idea that these locals were also of the same category. Now the being understood, light called the enlightened.

The Chosen in this region, as in others, had remained in solitude. They stood by passively while the greed flourished. It was the same story as everywhere the One had traveled. The chosen had been content in their lives. They wanted change, but were unwilling to give up what they had to get that change. They wanted their cake and to eat it, too. This attitude made them unable to smother the greed. Instead, they had been absorbed by the greed. The Chosen, too, had succumbed to the fear.

Now they were united. Now, things had all changed. With the collective, the greed would be the ones with fear. They knew what was coming, and there was no way to stop it. The elite, too, could read the numbers.

The masses began to arrive in the hundreds, maybe even thousands. Many species of the forest were present along with their friends, the chosen. They gathered around the tree looking upward. Most carried gifts from the land. Fruits, eggs, bread, and enough cheese for a feast. Their auras created a light across the hillside which reminded the One of the northern lights.

The gong rang in the background. The brother was the gong master. His collective soul made the music spiritual for all beings who could hear it. The sound traveled for fifty miles in all directions. Beyond that, beings could not hear its tones with their ears, but the sounds were present in their minds. The gong was connecting all the chosen.

It took a while for all the people to arrive. This area was spread over many square miles. People in the outer parts of the region took some time to show up. Regardless of how long it took, all the creatures had begun their journey with the first note of the gong. The sound had awakened all beings as the sun was cresting the mountains. Now, they all converged on this one tree and the beings that were inside it.

The One and sister spoke of many things during their wait for the creatures to arrive. They spoke of being small children and how they were made into lab rats. The greed had experimented on them and took from them their imagination. Things had been implanted in their bodies as children, and it had affected their whole lives. Early in their lives, they had thought that it was an alien abduction or something. It was at an early age that they realized that they had been wrong. They knew the truth and knew how to control it.

Their family had been put under control by the church and government collectively when they were small children. The entities knew about the chosen ones, and they were scared. These three children were unlike any they had ever encountered before. They understood from an early age. They had been born to this family with a cosmic push. Implanted into a DNA data bank to test the laws of destiny.

The three had been watched their entire lives. None of them had an interest in being a spokesperson for the humans or any other creatures. They were all content to live their lives as normal as possible. All the while, they were collecting information, and creating. The greed had seen that they were not posing a threat and had kept their contact to observation levels only. All the while, the greed thought that the implants which had been installed in the siblings was keeping them in check. They had been fooled. The three knew about the greed and the chosen. They understood the light and the dark and knew how to hide in either one. They understood that the light and the dark were just a cycle. The true evil was not darkness, it was greed.

The three, their entire lives, were preparing for this time. Preparing with the ever-present eye of the greed watching them. To the siblings, that eye was blind.

There had been humans that could break through the mental blocks imposed on them before. They were chosen ones who would speak the truth. Others would listen to these people, creating non-conformity. They called them prophets or messiahs, but the greed called them bothersome. They could not have people who spoke the truth about them. These prophets were always assassinated. All the prophets that had ever walked among the humans had been killed by the evil. Of course, their lies would cover it up. Blame would be pointed at an unsuspecting enemy.

Now the two knew the truth. It had all come back to them. There were different species of humans on this planet. There were offspring from many distant planets which had seeded Earth. The species of human that had survived the disease from the meteor were different than the ones who had perished. They had called themselves the chosen and they were correct. Their kind were an offspring from a nearby planet on the other side of the Sun. They had been sent here, tens of thousands of years ago, to help the humans learn about creativity. In their quest to share enlightenment, they, too, had been caught up with the wave of darkness that had followed.

These chosen were the ones who could see things for what they were. They understood while the other ninety nine percent went with everything they were given. The masses were of a species brought to this planet by the Science. They were brought as experiments and reproduced as experiments. As on other planets in the solar system, they had seeded their humanoid beings and watched what would happen. Every planet besides Earth had evolved quickly to the point of knowledge and wisdom.

The greed had changed it all. They were not here for experiments. Their pleasure came from control and destruction. Changing the natural course of things was the way. They were the evil.

The chosen had scared the elite, so the greed had to control them in a different way than all the others. Media and propaganda did not work on these people. They had fears, but not to the degree as the other humans. The answer to the problem was microchips. They had been implanted. It had been most successful on the chosen. Subliminal messages and orders could be sent through transmissions. They could be tracked and studied. They could be controlled.

The greed had been smart from the beginning. From the beginning, they had created race, sexual orientation and gender, politics, religion, police, and anything else they could think of to divide the people. Then they created patriotism to make it possible to create hatred toward any other people.

The greed operated solely on hatred. Without it, they did not exist. With the hatred, they could make people believe anything they said. They were rapacious. They were the ones who wanted it all. They were the power hungry. Addictive personalities caught up in a web of deceit toward the masses. All to feed their addictions and cravings for more.

The gong being struck in the background brought back memories for the One, like fireworks. The last time the gong was struck was after the man's brother had died. The man had struck the object that moonlit night with all his power. He had felt like a statue, his movements set in stone. A golden light had sprung from the gong, illuminating the entire hillside. The man had seen his brother's shadow in the light standing on the hill. It had called to him. It had showed him this very moment, in the tree house, listening to the sound reverberating through the land.

The One was snapped out reverence by the sound of his sister. She was standing at the railing of the tree house. Her form looked like it was one with the branch that she stood next to. The One thought about the form that his sister had taken on this journey. It wondered how she had come to reside in the body of an older person. The One thought with a chuckle about the different pods that the three had inhabited. There had been thousands. It truly had been a long, crazy journey for their clan.

The sister was speaking to the crowd. "My brothers and I have come from a very far place, over many moons. Two hundred and forty-eight moons have passed since returning to this place. We three were all located on parts of the planet, forming perfect triangles. We have been the keepers of the truth for many moons. Now, it is the time to share it with all of you. Total enlightenment is here. It is important that you listen to what my brother says. He is the One. The healer of our planet. By this light tomorrow, we will begin to build our device to contact our ancestors. All knowledge of your previous lives will be returned to you. The monoliths in our minds, implanted by the greed, are to be broken down. They will never return. We will all truly be free."

The crowd cheered and applauded the words of the sister. They wanted to be free. They understood that something was controlling them, and they had known it for a very long time. They had waited patiently for this day. It was the time to rid their lives completely of the greed. Once and for all.

The sister raised her hands, and silence immediately followed. The crowd looked up to the two beings, not as Gods, as heroes. They listened closely to what the sister had to say. "Today, our journey ends. Today, our journey begins. The end is the beginning, and it always has been. Since the dawn of the universe. Just as the beginning is the end. It is the way of things. The cycle. Now feast on the bounty that you have provided. I graciously thank everyone of you for the food and for bringing your energy to this magical place. Everything looks so very good. I am personally going to try one of everything. Now, let's say our prayers to Pachymama, holding hands," the sister exclaimed as she took the hand of her brother. She whispered to the crowd, but the sound came out amplified like a loud speaker. "I love you all," was what her voice boomed to the crowd.

As the sister climbed from the tree house, tears of joy filled the air. The people gathered had heard the stories of the three beings who were coming to make the change. The stories did not prepare them for the awesome energy that the beings brought with them. Their light was a pure one. Their light was ancient and powerful. The people had no doubts in these creatures. They knew in their hearts that these beings were the ones who would make the change. They knew these were the Ones.

The sister hugged every one of the people who had come to her. Every one of the humans wanted to touch one of the beings. They all felt the energy coming from the entities and wanted to get a little piece of it. They were human, after all.

The feast lasted for three days. The people were joyous and filled with hope. The last twenty-two years were a utopia, but now they were moving to the next level. The auras of the creatures feasting shined bright day and night. All kinds of folks were present. There were no divisions. All were equal. Nobody was looked at as being different. Sex, race, disabilities, all the people were equal. It was a time the One never thought it would see in the humans. Their species had always been filled with hate. The creature had to remind itself that these were different. These were the chosen. They had always gotten along. They had always had respect for each other and the planet. It was the other ninety nine percent that had ruined it all.

As soon as the aftermath from the meteor and disease were gone, the humans that were left had begun a new way. There was no need to forage through society's waste for food, these were people who knew the path. They knew how to grow fruits and vegetables, even without a sun. It had been hard for the first few years, but then the sun returned. Recycling was a thing they had lived their lives by, and now was no different.

There was no longer a purpose for the police or laws. Common sense was all that was needed, and the people all had that. All the problems society had created disappeared when the ninety nine percent went away. Crime was a word to be written in history.

Schools had been done away with. All the children had been taught by the people. When the children slowly grew older, the need for basic education completely went away. Higher learning was a sharing of information between all people. The collective learning was taught by all the people to all the people. It taught life lessons that would be important to the existence of the individual and the collective. Information now was essential to healing the planet and its creatures. Senseless knowledge was discarded like the rubbish it was along with fake information. Fake information had been created by the elite, to make everyone think that the greed wasn't as bad as they really were.

The forest and animals were common friends to the new humans. The children and adults were taught to show them kindness and respect. The children were even taught how to take care of the elders. Cooking and building came early for boys and girls. No sex was excluded from learning anything that they wanted. By the time they were fourteen, the children were ready to be on their own.

They were encouraged to take partners when they were ready. They were also encouraged to be free. Settling down with another soul only happened when it was meant to be. Everyone knew when it was meant to be. Marriage only happened between partners who felt the true soul mate aura. Their energies merged as one. Divorce was not heard of. Open marriage was accepted and encouraged long as both parties agreed. Jealousy no longer existed. People were not possessed by others. Without jealousy tainting people's heads, sex and love could be looked at as two separate entities. Mates were no longer looked at as possessions, just as companions to walk through life with. They believed that no one had the right to take away freedom from any creature.

Rights were not even discussed. All the people were truly free and living in harmony. There was no need for rich man ideology. This is what had made these humans strong. Gone was the fear. They could truly live in body and mind.

Their shelters were recycled materials from the time before. They lived in small groups. Most people had stayed put after the cataclysm. The meteor had created much damage, but not in this area. The virus had been the greatest destroyer. The ones who survived stayed in their homes at first, before moving on to meet others. They had no interest in all the newly vacated mansions. They didn't have to impress their neighbors, they just joined them.

Over time, the survivors in each area moved closer to each other. It made the transactions of food, clothing, and wares that each were providing more accessible to everyone.

This is when they used 'found materials' to construct their homes. Everyone helped build each house for their neighbor. It was truly a community. They all had one thing in common. They were the chosen. The one percent. They knew how to coexist with each other without control. They had compassion for their neighbors and all the other animals. Their greatest respect was held for Pachymama.

Daily chores were welcome. It was a time the people looked forward to. It gave them all the sense of being part of something bigger than each of them individually. It gave them a sense of purpose. Some grew produce while others raised bison. It was the one animal that had flourished after the meteor, and the survivors had gladly accepted it as their meat and dairy source. Some of the people hunted, some cooked, while others built.

All of them created.

They would work five or six hours a day. At the end of the work, the people would make things. Feasts from their bounty were enjoyed all night as the imagination flowed. All forms of creativity were greatly encouraged. The food would be consumed during this time. There was no need to sit at a table and eat. The people were alive. They would eat as the food became done. There was no patience to wait until all the food was done to fill a plate. Hands were the main utensil used for dining.

The people would sing and dance all night. Painting and drawing coexisted with pottery, stained glass, jewelry making, and so much more. Every medium of art ever created by humans was represented at these nightly feasts. The musical instruments, made by the people, would play until the last souls crawled off to bed. Alcohol was not needed by these beings, nor was tobacco. These humans had no time for man-made poisons. They all enjoyed the pleasures that marijuana brought. It was from the Earth and part of everything, just as they were. They saw how the herb opened the mind instead of creating blocks. Creativity blossomed, self-doubt withered.

It was on these nights that the humans felt closest to God. They were creating, just as their creator had done. None of them believed in the religious lies that had been fed to the masses by the greed. They saw the true gods. The Sun, the Moon, and Pachymama. Their whole goal, their life mission, was to be one with God. Creating was their way of doing just that. Fear had nothing to do with this way.

Cars and gas had been the first thing to be forgotten. There were many solar panels left behind from before. They were put to good use. The humans did not need much electricity, but for lamps and refrigeration, it was nice to have. Since the people did not work all the time, they could use their time and creativity inventing things and improving their lives. Things were getting better and better.

The chosen had salvaged the internet. Gone were all the corporate ads and viruses. Now it was just a tool of knowledge. A library at everyone's fingertips. Everybody did not have a computer. Just enough for each group consistent with the amount of people they had. The internet and computers had been changed drastically since the meteor. They had been more simplified. They were no longer the catalyst of the social media and the web of deceit. Now it was just a library of the information known to man. Any new knowledge gained would be verified and put on the internet. It was also the only form of communication between the different groups of humans. It connected all the survivors from the planet into one device.

The Chosen collective had worked together to make all this happen. Everyone worked towards the collective, with the focus still being on individuals. The people wanted to be themselves without judgment. If they wanted to sing as loud as possible while standing naked on top of a bridge, nobody would care. Except maybe to thank them for the performance. When everyone was being creative, nothing would shock them from somebody else's imagination.

There had never once been talk of a leader.

That had all changed months ago. The people of Mountain Ranch had heard rumors about the coming home of the One. None of them could envision the being that was spoken of. The rumors were that the entity had once lived on this piece of land but none of the locals could picture the face. The being had been a recluse while here. They had made no friends. This had been a place for spirituality and enlightenment. Creativity had enveloped their lives on this little piece of Earth. They had stayed to themselves, getting to know their inner beings and God. None of the locals had known the family, except the neighbors.

The changes began when the locals first heard the rumors of the arrival. Their peaceful minds and creative ways were interrupted by the coming. All their energy was shifted to the truth. The being that had been spoken of for so long was finally becoming reality. Now was the time for them to prepare the land and the house for the being. Now was the time to create an energy that the One would be proud to see.

The stories of the One had seemed larger than life. They had been spoken of on and off since the eighteen fifties. When the first miners had come to this place. Before them, the Miwok people of this area talked about three beings coming from the heavens and fighting a war against the dark. There had been over twenty different groups that had lived in this area over the last eight-hundred-thousand years. Every one of them told of the same prophecy.

Deep in the Earth, in a cave long ago buried, were cave paintings of the three beings glowing a green light. In the cave, light emanates from the painting, keeping all the shadows away. It has been illuminated since being painted millions of years ago.

Also buried deep in the Earth were devices that had been found by various tribes of humans who had come to this spot. This place was ancient and spiritual. Some of the oldest beings on this planet had visited this exact spot.

This was the same piece of Earth that the three siblings had arrived so many moons ago. When they had come to this planet, it was before the humans had been seeded. They had built their temples in Mountain Ranch over a period of millions of years. They had built their devices for the future. The prophecies had been clear to them.

Now, that future was here. Now it was the present. The work the three had spent for so very long was about to come into play. This is the time they had been preparing for since their arrival. Long before the parasites had infested this planet, the siblings were preparing for their eviction.

None of the chosen felt any doubt. The elders of Mountain Ranch had assured the youngsters that this was going to be the way. Doubt was not going to be put up with. The prophecies were not wrong. Change was coming. This was the new way and it was going to be beautiful.

Enlightenment was a sunrise away.

Chapter 39

The One perched itself in the tree house, reflecting on past thoughts. It seemed as if the people who had come were very joyful. The feast had continued throughout the last days. The being had not wanted to end it. It had not left the tree house the entire time, reveling in the happiness of the others.

The humans had not even rested the entire time. Their elation and all that food was all that they needed. The being had always enjoyed seeing other creatures happy. The entire collective had always felt a deep empathy for other beings. They had all felt at one with everything, and now they were the One.

The celebration had been a long time coming. Twenty-two years had passed since word of the One began to circulate among the survivors. Since that time, the people had devoted their time to creating. It had been a hard road of getting food back on the table at first. After the sun had returned, so did the bountiful harvests. The people had been patient in their wait. They knew there was a higher learning coming their way. They knew that answers to all the questions that their species asked were to be answered. The time of wisdom had come. The One was here with the knowledge. It was time to celebrate and get the souls ready for the next step in the journey.

The humans had waited a very long time for this day. They did not want the feast to end.

The gong rang through the trees the duration of the festivities. The brother had always been a strong soul, but its collective was mighty. He was the gong master. He was the One who brought enlightenment through song. The tunes had taken a hypnotic note, creating spells of healing. The One toyed with a singing bowl most of the time. The rhythms melted together somewhere between reality and the subconscious. All the beings who listened understood. They had been able to see before, but now they could perceive. Their sixth sense had come alive.

Many of the folks had brought food to the tree house. The being refused it all. "There is a cosmos in my being right now getting ready to explode. When it does, it will create our new reality. Food will just keep that energy quiet. Now is not the time for the cosmos to be mute. Now is the time for the wisdom to shout."

The air of the leaves filled the sinus of the One. It had been at one with trees since the time of long ago. All four beings of the collective had been truly in touch with these majestic sentinels of nature. Some had thought the family had been crazy with their level of respect for the forest. The four had almost worshiped them separately. Together, the One understood the connection that it truly had with trees. Now, that love of the wooded friend was the reality of the two beings becoming one. The tree was also a part of the collective.

The One climbed to the farthest twig on that massive oak. It perched its flesh pod were only birds had been before. It felt the approval from the spirit of the tree. They had become one. There was a flash of lightning that seemed to envelop the branches in an orb of yellow light. There were no clouds in the sky, the flash of energy seemed to come from the air around them.

The people on the ground all looked to the sky. The gong had stopped. The One felt the collective gaze of the people. The being absorbed some of their energy that the beings, inadvertently, sent its way. In return, the being's energy was absorbed by the crowd.

The masses stood in awe, beholding the sight. The One was literally standing on a branch that wouldn't even hold a bird. Yet the tree did not let the creature go.

The One had begun to metaphysically merge with the tree. It had first cast a warm glow over the oak in the form of the lightning. Now the light encompassed both creatures. The tree began to look like the One, and the One looked like the tree. The being looked like a cross between a tree and a biological creature. It moved like a person but was made of wood and leaves. The entire tree seemed to become alive like no other tree before. It moved its branches like arms and swayed its trunk like the giant hips they had become.

A low hum came across the small valley. The people turned and saw that the brother and sister were also at the top of trees. These perches were set in a perfect triangle in proportion to the tree of the One. They were about two hundred yards apart and were separated by the small valley. In the vision of the three beings, though, it appeared that they were right next to each other.

The siblings, too, were merging into the oak trees. The light around them was different than that of the One. The sister was encompassed in a blue light, while the brother was encompassed in a red light. Their beings, along with that of the trees which they were perched upon, were aglow with their individual light. The three primary colors were noticed by many in the crowd.

The trees formed a perfect triangle on the site. Inside the pyramid were all the people who had come to this place. They had split into three groups, each forming a line at an opposite angle of the triangle. The shape they created formed another triangle inside the triangle created by the siblings. This triangle was set in the middle of the other, forming a large six-sided star. Their numbers were six hundred sixty-six, a sacred number that had been bastardized by the greed. Two hundred and twenty-two people lined each side of the triangle. They did not split into these numbers on purpose, it was just the way of things.

The plan was falling into place. The people were going to supply the magnetism for the first stage of the truth. The triangle harnessed the energy and guided it to a source. The One knew how to manipulate the source and use it for good. It had dreamed the entire thing all those years ago at the sister's house in Minnesota. This was before the collective, but the memories persisted.

Many visions had come to the beings at the sister's house. Something had been feeding them knowledge the entire time. They had not known it then, but now with the knowledge, it was all clear. The sister lived on the Mesabi Iron range. This place was an ancient meteor strike, depositing the iron that was so avidly mined. It had struck at a time when the Earth's crust had still been cooling and was malleable. The meteor had impacted the planet at an angle and skid to its stop, thousands of feet under the surface.

As the Earth cooled, so did the meteor, becoming part of the terrain. The energy that this celestial body put off was still very much active. It was sending messages to all the people in that region through sounds and low vibrations. The people were too ashamed to admit what they were hearing. They would rather think that they were losing their minds. The One had heard the messages. The meteor and its entity had spoken. The extraterrestrial had a lot to say about the imprisonment it had been in for the last two billion years. This time in solitude had enlightened the creature like no other being that had ever lived on this planet. It had seen the whole evolution of the Earth and knew all its secrets. When the family had arrived, the entity was interconnected with their energy. The planet had told it of this prophecy, and now it was here.

The middle of the triangle created by the beings held a hidden treasure. The One had known about this artifact for a very long time. While they had been building their house, the man and woman had found a stone. It was a volcanic stone that had a quartz crystal embedded in the center of it. Only a golf ball size piece of the crystal was visible at the apex of the stone. The entire object was one square foot. It weighed over forty pounds.

The stone had interested the family when they had found it. They had known that it would be of great importance one day. The man had buried it in the spot in the field that had called to him. In fact, he had buried it in the exact spot that he had found it.

The stone had made the man lose his bearings that day. The directions had been lost to him. He forgot things as soon as they happened. The rock had a strange power to it, and it had affected the man. He had ultimately left it in the field and forgot about it until now. Now the stone was sitting in the center of the trees. Its form seemed to appear from nowhere.

The One began humming to complete the triangle. It started as a low, throaty sound but got more intense, like the sound from the singing bowl. The people below joined in. Their voices, too, began at a low pitch and built in crescendo. The sounds coming from the beings was in a wave kind of pattern. The sound rippled through the valley. The Earth began to vibrate and rumble. The people stood still. They had dreamed of this day for so many moons. Now was the time.

The light began to fade into a strange brownish light. The people all knew, a solar eclipse was just beginning. The moon had just begun to creep into the path of the sun.

The ground in the middle of the triangle began to rise. A solid beam of light was coming from the quartz eye embedded in the volcanic rock. The light was so bright, it made the humans turn their heads away, lest they be blinded. It stretched well past the atmosphere and into the heavens. The ground continued to rise. Dirt and debris now filled the air. The light shining through the dusty air was still too strong for the human eye. Rumbling and vibration filled their senses. It felt to many like Armageddon had arrived.

The One had continued the humming throughout the entire ordeal. The sounds put the humans at ease. Their worries floated away with the notes of the song.

The brother and sister also had joined in the song created by the being and the humans. The sound from the three siblings, and the trees that they had become, overpowered all sounds made from the crumbling of the Earth. Their sounds were one of hope in a land being savaged. The people had listened to those sounds and prayed with their own humming. They trusted the One. There had been no fear.

At long last, the sounds had gone away. With the restfulness of the Earth returning, the humming by all the beings subsided. Finally, it too was gone and only silence remained. The humans looked to the trees to see a sign from their leaders, but they could not be seen. All that were there were the faint shadows of trees standing through the thick haze of dust.

As the dust began to clear, their eyes were drawn to the object in the center of the triangle. There in the middle, was a giant piece of polished gold. It had miraculously come from the ground. The humans stood on three sides of the four-sided object. In front of them, was a giant pyramid. Each side must have been over three hundred feet long. The object seemed to be the same height. It was made entirely of gold, except for one small part. On its top was the volcanic rock, with the quartz embedded in it. The rock was at least ten feet across now and fit perfectly over the top of the pyramid. It formed a perfect black cap for the gold monolith.

The three trees encompassing the beings and the people formed two three sided triangles around the four sides of the pyramid. The full solar eclipse made the sun and moon perfectly in line with the triangles and the pyramid. The volcanic rock on top of the pyramid formed the last spot in the completion of the symbol.

This symbol was the symbol of the planet. Pachymama had just sent a message to the darkness that she was done with all of them. She was telling them that it was the end. This symbol was the beginning.

A charge could be felt coming through the feet of the humans. It passed through their entire beings, just to depart through the top of their heads, straight into the cosmos.

The species were connected to the cosmos once again. A line of energy went from the planet through all beings into the cosmos. This is the way it had been so very long ago. It had been thousands of years since the humans had lost the thread that connected them to the rest of the universe. The greed had taken it away from them. Now, their eyes had become wide open and ready to see. For the first time in generations, this species could perceive again.

The One and its siblings stood tall and proud as the oaks. Their forms swayed in tune with the wind. The One spoke to the crowd, in their minds. "Now you can see that I am not a God, nor are my siblings. We use our creativity and imagination to perform our magic. This planet is our God and always has been. We all have our own abilities, but we are all on the same level. We are all equals coming from different species. Look in each other's eyes. Now the true knowledge will arrive. I was merely sent here to show you the path. Now you will show others the path. Soon, we will all be a complete collective. Once that happens, we will all be going home."

CHAPTER 40

The story began. The One spoke with a whisper that sounded like thunder. All could hear. The minds of all the creatures present were connected in a common bond. They were connected to the present, the past and the future. These beings were the change as was the entire planet. All living things were the change. The change was here.

Animals began to emerge from the forest. They stood among the humans and were no longer frightened. All the beings were now on the same level. No one species was better than another. This was the first time in twenty thousand years that animals and humans had walked together. There were creatures' familiar to the humans and a few that were not. Animals that had long ago hid in the woodlands, away from the destruction of the humans, now were in the light. All species of the forest came to join the energy.

The sun coming over the mountains cast a warm light over the creatures and the entire valley. The sun cast a shadow from the One that fell across all its followers. Its words were soft and comforting, while at the same time very strong. The being spoke:

"The truth is here. Our ancestors were from another world. They came from a planet that was thriving called Krakatoa. Our people were sent to assist this planet and its young humanoids. They came to this planet about twenty thousand years ago. Our DNA was altered slightly so that we would be able to adapt quickly to the atmosphere of Earth. Immediately upon arrival, our species contacted the humans. They looked at us like we were gods. We already shared a common DNA with these beings, but they had evolved differently. This species had been seeded here over one and a half million years before by the same scientists that had seeded our planet and the entire solar system. While the rest of the humanoids progressed well on the other planets, the humans never seemed to get it. They had been slaves their entire existence on this planet to one species of extraterrestrial after another. Our people intermixed with these ancient tribes upon our arrival, but never mated with them. Our blood line has remained pure this entire time. Our ancestors taught the natives some of their knowledge, but the endeavor was quickly forgotten. Our elders realized right away that the humans held on to their ways. It was difficult for their species to accept change."

"During the ice age," the One continued, "our ancestors found ways to new lands. The native peoples had scoffed at our warnings and stayed in the cold regions. They couldn't adapt and were brought to the brink of extinction. The few hundred thousand human that had survived had been near the equator and south. Before the ice age, there were thirteen species of human on this planet. They had evolved in their one and a half million years and become subspecies of each other. Some of the extraterrestrials who enslaved the humans also mated with them, creating other species of their people. At the same time, other species had come to this planet for their own reasons, making it home for as long as they wished. Earth had always been abuzz with cosmic travelers. It was a nice stopping point in the universal realm of things."

"After the ice age, there were only five species of humanoid left on this planet. One of those was our species, the chosen. We had been a race that was very similar to the humans, but much more advanced. Our heads were much larger and our bodies smaller. We had long ago learned to use our minds over our bodies. We built machines that would do all our physical labor for us. Our ancestors spread out after the ice age ended. These people were not ones to take charge, however. Their existence was living in harmony with the planet and its species. Our species quickly evolved into the humans. After just three thousand years, the ancestors acclimated to this atmosphere and became indistinguishable from the humans. These ancients were nothing like the humans in their ways, however. They looked the same and their bodies were the same, but the thought was much different. They were the ones whom the greed and humans always called the natives, Indians, Aboriginals, savages, or many other titles. In truth, they were the keepers of Pachymama. These native peoples were the only reasons the humans had any bit of spirituality left. They were the only link between the humans and nature. The humans had murdered the chosen and pointed fingers at them. The chosen had become more distant once again."

"Soon after our people had arrived, they began to build. It was during this time that our people built the pyramid at Cheops and the Sphynx. They had been our first, twenty thousand years ago. At the end of the ice age, after they had spread across the globe, our people began to build monuments across dedicated to the stars and the planet they had left behind. They were colonists after all. There was hope that they would be going home, someday, to the world that they missed and loved, Krakatoa."

"At the same time, the humans were struggling for survival. The last great lord had left this planet more than ten thousand years before. It had created a vacuum in the lives of the species. They now had no purpose. They were a creature who needed a leader and without one were lost. They had freedom of a sort, but did not know what to do with it. They too, wandered. Only in their case, it was to find themselves. They were blind to the true way. Many migrated to the places where we built our temples. They mistakenly thought that we were Gods. They began to congregate where we were."

"The ancients knew about the stars and about their new home. They kept their population sustainable, and respected the Earth. They also respected the other twelve tribes of human. They interacted with these other species throughout time, but had little to do with them. The chosen were looked at as outcasts by the humans. Their ways were of sorcery and black magic. Humans had a side to them that no other animal on this planet had. It was greed. The humans wanted to own things, and they would do anything to have more than the others."

"The human evolution had already been written before the chosen had even arrived on this planet. It was not in the stars of destiny to speed that up. Nor did our people have a desire to enslave the natives of Earth. We could make machines to do all our work."

"Everything remained mostly unchanged until six thousand years ago. Another group of visitors from the stars arrived in the middle east area. This group was a shapeshifter and was very powerful. They had no reason to alter their DNA, but their appearance was a different situation. The visitors looked like large reptilian men. Their heads were small with large mouths and small eyes that were close together. Their arms and legs were short, out of proportion with their long bodies. They brought fear to the planet. The newcomers quickly had the natives thinking they were gods. This enabled the visitors to enslave the humans. They mined the Earth with their endless labor, and made riches at the expense of life. They built large temples to bask in the glory of their wealth. The visitors profited, while the people became their slaves. Two of the species of human could not be enslaved, and they were exterminated. The visitors had flying craft that they used to scour the planet for treasures and slaves. When they saw a monument, they would destroy it. Thousands of years of building monuments were destroyed in days. All relics of the past were laid to ruin. All the history of the humans erased by an angry breed. Our people had settled in what is now Egypt, England and the coast of Lake Titicaca. We protected our last temples and used their power to ward off the invaders. Other artifacts had been saved, but they were hidden deep underground. Just a few of our temples remain to this day. The pyramid of Cheops, the Sphinx, Moche Picchu, and Easter Island. It was these places that the greed claimed for themselves. They built their shoddy temples, using ours as their templates. They could never duplicate our monuments, so they simply claimed them as their own. All of our other offerings to the stars were destroyed or kept by the new elite."

"Many generations passed. The humans remained slaves to the visitors. Our ancestors remained hidden among the masses, at times slaves, too. The humans could gain some knowledge through evolution, or so the visitors thought. In reality, it was our ancestors who were giving the natives bits of truth. They would use it for their better. It was this time that the humans made their first language and became at one with the stars and arts. Many of their species took it upon themselves to become scholars and document the history of their people. The newcomers paid the least attention to what the humans were doing. Long as they were mining their resources, it did not matter. The visitors controlled all aspects of the planet. Their greed would take everything from this globe. Every mineral would be stripped clean, as well as the life. They had already done the same on so many planets before. When this planet was barren, they would simply move on to the next. In their wake, they would leave no evidence of life. Just like they had done with Mars. Just like they had done with all the planets in our solar system. All the planets except one. Krakatoa, our beloved home."

"The visitors put devices in people's bodies to control them. Everyone here today has one implanted in their bodies. Media and other forms of control did not work the same on the chosen. The greed knew that some were different and came up with the idea of the implant. We had not been controlled with fear like the other ninety nine percent, so they used a device, instead, to block the truth. This lack of control was what made our species different than the humans. It is why the chosen never fell for the games of the greed. They had been the ones who could see through the madness that government and religion would create. They had not fallen for the antics of the elite. Sometimes, the devices in the humans would malfunction, and the greed would have to reset them. They had been installed at birth. It was why they would take the baby out of the delivery room for ten minutes right after they were born. The nurse said it was to weigh them, but it was to implant."

"The devices had many functions. They tracked everywhere we went and everything we did. The visitors never knew the truth about the chosen. Their devices did their job in tracking us and watching what we did, but they could not control us. The visitors thought we were human like the rest of the slaves. Sometimes, throughout history, a chosen would speak out against the greed. They would preach to the others for change. These prophets were called problems by the greed. They were masters of getting rid of problems."

"A few thousand years ago, the humans began to get very organized and smart. They built cities and made communities. They became 'civilized'. The greed saw this as their prime opportunity. They infiltrated these communities and began something they called government. Religion was invented soon after. The worship of the stars and sun went away. The greed easily took over every community that popped up. Their control was complete. After borders were set, war was soon to follow. The greed had much practice in controlling the minds of the humans, and war was just another aspect."

"It was during this time that the greed also thought it best to rid the planet of any kind of visual history. Ancient libraries of the world, kept by loyal families for centuries, burned overnight. Temples and shrines that the chosen built were destroyed. Even temples that the greed had built were destroyed. They saw the benefit of destruction. It meant construction and an endless cycle of war and control. The next three thousand years were filled with destruction and death. A strange fascination of this species was with annihilation."

"During this time, our people forgot who they were and where we came from. The chosen had been integrated with the human population and nobody could see the difference. The two species still could not mate, there was one DNA strand off for that. They did marry though and coexist. The destruction of the history of the planet was complete. Our people, once coupled to the heavens, were now separated and alone on this celestial body. The connection had been lost."

"The greed had taken too much for the planet to handle. The last years saw the resources becoming more and more depleted, while the human population grew exponentially. Water and air had been so polluted that it was changing the DNA of all creatures. Earthquakes and deadly weather had been a byproduct of the devastation. The planet was running out of patience. The greed was in competition with their slaves for the remaining resources. The humans had also gotten wise to the elite. The human technology and knowledge grew so much in one hundred years, it made the visitors afraid. They had never seen an evolution in a species this fast before. It was time to get rid of the humans. They didn't need slaves on this planet any more. They had what they had come for. Now was the time to enjoy their riches."

"The Lunarks were the ones who had sent the meteor that wiped out the humans. The greed had made the moon dwellers think that they were going to be ridding the planet of their kind. They had been fooled. They had this weapon in their arsenal on their craft for such occasions, but had never used it before. The weapon was to disable the greed, but save the people. That hadn't worked as planned. Neither had the impact."

"One of the greed had been into the vaccination scheme to further control the humans. He had worked at the center for disease control and had come up with a virus that would kill all the humans. They had leaked the information to the Lunarks, making them believe that it was a virus that would wipe out the greed. It had been the idea of the creator of the virus for it to be placed on the meteor. This would keep the plants on the planet but rid it of the pesky humans. They just made the Lunarks believe that they were taking out the greed, and the plans were set in motion. Inadvertently, the Moon men wiped out their experiments, the humans. The greed once again sat back and watched the destruction they had created."

"The greed, in their arrogance, thought that they had exterminated the planet of all the humans. They had been too confident to see the wisdom of the animals and the spirit of the chosen."

"The device we are about to build will finally free this planet of the visitors and their destruction. Their greed has destroyed so much, including our friends, the humans. They will see very shortly the consequences of their actions. Earth again will be in perfect harmony."

The One had spoken.

Chapter 41

The greed had remained in the cities after the cataclysm they had created for the next twenty-two years. The first few years were a paradise. With no more humans, things were perfect. The greed could be in their normal shapes and not be cloaked. They had never adapted to the human ways. They had no desire to. They had no emotions or empathy. Cloaking was an inconvenience they had to deal with to mask their identity. Now they could be free again. The risk of any kind of uprising from the slaves had passed with the passing of the humans.

The greed had amassed so much wealth and commodities that they needed no more. The Earth had more to give, but they would take that when they needed to. For now, the creatures could wallow in their victory over the inhabitants of Pachymama. Everything was theirs all along, but now, they had to share nothing with the parasites of the planet.

Fuel was not a problem for the greed. They had learned long ago how to use the gravity of the Earth and electromagnetic fields in conjunction with each other. The vast amounts of quartz on the planet is what they had originally come for. Gold had mixed with the crystals, which was used for all circuitry; it was the conductor. This technology had been brought to this planet by the greed when they had come six thousand years ago. They had kept it hidden from the humans all along.

If the humans knew the truth, they would want to take their planet back. If the elite went around in their 'space ships', the silly people would think they were from other planets. Aliens and abductions had been created by the greed to mask the truth. All along, the sightings of UFO were the greed playing with their toys right in front of the humans. When they were seen, they denied it all. It was lie after lie, until the truth was buried in an avalanche of disinformation.

Oil had also been found by the greed. This, too, they had found thousands of years before. They had no purpose for the fossils and their sludge. Their energy came from the crystals, with absolutely no waste or byproduct. They had found byproducts of the oil and slowly gave the technology to the humans. It took less than twenty years, and the natives were addicted to their crude. It was one more way to control the masses. It also turned out to be a very good one. It changed the economy on the planet and made it easier for the greed to control the trade.

The pollution that the oil created was scoffed at by the elite. It made some difference in the atmosphere, but the greed did not care. When it would have serious impacts, they would simply get rid of the problem. Now, twenty-two years later, the atmosphere had slowly cleansed itself of the carbon and now was fifty percent less toxic than during the time of the humans.

The rulers had also given the people small bits of technology and knowledge. It made the humans think they were intelligent. The masses were so easily fooled; they believed that they were the most intelligent beings on the planet. The greed fed just enough information to the humans to pacify them and strengthen their beliefs in themselves. It had worked well for six thousand years.

Somehow, the oil had also accelerated the evolution of the humans. They began to believe in a collective thought, and it had worried the greed. The humans and the Earth began a bond. The people began to become intellectual and scientific. The humans took a pledge to save the planet. Their home. They made plans and put them into action.

However, the elite were not a species to be antagonized. They sat back and watched the silly humans with their collectivity. It was a notion their species could never achieve. The humans would never be fully united. Their kind could never fully omit the greed from their existence.

When the greed had first arrived, it had been easy controlling the natives. They used God as a weapon on these people. Many species in the history of Earth had done the same thing to the humans. They simply told them they were God, and the people dropped to their knees and began to bow and pray.

The greed had used their superior technology to build monuments and temples, art and writing. All with the use of human slaves and their imagination. If not for the human creativity, these temples and languages would never have been built. The greed was only good at one thing. Control.

Many temples were already in existence when the greed arrived. They had scoured the planet and destroyed every one of them, except three. There were magnetic fields intersecting these places that their craft could not fly through, and their weapons could not penetrate. Even underground temples and monuments that had been from very ancient people who lived millions of years ago were located and ravaged. They had searched and destroyed nearly all the history of the planet. Not a single soul had tried to stop them.

The greed realized quickly that the monuments and temples were all on energy spots of the planet. They knew that it took intelligent life to build temples which were on magnetic intersections. They could see the stars that the temples were aligned to and read who had built these places.

The greed was also a very ancient species. They had been traveling the cosmos for more than one billion years. They had seen many worlds and monuments. They had taken over some of the worlds with clues from temples left on other planets. These clues were like a road map of the stars, for any being that could read them. Good or bad. It pointed the greed right to the next intelligent solar system that they would devastate.

The greed built their temples on top of the ones that they destroyed. There were not enough of their species yet to inhabit an entire planet. They had played this role before many times. They had even been on this planet hundreds of thousands of years ago, as scouts looking for conquest. They would bring civilization to the natives, all the while enslaving them. They would take the resources and rejoice in the annihilation of an area and its people, wallowing in its riches. Slowly, they would spread out until they were the dominant species. They even made a word for it. 'Manifest Destiny'.

They would absorb all the people of these places and their treasures. The other species on the planet would be building their temples of gold, while the greed was just preparing to take it all away. As the number of the greed grew, so did their frontier. They spread until their control held entire planets in its dark grip. Every intelligent species on the planet would be the slaves. Most were too blind to see it, and let it all happen.

They would never destroy the Earth completely, though. They wanted to come back someday and do it all over again. It had been their way. After the complete conquest of a planet, the greed would leave enough of their kind behind to wallow in the riches while the rest would be off to new conquests. They were all just a wormhole away anyhow. These beings traveled between their conquered lands freely and efficiently. It is what had helped them spread throughout the universe. Once a planet was conquered, a portal would be erected, and the connection to any other star circle in the cosmos was complete.

When any of the slaves would protest or organize dissent, the greed would use fear to quiet them. If that did not work, death was the next step. People were just a number to them, and it was easy to erase a number.

The natives always grew more and more disenchanted with their false Gods. The greed was way smarter than the humans, though. They knew about control and manipulation. Without empathy, it was easy to treat the animals how they desired.

The greed created religion to put the humans into divisions. They just made up Gods and wrote prophecy that the humans ate up. With religion came wars. They created the notion that if someone was of a different religion from yours, they were your enemy. The masses all picked a side.

The humans were followers, the greed knew how to lead.

It had been obvious that the humans would not believe they were Gods for long whenever they arrived in a new area. Gods were supposed to be kind and think of all the people. They were not self-absorbed charlatans, just thinking of themselves and their powerful buddies. Gods certainly did not rule with fear.

Dividing the people worked so well, the greed decided it was the way. They created government to further control. Racism, sexism, and social class were the last aspects of the complete division of the humans. If they were divided, they were blind, was the way the greed saw it. Division created hatred among the masses. It was all directed at themselves. If their hatred was a collective, directed at the greed, the rulers would lose control.

Uprisings would occasionally occur, but the greed would make the people believe it was their neighbor who was the true enemy. Or another country was to blame because the greed told them so. The people had no idea they were being manipulated by rulers from another galaxy. They thought it was just the wealthy class that made all the rules. The common folk looked up to these beings and wished that they could have what they had some day.

These people represented the majority. They were the fools. Because of them, the greed had taken everything that the humans had worked so very hard for. While slaving away, they were thrown the scraps of food that their gluttonous rulers did not want.

Eventually, the human collective became disenchanted with the many things being done to them and the planet. Some began to wonder why the same families were always in power. More elaborate schemes were perpetrated on the humans. Oil was known to be the final phase of their existence.

The greed was monitoring and watching the humans the entire time they had been on the planet. They gained pleasure from creating hoaxes with the media to get the humans all fired up. It was easy to get them into war. The wealth that came from the wars was insanely large, but it did not matter to the greed. They did love to eat their good food and drink, and all their other wealthy pleasures, but they could have gotten that any way or another. War was so fun to watch for their species. They were ones who had to fight on other planets to complete their agenda. Sometimes they had been defeated in the past. Other times, like this planet, they could create wars among the slaves while enjoying the riches. All the while, everybody would be struggling. This was the entertainment of the greed.

The greed also made it appear to the masses that they were traveling to distant planets with their new-found technology. In reality, they had been traveling throughout space freely for millennium. The pictures that they would give to the people would be pictures of any planet they desired. The humans wouldn't know any better. Distant galaxies and nebula were only a scratch of what the greed really knew about. There was no need to let the humans have any more than the slightest bits of this information.

They had to show the slaves something, so the greed had taught the humans about telescopes. They had gotten bigger and bigger over the centuries as the slaves were starved for knowledge about their origins. Humans were asking for answers. The greed would give them what they wanted. Answers in the form of lies.

Throughout the reign of the greed, other visitors had tried to come to this planet. The greed had indeed been building things with the resources for space exploration. They had been building defense systems around the Earth. Satellites peppered the sky. They orbited the sky in grids, intersecting at prearranged intervals. These systems were the first defense if intruders came. The greed had always had a defense in place. The first thousand years, there had been no other visitors. By the time the first ones had arrived, the greed was ready for them. Their species was one of war. They were not ones who were afraid to fight.

At the end of the fourteenth century, a race of another species infiltrated the planet and its solar neighbors. They had been hiding in the moon for millions of years. Their craft had been built in a very distant star cluster not seen by the best telescopes on Earth. Their lunar spacecraft had been sucked into a black hole and ejected in the inner parts of the Milky Way. By the time it had reached this solar system, billions of years had passed. It had been weakened by its long journey and its beings who operated it were getting weary of travel. They had been sucked in by the Earth's sun, which was twice as large at that time. The craft had been flung from the sun's magnetic field like a slingshot and rocketed toward the outer parts of the solar system. It passed by the blue planet a bit too close, and its unusually strong magnetic field held the craft in its orbit. The Earth had a moon and the Space creatures had a place to rest for a bit. That rest ended up being for millions of years.

These visitors, too, came to the Earth during their resting period. They had explored the solar system and seeded the planets and moons with life. Their way was of experiments, and they brought along their own bacteria and spores to speed up the evolution of celestial bodies orbiting suns. After seeding a planet, they would just wait and observe. They would also genetically modify plants and animals that already existed within their experimental realms. Occasionally, they would go to these planets to check on things in person, but most of their observations came from their base inside the moon.

They had seen many different visitors come during this time to the solar system. They had to fight a few times, but it had never been to this degree. These beings, the reptilian, had visited Earth often. Now, however, their mission was different. Their mission now was not to observe, but to control. They had the intention of taking over the entire solar system. They went from planet to planet and took samples of all the life that they found. They captured beings from every planet and moon. Almost every celestial body in the solar system had multiple life forms on them. On Venus and Mars, their intelligence had surpassed that of the rest of the planets.

The grays, as they came to be known, gathered their information and analyzed it. When they observed the greed returning, they knew that they were going to be in for a battle. They had encountered these beings before and saw their destructive ways. They decided to remain in their moon and see what transpired.

At first, the grays just waited in hopes that the greed would get tired of this planet and go away. Every time these reptilians had come before, they had left. The Lunarks had high hopes. It never happened. After five thousand four hundred Earth years, it was time to intervene. The lunar creatures had powerful ships that resembled cigars with lights on top. They could travel at the speed of light and maneuver in any direction or angle that they desired. They began their formations across the planet in the year 1462. For three-year intervals, the moon men flew around the planet and observed. They had a cloak that made detection devices of the greed useless. The greed knew about the visitors through the stories of the slaves. They had been seeing flying objects. Some with cosmic powers. The greed thought at first that it was more nonsense from the humans until they, too, began to see the craft. They tried, unsuccessfully, to bring one of these crafts down.

The lunar creatures would come at intervals of fifty years for their main experiments. The rest of the time, they would fly freely in the Earth atmosphere. It was at these intervals that their numbers were the greatest. After they had been detected, they came as ambassadors to the elite. When that did not work, wars had broken out. Occasionally, the humans would observe these fights and think that it was angels versus demons. In truth, both sides were just fighting over control of the blue planet. The greed and the visitors.

In 1898, an experimental device took down a ship from the moon men in Russia, creating a nuclear blast. Two weeks later, a craft was hit in a small Texas town and went into a corn field. The impact was so hard, the craft burrowed into the ground to a depth of six hundred feet. The escape capsule on the top of the craft had ejected upon impact, and its occupant was fully conscious. The people of the town took the creature to a nearby farmhouse, which was promptly surrounded by the greed in their high-tech craft.

They used a beam of light to capture the gray through a small triangular portal in the bottom of the space ship. When the light was gone, so were the craft. Only one of the humans remembered any of the details later. It was a boy of about ten. He swore up and down to the townspeople about what had really happened, but they had ridiculed him. Eight years later, at age eighteen, the boy would join the army to get away from the bullying that had followed him since the incident in his grandpa's corn field.

The grays had realized the strength of the greed and resorted to fly missions only for research and reconnaissance. They were very secretive about these missions. They had altered their cloaking devices and were preparing for the next wave. It came in 1947. The lunar patrol entered the Earth's atmosphere in all directions on the globe. The numbers were not staggering. They were not looking for an all-out war. They wanted to negotiate with the greed and bring a show of power along with their ambassador.

The visitors had met with the greed in Washington D.C. with a delegation of twelve craft. Neither party agreed to the other's terms. There had been no resolving the differences. The moon men returned home with the news.

The Lunark had left some of their craft behind for more observation. The greed had nothing to do with that. They had used their previous weapons, which had been improved. Their craft had also been altered to battle with the long shape of the moon ships. The greed were the owners of the disc shaped craft. They had lights around the outside, and some were huge. As big as city blocks sometimes.

The greed had a battle with the lunar craft in New Mexico. Both sides took a beating. The moon creatures lost three ships in four days, while the greed lost one medium size craft. Four of the greed had been lost, while nine grays perished. The locals had taken the lunar craft to the town, and the greed swiftly swooped it up. They had made up a story like all times before. Some doubted like always, but most believed.

Ironically, one of the lunar craft crashed on the property of a sixty-year old rancher outside Roswell. It was the same man, grown now, that had remembered the crash in Texas all those years ago. Fifty years ago. He had kept the craft and its three occupants at his ranch for three days before driving them to Roswell. He had not been so ready for the ridicule to begin all over again.

During this time, the rancher and his sons buried one of the creatures that had not made it out alive. Its pod went into the family cemetery out back. The other two were wounded badly. One of them had abrasions and a puncture wound in its abdomen. It secreted an oily substance from its wounds. The other astronaut was burned severely. Both looked like they would have a hard time surviving.

The rancher and his wife nursed the two creatures for the full three days. All the beings communicated freely with their minds. The language was through thoughts that floated in the air in the middle of the four. They were as clear as English to the man and his wife. The being told them where it was from and what was coming. It told them about the greed. It also told them that the greed was tired of the humans, and they would be in very much danger. The lunar creature had a strange request. The entity persisted until it convinced the rancher to drive the two beings and part of their craft to town. The rancher and his wife tried to talk the Lunark out of this crazy idea, but to no avail.

As soon as they got to the Air Force base, they were surrounded with guns. The beings were left in the back of the truck while it was taken away. The rancher never saw the creatures or his truck ever again.

The greed interrogated the rancher and his wife. He had mistakenly taken them to their house in the wilds of New Mexico. The greed had no mercy. They had picked up all the pieces of the wreckage with their own craft, and were gone in minutes.

The men in suits and dark glasses quickly tired of the rancher, his wife, and their sons. The family would not tell them anything that they asked, anyway. They were murdered on the spot. The next day, when the reporters arrived to question the family, the man and his wife appeared on the porch. The greed was wise, and they were shape shifters. They could become anything or anyone that they wanted. There was no need to get the humans any more fired up than they would be. Once again, the newspapers were fed lies.

The grays continued to patrol the Earth and the remainder of the solar system. They were weary of the greed, and it was mutual. They had an unwritten truce that applied only for certain things. Again, in 1956, a lunar patrol was sent to the White House. They met with the greed for over six hours and reached a deal of tolerance. The deal was to be for sixty years. They could both use airspace, but it was very limited. Research on the humans and animals was allowed. The greed despised the humans, anyway. In return, the moon men would have to bring ten shipments of helium three. This was a mineral which had accumulated on the surface of the moon. All agreed. All lived up to the bargain for the next sixty years.

The grays had seen their weapon strike the Earth and watched its devastating aftereffects. They had tried to contact the greed one year after, when all the humans had already died. The grays wanted to renew their contract with the greed. The greed, however, would have nothing to do with it. The visitors had tried to eliminate them, and they were not ones to be done dirty twice by any species. They had the Earth, and they were going to keep it all for themselves. The lunar ambassadors negotiated for three days, but left with nothing more than insults and threats. The greed said they would even take the Moon if they wanted to. They warned the lunar beings to stay well away from their galactic space.

The end of the final phase of their plans worked out well for the greed. They had easily taken care of the planet with the human's simple greed. They had known their contract was up with the moon species and needed them no more. Their scientists held much wisdom. They had acquired large amounts of Helium Three, traded from the moon men. The Lunarks produced this valuable compound with the help of particles from the sun rays. They had learned to collect it and produce it into a very clean burning fuel. It would last forever with absolutely no waste.

The moon men were tricked by the greed. They had been observing, but the Earth's scientists had been developing weapons with the helium three. They had covertly made these weapons while putting up decoys looking like power stations. Now they had the weapons to take care of all the pesky space men too, along with the humans.

The last decades on the planet had been brutal at the hands of the greed. Their contempt for the humans was intense. They had given them bits of technology. They watched with their greed while the humans ate themselves from within. They gave them video games to control the children, for life. They told the masses anything they wanted with the media sources. They would believe it like the suckers they were. Computers made it easier to gain more technology, which made them unravel at an unnatural speed. The humans simply could not keep up with the technology thrown at them, and they lost their minds.

Then, the greed pulled out the card that they had warned the masses about since the beginning. The 'Anti-Christ'. This character was, actually, the internet. From the beginning, the greed gave this 'tool' to the humans to watch them suffer. Social Media blew up with the vanity of the humans, and it was over from there. The greed did not have emotion, so they would watch the humans destroy themselves with theirs. Cell phones made it possible to carry the internet in your pocket, and privacy was lost. Identity in the humans imploded. There were no longer individuals. The greed had succeeded in making an entire species into one word. Consumers.

Fear and hatred were now spread by turning on a device in your pocket. The greed had no reason to do this. It was some sort of strange entertainment to their kind. The greed had divided the people for so long, and now they united them in their last episode as the natives of the planet. They would let them share knowledge and make them think they understood. They would make them think they were one. A collective. Once again, the humans had been tricked.

The spread of the collective thought theory was one of a new way for the planet. It was a way for fairness and equality for all. There would be no more mega rich. Everybody would prosper. Everybody would also be in control. The internet would be used as a tool to unite all citizens of the Earth for the truth. All people would vote locally and nationally and worldwide in elections, which were conducted on the internet. All knowledge would be screened for accuracy. Hacking would be solved with the best computer people. Everything could change, you just had to get rid of the chump change. That is how it would have worked if the elite were not in charge of everything.

Utopia did not fit into their One world order.

The people of the Earth did not realize it. The One percent who were in charge were not the only one percent. The chosen had been hidden among the humans, undetected for thousands of years. When the internet arrived, it was the chosen who jumped to the activism and unification. They were the ones who were the most intelligent. They had been sent here long ago to help the humans, and now they were doing just that. But their help had very adverse effects. The chosen, too, had become lost with the passing of time. They had become blind leaders through the landscape of consciousness.

Finally, the humans had lost the ability to connect face to face with their species. All their energy was focused on something created by the greed. The humans were truly lost. The last small thread of energy connecting them to the heavens was severed. Their spirituality, mostly mislead, was now lost. The greed had defeated the souls of the humans. They had collected their thoughts and their energies through the internet.

As the humans were trying to connect, the internet was absorbing their beings. Long after their pods were gone, the greed would still own the souls and thoughts of the humans.

When they had every soul connected with their implants and the internet, it was easy for the greed to store all the spirits on just one-disc type device.

The home planet would be pleased upon their return. These explorers would be bringing home resources and souls for future slaves. Carrying around the souls on their devices made it easy to implant them into primitive beings and begin civilization. They had done it many times before with souls. Sometimes, like on Earth, they even reproduce at rapid speed and made more souls. The human beings were a species who created a new soul with the birth of each child. Many visitors to their planet had said the humans had been blessed by some distant God for having this trait. Others had said it was just another parasitic trait of the humans.

After they had the souls, the greed sent in the meteor. They had always been in contact with their planet in the Orion belt. Transporting resources and bringing more ships had been happening since their arrival. Now their home planet had made a weapon with the helium three and sent it on a small asteroid. The greed had concocted a virus that would wipe out the humans, and it was sent with the meteor. The meteor had been orbiting the moon for months before smashing into the Earth.

The Lunarks had taken notice. They had captured the asteroid in their magnetic technology and altered it into the weapon that would finally rid the solar system of the greed. They had no idea that it had been sent by the greed. The moon people guided the asteroid with their electromagnetic rays and shot it at the greed. First, they had concocted a virus that they thought would affect the parasite. When it had been installed, the meteor had been launched toward the blue planet. It was the same day that their treaty with the greed had ended.

The Lunark thought that the device had malfunctioned. There was a homing device in Antarctica. It did not attract the meteor as planned. The rock took a strange trajectory when entering the atmosphere and crashed in Kanab. There was a device there, it had been left behind by the One. The girl had found it earlier in a park in Bishop. She had accidentally left it in her back pocket. The device had fallen under the bed, undetectable. It was a homing device. Weeks after they had left the room, the device attracted the meteor and set into motion the destruction of the humans and half of the creatures on Earth.

The greed was not accustomed to malfunctions. They had planned, all along, for the meteor orbiting around the moon to be tampered with by the Lunark. When the moon people had launched the meteor, it was the intention of the greed for it to hit Rockaway Beach. The greed had reasoned that it would eliminate the light first, while causing them the least bit of problems. It didn't really matter to them either way where the meteor struck. It had served its purpose by destroying the humans. The Lunark were next anyway. The human energy had been wiped off the planet. The monitors of the greed showed no signs of life. There was not one human that had survived.

The greed had lost some of their own when the meteor struck unannounced in Utah. The eruption of Yellowstone had been unexpected and killed many more of their kind. They had no emotion for death. The greed understood. Your soul just went somewhere else. The rest of the greed remained in their bunkers that they had built long before. In some cases, where the damage was minimal, they mostly stayed in their big cities with their luxuries and air filtration. The humans, dying of their disease, had never been part of these buildings. The rulers had only let their own in the doors of the elite.

Now, the greed felt like they had everything. Their communications with the home planet were done with light, as was their travel. They had no time for radios, phones, or the internet. These were distractions they had thrown to the humans. Clouding the minds of the masses while theirs went unimpeded. While they were using the real technology for themselves, they were lying to the masses. They even put it all over their news and called it alternative news. That had been then. Now they could focus on the spoils of their campaign on this planet.

Food was not an issue. The greed had stockpiled everything they had needed to survive for hundreds, if not thousands of years. Around the strike zone and most of north America, it was a wasteland. The Eastern seaboard had survived completely unharmed, as did the rest of the planet.

Without the humans eating the animals, some of the creatures exploded in numbers. Others could not reproduce any longer and became extinct. Populations of predators exploded. They ate every living creature that they came across. They were also easy pickings for the greed. Their kind had always been expert hunters. Their travels throughout the universe had made them so. They had no time for cooking, though. They would kill an animal with their hands and mouths and eat it on the spot, in its natural form. There would be no skinning or gutting of animals. They were reptilian, after all. They had no time for cleaning food before they ate it.

Grains and other commodities were always at the ready. They had methods of preserving that would take the proteins and vitamins and condense it into a small tablet. This is what the greed survived on when they were not hunting. It was very easy to store all the nutrition that they needed. They only ate once a week, but feasted on that day. It was enough energy to last the week, or longer if needed. They had not needed to go hungry on this planet once. They had thrived.

The only other plant that they ate, besides grains, was a lichen that grew on the quartz rock. Their kind had known about this lichen before they had arrived. Older colonies had brought back this highly prized substance. When digested, the moss would be like a drug to the greed. They couldn't get enough of it. They had tried to cultivate the substance themselves but had been unsuccessful. The lichen took very long to grow, centuries sometimes.

As soon as the humans were eliminated, the Lunark came in. They had sent battalions of their star ships to investigate what was happening on Earth. They had quickly learned that the greed had activated defense barriers around the planet. They were of an electromagnetic field that the Lunark were not familiar with. For the first time since they had arrived, millions of years before, their ships were unable to penetrate the atmosphere of the blue planet. They had returned to their fortress, the moon, to regroup. Their scientists, too, were very wise and held much knowledge. They would know how to break down the force field.

The greed had waited for the Lunark to get safely back to their base before launching their weapon. It was a sphere the size of a basketball. The metal was platinum and gold. Inside the orb was housed a very lethal dose of helium three. The greed had figured out a way to cause an electromagnetic charge to the helium. The gold was the conductor. The platinum made the orb durable. The charge would be created with an impact from the object traveling at the speed of light or greater. Its effects were thousands of times worse than any nuclear bomb that the greed had made on Earth. This was a device that would destroy a planet but leave its formations and mineral. This device would simply vaporize any life form on a target planet. Or in the case of the moon, all life forms inside a celestial body would be vaporized.

This is the device that the greed struck the moon with. The weapon was propelled into space using a device the greed had that would accelerate any object at five times the speed of light. The small bomb hit the moon square in its largest crater. It penetrated the outer shell of the giant space station at its tremendous speed. It had been moving so fast, the device went into the center of the moon by about six hundred miles before exploding. It crashed through layer after layer of Lunark communities until it slowed enough to cause its intended wrath.

The bomb completely vaporized every inhabitant of the moon. Every living creature, and the experimental creatures they had gathered, were gone. Their plants and food sources were equally obliterated. This species' home base had just been erased from the memories of the universe.

The Lunark had retained ambassadors with a few of the other planets in the solar system. A few outposts here and there would mean that their species would possibly survive, however small. Less than one percent of one percent of their species had not been on the moon. The greed was aware of that fact. The Lunark were no longer a threat. Not that they ever had been.

After twenty-two years, things had changed for the greed. At first, they loved the solitude and peace that had afforded them after the Humans and Lunark extermination. Now they had lost all their entertainment. They were getting restless. The greed thought of the days when they had souls to control. Their species just liked to be in control of things. Their existence on this planet had worn itself out.

The greed thought about putting the souls of the humans into the wild animals. They had selected many species that they thought would be perfect hosts to make a new mass. They missed their slaves. The powers had decided this to be a bad idea. They were hunters and wanted freedom to hunt any animal they wanted. If they did not know which ones had human souls, they might inadvertently eat one of them. They had learned long ago not to eat the humans. Their souls would remain inside the greed, clouding their judgment with their silly emotions. The souls would never leave the beings once they were ingested. They were like pollution when ingested. The pollution would never dissipate. There was no cure. They had stayed well clear of any thought of eating the human scourge.

Manipulating another species did not seem feasible, either. The visitors had spent much time on the humans. Success was only achieved because of the simplicity of the species. They had just enough intelligence to manipulate. Their self-belief that they were better than the other species was arrogant and wrong. It had made them the perfect species to enslave. It would take thousands of years to genetically mutate beings of this planet to become intelligent enough to work and build. The greed had no time for this. Someone else had mutated the creatures of this planet long ago and departed, leaving behind the humans as their legacy. They had done the work for their rulers. The elite had simply come in and filled a position the humans so desperately needed. Someone to believe in.

The greed dreamed of returning to their home planet. They just could not bring themselves to leave the riches that they had gained on the Earth. They had worked hard manipulating this planet for six thousand years and now wanted to enjoy the riches. Greed was the emotion of this species. They were not about to change. The species was for riches, but mostly for control. The greed loved to manipulate things and control situations. It was like a board game to them.

Little did the greed know, their ways were about to change. In their arrogance, they had not cared about the survival of the chosen. They had never known this species to be a threat, but now they were preparing. The chosen were making a true collective. Not a fake internet connection perpetrated by the greed. These chosen were coming together and bringing their energy into one.

The chosen were being led by three other beings. Each of them were the One of wisdom. They were the knowledge. They had the voice to make the collective come together and be all powerful. They had the power to heal the Earth and the righteous beings who were its inhabitants. The three were about to shine the light for all to see.

The greed, indulging in their darkness, could not believe the prophecy. It was out-landish to think that three beings could destroy their kind. They left it as myth what the prophets had written so many moons ago. They were of a humanoid species, after all. The greed did not trust these humanoids. Their ways were not normal to their reptilian lifestyle. Their ways were odd. The elite had no regard for any humanoid creature nor its fables.

They had decided to ignore the prophecy. They had chosen to make their own destiny.

This lack of respect for the wisdom of the cycle was the beginning of the end for the greed. Their presumptions of greatness would be their downfall. Their insolence made them blind. Their rule over the planet was coming to an end. They saw it coming but could not grasp the magnitude of the change.

By the time they saw the light, beaming into the heavens, the greed would be wracked with fear. They would understand immediately the cost of their arrogant ways. There would not be much time to prepare. The One was upon them.

CHAPTER 42

The pyramid in front of the chosen shook with the intensity of an earthquake. It was not a strong, aggressive shake. It was a deep trembling, which rattled the entire core of the gathered beings. It felt natural and nurturing. The rumbling seemed to connect all the beings together in the triangle that they formed.

The intensity of the symbol created by the pyramid, the chosen, and the three beings was enough to make the entire planet tremble in what would have been measured a four-point earthquake. It was a message. All the other chosen left on the planet knew that this was the time. They had been waiting and now had gotten the signal.

The Earth had accepted the chosen immediately upon their arrival. Their planet and its species were ones of peace and nurturing. They had strong emotions and a sense of empathy like no other creature in the solar system. They had cared for Pachymama as if it had been their own planet. They revered the bounty of gifts that the planet provided. They had never taken advantage of the Earth, and the planet had taken care of them. Even when they had been controlled by the greed, the chosen had stood strong and resisted their evil ways.

The chosen were also a very passive species. They were not ones to tell others what to do or how to do it. They lived the life of complete self-control and self-respect. Whatever made them happy was acceptable and accepted. Crime had not existed on their planet. They were also not ones for possessions. Everybody was equal. They had never tried to become the rulers or controllers of any other species. They made it clear that they were not Gods. Harmony was their way. It was how they had fit into Pachymama so well when they had settled on it.

Harmony had also been what kept the chosen unseen by the greed for so many thousands of years. While so many humans had tried to make names for themselves and gain popularity, the chosen had no part of it. They saw the silliness in this. They wanted to fit in and be hidden. The last thing they wanted was to have eyes upon them. Enough people were always pointing their fingers at the chosen anyhow. Their disparities with the humans was noticed by the masses. The chosen had often been ridiculed for their absurd thought and behavior. In truth, they were just using their creativity, and the humans did not understand.

The imagination in the humans was taken by the greed almost immediately after their arrival. Not that it had existed much before. They were a species that had been enslaved by many different visitors over their history. They were not bad creatures, they just were not developed. Their creativity had been impeded so they could not think for themselves. They were just emulating their rulers, the greed. They wanted a piece of their pie and were misled into thinking they could have a slice. It was another part of the regulation. The corruption of the human minds was vast in the quest to keep control.

The chosen had lived among the humans in complete obscurity. They, too, had been fitted with the devices at birth. The greed was thorough in their mind control. However, their implants were made for the humans. They did not work on the chosen the same. Their genetic code was slightly different than that of the humans, and the devices were blocked.

However, the mechanisms did achieve one of its goals in the chosen. It blocked their memories of the past. Without this, the beings had to begin all over in their evolutionary quest for spirituality. Without their true spirituality, the beings lost their sixth sense, perception. Loss of these two things made them almost like the rest of the humans.

Their true-identity had remained hidden. Their numbers were counted and documented, but as if they were humans. Their genetic makeup was almost exactly like the humans and the greed could not tell the difference. To them, they were all human. They were the elite, and all other beings were their slaves.

The chosen had not fallen into the technologies that brought down the rest of society. They had been ones to stay true to the land and their families. They had searched for the knowledge and spread it when found. The truth was there. The greed was just very good at hiding it and destroying it. The chosen had been with the wisdom so many thousands of years before, but the greed had reduced their spirits as well as the humans. They had enslaved both and worked them until all knowledge of their individuality was lost.

Now, twenty-two years after the extinction of the humans, the chosen were about to be reconnected with the heavens. They were about to know the truth again. The grip of the greed was finally going to come to a complete end. The wisdom was about to begin.

The oaks stood proud and true above the chosen. They all seemed to grow with the merging of souls between them and the siblings. The trees now seemed to be over five hundred feet tall and hundreds of feet across. The chosen, in their masses, stood in awe at what they were seeing. The trees looked like giant humanoid wooden creatures. Their movements were that of a man.

The three spoke separate words, but they flowed into one story. The sounds emitted from the winds created by the blowing branches. It formed a song of sorts that permeated the souls of all those present. All their senses could understand what the three siblings spoke.

The rumbling of the pyramid had eased up, but there was still a vibration that brought warmth and strength to the chosen. The voices coming from the three beings comforted the gathered. This is what they had come for. The truth. The story was told to the acceptance of all. They had no doubt in the three creatures. The knowledge had returned.

The One and its siblings communicated to the masses. "Now you know the truth. Now you can accept the knowledge. The feeling of being different your whole lives is because you were different. You intermingled with the humans but kept our bloodline pure from theirs. We were never human. You are Krakatoa. Your planet will be back in the next cycle of Venus. The time is very near. There will be very much preparation."

The sister spoke with the wind. The people turned their eyes to the massive oak in front of them. "In the beginning, your ancestors helped to heal the human sicknesses. They had been badly treated by many separate visitors that had come to enslave the people. One species of extraterrestrial, from a nearby solar system, had recently come to take slaves back home with them. They had taken an entire species of human from the planet. They had come more than sixty thousand years ago and remained for more than thirty thousand. They had made their settlement in what is now Bolivia and Peru. The stories of Atlantis come from these visitors. They had seen the advanced state of the humans in the region, and had bred many of their kind for transport back to their planet. They knew how to manipulate electromagnetic energy with matter and travel anywhere in the universe they desired. It was all set up on a grid, and these creatures knew how to read it."

"Over time, the humans had grown tired of the visitors and their many years of enslavement," the brother interjected.

The sister continued, "During this time, as had happened many times before, the humans had been slaves at first. However, they were a smart creature and would begin to get restless. They would learn to protest, and then the system would all come apart. This time, the visitors had to leave in a hurry. The Earthlings had made a device that they had learned about from their elders. A former intelligence had taught the humans about this device. The humans called it a Vebana in their crude language of grunts and gasps. It had all been prophesied that the device would be used in this era. The humans had destroyed the home base of Atlantis with this weapon. The visitors that had survived made a hasty escape. The humans had erred in their arrogance, though. It had happened over and over the same for their species. The device created a hole in the ozone layer, letting in toxic rays from the sun. Many of the population of the Earth died from space viruses. The ones that survived were once again infants, mentally, on this planet."

"By the time the chosen got here, twenty thousand years ago, the humans were on the edge of extinction," the brother spoke. "The healing ways of your people brought the humans back their strength. In the process, some of our knowledge was passed to the humans. Your ancestors had the gifts of flight and telepathy. Their knowledge of the solar system and this planet was genius. This wisdom was passed to each of their ancestors for thousands of years."

"The stories of flying Gods and many other legends of this planet originated during this time," the sister said. "Most of the new Gods of the planet were just our ancestors being worshiped by a people who were always desperate for leadership and salvation. The previous masses and their history were long lost to these current humans. They were looking for anything to show them the way."

The voice of the One flowed through the wind into his sister's words. "The chosen ancestors lived a simple life as do we. The gifts that they possessed were perceived as magic. Many of the kind were branded as shamans or witches. All had become creators in their own special way. All were very different than the human, but very respectful. The chosen never felt nor acted better than other creatures."

"The chosen helped the humans build temples to our universe and teach them a better way. They at first seemed to grasp the importance of what we were teaching them, but time after time they went back to their old ways of war, pestilence and greed. After a short time, the chosen decided to stop teaching the humans any new technology. They went their own ways and founded their own communities," the sister spoke with her voice of a tree, flowing in the wind.

The One spoke, "It all changed when the greed arrived. At first, the chosen had decided to remain invisible and see what would happen. The greed swiftly took control with no resistance at all from the humans or the chosen. The humans had seen the greed as Gods, coming down in their fiery chariots. Their flash and appearance made them look like super humans. Some were over twenty feet tall, and looked like statues of stone. These images solidified, in the minds of the humans, that the Gods had landed. The control had begun at that very moment.

"The chosen had seen it all and knew that these visitors were no Gods. These beings had a darkness about them that worried the chosen. They had encountered beings of this nature before. They would use a celestial look and big words to influence the masses. When they had all the inhabitants bowing to them, the masses could be easily enslaved. The chosen tried to get the humans to listen, but once again their words fell on deaf ears. In the minds of the humans, the Gods had arrived. In the minds of the chosen, they saw the error in their way. Not standing up from the beginning had cost them their freedom."

The brother continued the saga, "The masses had all been gathered up and implanted with the devices, as were their offspring for the next six thousand years. The devices did not control us, nor could they track us, but they did block our subconscious. That in turn blocked our memories, perception, and ultimately our spirituality. The magic of flight and telepathy that the ancestors had possessed had been taken away. All our magic had been stripped away with our imagination. There was still a connection, but the devices made it thin. This thread has been repaired. Now, it is the cable that it once was, connecting us back to the cosmos and Krakatoa."

The three siblings spoke as one to finish their dialogue. The people had been in a trance, faces pointed toward whichever tree had been speaking to them. "All of you here, standing around this pyramid, are the bringers of the word. The true collective is here. Now, we must separate for one last time. You will all go in the direction that your heart takes you and spread the words of truth. The wind that we have created in this triangle will follow you to the corners of the globe. Many are waiting to hear the story. The voice is here. Your magic is being restored to you as you listen to the wisdom. The vibration from the gold is dislodging your implants. Your subconscious is about to wake up and meet your conscious. It is our gift to you, the chosen."

The One stood strong as it watched the brother and sister diminish into their normal forms. As shape shifters, the beings had always been able to take on any appearance. Their use of another living creature made their shifting simpler yet stronger. The two would simply morph into one being, becoming one energy. Like using the branches and the wind to speak when in the tree form. The two twisted and turned and were in their human shape in moments. They stood tall in front of the massive oaks that had seemed to double in size from their original. The trees stood strong and proud with the departure of the alien energies.

The brother and sister were now emanating a blue and red glow from their beings. They each seemed to look like they had when the three were younger, in their twenties. Both had taken on the appearance that the One had always known them. Their pods they had used to get here were shed and now they were back in their natural form. They were tall, almost eight feet, and had long black hair to the waist. They looked just like they had when they were in their prime. The trees stood tall and strong behind each of the beings, like sentinels protecting their kin. They had merged their energies and shapes together. The two entities had become one. Their energies would forever be connected.

The One spoke for the last time. "You will know what to tell your fellow chosen when you meet them. We are all related, after all. We are all Krakatoa. Our spirits are reborn over and over to walk the same paths with our people forever. All the chosen are familiar to each other. Your powers will become one with you again. The collective will be growing stronger daily. My brother and sister will be going to their places on the globe. Some of you will follow them. Some will stay here to prepare. Others will be off to find the other chosen. There will be a triangle formed on this Earth between myself, my brother and sister. We all three will be building our devices to enlightenment. The devices will contact our ancestors from our not so distant home. Our contact will be reconnected, and once again, we will be One. The bond will be back. The devices will be seen by the greed, too, of course. They will know immediately that they are not the only intelligent beings left on this planet. They will send their craft, but it will be useless. Without their mind control and tracking, they will be weak and ineffective. This is when we rid this planet of the greed forever."

The chosen held onto every word the One had spoken. Memories of the ways of the past were slowly returning to their minds. Their thoughts, shadowed for so very long, were awakening. Repressed memories were flooding back in. Where their brains were only allowed to work at six percent capacity before, just enough to survive, now they were creeping up to one hundred percent. Everything was beginning to become as clear as the sky.

As the One and siblings finished their dialog, the trance of the chosen had ended. Every one of them sneezed at the same time, in the direction of the pyramid. The implants were gone with the force of the human sneeze. They hit the pyramid and bounced harmlessly next to its base. The gold completely shielded any transmission from the devices. The chosen all blinked and shook their heads. Their sinuses felt clear. All their senses worked, including the sixth and seventh, telepathy.

All the beings took flight at the same time. They just floated off the ground and elevated to the top of the pyramid. They formed a circle and kept it true as they ascended the monolith. The circle got tighter and tighter as the beings levitated to the top. There was a joy in their hearts that they had not known for so very long.

The truth flooded back into their conscious. It had been hidden in the subconscious for so many generations. They remembered all their past lives. They remembered Krakatoa too, and their wonderful lives there.

The One watched with joy in its heart. Its brother and sister were there, forming the circle of their people. Both beings had retained their original forms. They looked like twins. Both were with long black hair. Their features were almost identical. Even their auras were identical.

It had been many years since the chosen had been one with the wisdom. Now, they were complete again. Their strength was cosmic. It had all been written in the past so many times. Now their people were off to spread the word.

The brother and sister drifted off in the two directions. Their path would be a perfectly straight line on the map, straight to their destination. They too could fly but slightly different than the chosen. The One and its siblings took on the shape of huge condors and flew as high as they liked. They could travel very long distances just on the currents of the wind. They wouldn't even have to flap their wings. They were twice as large as a California condor, with wingspans of twenty-five feet. With their strength, they could travel great distances in a short period of time.

The pyramid continued to pulse a warm vibration. The One completed its transformation back into its human form. The being felt a power from the tree and felt a power in the tree. These wooded creatures had many different power points and sources. They held multiple auras. They were connected to the electromagnetism of the Earth.

The two had truly merged. They had acquired each other's strengths. The One glanced at its skin as it separated. It was veined heavily like tree branches. Its skin was moving, slowly morphing from tree bark back to tattooed skin. They both knew that they were going to be allies in the days to come. They understood each other. The respect had gone back to the beginning of the trees, their ancestors, and the One.

The One came out of its trance. The people were all gone, including its brother and sister. Not a single soul remained. The solid gold pyramid was still there, but it had shrunk down to a size of about three feet on each side. It was a mere model of the monolith that it had been moments before, when it had covered over five acres. The brother and sister were gone. They had taken their followers to the distant lands on the other side of the globe. Time was not calculated any more, nor was it important. The cycle was repeated every day, and all things were with the cycle.

The One walked to the pyramid. The golden object put off a glow encompassing the being. It felt the weight of the object pulling at its very soul. The One knew it was time to begin building the device. The time had come. The stars had been correct, like they always had been. The full moon shined bright and red, like it did every night now in the post greed apocalypse. A full eclipse was just ending. The One heard a gong, faintly being struck in the distance.

The One merged energies with the pyramid. The family who made the collective had found this pyramid many years before, when they lived on this land. The boy and his grandparents had located the gold, and the niece had helped dig it out. They had found buckets of the shiny stuff. While digging, they found a small pyramid shape buried in the ground. It seemed too perfect to be natural. They were very happy to find such a good strike. It was the one they were looking for.

As they dug, they realized that this was an object on a grander scale than had ever been found before. It was huge and it had a very strong pull to it.

They had planned on excavating the pyramid some day when there was more time. In the meantime, they enjoyed the vibes the monolith put off. They had resonated through the family, originally forging the One.

The gold was always the conductor. The energy from the family was very strong after the string of deaths in their family. All four of the beings had strong energy already, but after the tragedies, they had exploded. The gold and the pyramid melted those energies into the collective.

It had begun here, and it was going to end here.

CHAPTER 43

The One set about its task. Destiny had brought the being to this place, and Pachymama was the force. The One began to build. It had the knowledge of the pyramids and all other great monuments that had been built on this planet. The chosen had been great builders on their home planet of Krakatoa and had built beautiful monuments on this planet. Their knowledge, with that of the One, would swiftly get their devices built and operating.

The One and its siblings had also built many monuments in the past. They had no need for slave labor. They had learned to manipulate the electromagnetic forces of the Earth. Their minds and energy were all the three needed to build. The beings had built temples and monoliths out of many resources from the mother Earth. Coral, quartz, limestone, and granite, were the most common. Gold had become a byproduct of the riches the Earth provided. They had not taken the gold for wealth, they had used it in their temples and artifacts. They built things, just to create. Creating was being One.

The One had been in different collectives when it had been building its monoliths. It achieved its greatness from the unification of four beings. The One understood. It had walked the path for a very long time. The brother and sister, too, had the knowledge. Their beings were the change. They were the truth. Together, they were the wisdom.

The One and its chosen began to build a device that would defy the magnetism of the Earth. It knew about gravity and magnetism. They were the same thing, just slightly different principals. All things revolved around the same basics of magnetism. Everything had a positive and a negative charge. All things were held together with this invisible force. Magnetism was the glue of the universe. It was also a power that was not realized by less advanced species. It was a force that was to be respected.

First the pine trees were to fall for the timbers it needed.

The One reached into a pocket and retrieved a small device. The being knew that it was there without thinking. The object was a small metal piece of about one-half inch square and one quarter inch thick with a wire hanging off it. It was the artifact that the boy had found at the Mississippi Mounds. Back then, the family did not know what the object was; but now, the One fully understood.

As soon as the object was in the being's hand, the wire that hung from the object became one with the creature. The object molded itself to the hand of the One. A bright light came from its center. The One knew exactly what to do. It had used this device many thousands of years ago, and now it had returned. It was a saw of sorts. It could cut through anything.

The One held the device at an angle next to the first tree. The sun would reflect off the object when the being had it in the perfect position. The light reflected off the gadget was like a laser. The tree would simply fall over with a loud crash. There was no abrasive saw marks or smoke from heat. The light separated the particles in that one part of the tree, making its connection non-existent. It would create a negative magnetic charge in the void and the two parts would push each of themselves away from the other, like two dissimilar magnets.

There was no trauma to the tree at all, except for the cutting of its lifeline. The trunk would regrow in this way of logging. Within three years, the mighty roots would produce another tree, which would have already grown twenty feet. It was truly sustainable logging. All nine trees that were needed were swiftly dropped to the ground. The limbs came off with a swipe of the hand, leaving straight timber.

The greed had the same technology, but chose not to use it. They had no cares for the Earth nor its creatures. Wherever they went, they took resources. They had no time to replenish them nor show empathy towards any creature of a planet. They were takers. All that mattered to the greed was getting more. Restore was not in their vocabulary.

The One had brought the box that the boy had kept his collection in. It had been in the vessel the entire trip, and now it was in the hand of the truth. The key appeared in the fingers of the One, with magic, and it opened the small metal box. The glow from the eye on the lid of the container flowed through the being. The two were one. The small metal moons on each side of the box began to rotate. The One remembered this box vividly. All the memories had returned to the being after the collective. This box, and its contents, had been the only items that the three siblings had brought to this planet when they had arrived. Now, it held all the powers they would need to protect this planet.

The One used the other objects acquired by the boy to move the massive trunks into place. The stone with the sun in the middle was a transporter. Beings could move any object to any place with this device. It had been made by the greed. The One and its siblings were the only beings ever, beside an elite, to possess the device. The apparatus not only had powers, it was also a tracking device that the greed would use to follow the family, before they had become the One. They were not happy that the three beings possessed their invention. They wanted it back.

Miraculously, there was another of these devices that had crashed in a Texas field in the late eighteen-hundreds. The small boy who had remembered the ordeal of the invasion that night had found one of the sun stones in his pocket in the morning. He never showed it to anyone. He knew it protected him from something bad. In Roswell, when the craft had crashed on his land, the man had finally showed the object to another living being. One of the pilots from the crashed saucer. The extraterrestrial told the man to bury the device in a local lead mine. It would be safe there. The eldest son of these people, who was grown and in the Air force by the time of the Roswell crash, was the same man that the family had met at the Grand Canyon and along their journey.

The One knew exactly how to use the tool. The device spoke to the One. The being could see the words spoken to it from the sun stone. The One pressed the sun indentation from the stone against its forehead. The eye in its head cast a glow as the object neared. The stone stuck to the head of the One, amplifying the eye in the center of its being. It could see in a different spectrum. Other dimensions, alive and well all around, were clear. The One had become a part of everything.

The other device in the box was the metal tube they had found at some lava beds. As soon as the object was in the hand of the One, the magnetic force was complete. The metal object was powered from the sun stone and its energy. It could only be energized by a being with the knowledge. Now this tool was in full working order. The One easily moved the large logs. It arranged the logs in a position throughout the valley that had been told to it from inside. It knew exactly what to do.

The One erected the massive logs into vertical positions. They each stood exactly fifty feet tall. It positioned three in each spot to form a triangle that met at the top. There, copper wire was spun around to hold the three poles in place. They looked like poles set up for massive tipis. As the One had been transporting them, the trunks had been smoothed by the magnetic field they had been encased in. The bark and nubs of the branches had been stripped away. They were now smooth pieces of wood that tapered from the bottom to the top. When the being was done, the logs formed a perfect triangle in the open expanses of the valley.

A large piece of granite was the next thing to be cut. It was directly in the center of the triangle that the poles had created. Again, the device attached to the hand of the One was used to separate molecules in the massive stone. It was easily separated from the other stones around it. The One lifted the block of granite from the ground using the stone and the tubular device. The behemoth stone rose from the ground with a shaking and the sound of moaning. It was lifted by the being and its tools until it barely cleared the surface of the ground. Then, the One pushed its hands at the monolith in a sweeping motion. The stone glided hundreds of feet, just inches off the ground. It floated through the space like a feather, coming to rest on the far side of the meadow.

What was left behind was what the One had come for. In the hole where the granite had been, there was a solid core of pure quartz crystal. This single piece was over a hundred feet across and just as deep. It was perfectly clear and flawless. This stone had remained hidden from the greed for thousands of years. It was the final piece to be found. The One had known about its existence for a very long time. It is why the final collective was to migrate here so many years before. They had come to this place for a reason that they didn't understand. It had been because of this piece of quartz and the pyramid. This place had been spiritual to the One and its siblings. This was the place they had arrived on this planet for.

As the One worked, the animals of the forest came to keep it company. Fellow beings, the deer, bears, fox, coyotes, mountain lions, hawks, and many others came for the energy that was being created. They were all curious about what was happening in their forest. The One could now openly communicate with the other animals. They could speak with their minds. The third eye in the being's forehead was amplified by the sun stone. They were all part of the collective. They were all part of Pachymama.

The animals spoke to the One. They told the being about how they had been in fear of the humans for so very long. When the humans had first arrived, the animals had gotten along fine with them. They had interacted with them, like they had with all other beings. Then, over hundreds of thousands of years, the humans changed. They had been enslaved by species after species coming to this planet. They had changed and evolved with every visitor that had come and left behind some of their traits in the humans. The DNA of the people had been altered so many times during this period, the humans were no longer animals like the others on the planet. They were hybrids that did not fit in with all the other creatures.

The animals also knew and understood the chosen. The animals embraced these beings. They had shown empathy for the planet and all its animals. The chosen had been accepted by all creatures. The beings had been the only reason more of the animals had not become extinct. They had fought for the survival of all species while the human and the greed could have cared less about anything except for themselves.

The animals spoke to the One about an ancient creature who walked the planet. It was a creature that had bridged the gap between the animals. It had many names. All the native people had contact with this creature, as did all the animals. It was mostly known as Sasquatch. This creature was the one to keep peace in the entire animal kingdom. It was the judge of no creature. It was at one with all living beings. This animal was the true shaman of the planet for millions of years. The beings still are to this day. Their kind remained hidden for so long, in fear of retribution. They are the higher beings, which frightens other higher beings. Many visitors who came to this planet would never had let this species exist, had they known about it.

The animals talked about how everything had changed when the greed had arrived. They had persecuted the humans and the animals. The once proud creatures of this planet now cowered in fear. The greed had rained terror on all living creatures since their first arrival. They had destroyed our beautiful garden for their sick pleasures. The animals knew that it was a sickness that the greed possessed. They had been so ready to control the masses with sickness and addiction. Their kind had been suffering from it all along. It had made them weak. Most could not see. It was clear to the One.

The greed made the greed weak. It controlled not only the masses, it controlled the greed as well.

The One continued to raise the pillars and prepare them. The being could get the work done and communicate with friends all day long. The energy that the animals brought were a bright charge to the soul of the One. They had fed the being. The copper wire that the One had acquired on the road was now put to good use. It was wrapped around each pole, from the ground to the top. Ten layers was the desired wrap.

The metal rods that the being had acquired also were used. They were put in the center of the wooden poles, using the tubular device in the hand of the One. The object shot a solid beam of light and drilled a perfect hole in the middle of the poles. The rods were a perfect fit.

The copper wire outside, and the metal inside the wood, made a complete circuit. A chunk of gold in its raw form was taken from the bucket that had been mined many years before. All three varied in shape, but all were of a hand size, roughly twelve pounds each. Each gold nugget hung from the center of the poles. The copper wire suspended the nuggets and connected the gold to the rest of the device. All the poles were set at a slight angle, toward the center of their triangle. They were all leaning toward the crystal vein in the middle of them.

At the base of each device, the One placed an agate that they had gathered on the beach. The three objects created an energy within the crystal. The gold pyramid, to the side of the crevice, began to, once again, vibrate and hum. The object now looked like a doorway into another world. It didn't seem to be solid anymore, more like a portal of golden light. It gave off a warm glow.

The devices were complete. They were ready to power up with the energy created from the crystal.

The One knew that it was almost time. The others would be at this same stage. The being thought hard about its people. It was time to reunite them and fulfill the destiny. Mother Earth had spoken and told of the path. The One and its siblings were the healers. They had been sent long ago for this one purpose, at this very time, in the history of an ancient planet. Their time had finally come.

Night had taken the land. The moon lit the fire in the One. A lunar eclipse was slowly happening. It was the first time in six thousand years that a solar and lunar eclipse happened on the same day. Magic truly was returning to the planet.

The One held its ancient box in strong hands of stone. The moons on the outside once again spun slowly at first and sped up with the increase of intensity from the One. They would become crescent throughout the cycle of full moon, these little orbs. They were constantly changing cycles on the top of their enchanted box.

The One began to pulse a thought wave in all directions. It was like the aura of the One was reaching out to the chosen, amplified by the moons on the box. The first to hear were the three women who had traveled with the being to Crescent City. The leader heard the faint calling before any other being. She told the others to listen. Soon, the provider and the protector, too, heard the calling. They spoke to all the others. They, too, could hear.

The women gathered up the rest. There was no need to take things, the Earth would provide for them. The three had given birth earlier in the day. They had only been with child for five days, and now they were born.

The babies were like no other born of this planet in the past. By day's end, the three newborns had reached full maturity, and were now grown adults. There were nine of them. The women had each given birth to triplets. Six boys and three girls.

As the children had grown in one day, the women and their bodies also healed in the span of one sun cycle. By day's end, they were fully healed and on the road with their offspring.

The twelve would lead the group. The other chosen followed behind with joy in their hearts and song in their step. The time had finally arrived. They were now truly going to know the truth.

The One needed more help. The chosen were a kind species and knew about building things, but the One needed more. It needed thinkers on a grander scale and beings who could take charge when it needed to be. It was not thinking to put anyone or anything under control.

The masses might need guidance, though, and the One would need ambassadors to fill that role. The nine had been born for just this occasion. The bloodline was now mixed with the chosen. It was all part of the prophecy.

When the nine beings would arrive, the One would revere them for what they were. They were the new beginning of a time coming after the end. They were the ones who would ensure the evolution of all species. They were the evolution. The nine were to hold the greatest trust. The planet and the universe needed them at this very moment. Their path was clear.

CHAPTER 44

The sun cast a purple haze as it breached the mountain peaks. The aura from the One was still emitting like the pulse of the gong. The sound was permeating everything, as was the aura. The being could feel the chosen getting closer. The energy level in the One was high. It was waiting to meet the next generation. The feeling was the same as the family had felt when getting closer to the sister's house. As the family got closer, the energy grew.

For the first time since becoming the collective, the One felt an excitement. It was looking forward to what was to come. The truth became brighter as the beings got closer. It could sense their energy from hundreds of miles away. The One had even felt the knowledge of the birth of the children. They had all been born in unison. All three women gave birth to the first child at one eleven. The second child was born to all three women at two twenty-two. The third was birthed at three thirty-three.

The being had known the exact moment that the others had left the coast and headed southeast. They were connected. There was a bond of energy that was the same connection that a soul would have with its pod. These ten beings were all part of the Wisdom. The One felt the other nine like they were lightning bolts of energy.

One of the children was different, though. Its energy was either farther away, or it was not of the same caliber. This being part of the nine, was the One of their group.

The One prepared diligently for the arrival of the family and the others. Chosen from all over North America, they would soon be arriving. The word would be passed.

The brother and sister would be preparing for the same in the regions they were. The brother in Bolivia, at the ancient site of Tiwanaku. The sister in England, at Stonehenge. These were the first three places on the globe that the beings had inhabited after arriving on this planet. These had been their sacred sites ever since. They had built temples and monoliths to show their respect for Pachymama and the stars. At these sacred spots, the beings had become One with the Earth.

When the greed had arrived, the One and its siblings had to hide their sacred spots underground. A little manipulation of the electromagnetic field around these places, and their secrets were safe from the greed. The elite had found what was on the surface at these locations, but not what was beneath. The temples on top were built by visitors who had visited earth sixty thousand years before. This species, showing no regard at all, had built their temples on top of those already there. Ancient sites, built by countless visitors, were desecrated by this species around the globe. They had been a species of dominance. They came and took over, left their mark, and were gone. Just another visit from a wayward traveler who had decided to leave their signature and enslave the humans to do their bidding.

The One had known of the prophecies. It knew of the coming of the greed. The temples on top of theirs would further act as a shield for the truth. Watching them destroyed was meaningless to the siblings. The species who had built them were not kind souls. They had tried to dominate the planet, but Pachymama had revolted. A virus had sprung from the trees and wiped out many of their population. The humans had also tired of their enslavement and retaliated with a weapon that was far too advanced for their species. The remainder of the visitors had swiftly left, back into the cosmos of history.

As was the case many times in the history of the planet, the humans and other inhabitants were happy to see the visitors leave. Their visit had been a short one, but was long enough to enslave entire regions of humans. They were put to work building temples to destroy the history of Pachymama.

When these temples had been destroyed by the greed, the One and its siblings watched with mixed awareness of what was to come. They had known that these newcomers were not good creatures. They had come to control. They had annihilated the artifacts and history of this planet. The temples to the true God had been destroyed. It did not matter to the three; what was below was of far greater importance than the surface. The future of Pachymama was everything.

The One worked toward the mission. Three iron plates that were six feet in diameter each had been built from scrap that had been collected by the neighbors. The chosen had been busy in the absence of the One. They had known with an inner knowledge exactly what to acquire. The plates were placed in between the three sets of posts. They were placed exactly in the middle of the space, but more toward the center of the triangle, by over twenty feet. Their shape formed another triangle inside the triangle.

Many ideas and plans were coming to the being in its reverie. It knew the reasons. It would be impossible for any creature to retain all their information in the conscious alone. Some had to be stored in the subconscious. When information would be needed, the knowledge would return in a vision.

The biggest project this day was to get the wheel centrifuge working. It looked very makeshift, having been made of found items. The One was confident though; the device had come to it in a dream. The plans, blueprints, and complete operation had come with the vision. There was no doubt that it was going to work.

The hole where the granite had been being to be the setting for the centrifuge. The quartz would be beneath the device, providing the power needed to run it. It was simple; a wheel looking device held in position with an iron rod and capped with another wheel tilted on its side. They were situated at a ninety-degree angle to each other. The wheels were made of solid iron with small boxes attached to the spokes. They had huge rings around the outsides of them made of solid twenty-four karat gold. All four rings were six inches thick, two feet high, and fifty feet in diameter. The gold had been mined here so long ago and cached in a deep underground chamber. It, too, had survived the prying eyes of the greed.

While digging holes for its devices, the One found a vein of gold that was forty feet wide and over fifteen hundred feet deep. It was the most gold the creature had ever seen in its life. It had only been ten feet under the ground, but it had been hidden under a large boulder of volcanic rock. The volcanic rock itself was full of bits of perfectly clear quartz. It was in a pattern that was certainly not random. The entire vein ran more than a thousand feet long. The One knew this gold was here for a reason. It was in a line that was perfectly north to south. The line was straighter than nature could have possibly been. It was about two thousand feet away from the pyramid, but it contained much more gold than the monolith.

The device fit perfectly in the hole created by the missing boulder. It was set on the solid crystal below it. In between the centrifuge and quartz, the One placed the metal ball that the boy had found back in Texas. It had been in the corners of the box the entire trip, but now it was whole again. Now, it was the support for this massive electromagnetic machine. The entire contraption pivoted on the small orb. Now that globe was the conductor. There was only one of these devices in this part of the universe. It had been imbedded in the man for safe keeping.

With the help of the few chosen that had stayed to help the One, the last of the copper wire was wrapped around the wooden poles. The chosen had acquired large amounts of copper wire in the last twenty years. They had taken any kind of wire that they could find, and it was abundant. Without electricity nor the want of it, copper wire was everywhere.

The pine poles, covered in their wire, were finally connected at the top with strands of copper wire. The thinness of the strands, and the complexity of the weave, made it look like a robotic spider had made the connection. Strands of wire also hung to the iron plates, which were hundreds of feet away. The two metals made a connection like guide wires holding an antenna on top of a building. The only difference was that this was a conductor. The distance was massive. The amount of copper wire was thousands of tons.

The One could hear the rumbling coming from inside the poles. Electromagnetic energy was beginning to project into the air around them. The being could see the sun rays entering the triangles, bouncing off the pyramid, and reflect on the copper wrapped poles. The coils would pulse with added energy with the combined forces of the sun rays. The poles breathed with an energy fueled by forces of the cosmos. The One had known about the forces of the universe for eternity. Now it was putting that knowledge into action.

There was only one more part of the device that needed to be complete. The One held those in its pocket. They were agates that the family had found on the journey. Each of the four stones were in tune with the being that had found it, or it had been gifted to. Each of the stones looked like a small fossilized skull of an extraterrestrial species. Each of the stone's names was Toomey. The One held these stones close. They were the key to getting it all started. They had been allies of the siblings for eons. When the time came, all was ready.

It was some time before sunset, so the One decided to go fishing. There was a pond that was walking distance away. The collective memory remembered this spot. They had been there before. Some fresh fish for the arrival of the family would go over well. It would also give the One some time to reflect on the work that had been done in such a short time. The chosen had helped a lot, but the One had accomplished most of the tasks. It had known exactly what to do and had the tools to do it.

The centrifuge was built entirely by the One, using its cosmic devices. Some parts had been made millions of years before, while others had been built by the chosen. All parts were ready for assembly, with plans drawn from the being's dreams.

The One picked some blackberries and tubers to go with the fish. A few acorns and quail eggs, and the meal was complete. The family had liked to cook before, and now the collective was the same. The fishing had been wonderful. It was obvious to the One that the demise of the humans was beneficial to the other animals and plants. It had been good for the planet. There had been too many of them. At the same time, the One also thought that it had not been necessary to kill all of them nor other species.

The feast was prepared. The One had not used this dwelling in so very long. The being had created many things at this place. It was covered in paintings and other quirky art projects. The family had been creators. They had known the way.

Now, the old familiar barbecue was back in use. The mini keg had weathered the cataclysm and the weather. The smell of oak burning wafted from the top vent. The One was happy to be back to this place. It brought back good memories of a time so very long ago and again in the recent past. The One had begun here, millions of years ago. It had remained at this place while the sister went to England and the brother to Bolivia.

Just forty years before the change, the collective had returned to this place. As the numbers will always line up, and the cycle is always fulfilled, the family moved to this very same spot. They had been part of the collective for endless time. What had brought them to this place, to build a house, was the cosmic order of things. The emotional pain thrown at them was a test of their strength. It had been many events lining up to make the outcome the way it was. It had prepared them for what was to come. Their minds had been open. They could see clearly. They had gone on the journey to gain strength as the collective. On the coast, they had become the One.

All the events had been written like a novel in advance. This story had indeed been written in numbers billions of years before any of these species even existed. There had been just as many species then, maybe more. They, too, were in battle with each other at times and coexisted at others. It mostly depended on the demeanor of each species. One thing all the intelligent life in the universe had in common, was that they all liked to travel and inhabit other planets. The cosmic highway was full of more species of beings than there were stars in the sky. Extraterrestrial tourists were the explorers of the universe.

The sun began to set as the food was cooked. The One sensed eleven strong souls coming. Where was the ninth child, the being wondered. The answer came back to the One immediately. It had known all along. The being had been told the prophecy by the ancients, long before leaving its own beloved planet. It was more of a truth than a prophecy. The lining up of numbers to create the natural flow of things.

It could not detect the ninth child, because the One was the child. The child was the One. As always, things had come around full circle. The dimensions flowed through space and never stopped. The immensity of the universe was millions of times larger with all the dimensions which used the space as its own playground. The One knew the end was coming. It was the only way. Without the end, there could be no beginning.

The dimensions were beginning to come together in this little place in the mountains. They were crossing around each other throughout the triangle shapes that the One had created. The One could see it all. Dimensions were clear to the being. It could now see sixteen spectrums of colors. Beings were all around, invisible to most.

The stone, still attached to the head of the One, was all seeing. It was the truth.

All was about to come together. The One was ready, as were the chosen. They were ready to ride the waves of dimensions like a carnival ride if necessary. The One knew it was not going to be easy. Many bad things were going to happen. Many lives would be lost, and many would be betrayed. It was the way of the way. The story had been written long ago.

The One focused on the cooking. Its mind needed to be clear for the night and days ahead. Much energy was coming their way. Change was upon the creatures of the planet. Now was a time to relax the mind.

The fishing had been helpful. The One had caught twelve trout, all the fish weighed exactly three pounds. The One had cleaned the fish and fed the remains to a family of black bear that had taken up conversation with the One. They had enjoyed the extra fish that the One had caught, as well as the guts of the ones it was cooking. The bears knew this being. Their kind had stories of the One that went back to their beginnings on the Earth.

Now the fish were all wrapped and the tubers cleaned. The One was ready for this day and this moment. It was a favorite pastime of the family, barbecue. Now, their new family would be coming, and all would be uniting. When they arrived, the family tradition of this spot would be upheld.

The feast would begin.

CHAPTER 45

The One had built a bonfire near the house. Years before, the family had dug this fire pit. They had lined it with bricks from the brother's house. They had taken them from his house after he had died and made this monument in his memory. Every time they would bonfire, they would think of the brother and his family.

The fire lit the evening sky. The chosen had gathered around the warmth and reveled in the glow from the fire and the One. They looked up to this being. They knew that the entity said that it was not a God, but it was a leader. It was the leadership their kind had been dreaming of for thousands of years. It was the leader that was bringing them back to the beings that they had once been. All the things taken from them by the greed was being returned by the One.

The women were the first to arrive. The One had known they were near. It had felt their presence. The being had sent some magic toward the family, and a portal had been opened. Crossing through the wormhole, it took just hours to pass hundreds of miles.

The three arrived on horseback, without saddles. There was no longer a need for saddles. All the creatures were at one with each other. There was full trust among all beings. The women all wore flowing dress of cotton that had been tie dyed. Each of their dresses was completely different than that of their sisters. The women were individual after all. The One expected them all to be exactly who they were. The three wore fresh lilies in their hair, all a color to complement their skin. They flowed into the camp of the chosen like flower petals in the breeze.

The chosen, who were present, all stood in awe as the three women rode by. Their hair was long and flowing, intertwining with the colors of their dress. They revered the three as goddesses. Their aura was one of complete light and good energy. A few of the chosen dropped to their knees in respect, but the others around them would pull them up. These women did not want to be treated as Goddesses. They knew who they were and were not trying to be something more. It is one of the main reasons they had been selected by the One.

The leader approached the One first. She had been the closest to the being. Their bond stretched beyond the comprehension of time. Their souls had connected throughout many lifetimes, stretching eons. The two beings stood next to each other at the fire. They did not speak, but talked about so much. The fire was the conveyor of their words and thoughts. The crackle told the other exactly what needed to be said. Their minds flowed as one.

The provider and protector arrived a short time after. They had tended to the horses and acquired food for the group. It had been a long journey. Energy had been depleted. When the two women joined the other two, the circle was once again complete. They stood on each side of the fire, each facing due East, West, North and South. The provider gave fruits and cheese to the leader and the protector, but the One would have nothing to do with the nourishment. It had something far more important on its mind.

The three women ate in silence as the One chanted. It was a chant that came from the being's throat and resonated through the camp. The sounds coming from the being were mellifluous. The women stopped their feast to listen to the strange tune. The trees even seemed to take notice of the odd melody.

The eight-offspring arrived on the notes of this song. They just appeared and were there, in the glow of the fire. Their beings stood around the other four, slightly to the outside. They, too, formed a perfect circle. The One noticed the size of the beings. They were very large. All the newcomers were carrying gifts of the Earth. There was salmon, fruits, vegetables, bread, honey, and so much more. They had acquired these items from the chosen along the way. As they had passed by each community, they had acquired more chosen and more bounty of the Earth.

The One felt the hole in the circle. The being knew the answers to the questions, so therefore did not have to ask. The ninth child was still in the darkness, just beyond the circle. This being was a shy one. It had time for thinking and learning, and little for interacting. This being was on a mission, and there was no time to waste. The One called to the being to step into the open. While the others had all been about nine feet tall, this creature was the same size as a normal person. The One noticed as soon as the being stepped into the light of the fire, it was his doppleganger. This creature looked just like the One, and even had the same mannerisms. The One had known the prophecy, but seeing it was still amazing. The being was looking at itself.

The ninth child stepped into the group, completing the circle that had been formed. A light was projected from the fire pit, amplified into the heavens by the forces encircling it. The beings were all greeted warmly by the One. The entity was amazed at the size of the offspring. They had a knowledge about them, yet still a simplicity. They were humble and ready to absorb knowledge. There was extreme confidence, but not a thread of arrogance. There was a familiar closeness between these nine beings, their mothers, and the One. These souls had been with the One before. They had traveled together before on this planet. They had always been allies.

These beings had been originally orphaned on this planet more than one million years before. The One and its siblings had rescued them after the rest of their species had been killed upon entry into the Earth's atmosphere. These nine beings had been raised and befriended by the One and its kind. They had been in the human form when they had first arrived. They had lived for over a hundred thousand years on this planet before the humans had arrived. These creatures had stayed well away from the humans and lived far away from them.

The first human like creatures had been brought to this planet to mine a mineral that no longer existed. They had been thorough in their mining. The beings had been left behind when there was not a need for the resources of this planet anymore. The nine saw the whole evolution, revolution, and destruction of the humans over and over again. They had remained passive voyeurs of the destructive race. When the greed had come, they had hidden their knowledge and went underground. Their energy had been lying dormant in the sacred spot ever since. The sphinx held their secrets well.

The One had awakened these nine entities once again. The three siblings had been the ones to hide them when the greed had arrived. The being had been there at the end, now it was there at the beginning. The One had once again been their friend.

The feast the One had prepared was enjoyed by all. The thirteen beings sat outside under the stars, and feasted around the bonfire. The One refrained from the call of the food. Its mind needed to be clear of the clouds created by the stomach. The chill was kept down by the flames and set the mood for the story to follow. The chosen gathered around the family and listened with awe for any word spoken by the spiritual being. The food had been plentiful. It had come from all over the west coast. None of the people present could ever remember having a better meal.

The ninth child had slipped away during the feast. It did not need much food. Its mind was occupied with the things that had to get done. They were so close. The child had been cordial to the others and had a great respect for them all, especially the One and the leader. They were like parents to him, after all, in a cosmic way not understood by any but their circle. The child spent the time in the stream and any other place where the One had been building its devices. It knew exactly what to do with them.

The ninth child knew he was different than the others. He was born with a knowledge of the science of the universe. There were no mysteries to the being when it came to the planet or cosmos. It could also remember past lives, and go back to those lives. Or if it pleased, it could go to the future existences. It could learn so much about everything by doing this. It also understood quantum physics and knew how to put their principles into use. It was how the being could travel to its past and future lives. Math and the stars were built into the being like a computer. The knowledge of the wisdom was imbedded inside this creature.

The ninth child had a mission to finish. He had been the first to become One without the collective. The three siblings had been the combination of four other souls, making the collective. This child did not need the other three souls to be complete. This being was the Wisdom. It knew that the chosen were all going to be consolidated soon. Their energy was about to combine into less flesh pods with stronger energy. The knowledge would be extraordinarily high among these beings once they were the collective. It would be their true state. It is what they would have to become if they were to return to Krakatoa.

The child strengthened the copper tubing on one of the poles that the One had erected. One of the metal discs was also slightly adjusted. This being, too, had found some stones on the journey to Mountain Ranch. They were in the form of a skull, and were of a fine quality green jade. All three stones were the same size and shape, although they had been found hundreds of miles away from each other. The being pulled the stones from its pocket. They fit in its hand perfectly, so as not a bit of skin was showing through them or around them. They, combined, were the exact size as the ninth child's hand. The device began to power up when the three stones were held. The centrifuge in the middle began to slowly spin its wheels and dynamically move its weight. The child casually dropped the stones back into its pocket. It was not time for this yet. The destiny was being fulfilled, but there were things that had to be done first. The being had restraint. It was the only way to get exactly the outcome you were looking for, patience.

The ninth child had powers that matched those of the One. Its creation had been to help the One and in doing so, to help this planet. When they had arrived on this planet, the nine beings were apprehensive about their new surroundings. The three siblings had taken them immediately under their wings and befriended the newcomers. The ninth child had always been the smallest. The One and the boy had bonded like none of the others. They had walked the planet together for a million years as best of friends. Now the child understood. When they had been sent to this planet a million years before, it had all been part of this destiny. It was in the prophecy to meet the siblings and befriend them. Every event that had happened since their arrival, had been leading up to this event. Now was the true beginning. The end was very near.

The ninth child moved the angles of the wood columns ever so slightly. They were just a slight half degree off their intended position. Its eye could see the grid set up over everything. It started with the smallest grain of dirt and went all the way into the far reaches of the universe. Everything was a grid. That is why the numbers would always come up in conjunction with each other. It was part of the cycle of everything crossing paths on the grid of reality.

The ninth child thought about the One as he went about its work. Its mother, the leader, had spoken very highly of the One. The child knew that the being was not its father in a traditional sense. The One was his father in a spiritual sense. The two were One. The being had freed the soul of the nine from their long hiatus. All the memories were clear to the child. The entity cherished the friendship it had with the One and its siblings.

There was a coming together on the planet, and it seemed to be centered around the One and its brother and sister. The ninth child knew that it was a part of it, too. It had been having the same dream for the last six thousand years. The vision persisted since waking from its long slumber. It had been a vision of living in a garden again, a Garden of Eden. There was peace and no thought of violence nor crime. Religions had been done away with, and the people understood the true god. Earth. The planet had healed itself with the healing of its beings.

The ninth child continued its work into the night. It did not need light to help in its labor. The being had the vision of a cat. The oak trees swayed strongly as he worked. This was a task of the highest power. The ninth child knew of its importance and did not take it lightly. This prophecy was very old. Bad things happened if the prophecy did not get fulfilled.

The full, red moon was rising when the ninth child returned to the bonfire and the others. One of the chosen had made fresh peach pie. All the creatures except for the One were enjoying the desert. The One chanted its melody. It seemed to be calling to a force that only it could see. When the child approached, it knew exactly who the One was calling to. The being was speaking with its brother and sister, both halfway around the globe.

The child sat among its people. They, too, knew that the being was different than the others. This creature was like the One, but different than it at the same time. The family and the chosen saw something special in this being. There was a trust toward the child that was unequivocally genuine.

The One welcomed the ninth child back into the circle. A space had been empty next to the being for the whole night. It was awaiting this special friend. The One had many things to say to this creature. The ninth child took his rightful seat and the pie that was offered. He looked to the stars and ate the first pieces of the pie directly from the tin. The meteors were particularly active this night.

"What do you remember about your birth and your past?" the One asked the child.

"First," replied the ninth child, "you are not my biological father, yet you were present when I was conceived. You freed our souls. We had been trapped for so long in limbo and your collective, along with our mothers, brought us back into a flesh pod. Now we can walk amongst you, my friend, like it has been since the beginning. Our nine are ready for the end and anything you need from us. Once again, the beginning is going to be beautiful. Our nine are the first on this planet to ever be born of collective energy. Normally, a collective cannot reproduce, it is the way of things. This time was different. These days are different. This is the prophecy, and it will be what it will be."

The ninth child continued, "Our mothers believed that they had conceived and given birth to us in less than a week. They also think that we aged twenty-two years in just days. This is not true, though. Their memories have been warped. It was a different dimension that we had been conceived and born in. Your family had passed through the area all the years before in your car. You opened a dimension that had allowed our conception to come through. My siblings were born twenty-two years ago. They were the first and only chosen that have ever been born after the meteor strike. The conception was a prophecy from the ancients. Now, we are here to fulfill that prophecy."

"My birth had been different, though. I had been conceived at the same time as the others, but I had not been born until just a few days ago. I had remained a fetus inside my mother, the leader, for twenty-two years. All this time in the womb, I was in a different dimension almost every day. I had seen the truth of the universe and had traveled a few of its dimensions. I would die at the end of each of these experiences. Every day that my mother awoke, I would awake, too. She did not even know that I was still inside her. I was just a soul, flesh had not come to me yet. It is with these inter dimensional travels that I have already been born with the knowledge. You asked me how I was born, but I cannot remember. I know I was separated from the leader by a being that had come to our people. It had come in the middle of the night when the moon was just a sliver. The being had come to the leader, and I was joined with its pod. That being was you. We are now One, but we are two at the same time. Your species were here for so long, and you took care of me and my siblings. Once again, our energies are back where they had started. Our ending had come, now we can begin again. My father, though, and my mother, are a species long ago wiped from the history of the universe. When our people had come to this planet, it was the last-ditch effort of a species near extinction. All the other attempts at colonization had failed, including this one. Only the nine of us survived, and we were unable to carry on the bloodline of our people in the pure form. We had no choice but to mate with the humans. It was the only way our species could survive."

"Very well," said the One, "I see you already have knowledge. Do you know why we are here together, though? Two beings with great power who look exactly like each other, sharing the same dimension. Do you know that it is the first case in the history of the Earth that two doppleganger co-existed in the same dimension at the same time?"

"I have thought about this since our arrival," replied the ninth child. "Our energies have been superimposed on each other. We are One, but we are separate at the same time. Our paths can cross because I have a single soul, while you have four. If I had more souls, or you had less, we would not be able to co-exist. The consolidation of souls is coming back to the chosen. They will soon be going back to their normal shape. They will also be going back home. Their time on this planet is almost over."

"You have knowledge my friend" spoke the One. "There is more that you need to know about the chosen though. When they first arrived on this planet, each of their flesh pods held sixteen souls. It was the way for them to travel great distances with as many souls as possible. Colonization took multiple beings to make it work smoothly. After their arrival, the chosen had found suitable humans to merge energies with. They did not breed, they just became allies. Having been slaves for hundreds of thousands of years, the humans had revered the empathetic chosen as Gods, and let them into their communities. They were still a very barbaric people, the humans. They had been civilized and decimated time and again by visitors to this planet. The chosen selected a people of Mesopotamia, who called themselves the Annunaki. The chosen had used the pods of these ancient people to fill with their souls. A neighboring tribe of humans, the Aliouninions, were chosen for the next round of separation and now each chosen held four souls. This had been in North Africa. Two other groups of chosen found themselves on other parts of the planet. One group was in Peru and the other in Cambodia. They, too, had merged their souls with those of the local inhabitants. When the greed had arrived, the chosen had split their souls into one aura for each flesh being. This way, they would be able to fit in with the humans easier and not be detected. They had merged with the Egyptians, Chinese, and Rapa Nui in this era. The chosen had already built their temples thousands of years before, and traveled the planet in exploration. The humans had naturally migrated to these monoliths built by the superior beings. They had built their cities and communities around those of the chosen. The chosen did whatever they could to keep the humans away, but whatever it was, it was not enough. Now, the chosen had been mixed with the human for so long in their single soul existence, they have lost touch with who they were and where they are from. The chosen had known they were different than the other humans, they just didn't know why."

The One continued its story. The ninth child was sitting close to the being, listening to the words spoken. The child knew all this story and so much more. It didn't want to interrupt its friend. The child also knew that the other chosen were all within the circle, listening closely to the words of knowledge that the One was speaking. The only other sound of the night was the popping of the fire in the pit. "There were three groups of eleven thousand one hundred eleven chosen who arrived on this planet. Each of those beings had the wisdom of the heavens. As their souls went in different directions, so did their knowledge. That is why you see so many familiar faces out there. The souls of the chosen are all tied together like a spider web covering the planet. They are all truly connected with their main souls. Theirs is a race of One."

The group sat silent as the One spoke. The story was about to unfold. This was the key to their existence, and the One held the wisdom. Their people had been robbed of the knowledge that had once been theirs. The greed had taken so much from everything. History, creativity, and hope was all stolen. It had been replaced with fear. It was the way of the control. Now that fear was being returned to them a hundredfold.

Now the chosen were ready. They, too, like all creatures of Pachymama, had it bad under the control of the greed. Now it was all changing.

First, the knowledge would feed their enlightenment. Once they were enlightened, they could once again walk the planet with wisdom in their beings.

Once again, they could be whole.

CHAPTER 46

"**A**s we sit around our fire, there are other chosen who know the truth. They are spreading the knowledge across the globe. There are others preparing, just as we are here. They have made the same devices as we have built here. As we gather at the flames, so are they. Their story begins exactly when ours begins. The chosen are a species of One. All are about to see the connection they hold with their fellow chosen," the One spoke. It paused while poking at the fire. Shapes had been forming in the smoke and flames, twisting in their own existence. All the beings around could see. The One was stirring up spirits in the bonfire. The being was speaking to all creatures.

The story began: "The chosen come from a planet that also orbits the sun in this solar system. This planet is called Krakatoa. This word has popped up in human history on occasion, but it had always been a mystery to the humans. The word had been lost in the tyranny perpetrated on the planet. A memory that had been taken away by the greed. Krakatoa and Earth are only visible to each other every five thousand two hundred twenty-two years. At one time, all the other planets in the solar system had intelligent life. The planets had an alliance. Resources and knowledge were shared freely among worlds and species. Earth was the only planet that did not join this alliance. The intelligent beings on this planet were slaves to whatever being came along. The other planets watched as visitor after visitor came to the blue planet, and took away what they wanted. The alliance had made a pact among themselves to let all planets and species evolve naturally. The Earth was left to its own destiny. The humans were the youngest, in terms of evolution, among the intelligent beings in the solar system. They had not progressed intellectually yet. It was an experiment by the alliance to watch the humans evolve. None of them knew what would happen."

"The alliance became distraught with the idea of so many visitors coming to the Earth and taking advantage of its people and resources. The humans were not having the chance to evolve naturally. Whenever they were left on their own for any amount of time, they would make progressive results with their evolution. When they would begin to thrive, another species would come and destroy everything they had worked for. It had been like this since the humans had arrived on this planet, more than nine hundred thousand years before. Other species of hominids were already present on the planet when the humans arrived. They had been leftover species of other planet's beings who had mixed with the creatures of the Earth, making hybrids. These were the first creatures to walk upright at this period of the Earth's history. The planet has a much deeper and ancient history. It has been used as a base by extraterrestrial beings since it first cooled, more than three billion years ago. These varying species all left a little seed or something behind. The Earth has changed geologically many times since, altering the face of the planet, and the life on it. Many times, in its history, the planet was struck by objects from space. They had destroyed the planet time and again, but had also seeded it many times in its long history. Life had been on Earth for billions of years. At times, that life had been very intelligent. Other times, the inhabitants favored war, while at others were like primates. Whatever the case, trillions of species of creatures had made Earth their home at one time or another. Nothing was left of these early Earthlings; the changing planet had erased all memory of them and their kind."

"Almost twenty-one thousand years ago, the alliance was done watching the Earth being taken advantage of. This is when they made up a plan. When Krakatoa passed near Earth on its next cycle, the chosen would hop onto the blue planet and provide a little extraterrestrial help. The beings of the solar system knew that the only way to enlightenment was through creativity and imagination. Their hopes were that the chosen would bring this to the humans of Earth. The chosen were selected because of the shape shifting characteristics and their emotional yet rational ways. The craft were sent out, and they landed on the sacred spots. The energy grid of the Earth had long ago been mapped by the alliance. The chosen landed on three of these spots."

"The chosen eventually broke into twelve different tribes around the planet. The solar system is comprised of twelve bodies. The twelve tribes began to build monuments to the heavens. Each of the groups were in tune with a certain celestial body. Its temples and monuments would reflect these connections. After the ice age, the people began to connect with the chosen and learn some of their ways. It was now that the humans had learned farming and cooking from the chosen. While the humans were busy with their chores, the chosen built their temples. The people gladly gave the chosen whatever they needed. They eventually saw them, not as Gods, but more as brothers that they looked up to. The chosen had taught the mortals that all beings had their own place in the cosmos. Every being had a purpose, and that purpose must be fulfilled. Eventually, the humans understood. The chosen had taught them respect. They could now grow as a species. The humans took care of the chosen, while the chosen took care of them in return. Both species treated the other with respect. The chosen also taught the people language, music, and culture. The humans were truly becoming intelligent and civilized. Life was euphoric for four thousand years. The humans had grown into a species of beings who could be trusted. The war that had been prevalent in the past was a thing of history. Goddesses ruled the planet, in touch with the stars, the seasons, and all the people. The women gave birth. They were the true creators in a species of creators. All beings during this time lived in harmony. Creativity propelled the humans faster towards their evolution."

"Twice in this time, visitors from Krakatoa had come. Their mission had been to reassure the chosen that they had not been forgotten on this planet. Their souls were one of rebirth, over and again. The souls of the chosen were the same as had originally come to this planet. They loved their planet and remembered it fondly. The visitors would also bring news about the home planet. Communication had been banned from the chosen. The alliance had not wanted the humans to know that these beings were from elsewhere. It could have disrupted the entire evolution at this early junction of the human species."

"Everything changed with the arrival of the greed. They were not content with taking over Earth. They had already visited every other planet in the solar system. They had destroyed the alliance. All other life in the solar system was destroyed by the greed. They had been watching this sun and its orbs for a very long time. They had witnessed what the other planets had to offer, and they would take it. That job would be much easier after they got rid of any life forms that might put up resistance to their plan. Then they could seed it with their slaves and genetically mutate any species which might have survived. It would take many thousands of years. Planets that had once thrived with life were now wastelands. Some were turned into giant balls of toxic gas. Whatever it was, the Earth was left an orphan."

"Krakatoa was saved. The greed had not seen it when they had been scouting the solar system. The massive green planet was on the far side of the sun, out of reach of the greed. It had been fortunate for the chosen. They were not equipped for war. Neither was the alliance prepared for a war of that magnitude. The greed had come from a wormhole, through a black hole. They had come from Orion and swept through the solar system with their advanced weapons. They had researched each planet, and figured out the best way to destroy each without destroying the resources. Mars was hit by a small device that destroyed everything on the surface of the planet. It had become a rocky desert overnight. Jupiter was hit with a device that changed its oxygen rich atmosphere into helium. Its beings had all suffocated. Pluto was struck with a device that turned it into a solid block of ice. Every planet was hit with a diabolical weapon. The greed had no empathy. They lived to see the misery in others."

"Earth had been saved purely out of recreation for the greed. They had briefly come to this planet once, many millions of years ago. Another species had been in control and they, like the greed, were very adept at war. After many battles and skirmishes, there obviously was not going to be a winner. The greed, being the newcomers, made a treaty with this species and went on to the next solar system. They had remembered the humans from their earlier encounter. The people had joined with their masters and fought against the visitors. The greed had not taken kindly to an inferior species such as the humans waging war with them. They had promised themselves that they would come back someday and handle these anthropoids. That day finally came, six thousand years ago."

The last passing of Krakatoa was uneventful. The planet sent no emissaries this time. They were in fear of being discovered by the greed. The Krakatoans had watched the greed destroy their neighbors less than one thousand years before. It had not been a nice thing for them to see. They had been helpless, as they observed the slaughter. The chosen had long ago devised a means of cloaking their planet. The device had worked well. The greed had no idea that there was another celestial body in this solar system. When it had been closest to Earth, Krakatoa was less that one hundred thousand miles on the far side of the moon. This was the prime spot for the beings to travel between planets. This traversing of planets was not possible with the greed in control of Earth. They would detect the visitors from Krakatoa and destroy their planet."

"The chosen remained passive for thousands of years. They watched as the greed controlled the minds of the humans and their own. They also lived among the humans, away from the prying eyes of the elite. The greed were the rich men, who held the power on this planet and made all the rules for everyone else. They had destroyed so much in this solar system and throughout the universe. The solar system, however, had been around long before the greed, and it would be around a long time after they were gone."

"Earth aligns with Krakatoa in three days. It will only be visible to us for twelve days, and then it will be gone for another five thousand two hundred twenty-two years. We must be prepared for its return. Our beings, here now on this spot, are going to combine energy with the others, and we are going to stop the greed. Their time on this planet and this solar system is well worn out. We are going to restore both to their healthy ways of peace and harmony. Then, our people can live freely again without the worries of a destructive breed."

"We will be calling with our signal. We are going to broadcast to the greed where we are and what we are about. They will come to destroy us, but it is not the way. Our power is strong. The destiny has been written so many times over and over. The outcome is always the same. The light is always more powerful than the dark. Our power is strong. It is the strongest collective that has ever been assembled against the greed. The full collective is all the living creatures on this Earth. We are now united. Soon, we will be reunited with our fellow planet. The healing has begun."

The ninth child spoke, "There is just one thing that you are leaving out, my friend. When the greed came to this planet, they came as light. They came with the brightness of the stars. The humans were fooled into thinking that they were Gods, because they were the light. They had masqueraded themselves as the light. They had in truth, come from the darkness. Their black holes that they manipulated were the darkest places in the universe. Of course, the humans, being a young species, did not know this. The chosen did, however. Their species knew exactly where these beings came from, and how they came as the light out of the shadows. They could have changed things then, but did not. Now they will be getting a second chance. Now, we will be relying on their species like never before. Now, this planet is going to be cleansed."

The ninth continued, its voice never changing its pitch, "The stars are all aligning again. Our time is here. The path is clear. Let's join hands now and rejoice."

The thirteen beings held hands around the fire. Electricity passed through the union. The group began to sing. A gong echoed through the night, resonating its melodious tone.

The chosen, gathered around the thirteen, began to sing along with the beings. Their numbers were an example of all people of the Earth. Every color, sex, and height was present. The chosen had understood the power of One. One meant all beings. Color of skin was meaningless. Color of the aura was everything.

Light flowed from each of the beings. Their auras united. The One and its twelve watched the aura dance through the air like the northern lights. The being and its kind knew. The chosen were there. They once again held the wisdom.

The gong made the rhythm, the voices made the song.

CHAPTER 47

The thirteen beings sang all night. Their dulcet punctuated the darkness with the gong reverberating in the distance. At daybreak, they could see their breath in the cool air. The chosen had chanted along with them, but the others had one by one made their way to shelter. The summer days had been very hot, but the nights were cool. None of the chosen were prepared to be outside in those conditions. They had returned to the comfort of their abodes.

The few that had stayed all night would later go back and tell the others about the spiritual awakening that had happened.

Sometime in the early morning, the gong had abruptly stopped its ringing. The sound had been constant all-night long. At the exact moment that the gong stopped, so did the singing. Light rays came from the twilight and covered all the beings present. The sky was a complete rainbow of color stretching from horizon to horizon. The colors coated every surface touched by the morning dew.

The chosen who had remained behind would later tell others that they had been touched by the Hand of God. They had been shown the universe and its complexity. They had been enlightened.

At the request of the One, the women formed a triangle around the being. The nine children formed a circle around the group. This was the ancient symbol of the universe. The One and its siblings knew well the ancient meanings of this pattern. "This is how our monuments had been originally configured," the One said. "Stonehenge, Tiwanaku, and here, Mountain Ranch, are the monuments we make with our beings. These are ancient to our people. Concentrate now, hard, and bring our energies together. We are all one being. It is time to come together once again. It is time to believe."

The Earth shook and began to fall away under the thirteen beings. The soil seemed to liquify along with its rocks and drain into the center of the Earth. More than fifty feet of soil disappeared in the chasm created by the planet. The thirteen beings were left standing on stone pillars; each of them on their own column. The stanchions had been made by the One so long ago. Millions of years ago. It had used its technology of electromagnetic forces to quarry the stone and build this temple. The entire structure went below ground for hundreds of feet and was over a thousand feet across. The part they were standing on, was only the top. It was a perfect replica of the entire Solar System.

The air pulsed with energy. There was a powerful light coming from the chasm that made it seem as if the Earth was emitting sun rays. The sky was a pure blue tone. The ground shook gently under the feet of the beings, making the columns sway back and forth slightly. The beings were all about forty feet apart from each other.

A large brown crow flew overhead. The One saw the bird with its third eye before catching sight of the creature. When the being looked to the sky, it was already greeting an old friend. The crow and One held each other's gaze for over a minute. Suddenly, the bird swooped down like it was going for some prey. It caught its large wings about twenty feet from the ground and softly fluttered down to the shoulder of the One. Both creatures had a deep respect for each other. Both had walked this planet many times before.

The One understood the crow, just as it understood all creatures. They too had a soul, just like the chosen and the humans. When the pod would be depleted, the soul would be reborn into another pod of the same species. Different species were never mixed. The soul you had was the soul you were to be for eternity. Unless your soul was destroyed or even worse, captured. Like the humans. Energy did not die on its own, but it could be destroyed or absorbed.

Some souls would cross paths with familiar souls throughout lifetimes. Therefore, it is why some people looked so familiar at times. All beings had a family, they remained with that family for eternity. The paths created by creatures with common DNA was forever bonded.

The chosen began to arrive. First, the ones who had slept earlier, the night before, came out to see what they had missed. Some spoke of regret for the things they had slept through. The ones who had stayed put them at ease with the talk of so much more knowledge to come. They had missed some, but little compared to the next days. This group gathered in a large circle around the thirteen. The energy was becoming complete. The rest of the chosen arrived. They did not trickle in or stroll up one by one. Their mass came all at the same time. The hillside had been covered with the souls of all ten thousand of their beings. The one thousand, one hundred and eleven that were here already completed the group. These were all the original souls that had landed on this spot twenty thousand years ago. They had come back. Now they were reunited.

The creatures had rejoined their collective and became one being again. Their destinies had put them with the right people that were the original parts of their overall aura. When they had split their souls all those years ago, they were still connected to each piece of it. The numbers brought them all together. They were once again at their original power and knowledge.

When the beings had separated, it had been out of friendship at first. They had helped the humans and built many communities and temples. Then, they were forced to split under the control of the greed. The more pods that their souls inhabited, the less knowledge each of them had. When they were split into sixteen souls, they were no more intelligent than the humans. The difference was, though, the chosen always had a great empathy for all creatures and the Earth. Much more than the humans ever had.

These chosen had come from all over North America. Along the way, the souls had become the collective, just as the One had become. These beings had acquired the power of their people back. They had not known this power and knowledge since just after their arrival on the planet. Now they were whole again. Now, they could mend this planet and maybe even go back to their own. It was coming by in three days, the One had said, and they would love to skip over to it. Earth had lost its appeal to the chosen. They were ready to leave it behind. This experiment was over.

Light trails followed the chosen on their path, as they crossed over every hill in every direction. The sky lit up with solar flares that none of the chosen had ever seen before. There seemed to be fireworks coming from space. They would burst in the sky, these fireballs of light. When they exploded, there was a light like the sun had been brought to Earth. The intensity was for the briefest of moments, then it would fade away. The sky was alive with countless numbers of these fireballs.

The chosen pulled closer to the monument and the beings perched on top. Their recollections of the past had all been coming back to them. The blocks put in by the greed mattered no more. The chosen now knew who they were and what their purpose was. They were now reunited with their original clan. The same beings they had come to this planet with so very long ago.

Other creatures began to arrive. The crow had been spreading the word among the animals, as the chosen had been spreading the word through their own kind. A lost tribe of very early beings arrived. They had been a hominid species but had come from nowhere near where the humans had come from.

This humanoid creature present now had been different. Its species had come to this planet hundreds of millions of years before. Their kind had walked with the dinosaur. They were the oldest intelligent species on Earth. They had remained hidden on this planet for so many moons. Throughout their history on Earth, the being had seen countless visitors come and go. Most had found the Earth not to their liking or unable to support their species. The ones who had stayed behind had generally been bad for the planet. These creatures knew of the dangers of the visitors. They had come from a very distant solar system in a far-away galaxy. From the beginning on this planet, they had been healers. They healed other beings and the planet. They were the Sasquatch.

They had known all about the parasites from the greed's previous scouting visit. The Sasquatch knew well to remain hidden. They already had problems with humans over hundreds of thousands of years. The humans thought it a good time to hunt these creatures. They did not eat them, the humans killed the Sasquatch just for bragging rights. The beings had remained hidden from the humans, the chosen and the greed. The grays had encountered these beings many times but had left them alone. The Sasquatch was a powerful creature. It had shape shifting capabilities and could cloak itself.

Millions of years before, a few of the beings tore apart five grays one night. The Lunarks were trying to experiment on a young Sasquatch, and some of its kin had sneaked up on them. They had torn the grays apart. Only small pieces of skin and their cartilage exoskeleton, in millions of pieces, was left. The Sasquatch had sent a definitive message to the Lunarks. They were not to be experimented on. The grays had shown nothing but respect to the Sasquatch ever since.

The chosen knew very little about this creature. Their contact had been very sporadic and accidental. The Sasquatch could detect the difference between humans and chosen. Their auras were completely different, and the chosen did not smell like the humans. All the chosen really knew about the Sasquatch was that they were a gentle species who wanted to be left alone. The chosen had done exactly that for the last twenty thousand years. Never once did they attempt contact with this mythical beast. The Sasquatch had remained hidden from the chosen only because they lived among the humans. They were concerned that their identities would get out through the chosen.

"We are all gathered here now. All the creatures from this area of the planet are represented here." The One spoke from its perch in the center of the massive monument. "Many changes are coming our way. We will be a part of it all. Before we continue though, there is one more history that we must hear. It is the story of this planet which is known by only one creature. Now it will tell its tale. Now, we hear from the Sasquatch."

The leader of the lost tribe appeared next to the One. The crow cawed its call as a welcome to an old friend. Unlike the chosen, the One was very familiar with the Sasquatch. Especially this one. When the One and its siblings had first arrived here, the Sasquatch had been a mentor in the ways of the planet. The beings had quickly realized that the One was not like other visitors. They had not come here to rape the planet. They had come here to coexist with the other creatures. The One and its siblings understood all beings, including the Sasquatch. The two clans had built a friendship that had lasted millions of years. They had been witness to so much evil on this planet together. They had to endure the sights of so much death and darkness while being unable to do anything. The prophecy did not allow it.

A strange aura surrounded the Bigfoot. It was flowing like serpents and pulsed with a pattern that seemed binary. The richness of its aura surrounded the ten-foot tall behemoth. The Sasquatch spoke in a language unknown to the chosen. The being made guttural sounds with its throat, which came out more like grunts and whistles. The chosen, however, could understand everything the creature was saying in their minds. All the beings present were facing the Bigfoot. The Sasquatch began its story.

"Our species came to this planet, which we call Pachymama, over one hundred million years ago. When our kind first arrived, the planet was full of life. Dinosaurs roamed freely among the evergreen forests. The climate had been a little warm for our species, but we adapted. Our planet had been dying due to overpopulation. It was not our species that were overpopulating. We had been on that planet for over one billion years and treated it as the God that it was. A different species had arrived and decimated our planet. They had been reptilian creatures who sucked the life from our garden and enslaved its beings. There were hundreds of intelligent life forms on our planet when they had arrived. Within ten thousand years, all had been enslaved except our species. The visitors had encouraged procreation among our different species, and they had succeeded. Within a very short cosmos time, our planet was destroyed by overpopulation. It became a wasteland. War, never even known before, became common when the resources became less. The visitors had simply watched it all while they were gloating extravagant lifestyles in the faces of the slaves. When it was over, they boarded their spacecraft and went to the next solar system. These visitors are the same ones who now have infested this planet. They were and are the greed. They masquerade as the light, but they are some of the darkest beings in the universe. Pretending to be Gods is just another of their evil ways. These parasites have once again ruined our way of life. This time, on Pachymama."

"On our home planet, we were the only ones who had seen the destruction coming. As creatures of the forest, we watched as so-called civilizations came apart and destroyed each other. We had all shared the technology as a unified planet. Every species, and our planet, benefited from any breakthroughs in science or any other facet of a productive collective. The collective had been strong. We had built ships that could go far into the universe but had voted against traveling and exploring. Our own solar system was large enough that we did not need to search for more. We did not desire control nor riches. We were also a gentle planet who had no ambition of spreading our influences elsewhere. We took care of our solar system and it, in return, took care of us. This went on for more than a billion years. We lived on a virtual utopia. It all changed the day the greed arrived. We were not prepared for the space craft and their weapons. They had struck the planet quick and controlled the masses from there on out with fear. The greed had learned long before that fear was the best control weapon of all."

"Our planetary collective had discovered worm holes and had mapped them out and the entire universe they were a part of. They had seen what was beyond the universe even. This collective used all the energy from our planet and its beings to focus and meditate as an entire group. Not a single energy was left out of these meditations. Our planet was truly One with all the beings at the same time. The collective subconscious was very strong. We had learned to bridge the gap between conscious thought and subconscious thought long before. Our planet was one of intellects. They were ones to solve problems and learn about everything. The subconscious took the collective to all reaches of the cosmos. This is how they had mapped out the universe. Basically, they had meditated as a planetary group."

"Our ancestors had chosen the best spots for our new habitation in the universe. We were not ones for war, so they had decided to protect a few with escape ships rather than fight. There were multiple galaxies, and most of them had life or could support it. They, however, were looking for a planet that was relatively young and whose inhabitants were not of a higher intellect. They wanted a place where they would not have to be worried about being exploited by a so called superior race."

"Before the control of the greed was complete, the elders sent twelve ships into wormholes. The wormholes they had discovered threaded through parallel dimensions. They were the fabric which made up black holes. They were just large interwoven tendrils of wormholes. Through these portals, beings could, and did, travel throughout the universe, and even time. It is how the greed also travels. Our group, one of the twelve, ended up on this planet."

"When we arrived, our people decided to live like we always had. Hidden in the forest. The dinosaur and other animals had been dangerous at first but we quickly learned their ways and befriended them. They became our allies and protected us against the constant visitor from space. The wormholes were busy places. We used stones for our monuments, which were tributes to our species. We had no use for possessions. We lived in small communities which easily blended in with the forest. We also had a way to blend into our background, making us invisible to all but a few creatures. There were only one thousand one hundred and eleven of us when we arrived. We had dispersed immediately upon our arrival and spread to all parts of the globe. This was a time when all the continents were very close to each other. Ice and our uncanny swimming abilities had made it simple to cross to whichever land we desired. Our species procreated, but at a slow pace. We had learned from the mistakes on our own planet and did not want to make a repeat. We had never been ones to overpopulate, anyhow. Even when the rest of our planet was falling into the ways of the greed and overpopulating, our kind stayed the same, and hidden. More than ninety percent of our kind had still been decimated by the destruction. The other ten percent was all that was left when we departed our twelve spaceships."

"Many beings have come to visit on this planet. Most have left within a couple thousand years, but others stayed much longer. A few had come and never left. A couple species had brought with them weapons that had destroyed most living things on the planet. After there was no resistance, the beings would come in and take a mineral known only to their people. It sometimes would be in small quantities and others plentiful. It would always be highly prized by the beings."

"All of the beings that had come to this planet had left something behind with them. A seed or a new species, subspecies, or any other mutation. Some had spliced DNA with beings from this planet while others had mated with some species. Many had brought the food of choice on their planet to begin their new life on this planet. We, the Sasquatch, just sat back and watched it all. We kept a written record of the entire history of this planet as we saw it. From the perspective of a creature who wanted nothing more than to survive and think. We never intervened, nor connected with any creatures who had come here until the One had arrived with its siblings. They had detected us, even in our cloaking mode. They had approached us with the wisdom, and we had warmly accepted them. They have remained our friends since. The prophecy tells of this time, with our beings as one."

"About one million years ago, a species arrived in a large spacecraft and began to orbit Pachymama. The entities from this orb began to experiment with the creatures of Pachymama. These beings were of a scientific species which collected data on the beings of the universe and profiled where these beings could be adapted to. They would take their DNA to different solar systems and implant their experiments on each planet and moon. Then, they would watch and monitor the effects. They would come back over time and monitor the progress of each creature that they had created. The superior beings would be taken aboard large craft to the place where they would be sold as slaves. These creatures had slave gardens growing all over the universe, and would use them to fill their demands. They had come to this solar system with their experiments in mind and went about their task unimpeded. They genetically changed some animals which created an effect the humans called evolution. They captured some gorillas, monkeys and other hominid species that had come to live on this planet. The humans had been born. The visitors had not been able to see our species so we had remained safe. They were not ones to discount nor take lightly. These scientists did not care one bit about their experiments nor the outcomes. They just wanted to see what would happen."

"The terrestrials never departed this solar system. Their glowing spacecraft in the sky is a constant reminder of their presence. They brought many of their creations back with them but left some behind for future purposes. The human creatures populated at a rapid pace and could be harvested often. The Lunark used these harvested slaves to mine the helium three from the surface of the moon. They would also use them in trade to other species throughout the cosmos for whatever they desired."

"The humans also mixed with some of the other hominid species, and there were then sixteen humanoid species on the planet, including us. We are not human, but we do share a common thread of DNA with the species. The population of the planet was brought to near extinction countless times because of cosmic wars and natural disasters. The humans thought they owned the land when they were free. Their mindset had become like the greed that had controlled them off and on their whole existence. All they owned was their own arrogance. If they would have been united and used the collective from the beginning, the species may have had a different outcome. They had been strong and forceful toward the others in their species, but when visitors from space came, they had bowed down and were enslaved with the wave of a hand. Countless times these beings had been enslaved by greed. Visitors from other planets all had come for their own reason. Some for vacation, others mined, while others used the resources for sports. Whatever their purpose, greedy creatures always needed servitude."

"The other planets in the solar system were also seeded with this DNA. They had all evolved in their own way, and some already were populated with intelligent beings. The scientists had to hide their arrival at these planets. Secretly, they would abduct the citizens of each planet and insert their DNA in each of them. A few planets had detected the visitors and stopped them from infecting their planetary species. They had alerted the other species in the solar system, but it was too late. The scientists had already infected the entire solar system. The humanoid DNA spread throughout the solar system, changing the creatures there. Over a million years later, all the creatures from the eleven planets shared the same DNA."

"We saw the changes of the creatures of this planet and the evolution that they went through. We also saw the shift in the ways of the beings. Benign before and happy to hunt and gather, they were beginning to have cognitive thought."

"Our species had chosen to remain hidden all this time. We had seen times of peace on Earth before, but it had never endured. Long before the humans, there were one species after another coming to our beloved planet, inhabiting it and leaving. Our kind can teleport quite easily. That, and the gift of cloaking, made it simple to remain hidden from other eyes. All eyes except for our friend the One."

"Everything changed after the greed arrived. Peace crumbled in a very short time. They enslaved the humans and made them kill each other to gain their possessions. The greed had brought a technology that was far greater than anything known in this solar system. They were very good at war and weapons. The greed captured a couple of our beings and implanted them with their devices. They developed special tools that they used to see our kind. Eyewitness accounts had alerted them to our presence, and the greed wanted to control all beings. They could also see into different dimensions, but could not travel to these other realities."

"The greed had sensed our beings before, but had not been able to detect us. This time, they had worked out that problem and brought glasses that would make us visible. They had implanted devices in three of our being, which altered their gene, and eventually the genes in all future generations. It had been a gene that did not allow us to reproduce. The greed had no interest in enslaving the Sasquatch, they had the humans for that. They had just wanted to experiment on and exploit us like they did all other beings. This is the last of our people. We are the last of the mighty Sasquatch humanoid."

"We are here to help heal this planet. Pachymama has been our home for so very long, and we want our paradise back. We see that the chosen have the same love of Pachymama as we do. We want to help you rid her of the parasites. The One and its siblings will lead us. They are the way. The prophecy says it. Our planet is going to be healthy again. All of her beings will live in harmony once again."

The crowd started a low hum, which made the Sasquatch feel welcome. The beings walked into the group of chosen and other creatures. They became one with their new friends. It was the first time ever that the chosen and the Sasquatch had held a trust in their hearts. The Sasquatch had been in harmony with every other creature present while remaining in solitude.

The leader of the Sasquatch appeared in the group, standing among its peers. The chosen souls enveloped the beings and spread a warmth that was illuminated by a dark red aura which had amassed above the masses. The chosen, mixed with the Earth's animals, filled every hillside in view.

The crow flew from the shoulder of the One. It made an aerial reconnaissance of the group. The birds eye was seeing what the One was perceiving with its third eye. The being could clearly see the sea of bodies below. It also saw that they were standing in a perfect circle with four straight outcrops pointing in each direction on the globe. They formed the sacred symbol. No one had told them to stand like this. It had just happened.

The One knew of this symbol and its meaning. It had used this symbol its whole existence and seen its use and power throughout the universe. It was the sacred symbol of the One. This had all been in the prophecy. The sacred symbol would be created from the creatures, signaling the end. All of this had been written so many years in advance. Billions of years, maybe more. No one really knew who wrote prophecies, they were just there and they always came true.

The nine children and three women began to levitate off their monoliths. They, too, were transported to the masses by an invisible force. The ninth child lagged. There was something the child needed to do. The One appeared by the side of the child. The two looked at each other and knew, without words. The prophecies were correct. The end was near. There was much to do.

The other eleven walked among the masses and spread the word of warmth and care. Fear was the farthest thing from any of the creatures' minds. The time had come. They had been enlightened, and now they were among their beings. The collective was forming. All beings were going to be needed to fulfill the destiny and rid the planet of the greed. All beings were going to have to be strong.

As the children spread the word, the masses listened with respect. They all knew, without a doubt in their hearts, that everything was going to be alright.

CHAPTER 48

The One walked into the forest with the Sasquatch. It had been many moons since the two creatures had walked in this forest as one. The other giants followed behind their leader and the being they had heard legends of.

The Sasquatch had roamed the Sierra Nevada mountain range as its main habitat for tens of millions of years. Their roaming range was a very extensive one. North America had provided the perfect survival ground for this majestic giant. Its mild climates and plentiful food were exactly suitable for the Sasquatch. The abundance of trees and plants kept the humans and the greed away, while providing cover for their species.

The creatures on the other continents had not fared as well as the North American clan. A few had survived in Russia and some in the Himalayas, but most could not adapt to the Earth's climate.

The One asked the Sasquatch about its numbers. The meteor had destroyed much of the western part of America, which was where the Sasquatch called home.

"We were once many thousand in numbers," the creature responded with its clicks and whistling language. It raised its hands and waved it in the direction of the others in its clan. "Now this is all that is left. Twenty-two souls left of a once proud species. Our life spans are thousands of years, but we are at the end. We were the last Sasquatch born to our ancestors. We are the last who carry those souls with us. When we are gone, there will be no more Bigfoot in this solar system. The souls of our ancestors and their knowledge is our purpose for life. The knowledge of the planet and the universe is with our creatures, but it will be gone when we are. There were just over a hundred of us when the meteor struck. We were the only ones who survived. Our brothers and sisters perished in a hateful act perpetrated by the greed and the Lunark. It was devastating to our kind."

"You are the link between the chosen and animals of this planet," the One said to the large hominid. "The chosen have regained the trust of the animals and the planet. All of them will need your help. Even though your numbers are small, your role will be very large. Your energy is a special one that was sent here long ago for this destiny. Now, our energies will combine with that of the chosen and all other creatures of Pachymama. Together, our collective is going to be stronger than the Universe has ever seen. It will take this energy to send the greed away. We are not using weapons to fight theirs, everyone knows how that goes. We are using our combined knowledge to form the true light. Not the light that the serpents have hidden behind all these cycles."

The One showed the Sasquatch the large vein of gold it had found. The being had unearthed much of the vein with its devices. Laid bare, it radiated in the rays of the sun.

The One had found a very large piece of quartz in the exact middle of the glimmering line. It had used a device that was built out of a long metal rod wrapped with copper wire. When the One waved the wand over the gold and quartz, the rock vibrated and hummed. After only seconds, the enormous stone levitated out of the gold and was gently placed on the side. It left behind a large hole in the absolute middle of the vein. Clean water began to immediately flow into the cavity from the small stream running the length of the vein.

The One knew that there was another gold deposit, running due east to west, that was four hundred and forty-four feet below the surface. The two together formed a perfect cross pointing to the different global directions. Still further underground to a depth of six hundred sixty-six feet, there was a perfect circle of gold. This massive ring was fifty feet thick and five hundred feet in diameter. The One had discovered this symbol imbedded in the Earth when it had first arrived. It had always assumed that the behemoth gold symbol was created by Pachymama.

The quartz was valuable to the One and its siblings, and they had scouted and found what they had needed. They had stumbled upon this ancient monument built to the heavens but had not unearthed it. It had been sacred since a time long ago, before the knowledge of the One. It was sacred to the planet. The three had respect for Pachymama and would not take more than what was necessary.

The One next showed the Sasquatch the large iron deposits it had unearthed. The iron covered a three hundred and thirty-three-acre spot, but the One had only unearthed one acre. It was all that would be needed to allow the electromagnetic charge to enter and exit it. The parts underground would be held in place by the Earth, which would be creating a large, natural grounding rod. The Earth had provided everything the One had needed. Pachymama was their true ally.

The One told its large friend, "these three elements are very important together. This iron comes from a volcano that erupted long before we came. Our guess is two billion years ago. It exploded with force and left this huge deposit straight from the core of the planet. The gold is the conductor that we will need for our devices. It will create the energy necessary to power up the iron and make it into a giant electromagnet. It is going to be very powerful. These metals, along with our devices, are going to produce a pulse of maximum intensity. The quartz is going to amplify it by untold amounts"

The Sasquatch answered, "I am sure you have considered the actions of the greed. They did not just experiment on the creatures of the planet, they also experimented on the planet itself. They had sent nuclear devices to the core and atmosphere. They had also used these bombs in the oceans. It altered the core of the planet. The bombs shocked the inner parts of the planet and made the internal spin slow down, drastically. The planet slowed its magnetic pulse in conjunction with the slowing of the core. This is what began to alter the human's perceptions of things. When the Earth's core slowed, so did the thinking of its creatures. They were much easier to control like this. Now, will the slowing of our planetary core influence your devices?"

"Our device is going to right all the wrongs done to this planet." The One said. "The greed are destructive scientists with no care about any creatures but themselves. Their experimental games on this planet are over."

"What is it that you need from our species?" Asked the Sasquatch.

"Your kind is the true shaman of this planet. All the other animals know this. Your kind has been here longer than any other creature, yet you have left not a bit of a footprint. You are the true ancestors of Pachymama. You were treated badly by the humans and worse by the greed. But our three have always been with you. Now I need you to do something that will take great strength. There is a monument here which we will need raised. This monument was here before your species arrived. It was built by an ancient species of visitor to this planet. Many had come. It has been billions of years that this planet was habitable. Many had come to this very spot. Drawn by the gold and the quartz. The other places, where my siblings are now, were two places just like this one in that regard. They were rich in gold and quartz. What we found upon our arrival was that many visitors had mined the gold. Some had built temples and monuments out of it. Their offerings were either deep underground or just in dimensions that the other species could not see. The temples to the stars were there just the same. While the rest of the planet went through cataclysm and complete annihilation, these three spots remained untouched. They have existed like this for over three billion years. Even your species, the mighty Augnelach, were drawn to this place."

"You are the first to speak our true name in millions of years. The souls of my ancestors are thankful. You truly are my friend and a friend of all who is light." The two beings embraced in a hug of long lost friends. The One grew to the size and appearance of the Sasquatch as the tight hug lasted more than five minutes. The two passed knowledge through their embrace. The One communicated with the ancestors of the being, while the Sasquatch learned of the destiny to come.

When they broke the embrace, the One went back to its normal size. It did not want to give any impressions of being a God. Size had a way of making people think different. They did not need Gods. They needed each other and the collective creativity.

The One took his friend to the pyramid. The gold had been dug from the spot and built with the knowledge of electromagnetism. It had been pulled out of the ground, in the shapes necessary, and stacked together. All this using the planet's magnetism. It had been hidden here all along, in a dimension slightly parallel to this one. The collective had made these dimensions converge.

"The pyramid is not very large right now. It has properties that I do not fully understand. Its builders were from a far-away galaxy that does not exist anymore. Somehow, some of their souls are still here, inside this monolith. A few of them survived the fate of their species. That had been the story over and over in the heavens. Destruction would create a migration to other worlds for survival. Some species made it and some didn't. All of them tried if they knew how. All species in the universe had one thing in common: Survival." The One told the Sasquatch, "Your powers and your species collective will make this pyramid grow again to its epic proportion. Your energy will combine and bring this craft back to its full strength."

"You were right about being drawn to this place," replied the Sasquatch. "We could have gone anywhere on this planet, but this place called to us. The continents had all been connected when we arrived, and travel was easy. Our ancestors were much taller, too. When our species first arrived on this planet, we were sixteen feet tall. Our kind could move around quickly. Being in harmony with all creatures made travel easy. We had been nomadic our entire existence on this planet and moved wherever the wind would take us. The trees and plants told us things about what to eat and how to eat it. They would tell us stories of other creatures and other places. They would share their knowledge of plants for medicine, also, and hallucinogens. We were in perfect harmony with nature. Throughout these eons, our kind have always wandered over a very large region. The ones who had remained on the other continents, as they slowly drifted away, had known the consequences. They would be on their own. Less than one hundred of our clan stayed there, while we all came here. We never saw our brothers and sisters again in person. They were long ago wiped out by the greed. Humans and their Gods had encroached on their lands long before they had on ours."

The Sasquatch continued, "This spot, as you see, was always sacred to us as well. We, too, have built our monuments. But we built them in a different dimension. The greed, humans, nor chosen, have ever been able to see our monuments. Even you, the One, cannot see them just yet, but you will very soon. We built our temples for the planet. Out of respect for our beloved Pachymama. It was the only one who had to know the love that we had. With our ability to cross into other dimensions comes being able to teleport. They are completely connected. At one time, our species could bounce from any dimension they wanted into the past or the future. The last couple of thousand years have been changing, though. The past dimensions narrowed until they completely closed. The future dimensions no longer exist. Before, we had perfect communication with any of our kind. No matter when they lived, in the past or future, we could be in contact. Our souls went on forever in different dimensions, and we knew how to use this gift for eternal life. Now, even those dimensions are closed to us. We cannot bounce back and forth at will. We can still see eight dimensions, but none with our ancestors. It is one more wrong that the greed perpetrated on us. They have made us mortal."

"The greed used the humans to do their evil, all the while telling them it was the righteous way. They were the true evil," said the One. "Our collectives did not fall under their control, and were looked down upon by the mass. Creativity and imagination were not part of the plan. I am sorry for what has happened to you, my friend. It is sad, but it has happened to all creatures on this planet. The humans are extinct, their souls in the banks of the greed. We are all Pachymama, and we have all been done dirty by this evil greed."

The One turned to the Sasquatch, but the creature was no longer by it. The being instantly knew that the giant had teleported. Splashing of water down the hill caught the attention of the One. The being was very joyful at the sight it saw. The Sasquatch was splashing about like a child in the golden pool. The entire basin had filled with the slow trickle of water. The One ran down the hill toward the watery bath.

Memories from the time when the collective lived here as a family and played in the forest came rushing back to the being. The thoughts filled the heart of the One with strength. The happiness of the Sasquatch, splashing about, filled the One with elation. How long had it been that this creature had been so happy? Its last thousands of years were filled with pain and suffering, not happiness. Now, the being was swimming in a golden pool, letting all the darkness wash out down the stream.

The One watched as the Sasquatch took on the same color as the basin. Its fur turned a vibrant golden color. The sun reflected off the wet fur, and the golden basin intensified the effect. The One had never seen an aura like this one. The entire being and the surrounding forest were painted in a solid gold color. The sight was spectacular to behold.

The forest, too, began to change as the golden light spread throughout it. The One could see stone dinosaurs of life size proportions. More than a thousand stone Sasquatch heads dotted the hillside.

Some seemed to be hundreds of feet tall. When the vision began, the monoliths at first looked like shadows created by the trees. As the golden light spread, the stones began to cast shadows on the trees. Thousands of the stone dinosaurs were scattered among the gigantic heads. The One was impressed that the Sasquatch had built these massive monoliths. The detail seemed so lifelike. It looked like actual dinosaurs and giant Sasquatch had been frozen in stone. Sentinels on this sacred spot.

Strange animals, ones the being had never seen before, bounded through the forest and among the monoliths. There were deer the size of your hand and reptiles the size of small trees. Hundreds of animals were about. All seemed to be in harmony with one another. The forest also seemed to be different. Ferns as tall as a house filled in the spots in between gigantic oaks. The forest was alive with sounds, as the sky was alive with the gold.

The One was broken from its vision by being pulled into the pool by the hands of the Sasquatch. There was no hope, the beast's hand fit all the way around the being's leg. The One emerged from the water, laughing. The Sasquatch joined in. It had been a very long time since the Sasquatch had laughed. Now things were different. The One had brought the word of hope. Now, maybe it was truly a new time.

The Sasquatch told the One about being immersed in water that sits in the golden symbol. It told the One how it would open your mind's eye and you would be able to see more dimensions. Even the glow from the pool had allowed the One to see into another dimension. It also spoke of the responsibilities of not disturbing those dimensions by leaving something behind. "Not many creatures could physically cross over dimensions, but if you do, be careful."

The others were drawn to the laughter coming from the stream. The ninth child came running down the hill at full speed. He hooped and hollered all the while before diving head first into the pool. The One looked on with wonder as the child dove into the shallow waters and disappeared in the golden glow. The water was only about four feet deep, but his lookalike was gone.

The Sasquatch eased the mind of its friend. "This One is special. His mind's eye is like yours and can see the truth. You two are connected. He is going to be a big part of the coming days. Now the child is in one of the dimensions I was telling you about. He crossed over and will cross back when it is the cycle. His energy is strong, and we are going to need your bond. He is the key to saving Pachymama from this curse."

The ninth child broke to the surface. His eyes were very large and solid black. He was naked and covered in tattoos. Even his head had tattoos. On the child's forehead, there was a fresh tattoo of an eye. It was bleeding from the golden water that was dripping from the being. Everything around the child looked to be coated in gold, but this being was in normal light. The tattoo dripped a thick red blood. It blinked open, like it had been asleep for a very long time. The eye underneath was pure white with an amber iris. It blinked five or six times and then became wide open.

"Finally, I can see." Said the ninth child in the voice of the man. The One made the connection immediately. Their third eyes looked directly at each other.

They both understood.

The two were One.

CHAPTER 49

The ninth child now understood the dimensions. His third eye had been opened, and the truth was clear. He had known before about the different dimensions and the parallel planes that they existed on. This, however, was the first time that the being had seen these dimensions in all their clarity. This being, and its siblings, were of a species that could see six colors of the spectrum. This enabled them to see many things that other species could not see.

The humans had been able to see only three spectra, while the chosen could see four. That extra spectrum was what enabled the chosen to see the aura of other beings. It also enabled them to see spirits and wayward energy. The cloaking devices on the craft of the greed did not work the same on the chosen. Their species saw UFO all the time, while the humans were tricked.

The One could see sixteen spectra, but only on command. Its normal vision consisted of six, like the nine children from the lost galaxy.

All the beings in the bath could now see in sixteen spectra.

As the ninth child stood in the water bathed in golden light, it could see color spectrum that was lost to most species of the universe. Seeing all the color made the dimensions clear. The being could see eight different dimensions all in the forest surrounding the pool. Everything had merged together, forming a universe in front of his eyes. The being did not know such beauty existed. It was truly a garden of Eden. All the while, the ninth child knew there were other dimensions that remained hidden to his eyes. There was so much for one brain to take in. It made the being grow dizzy with a sense of overload. It felt like a giant weight was lifted off its being, while being replaced with another.

The masses had gathered around the golden pool and were watching the miracle take shape before their eyes. The ninth child was coming alive like no creature before. A light radiated from the eye in his forehead, covering all the chosen in a warming beam of light. It gave the chosen and the other creatures of the forest a sense of hope and connectivity. It made them closer to the collective.

The ninth child now knew the secret of the gold. The refractions from the metal was what opened his eyes. The greed had not known this secret place. If they would have known about this, their powers would be unstoppable. The Sasquatch had kept their knowledge hidden well. The secret of the dimensions was here, and the beast was the caretaker. The gold was the key.

Along with the masses stood their exact doppelganger. Some had as many as eight exact beings standing within its circle. The ninth child reasoned that it must be one for every dimension present. Some of the masses had only one or two doppelgangers. Even the animals present each had exact twins by their sides. A few of the beings had no doppleganger. The child thought that maybe they had died in their other dimension, and their energy no longer existed there. It had moved on to another dimension, maybe one not even known about.

The One had thirty-two doppelgangers around it. It was a collective of four who all had eight living souls in other dimensions. These beings stood in a pattern which made the symbol of the universe. The One was in the middle of its lookalikes, at center in this dimension.

The Sasquatch, too, had doppelgangers. Their numbers were over a thousand. All the souls of the Sasquatch from all the time on this planet were visible. They were a different species than all the rest of Earth's inhabitants. They were truly at one with everything. In the past, they had mingled throughout time with the use of the dimensions. Since the greed had closed that bridge, they had learned to be very self-sufficient. Today, though, the ninth child had brought all the dimensions of the Sasquatch together. It had been a very long time since all the species had been as one. Most of the souls that had first come to this planet were present.

Sadly, none of the Sasquatch who had remained on the lost continents were there. Their souls had been lost to time.

Animals not known before were everywhere and in abundance. All the species interacted as one. These beings had all come together with the aid of this healer. Now they were all part of the collective. More monuments had also appeared, attesting to the spirituality of this place, and confirming how much intelligent life had inhabited this planet in the past. There were monuments of native granite, some of quartz, and many of gold. Their sizes ranged from less than one foot tall to behemoths that blocked the sun in places. Mountain Ranch was alive with the life that had always been here, but never united.

Two large snakes of immense color were twisting together in and out of the pool. The child had a recollection from past lives of seeing these exact serpents. He knew they represented DNA. These serpents were the cosmic. They were the wisdom of the universe. They also held the keys to all life on Earth and the universe. These twin ropes were inside of everything organic in the universe. Now, they were making themselves visible, once again, to the child. Their dimension was the one of truth.

The child could also now communicate with the trees and plants. They spoke of the longing to have clean air and water again. They also spoke of the destruction of their species at the hands of the humans, controlled by the greed. They just wanted to be in harmony again with everything, like it had been so very long ago. The ninth child assured the forest that the healing was coming. Healing for the entire planet and every being on it. Pachymama was going to be strong again. It no longer was going to be a world that leaned toward the dark. It was time to bring the true light back to the planet.

The ninth child levitated out of the golden waters. The being came to rest on the side of the pool, looking out over the land. As soon as it was out of the water, the visions of the other dimensions disappeared. Only the masses remained, without their doppelgangers. The forest returned to the way it had been before.

The One slowly pulled itself from the pool. Its strength had dwindled to nothing, and it needed to accomplish so much. How had this happened? The being had been so strong only moments before. When the dimensions had opened, the fatigue began. Now there was nothing but weakness.

The ninth child approached the One and took its hands in his. The light from the child's forehead focused directly on the being in front of him. The light fell right in the middle of the forehead of the One. Their third eyes became connected with the light coming from the head of the ninth child. The man spoke to the One, "It is against the physics of the universe to coexist in the same dimension alongside your doppelganger. This is the first time in all history of the planet that this has happened. You were also the first collective being in almost six thousand years. Your collective, too, went into hiding when you and your siblings hid me and my eight brothers and sisters. You waited patiently for the time, which was part of the prophecy. Your collective was the end. You brought it about. Now is going to be the beginning. Now your four souls are to merge with mine, and we will still be four souls. Our souls are one now and will remain the same. Our collective will be the strongest being the solar system has ever encountered. This energy will spread throughout the cosmos, uniting all beings in harmony. You entrusted myself and my siblings with a great trust. We will not disappoint you. Now go, ancient one, return to the ancestors with our song of change."

The One closed its eyes for the final time. Electricity merged the pods of the child and the One. Their collective was now complete.

The pyramid was in place, as was the collective.

The Sasquatch lifted the lifeless pod of the One. It had a joy in its heart that death was not usually a part of. The creature knew this being never died. This was the beginning. It would never exist without the end. This being's existence just kept going on forever.

The Sasquatch carried the One to the golden pyramid. The masses all cleared a path for the creature. The entire group began a soft humming as the Sasquatch passed through their numbers. All the creatures wanted to lay a hand or paw or talon on the pod of the One. This had been a sacred vessel. They looked at it like it was a temple. Even in death, the energy of the One was strong.

The Sasquatch laid the One on the point of the pyramid. Its other kind gathered around, as if to protect the pyramid and the One, who was bent over backward around the top of the monolith. The pyramid slowly began to levitate. The Sasquatch gathered under the pyramid in a square shape. The sky began to turn a dark purple. Lightning began to flash through the air, coming from the top of the pyramid and through the body of the One. The lightning was constant and lit up the dark skies with a blinding light. The pyramid began to grow. The ninth child, still by the pool, had a perfect view of what was going on. The being was the only witness to these cosmic events. The light blinded all the other beings. They all had to look to the ground to save their eyesight.

As the pyramid grew, the Sasquatch always remained on its edges. It was almost like they were merged with the golden monolith. The expansion of the monolith pushed the Bigfoot outward. Much time passed. All the while the lightning continued to flash. The sky continued to swirl with dark purples and grays. It looked like a tornado could touch down at any moment. The pyramid grew to the size of over five acres. The Sasquatch stood at each corner and four on each side. The leader of the Sasquatch and its mate stood directly under the monolith, right in the middle. The large beings stood like strong pillars, holding their temple as an offering.

The top of the temple exploded in lightning.

The ninth child had now become the One. The being focused its attention on the light coming from the pyramid. The entire structure was lit up from within. It was giving off a very strong aura. The One realized that the pyramid was alive. Only living creatures gave off an aura, and this one was giving off a very bright one.

The lightning from the top of the pyramid got more and more intense. It was soft and comforting, but also brought on a sense of impending dread. The lightning began to form into a solid beam of energy that went straight into the heavens. The purple clouds were moving in strange patterns. They began to form into objects. The lightning danced around the objects like movie props.

The One had known all along that the clouds were the spacecraft of the greed. It is how they would always arrive, amidst their purple tempest. The craft were enormous. Each of them was over three acres in size. The bottoms looked like organic cities. They were dark and foreboding. A darkness permeated from these craft. There were more than ten craft visible through the clouds, which were quickly dissipating.

A dark light from the first craft shot toward the Earth. It met with the white light of the pyramid. The two created a strange vortex that made the sky spin. The craft of the greed seemed to be multiplying, as their dark light overtook the golden light. Soon, their craft blanketed the sky.

The entire valley was cast in the shadow from the craft. The light from the pyramid began to diminish, as the darkness overtook the entire scene. The masses looked to the One, floating above the golden pool. Their gaze was one of questions.

The One gave the answers. "It has begun. The greed has arrived. We caught them by surprise with our announcement, but they are very powerful. Now, everyone must take their place around the pyramid. The symbol cannot be deviated from. It is all important. Today is the day."

A large bolt of lightning hit the pool. The energy flowed through the water and reached its tendrils straight into the air and through the pod of the One. It began to emit lightning all around its being. It pointed to the craft, filling the sky, and spoke in the minds of the masses, "We were wrong. The greed has known about us all along. They did not know about this place, but now they do. They just tried to take me out with their weapons, but will not succeed. They have really made a mistake now. What they didn't know was that I knew that they knew that the chosen still existed. Many things I said were for the benefit of their spies. The greed always had spies, since their arrival. These times are no different. They did not think that anyone or anything was ever going to be powerful on this planet. They thought they could do whatever they wanted without any consequences. They fucked up. This is not the way of the universe. Every breath is an exhale. Every pull has a push. Contracting happens alongside expansion. The Earth and the cosmos would never allow the ways of the greed to happen. There have been laws of nature all along, and all beings must follow those principles. Now the greed will find out what happens when you do not abide by the rules."

Lightning shot from the hand of the One. It hit all the craft at once, making them all briefly shine a golden aura. The craft flew erratic for a moment. They seemed to expand as a group, like they were building up a secret energy. All at once, the craft emitted a beam of solid gray matter that merged with the light directly above the One. The dark matter built in intensity above the being as it hovered, awaiting its turn of destruction.

The One held an object in its hand toward the heavens. The darkness shot its full strength toward the entity. The dark ray was fifty times wider than the form of the being, but was reduced to the smallest of rays by the object that the creature held in its hand. The object not only absorbed every bit of light coming toward the One, it seemed to suck even more energy from the ships producing it.

The One held the object in place until the light flashed off. The One could feel the energy strain that the device had just put on the greed and their craft. The being sensed fear coming from the extraterrestrials.

The being looked at the object in its hand. It was the stone that had been given to the family so many years ago. Their friend the crow had gifted them this object, and they had taken it with them as a family heirloom. The sun in the center of the stone glowed the same gray that the spacecraft had given off.

The entire being of the One was trembling with the energy from the stone. It looked to the ships above it and held the stone high. "Now I have the final power!" the being shouted with its mind. "Now I control you."

Chapter 50

The sky was filled with the craft like blocks of a building. The shapes fitted together until there was nothing visible except their ominous ships. The chosen all felt a common dread at the sight. This had been built into all their subconscious by the greed. The implants had been installed at birth, and this was one of the main reasons. Everyone with the implants had witnessed this in their subconscious many times before. These monoliths filling the mind.

The greed could control all animals they had implanted. The devices were of a type that created fear in its host. This is where the feeling had been coming from since they were young. The implants were strong from the beginning.

The greed knew they were in trouble. The devices did not work the same on these humans. They had known there were small bands of humans left, but they had not been worried. They would be needing slaves again in a short while anyhow. They knew that these beings were not humans. Their devices had not been able to control them. They could inflict fear in the beings, but not like it had worked with the humans. These beings had learned to block the fear as they had gotten older. They had torn down the monoliths inside their minds.

The chosen stood strong. Many of the greed were now standing near the group in a ghostlike form. They were in their natural state. Large, seven-foot tall reptilian humanoids. They were an ugly group with slithering tongues that did not like to stay in the mouth. They had no ears, but a kind of gill on the side of their heads. Their eyes were long slits and solid black. Their arms and legs were very short in proportion to their torsos. They each had four toes and three fingers. Their short tails almost made them look silly.

The greed was appearing in waves. They were strong, but there was a confusion brewing in their ranks. They had no control over these beings. Something was blocking the implants. Without control through fear, the greed could not fully solidify into reality.

Their beings were ghostlike and pale. Some came close, but none fully took on a physical shape. They all remained shadows.

The other creatures from dimensions unseen were also appearing. Their strength was strong in the light. They took on physical shapes that covered the valley. The area looked like an intergalactic concert with millions of guests. The creatures all stood as sentinels around the pyramid and its beings. The energy of all the beings present became one. The collective was strong. As it continued to increase, the energy made the darkness decrease.

The greed was relentless. Waves of their soldiers flooded the area all around the chosen and the creatures of the light. They covered every hilltop as far as the eye could see. Their collective was one of a dark shadow that had spread across the land. From the hilltop to the horizon, the shadow cast its evil darkness.

The light remained strong from within the valley. More and more beings were piling into the circle created around the pyramid. Dimensions were opening and allowing the integration of time and space. The heavens were opening. Pachymama was fighting back.

The One had been building the energy from the pool within its being. It shook with the power that was absorbed. The dimensions had all opened as soon as the feet of the being touched the water. As it descended further into the golden depths of the water, more dimensions had opened. Energy from all dimensions intermixed in a cosmic river. Everything flowed together as one.

The being sensed its brother and sister in other parts of the planet, standing ready just as it was. It was the exact same scenario that they were involved in.

They were connected, yet so far apart. Their energy formed at an apex on twelve different spots of the planet. The three beings, creating a triangle of energy, used the magnetic energy of the Earth to create a force of gravitational pull. Their minds were all three connected as one. The distance was great, but it felt like they were standing next to one another.

"Now," whispered the One. The being lifted the stone that was held in its hand. It held the energy from the greed at the same time as holding the energy from the light. Both their powers were contained in the small object. A large ball of energy shot from the stone while the One was waist deep in the water. The energy collected by the being from the pool had been explosive. The burst shot outwards and flowed into the devices the One had built. The three triangles, wrapped with copper wire, were the recipients of this blue ball of fire. It hit the first and wound its energy throughout the careful wrap of copper. The energy shot out of the first pole in a yellowish tint and raced to the next pole where it once again spun around the copper wire. On exit from this contraption, the light had turned to a bright red.

The power created by the One had intensified hundreds of times through the electromagnetic conductors, which had been carefully placed inside the triangle. The energy twisted through the air in the middle of the poles, creating its own lightning storm. It shot forth like a laser as all three beams converged to one. The color created by those three rays created every spectrum of color known in the universe. The beam raced out and connected with the pyramid. The two were bridged by the light for over a minute. The ground shook the entire time. A light was produced from the top of the pyramid that glowed like a nucleus. When the entire monolith was alive with this intense light, the structure pulsed. Electromagnetism shot off in all directions, the strength like many nuclear warheads being detonated at the same time. The air had a shock wave of intensity that none of the creatures in the light felt. It passed through their beings harmlessly.

The only thing affected by the pulse was machinery. Organic beings were not harmed by the electromagnetism of the Earth, no matter how much it was amplified. The only thing mechanical was the ships that the greed invaded with. Like their implants had infected many minds of creatures before, now the collective was infecting their warships. The craft began to disintegrate into thin air. Light began to appear as the vessels became no more. The single pulse had not only evaporated the ships of the greed, the beings themselves were dissolving into thin air. The light from the pyramid and its circle spread over the valley and all the hills. The shadows retreated with the power of the light. There was a smell of purity in the air.

The pyramid vibrated with a resonance of celebration. The joy of the planet and its creatures flooded throughout all the beings present. They had created the collective and defeated the disease. They had taken their planet back from the parasites who had treated it so badly.

It was the same scenario across the planet. The force from the other electromagnetic pulses had combined, wiping out a huge portion of the greed. Their rape and rule of the Earth for the last six thousand years was over. The beings rejoiced. The beginning was here.

A rain began to fall all over the planet. The sky, even where cloudless, rained over the lands. A bright light had appeared in the heavens. The chosen knew. It was Krakatoa. They were going home. Their planet, long lost to this colony, was coming back for them.

The Sasquatch emerged from under the pyramid. Their fur emitted a golden glow that the light clung to. The beings looked like gods sent from the heavens. The creatures quickly formed a circle. They were all gathered around one of their kind. They looked on with awe. She was pregnant. It was a miracle. The One had been correct. The greed had been defeated and now the first Sasquatch in many moons was pregnant. Their species was to survive.

The One lay motionless by the pool. The energy it emitted would have killed most beings. Now, the One reflected on the road they had taken to arrive at this spot of time. So many miles they had traveled for this very moment. A tree branch dipped down and fanned the One. The giant oak felt the connection with the being, as did all the other creatures of the forest. The being had been thrown from the pool with the energy ball it had launched. The other dimensions had closed as soon as the entity had left the water.

Now, all the other creatures had gathered around: The chosen, the deer, bear, birds, insects, and all beings. The Sasquatch stood closest to the One. They knew how to give their energy back just as well as how to take. They, as a group, were giving back to re-energize the being. The One sat upright. "We are not done here yet," it said. "These creatures are powerful and will not give up easily. We surprised them. We just handed them a serious defeat. They have lost the last thread of control over the beings of this planet. Their kind are not pleased. They are not used to defeat. They will be more pre-pared next time, but it will not matter. We have more surprises for these bastards."

The One instructed the other creatures to climb to the pyramid as far as possible. There was just one more thing that was needed to be done. "The final cleansing is here," said the One.

All the creatures climbed onto the pyramid. The animals and the chosen stood as one being. The rain continued to fall, but the creatures on the monolith remained dry. The pyramid began to pulse a very loud sound. It would be deafening to all, but was unheard by those on the monolith. They simply heard a low rumble and smelled the gold in the air.

The sound was deafening to the greed. It was a sound that would make them lose their minds. Their kind, worldwide, writhed in pain and terror. Their machines defeated, they were helpless.

The centrifuge, built by the One, collected power that was still racing through the three copper coils. The power shot down into the agates that the One had placed so carefully. It bounced off the stones and arced into the iron plates put up in the pattern of the symbol. The electricity was a sign to the heavens with the pattern that it created. The lightning came off the iron plates like tubes of energy, shooting into the middle of the triangle. They came into direct contact with the centrifuge at the three points of the plates. The two pieces of the centrifuge began to spin rapidly and picked up speed until the two parts were a blur. They looked like one giant ball of energy when both wheels were spinning at full speed, in different directions. A vortex of energy began to open above the spinning object. It gradually got bigger until it covered the entire sky. The light was as if the northern lights and lightning were mixing with rainbows. When it was at its maximum intensity, the vortex pulsed once and went into all directions, as a powerful burst of electromagnetic energy. This was a different type of energy than the planet had ever known. The One had been shown this device in a dream so many moons ago. It had never forgotten.

The centrifuge did not slow down; it stopped. The ground shook with the intensity of the shock as the behemoth suddenly halted its movement. The stars were visible, like none of the Beings present could ever remember. The heavens had been blocked by the greed for six-thousand years, and now they were completely clear. Many galaxies were visible in the evening sky, as were the three moons.

The rain began to fall in bigger drops. Then, the water began to change to an oily black substance. The bodies of the greed followed soon after. Their beings had been melted by the powers emitted from the centrifuge. The brother and sister had built the same exact device in their spots. They, too, had dreams of the blueprints. All three of the devices had powered up at the exact same moment. The greed perished in their last attempt at control.

All the beings on the pyramid were shielded from this black rain. The lands all around were peppered with the debris of a dying species. The oily residue covered the land. The rains lasted for hours. The greed had infested this planet much more than anyone had thought. Their numbers were in the tens of millions. There was no way any of them could have survived this power. It had all been destiny.

A few of the greed had survived, though. Deep in Antarctica, the true rulers of the elite made their home. Their lairs were dug deep into the canyons and mountains on the mostly unexplored continent. They had remained safely hidden there since their arrival. These beings were the first to come to this planet to take over. When they had established themselves as Gods, they had brought in their generals and other lesser beings. After they had their minions in charge of the mayhem and slavery, they could simply sit back in their kingdoms in a faraway land and reap the riches of their greed. The misery of all the other creatures. They enjoyed their mayhem, as they dined on the souls of the humans.

The Earth quickly absorbed the raining mess like a dry sponge. All around, plants were already coming up where the goo was absorbed. The body parts that made it to the ground were quickly broken down and composted. Minutes went by as the Earth took advantage of the parasites that had infected her for so very long. The greed was to provide a great fertilizer to a planet they had abused for so long.

Before the last of their kind had been absorbed by the planet, the five original rulers of the greed had boarded their spacecraft in Antarctica and were rocketing off into space. Their home planet was just a wormhole away, and all would be well again upon the return. The beings had tried to come across as calm to their counterparts, but all five were having a strong sense of fear. This was not a feeling the beings were familiar with. Theirs was a species of dominance, not of fear.

"The greed is gone," stated the One as it pointed toward the trail left from the escape craft overhead. "Their time of destruction on this planet is over. Now we will reunite with our ancestors and rebuild this planet. The end has come. It is now the time of the new beginning. It is a cycle that has repeated itself again and again. It will repeat itself many more times in the future. Celebrate now, my friends, we have much to be happy about."

The greed had not wanted to fly over the One on their departure, but the window to leave the planet's atmosphere left no option. It had all been a part of the destiny anyhow. When the centrifuge had been twisting, the two small metal balls underneath were containing all the energy. These two small orbs held the power of a thousand suns in their small metal enclosures. As the saucer of the greed flew overhead, the two spheres flew magnetically into its flight path and attached themselves on the bottom of the ship.

Unbeknownst to the greed, they had picked up a device that was strong enough to destroy entire solar systems. When they got back to their home planet, annihilation would follow. Their terror throughout the universe was to be swiftly ended. Their outposts, reliant on the home planet, would quickly come to an end. There would be no more of this species in the entire universe. They had done their crimes against others, and now they were to reap the punishment.

The One had regained its feet and was among the Sasquatch. The pyramid had shrunk down to a size of about one square yard. As it got smaller, all the beings were left on the soil, in a predetermined space. They made the symbol of the One. The large circle with four arms pointing into all four directions. They had not made this symbol on purpose; the pyramid had left them like this.

The One had changed appearance. The eye in its forehead was now twice the size of a normal human eye, and it was a golden amber color. Its other two eyes were further apart, and the angle was different. The face, overall, was now the shape of an almond. It was still the One, it just looked different.

The being walked among the people who had stayed in their spots, showing homage to the One. It spoke to the chosen with its mind and as a collective.

The beings were truly connected again. They were back to the original people as when they had first arrived on this planet. The implants had disintegrated along with the greed and their craft.

The true wisdom could now come back to the chosen.

Now they would be able to truly use their free will.

Chapter 51

The light in the sky had been getting progressively brighter. The blocks put in by the greed to mask the stars were gone. All beings could clearly see the heavens once again, like it had been before the reign of shit.

Krakatoa was on its farthest orbit of the sun. Its elliptical rotation brought its path in proximity to Earth. The time was now. The chosen were in an animated mood. They spoke excitedly about their new freedom. They spoke of the beginning, without the greed. Since the arrival, and especially since the extinction of the humans, the chosen had been kind servants to the Earth. Their kind had always lived in conjunction with the planet, but they had become lost. They had become human. Now, they would be going back home. Now, they would be Krakatoa once again.

The One had been silent for a long time. It watched the other beings celebrate the beginning in solemn thought. The being knew too much about the universe and its species. There was much dark in the universe, just as there was much light. The balance made up all living things. Without one, there was not the other. Everything in the universe had a plus and a minus. Just like the coils that the One had built to ward off the greed.

The One spoke to the chosen. Its voice was a whisper as it exited the lips but was amplified by the time it went in the ears of the gathered. It spoke of a darkness. The darkness that the others had thought that they had left behind. It was here, in their faces, like always. The One spoke, "War had broken out on Krakatoa. The greed had infiltrated a lower intellect species and made their experiments once again. The outcome of their invasion had been the same as on Earth. The lower species quickly became powerful and emulated the greed. They looked to the beings as though they were Gods. They wanted to be just like them and aspired possessions. Over time, the greed had given these beings more and more technology, until they had power over the other beings of the planet. This power grew into an addiction. Greed and deceit walked hand in hand. They would stop at nothing to acquire wealth and power. The same exact thing that had happened on Earth. The beings were too stupid to realize that they were just puppets to the greed.

Experiments that were watched for the enjoyment of the superior beings. They were the true power. They had fed the masses false beliefs on planet after planet. The greed would make beings think they were in control. They were actually being controlled by the same beings casting their experiments and doubts on them."

"The greed was aggressive and strong while the chosen were passive. All the beings on your planet had been passive souls. It is why you were chosen to come to Earth all the moons ago to help the humans. The genetically altered beings of Krakatoa reproduced at an alarming pace. Soon, within three thousand years, they had overtaken the planet. They were a parasite on Krakatoa, just as they were on Earth and every other planet they visited. Krakatoa, too, has been ravaged by the greed. This was the true reason the ancestors did not come to Earth five thousand years ago. They had been under siege. Their persecution was equal to that of Earth. The only difference was that Krakatoa did not fight back. Earth did."

The chosen understood about their planet now. It had all opened in their minds as a collective. All thirty-three-thousand, three-hundred-thirty-three of their souls across the planet all woke up at the exact same moment. The stars opened in the sky, but the sun was bright. The true vision had returned. They were now truly one. They were the chosen, and they were all that was left of their once proud species.

A collective hum began to emanate from the mass of chosen. The sound could be heard across the planet. It met the sounds coming from the chosen, who had gathered in the other two sacred spots. The melody that the sounds made when they met was angelic. The song was one of hope. The rhythm of gongs joined in, and the entire planet rejoiced. Pachymama, captive for so long, was now free of all the parasites. Not just had the greed been taken care of, the Lunarks had also been brought to near extinction. The greed had been merciless on this species. All that was left of the Lunarks in the solar system was their burned out, red spacecraft the humans had called Luna.

There had been survivors on other planets. The greed had no time to document the different species who had made it through their terrible onslaughts. The few who survived would not be a problem for a very long time.

The natives of the planets in the solar system knew all about the greed. Most of their species had been brought by the Lunark in the forms of DNA that they had spread throughout the universe. All for their experiments and slavery. They had known that the greed would be coming back at some future time, and they had. They also knew that the time would come when the greed was tired of the species of each planet and would destroy everything. It had been in the prophecy.

The beings inhabiting the planets in the same orbit had been prepared as best as possible to ensure the survival of the species of their planets. They had built huge intergalactic spaceships, and even deep underground bases on asteroids thought to be lifeless.

They had put their DNA and their planet's species, creations, and technology on deep space travelers; a genetic bank. Their planets were uninhabitable now, but other planets that they encountered would be. They would land somewhere and adapt to their new environment. It was the way of the universe.

The devices that the One had built began to vibrate. A rainbow of colors swirled between the poles, once again focusing its energy on the centrifuge in the middle. The device powered up again with the most minimal of energy. It was at full charge already. The rings of the device were solid gold and held its charge, making the energy grow greater within its cells. The colors danced around the center of the triangle. The One, standing within its confines, was bathed in the spectrum's rays. It raised its hands to the masses and the light flung from its palms, coating the chosen and all the animals.

The feeling of euphoria was overwhelming to the beings. As the light had touched them, so had the feeling. It was like none of them had ever felt before. They truly felt like they were all in heaven.

The One spoke to them all in their minds once again, "You are in heaven," it said. The chosen crumbled to the ground along with the animals at their sides. Their humming, strong enough to rattle the tree limbs, never ceased.

A portal appeared above the centrifuge. It hung in the air over the golden device, like a cosmic storm cloud made of a rainbow of colors. As its strength was intensified, the colors began to merge, until it was a solid light of the purest white. All the colors came from this light, as did all energy.

A figure appeared in the middle of the haze. The being was silhouetted by the bright white aura which emitted from the portal. The creatures present were all on the ground, like they were worshiping the coming of a long-awaited God. Their strength had been zapped from the energy emitted by the One. Now they could just look on in awe at the spectacle in front of them. All the creatures, except the One and the Sasquatch, had been zapped of strength when the energy had been emitted. It was quite the opposite for these two species. The One, along with its twenty-two friends, the Sasquatch, had absorbed the energy depleted from the other creatures. As they were laying weakened, the twenty-three were standing tall.

The gong continued to beat in the distance. The One knew the source. The eight children, its former travel mates and siblings, were at each corner of the map. Their metal discs were in perfect harmony with each other.

Their three mothers were in the same place they had been for days. They held the tree house in their care. The three-singing bowls that they had acquired kept rhythm with the gongs and the chanting from the chosen. All the sounds, sights, smells, tastes and feelings were in melodious harmony.

The being coming from the portal was just a shape at first with the bright light behind it. As it came further through the dimension, the entity took shape. It was fully dressed in a black garment that was a stark contrast to the light of its aura. As it got closer and the others could see its features, they were all surprised to see that the being was the One. Its eyes were gone, only blank sockets remained. The mouth was obscenely stretched into a grin that filled most of the lower face. The being looked straight ahead as it became physical in this reality.

The portal twisted behind the creature but remained unchanged. Even when the being was fully solid, the portal and the centrifuge did not stop. It did diminish in its power output. This was evidenced by the return of the rainbow of lights as the white light broke into multiple spectrum.

The being from the gate appeared in front of the pyramid as it began to speak. Its wide grin moved grotesquely as it uttered its speech. Its words thundered across the small valley. "All is never exactly what it seems to be. All positive has a negative. Your people, the people of Krakatoa, have been good tenants on this planet. You have spent your time here in a productive and creative manner. You have lived in harmony with the fellow beings of this planet and did not fall for the tricks of the greed. You have defeated this scourge from this planet and the healing has begun. However, there is so much more that you don't understand yet."

The being continued, "The greed knew all about your people from the beginning of your existence on this planet. It was all part of their experiments. They could easily see that you appeared like humans and even had human DNA. Your species were much smarter than the humans, though, and you had a strong sense of empathy. Your free will and creativity overshadowed that of the humans. The greed was curious about you and your kind. They wanted to see how experiments with the same DNA from different planets would interact. The greed also knew about Krakatoa. They had first seen the giant green planet when your species were first sent here. They had seen the ships leave Krakatoa and enter the Earth's atmosphere. The greed did not have any outposts on Earth at that time. They had scouted the planet for resources and slaves and would come back when they were ready to exploit. They did have observers, though, that were based under the oceans of the blue planet. They would watch what was happening on the planet from their watery depths. Their reports back to their home planet were detailed instructions on planets to conquer. When all preparations had been made, the greed would strike. It had taken them about fourteen thousand years to return to this solar system after their observers saw Krakatoa. They had waited patiently and prepared for their armada's return to the milky way galaxy."

"The greed had allowed your kind to flourish on the planet. The chosen were not interested in being in charge, just creating and using their minds. The greed had seen this and were fascinated. They had never observed or experimented on a species like the chosen. They were intelligent, had no time for war, and cared about each other. The greed thought it best to control your people along with the humans. Their implants worked on you in a different way than the humans. It was their intention all along. They had fed you and your species disinformation, like they had the rest of the masses. While they were distracting you with media and religion and war, the reality was far greater. They were fighting galactic battles of destruction with their high-tech weaponry. Whenever the masses on Earth would see any trace of these devices, they would be lied to with a lie about a lie covering a lie. Reality on Earth was in truth one big lie. The greed used this as another one of their experimental tools. They liked to deceive and hold back the knowledge. They thought they were the most powerful beings in the solar system. They had no fears."

"The greed invaded Krakatoa quietly but efficiently. They knew all about our plans here to rid the planet of them. It had been in the prophecy. They had been preparing for this battle on Earth for twenty-two years. They came with confidence of battle but we came with the wisdom. I know this battle seemed like it was short lived, but it was not. We gather in this spot over and over for eternity. This place has been sacred to this planet since its birth. We have used this energy combined with the collective to destroy the greed. After all our labor, we are finally victorious. The end was quick, but the beginning had occurred six thousand years ago when the greed first arrived. Now, every living creature on this planet has brought about the beginning."

The figure in black continued, "Now the creatures are weak, just as you are. Our defeat of them on this planet has also weakened them on Krakatoa. The One sent a device back with them that has successfully destroyed their entire domain. Hundreds of planets and ten suns were destroyed, but the universe is almost rid of the greed. Soon you will be going home. You will carry the knowledge of the devices with you, along with the collective wisdom. You will be prepared to take your planet back from the greed and begin your own healing process. They have terrorized this solar system too long. We have already put fear into their souls. Their ancestors and species have been annihilated. They had always wanted to know feelings, now they know the feeling of fear and destruction. It is the only emotion their heartless greed will ever know. Now that we have beat them, others in the universe will have hope against the invaders. Without a home base, their outposts will be weakened, making them very vulnerable. They will be destroyed easily now. Word will pass through the cosmos like lightning, the greed can, and will, be defeated."

"There is one more thing I must tell you. The truth has been hidden from you. My brother and sister and myself are not one of your species. We are not from Krakatoa. We came to this planet more than fifty million years ago. Life was much different then.

We contacted the Sasquatch, but the other intelligent life forms on the planet were of a warring species. We had no time for war nor destruction. We had come from a galaxy that was destroyed by war. The different species had built more and more advanced weapons. Every time one group would make stronger weapons, the others would have to follow. They could not think to let another group be more heavily armed than they were. After time, the destruction became constant. Planets and solar systems were being wiped out constantly. The groups had even devised weapons that would erase the souls of the beings as their pods were defeated. Their entire existence would come to an end. Before the end, the three of us had devised a device that combined electromagnetic energy with white light. The fields that were created allowed our kind to travel throughout the universe at will. We were ambassadors to this planet. We were the only beings to make it out of our galaxy alive. Our beings had not been part of the wars. We were intellects who were interested in the wisdom and nothing else. Creativity and learning consumed our beings. We had pleaded with the others to stop the destruction, but it was of no use."

"Once getting to this planet, we instantly knew that we had found a new home. We have seen the entire history of this planet for the last fifty million years. Evolution to destitution, we were there for it all. Like you, Krakatoa, we could separate our souls and explore more. Together, the three of us made twelve. Different species came and went on this planet. Some destroyed themselves while others left. Many species were accidentally left behind by space junk or the inadvertent leftover spore from a visiting spacecraft. The three of our beings would try to contact every one of these visitors. Being able to shape shift, we would get into their inner circles in the shapes of familiar animals. Once we knew their ways, we knew which shapes to take to approach the visitors. Sometimes, we stayed well away from a species that had arrived. The darkness would permeate everything in its presence. Other times, like with the Sasquatch, an instant friendship would begin. Most of the species had come here with one intention; to dominate the planet, its species and its resources. In these cases, we learned the best way to dominate and influence those creatures. Our wisdom has been around a very long time. Other beings were never difficult for us to analyze and influence. They were just one more parasite on our garden of Eden. Since our arrival, we had made a pact with Pachymama and the Sasquatch to help protect the garden and the planet. At all costs, Earth was to remain pure. When you, the Chosen, arrived, we just thought it was one more parasite infesting our forests. We observed your ways and saw your lack of seeing everything the way they really were. You thought you could see, but you could not fully perceive. After the takeover, the greed was only letting you see disinformation. The truth was hidden from your eyes. The greed had tried to interbreed your kind with the humans, but it did not work. They would allow marriage between the two species, but you could not reproduce."

"The chosen were the prophets for the humans. The historical speakers were Chosen who were trying to teach the humans the way. The humans had begun to understand at the beginning and were becoming one with nature and the cosmos, but then the greed had stepped in. They took all that the Chosen had taught the humans and bastardized it. Prophets that taught the humans about the ways of the stars and Earth were now changed into religious stories. Poets and philosophers all spoke of the need for government and control. The greed permeated every bit of creativity that the humans had acquired. They had taken away everything the chosen had taught them. The truth speakers were now called the son of God. The greed would let these prophets speak until they would have a large following. When the people would be chanting for their savior, the greed would cut the holy one down with a vengeance. It was all a part of their game with experiments. They gave the humans hope, just to have it ripped away from them. It all fit into their evil plan of control."

"All this time, we had befriended the Sasquatch. We arrived many millions of years after these gentle creatures. We had made an instant friendship when we arrived. We could see the Sasquatch in all their glory. They had a kindness to their souls which attracted us. Their intelligence and knowledge of all living things was something that we shared. Our three and the Sasquatch had remained the only intelligent species who were allies on this planet."

"When the greed arrived the first time, we had approached them like we did with all visitors to this planet. The greed had come to control and destroy. They were uninterested in any of our knowledge nor friendship. They had not heard of our beings in the universe and did not care what we had to say."

"The Lunark were also very strong. We were helpless against their experiments and their ways. We had watched as they implanted their human DNA and souls into the animals of this planet. The Sasquatch had known to stay hidden from these creatures. Their kind had known about the greed and the Lunark. They had even known that visitors were coming and when. It had all been in their prophecies."

"The Lunark had departed soon after, leaving their seeds behind. They also left a colony behind to monitor the activities of the solar system. It was their way to seed a planet and check on it anytime they wanted."

"When they were sure the humans had gained a sense of intelligence, they moved in and put their plans into action. All the while the humans were evolving, other visitors came and enslaved them. A couple of species even brought humans back to their home planet with them. When they explained this to us, they said that they needed a slave species on their planet also. The humans were bred to be slaves. It went on like this for tens of millions of years. The humans would evolve and be crushed by visitors. All the while, the evolution of their species continued."

"When the greed arrived the last time, they approached myself, my brother and sister. We knew how strong they were and were weary of any contact. We had avoided this species every time they had come to Earth except the first time. Now, they looked for us. They had no fear of us but held a respect for our kind. They knew that we were the ancient ones on this planet and held all its knowledge. They wanted things from us, but knew that we were not a being to be controlled through fear. We were not a species of possessions nor of wars. We were just ones who wanted to co-exist with everything and search for the knowledge. The greed could not leave it at that."

"They knew about our knowledge of electromagnetism. They had seen the temples that we had built on the three sacred spots. They had encountered our force fields while trying to destroy these holy places. They had known that we did not use slaves for this. We had used our minds. The greed was very curious of us and our ways. This visit, they wanted to exploit us and take our knowledge. They promised war and destruction of our three if we did not cooperate. We scoffed at their talk and their fear tactics. The greed was meaningless to us. We did not want to have anything to do with them, but destiny was what it was. This had all been part of the prophecy. We got the greed to finally leave us alone and never contact us again. We had made a deal with them. We knew that they were the dark and knew better than to make deals. But, the human ways were created by the species emulating their rulers. We thought that it was the way it was. With our knowledge of the creatures of the planet, we devised a device which could be implanted in every living being. We made it so the beings wouldn't know they were implanted, while being under complete control of the visitors. At first, they just put them into the humans and the chosen. Then the greed began to capture wild animals and implant them too. They were building an army of the creatures on the planet. They were not going to give up Earth to any visitors again."

"So, you see, in light there is dark. As I said, we are not Gods. We are just other beings from a planet far from here, trying to survive in a universe full of bipolarity. When the greed returned, we knew that the planet was not going to stay in harmony long. We signed a treaty with them allowing six thousand years of occupation. When the time was up, they did not leave. They just kept getting worse and worse. They persecuted the humans and the Chosen alike. When the time was up, the greed had already wounded the planet and its species to the brink of complete destruction. It was time to step in and stop them. We knew our plan all along and were waiting to implement it. We were going to get rid of the greed forever."

"You have been deceived all along. We used your species to rid the planet of the greed. They wage war with what is left of your planet as we speak. Your fellow Krakatoa need your help. You now know how to defeat the greed and will bring the knowledge back home with you. Now, climb into your golden pyramid. This is the ship your species came through twenty thousand years ago. This is a bridge between worlds that was erected in the early hours of Pachymama. Its portal will take you back to Krakatoa, where you will fight the final battle against the greed in this solar system. This time, that fight will be for your planet. You know in your souls now what to do. My devices and your wisdom will eliminate the cancer on your planet, as they have on this one."

"Two other pyramids are preparing now in the other sacred spots. All thirty-three-thousand, three-hundred-thirty-three of your souls will return and you will be victorious. It is in the prophecy. I am sorry that we deceived you and your kind. It was wrong what we did toward your species. As you can see, this all had to happen to defeat the greed. You, the Chosen, were all part of this battle from the very beginning. Krakatoa and the rest of the solar system were all combined for this time. Your brains were different than the humans. We devised the implants so they could not control your free will. That is why you chosen always were the creative species on this planet. You saw the true God. Pachymama. The humans had been the slaves. We are the keepers of the knowledge and history of this planet. We must protect it any way possible."

The being finished its speech and stepped aside. During the saga, the pyramid had grown once again, until it was half its full size. The creatures eyeless gaze pointed to the heavens. The chosen passed by the being. Those who looked at the entity looked on with disgust. The One and its kind had done their people and the humans very wrong. Their species had been used by the three beings and the greed. They could have been on their planet taking it back from the greed. Instead, they had been lied to so they would stay here for the fight on Earth.

Some of the chosen walking by had so much anger, they wondered why they had even gotten rid of the greed in the first place. They possessed mostly what they wanted and had to work a lot, but it was simple and mindless. These chosen thought that the union between the greed and them was one of convenience. It was exactly how the humans had thought.

These beings and their negative thoughts had been with the humans for so very long, they were still thinking like them. If they only opened their sixth sense and understood. The truth was right there. Some could not see it yet.

The Sasquatch re-appeared from the forest and walked behind the chosen. They stopped before entering the pyramid. The large creatures formed a square around the One. When the last of the masses had entered the monolith, the One looked from the heavens to the door of the pyramid. The last person to step inside was the leader. She, too, had been one of the Chosen. The protector and provider were standing behind the woman. The One held out its hand to the leader and dropped a stone into the woman's hand. The three women were weeping softly. They had known the One and had known the truth. This being was the true light. Its only purpose had been to save the Chosen and the rest of the creatures from the planet.

The leader looked to her hand as the door began to rumble. In her palm was the stone that the One had been gifted by the crow so very long ago. The sun carved in the center gave off a very strong glow of golden yellow. The One used its mind to tell the three women that the entire population of human souls from this planet were inside the rock. It told them that they would know what to do when they defeated the greed.

"How did you get their souls?" asked the leader.

"When the greed was defeated, I used this device and took the souls back. Before their escape pods could return to their home, I reclaimed these energies using one of their own star gates. They had tried to use their weapons on us, but I had reversed it and sucked all the souls into the very device that was the defense against the greed. The knowledge of the dimensions is complete now in my thoughts, and retrieving the souls was simple. It took all of one Earth minute. The humans might be a slave race full of war, but they do not deserve the fate of the greed. Maybe you and your species can free them once and for all. Maybe the humans will finally have free will and think for themselves. All species deserve this, even humans."

The door slowly slid closed. The One stepped back ten feet. The Sasquatch never left the square shape they had created around the being. A gold pulse of light emitted from the devices built by the One. The energy from this pulse concentrated on and were absorbed by the pyramid. In a flash, the pyramid shot a solid green light to the heavens and silently exploded into trillions of particles. The rumbling of the pyramid immediately stopped, and the valley became silent.

The air seemed to take on a golden hue. Gold was permeating everything and coating every surface. This small pyramid had just turned to gold dust. Its particles refracted the sunlight, creating creatures not unlike when the sun would shine through smoke.

This creature being created, however, was one of pure light. The gold became one with all the beings present, casting them all in a golden glow.

The Sasquatch picked up the One and flung it into the air. The being disappeared in a flash of golden luminosity. Laughter overtook all the beings.

Tonight, was to be the real celebration.

Chapter 52

The sky became a turbulent mass of colors. The land was now bared of the monolith and the Chosen. The centrifuge was all that remained, centered in the middle of the three copper coils. The device had kept emitting its power after the pyramid had vanished. The portal slowly evaporated above the machine, taking its orator with it. As the portal was no more, it was the same for the being who had come through its doorway.

The Sasquatch stood in a circle around the One and felt the energy flow from the centrifuge. The twenty-three beings were the only ones visible. The other eight children stood at a further perimeter around the beings. Their gongs never missed a note. The animals, too, had disappeared back into the forest. Their way was not with the self-proclaimed intelligent beings. The animals were all intelligent creatures themselves. Each creature held its wisdom in different ways.

All creatures left on this planet understood the equality of all beings. The only beings who thought they were better than the rest had been eliminated. Not only was the Earth set to heal, so were the species who inhabited its sphere.

The centrifuge continued to swirl. The sky became mixed with a combination of dark colors and light. Shadows played through the atmosphere, along with the movement of the cosmic clouds. Lightning was striking, but not a normal type. It was scattering across the sky like spider webs. As it met at intersections, the lightning would zigzag down to the Earth. Most of the rays were absorbed by the coils. The rest was going into the ground and being absorbed by Pachymama. She was recharging herself and the rest of the creatures.

Two strong, solid bolts of lightning struck straight to the planet. They were about the width of a semi-truck and extremely bright. The bolts both hit where the pyramid had stood moments before. The ground shook when the light made contact. Bits of rock and soil went flying in all directions. A dust cloud was created by the impact. When the dirt had settled, two shapes were seen walking toward the group. The One had already known, as had the Sasquatch.

The brother and sister had arrived.

All three collective beings were reunited. The centrifuge that had been built by the One had been copied by the other two. They had built a force field that had connected all three spots on the Earth along with all the energy points. It had created an electromagnetic grid pattern on Pachymama which had given its core a serious boost. The molten center of the planet once again sped up to its normal spin. The planet was immediately being healed. This was medicine for celestial bodies.

Along with the boost for the planet, the energy had brought all three beings back together. Teleportation was a byproduct of electromagnetic fields, along with so many other side effects. It was what made the universe active. It was the universe.

The centrifuge slowly came to a halt. The sky cleared almost immediately, showing the sun in mid sky. Another celestial body, further on the horizon, meant that Krakatoa was very near. The One wished well for the Chosen and even the souls of the humans. They all deserved a beginning. If they had paid attention, they would be building their own devices and destroying the greed on their planet. It had been in their destiny to take this knowledge and save their planet.

The air seemed cleaner and brighter than ever before. The pollution, what was left after twenty-two years, had collectively gone up into the lightning that had brought the brother and sister. The toxic gases had been collected into a small device that looked like a metal tube with hieroglyphics on it. It had been the device that the collective had found on the road many moons ago. The One chuckled to itself at this thought. The path had been truly laid out for them. They had held the knowledge. The secret had been so simple. It was creativity. Every being had it, but many wasted it. The ones who used it were the truth. Creativity had paved the way to every moment in the life of the three.

The One took this device and flung it to the large planet in the sky. It left his hand like a rocket and instantly disappeared. This device was for Krakatoa. The friend of the One, the leader, would be getting it and would know what to do. These toxic carbon gases that the greed had so nonchalantly produced were now going to destroy them. The Krakatoa were going to get this device on the main ship of the greed, and when they left the planet, they would be taking a plague back to their other kind. The greed who were left would be congregating to prepare for their revenge. They were not going to take defeat of their species well. They had other secret bases in the universe that they would use to regroup. The other beings in this solar system had figured out their ways and how to destroy them. Now, the greed would be hitting them with everything they had, as soon as they regrouped.

With the stars lining up just right, the device would be the end of the greed and their entire race. The pollution that they had created on Pachymama was going to be the virus that spread among their numbers and wipe them from the stars. They would never terrorize any planet in the universe again. If it failed however, the full wrath of the greed would come down on Krakatoa and Earth. It was a chance that had to be taken, though. The time of the greed was over. It was the time of enlightenment.

The collective energy from all the living creatures on Earth had been very powerful. The greed had infected this planet too long, and now they had been cast into their dark shadows. Now they were gone. Rejoicing was coming to the true beings. There were still many extraterrestrial beings living on this planet. Many meteors, and many visitors had come to this planet. All life on this planet had formed from these seeds that had come from distant visitors. They had evolved into their own different species as they had adapted to the Earth. All these beings were intelligent, even a blade of grass.

The humans had thought that they were the only intelligent beings on this planet, but in their arrogance, they had been so very wrong. They could not look at animals and plants as equals to them. It had been built into their DNA. They always thought they could do what they wanted with no regard for the planet. Anything bad they did, they could go to their buildings and get forgiveness from their imaginary Gods. The Gods that they had embraced were, actually, the elite controlling everything for the benefit of themselves. They were nothing like Gods. God did not control with fear.

The greed had programmed their slaves well. If they thought that they were better off than other creatures, then they would work without too much protest. Giving them that little bit had enabled the greed so very much. The humans had been so easy to trick; they even used color of skin to turn souls against each other. It was the same thing, give one group a little more, and the other wants it, too. The ones who get all the perks are content, because they think they are better. The ones who get the least have contempt for those who get more.

The One walked the twenty feet to the golden pool. Its strength had not only returned, now the being felt like it had all the energy from the universe in its mind and body. The wisdom had returned to the planet. The energy that humans had absorbed for so very long was now open to flow into all beings. All creatures remained as the collective. This is how it had always been before the greed. This is the way it would be into the future. When the individual minds were strong, the collective was the wisdom. Without individual strength, the collective was nothing.

Now, all things were going to unify. The planet would be whole once again. All its beings were once again going to know their true God.

The brother and sister were on opposite sides of the pool. The three beings formed a triangle as they stood facing each other. They shared their thoughts and the happiness that it had all ended. The greed and the other parasites were now gone. Now was the beginning.

The three beings levitated into the cool waters. Their triangle grew smaller as they approached each other. When they were at arm's length, the three abruptly stopped. They stood looking at each other with their third eyes. The brothers were a bright green, while the sisters were blue. The One had an eye of amber. The three beings stood locked in their gaze for some time. It seemed to the beings like days were passing as they spoke of the truth. They spoke about how the wisdom had returned to the planet. Knowledge was now something that was shared freely, like it had been in the past. The sun did not move much in the sky as the three communicated, indicating not much time had passed.

They all three turned to the outer parts of the pool so their backs were facing each other.

The three siblings all began to chant in their language known only to them. The dimensions opened around them and the countryside. Their minds melted into one as they became One with everything. The beings could understand the insects and the plants. Even the rocks and the dirt had a story, and the entity was listening with all its senses. Many more of its senses were open in this multidimensional atmosphere. All the senses present in the Earth's creatures were now harmonized in the being of the One. The creature truly had become One with all. All had become with the One. They had a mental contact with all the things around. A low pulse in the collective was naturally deciphered into the knowledge.

Krakatoa was very visible in the daytime sky. It looked like the moon, but ten times larger. There were now four moons in the sky revolving around the near planet. The color of the sky had taken on a magenta tone. It was laced with many shades of blues and yellow. The entire sky looked like a rainbow around the celestial body, setting in the North. It looked like an amazing sunset that was covering most of the sky, but it was the middle of the day. The sun was high in the sky.

The monoliths that had been built by the Sasquatch were visible once again. Other monoliths and temples were once again visible. Many more were in sight which had not been seen before. Those dimensions had not been opened yet. Now they were all in plain sight of the three beings and the Sasquatch, who had taken up spots surrounding of the pool. Many creatures were present in these other dimensions. Beings of all nature came into view. None of the creatures seemed to care if they were being seen by other beings. All these creatures were in harmony. This planet in all its dimensions had been truly healed.

Movement from the giant stone Sasquatch head drew all eyes. The mouth of the monolith had opened, revealing a dim green light. The space was quickly filled with the large shapes of Sasquatch. The beings had built these portals as a highway to traverse dimensions, but the greed had blocked them. They had been unable to contact the others in over six thousand years. Now the clan was reunited. The Sasquatch from the pool raced down the small hill into the valley. The other beings, coming from the portal, raced up the hill toward the same point. The two groups met with a tumbling, wrestling, and throwing each other celebration. The beings had been apart for so very long. Their happiness was shared by all the creatures present. Forty-four of the beings had come through the portal. Two different dimensions opened where the Sasquatch resided on this planet and twenty-two had come through each. Now they were sixty-six strong, and growing. Each of the new groups also had one pregnant female. The Sasquatch had already begun to heal.

A very ancient Sasquatch approached the One and embraced the being. These two had been friends since the beginning. They had been the first two to make contact. The embrace was one of brothers. A trust that was true and undying. When they separated, the One reached into a bag that had been tied to its side since the Oregon coast. He slowly opened the leather sack and presented the gift to its old friend. It was the singing bowl, made of Moldavite, that the being had picked up at the second reuse store in Oregon. This Sasquatch was the maker of the bowl. It had lost it to hunting party of humans, thousands of years before. It had passed through many hands through this time slowly losing its importance to history. Now, it was back in the hand of the creator. The Sasquatch cried as its large hands gripped the flawless green bowl and began its melody.

The three siblings celebrated with the Sasquatch. They all marveled the fact that they were once again in multiple dimensions. The glow from the three beings reflected off the bottom of the pool and cast a brilliant light into the heavens. It was a sign that all was well.

The Sasquatch slowly regained their position around the pool and the beings. Their energy combined with that of the siblings, and the energy reversed its course and went directly into the ground. The Earth rumbled with the force of the pulse. It instantly absorbed the positive electromagnetic energy the creatures had created. The pulse flowed through the planet and exited on the exact opposite side as the negative discharge. This was where the two poles of Pachymama would exist for the next one hundred thousand years.

The water evaporated from the pool. It had been absorbed by the Earth, along with the energy created by the entities. The three beings levitated to the corners of the pool and stood next to their allies. The siblings need not talk. They were ones who could communicate with their minds. They only used words with each other when they were particularly worked up about something. Then, the language was one of song, like no other on the planet.

The Sasquatch spoke about the abundance of food in the other dimensions. Berries in all forms grew to sizes as big as a basketball. Nuts, fungus, and other edibles only known in those dimensions were plentiful.

The Sasquatch spoke about how this abundance of food had kept them in existence all these years. They also spoke about the encroachment of the greed on the other dimensions. They only had the capability to enter a few dimensions out of hundreds, but it was enough to destroy the beings there. The Sasquatch had been infected in all three of the dimensions they inhabited. The infection which had been implanted by the greed had spread to the colonies in the parallels. Their beings were ones who traveled freely throughout all three of their dimensions to retain their family value. The importance of family was what had spread the virus among the Sasquatch.

The pregnant Sasquatch was very revered. The other beings knew how important it was to keep their species going. They were not ones to worship each other, but the mothers were being treated like queens. These pregnant beings were thousands of years old themselves. They were way past the time of having babies, but here they were. It had been a miracle. Now was going to be a new start for the creatures. Now, their kind had a chance.

All the beings began to walk into the triangle created by the devices. The energy from the shape was drawing the beings into it. The eight children also appeared, gongs in hand. They formed a circle within the triangle. As the others entered, the Sasquatch stood twenty-two on each side of the line created between the poles. The Three stood next to each other, their backs to the centrifuge.

The brother asked the One how they would know if the chosen had made it to Krakatoa safely. The One told him that they had already made it and were building their devices. The being also told it's sibling that the chosen would understand soon why the siblings had done what they had done. The chosen had thought that they had been betrayed by the three, but the One assured the other that they would have the knowledge.

The One also told the brother that a device had been sent to the allies on Krakatoa. It was a device that was going to be sent back to the main bases of the greed. It was not going to kill the greed, it was going to infect them. After they were infected, their pods would be open to the encroachment of other souls. When that would happen, the souls of the humans would be let loose in the colonies of the greed. They will merge with every soul in the species of the greed. Every one of their outposts will be infected. They like to experiment so much on other species, now, the One was experimenting back. They had treated the humans like nothing, now they would become partly human. The beginning of their end was here. Now the humans would be taking over the greed, from inside their beings.

"The best interest of Pachymama is and always has been first, above all beings," the sister spoke. "We may have made a mistake using the chosen like that and letting the humans perish, but it was the way. All beings make mistakes at times, just like us. In the end though, we achieved our mission. The end has finally come. Now we are in the beginning. My blessings go out to the chosen in their quest to rid their planet of the greed."

The Sasquatch began to sing a very strange tune. It was somehow very familiar to the One, but it didn't remember why. It consisted of clicking and whistling, which came from the creatures' throats. The pregnant females were standing two steps in front of the other beings, directly in the middle. All three were standing on the stone pillars that had been formed earlier by the crumbling soil. All three Sasquatch opened their mouths at the same time. A beautiful melody emitted from the beings. "It sounds like paradise," said the brother.

The tone coming from the pregnant females was a melodic wave of tones. It seemed to appeal to the other creature's senses. All the species were facing the females. The three siblings had taken up a position on three sides of the centrifuge, standing high on the pillars the Earth had created. The triangle they formed was at a perpendicular angle as the females. The six beings formed a six-pointed star.

The melody had a message in it which flowed right to all the creatures. Again, animals from the forest gathered around the perimeter of the devices to see what was happening. They too were being called by an invisible energy.

The song spoke of a new time on Pachymama but a different time. The message spoke of the planet being reset every so many millions of years. It also spoke of how we passed through dimensions and passed through lives only to be reborn in the same life with slight differences. The planet was the same cycle. It was reborn over and over, just on a much larger scale, and over much longer time. The end was always the beginning, and the beginning was always the end.

The song was sung over and over, like one long continuous tune. The three beings felt almost hypnotized as they listened to the message. The Sasquatch had always been friends with the three, and now their ending was creating a beginning together.

The beings stood atop their temple pieces, around the centrifuge. Darkness had fallen as the song went on. The eight children beat their gongs at rhythmic times. All the beings looked to the stars. The milky way and stars were clearly visible, as was Krakatoa. The green planet no longer looked like a moon. Now, it was visible as the Earth was from space. Only Krakatoa looked different than Earth. It was sixty percent land and forty percent water. The water and the land were lush colors of green.

"Now," the sister whispered. All eyes went to Krakatoa as a bright light appeared on its surface. The light grew brighter, until it pierced Earth's atmosphere and bathed the three beings in its green glow. The light was filled with life. It completely encompassed the One, its siblings, and all the area in the middle, including the centrifuge. It sent a message of peace and understanding. It thanked the One for its devices and Knowledge of defeating the greed. A full year had passed in their Krakatoa time in the span of only one day on Earth. Their battle had not been easy, just as on Earth. They had lost many species to the greed over the years, and this had been the final battle. "The greed had the same fate on both planets," the light told them. They had known about the mother ship, thanks to the three women sent from the One. The woman they called 'leader' was the one to make the implant. When the greed scrambled to their rescue pods, she had slipped the device into one of their saucer craft. The humans had once again been planted in another species.

The chosen, through their light, also communicated their gratitude to Pachymama for their stay. It had been a spiritual time for the chosen, and they hoped to return some day. The One communicated back that they were welcome any time to come back. Their species were part of the history of this planet. The One also spoke about the importance of rebuilding their planet. They had been part of a prophecy that repeated itself over and over. They had been spared to fulfill that destiny. Now, they were the seeds back on their planet that had been infested with the greed and the humans. Now, these were the only true chosen left. Their cycle had come all the way around.

The chosen communicated to the One about a gift that they were sending back to Earth. They had collected the DNA of many species on Earth before the greed had taken complete control. These samples were twenty thousand years old. Life forms long extinct on Pachymama now could be reseeded. The centrifuge began to spin once again. The green light began to take on a brightness like that of a supernova. It was not blinding to the beings, though. It was of a spectrum that would not destroy their retinas.

The centrifuge began to fade in and out of existence. It was connected to Krakatoa, but its purpose was almost over. Krakatoa would soon be out of range for the next five thousand two hundred years. The device became ghostlier with every spin of its mighty wheels. As it faded from sight, so did the Earth begin to fill in around the pillars. The song from the Sasquatch continued the entire time.

When the song ended, the entire scene was different. All the other dimensions had closed. The centrifuge was gone from sight, as was the hole it was in. The land around the pillars was completely solid, as was the golden pool. It had all been completely buried back into the Earth, hidden for future generations of caretakers.

As the Earth was shifting, Krakatoa was fading from sight. It just became smaller and smaller, until it faded to another star in the sky. The four moons of the planet had stayed behind. They had been another gift from the green planet. The celestial bodies had adapted well to the Gravitational pull of Earth, they seemed right at home.

These moons also contained life forms from the entire Solar system. Their cache had been hidden from the greed. They were all friendly species, and the Earth would need a new population. Even if they were just visitors. The new moons were the true testament to the new beginning. Everything truly was starting over.

There was an object in the spot where the centrifuge had existed. It looked like the hull of a submarine, but of a shiny metal. The object opened in the middle, and a light appeared from within. As the light grew brighter and greener, shadows began to form from within. The entire object was maybe fifty feet long and twenty feet tall. The shadows grew to massive sizes as they passed through and from the device.

The Sasquatch leader approached the object from Krakatoa. It walked right up to the open door and held out its large hand, in welcome, to the first shadow solidifying. The being was a wooly mammoth. Its mate followed closely behind. Sabre tooth tigers, dodo birds, and thousands of other species all came from the craft. This is where the stories of Noah's ark had come from in the bible. There had been a collection of all Earthly creatures. They had been taken by the chosen and safely stored in this time capsule. It had been flying through the cosmos for twenty thousand years, the humans had called it Halley's Comet.

The last two creatures out of the ark were a pair of humans. A man and a woman. Both were of a dark skin, and both were covered in tattoos of patterns with a cosmic message. As the last two were out, the light from within faded. Quickly, it was extinguished, only to be replaced by a bright yellow light. This light caught the attention of the eight children. They all walked toward the brightness, like a magnet was pulling them. They did not even look back. All eight beings walked into the portal. The Sasquatch waved its hand, and the craft swung closed. It, too, began to fade out of existence, until there was nothing in sight.

The creatures that had come through the portal scattered in all directions. Some stayed close, but most went off to explore. These beings were all happy to be home. They knew that they had been frozen in stop animation and condensed into atomic size, but they did not understand the physics of it. Like most creatures in the universe. They went right to feeding and exploring. The planet had changed very much since the last time they had roamed it.

The two humans approached the One. They both looked at the being and knew. This was the wisdom. They both began to bow to the being, but the One stopped them. It explained to them that it was not necessary to worship any other being. True God lived within us all. We were all God. Creativity was our way of using the powers of a higher existence.

These humans seemed different than the ones from the previous cycle. These ones seemed to have a slight understanding of what was going on. The One instilled in them to be good to the Earth and to all creatures. It told them to use their imagination. It also told them that all their actions would have a reaction. It told them to make decisions wisely. The One told the humans to pass this knowledge down to all their ancestors. These were the words.

The One looked to its siblings to reiterate its words. The other two were no longer there. Neither were the Sasquatch, nor any other of the beings from the forest. The One had not seen them leave. Now, it stood in the middle of this valley with two naked humans. The One understood it all. It was the same as it had been before. The others were gone, and it was on its own in this little corner of the planet. It was time to begin writing. There was another story beginning, someone would have to write the prophecy.

The two humans once again began to drop to their knees and pray to the One. The being stopped them, and told them gently to heed the word. This was the knowledge. The humans nodded their head in agreement.

The One saw it all. The two humans did not understand. They were putty waiting to be molded. They were the first of many fools to quickly overpopulate this planet. It was all like it had been before.

What had the being and its siblings really changed.

The One spoke in a whisper, but it was a shout to the forest and surrounding area. "Go."

The experiment had been reset.

CHAPTER 53

The group was awakened by a sonic boom. The boy exclaimed loudly from the backseat, "What the fuck was that?" He had been having a most peculiar dream. In it, the group in the car had merged into one soul. They were in a battle against aliens, but the memory of the dream was vague and fading. He had remembered the feeling of being free. Dark shadows had ceased to exist in his dream. Whoever they had been battling, they had defeated them.

"It was a UFO," said the man wearily. "It just came over that hill and buzzed us." The craft flew by again. The boy noticed that it was very large and flying fast. Fast enough for a sonic boom. The object passed in and out of sight multiple times over the next thirty minutes. Every time the craft passed, it seemed to be going slower and slower. After the twelfth pass, the flying disc slowed to a pace that was in pace with the car. A large brown crow was sitting on the hood of the car as it wound its way through the hillside. Everything, to the boy, seemed so familiar, yet so strange this day.

It had seemed like years since the trip with his grandparents had begun. In truth, it had only been four days on the road. They had picked up a hitchhiker this morning, some miles back, and now the girl shared their path.

Strange lights had appeared to the three the night before. They had been camping in the desert. A bright light had come over a hillside and flew erratically above them. The grandpa seemed very concerned about this. The boy had never seen the man scared, but there was a certain apprehension in the elder's face. The man played his gong all night long, while keeping a watchful eye on the lights in the sky. They had flown throughout the night and into the early dawn hours. By morning, the boy understood the expression which his grandpa had held all night long. It was not one of fear. He looked angry.

As the boy looked to the morning sky, he could clearly see the origin of the lights throughout the night. The large flying disk blocked the sun. The entire valley was covered in a dark shadow created by the enormous size of the craft. It was of an organic kind of metal on the bottom. The entire undercarriage of the ship looked like a giant living city. A bright red light was shining from the center. The whole thing looked to be over a mile wide. The object gave the boy a very uneasy feeling. He had this same feeling as a child sometimes, when he laid down at night. The bad feeling was oh so familiar to him. It made him feel ugly inside. He wished that he could hide from this craft, but it would be of no use. He had tried that many times before with no success.

They had left while it was still early in the morning. The saucer had finally shot off to space, and the family could once again start their car. They had packed up the camping gear and got out of there in a hurry. The woman checked her phone when they were in the car and was shocked to see that an entire day had passed. They had been at the same spot for thirty-six hours. She was certain, as were the others, that they had only camped one night.

Some miles down the road, as their nerves began to calm some, a hitchhiker brought the family to a halt. The tie-dyed shirt was like a beacon in the desert, drawing the family toward her presence. The girl looked very familiar to the three. As soon as they stopped, the look on the blonde girl's face told them that she felt the same. They all had crossed paths before, and they all knew it. None of them spoke as the girl climbed into the back-seat, next to the boy.

More than a hundred miles passed without any conversation. While the man drove through Death Valley, the others took a much-needed rest. The woman and boy had been up all night with a vigilance against the visitors. Sleep was now their reward for their bravery and perseverance. The girl also slept soundly in the back. The man looked in the mirror at the girl's features. He could not get over the feeling that they knew each other well. She seemed like an old relative that they had planned to pick up in this very spot. Everything had seemed so preordained.

The first sonic boom from the flying disc woke the others. The man had seen it fly overhead before the thunder that had followed. By the second pass, mere seconds later, the others had all sat upright and were looking out the windows at the dreadful sight.

"What do they want?" asked the boy.

"They want back what we took from them," answered the man. "They are not ac-customed to defeat and do not take it well. Also, we have one of their kind, and they want it back."

The girl, with a trembling voice, said "They have been following me for a very long time. I saw them one night when I was very young. Ever since that night, I can clearly see their species. They are ones to cloak their identity. Most people would not even know they were walking among an extraterrestrial cloaked to look like a human. They do not like it when people can see them. Only a few of our kind can see them, and it worries their species. They control with fear. Their control over me does not exist. I have their knowledge. They want it back." These were the first words that the girl had spoken.

"What are you scared of then?" asked the boy. "Your voice has tones of fear in it."

"These beings are capable of so much destruction. I am not scared of them, but I do hold a dark respect for their ways. They have controlled the beings of this planet for so very long. It is an addiction to their species. Their whole mission is to experiment. Controlled experiments could not happen without complete control. Now their control is slipping away. A new time is coming to this planet, and we are part of it. The time of control and greed are coming to an end. All beings deserve freedom and happiness. True aspects of these ways, not the make-believe freedom and happiness the powerful have pushed on all living beings."

The man said, "Now is the time we stand tall. The path we are on is one of enlightenment and healing for our souls. Our new addition has been part of the destiny from the beginning. On our quest, we have encountered the change. Now, we must embrace it and stand for our beloved Pachymama."

The man pulled the car to the side of the road. The four beings exited the vehicle at the same exact moment. The crow, still on the hood, began making clicking sounds while bobbing its head up and down. The bird's movements became more frantic, as did the sounds emitted from its beak. The noise intensified until it was deafening. Thousands more crows began to arrive. They covered the area around the humans and their car. Some even perched on the beings. The boy had a crow sit on his head. The air was filled with the soft caw of the creatures.

The sky began to rumble like a slow thunder. The sand under the feet of the group began to swirl and liquify, but their pods did not move. It felt like they had roots that held them firmly underground, holding them tight against the evil pull of the visitors. "I don't think they are very pleased with us," said the woman.

The vessel was so large and near that the sky was completely blocked out by its magnitude.

Lights began to spin on the bottom of the spacecraft. They sped up their motion until the lights all seemed to concentrate around the bright red light in the center. As they became a blur, the light in the middle began to change. As it had been solid, now it was of a watery look. Its flickering intensity looked like a bright red portal.

A bright beam of red light shot from the concentrated light and went straight for the humans. The light came to within two feet of their heads and seemed to be deflected by an invisible dome of about thirty feet diameter. The red light flowed around the sides of the invisible barrier. Its appearance was one of red lava pouring out of the light and coating the outside of the protective bubble. The four could see tormented souls, crying in agony, within this flow of lava light.

The crows within the dome began a cawing that was almost melodic. The crows on the outside of the dome were sucked up into the light until they, too, became one with the red glow.

The spinning lights, as well as the red portal, grew more intense. The lights seemed to move faster still, until they were one solid light around the craft. The red beam of light grew more intense and heavier. It pulsed every so often in a rhythmic pattern. The dome of protection over the group did not sway. The energy of the combined beings was a strong one. It was also an ancient one and held the knowledge.

This whole story also had been written so very long ago. This destiny played over and over through the particles of time.

"Raise your hands in unity," said the woman. Her voice could barely be heard over the sound the crows were making.

The four creatures raised their hands. In the hand of the woman was a stone with a sun in the middle. The symbol went completely through the object. Energy raced from the hands of the four and concentrated on the rock.

The object was pulled from the hand of the woman by unseen forces. It hung in the air, about a foot above and in the middle of the four beings. Their energy pulsed into the stone like lightning. The stone began to emit a bluish aura. Soon, the aura filled the inside of the dome and all the objects inside its confines.

The crow and its species became silent. The dome increased in size, pushing the beam from the spaceship back to its source. The craft began to shake and rumble. As the beam disappeared, the spacecraft broke into millions of pieces. They floated away like ashes from a bonfire.

The sky cleared briefly but once again turned black. The crows had taken flight from the red light that had imprisoned them. They were eating the pieces of the disk as they floated with the wind.

The beautiful melody of the crows filled the valley of death.

Chapter 54

A loud noise and shouting woke the family. They had been at this hotel three days waiting for a hurricane to pass. The girl had been in a very strange dream. She had dreamed about being chased by other beings. They had been closing in on the group, and now they had found them. The dread encompassed her dream and carried over to the conscious.

She had been slammed back into consciousness. The sound of gunfire permeated the small room. Something was happening next door. The barrage stopped, and all that could be heard was a woman crying. The girl was trying to remember where they were this day. They had been on the road for some time and had been holed up here for a few days, but nothing seemed familiar to the girl. It felt like she had never been in this room before.

"What just happened?" asked the girl.

"We're about to find out" answered the man. His words were punctuated by a loud banging on the door. The man jumped from bed to answer the knock. A large man dressed in black was lurking in the doorway. The guy's face looked odd to the man. The mirrored glasses concealed the intruder's eyes.

"Sorry folks, but you're gonna have to leave," the figure in the doorway said. His voice was one of a cop using their power voice to create fear. The man did not like this situation one slight bit. He did not like it one bit when anyone tried to instill fear in his being.

Something was seriously out of place here, the man thought to himself. All he could see was the intruder and the bright light that framed him. The stranger seemed to fill the space and their minds with his presence.

"What's going on?" asked the man. He was expecting a reply of intimidation but got the answer he was looking for instead.

"We've been tracking this guy since Gallup. We finally got our opportunity to take him down. He killed his whole family back in New Mexico and ran off with his lover. He killed six members of his family and has killed two families on the road here, to

Louisiana. He had met both these families at the hotel he was staying at with his lover. They are Satanists or some silly shit like that. They have been hiding out here for days. Now he is dead. The end of this story is near." The cop finished his tale, and then his words got harsh once again. "Now, please just gather your things and leave," he scowled at the family.

"Fair enough," answered the man. Many strange things had happened to him before in his crazy life, but nothing like this. Staying next to a serial killer for the last three days with the threat of being murdered always one snap away. The man had known something was unusual about the neighbor and his girl. He had only seen them once when they had been entering their room. The man had gone for ice, and when he came back, the neighbors were going through their door. They both had looked at the man and saw that he was different. They had a fear of the man and his family.

The man had given them both a small head nod but it was not returned. He had seen the aura of the two beings and perceived that it was very dark. These were not people to be trusted. He had spoken with the others about his concerns, but they had all said that he was crazy. "His imagination was running rampant like always", they had told him.

The family quickly gathered their possessions and loaded the car. As they were getting into the vehicle, the officers were bringing the woman out of the adjacent room. She froze when she saw the girl standing next to the minivan. "That's her," the woman shouted while pointing at the girl. "That's the witch I was telling you about. She is the evil one. She is going to ruin everything for the humans."

The woman was shouting hysterically. She had been handcuffed behind her back, which made her entire torso pitch forward with her words of hatred. She began to shake and tremble with the intensity of her tirade. The woman became so angry, veins were popping out on her forehead, which had turned an angry shade of red. She could not stop her rant, even when one of the officers hit her with a taser. This seemed to really anger the woman. She gave a roar and yanked her hands free of the handcuffs. Her wrists were bleeding profusely as she tore off after the girl, all the while yelling her battle whoop. She had absolute hatred in her eyes.

The girl nor the family moved. They were shocked by what they were seeing, but mostly they were not afraid. Too many things had happened to them, and fear was not a part of their lives because of it. The cops by the hotel room door were at a ninety-degree angle to the frantic woman and had drawn their guns.

The woman had not been very big. Maybe one hundred twenty pounds. The police opened fire on the woman when she was just yards away from the family at the minivan. The first few bullets did not stop her. After being shot eleven times, she stopped in her tracks. The large man who had originally come to the door that morning was immediately behind her and looked like he was going to handcuff her once again. Instead, the man reached up and pulled something from around the woman's neck. With his other hand, he brought his nine-millimeter to the back of the woman's head and fired once. Brains and bone peppered the girl standing ten feet in front of the lunatic.

The woman finally dropped. She lay bloody and crumbled at the family's feet. The figure who approached the family's door now came to the girl. He leaned in close and said, "We know all about you and the others. This serial killer also knew about you. It was the mission of these two parasites to take out your entire family. They had killed two other families, just like yours. You are not alone on your quest. Others have had the same calling. Soon, your paths will cross, and the true change will come. This day was not the day for your energy to end. It is not in the destiny. Go now, continue your path. Look for others like yourselves. They are out there. Just remember, there are those who are watching you and know your every movement." The man dropped the necklace from the killer into the hand of the girl and closed her fist around the bloody object. He was gone as suddenly as he arrived, going back to the death in the parking lot.

The girl got in the car. Her clothes and face were sprinkled with blood and bits of flesh. "Can we go now, please," she said with a sadness in her voice. She was already pulling off the hoodie she had been wearing and was wiping her face with the colorful fabric. The woman dug through her purse and handed the girl a few hand wipes.

The man was out of the parking lot as fast as possible. They needed to get away from this place and its bad energy. Dealing with the cops had normally been unpleasant for the man, but this had been something entirely different. They had seemed to know what was going on. These police officers were part of whatever mission they were on. It was all part of the destiny. When they had gotten back on the highway, the man asked the girl, "What was that all about with that lady? She sure seemed to know you, or think she did at least."

"That lady was a friend of my dad's," answered the girl. "She was a very bad person, and in some ways contributed to my dad's death. I have been following her around for the last two years and finally found her in Gallup. She knew I had been following her and set her new boyfriend on me. I told him all about her evil ways and to beware of her presence. That night, he killed his family. The police did not kill the Succubus, just her flesh pod. Her evil is old and will live on forever. I know who she is and that scares her. Now, I also have some of her powers in this."

The girl held the long chain that had been gifted to her by the cop. It was of a strange metal that looked like woven hair. The amulet was a solid piece of clear quartz about two inches wide and one inch tall. Inside its clear interior was a solid blue eye. The eye seemed to look at the girl and the rest of the family as it was held in the car. The girl pulled out a small leather pouch from her side and dropped the object into its darkness.

The metal made a clinking sound when she placed it in the sack, like there were other objects inside its magical enclosure.

"Most cannot see the Succubus for what she is, but I can," the girl continued. "She is the eater of souls. She is a being who came to this planet over a hundred thousand years ago. Most would call her a demon, but she is really an alien. She can take any form of any animal in her presence. She makes the males of any species fall in love with her, and then she eats their souls. This creature had targeted my Dad. He had come across her presence in his trading. He found this necklace and had to have it. He would have given anything for it, but not his soul. By the time he had realized who he was wheeling and dealing with, it was too late. The Succubus already had her talons embedded in his being. He had been just as strong as the creature. They had been in a battle over who could eat the other's soul first. Neither had won, my dad had died in the struggles, but only his pod. His soul is alive and well."

The others sat in silence, pondering the girl's words. How had their paths crossed back in Roswell? The girl had approached the family at the UFO museum, and they had struck up a friendship. This girl had seemed like an old friend to the family. Their paths had crossed for sure in a previous life. How much did they really know this girl, and why did she seem so familiar to all of them? When she had asked them for a ride to Mississippi, it seemed perfectly natural to say yes.

The crows began to appear. First there were a few, but soon thousands. Their flight was a choreographed rhythm that seemed to spell out a message. The message was not clear now, but it would be soon. "How did our paths cross?" the man asked the girl.

"This whole trip is a preordained destiny for all of us. We have all been through some terrible times. Most would not have made it through these hardships. Now is the time for us to combine our energies and make it good. It is the time to get rid of the dark shadows and replace them with the light. We are passing through many dimensions now. You cannot be aware of it all the time. Sometimes things happen to us, and our existence in that dimension ends. However, we exist in multiple dimensions and are reborn in a different dimension every life cycle. Some things come back to our memory, but most do not. Our subconscious blocks us from knowing about our previous lives. It also blocks any memory from the different dimensions. I look familiar to you, because I am your family. I am your niece."

The man stomped on the brakes. He got out of the car and flung the back-passenger door open. He stared intently at the girl. Her eyes looked exactly like his. Could it really be his niece? "If you are my niece, then tell me about the last fourteen years. My niece was abducted from her bedroom when she was six. The only witness had been her seven-year old brother, who said that a group of small men took her. He had said there were three of the beings, and they had arrived in a light and left in the same light. It was the only clue ever found. My brother's family, police and community never gave up looking. The sadness had never left the family. Eventually, they had all died of broken hearts."

"I was taken when I was six, but I was returned the same night. I was there with my family all along, in some strange parallel universe. I could see and hear them, but they could not see me. I even saw the cops and their investigators trying to blame someone in my family. I watched my parents and brother search for me and slowly lose their minds. Sometimes, I could get their attention by breaking something or knocking things over. Mostly they thought these were from bad spirits that they thought followed them. Like a dark cloud. Sometimes, I would go places with my family. Some people even saw me, but most didn't. No one ever saw me when I was with them, only when I would wander off by myself. I was there when my family all died, but I was helpless to stop it. I had been cursed by whatever had abducted me. I was with my family, but not with them at the same time. After their death, more and more people could see me. After just a couple of weeks, I was fully in this dimension again. It is when I decided to hunt down the Succubus who destroyed our family. I figured after I took care of that bitch, I would go after the greed, who had abducted me all those years ago, only to imprison me in the walls of my house."

"What is your name?" asked the man. Everything the girl was telling him made complete sense. He had known about the visitors. They had visited him and his brother and sister when they were small children. They had tried their experiments on the three siblings, too, but their collective energy had been too strong for the visitors. Abduction had not happened. Instead, they had terrorized the minds of the three. Fear had been implanted with spirits and demonic possession. Being small children, the fear enveloped them.

The greed, however, did not see the side effect of this. The three beings were frightened repeatedly until they became immune to the fear. Then, they became aware of death and did not fear it, either. With no fear, there had been no control.

This is when the greed began to really watch the siblings. The three had always been able to see into dimensions where other humans could not. The greed had known that the three siblings were different and defiant. The three were going to be a problem for them in the future.

When their control through fear did not work, the greed went to work to control the siblings by religion. Their mother had been very religious as a youngster and passed her ways to her children. Once again, the three scoffed at the idea of any form of control. They were truly free spirits with knowledge of creativity.

Throughout their entire lives, the greed had sent many different attempts of control on the siblings. They had all failed, but were a burden on the three. Many bad things had happened to the family over their lifetimes at the hands of the greed and their attempt to control.

Even the niece's abduction, fourteen years before, was a deed perpetrated by the greed to control the siblings.

The girl was looking at the man with respect. She knew her uncle well. Before her abduction, their families had gone on holidays together. She had grown up knowing her aunt, uncle, and their son. They had always come over to the family house and were true family. They had helped his brother look for the girl. They had been there with their family in the time of their need. It was how it was supposed to be.

The energy from a family was like nothing else. They could either heal each other or destroy. In a time of hardship, unity in a family was the key to healing. No other beings could help you the same.

Other members of their family would also come around, but it was different. They all seemed to want something from her parents. They had both lost a piece of their soul and needed comforting. The uncle had been the only one there just for that.

The girl had joined in their talks many times, the others had just been unaware of her. This did not stop her from being part of the family. She acted like everyone could still see her. She was there, and she held the knowledge.

The man repeated the question. "What is your name?"

"One" stated the girl. Her deep hazel eyes looked directly to those of her uncle.

The man grabbed the girl and embraced her. Tears flowed from his eyes.

He had been waiting for this moment for fourteen years.

Chapter 55

The window opened in the sky. There was no other way to explain what the woman had seen. The others had been asleep for miles. She was the driver. At first, it appeared to be a black line in the sky. Almost like a shadow stretching from horizon to horizon. Then, the line had opened and the woman could see the stars. A bright light seemed to be in the distance, pulsing a green luminous orb.

"What the fuck is that?" exclaimed the woman as she stopped in the middle of the road.

The others all woke up quickly. They had been accustomed to waking up quickly on this trip. So many things had happened, they were always at the ready. None of the others needed to speak, they could see the strange occurrence happening in front of their eyes. The sky had indeed been opened with surgical precision. The line was opened like an abdomen. Not only were stars visible, so were galaxies. The green light grew very bright until the group could see nothing but the strange vibration. It filled the void in the sky. Only a little bit of space was visible, directly in the center of the light. The entire opening now looked like an enormous green eye.

The car seemed to be hovering above the ground. Then, suddenly, they were whisked into the hole in the sky at warp speed. Lights and stars flew by the group as they were plastered to the seats of the minivan. The movement of the vessel, occupants, stars and galaxies all whizzed by at the speed of blur. "What's happening?" yelled the man. He was still coming out of his sleep and now was flying through space.

"Tornado" shouted the woman. The van continued to speed through time. The force kept the family from any movement. Shouting was barely heard over the speed they were traveling. The voices sounded like a worn-out record on slow speed.

The next hours were a haze to the group. When they were fully aware again, they were stopped at a park. They all had a recollection of the passing through space and time. It all seemed like a dream to them now. No other persons were in sight. The family got out of the car and walked. They needed to figure out what had happened and where they were. Thinking was not coming so clearly for any of them.

The man walked around the minivan to check for damage but miraculously, there was none. He also checked his body over and told the others to do the same. All of them seemed to be okay. The man did notice a small scratch on the back of his neck. It seemed familiar to him though. He couldn't remember when he had gotten the mark, but he remembered having it.

The entire town seemed to be deserted. The man said it reminded him of a twilight zone episode.

The four walked for some time before they found a plaque imbedded in stone. The plaque said 'Joplin, Missouri. Population 3333.'

"How could that be?" asked the woman. When we hit that tornado, we were in Texas. That's over one thousand miles away. How could we have ended up here?"

The man remembered Joplin and told the others the story. "A few years ago, there was a terrible tornado in this town. It had destroyed every soul and every structure. The entire town had perished. My sister and her husband had come here as rescue workers. They had told me about the destruction and death that had been laid upon this small burg."

"How did we end up here then, and why is the town in perfect condition?" asked the woman.

The man was about to answer with a question. His thoughts were interrupted by the sight of a figure sitting on a bench across the street. The figure wasn't moving, but it was obviously the shape of a human. The four strode towards the figure knowing for sure that things just were not right. The dogs would go nowhere near the seated figure.

The family stopped when they were about a yard and a half away. The creature was sitting in its black suit and hat with its head slumped. The creature could have been dead or alive, the family could not tell.

"Excuse me," the man said, "we are lost. Can you give us some information please?"

The figure sat motionless. The man persisted. "Hey, can you hear me?"

The figure slowly raised its head. The eye sockets were vacant. It opened its grotesquely large mouth and a loud siren sound came from it. It filled the air with a pitch of dread. The sound was so loud and abrupt, it knocked the family from their feet. They quickly bounced back to a standing position at the ready.

The sound was quickly blocked in their minds by the complete control they had achieved. Weapons like this would easily harm most humans. These four were not most humans. They had been caught off guard by the strangeness of the situation. Now they knew. This creature was not going to surprise them again.

The scream ended as fast as it had begun. "What is this" said the man calmly to the figure seated in front of them. This being looked very familiar to the group. They had encountered it before. It had tried many times to bring them fear, but it was powerless in doing so. This being had known defeat at the hands of the four. All the creatures present knew it. The four had no fear, only impassiveness.

"You know what this is all about," the figure answered through telepathy. "You and your group think that we are blind to your ways and would just let you continue on your path. You were wrong. We have controlled this planet for a very long time and we are not just going to hand it over to a few who want it all. We know all about you and your destiny. We wrote the rules here and we write the destiny. All you humans are so stupid. We have made you believe lie after lie. All of it nonsense. We are the ones who make the masses work. We are the ones who give them beliefs and hope. We are their true Gods, at least in their minds."

The streets had filled with other figures in black. From the air, the streets would look solid black with the dark beings. "Look around you" said the figure while waving at the dark figures which had amassed. "Your path stops here, today, in this place. We have been following you for many miles through many different dimensions. You knew how to manipulate those dimensions with death. We see that you four are different than the other humans. You know about death and dimensions. You have been running from us for a very long time in search of your treasure. Now, it is over."

"You have seen things very much wrong. That was always the problem with your species." The entire family said in unison. The figures had been approaching the group but now they all stopped where they stood. The four voices, together, brought a fear to the beings. The greed numbers were strong as was their technology but these four beings were different. These four creatures held the wisdom. They continued. "You and your group convinced the humans that you are Gods, but you are not. You are visitors traveling through the universe just as we are. Just as many other creatures in the cosmos. We also do not want this planet to ourselves. We did not come here for treasure nor power. We just want to rid Pachymama of you and your kind. You are the evil, the darkness. The planet is the good, the light. Both cannot exist without the other, but both do not need to exist together either. It is time to rid the light of the shadow you have cast."

"Your other mistake was to think that we are human," the family continued. "We are far from being human. Your implants have never been effective on us. We have inhabited many flesh pods on this planet and many had your silly devices in their brains or their bodies. We scoffed at your childish ways of playing scientist. Your species truly are pathetic. You thrive on the misery of others while living lavish lifestyles. This planet and all of its creatures are going to rejoice when you and the rest of the greed are gone."

"You are fools" laughed the seated figure. The shadow figures converged on the family as soon as they stopped talking. Their presence was dark and dreadful. The four did not let them faze their armor. They stood strong as a group and were ready for the dark clouds. They had spoken about this moment often. Many times, after the death of their family, the man and woman had spoken about the dark clouds that had come. They had been following them ever since. These dark times had prepared them for something in the future and that something was now. They had encountered darkness before and got through it. They would do it again.

The girl produced a stone from her pocket. On it, the engraving of a sun. The stone emitted a strong blue beam of light as soon as the sun rays touched it. The stone felt hot to her touch. It vibrated a strong energy through the girls being. Her senses were stimulated by the object and its light. This mini monolith was magic. She had somehow remembered getting this stone as a gift but that seemed like so many years ago. It was in the distant parts of her brain, filed away to make room for all the new memories from the journey they had been on.

As soon as the dark figures saw the stone in the girl's hand, fear encompassed their beings. There had been rumor among their people that the four had possessed one of their sacred stones, used only by their shaman, but it had been a myth. Or so they had thought.

The girl held the stone above her head and shouted, "ONE!" The light from the object pulsed its blueness outward until it connected with the sky. The light and the blue of the sky became one, covering everything in the area with its cool glow. The two shades merged into one spectrum, coating everything in a Prussian blue spectrum.

The sky began to fill with darkness. The light had awakened millions of crows and now they were all taking flight at the same time. At first, some of the birds seemed to be coming from buildings, trees and even some forming from the Earth. Then, as the numbers got greater, the azure of the sky seemed to be transforming into the dark birds. The crows emitted a cawing, in unison, that made the ground rumble. The flapping of their wings sounded like thunder.

A gong like sound came from the stone in the girl's hand. The figures in black began to retreat from the group. Another pulse from the stone and a loud gong sounded explosively. The figures, except the seated one, were instantly gone. They were broken in billions of little pieces. They floated in the air like ash. The crows swooped through the pieces catching the remnants of the beings in their beaks. They seemed to be in an orgiastic state as they feasted. As the birds got their fill, they disappeared back into the air and the Earth. The sky was blue again. All the crows except for one had gone back into their dimension.

The seated figure was the only one to remain. The family, once again as one, spoke to the cowering being. "Go now and tell the others. You may be strong and use nice magic, but we are the ONE. Our destiny was written long before the arrival of your species and your human seeds. You may think that the prophecy is made up, just like all the information you made up and fed to the masses. You are wrong. The prophecy is very real. It is why you keep losing. It is the way. You are only Gods in your own minds. It is a dangerous attitude to have."

The creature in black slowly lifted its head to look at the four beings. It tried to make a sound from its grotesque mouth, but not a single tone came forth. The being had been defeated. There was nothing left except for this pod. Its soul had been devoured by the crows. It was another message that the greed would be getting. Not only were they being defeated, their souls were being eaten by the One also.

The family knew all about the greed creating fear in the Earth's creatures. Fighting fear with fear was only appropriate. After all, the greed were the ones who had wrote "an eye for an eye" in their false religions.

The girl stuffed her stone in the vacant eye socket of the dark figure. The light from the object enveloped the being, concentrating until it shot into the heavens like a comet. The figure was gone. All that remained on the bench was the stone the girl had produced from her pocket.

"How many times are we going to go through this?" asked the woman. "The greed are the kings of mind control and manipulating the situation."

"Sometimes, I don't know what is really happening and what is made up by the greed," said the girl. "They have changed reality before for their benefit. Why would we not think it is what they are doing now."

"It is almost over now," replied the man. "They know about us and are scared. We know the greed are powerful and we also know what they are capable of. However, we need to remain focused on the mission. We are stronger than them. The final battle will happen at my sister's house. It will truly be the end."

As the four walked back to the minivan, they noticed that the pristine town was no longer so. It was destroyed now like an atomic bomb had struck. They all knew what had happened. They were here two years later, on the exact day. This had been all part of the destiny.

Joplin had not been destroyed by tornadoes, it had been destroyed by the greed. They had been testing a new weapon and made it look natural. Nothing had been natural about it. They had covered it up with their disinformation and lies. It had been business as usual.

The humans believed every lie fed to them by their rulers. The humans were true puppets to the greed. The one who suffered the most was Pachymama. It was the light, and the dark had infested its being. Now it was time for a new beginning.

The One was going to bring upon the end.

The greed was to be no more.

Chapter 56

The trip to Minnesota was a haze for the group. They encountered not a single other soul on the long journey, except for the crow that guided them on the way. Driving through town after town that was deserted was unsettling to the family. The man spoke of the masses knowing something was coming and being scared. They stayed locked indoors, hidden away. "It was the way of the humans. Stand for nothing and fall for everything. They truly are the parasites on this planet," said the man to the others.

Gas and food were easy to come by. The workers at the stores had abandoned their businesses and hadn't even locked the doors. They had obviously left in a hurry. The family still left behind money for the things they had taken. They were not thieves even in this hour of the human turmoil. It was only right to pay for what they needed. It was the righteous way, and that was their way.

At one gas station, the television had been left on, and the man and woman caught a glimpse of it. The news, and everything else, on the box was about the reality star turned president. He stood there talking his words of hate and false truths while criticizing others for what he was. The family saw right through this and all the other propaganda that the media threw their way. It was all smoke screens for the greed to continue with business as usual and give the rest of the slaves their just reward. More work to feed the family.

The man knew the truth about this new party that had suddenly came about in American politics. The Nazi rulers had been defeated and their armies and navies disbanded. Even some of the high-profile mass murderers were hunted down and brought to trial. But the true greed that had perpetrated it all had walked away with all their riches, awaiting the day to get strong again. They sat on their treasures for seventy years, while infiltrating their influences back into the global economic scheme. They became more and more powerful all this time, and when it was time, their man was in power of the country with the most weapons and influence.

These same bankers and financiers, whose hands did not know the feel of dirt, now were going to instill their agenda all over again.

While the whole planet debated and then went to war, the true elite would be sitting in their nice warm bases in Antarctica. Their feasts would consist of the terror perpetrated on the humans and the planet. They would not get their fill until mayhem encompassed the entire globe.

Back in the car and on the road, the family did not talk about politics. They were trying to put the outside world behind them for this trip, and make their own existence inside their small bubble.

The four spoke excitedly about the next part of their journey. They were to be reunited with their people. The energy grew more powerful with each mile. The group grew more excited as the energy grew. They all felt the draw that the sister's house was having on them. There were forces which drew them near. The crow, flying low over the car, knew the exact way. No maps were needed on this day.

The family spoke of the journey which had led to this trip. The multiple deaths had taken its toll on their energy and now they were beginning anew. Darkness had enveloped their lives for the last two years, and now it was time to bring back the light. It was time to stop dwelling on past events and accept the destiny for what it is. The perforations of the heart would always remain. Time was what would heal those wounds, while scars would remain. "Time is the most valuable thing any of us have," the man had told the others.

They spoke about how all the things that had happened to them in the last years, and over the course of their lives, had put them on the road to this moment. How every decision they made before, in the past, affected this very moment. They had all chosen this destiny by making the right choices along the path. Even bad choices were made by all beings at times. How you dealt with those bad choices affected everything. Also owning up to those faults and not denying your mistakes, made it much easier to make right decisions. Every action of life trickled into the future.

The storm began almost as soon as the family got into Minnesota. Black clouds had swooped in over the horizon. Now they were dumping their full load and punctuating it with lightning. The niece said it was the worst rain she had ever seen. It was relentless. If there had been other cars on the road, the hazard would have been great. As it was, the man kept the speed down to about thirty miles an hour, and safely made their way through the downpour.

Just east of Duluth, the tornadoes began. The last rains were nothing compared to this onslaught. The man gripped the wheel with white knuckles through blinding rain and whipping winds. A few times, he could feel the car lifting from the road. The energy in the car, however, was one of togetherness. They were one in this car, and they would get through this ordeal together.

The boy used his Bluetooth to get his playlist on the stereo. The next time the car left the ground, the boy played 'On the road again' at full volume. The sound pounded even above the cacophony of sounds permeating from the winds. The family all laughed, drowning out the sounds of dread and replacing them with ones of light and hope. The car was pulled by unseen forces back to the ground, where it jolted to an abrupt stop.

"You guys all handled that very well," said the man. "The greed is all around us. You can see their shadows through the storm. They are just trying to scare us. Their fear does not work with us. They obviously see it. We are laughing in their faces. Good joke, boy, with the music. Our energy is strong together, and we must keep it that way. Pachymama is also one with us. The greed will never get control of us."

The man's words were punctuated by the boy striking the gong from the back seat. The girl followed seamlessly with the melodic song of her singing bowl. The man was filled with pride. The others understood fully. The man and woman looked at each other and smiled. Theirs was a unity that was going nowhere but toward the light.

The rain pursued the family the entire way. Ten minutes from their destination, there was a loud thumping coming from under the car. The man had no choice but to pull over. The second he exited the car, he was soaked, like he had fallen into the lake. The rain did not bother the man nor his senses. It had qualities about it like everything in nature that made it beautiful and unique.

Now that the man was outside the car and not moving, he could see the shadowy figures all around them. Only semi-hidden from the rain, their numbers were countless. The energy from these creatures was one of dread and darkness.

The man thought hard about the light. The true light. Not the false light like these creatures had portrayed themselves as since their arrival on Pachymama. He thought about its beautiful rays being just past the clouds and trying to break through the turmoil of the weather.

The beings seemed to be standing still, observing the man and his actions. He could see a strange aura coming from the figures. It was menacing, but the man was not scared. The family's power had become stronger then the being's, the man knew it with confidence. The man felt a power with the others that brought fear among the shadows.

The wind was whipping all around, but the tornadoes were not near the family. They seemed to be drawn away from the group by a force field of some kind. The greed and their power had no control over these four beings.

Kneeling on the ground brought stability to the man. He had become a bit light headed from the torrents of rain and wind. The watchers who were all around were also draining his energy somehow. Their powers were many and strong. They had ways that would be considered magic, but it was their knowledge of manipulation. The man peered under the vehicle. Whatever he had hit, it was stuck under the car. At first, he could not tell what the thing was; it was dark from the storm and darker under the car. When his eyes adjusted, and he wiped them dry, the man could clearly see.

There, crumpled into the shape of a ball, was lodged an alien humanoid creature. It was just like in all the drawings, paintings, and movies that the man had seen on visitors. Large head with large eyes. Small body with long arms and short legs. This creature had been mangled badly. The man tried to think when he could have hit the entity. Its arms and legs were twisted in odd directions. The few scrapes it had were emitting an oily looking substance that reminded the man more of grass than of blood. Its skin, torn away in pieces, was mostly intact and grayish. It looked like scaly leather, but it was difficult to make out in the dim light.

The being was moving. It was still alive. The man noticed the extraterrestrial was trying to grasp something that was tied around its neck. It was a roundish object about three inches across and maybe one inch thick. It had a symbol resembling a sun cut through the middle of it. The man couldn't tell if the object was stone or metal. It looked very familiar to the man, but he could not place it. The object seemed to give off a slight glow that illuminated the bottom of the being's face. It was scared. The being was being very protective of the amulet. The man could sense that the being had no fear for its own life. Its main concern was the device around its neck.

Just before the alien's long, sucker like fingers touched the stone, the man shot his hand under the car and snatched the object from the creature's neck. A cord made of organic material snapped with the sound of glass breaking, releasing the object into the man's hand. A powerful shot of energy raced through his body. It was followed by an immense feeling of pain, pleasure, joy, and sadness. All at the same time.

The wounded creature let out a blood curdling cry as soon as the chain had broken from its neck. Its shock that the amulet had been taken was perceived by the man. It also perceived the anger in the scream of the parasite. The piercing sound was a siren to the other creatures following the family. This human had just stolen their sacred stone.

The man sprang to his feet, shocked. Suddenly, he knew; the object was the key between dimensions. It was also the key to the knowledge of those dimensions. He had held this object before. It had been another of his lives, in a different dimension. Things would happen very similar in each dimension with minimal changes. He couldn't remember any of these lives in other parallel places, but he knew they existed. He knew somehow, that with this device, he would be able to remember those other lives and re-live them at will.

He could now clearly see the other beings through the pounding rain. It was still coming down very hard, but now the showers were invisible to the man. His eyes had slowed down time, where he was moving much faster than all other moving things. It was the way in this dimension that he had just bounced into. When he had snagged the amulet from the extraterrestrials neck, an explosion had killed the man and the entire family. The explosion had been so great, it had taken out Northern Wisconsin and all of Minnesota. The great lake had gotten much bigger.

That had been that dimension, now they were in this one.

The beings had gathered closer around the minivan. They could clearly see that the man could clearly see. These beings were very angry at the family and wanted only revenge. It was one of their kind stuck underneath. The man had taken the sacred object, and they wanted it back, along with their brother.

The problem was, the man had no intention of giving the object back to the beings. It was his; he had carried it from other dimensions. That device, his family, and his tattoos were all that was transcended from dimension to dimension. He was not about to give up any of them.

The beings simultaneously pointed their long fingers at the man and emitted a high pitch scream that made trees topple. Creatures raced from the forest as the small gray lizard like men shouted their obnoxious pitch. The man could hear nothing coming from the grays. All he could hear was the melody of the singing bowl, punctuated with the gong. His niece and grandson were playing their righteous melodies of light from the backseat of the minivan.

The rain instantly stopped. The man sensed the large craft blocking the sky. It had been up in the clouds, hidden by the rains. It was the rain and the storm. These beings had abilities of manipulating weather. It had been apparent with the deluge of tornadoes.

The man had seen this vessel many times before. It, too, was present in so many of the dimensions. A bright light came from the vessel directly at the man and his family. It hit the amulet in the man's hand and made a storm of energy above it. The light shot off into so many directions that it seemed to be solid. It covered everything visible to the family. The four could smell, taste, feel, hear, and see the light. Mostly, they could understand the light. All the visitors disappeared into the brightness. They were gone in a flash, and then the light was gone, too.

The rain returned. The man looked about, but the creatures were gone. He looked under the car and saw that the mangled being was still there. He calmly opened the back of the car and removed the dog kennel and a fishing pole that they had brought along. The boy asked if he needed help, but the man said the gong was the best help that they could get right now, along with the singing bowl. The man used the pole to dislodge the alien. He was careful not to touch the being with his hands. He didn't like the smell coming off this creature and did not want any of its bacteria on his skin.

Once he got the extraterrestrial free from the undercarriage, he used a stick to stuff the being into the kennel. He slammed the door shut. It was a tight fit. The being barely fit. Its large black eyes looked pleadingly at the man, trying to communicate through the minds. The man felt the creature knocking at his thoughts, but blocked them completely. He remembered it all now. These beings had been coming around his life since he was very small. They had done all kinds of things to him, but his body had rejected it all. Now, he had one of the little bastards captured. He laughed at the pathetic attempt by the creature for mercy. They had never shown him mercy.

The man stacked the crate into the back of the van and piled the suitcases on top. The being was buried under the cargo. He had a spring in his step and was whistling as he went back to the driver side door. "What are you doing with that thing?" the woman asked as he got into the car. "It stinks".

"Don't worry," said the man, "It will serve us a purpose. We found a living book, and now we are going to read it."

"I've been looking online, and it says not to have any contact with those things if you encounter them," said the woman. "While you were out there playing with your buddies, I was doing some serious research. They said never to take their amulets or jewelry, as they can create rips in the space time continuum. They said whatever you do, do not capture one."

"Too late," replied the man as he looked at his wife with wonder. Her words were so odd. "I've done both of those things. I know it pissed off the grays. They deserve everything they get. This has been coming their way for a very long time. They have controlled things on this planet for far too long. They have manipulated minds and nature. Now, I have one of their amulets, and I already know about its powers. It has been in our possession before. This trip we are on, we have made countless times. Every time, in every dimension, it is slightly to drastically different. These beings are worried about us, and now they are in fear. We have turned their own tactics back around on them. Now, we have the control. Silly thing is, we don't want control over anything. But, at the same time, we are not going to let the control go on anymore. The end of the greed is near."

"I know the truth about the grays now," the man said to the others. "Their stone that I took told me all about them. They are not what they seem. These grays, or visitors, or whatever people call them, are not coming from other planets. They are in truth the greed. They just shape shift into anything they want to create the most fear in their adversary. They were the creators of 'civilization' and the destruction that it brought with it. They built bases on Mercury and Mars to be able to have a convenient escape if things went wrong. Their existence is one of manipulation of reality, creating fear so that they have complete control. They are the ones to create the illusion of alien visitors to make smoke screens for their flights of their space craft, while instilling fear at the same time. When people see their advanced warships, they think it is an alien from another planet. They just make up scenarios to make the people look crazy. When the greed first arrived on this planet, they put satellites around the planet, blocking it from any visitor coming into its atmosphere. Any craft that comes closer than the moon is quickly detected and brought down by the defenses on the moon. The satellites are a last resort. They have controlled everything since the day they arrived, like a giant video game. It is why the numbers always line up. They mapped it all out on their computers long ago; we are living their next level."

The remainder of the trip was easy and smooth. The family all sat in deep thought over the words of the man. The rain continued, but the tornadoes had stopped. They had kept the speed slow again and caught their breath on the short drive to the sister's house. The woman spoke to the man, "I think you are crazy to fuck with these aliens like you are, but, I trust you like nobody ever before. I knew from the beginning that you were different. You have proven that so many times. Now, like always, I am one hundred percent by your side."

The man reached over and grabbed his wife's hand. Their unification was a strong one from the beginning. Through the years, so much turmoil in life had brought them even closer. They stood by each other, even if the other was starting a war with aliens who had controlled the humans for six thousand years. One thing the woman knew for sure, they were always in for some adventure.

Pulling into Hoyt Lakes was very odd. It looked like they were having a parade, but there were no people. Floats and banners were sitting idly in the street waiting for a manned crew. The festivities were soaked from the rain as it began to accumulate in the streets. A small river had formed down the center of the main avenue. They reasoned that this was maybe the reason that the people had abandoned their parade. The man knew better. They were all inside. These people, like the ones on the road, were hiding. They knew the end was near.

The family finally pulled into the sister's house. Their energy was at an explosive level. Parking in the driveway, they were not altogether surprised to see the sister's house bathed in sunlight. It was the only sunlight in the entire downpour, and it was right on her house. The driveway wasn't even wet in the least.

The family made their way to the door to be greeted by the sister's boyfriend. The family had never met this man, but they instantly all got along well. The group could all tell that this guy was a stand-up fellow and was going to be a much-needed ally in the days to come.

The sister appeared from behind her man with a warm glowing aura. True family hugs were abundant. The sister commented about the amulet the man was wearing. She asked him where he had gotten it, but he did not answer. The look he gave her told the story.

These two were connected. The same things had happened to each of them throughout their lives. The sister produced the same exact amulet. "I got mine at Lake Superior. Weird things going on over there. I had to go investigate, and well, you know."

The man replied, "I got mine about ten miles back on the road. Weird things going on here too. We have a lot to speak about. Many things are lining up. Numbers that haven't lined up for a very long time are coming into sync. The numbers are what the destiny is made up of. When the numbers line up, destiny is flowing like water. Things are about to happen to fulfill the destiny of this planet. But first, how did you get your amulet?"

A male voice from inside the house thundered through the walls. It spoke with a confidence and a familiarity that brought tears to the man's eyes. "The same way you got yours and I got mine. We took them. Just like always, since we were little kids." Out of the shadows appeared his brother. Around his neck hung the same amulet that the other siblings had. On his shoulder was perched the largest crow the man had ever seen.

The bird had bright green eyes.

Chapter 57

Ever since he had entered the light surrounding his sister's house, the man had felt a strong sense of euphoria. It felt as if he were on a natural drug. His senses told him that this was the healthiest his mind and body had ever been. This very day, power seemed to flow from the man. His energy was so strong, the flesh pod could not contain it all. The man's aura danced around the room, combining with that of his brother's and sister's and the other multitude of spirits present.

The last hours were crazy, but the man had somehow gotten a strange rush from the events. The sister's house, and it's light, was a welcome sanctuary of peace after the cataclysm they had just drove through.

The niece was laying on the couch in a daze. She had nearly fallen over when she had passed out. Seeing her father, in the flesh, made her head spin out of control. Luckily, the boy had been there to catch her.

All the others had stayed in the front room around the girl. The brother stood in the middle of the room with a wild look in his eye. The crow, still on his shoulder, seemed to be whispering something to him. The creature was making faint clicking sounds next to the ear of the sibling.

"I knew you were going to be here," the man said to his brother.

The brother spoke, but his mouth did not move. The man could clearly hear what he was saying, but the others could not. His brother's words were only for him. "I am happy that you listened to my words, brother. They have brought you far, as I knew you would go. The One is complete again. Look around you, our people are all here. There is so much we must speak of, but first, let us rest. You have been on a very long journey. The beings that have followed you are only joining the ones that were here already. They followed me too, when I arrived here at our sister's house. We will deal with that later, too, after we get to full strength."

"I'm already at full strength. You and sister have just recharged my batteries," the man spoke with his mind back into that of his brother's. They were connected, along with their sister. They always had been, every existence, as they walked through the histories of time.

The man had noticed the shadows as soon as they had entered the light. They were all around his sister's house, inside the light. These shadows weren't the same as those he had seen on the road coming here. These were of a positive energy. They made the man feel good and safe. He realized that these were his ancestors and his people. All the shadows were so familiar. The man could detect his parents. There was his sister's and nephew. His grandparents and aunts and uncles were all present. It was like they were having a family reunion in an equidistant dimension. That parallel so happened to be his sister's house.

One of the shadows stood out more than any of the others. It seemed to stay a short distance from the man, always keeping the same buffer zone. The man tried to move closer to the shadow, and it would repel like opposing magnets. He realized who this shadow was. It was the most familiar of all. It was him, but not in this dimension. Interaction between the same being in different dimensions was impossible. The negative and positive charges would completely block the being from meeting with itself.

All the family members had a shadow presence in the room. The same was the case for all of them, their shadows did not get near them. The only one who did not have a shadow was the brother. The man knew. In that dimension, the brother had died. In this dimension, the one they were in now, the brother was alive and well.

"Sister," the man said, "it has been such a long journey and we are so very hungry. Do you have a barbecue or something? I'll take care of all the cooking if you show me where your stuff is."

"We have a barbecue and plenty of charcoal. It's in the garage. Unfortunately, we have nothing to throw on the barbecue. We have been unable to leave the house for a while now. The rain outside the circle burns our skin. The town has been deserted for months, about the time the rain started. It hasn't stopped once since it began. We have plenty of rice and beans if you would like, just no meat," the sister said sadly.

"Don't worry, we brought our own meat," said the man nonchalantly while he looked blankly at his sister.

The man's wife shot him a questioning look. She knew that they had brought many supplies with them, but no meat. Something in the man's voice told her he meant more than just groceries were to be consumed this night. "I love you," she said, as her husband was going out the door. "Be careful," were her last words as the door to the garage closed behind the man.

He had also grabbed his brother and the boy, and all three of them had gone on a mission to the garage. The man and boy were almost dancing with excitement as they walked through to the car. The large crow was sitting silent on the brother's shoulder, but its green eye had not left the man nor his actions since they had arrived.

The three got to the car, and the man told the others to stand back. The crow cawed once, loud enough to sound like a bark. The man opened the hatch back and threw the suitcases on the ground, scattering them throughout the small enclosure of the garage. After all the bags were gone, the prize was about to be taken.

There, cramped in its little doggy kennel, was the gray. Its eye was pressed to the bars, and it was glaring at the man. There was absolute hatred in the eye of the being. At the same time, the being had a look to its eye as if asking for help and kindness. The man felt no empathy for this creature at all. He had been on a long journey in this lifetime and others. These creatures had always been there to inflict fear, in every dimension and existence. Now, he was just returning the terror to one of their kind.

The brother looked astonished. "What have you done," he asked the man in a booming voice.

"Pissed off the greed," replied the man, casually. "Now, we are going to continue to rain fear and terror upon their species, just as they have done to the humans and this planet for all these years. I have them just where I want them."

"You're crazy, grandpa," the boy said. There was a strange glow of excitement in the boy's eyes. His words said one thing, but his look was one of admiration and respect. He was ready to go along with whatever his grandpa was to ask of him. This was his family, no matter how crazy things always got when they were together. It was what he had. His people meant everything to him, and he was one hundred percent behind them.

The man found a chain hanging from the wall of the garage and hooked it to the handle on the top of the cage. The gray made a hissing whistle sound that would have unnerved the man in the past. Now, it just made him laugh. The boy and his uncle exchanged an odd look. It looked like the man was going crazy. He pulled up hard, and out came the kennel. The captured being landed on the pavement with a rattling thud.

The creature hissed in pain at the brutal treatment. Its sounds were evil, the boy thought in his head. He was not scared, though; the boy trusted his grandpa. If the elder wasn't scared, then he wasn't either.

The three men could see the other visitors just beyond the perimeter of the light. The watchers were weak and powerless to stop what was happening before their eyes. The man could sense their anger. There was another energy coming from the beings that was stronger than any other. It was fear. His plan was working, and it was most enjoyable.

"Maybe you should think about this," said the brother. "This is not part of our destiny. This prophecy has never been written. No one has ever broken through like this. I knew you were always crazy and more carefree. I told you so many times before. I also knew that it wasn't insanity that infected your head. You held the wisdom. You were the

One and you still are. The time is near. Choose your way carefully now brother. These next decisions will affect the entire universe."

"Brother," answered the man, "you are the writer of destinies and religions. You were the one who created so many languages with your chanting. Most thought you were being silly. I knew the truth. I know the role you have played in this long saga. We have been part of it for millions and millions of moons. However, as you know, there are many destinies. Just like books. You can read more than one, and everybody has their own interpretation. I understand how every little action changes the path of our lives. Our destiny has been written for us, and there is no deviating from that. However, if we combine different destinies of our own from parallel dimensions that we reside in, then maybe we can make a soul that can transcend through all space and dimensions. A soul that would be all seeing and all knowing. This being could change destiny and create its own destiny. It would be a being that was free of the laws of other creatures and even the universe. This being would be seen by most as a God. In truth though, this being would be the wisdom. Everyone who was close or smart enough would want to be around this being to absorb the knowledge. Creativity would once again permeate the universe. Destinies and destruction would be put in the far corner, to be brought out another day."

"I accept what you choose," the brother replied, "just remember what I said. You are going into unfamiliar realms of consciousness and space. Our beings have never even considered to do what you are about to do. Again, I follow any decision you make. We are 'The One'."

"Me too, Grandpa, I'm ready," the boy said with respect.

"Oh, don't worry. I have had many miles of traveling to think about our next actions," replied the man. "I had visions after you died and saw every bit of what is happening right now. Every detail was in my dreams. Now, that prophecy is coming true. The prophecy from my mind. The destiny that my creativity created for myself. My grandson was all part of it. I could tell you exactly what he is about to do, but I don't want to ruin the action. It's going to get pretty damn crazy around these parts of Minnesota real soon."

The man laughed a sinister laugh as he pulled the stone from his pocket that made the other two in the garage look at each other. The boy and his uncle tightly embraced. Their relationship, too, had been strong. Their mutual respect and trust had prepared the group for this moment. The collective was together, once again.

The man approached the cage with the solar stone in one hand and a towing chain in the other. The being in the cage was glowing with an intensity of its hatred. It was powerless, like the rest of their swarm, against the family in the light. The stone had given the humans another weapon against their kind.

He opened the kennel and hooked the chain around the alien's neck in one quick movement. The man had not even told his grandson or brother before opening the enclosure. He had simply popped the latch and freed the being into captivity. Just like they had done so many times to the humans. The being struggled strongly at first. The man held the chain with a tight grip, but the extraterrestrial was no match in strength to a human. They used their minds to do all their work, and their minds did not work on this group, nor inside the light. Their bodies were weak. That, combined with the man feeling stronger than ever this day, weakened the being to exhaustion in seconds. The man had not even broken a sweat holding the twisting being in its chain tether. The visitor's battle was quickly lost.

Of course, the man knew all about these beings and their ways now. The stone had told him everything about them and their control. This was the greed. Their minions could shapeshift into any creature they wanted to and fulfill any doctrine from the elite. In this case, beings that would normally be in the form of cops would shape shift into extraterrestrial gray beings to make the humans think there was an alien invasion. The rains and weather were easy to control, and the beings in its shroud could take on their familiar shadow shape. Fear had easily been spread among the humans.

Dragging the creature through the garage, the man swooped a machete from the wall. The being had unfolded as it had come out of the small square enclosure. As it was being dragged, it stretched out. The boy looked at the creature as it was being dragged past him. It was massively wounded from the car and the subsequent imprisonment. It was covered in large gashes, and places had complete chunks missing.

The being looked to the boy as if for empathy. The boy had nothing but hatred for this creature and its kind. His grandpa had told him about the terrible role they had in creating fear around the planet. They were the ones who had created money, government, and control. All in the name of experimenting, while pretending to be Gods. The humans had been nothing more than their lab mice. They could care less what happened to them, long as it was entertaining. Now, the boy thought, the tables had turned.

The boy followed his grandpa into the backyard. The man spotted a dog spike cemented in the yard and tugged the creature toward it. He hooked the chain to the clip on the dog spike and backed up a bit to look at his handiwork. The creature could barely move. Its head lay on the ground in a pitiful manner, looking at the man. It did not matter; these beings did not feel emotion. Only fear, anger, and a strong desire for control.

The visitors beyond the light had increased in numbers. They seemed to be on top of each other and very deep in numbers. The man could sense their anger, but also, the horde was filled with fear. The man had never sensed fear in the visitors before this day. They had always seemed so in control of everything. They would manipulate any situation in any way they chose. Fear and terror were their tools, not their crutches. Until today.

When the man had captured the amulet, things had all changed. Normally, the grays would have used the amulet to switch dimensions or erase the memories of all who had seen. It was their tool to sneak into people's houses and mind control them some, while implanting their experiments in them. They had done it since they allowed humans technology. It had been another way to keep them in check.

Sometimes, the amulet would have even been used to transport the human to the mother ship for more experiments and implants. Many humans had been taken and never returned. They were simply replaced by a hybrid that was built with their DNA, but mentored by the greed from birth for total inclusion. Sometimes, the people weren't even replaced. These cases would be closed on a verdict of vanished.

The grays watched helplessly as their brother had been stuck in the dimension with the family. They had been warned of this group and had been following them. Their commands had clearly been to desist the targets. This place in the Minnesota iron belt was going to be the extermination. Somehow though, their powers had been worthless on the four. Their collective was strong. Stronger than anything the greed had ever seen. The worst fact to them was that the man had one of their kind in his possession, along with its sacred amulet.

This had been only the fourth gray to be in the possession of humans ever. This was the first time it had been captured like this, though. Hunted almost. The other time had been in New Mexico. One of the craft of the gray had crashed in the desert after being hit by a meteor. Some farmers had recovered the wreckage and three bodies. The military leaked information to the press, and the cover ups had begun. In truth, when the greed had come and picked up the 'alien' bodies, they were picking up three of their own pilots.

The pilots would take on this form because of the way their molecular makeup would accept space travel. It was basically their flight suits. When they had been hit by the meteor that one time, their identity had been released to the public. From then on, it had been a campaign of disinformation on all UFO. They did not want the masses knowing that all those strange things in the sky were their intergalactic craft. The truth would have ruined everything for the greed.

It had been different that time, when the creatures had been captured, then this time in one major regard. The beings who had found the visitors then had quickly turned them over to the government. The greed had swiftly recovered their own. This time, humans had their brother and had no intention of returning the being. The visitors were not pleased. To the beings who looked at themselves as Gods, the humans were mice. No better than lab rats. Now, four of these rodents had captured one of their scientists.

The man had no intention of giving the creature back to its species. As a matter of fact, the man thought, terror was about to rain down on the being. The gray and all its kind were about to get punished for their evil ways. The first punishment was going to be the extension of fear that the man had already invoked in the greed.

"I can hear your thoughts," his sister's voice said in his head. She, too, was now in the yard next to the brother. The niece and woman had also come out to see the madness the man was perpetrating. They formed a square around the man and the being. Each of them stood with their back to a direction on the globe. The boy stood next to his grandpa. The man had been preparing his grandson for this day since the boy was months old. The boy knew how to handle a situation like this. He had done it many times before.

"I can hear your thoughts, too," said the woman. The same was repeated by the brother, niece and the grandson. All the beings were interconnected with their thoughts and knowledge. The collective was again united in the sacred symbol of this family. It beamed from their beings into the cosmos. It was an ancient symbol. It had been a protector for millions of years. It was the symbol for the ONE.

The man passed the machete to his grandson. The boy lit up when the object was in his hand. His grandpa had bought him his first machete when he was six years old. This tool was all too familiar. The boy raised the weapon high above his head. Like he had said countless times in the past, just before he swung the blade, these words were shouted from his mouth. "You killed my family!" The words were punctuated by the boy bringing the machete down upon the shoulder of the alien. He had not aimed for the head. He knew his grandpa too well and was familiar with the animosity that his elder held toward these beings. He wanted this entity to suffer.

The boy repeated his war whoop with each swing of the machete. There were four of them. Each blow brought a scream from the extraterrestrial that would be piercing to the ears if it weren't music to the six beings present. The strength of the human's hatred flowed through the boy as he systematically chopped off the alien's arms at the shoulders and legs at the hips. Each blow was enough to lop off a limb. He struck the being with the collective of hate, all the while shouting, "You killed my family, alien."

When the limbs were no longer attached to the being, the boy gave the weapon to his grandpa. The man swung it around a few times over the twitching torso of the alien being. Its arms and legs missing, the being was tortured beyond senses. Still, the man did not care. The boy had always said this same rant of destruction his whole life because of this day. His memories of other lives were what he had channeled while swinging his weapon. It was true, these beings had killed their whole family during their twisted experiments. They had killed all the humans for that matter. Sucked the life from them slowly and methodically. All in the name of experimentation and control. They deserved everything they were going to get.

The being looked to the man with one last look of salvation. Its companions, outside the light, were milling about, making sounds of anger and fear. They were helpless, while the human and its boy were killing one of their own. The man raised the machete high and looked right into the eyes of the being. "You killed my family," the man said between clenched teeth. He swung the blade with all the force and hatred of the humans combined. The being had given one last scream when it had seen its fate. This scream was the most beautiful sound the man had ever heard. The second-best sound was when the blade split the alien head and torso in two. The entire being fell perfectly in half like an avocado. The man made one more blow on the creature, severing its neck from its torso. Now, the entire being was in eight pieces.

The stench was terrible. It smelled like rotten eggs mixed with manure. The boy asked the man what they should do. The creature was obviously dead. Its innards consisted of an oily, grass like substance. It was what the flesh was made of and the blood oozing onto the ground seemed to be the same material. Its body parts had already begun to turn a mottled black color. It was certainly beginning to decay rapidly. The man unzipped his zipper and pulled out his penis. The boy followed suit. The man and boy each pissed on one half of the torso and two limbs each. They were careful not to get any on the head. They had been holding it for a while. Their urine covered the death in front of them. The smell instantly went away. The flesh from the alien began to decay even faster, quickly becoming part of the Earth.

Outside the light, the tornadoes had begun again and were now destroying everything outside of the sanctity. Houses were disintegrating into sticks. Trees were blown into millions of pieces. The tornadoes ripped at the light but could not penetrate its brightness. The beings on the outside had also become very full of turmoil. They were hitting the light with all kinds of craft. Many of their beings charged toward the man and boy but were held back by the electromagnetic pulse that the beings were creating. The few beings and their craft that did manage to penetrate the outer ring of light were instantly vaporized. They were powerless against the charge that had been made around this spot.

The visitors knew all too well that this spot was also an energy spot on the planet. It was also home to a very large meteor that had hit the Earth billions of years ago. The celestial orb had left behind a vast amount of iron in the ground. The sister had learned how to tap into its magnetic properties.

The other four joined the man and boy. The alien was nothing more than an oily mess on the lawn. Except for its head. The cranium, split in two, showed no signs of decay, although it was visibly dead.

The creatures outside the light were in a frenzy to see what the ones inside its sanctity were doing. The man said to his niece, "I knew exactly who this being was. It had been assigned to me at birth and has continued with my path through my life. The being has always been there, hiding in another dimension. They had made most of their experiments think that it was their guardian angel following them around. It was one of the reasons they had created religion. They made others think they were getting abducted by extraterrestrial beings. They were not friendly. They implanted the Earth beings with their devices at birth, and then controlled them throughout their lives. All in the name of their sciences. They never fooled me, though. I've known for a very long time. This fucker was my demon. They gave one to all of us just to control us if we got out of control."

The man picked up both halves of the head and held them together. He told the boy to get the amulet out of his pocket and hold it over the alien's head. The boy did as he was told. When the amulet was about one foot above the severed head, a light came from it and covered the head in a warm gray light. The man had been holding the cranium together off the ground, but now let go. The light held the head in place and together. The boy had animated the dead alien head, hanging it in midair with his magical light. The being's eyes showed life again, and an anger that the man had never seen. The being tried to communicate to the man about what he had just done, and the stupidity of his actions. The man would have nothing to do with it. He told the visitor with his mind that it was his turn to speak. They had their time and now it was the man's.

The other beings, outside the circle, could clearly hear the thoughts of the man as he spoke through their brother. They also felt the pain and anger that the being, now decapitated, was projecting. The man spoke to the greed, "I have known about you for so many years. Almost from birth, I knew about you. You had put your devices in the brains of myself and my siblings. All three of us had rejected the implants that you had given us. We were not to be controlled by your kind. You and your kind fucked up. Our species are not human, and you have never had control over us. You had tricked us and implanted us against our will, but it did not work. You just made us forget for a time, but the knowledge has returned."

"Our species have been on this planet much longer than yours. You came here and took from our true god, Pachymama, and enslaved its creatures. You gave nothing back but fear and destruction. It is time for you and your kind to go. This is the end of your end. I know all your kind are hearing me now. So, go in peace, or go in pieces. That was your only warning. I have your key, as does my brother and sister. We know your secrets and weaknesses. Your days of control are over. Destiny gets merged today, and you will be the losers."

The man looked to the boy and said, "Do it". The boy was a blur as he chopped the alien head into pieces. The boy became more of a butcher and less of a slasher. The pieces of the head began to pile up next to the barbecue that the man was tending. It had a different texture than the body. This flesh looked more like it was a fungus or membrane.

It was nothing like any of them had ever seen. The man and boy did not care. They were hungry. As the boy threw the steaks on the grill, he asked his grandpa how he thought the meat would taste.

"Like chicken" the man said, and they both laughed loudly.

The others were gathered around and getting into the festive mood that the man and boy were setting.

The woman and niece had brought singing bowls and were creating their melody. The brother chimed in with the gong and the melody was set. The sister's husband had joined the others and began a slow song that continued throughout the dinner. "His voice is one of beauty," the boy had told his grandpa as the elder agreed.

The energy in the light was completely the opposite as that outside the light. It was calm and confident inside. It was hectic and unsure outside.

The man said more seriously, after they had been cooking for a bit, "I think it will taste like whatever we want it to taste like." The meat made a weird sizzle sound as it cooked. It seemed more like wood than meat to the boy. The smell was fantastic, though. His grandpa had barbecued every kind of meat known for the boy, but he had never smelled anything like this. The man went to the sister's kitchen and got her maple syrup. The man told the boy that in Minnesota, everybody had maple syrup in their fridge. Again, they all laughed. It had been a long time since any of them had anything to laugh at, and it felt good. For a moment in the storm, they could forget about the turmoil and be a happy family once again.

The man poured the syrup over the meat on the grill. He sensed helplessness in the beings outside the light. No longer did he sense their anger. Now there was only fear in their thoughts. They also projected a sense of needing, almost like a small child.

The man knew all too well what was going on. They were the kings of manipulation. They were trying to get pity from someone in the family. If they could sway just one, they would have a chance. It was useless.

These beings always did the same thing. They would destroy and kill and then look for sympathy in any way they could get it. They were also beings who would do their evil deeds and then make others take the blame for it. All of this with no pity nor even the slightest regard for the humans nor the Earth. Their disdain for this planet and its creatures had been obvious.

The disdain went both ways, as it normally does. The humans hated the greed for taking all the riches from the hard-working people while they never once even got their hands dirty. They would also be lacking any regard when the greed was at the bottom and the people lived in harmony with Pachymama once again. Sympathy was a thing the greed could beg for while they were reaping the rewards of thousands of years of hatred.

There would be no pity for the beings nor their minions. They were all cosmic criminals who were deserving of every bit of misery coming their way.

Every hand that was about to come down on their tyranny was going to be shouting the same thing, "You killed my family!"

Chapter 58

The meat had cooked quickly while the man and boy stood by patiently. It had been a long day, and they had been through so much on this journey. Hunger had overtaken their senses and was all they could think of. They needed to rebuild their strength. The two talked about barbecue and how they had cooked and tried many different species of meat. The talk made their mouths water.

The meat had a texture of mushrooms but the flavor of buffalo. The man and boy devoured the flesh. The dogs, too, made a fulfilling meal out of the slaughter. The others were reluctant to try the meat. There was worry in their eyes. The woman told the man that maybe he had gone too far.

The words fell on deaf ears. The man could not stop eating the flesh, even if he had tried. Not only was the meat delicious, with each bite the man seemed to gain the knowledge and strength of the alien. All the while, outside the light, the other visitors cowered in fear. Confusion was among their masses as they tried to figure out what to do. They had never seen a human eat one of their kind.

The man felt as though he had reached a higher existence than the alien species. He knew all about their powerful ways and now he had absorbed them. In his mind, he never seen himself superior to any other species. This was the first. He had crossed dimensions and brought one energy into another. The man felt invincible.

The actions of their brother worried the others. Even the boy had backed off when the man had begun eating the flesh like a wild animal. The things he was doing were very irrational to them. At the same time, the man seemed very focused and sure of what he was doing. His confidence made the others unsure of their convictions. The shadows within the circle of light all converged on the man. It seemed as if hundreds of kindred souls were being drawn to the energy emanating from the man. They seemed to be dancing around the being and his feast.

The solo feast did not end until even the smallest of scraps was devoured. The man had made animal grunts and whistles while tearing at the flesh with his teeth and fingers.

Even after his meal had ended, he got down on his knees and sniffed around the ground for more. The others continued to look on alarmingly.

The man was done. He had enough excitement for one day and fell to the ground in exhaustion. His mind was a whirl of thoughts. All the visitor's cogitation was now flowing through his head. They were a race of creatures with no empathy. They traveled the galaxies looking for life that they could manipulate and make experiments on. They had no connection to this planet except for the experiments they had conducted on its beings for so many years.

These beings had taken what they wanted from one planet after another. For their amusement, they watched the events that they had seeded unfold. They would set in motion evolution and destiny. They understood the numbers and manipulated them to their benefit. They were truly an evil species.

They were also a species that clinically reproduced. Their DNA was closer to that of plants than to animals. They were very intelligent beings but lacked any spirituality. Their main objective, wherever they ended up, was to take everything and control it all. Create civilization and watch a species implode from that point on. They were true rapacity. Their race numbered in the trillions, and they inhabited almost every corner of the universe. They were the cockroaches of the cosmos.

"We need to talk," the man said to the others. "We now have the knowledge from these beings and their keys to the dimensions. It is just about time to rid this planet of them forever."

The brother spoke through the mouth of the crow on his shoulder. The bird had not once left the man's shoulder since the family had arrived. The crow, moving its beak open and closed, spoke its tale for the brother. "First, we must discuss the past before we can enter the future. Many years ago, I spoke these words to you, but I felt you could not hear them. This all began when we were small children. We were on vacation with our family, passing through Arizona, when the water pump on the car went out. Dad had pulled into a farm and knocked on the door of the farmhouse. A weathered man with fire in his blue eyes opened the door with a shotgun pointed at Dad's face. We were in the car, terrified at what was happening before us. After what seemed like an eternity, the man slowly lowered the gun and disappeared into the house. Dad followed the man inside."

The sister continued the story, "When dad got back to the car, two hours had passed. Something looked very different about him when he put his face to the window. There was a different tone in his normally confident voice. Whatever had happened inside that farmhouse, we knew, it was not good. He said he was getting a ride into town by the farmer to get a new water pump. He also said we were to stay in the car and for no reason at all even open the doors. He even wanted us to roll up the windows, but mom said we would be dead in minutes in the hot sun. He also said that the farmer had told him there were strange occurrences happening around here. "The boogie man lives around these parts," Dad had said. "This place is very dangerous," he reiterated again and again. "Do not leave the car." As he was walking to the farmer's truck, he turned back four separate times and pointed at us, silently telling us to stay put. Shortly after he left, Mom seemed to doze off in a trance of sorts. Most of the other kids succumbed to this same trance. The three of us were wide awake. We were different than the other four kids. Our minds saw things that most adults would never even imagine. Our parents did not understand us the same. We three were unique. We had been born with the ancient souls of who we are. We once again were born into the same family, fulfilling our path like it had always been. But our other siblings were nothing like us. Being kids in that hot car made it difficult to sit still for too long. Especially when the others were all passed out. It didn't take much coaxing from brother to get us two to follow him."

The man's words followed seamlessly with his sisters. All three siblings had joined in the telling of the tale. "The large red barn with white trim was only about twenty feet from the car. We entered the structure and immediately noticed a bright light that was coming from one corner. We got closer to the energy and a large black figure appeared from its brightness. We instantly saw that it was a humongous man dressed all in black. The creature's eye sockets were empty. Around his neck, he wore an amulet that was glowing a strange green light. We were frozen with fear. We were only five, after all. The being was upon us in a flash, and grabbed me by my shoulders. A beam of light flashed from his amulet into the heavens, until we were encompassed by it. I felt an unseen force slowly lifting me off the ground towards the heavens. Suddenly, the light and the man in black were gone. I lay crumpled on the floor of the barn. Looking up, I saw you, my brother and sister, standing over me. You had empathy in your eye for me. In your hand, brother, was the amulet. You had snatched it from the being. It is what had made the creature vanish."

The brother continued, "When Dad got back, we had already sneaked back to the car, and it seemed no one was the wiser. He fixed the car while the farmer stood on the porch with his shotgun at the ready. The old man seemed to be staring directly at the three of us, like he knew what we had done. We sensed fear but it was not from us, it was from the farmer. Our fear had ended that day."

"Dad seemed really happy when the car was fixed and pulling away. As we were leaving the farm, I looked behind us at the sign hanging over the dirt road. It said in large red letters on a black sign, 'Stardust Ranch'. That is where it all began. It is where we began to take back our souls and our rightful place on this planet. The inferior greed would never be in control of our species."

"We each have one of these amulets coded to our DNA and energy field," the brother continued. "The greed uses each one to control us individually. Each visitor is assigned many beings to control. Almost like a board game. Whatever it is, it has always just been a game to the elite. I took back my amulet just as you have and sister has too. We long ago rejected our implants, shedding that avenue of control. They had been effective in blocking our memories of the past lives, but that has all returned. We all three have the amulets now. We are the One."

"How did you get your amulet?" the man asked his sister.

"I woke up in the middle of the night once, and one of those little bastards was by my bed. My cat went for the creature's eyes, temporarily distracting it. They hate cats. While the being was distracted, I grabbed the stone from its neck. Their monitoring of me and following my every movement ended then. They are still all around us now and many other times. They cannot lay a finger on us, though. They can only look at us like we are in the zoo. Our light is our force field against them. It emanates from inside our beings. We are not trapped in the light, it follows us wherever we go. The greed is destined to live in the shadows outside our sanctity. We are the only three in all of history who have recovered their own amulet. The destiny of the greed was not written with this outcome. Nothing like this has happened to their species before. We are in complete control of our souls, like we always have been. The fact that we are brothers and sister frightens the visitors. They feared us before, but fear has consumed them since you acquired your amulet. On top of the amulets and the power they give us, you are the first being on this planet to ever kill a visitor, let alone eat one. Their final battle now is with us. The fate of the planet and its people are ours to decide."

"The visitors will know soon," said the man. "Our destinies are being written and rewritten as we speak. The numbers of the universe are all coming together. We now know how to use the dimensions to our benefit. We have their keys to the other realms and to their knowledge. It is our time. Look around, we are all here. We are the One."

The shadows outside the light grew more solid as the words passed. The man saw all the ancestors present inside the light. This showdown had been coming for a very long time. This family had come together to form the Collective.

It had been in their DNA.

They were the spiritual. They, together, were the ones who could defeat the parasites and rid the planet of their harmful ways.

The siblings were once again together. They were the One.

CHAPTER 59

The man had become disoriented. He knew in his mind that something was not right. Reality seemed to be folding in on itself, allowing fantasy to persevere.

He looked to the others but saw the same strength in them as before. The brother and sister were looking at the man strangely. He knew that they knew what was going on. Even when they were kids, the three had been interconnected with a psychic energy. Their souls, separate, intertwined with one another.

As their parents had been, the three also had precognitions of the future. They could sense when something was wrong, but each sensed different forms of dread. Their precognitions were like a blanket, covering all aspects of what might go wrong.

"Are you alright?" asked the sister. "You look like you need to lay down."

"These visitors have tricked us again," replied the man. "They let us get so close, and then break down our realities. Space and time have been warped around us again. We have fought this battle hundreds of times in the past, always with the same outcome. The greed always gets what they want. They control everything, including the governments of the world. They are the creators in the sense that they have created all this madness for the simple reason of just watching the humans try to figure it out. How did we think we could defeat them? They fit the image that every being has of God, because they created that image."

"You are wrong," said the sister. "It has taken a long journey to get to this point, and we are not going to slow down now. Why don't you go inside for a bit and rest? Then, maybe you can regroup your thoughts. We really need you right now."

The man's ears felt filled with cotton. It seemed as if he was in a tunnel looking through to the other side. The man knew he was about to pass out. All his senses became skewed.

The boy was there quickly, by his grandpa's side. He steadied the man and helped him into the house. A blue glow was emanating from the living room. The boy let the man lead him toward the strange light. The room looked like a murder scene. Everything seemed so surreal. He wasn't sure why he was having these thoughts, but it was there.

The blank, blue screen of the television was the source of the blue glow. Nothing was in its right place, although his sister had kept her house very neat. All the furniture had been moved around, and nothing sat square against a wall. Half of the pictures on the walls were either broken or laying on the ground. All the knickknacks that the sister had were broken in the middle of the floor. The man turned to look at the boy for his reaction, but his grandson was no longer by his side. He was alone in this turmoil.

A large black figure in the hallway overpowered the man's attention. The figure was standing so very still that it looked like a statue. The man decided to approach it. Throughout all this doubt, he still had no fear. The things that he was going through did not deal with fear at all. They only dealt with trying to figure out what was real and what was not. Every step the man took, the figure retreated. He followed the stranger down the hallway and was led into one of the bedrooms. The walls of the room were bathed in a red light. Through the window, the man could see the setting sun. It was as crimson as he had ever seen it. This, he saw, was the source of the fiery glow on the walls.

On the bed were laying two people. They were laying on their backs, stiff as boards. The man looked closer. The people laying there were his wife and himself. He did not recognize the plain white clothes they were wearing, nor their dark black hair. Both these figures also had no tattoos. They seemed to be empty pods, waiting to be implanted with souls. They were both lying in a coma-like slumber. The red glow on their faces made them look angelic.

Movement to his side caught the man's attention. The dark figure was again in the hallway, silently beckoning to the man. He followed the figure to another bedroom. This one was bathed in a yellow glow. On the beds in this room were his sister and her husband. They, too, were perfectly still on their backs, as if in a coma. Their clothes and hair were the same as the two beings in the other room.

The full moon shined brightly through the window, casting its yellow hues. The room seemed like a light was on, but it was dark outside. The color made the two figures look very serene and at peace. Again, the two looked like empty pods. Soulless beings waiting to be animated.

"What does this mean?" thought the man. He didn't understand how the sun was out one window while the moon was outside the other. He had felt as if he were in a movie ever since opening the door to the house. He grabbed the wall for support. Everything around him seemed to be spinning.

The sound of a singing bowl brought him out of his trance. He followed the melody back to the living room. The mellifluous sound was the only thing keeping the last threads of sanity together in the man's head. Besides the song from the bowl, the room was completely silent.

Across the room the man saw the source of the melody. Sitting in a rocking chair, illuminated by the blue from the television, sat his brother. The singing bowl was in one hand, producing a sound by itself. In his other hand was a crystal ball that the man had given his brother as a gift. He had acquired it in Brazil many years before and known it was perfect for his brother. The orb seemed to be filled with a kaleidoscope of colors, stirred up in rhythm with the song from the brass instrument. The brother was staring intently at the man, as was the large crow sitting on his shoulder.

"What's going on here?" the man asked. "You guys trying to drive me crazy?"

The brother spoke, "You're a knucklehead. You don't remember what happened, and now your mind is making up story upon story. You truly don't remember what happened to you?"

"I remember coming on this trip to heal our souls. You died, as did most of your family. Death had overtaken our family. We needed to get away from all that and start anew. We have been on that healing mission for months now, maybe even years. The journey never seems to end."

"But how did you get here?" asked the brother.

"That's easy, we drove here," replied the man.

"Okay then, tell me one part about your trip here."

The man stood looking blankly out the window. There was nobody in the yard, and the sun was shining bright. Some neighbor kids rode their bikes by. The man thought that it reminded him of being in the Twilight Zone. Everything was too perfect here. He had no answer to his brother's question. He couldn't remember one single detail of the trip to get here. "What's going on?" he asked his brother.

"None of this is real," replied the brother. "This is all in your head. You have been in a mental ward for the last twenty-two years. They locked you up after you killed all those people down in Gallup. You had buried twelve bodies around your house, and your neighbor dropped the dime on you. You swore your innocence to the authorities. You kept telling them that you had dreamed about burying the bodies and gave them many details. You swore it was all from your dreams. They never found any of your DNA connecting you to the murders, but your story about the dreams made you seem crazy; and guilty. They never once even thought to investigate the neighbor. You were guilty, all along, in their minds."

"They locked you up and said you were the worst serial killer ever in those parts. They put you in a cell with no windows and didn't let you out, ever. You lost your mind in that cell. You painted all the walls with your own blood. You worked your fingers and hands into bloodied pieces of meat, making your cryptic messages on the harsh concrete.

They had to put you in a straight-jacket for a while and kept you on drugs. This has been your mental state for the past twenty-two-years."

"How are you here to tell me this now? I remember those dreams. They had been terrible. I thought I had lost my mind. They seemed so real. It wasn't me, though. The neighbor had murdered all those people. He had ratted me out to save his ass. I had confronted him about my dreams, and he had panicked. The only thing to do in his mind had been to burn me to save his own freedom."

"None of that matters anymore. It all happened long ago, in the past. They will never let you out of here. I am not, really, here with you. You are at the mental hospital and me and sister are at her house in Minnesota. They decided to try a new therapy on you and brought in myself and our sister to assist. They knew how we were psychically connected and thought we could come in and explain to you what happened and what is happening. They thought that if you could understand, then maybe you would get better."

"Who are they?" the man asked, with serious irritation beginning to creep into his voice.

"You know, man. The government, the authorities, the church, and all the others who are in control. The greed. You did some bad shit, and now they want you gone forever. They say you are a menace to this planet. Now they just want to lock you away forever. They are curious about why you did it and if there were more bodies. That is why they sent me. If you were getting better, you might give them the information that they want," the brother said calmly. His voice was more like he had rehearsed his words many times over. His voice was not that of the man's brother.

"How did they get you to say this to me?" asked the man.

"They just want to help you," replied the brother.

"They only want to help themselves," said the man. "It is all they are ever interested in. They control everything and warp all events into their own benefit. Now, obviously, they control you, too. I never thought I would say those words to my brother. You were always so strong. When you died, it crushed us. We needed you way more than you ever could have imagined. Was that even real?"

The brother began to fade away. The whole room and house began to defragment before the man's eyes. All the detail of things faded away until only white remained. Everything was white, not even a single shadow. The man couldn't move. He was strapped in a mechanical device and chained to the wall. He looked around in confusion. Tubes around his head were the only things visible to him. His brother's words echoed in his head. "How, indeed, had he gotten here?"

A door opened into the white. A large, dark figure filled the empty space. Its eyes seemed to be lost and distraught. They were solid black with no white. The mouth on this figure, too, was grotesquely twisted into a menacing grin. Most of the teeth were visible. The being wore all black, but the man did not recognize the style of clothing. The figure was simply wrapped in black material.

"We've been waiting a very long time for you to wake up," said the being.

"Who are you?" asked the man.

"You know who we are. You have been in our care for a very long time. In the adjacent rooms are your brother and sister. They are in the same state of mind as you are. They, too, have just awoke from their long slumber."

"But why?" asked the man.

"When you were children, our people saw something in the three of you which brought fear among us. There had been a prophecy about three humanoid triplets being born and destroying our kind. We tried to control you like the others on this planet, but it did not work. Your spirituality and creativity put you three into a class of your own. You understood people's energy. You could have amassed the humans and showed them the way. Instead, we took you here and have had you since you were children. We captured the three of you in Arizona, at one of our bases, more than forty-five years ago. The three of you were drawn to our energy, and we took advantage of your curiosity. Your parents nor the authorities ever stopped looking for you. You three will never be a threat to us. We have you just where we want you. We even control your thoughts with dreams and ideas that we plant into your head. Your entire lives and memories have been created by us. Everything that has happened to you in the last forty-five years has not really happened. We brought you here, and you have never left. It is the only place we could control you, here, in the confines of our laboratory. We are eight hundred feet below the surface of the Earth. We have given you drugs and kept you in comas for forty-five years. We could not control you on the surface, so we brought you here. This is a sacred place for us. Our people built this facility thousands of years ago for someone just like you. When the prophecy came true, we had been ready. You three are the only ones who have ever been here, physically in this place. I am not even here. I am in a building on the surface of the planet. My thoughts and words are only in your head. Your brother and sister are being told the same thing right now."

It was all too much for the man to process. Once again, he was alone in the room. A liquid was running down his face, originating from his forehead. It tasted like tears. The pressure in his head felt as though it would burst. It felt as though a fire was burning all around him, and inside his being. All his senses became blurred into his subconscious. For a moment, he felt whole again. A feeling he had not had since he was a small child.

His restraints were suddenly gone, freeing his aching body. It was like they had simply disappeared. The whiteness around him began to morph into colors and shapes. In just moments, a forest had developed right before the man's eyes. The clean, cool air brought his senses back into reality. It felt like he was one with the wilderness. A large crow flew overhead, casting its shadow on the man.

The crow seemed to be pointing a direction to the man. He followed the bird's lead around a small hill and a grove of trees. This is where he had found what he had been looking for.

On a fallen tree, covered in moss, were sitting his brother and sister. Each had a singing bowl in their hand and were playing a separate melody. The two talked in tongues as their song unfolded. The siblings looked to the newcomer. They had been waiting for him.

The crow flew overhead, making a strange sound of clicks and whistles. The three beings looked to the bird but were blinded by the sun. Everything seemed to turn pure white from the intensity of the light.

A gong sounded in the distance.

Chapter 60

"Where are we now?" the man asked his sister.

"We are almost back to the beginning," she answered. "Our journey has brought us back around full circle. This is the end, which will bring on the beginning. We will do it all over again. It's all found in the numbers. Our destiny has been written over and over. Just like all living creatures. Anyone who can read the numbers can read their way. It is the wisdom."

The brother spoke, "I tried to tell you on this long trip we have taken together. We are just energy, souls inhabiting the flesh pod of one being, until we move onto the next. Every life we live is scripted in numbers. Some may seem so different, while others are almost identical. No matter which it is, our lives and dimensions run parallel to each other. We skip across them like a flat rock on a pond. Some lives last for days, while others last years. Sometimes they last way too long. You must know when it is time to skip to the next. Mostly there is no choice. The numbers decide when it is time to end. Then the new life will begin."

The sister spoke, "The three of us have traveled through time together. This forest is the place of our birth. The first awakening on this planet for our souls. We lived here for many moons, peacefully with the other creatures. We had all become friends. Our beloved friends, the Sasquatch, showed us many ways of Pachymama and how to survive. When it was time to leave our paradise, the crow showed us the path. Now, they come again to welcome us to the new beginning. The next book is about to be written. Again, the crow will show us the way."

The Sasquatch appeared like shadows from the forest. There were maybe twenty of the beings. They did not walk out of the forest, they just became from the forest. They had been there all along, cloaked in the ways of their species.

Crows swooped in numbers from within the grove. They seemed to form from the branches and leaves. Their flight took on a dance of sorts, as they made shapes in the sky. Their flight was a murmuration of beauty. Their choreographed movements rustled up a wind from their strong wings.

All the Sasquatch gathered around the three siblings, while the crows danced above. All were very familiar to one another, like close relatives. The Sasquatch spoke to the three in its throaty language. The thoughts were clear in the siblings' heads, as were the words coming from the giant. It spoke about the ending passing, and the beginning being upon them. It spoke about how this is normally a time of celebration, but something was very different this time. Their numbers had been decimated by the greed of the planet. Their species were in danger of being wiped out from the humans and their ways. There was a sense of dread among the Sasquatch. The last cycle had begun almost the same, this time it was much worse. There was a disease on this planet from a species who liked to be in control of the rest. The same story played over and over, just with slight variations. Sometimes there were huge differences. However, it was all about the skip. Just like the souls of all creatures, if it was on Pachymama, it was all part of the One. Altogether, the planet and its beings were the One. The One had been persecuted once again. Business as usual was the way of the greed. It was their game. They were the control.

"How else could it ever be?" said the man to the Sasquatch. "Reality is always changing, just as the seasons, but the seasons return every year. Everything in the universe is on a giant cycle, just like the planets revolving around the sun. Everything in the universe also is on a cycle. We all have our cycles, over and over. Always ready for the next one. Just like our new lives. Sometimes the seasons are gentle and sometimes wrathful. Just like our lives. We just keep going on and on. Soon, my friend, the season will be upon us when we rid the planet of the greed. Soon, we will once again restore our garden."

"Your species will remain like it always has," the sister said to the Sasquatch. "You have been the caretakers of this planet for hundreds of millions of years. When new species arrive and others evolve, your numbers will slowly grow to a sustainable amount. Your kind will always remain hidden from other creatures. Now, it is a new cycle. This one is going to be different than the rest. This time, change is really going to happen. Your species will be very important in that change. You are here for Pachymama. Now heal your species and heal the planet at the same time, my friend. It is your destiny."

The Sasquatch faded like shadows back into the forest. The crows were in a frenzy of flight. They converged on the three siblings and took hold of them. Every part of the three beings' bodies were covered with crows. They looked like giant crows themselves, as the birds took flight with their passengers. The birds flew higher and higher, their numbers in the thousands. The three beings could not even be seen in the cloud of black wings. They were joyful of this experience. It had been a long time since they had taken flight. They flew so high the oxygen became thin, and the sun blocked out everything except for the flutter of wings. All they could see was the bright light which was becoming more and more blinding. Eventually, the light overtook all their senses. They became the light.

The sense of falling woke the three out of their dreams. The white from the sunlight had once again become the white room. The man was lying on an inclined table with tubes hooked up to his head. He couldn't move. He sensed a strong sense of emptiness all around him. He didn't feel the energy from a single soul. There were no sounds, either. The only smell was a strong chemical one. Dread filled his being.

Panning his eyes around the room, he noticed many cameras pointed at him. Also, there were monitors all along the walls flashing images and videos. There were hundreds of monitors along the wall. All of them were facing the man. The device his tubes were hooked to was out of his field of vision. The tubes themselves seemed to have blue electricity running through them. He could see nothing else in the cell.

He focused his eyes on one of the monitors. On it played a video of him with his brother and sister as kids. Another monitor was playing videos of him and his wife. There were videos of his son and other relatives. There was one monitor playing a road trip. They were all scrolling through video after video.

All of them were of the man's multiple lives and existences. They were playing every second of the events in the man's life. How did they have all of this, he wondered. They would have had to have been recording from his existence, from his own being.

He was trying to figure out what was happening to him when a tall dark figure appeared from nowhere. Suddenly, the being was in between the man and the monitors. Its empty eye sockets bore into the man's skull. His thoughts were flooded with images from the dark being, like an avalanche. The thoughts were not good ones. They were just of darkness and destruction.

The man was absorbed by the darkness in the other being's eyes. He could not look away. The darkness began to take over everything in the man's senses. He seemed to become one with the dark. Everything was encompassed in its icy grip. The shadows even took over the bright light from the room and monitors.

Everything in the man's being went completely dark.

CHAPTER 61

The loud sound of a horn from a big rig shook the man awake. He opened his eyes just in time to see the truck sliding at an obscene angle, just inches from their car. They had barely skirted certain death. It was not the same for the minivan coming up to their left. They hadn't seen the diesel truck and were on a direct collision course with the large cab.

The music was still blaring in the car. The man must have dozed off for a moment. He couldn't understand how he had slept with the thumping from the speakers blaring away. He watched helplessly as the minivan hit the diesel at full speed. They hadn't even braked in the least. The man had seen four heads in the car just before impact. One of the faces turned and looked at the man ever so briefly. It was a boy of about fourteen. Their eyes had met. It had all seemed so surreal.

The truck and minivan exploded into a fireball, the car puncturing the truck's fuel tank. Shrapnel flew in all directions. The man knew instantly that there would be no survivors.

The friend swung the wheel madly to miss the mayhem in front of them. They fishtailed around before coming to a stop, facing the destruction. As soon as they had stopped sliding to a stop, the man hurled himself from the vehicle and ran towards the wreckage. They had come to stop about sixty feet away from the inferno. Even at this distance, the flames were terribly hot. It felt to the man like his skin would peel off. He had no time to think about his own safety. His adrenaline was pumping wildly. These people might need his help.

The man had to stop halfway to the wreckage. The heat from the inferno was extreme, but what really made him stop had nothing to do with danger. The man had long ago sworn against fear. What he saw was what had made him stop and assess what was happening. There were no bodies in the minivan. Not a single person was in the car. The man knew for certain that he had seen four souls, but now they were not there. The truck driver had obviously died on impact and was burning like a wick. Flames covered both vehicles, making them one with the inferno.

The man shook his head and looked around. A large figure was running towards him through the haze of the fire. As it approached, the figure shifted into the form of a very large brown crow. It flew over the man and dropped something from its talons. The bird and man's eyes met in a mutual gaze. The blaze seemed to be fueled with the wind created by the crow's wings. The whole thing reminded the man of a phoenix, and a new beginning, as the bird flew toward the sun and out of sight. It had followed the heat haze until it was no longer visible.

The man's reverie was broken by an object in his shirt pocket. The bird had dropped something, and it had landed directly in the garment's pouch. The man could swear that he heard the crow caw three times, fading in the distance, as he looked in the pocket.

A small explosion brought the man's attention back to reality. He looked to the mini-van and saw that there were now four occupants in it once again. Something was very out of the ordinary. Although the riders in the van were engulfed in flames, the bodies seemed to be alert and smiling in some strange way. The man would swear later that they looked as if they were singing along to their favorite song.

Other people had begun to arrive with their portable fire extinguishers. The fires had died down as the fuel burned away. Now, there were skeletons of cars with their intact passengers. The man told the people to stay away. Their fire extinguishers were of no use. These five souls were not going to make it.

By the time the highway patrol, fire department, and ambulance arrived, there was nothing left but a heap of twisted metal and five charred corpses. One of the officers was familiar with the man. He had tattooed her on multiple occasions, and they held a mutual respect. The woman could see that the man was visibly shaken. She had never seen him like this. He was one to always be in control and now he seemed anything but.

"What happened here, Man?" the officer asked.

"I'm not sure," he replied. "My friend over there was giving me a ride to the airport to pick up a rental car. I must have dozed off, because I woke up to loud music and destruction. I saw the van hit the truck and explode, but I didn't see what led up to it. All I know is, that was some bad shit to wake up to."

The man thought it best not to tell her about the lack of passengers immediately after the accident. Spending the first day of his vacation in a mental ward did not seem like his way. Nobody would believe any of that. He wasn't sure if he even believed it himself. Maybe he had been still waking up, and his mind had been playing tricks on him. This is what he tried to tell himself. The problem was, he didn't believe that. He was not one to ever fabricate things before his eyes. His sense of observation was acute and always active.

The officer asked the man if he was going to be okay. There were other people to interview. "Yeah, I'll be fine. This is not my first time to see death happen in front of me. I have seen it too many times and am too familiar with it. I know how to deal with it. Thanks so much for asking me." The two hugged for an extended time in the middle of the freeway. The man had always known that this woman was one who understood. She was like him. She was a seeker of the knowledge.

The woman strode off to question the friend. The man was approached by another woman in her thirties, wearing flip flops and green shorts. Her sunglasses were too big and her pink shirt contrasted her aura. The look on her face was very distraught. "Excuse me sir, may I ask you a question or two?" she asked the man. There was a tremble in her voice that told the man that it had taken all her courage to approach him.

"Sure," he replied. "What do you need?" His voice, too, was uneven, obviously rattled to the core himself.

"Are you okay, sir? I saw you were the first one there trying to help. I respect what you did. Nobody else even got out of their vehicle, except you and your friend. Some drove off as soon as the show was over. You are a hero, sir," the woman said.

"I will be okay," the man replied. "You are mistaken, though. I am no hero. I saved nobody and watched helplessly as they were all meeting the end. However, that is the way of things. I embrace the fact that we are all dead already. These lives just ended, but there will be a beginning. They flow together like seasons. This may seem like a tragedy now, but with life there is death. Neither exist without the other. Life brings death, and death brings life. It is the way."

"But sir," the woman continued, "when I saw you silhouetted against the flames, I could see a huge dark shadow around you. It seemed to morph into a large bird and fly away. I also noticed there were no people in the minivan after the crash. When the bird flew away, there was a small explosion inside the burning vehicle. All four of the people reappeared at that exact moment. I ain't never seen nothing like that. What's going on here?"

"I'm not sure what happened. I saw something similar, but thought my eyes were tricking me. Everything happened so quickly, I'm not sure what I saw. It looked like they were singing and having a good time. They were not there, and then they were. It was like they were fading in and out of this dimension or something," the man told the woman.

The woman was swiftly walking back to her car before the man had finished his words. She jumped in so fast, one of her flip flops fell to the ground. The woman disregarded the lost shoe as she yanked her door shut. She tore off, kicking up a dust storm as she sped off. A volley of police officers, standing along her path, frantically waved their arms to get the woman to stop. They did not need another death here today. Their actions were useless. The woman zigzagged through the uniforms and made it to the open highway. As soon as she was clear, she sped off.

After what seemed like hours, the man and his friend were back on the road to the airport. The man had witnessed the extraction of the bodies from the wreck. Miraculously, the family of four lost most of their charred flesh and now almost looked recognizable. Their eyes were gone, leaving empty sockets. Their mouths were twisted into large grins that spread across their faces, exposing their teeth. Besides their faces, their bodies were still covered in the black char of burned flesh. The man had thought to himself that they looked like they were wearing solid black garments of some futuristic race. The man could tell that there were two women and two men. Also carried out of the wreckage were two small dogs. As one of the victims was being taken away on a gurney, the man thought that he looked oddly familiar. He looked a lot like himself.

In the car, the friend struck up conversation with the man. They were both shaken and looking a little pale. "Wow, that was a close one. We could have died back there. Especially you when you ran toward those flames. I thought you were crazy or had a death wish or something."

"We are already dead," spoke the man. "My brother always said that you cannot kill what is already dead. He was one hundred percent right. How else could we truly love life unless we understood this. How can people be truly happy who are always in fear of dying. They are already dead, too. They just can't accept it. Maybe we died back there and now we are continuing in a parallel dimension. How would we know? Nobody can ever remember what happens after death. It just ends and then begins again. If we did know what happened after our demise, there would be a lot more cases of suicide on this planet."

"You always talk some deep, crazy ass shit, Man," the friend said.

"It is because I have been through deep, crazy shit my whole life. Spirits and other strange phenomena have always been a huge part of my life. My parents were gifted in the same way, as were my brother and sister. Our children have been passed the same gift. We can see things others can't and speak with spirits. Most thought we were crazy, so we kept it to ourselves. The world and its madness told us a different tale than the masses. We saw the truth. The wisdom was one, with us and our kind."

"There is something I need to tell you that I don't speak of often," the man continued. "I lost six members of my immediate family in the last two years. It has taken a serious toll on our family and crushed our spirits. This trip we are taking now is to begin new chapters in our lives. It is time to put an end to it all. We are leaving our dark times behind us and searching for the knowledge of the light. We will be reborn when we arrive back at the coast. That is where it will end. That is where it will begin."

"Why didn't you tell me before? You know I would have been there for you," said the friend.

"It is not something any of us talk about. Our people have gone to the next life, and we feel a deep loss for them. It is like having a hole in your being. We do enjoy the fact that we will be with them and all our ancestors again. Our energy is interlocked like the same DNA that we share. Our energies never truly separate. We are One."

The friend was shaking his head, as they pulled up to the air terminal. He was looking at the man with disbelief. This ride to the airport was not what he had signed up for. The near accident had been terrible, but what the man had just told him was equally as bad. He cared for the man. He was not one to hand out respect, but the man got his. It was a mutual respect. The two understood each other and had become friends because of it.

As the man grabbed his backpack from the back seat, the friend jumped out to assist. Their two souls had just bonded. Their energies had merged once again. The first time had been with the body suit that the man had inked. The second time was near death and a story of stories. The friend felt that the man had just given him a piece of wisdom.

"Thanks for the ride," the man said, "I really appreciate it."

The friend was next to him with an embrace ready. His larger size was enough to pick the man up and embrace him with all his might. "You are a crazy motherfucker, but you are my friend. Be safe in your travels. I will see you soon."

As the man walked towards the rental car terminal, the friend drove by and gave a friendly beep from the horn. A large crow was sitting atop a light pole looking at the man. The man looked back and gave three clicking sounds with his tongue. Their eyes seemed to meet for an extended time. The eye of the crow was a grayish blue color. Its large size made it look like a vulture. The crow clicked back three times and flew off. The man smiled to himself. This was a good omen. They had an escort to show them the path.

These thoughts came to the man out of nowhere. He did not know where the thought of the crow being their guide came from, but it seemed so natural of a thought to him. He knew it to be true in his heart.

Suddenly, the man remembered the object in his pocket which the crow had dropped earlier. He already knew what he would find, and he also knew that this bird on top of the light pole was the same one from the wreck. It had flown from the ending to show the beginning. It was their friend. The man did not know how, he just knew.

He fished in his pocket and pulled out a small oval stone about two and a half inches by two inches. It was about an inch thick and brown. In the center of the stone, carved all the way through its thickness, was a sun. This symbol looked very familiar to the man. He prided himself in his knowledge of ancient symbols but could not place this one. He could not remember where he had seen this symbol, but he knew he had seen it before.

The stone seemed to give off a warm energy that permeated his being. He thought to himself that he would never leave the presence of this stone again. The two were now attached.

The man dropped the rock into his pants pocket and walked into the terminal. He was the only one in the building, except for the clerk at the desk. He looked at the large clock, on a pedestal in the terminal, and was shocked to see that it was ten at night. His friend had picked him up at noon. When he had been dropped off, it was still light outside, maybe six. The man checked his watch, but it had stopped at five fifty-five. He pulled the phone from his pocket and saw that it was indeed ten minutes after ten. He had lost over four hours since he walked into the airport. He saw that he had many texts from his wife. She was worried about him. She had not heard from him since he left the tattoo shop at noon. Ten hours before.

The man texted his wife to let her know he was okay, and that he was at the air terminal getting the car. He would explain it all later, he told her. It had been a crazy ass day, and he still had a three-hour drive to get home.

The man at the counter added to the madness. His blank stare and demeanor were unsettling to the man. The clerk already had the paperwork there and the key ready. As the man approached, the other gave him the key and paperwork to sign before they even made a greeting. Signing the papers made the deal complete. It had never been this easy to rent a car, the man had thought. Doing everything online was key to an easier transaction, but this guy hadn't even asked to see his identification. It was like the clerk knew the man like a frequent renter.

The man was at the counter for less than thirty seconds before walking away in order. He told the representative to have a nice day, and the gesture was returned. The guy behind the desk sounded like a robot to the man. Something in his voice seemed so familiar, but the memory was just out of grasp.

The man was happy to be walking away from the counter for the rental car. He reflected on what had just happened with the clerk and the time. The accident from earlier weighed heavy on his mind. The family had planned this trip to heal their wounds of the soul, and now it had already started just as the last two years had been. He felt like he was trapped somewhere between the conscious and subconscious.

The man decided to try and forget about all the strange things that had happened to him this day. He and his family had been waiting and preparing for this trip for so very long. The journey to this getaway had been a long, sorrowful one. The last two years had been a journey through the darkest of times. A black cloud had truly hung over the family's head. All the heartache they had gone through was punctuated by this day's events.

That was then though. This was now. The man sensed that it was truly over.

They had reached the end.

This was the beginning.

The trip had begun.

EPILOGUE

Six months had passed since the family had returned from their trip. As the man had known before they had even left, the time and memories would fade quickly. If not for the journal that the man had kept, the memories would have long ago faded into nothing. The pictures and written story were the only confirmation that the events had even happened.

The man had been hard at work with the story after their return. Their adventures had been documented well along the journey, but now it needed to be properly written. There were many more things to say that hadn't been possible with the limited time on the road. Reading his writings and typing them helped the man recollect whatever he could of his faded memories.

The story seemed like it was a tale about someone else and their adventure. A few of the events were slight memories of dreams that the man had. It seemed so real somewhere deep within his being, just not in the conscious. This story had come from his subconscious. He understood now. He had written this book when he was in a dream state. Somehow, his body had written it and been animated while he was sleeping. Like sleepwalking or something.

After their return home, the tale had taken a full six months to type into the computer. The finger numbing process was a daily task. The man took all his undertakings seriously, though. If he had an idea, he was going to see it through until it was finished. Every day after tattooing, and much of his off time, were spent weaving his epic saga.

After the third month, the man realized that the story of the trip was a merging with the other book he had written. The book of the truth had been written late at night when everyone else went to sleep. This was the story he had told none of the others about. Its writings coincided with everything that the other book said. He obviously wrote until falling asleep, and then his subconscious took over the story of the adventure.

After this epiphany, the book began to take on a prophetic nature. This was the story he had originally set out to write. This was the true purpose of it all.

His hope was that a few humans would read the writings without their biases and beliefs. They might open their eyes. Once people started waking up, things could change. Until then, humans were destined to walk around in the darkness that encompassed their beings. Maybe the book could help a few of them, the man had thought. His hopes were shadowed by his serious doubts.

While his fingers were tearing up the alphabet, the small stone, Toomey, hung out on the keyboard. The being gave its input the entire time, to a story which had been written over and over. The saga had also been destroyed countless times, only to be rewritten when the time was right.

The man thought often that he was not even writing the story. He was just rewriting a tale that had been told to him so very long before. It was a saga created to help the humans regain their spirituality. It was a book that exposed the greed. Whenever the greed had found the book, they had destroyed it and any of its copies.

The manuscript warned future generations of the greed and how to keep them at bay. Many other such warnings had been created around the planet for the same reason. Prehistoric hieroglyphics, around the world, were all similar, because they spoke of the same warning. Creatures had come from space, pretended to be gods, and enslaved the planet. Most humans did not heed the warnings. They looked at the ancient signs like they were scribbled by primates.

The original book of wisdom had been bastardized by the greed before they had destroyed its teachings. They had borrowed much from its words and translated them into the new religions that they were forcing on the humans, as if they were gods. Eventually, they put titles on their religious books that they had created from the saga. It soon became meaningless to all who knew the truth, while others bowed and committed their souls.

The true wisdom was inside of everything. The book's original purpose had been distorted by the greed.

The words in the journal became almost unreadable at times. Sometimes, the man had a difficult time discerning if it was even his own handwriting. A few of the pages seemed to be in a totally different language, which the man was not familiar with. He did not need to be able to decipher the words, though. His mind knew exactly what they said.

One page in the diary was all symbols, like the ones he had seen in Roswell. He had a dream of finding a spacecraft in the desert. He had found wreckage with strange symbols. The man had photographed these symbols with his mind. He remembered seeing these same markings in photos of the Roswell crash. Now, they covered an entire page of his writings. There were many more characters filling the page than he had remembered from his dream. It reminded the man of an ancient form of Egyptian Cuneiform style writing.

Another page was covered in parallel lines of numbers. The first half of the page consisted of ones and zeroes only. The bottom half were a series of seemingly meaningless digits. When the man read these numbers, however, they were anything but nonsense. These digits were the numbers of his life. Series of phone numbers, social security, addresses, birthdays, anniversaries, and so much more were present. To everyone else, these numbers would be a cryptic code, impossible to crack. To the man, though, it was the story of his life.

The man had finished typing the novel by the end of the year. Like all extensive projects, it would consume his time. Something else would have to be given up. In this case, it had been painting. The man had finished the mask book at Thanksgiving. It had been too important not to keep up on. Page one hundred fifty-five had been bittersweet. It had been such a long process, covering many hard times. In the end, when the book closed the last time, the feeling of the man was mostly one of indifference.

At this same time, the man had begun to read books about UFO and extraterrestrial. At first, the fascination was profound. His interest had been piqued once again on the road. The man had seen many things in the sky that were very unusual in his life. He had no doubt of the existence of UFO and life beyond this planet. He thought it silly to think that humans were the only ones flying around inside and outside of the stratosphere.

The more he read these books, though, the more he began to doubt them. Not the UFO; the books were what he was skeptical of. It seemed like they were written as another smokescreen. Another lie perpetrated by the greed to convince humans that maybe there was a cover up of something that maybe existed. They were the kings of this manipulation. Everything they taught us or told us was a warped version of the truth.

While the greed was flying around in their electromagnetic craft, at times in battle with otherworldly beings, they manipulated people's minds into thinking they were the visitors. They even abducted people, made crop circles, and mutilated cows to keep up with the deception. All the while discounting the sightings as people's imagination or illusion. It was another way to control their slaves and keep them blind to the reality.

The months of Autumn had passed in a story. Chores during this time of year were minimal. After going to see his mom every Sunday for the last ten years, this new free time was unusual. The man had not been home on Sunday for a very long time. Spending time with his wife was much needed for both. Life was getting back to normal.

Writing was the enlightenment that the man had been searching for. It took his mind off all the sadness, and made him once again see the light. His brain and soul were finally healing from the trauma that it had endured.

The grandson had settled in well in Crescent City. Beginning high school in a coastal town was going to work out well for him. His interest in sports was solid. The man and woman had already gone and picked up the boy once in this time. The coastal area was beautiful. The family all looked forward to spending time together in the majesty of the redwoods throughout the next four years. Their bond was to remain a solid one.

The girl, too, had done well since the return. She had gotten enrolled for the next semester in college while on the road. Her grueling schedule was hard, but she still made the effort to get a job. Work filled her free time. It gave the family less time to see each other, but it was the way of life. The girl knew your path was the way you chose it. She was choosing wisely.

The new year had come and gone. The man had told his friend in Wisconsin that he would be coming out there for tattoo sessions. That first session came in Mid-January. The man had purchased a ticket, months before, and the day had arrived. The weeks before had been hectic. The man and woman had just driven their grandson home the week before. There would be no rest for the man. It was something he was used to, at least. Rest had not been a word that applied to him since he was a youngster.

The man had spent the last few months researching the different options for publishing. As the book progressed, he knew that it was written with a purpose. For anyone who read it and understood, they would awaken and heal. They would be on the path to the truth. He also knew that it would piss off a lot of people. Humans did not like it when you didn't agree with their beliefs. When you exposed their beliefs like lies, the haters would get monstrous.

Dealing with death was not an easy thing. It had been the hardest times the family had ever been through. There had been no guidance or assistance. The family that remained had to handle things on a day by day basis, without any outside help nor spiritual kindness. They had been abandoned by the community which boasted about their tight knit ways. Their friends, too, had stayed away like they had the plague.

The man had fully awakened with the journey of death among life, and the story. Now, his writings could possibly help another family in spiritual need, under similar circumstances.

The man was thinking about these thoughts associated with the book as he walked through the Phoenix airport. The story was what consumed most of his thoughts these days. The trip to Wisconsin had begun early from Fresno. Six in the morning was when the flight had departed. It would be a full day of travel to get to the tattoo destination.

There had been so many houses and buildings when they were landing. The masses were thick here in the desert. The airport was no different. Large pockets of the herd were sprinkled with small pockets of solitude. It was difficult and took some time, but you could find a few terminals with minimal passengers. These were the places of seclusion that the man looked for.

This was also where he got a shock. While browsing through books to read in the bookstore, he saw one with the same title as the one he had been writing. It had been difficult coming up with a title that hadn't been used for books already published. He had spent months to come up with the perfect one, and now it was here in front of his eyes.

The man picked up the book out of spite. He turned it over to see what the lame ass story was about. He read the paragraph three times before opening the book randomly. He read the first page that he had opened and flipped to the second, speechless. His mouth was hanging open in disbelief. This was the same exact book that he was writing. Word for word, it was exact.

The man was furious. Someone had stolen his story. Someone had stolen his soul. He tore the back cover a bit while pulling it open. He had been rougher than he thought in his sudden anger.

"You gonna buy that now sir," the robotic clerk said to the man. His wallet was out as she was finishing her words. He had already intended to purchase this book. It was going to take more investigating. Before he read any more, though, he needed to sit down.

As the man staggered to an abandoned area, many eyes were upon him. To all the people present, the man was no more than a shadow. His features were not discernible. Everyone got out of his path. It was like death itself was passing by.

As soon as the man was seated, he opened the back cover once again. He had already seen it once, but now it was confirmed. The picture of the author was a picture of him. It was a picture he remembered, taken while he was in the Navy. Underneath the photo, in its nice font, was the name of his brother.

Upon takeoff, the man realized that he did not remember getting on the plane. The time was a vacant spot in his mind. He felt as if the last thread of sanity had been broken. It had been stretched thin for a very long time, but this was the breaking point.

It had taken all the will of the man to keep his head somewhat straight for the last couple of years. It had not always been an easy thing. Keeping sane was hard work. Losing it all would be so easy. In the last months, it had been getting easier and easier to keep on the right path. The trip had been therapeutic and enlightening. It had begun to heal the wounds that had been cut through his soul.

Since the trip, the story had fully set his mind in the right direction. His relationships with others were improving as his mind got straight. He had still shied away from friendships and other exchanges of energy. He was more than content to just hang out with his family. They were the energy that brought strength and creativity.

The other half of his life, the tattoo shop, was filled with other souls and their energy. Being alongside his son every week was what brought the man and woman back every week. They very much liked to hang out with the son. He was part of their circle. It would have been easy to walk away from it all if it weren't for him and their other coworker. Dealing with the customers took all the willpower from the man at times. He had pried himself away from strangers in the last couple of years. At the tattoo shop, there was no choice but to accept these foreign energies.

The flight attendant spilling a cup of water in the man's lap is how he woke up. He was in a daze for a few minutes as the woman patted his shoulder and chest with small airplane napkins. He looked around bewildered. He had been thinking about tattooing and the tattoo shop, which always filled much of his thoughts. He had been staring out the window, lost in his thoughts, when he had seen a bright green orb about the size of a basketball next to the airplane. He had shifted to get a better look, and the next thing he remembered was now.

It had been light outside earlier, and now it was dark. The man looked to his watch and saw that three hours had passed since they had taken off. It had seemed like ten minutes or less since they had been airborne.

Sitting in his lap was the book that he had purchased back in the terminal. It was open, face down, on top of his seat buckle. He had to grab it as the flight attendant frantically wiped. It was open to the midway point.

The man could somehow remember reading the book. The thought made his head swim. He didn't even remember hours of flight, but he remembered reading the book. He knew for certain that it was the exact same words he had written. The paradox of thoughts was almost too much for his unbreakable, yet fragile mind.

The man did not know how or who, but his book had been pirated. They had not even bothered to change the title nor the words. The punctuation and spelling was all correct. It was like they had taken his draft and professionally published it. It had been a dirty deed.

He was finally fed up with the flight attendant. She seemed to be drying him a bit excessively. He shooed the woman away with a wave of the hand. The anger was obvious in her face. The other passengers in the vicinity absorbed the hatred from the uniformed woman. They all glared to the man with anger that they didn't even understand. They were sheep, like most, thought the man. Anyone slightly in charge, the masses would follow.

The man looked out the window shade to the darkness. A light that seemed to be blinking in the distance was the light from the wing. He had seen it countless times on his travels. He fixed his eyes on the beacon while clearing his thoughts. Its steady pulse was comforting to his troubled mind.

Another light, farther in the distance, was moving strangely. It seemed to be flying next to the aircraft at times and other times around it. After a few minutes, the light began pulsing towards the aircraft, and then away at a distance of maybe thirty miles. The man could see the distinct red light paired with the solid white light on its near collisions with the aircraft. Then it would swoop away just as fast.

The man looked to the other passengers and saw that they were all looking down at their laps. They looked like robots. Every person on the plane, even the flight attendant, were in their seats with their faces glued to the book they were all reading. The man could see clearly the cover of the books in his vicinity. They were all the same book that he was reading. The same one he had written. Now he knew that sanity was slipping. Not only had his book been pirated, everyone on the flight was reading it.

Consciousness seemed to be fading from the man. His thoughts spun out of control. He had thought that he was dreaming, but this was no dream.

It had all started over again. He was trying to remember why he had come out here in the first place, and now it came flooding back. His sister had died. Her boarder had choked her in a jealous rage and made it look like she had hung herself. The roommate had been slowly poisoning her boyfriend until the gentleman had died a month before. The man was going out there to take care of his sister's affairs and to torture her boarder. Bad things were coming his way.

The light outside was getting brighter and faster. It moved away and back again in the time between blinks. The man looked to the passenger next to him, but the woman's face was blank. She had no eyes in her empty sockets. Everyone in the cabin had the same absent stare.

Looking back to the night, the man noticed that it was not one set of lights playing its game with the aircraft, it was four sets of lights. They were now on each side of the plane. All the lights were pulsing along with the movement of the craft.

A large shadow began to interrupt the lights at intervals. This shadow was from the mother craft. It was huge. He had seen this vessel so many years before, with his son. Now, it was here, flying over the heartland of America.

The lights seemed to be making up the sacred symbol. The man sensed it as it was formed around the aircraft. The vessel became part of the sign. Together they created the symbol for the One. These craft were here on a purpose. The man understood.

He realized what the other passengers really were. They were nothing more than flesh pods, awaiting souls. The man was with them to show them the way. He had made the journey, now he could guide others.

Once again, looking back to the darkness, the man knew. The large craft, with its solid white and red light was the craft that took care of the souls. They were the ones who gathered and distributed the souls when they became free of their flesh pods.

The large vessel began to fly circles around the aircraft. It picked up speed rapidly as it flew in its perfect orbit. The plane had seemed to stop in midair while the larger craft created a blur of light around its fuselage.

The man was thinking to himself that this story was about to end. It had been a nice journey, but just like a good road trip, it had to be over eventually.

He was not scared. His heart beat a thump with the adrenaline of what was coming. He had lived a great life. There were no regrets. It was his time.

A bright flash of light was how the transition worked. It was the last thing you saw, and the first thing at rebirth. There was no pain. It just happened.

No one ever saw the man again. The light had been his end. His aircraft had been lost in a storm over Lake Superior. No wreckage nor passengers were ever found. As is the cycle, the ending brought the beginning. The light was the rebirth for the man. The cycle had been complete once again. For his soul, it had begun.

There would be talk among his family for the rest of their days, but no proof. The man had written a cryptic message to his niece before going to the airport. It had been a premonition of the doom that was coming. She had followed through with his request to finish the book. It had enlightened her being, just as she had enlightened the book.

As with all tragedies, time would heal. The woman would be hit the hardest, but the other members in their support group would all pull their energies together and help her get through it. The man had meant a lot to his circle. Be it husband, father, uncle, grandpa, or brother, they all knew that he would want them to continue and do well. Just like when he was alive.

With the death of the man, along with his brother and sister, the trinity had been ended. The cycle had once again been complete. This time, however, it had all been written down. The story, after being finished by the niece, had been passed to the man's son and his sister's son. The two of them, with the niece, completed the triangle once again.

The energy returned to the one.

The One returned.

It was the beginning.

Author Biography

Hailing from California's Gold Country, Sol Gatos is an artist who works in several media: he creates poems, paintings, drawings, tattoos, and sculptures. He also engages with philosophical theory in a quest to understand life.

www.ingramcontent.com/pod-product-compliance
Lightning Source LLC
Chambersburg PA
CBHW080721020726
47503CB00010B/2742